SEAL OF PROTECTION
COLLECTION 3

PROTECTING MELODY / PROTECTING THE FUTURE/PROTECTING KIERA/PROTECTING DAKOTA

SUSAN STOKER

PROTECTING MELODY

SEAL OF PROTECTION, BOOK 7

Tex gave everything he had to his country and his SEAL teammates. When an IED took away part of his leg, and his career, he devoted himself to his country and friends from behind his computer. He's always been the man who can find anyone, who uses his computer skills, legal and illegal, to keep people safe and to put the bad guys behind bars.

But behind a computer is a lonely place to be. While he might put on a good front, Tex can't help but feel he's missing out when he sees how happy his friends are. But when the woman he's been talking to online for the last six months suddenly disappears without a word, Tex knows it's time to step up, and use his skills for himself this time.

**Protecting Melody is the 7th book in the SEAL of Protection Series. It can be read as a stand-alone, but it's recommended you read the books in order to get maximum enjoyment out of the series.

To receive special offers, bonus content, and news about my latest books, sign up for my newsletter:

www.StokerAces.com/contact.html

PROLOGUE

*S*ix Months Ago

Tex:Hey, I haven't seen you in here before. Your username struck me as interesting, so I thought I'd shoot you a private note

    Tex:Swear I'm harmless

    CC_CopyCat: Hey Tex. I mostly lurk

    Tex:Don't blame you, it's better to be safe than sorry

    Tex:You wanna talk?

    CC_CopyCat: About what?

    Tex:About whatever

    CC_CopyCat: That's kinda vague

    Tex:Well, we could talk about the weather, but that would be cliché.

    CC_CopyCat: LOL

    Tex:Made ya laugh!

    CC_CopyCat: Yeah, you did. Thanks

    Tex:Thanks?

    CC_CopyCat: Yeah. Thanks

    Tex:So . . . how's the weather where you are?

    CC_CopyCat: Crappy, you?

    Tex:Sunny and beautiful

CC_CopyCat: You're one of those aren't you?

Tex:??

CC_CopyCat: One of those annoying people who see the good side in everything

Tex:Actually, no. Not even close

Tex:You still there?

CC_CopyCat: Look, I'm not sure this is gonna work out

Tex:You just met me, I couldn't have pissed you off already

CC_CopyCat: I'm not here to find a best friend, I already have one of those

Tex:Then why ARE you here?

CC_CopyCat: Just passing the time

Tex:Then why can't you pass it with me?

CC_CopyCat: Because you're probably either a 14 year old boy who wants to find someone to sext with or you're a 50 year old pedophile looking for sex from a 16 year old teenager who doesn't know any better than to talk to people who spend their time in a chat room on the Internet.

Tex:Same goes for you. You could be anyone. You're probably an undercover cop looking to catch bad guys who use chat rooms to lure people to their death

CC_CopyCat: ARE you a bad guy Tex? Are you even a guy?

Tex:Are you a woman CC?

CC_CopyCat: I shouldn't say one way or the other

Tex:No offense, but I don't want to chat with a dude. I'm not looking for a relationship, I'm not looking for sex. I have male friends I can talk to

CC_CopyCat: What ARE you looking for then?

Tex:Just someone to chat with. My life is stressful. I'd love to talk with someone who doesn't want anything from me. Who just likes to chat with me because she thinks I'm interesting

CC_CopyCat: You never answered my question. Are you a bad guy?

Tex:I'm a 35 year old retired military man who lives on the east coast. I'm good with computers and spend most of my time with them. I'm not hideous looking, but I've found that I'm also not the guy women want to take home to meet their family. Swear CC, I'm harmless.

CC_CopyCat: You know that's what serial killers say

Tex:LOL. You're right. But you can trust me

CC_CopyCat: Yup, they say that too

CC_CopyCat: You still there?

Tex:You gonna diss me more or are you going to tell me about you?

CC_CopyCat: Sorry. I was kidding. Yes. I'm a woman

Tex:Thank you. What else?

CC_CopyCat: I don't really know you, that's all you get

Tex:I'll take it . . . for now. You gonna tell me about your handle?

CC_CopyCat: I gotta go

Tex:Okay, I'll be here if you wanna talk again

CC_CopyCat: How will you know when I'll want to talk again?

Tex: I don't, but I told you I work on computers, I'm always here

CC_CopyCat: Okay, maybe

Tex:I've enjoyed talking to you CC

CC_CopyCat: We haven't even talked about anything interesting

Tex:Yeah, but you aren't afraid to tell me what you're really thinking. I like that

CC_CopyCat: Most men don't

Tex:I'm not most men

CC_CopyCat: Whatever. OK, I'm logging off

Tex:Bye CC. Later

TEX SAT BACK and smiled at his computer. He didn't usually engage people he met online, but he'd been visiting this particular chat room for a while now and noticed *"CC_CopyCat"* lurking. He'd taken a chance and sent the private message, hoping he was messaging a woman. Tex had been honest with her, he wasn't looking to start up an online friendship with a man.

Call him sexist, but Tex was more comfortable talking with a woman than a man. Maybe it was because he was around men all the time. It was just . . . different, speaking with a woman.

Ever since he'd lost part of his leg to an IED while on a SEAL mission, Tex was more comfortable talking to people behind his computer or phone. Before he was injured, he'd never had a problem attracting the ladies. He was in his mid-thirties now and still worked out every day. Physical fitness was too ingrained in him to give it up after he was injured.

While Tex knew firsthand, on the surface, women still found him attractive and they'd gladly go home with him, after getting weird looks and two less than satisfying sexual encounters, he found it more comfortable for everyone to not bother. He now took care of his needs himself. Tex knew his friends all thought he was still sexually active, but the awkward explanations about his injury and the pity fucks got old fast.

He tried not to care what people thought of his leg, but when he connected with people via his computer, he could be anonymous . . . whole. Talking to CC was refreshing. Tex liked it.

He hadn't lied to the woman on the other end of the computer. She intrigued him. She wasn't fawning all over him, as some women Tex had messaged in the past had. She was cautious, but he could sense her humor under her stilted words. Tex hoped she'd log back in and they could talk again, but if she didn't, he wouldn't lose any sleep. There would be more women, and he'd keep busy living vicariously through his friends' lives.

Four months ago

CC_COPYCAT:*Hey Tex. How are you?*
    Tex:*Hey CC. I'm sorry, but I can't talk right now*
    CC_CopyCat:*Oh sorry*
    Tex:*It's not you. I'd rather talk to you than anyone else, but my friend's woman is in trouble and I'm trying to figure her situation out*
    CC_CopyCat:*That sucks.*
    Tex:*Yeah, her man is overseas and can't get to her. So I'm trying to get him home and keep her safe*
    CC_CopyCat:*OK, go do your thing. If you want to talk later, I'm here*
    Tex:*Thanks CC. I needed that. Later*

TEX HATED to put CC off. They'd been talking pretty regularly for the last two months and Tex really enjoyed their conversations, but Fiona was counting on him. She was obviously having a mental breakdown after whatever had happened in the shopping mall. He was calling her every four hours. It was heartbreaking to listen to her try to figure out what was going on—trying to decide what was real and what was imagined in her head. She was so scared. Tex turned back to the computers and typed frantically to try to get Cookie home and to his woman.

The next day, after the entire situation with Fiona was finally over, Tex tried to see if CC was around.

TEX:*You around?*
    Tex:*Guess not. If you come back, I'm here*

TEX RAN a hand over his face. Jesus. Fiona had just about broken his heart. He hadn't ever met her, had only met Caroline, Wolf's woman, but Fiona was just as tough, yet vulnerable at the same time, as Caroline was. She'd done exactly what he'd asked of her and every time Tex had called, she'd answered. Tex had no idea what he would've done if Fiona hadn't picked up the phone. She was in California and he was in Virginia.

Tex knew his friends had a lot of faith in his abilities, but if something had really gone wrong, there would've been nothing he could've done. Tex cursed his leg, again. Not a day went by that he didn't wish he'd have done something different on the mission that took his leg. Not a day went by that he didn't wish he was whole and the man he used to be.

He was good at the computer, but he wished with all his heart he could be on the front lines, with his friends, saving lives and serving his country. Tex looked down at the box blinking at him in the corner of his computer screen. CC.

CC_CopyCat:Hey Tex, I'm here. You there?
   Tex:Yeah CC, I'm here
   CC_CopyCat:Everything go OK with your friend?
   Tex:Yeah
   CC_CopyCat:I know we've only been talking to each other for a little while, but you're not your usual self
   Tex:CC, you have no idea
   CC_CopyCat:You wanna talk about it?
   Tex:You sure you want this? We can keep this light and fluffy and superficial. We can say hi every now and then and go on with our lives as we have been. But I'll tell you. I've had a tough few days and could use more than that. But if we get deeper, I can't go back to light and fluffy. You choose.
   CC_CopyCat:I don't like that you've had a shit day, and I'd love to talk to you about it, but I can't give it back to you. I want to, I just can't.
   Tex:It's OK. We can keep it light
   CC_CopyCat:NO! Dammit Tex. You need to talk about stuff. You can't keep it in. I didn't mean that I didn't want you to talk to me
   Tex:I don't need a therapist, I need a friend. I get that you're cautious and it's smart. I get it, but CC, I've enjoyed our chats over the last 2 months, but I'd like to be more real with you. We'll never meet, so I feel safe talking to you about

stuff. You can't share my secrets 'cos you don't know who I am. I can't share yours because of the same thing. Please, tell me something, <u>anything</u>, personal about yourself.

TEX SAT BACK and held his breath. He didn't know what it was about CC, but he really wanted to talk to her, *really* talk to her. He hadn't lied. He *had* enjoyed talking to her. They'd talked about their favorite foods (she liked Mexican, he liked Italian), favorite colors (hers was pink, his was blue), and many, many other superficial things. She'd even asked what his favorite Disney character was at one point. He'd thought it an odd question, but had answered her anyway.

But now Tex was at the point where he needed their relationship to be deeper than it was. He didn't really know why, but he wanted to get to know her better. He liked her. She was funny and interesting and even though they hadn't really talked about anything personal, he thought she'd be the kind of person he'd like to get to know better. He wasn't satisfied with the superficial stuff anymore.

Tex waited another few moments and when CC didn't respond back, he leaned forward and typed out a terse note, ready to log off and talk to her some other time.

TEX:OK then, I gotta go

    CC_CopyCat:My name is Mel. It's short for Melody

    Tex:Thank you, Mel. You have no idea how much I needed that. Thank you

    CC_CopyCat:Tell me about your shit day

    Tex:A while ago, my buddy's woman was kidnapped by Mexican slave traders. She was rescued and doing great. But recently she had a flashback and ran.

    CC_CopyCat:Jesus, Tex. But she's OK?

    Tex:Yeah Mel, she's OK. But for three days all she had was me. I called her every 4 hours to make sure she was staying put in the hotel. I listened to her go back and forth between reality and the shit that was messing with her head.

    CC_CopyCat:I'm proud of you Tex

    Tex:Don't be. I've done some horrible things in my life

    CC_CopyCat:Hasn't everyone? Seriously, get off your high horse Tex. You aren't the only person that wishes they'd done things differently. You aren't the only one who has a crap background, or crap childhood, or crap marriage. You just keep moving forward. You learn from the past and keep going. Sounds to me like your friends are lucky to have you on their side.

CC_CopyCat:Tex? Shit. Too real? Not fluffy enough?

Tex:NO. Not too real. I'm just thinking.

CC_CopyCat:OK. Let me know when you're done

Tex:Smart ass. You're right. But I think the things I did are worse than the run-of-the-mill crap background.

CC_CopyCat:So what. Are you going to go off and continue to do those horrible things? Sounds to me like you're trying to change that. That you're doing good. I'm sure your friend would agree with me

Tex:Maybe

CC_CopyCat:No maybe about it

Tex:OK, you win

CC_CopyCat:Of course I do

Tex:Mel?

CC_CopyCat:Yeah?

Tex:I'm glad you didn't choose fluffy

CC_CopyCat:Me too

Two Months Ago

Tex:Last time we talked you said you were scared all the time. I don't like that.

CC_CopyCat:I don't like it either

Tex:What are you scared of?

CC_CopyCat:People watching me. Getting shot. Getting kidnapped. Being sick. Being alone. You name it Tex, I'm scared of it.

Tex:Do you have depression Mel?

CC_CopyCat:No, why?

Tex:Most people who are scared of all those things are mentally ill

CC_CopyCat:So you're saying you think I'm crazy?

Tex:You know I'm not. But I do want to know if there's something really going on with you.

CC_CopyCat:I'm not crazy or depressed

Tex:Then what?

CC_CopyCat:Never mind

Tex:No, not never mind. TALK to me. Why are you scared of those things?

CC_CopyCat:I just am

Tex:Don't bullshit me

CC_CopyCat:You ever get the feeling that you're being watched?

Tex:No

CC_CopyCat:Well, I do. And it scares me. And thinking about that makes me think about the other stuff too. It's a never-ending circle

Tex:Never take the same route when you go about your daily business. Always walk with your keys in your hand. Walk with your head up and look people in the eyes. If you get in an elevator, don't turn your back to people. Never stay in an elevator if it's only you and a man you don't know. Tell someone when you expect to be home.

CC_CopyCat:You know a lot about this

Tex:Mel, I told you I was a Navy SEAL. We spend way too much time learning this kind of shit. If you get cornered or someone attacks you, go for their eyes, or their throat, or their balls. Don't get in a car with someone if they try to take you away, you're better off in a public place.

CC_CopyCat:Tex, I got it. I'm probably just imagining it anyway

Tex:I bet you aren't. Anytime I got in a situation where I felt weird, in 100% of the cases, it turned out I was right.

CC_CopyCat:OK, I'll be careful

Tex:If you need me, you shoot me a note, I'm here

CC_CopyCat:But we don't really even know each other

Tex:Don't care. Just agree

CC_CopyCat:You're awfully bossy

Tex:Agree

CC_CopyCat:OK

Tex:Good

One Month Ago

CC_CopyCat:Tell me about your friends. You talk about them all the time, and it's obvious they have some seriously awesome wives and girlfriends.

Tex:Yeah, they're all great. You know I was a SEAL. I worked with some of them when I was in the Navy, but after I retired they found themselves in need of my computer abilities. I can usually get them what they need faster than going through proper channels and with the issues their women have had, thank God that I can.

CC_CopyCat:What are their names again?

Tex:Wolf, Abe, Cookie, Mozart, Benny, and Dude

CC_CopyCat:I'm sure there's some good stories behind those names

Tex:Of course

CC_CopyCat:Who do you rely on?

Tex:What do you mean?

CC_CopyCat:When you need someone, or something, who do you rely on?

CC_CopyCat:Tex? Shit, sorry. Did I overstep?

Tex:No

CC_CopyCat:Forget I asked. I'm sorry

Tex:As weird as this might sound. You.

CC_CopyCat:What?

Tex:You, Mel. When I've had a crap day, I get on here and talk to you. You don't judge me, you don't ask me for anything, you just talk to me.

CC_CopyCat:I won't be around forever Tex. You need to get out more. Find someone there you can talk to.

Tex:People don't "see" me as you do Mel

CC_CopyCat:Maybe you don't give them a chance

Tex:No. I live in a military town. Most can tell by my limp that I'm not whole. They pity me. I can't stand pity. I was a fucking SEAL. And if I'm wearing shorts? Forget about it.

CC_CopyCat:Not whole? Tex. Over the last months of me talking to you, I can tell you're one of the most alpha men I've ever met. You're bossy and you tell me what to do all the time. But at the same time you're compassionate, you worry about your friends, and you drop everything to help them, even when they don't ask. Believe me when I say that those people who see the surface that is you aren't seeing even one tenth of who YOU are. Fuck them. See yourself as I do.

Tex:Shit Mel

CC_CopyCat:No, I'm not done

CC_CopyCat:I think your friends take advantage of you. They're always calling you to help them. To help their women, but you haven't talked about them coming out there to see you. To thank you in person.

Tex:Mel, listen

CC_CopyCat:No

CC_CopyCat:You listen

CC_CopyCat:Tex, If you were my friend I'd never take advantage of you. Ever.

Tex:You are my friend

CC_CopyCat:Damn straight

Tex:Thanks for making me feel better

CC_CopyCat:Anytime

Tex:What about you?

CC_CopyCat:What about me what?

Tex:What about your friends?

CC_CopyCat:I've got friends

Tex:Who? You never talk about them.

CC_CopyCat:Amy. Amy is my friend

Tex:Just Amy?

CC_CopyCat:Yeah. I trust her with my life. I miss her though. I've been away and I haven't been able to talk to her as much as I'd like

Tex:Why?

CC_CopyCat:It's complicated

Tex:You see me going anywhere?

CC_CopyCat:Amy's back home. She has a husband and two kids and works for a contractor. She tells me all the time that her company builds stuff that kills people, but her job is to finance it. I have no idea what that means, but I laugh at her anyway.

Tex:She sounds funny

CC_CopyCat:She is! Sometimes we have complete conversations using hashtags

Tex:#likethis?

CC_CopyCat:#yeah

Tex:So why don't you talk to her much?

CC_CopyCat:Well, she's home, and has a life to live. And I'm not there, so it's just hard.

Tex:I won't push, but that sounds like a cop out

Tex:I know you're not telling me the entire story, and I don't like it. But as I said, I won't push. But I AM going to send you my cell phone number. You don't ever have to use it, but I want you to have it in case you want to ever talk. I think we're good enough friends now that we can move our online relationship to the next level. I'd love to hear your voice sometime. I feel like your friend too. So, what are you doing today?

CC_CopyCat:Well, you know I work from wherever I am, so I've got two jobs today and otherwise I'm just hanging out. You?

Tex:I'm going to check in with my friends and make sure all is calm there, then I think I'm going to do something crazy today.

CC_CopyCat:What's that?

Tex:There's a new thriller out I've been meaning to read

CC_CopyCat:LOL. Crazy day for you

Tex:You know it

CC_CopyCat:Seriously Tex, you need to get out and interact with people more

Tex:Pot meet kettle

CC_CopyCat:Yeah, but you're you. I haven't seen a picture of you, but I bet you're beautiful. You're probably tall and built. Your hair is probably a bit too long and there's not one woman who passes you who doesn't take a second look.

Tex:Men aren't beautiful

CC_CopyCat:The hell they aren't

Tex:Well, I'm not. I don't think my hair is too long, but the only reason women take a second glance at me is to pity me because of my injuries

CC_CopyCat:You're wrong. I'm 100% sure you're wrong. Next time you're out, look. REALLY look. I bet you'd be surprised.

CC_CopyCat:Hey, I hate to do this, but I gotta go. I have a thing in twenty minutes and I have to get ready.

Tex:OK Melody. As usual I've enjoyed talking to you

CC_CopyCat:Yeah, me too. You have no idea how much. I was serious about what I said Tex. You need to get out more. Find that woman who's meant to be yours. You deserve it just as much as your friends and I'm sure they'd say the same thing.

Tex:I'll try. Talk later?

CC_CopyCat:Yeah

Tex:OK, bye. Have a good day

CC_CopyCat:You too. Bye

CHAPTER 1

*T*ex paced his apartment. He wasn't happy. He couldn't get hold of Melody. It wasn't unusual for them to go a couple days without talking, but it had been a week. Ever since he'd first messaged her all those months ago, they hadn't gone that long without touching base. Tex looked down at his computer screen. The words there mocked him.

Tex:Mel? Are you there? Haven't heard from you in awhile
  Tex:I'm worried about you. Please. Talk to me. I miss your sarcasm
  Tex:If you don't answer me, I'm going to have to make <u>sure</u> you're all right. I know you never wanted to talk on the phone, or exchange photos, but I have to know you're okay. I've already given you my cell number, please call or text me.

Tex had no idea when Melody had become so important to him. There were many nights he'd stayed up late talking with her online. She was funny and sarcastic, but she got him in a way his Navy SEAL friends never would. Tex had opened up to Mel about how insecure he felt around women after his operation and how he hadn't taken off his prosthetic in front of anyone other than his doctors.

Tex knew it was the security of typing rather than talking face-to-face or even on the phone that made him open up to Melody. There was some safety in the anonymity of the Internet and writing what he felt rather than talking about it. Even the Navy shrinks had tried to get him to open up and he couldn't.

But with Melody he was able to, and had. She knew everything about him. And now that he hadn't talked to her in seven long days, Tex was realizing how little he actually knew about her. He'd blown it off in the past, not really thinking too much about it. He knew Mel got very defensive every time he tried to get her to talk about herself, so he'd dropped it. Tex didn't want to scare her off, he enjoyed talking to her too much.

But now, he was kicking himself. He knew almost nothing about her, and he was worried.

Tex looked back down at his computer screen. He clicked some buttons, then just stared at the chat box he'd just been using to talk to Mel.

User unknown.

Tex sat up abruptly in his chair and frantically clicked more buttons. He swore long, using some of the more inventive words he'd learned during his time on the teams. Melody had deleted her account. She wasn't just logged off; she'd severed the only connection they had with each other.

Something was more than wrong. While Tex didn't know the specifics of her life, he knew enough to know she wouldn't just up and disappear without a word to him . . . unless something was really wrong.

Tex tried to remember every piece of information she'd let slip over the last few months. He opened a new document and started typing.

PINK
Mexican food
Disney?
Friend named Amy - works in contracting - govt?
Works from home - jobs that start at specific times
Time difference? Job starting at 10pm my time
CC_CopyCat - has to mean something, but what?
Being watched? Scared

TEX SAT BACK and stared at the list he'd made. It wasn't a lot of information. Hell, it was shit. But he didn't like what it was adding up to. His Mel was on the run. He had no idea from what or who, but it was suddenly as clear as if she'd whispered the words across the globe and they'd landed in his ear.

Mel was cautious, not wanting to tell him anything about her. She didn't talk to her best friend, even though it was obvious she was longing to. She was scared and felt like she was being watched. Whatever she did to earn money, she was able to do it on the road, she didn't work a traditional job.

Melody had his phone number, but Tex didn't think she'd use it. She was too concerned about taking advantage of people and was too scared of something. And if she wouldn't call him, and Tex figured if she hadn't called her friend Amy so far, she wouldn't break that pattern now. Mel probably wasn't in contact with her friend because she was afraid whatever situation she was in would blow back on her.

Tex rolled up his sleeves. Fuck that. He'd never felt like this about anyone in his entire life. He felt like if he didn't find Melody, a huge piece of his life would be missing. Over the last six months she'd come to mean a lot to him. Tex didn't know how it happened, but it had. He had no idea what she looked like, but knew it didn't matter. She could weigh five hundred pounds or be sixty years old, but she was his friend and Tex needed to find and help her.

It was as if his entire life he'd been leading up to this moment. He'd found his friends' women, he could find Melody. For one of the first times in his life, Tex was going to concentrate on himself. He wasn't thinking about his friends, he wasn't thinking about his leg or the constant pain he felt. He had to find and help Melody.

* * *

Tex rubbed his hand over his face. What time was it? What *day* was it? He had no idea, but he thought he'd *finally* tracked down Melody's friend, Amy. He wasn't sure, but it was worth a shot. He'd combed through contracting agencies throughout the country trying to narrow them down based on what Melody had told him Amy did. Tex hadn't been surprised at how many Amys worked for the government. He'd called about two hundred so far and while some people would call him crazy for thinking he could find a needle in a haystack, he felt good about *this* Amy.

Tex picked up the phone and dialed the number he had for Amy

19

Smith. It was almost cliché with her having the surname of "Smith." It had made it that much harder to pin her down.

"Hello?"

"Is this Amy Smith who works for Key Contracting?"

"Who the hell is this?"

"I'm a friend of Melody's and . . . hello?" Tex looked down at the phone in his hand when suddenly all he heard was the dial tone. He couldn't help but be impressed and he felt in his gut this *was* Melody's friend. All of the other Amys he'd reached had spoken with him politely and had said they didn't know anyone with the name of Melody. But *this* Amy had hung up at the mere mention of Mel's name.

If Melody was in as much trouble as Tex thought she was, her friend had done the right thing, but that didn't mean it didn't still piss him off. He immediately dialed the number again and wasn't surprised when Amy didn't pick up the phone. He left a quick message.

"My name is Tex. I'm a retired Navy SEAL. I've been talking to Mel online for the last six months and she's told me about you. I'm afraid she's in trouble. I haven't talked to her in ten days and I'm worried. Please call me back. Hashtag, your friend needs help."

Tex had no idea if what he'd said was enough, but he gambled that Amy hearing he was a SEAL might change her mind toward him. But if that didn't do it, maybe his last hashtag comment would.

His phone rang six minutes after he left the message, he'd been counting. Tex picked it up, recognizing the number.

"What the hell is going on?" Amy didn't waste any time with niceties.

"As I said, I've been talking to Mel online for a while now. She never told me anything about her personal life, but I'm worried about her. We usually talk at least once a week, but I haven't heard from her in a week and a half."

"Look, no offense, but I don't know you. How do I know you aren't the one stalking her?"

"So she's being stalked?"

"Fuck."

Tex heard the disgust in Amy's voice. She hadn't meant to confirm anything. "Look. . ." Tex paused and thought about what he could say to try to reassure Melody's friend. "I know she's scared. She admitted as much to me. She talked about you when I asked about her friends. She said she misses you. Amy, I need your help. I need you to tell me everything you can about where you think she is. She's obviously in trouble and she needs help. I can help her."

"Give me your name. I'll check you out. If I think you're legit, I'll call you back."

Tex didn't hesitate. "John Keegan. I was medically retired a few years ago from the Navy. Do you need a reference?"

"No. I'll find you if you're telling me the truth. I have my own connections."

Tex put the phone down. Amy had hung up without saying goodbye once again. He didn't care. All that mattered was Melody. Now that he knew he had the right Amy, Tex bent over his computer again. He could find out a lot of information now that he verified where Melody was from.

Thirty minutes later, Tex's phone rang. Impatiently he picked it up and answered the call, figuring it would be Amy. She obviously *did* have some good contacts if she was already calling him back and had checked him out this quickly.

Amy didn't bother saying hello. "My friend, Melody, was the nicest person you could ever meet. She was the type of person who would come over and watch my kids for free, and, in fact, beg me to be able to do it. She babysat my kids all the time and they loved her. She worked hard at what she did and she was good at it. She didn't bad mouth others and was way nicer than she should've been to people."

"Why are you talking about her in the past tense?" It shouldn't have struck Tex as so wrong to hear Amy talking about Melody as if she was no longer alive, but it did.

Amy's voice softened for the first time. "I didn't even realize I was doing it."

"How long has she been gone?" Tex tried to ease up on his take-charge attitude. Amy was obviously hurting too.

"About seven or so months."

"Have you talked to her much since she's been gone?"

"Not really, and it sucks. I miss her. My kids miss her. Her parents miss her. Hell, her *dog* misses her."

"Her dog?" Tex didn't remember Melody ever talking about owning a dog in any of their past conversations.

"Yeah. She asked if I would dogsit one day because she had to run some errands in Pittsburgh. So I took Baby for the day and Melody never came back."

21

"Her dog's name is Baby?" Tex could hear that Amy was getting emotional and he wanted to have her concentrate on something else for a moment before she continued telling him about Melody.

"Yeah. Baby is a fifty pound coonhound. Melody adores that dog. Every time I've spoken with her since she left, which isn't very often, she's asked about her dog. Baby misses her too. It's uncanny. She lays on the floor each night and keeps her eyes on the door. She knows. Even after all these months, Baby knows her mom is missing and is still waiting for her to walk back through the door."

"What happened? Why did Melody go? What's she told you?" Tex knew he sounded gruff, but he couldn't help it. He needed all the information he could get from Amy to help him find Melody. And the thought of Mel's dog pining for her made his stomach clench and hurt him more than if Amy had described how much she herself missed her friend.

"I don't know all the details because Melody won't tell me, but from what I can gather, she'd been receiving weird notes for a while. Not necessarily threatening, but not friendly either. Then they changed. The messages got mean. Melody didn't tell me exactly what they said, but I think they started threatening her parents and even Baby. She told me once that if it was just her, she never would've left. And I believe that with all my heart."

"Because if it was just her, she wouldn't care, but threaten someone or something she loves, and all bets are off." Tex could see Melody being that way. Again, he'd only been acquainted with her for a short while, but with the way she supported him and stood up for him when she didn't really even know him, Tex knew she'd be horrified by the thought of someone getting hurt because of her.

"Yeah." Amy's voice was low. "You *do* know her."

"Yeah. I know her."

"I'm worried, Tex. I haven't talked to her in about three months, and the last time I spoke with her she didn't sound good."

"In what way?"

"Usually she tries to be happy and cheerful when she talks to me, but last time she didn't try to hide her feelings. She was scared and depressed. She told me over and over how much she loved me and the kids and told me to give Baby extra pets for her." Amy took a deep breath. "When she said good-bye, it sounded different than any other time."

"It sounded final."

"Exactly. I tried to keep her on the phone, but she said she had to go and she hung up."

"I'm going to find her, Amy."

"She's going to be scared when you do. Someone's after her. If you're telling the truth and she doesn't know what you look like, she's gonna run."

"She won't run when she sees me."

"You sound sure of yourself."

"I am." Tex didn't elaborate.

"Please bring her home."

"I will. Can I ask a favor?" Tex knew what he was going to ask was highly unusual and Amy would most likely need some convincing, but after speaking with her he knew it was the right move and something he had to do.

After Amy agreed to his favor, with a few conditions, Tex hung up. Amy had given him a lot of great information, including Melody's last name, Grace, and Tex knew it was only a matter of time before he found her. And when he did, he'd make sure she was safe and could go home again.

CHAPTER 2

*T*ex smiled over at the coonhound sitting next to him in his truck. Baby was sitting on her haunches, almost like a human would, with her nose in the air sniffing the breeze coming in through the open window. Tex wasn't a dog expert, but for some reason he *needed* to pick up Baby and bring her with him on his quest to find Melody.

He had a connection with Melody, and having her beloved dog next to him made Tex feel closer to her. Besides, Baby was the cutest thing he'd ever seen, it wasn't as if it was a hardship to have her along for the ride. She had legs that seemed too long for her frame. Her paws were big, but she was lean. She was tan and white, with most of her belly being white and the majority of her back and head being tan. Baby's ears hung low, not quite as long as a basset hound or bloodhound's might, but they made her face look perpetually sad. But it was her eyes that had solidified Tex's decision to take her with him. They were a unique shade of brown, if Tex had to describe it, he'd say they were the color of amber. Every time she looked at him it was as if she saw right through him to all his fears and insecurities and could somehow make them all disappear.

Luckily, Baby had taken to him right away. She'd walked up to him as if she'd known him her entire life and had sat down right on his foot. Tex ruffled her ears and Baby looked up at him with the most trusting look Tex had ever seen. It was as if the dog knew Tex was there to take her to Melody.

On the phone, Amy had agreed to let him take Melody's dog, but it had taken some convincing once he'd arrived at her home. Tex had told Amy he'd drive up to Bethel Park, Pennsylvania and collect Baby. After he'd arrived, Tex spent an uncomfortable two hours with Amy and her family. They'd asked a million questions, and given him a thousand directions on what Baby liked and how to care for her.

When all was said and done, Amy had given Tex a hug and simply whispered in his ear before he left, "I'm only letting you take Baby because I know you're gonna find Melody. Bring my friend home, Tex. Please."

So here he was. Tex had packed two laptops, a large duffle bag and headed north to Pennsylvania. Now he had a large bag of premium dog food, an assortment of dog toys and snacks, and a dog to add to his belongings.

Tex was headed to California. It was a long drive from one side of the country to the other, but he was used to small amounts of sleep. He didn't plan on making very many stops, counting on arriving in California in about three days. He wanted to be there immediately, knowing every day that passed with no communication with Melody meant one more day she could be in trouble. Making the stop in Pennsylvania meant Tex lost a day, but he didn't want to leave Baby behind.

His sixth sense was screaming at him to take the dog with him, and he never ignored that feeling. It had saved him and his SEAL teammates more than once. Tex had no idea why it was important, other than the fact he knew Melody loved her dog.

His plan was to take Interstate 70 across the United States until St. Louis, then cut down to Interstate 40 to Barstow, California, then finally head south on Interstate 15 into the Los Angeles area.

Tex was more certain he was on the right track in finding where Melody was hiding after his trip to Pennsylvania. Putting together all the things he'd gleaned from his conversations with Melody herself and from talking with Amy, he believed she was hiding on the west coast.

He'd done a lot of research online before heading to Pennsylvania and Amy's house. He'd tracked Mel's movements when she left home. She went south first and then west to California. Most of the things he'd done to get that far weren't legal, but Tex was used to getting what he wanted, and covering his tracks while he was doing it.

Los Angeles was a huge city, and it was a long shot that Tex would find her quickly, but he was going to start with the Anaheim area. Melody had asked about his favorite Disney character, it had been an odd thing to ask out of the blue. Tex had asked Amy if Melody had a "thing" for Disney and she'd said no. So Tex could only conclude that Melody asking, had to have something to do with what she was seeing on a daily basis.

Amy had also told Tex that Melody was a Closed Caption reporter. It fit. She could work on the road from anywhere that had an Internet connection. There weren't that many CC companies in the country and Tex knew he could further track her that way. While it'd be more difficult because Melody was obviously using public Wi-Fi to connect, Tex could still narrow down the area where she was by backtracking the connection.

Tex was also happy to be headed to the Los Angeles area because he'd get a chance to catch up with his friends and to meet all their women. He felt as if he already knew them, and he couldn't wait to meet them face-to-face. While he wanted to rush and find Melody, he also knew he'd have to take at least one night's break to take care of his leg. Tex figured he'd drop down to Riverton and visit with Wolf and the rest of the team before heading back up to LA to find Melody.

He'd called the night before and told Wolf he was on his way west. Tex smiled remembering the shriek of joy that had come out of Caroline when Wolf had told her he was on his way to California.

Tex remembered Melody commenting on how she thought his friends were taking advantage of him. He knew that wasn't the case, but it felt good to have Melody looking out for him. Wolf had told him everyone had been planning on flying out to Virginia in a few months to visit. When Tex had asked who "everyone" was, he'd been shocked to hear it was *all* of them. Wolf, Caroline, Abe, Alabama, Cookie, Fiona, Mozart, Summer, Dude, Cheyenne, Benny, and Jessyka were all going to take a week off and come out to Virginia to see him. Tex almost couldn't believe it. It was ridiculous for all of them to fly to him, when he could more easily go out to California to see all of them.

Wolf had just laughed and said, "Try telling our women that."

Tex loved his friends' women. They were tough as hell, but more importantly, they made his friends happy. Tex felt proud he had a hand in keeping them safe, and he'd continue to do it as long as they'd let him. He knew he came off as somewhat of a hard-ass on the phone when he'd had the pleasure of speaking with his friends' women, but he wasn't sure what to expect when he met them in person. While he was still a SEAL and knew how to kill someone with his bare hands, losing part of his leg had changed him fundamentally. Over the phone or on the computer, he could be the man he used to be, but in person, he couldn't help but wonder if people thought he was weak. And that uncertainty had seeped into his psyche.

Even with Tex's excitement in being able to see his friends again, he had mixed feelings about this trip west. There was no doubt he'd have a great time with the group, but his main goal was to find Melody and figure out what was going on with her.

Baby woofed in the seat next to Tex.

"Need to stretch your legs, Baby?"

Baby just looked at him, head cocked.

"Yeah, okay, let me find a place to stop. I could use a break too."

Tex pulled over at the next rest area along the Interstate and clipped a leash onto Baby's collar. There was no way he wanted to risk losing Melody's dog. Tex knew hounds were prone to follow their nose instead of commands and because they were in the middle of Indiana surrounded by trees, Tex didn't want Baby to get the scent of a rabbit and take off.

Baby jumped out of the truck after Tex and happily trotted after him as they walked around the grassy area. Baby did her business and didn't protest when Tex steered her back to the truck. She jumped into the cab as if she'd done it a million times before. Tex unclipped the leash and left her in the truck with the windows cracked so he could go inside.

When he came back outside five minutes later, Baby was sitting in the passenger's side of the truck as if she was waiting for him.

"Ready to go find Melody?" Tex felt silly talking to a dog, but as if she could understand him, Baby woofed once and put her paw on his arm. Tex scratched behind Baby's ear and started the truck. They had a long way to go.

* * *

TEX PULLED into Wolf's driveway and shut off the engine. He was tired. His leg hurt, well it always hurt, but sitting in the truck for three days straight hadn't done it any good. As much as it'd pained him, Tex had bypassed Los Angeles to head down to San Diego to see his friends and their women. It wasn't much of a detour, and even though Tex wanted to see Wolf and the others, it was tough to put off his search for Melody for even one day, even though that had been his plan all along.

Tex ran his hand over Baby's head, which was resting on his thigh. Tex never had a dog growing up, but over the last three days he'd fallen in love with Baby. She was an easy dog to love. Mild-mannered, non-demanding, and she minded surprisingly well for a hound.

"We made it, Baby. Ready to meet my friends?" As had become his habit, Tex told Baby everything they were going to do before they did it. Tex opened his door and Baby was immediately ready to go. She sat in the driver's seat until Tex clipped the leash onto her collar and then happily jumped down next to him.

Tex limped up to the front door, realizing suddenly that he probably should've stayed in a hotel for one more night rather than bothering his friends at this hour, but it was too late now. The door flung open and Caroline was running toward him.

Tex stopped and braced himself, ready to catch the woman hurdling herself at him, but Caroline didn't bowl him over. Baby shifted until she was standing in front of him and growled, a low menacing sound that Tex had never heard out of the dog in the time he'd been around her. Caroline stopped suddenly and Tex looked down in bewilderment. Baby had never shown one ounce of aggression toward anyone in the last three days. She'd sat next to him for thousands of miles and hadn't growled or barked the entire trip. They'd seen countless of strangers along the way and Baby had never cared. There was even one rest stop that was crowded with rough and mean looking bikers, and Baby hadn't even spared them a second glance. But she certainly cared now.

"Holy cow!" Caroline said breathlessly, then Wolf was there. He curled one arm around Caroline's waist and pulled her behind him, and away from the growling dog.

"Baby! No!" Tex commanded gruffly.

The coonhound didn't completely back off, but she did sit down on top of Tex's foot. He could tell she wasn't relaxed. Every muscle in her body was ready to attack, to protect.

"Nice dog you got there, Tex," Wolf said sarcastically.

"Sorry about this. She's been perfectly fine the entire trip."

"I ran up at you, Tex. She's protecting you. You've trained her well," Caroline said humor lacing her voice.

"She's not my dog and I didn't train her. I just met her three days ago." Tex couldn't understand why Baby was acting like she was, but he couldn't help but be flattered. Apparently Baby had adopted him as a de facto master. Her loyalty to him felt good.

"Well, it looks like the time you spent with her on the road cemented your relationship in her mind. She's certainly claimed you, and I agree with Ice. She's protecting you," Wolf noted dryly.

Tex leaned over at the waist, knowing if he crouched down he'd never be able to get up again with his bum leg. He took hold of Baby's scruff with one hand and put the other under her chin and forced her head up so she was looking at him. "It's okay, Baby. These are my friends. They'll be Melody's friends too once we find her. You can't bite them. Hell, you probably shouldn't even growl at them."

Tex ran his hand over the dog's head as he let go of her. Baby licked his hand once, and her tail started wagging again.

"Do you think I can give you a hug now or is she gonna go for my jugular?" Caroline joked.

"Come here, woman," Tex told her in response and reached out and pulled Caroline to him.

When Baby didn't growl or in any other way show aggression, Caroline relaxed in his arms.

"It's so fucking good to see you, Ice. It's been way too long. You keeping Wolf in line?"

"Hell, Tex. You know that's an impossible task," Caroline joked back. "Come on, let's go inside and get you settled. I'm sure you're tired and want to crash for a few hours. We've got the basement all ready for you."

Tex pulled back and smiled at Caroline. She was always wanting to take care of people. He snapped his fingers at Baby as he started walking. Even though he had the leash in his hand, he was trying to teach her to respond to his nonverbal commands. So far, Baby was doing a hell of a good job at it too. The dog was smart. Very smart.

As they walked, Wolf clasped Tex on the shoulder. "Good to see you, man. Drive out okay?"

"Yeah, long, but good."

The two men looked at each other and Wolf recognized Tex's sign of "later." Tex didn't want to worry Caroline about how he was really feeling or about Melody either. Tex had told Wolf a little bit about what he was doing in California, but not the entire story.

They entered the small house and Baby trotted alongside Tex as if she'd known him her entire life. He unclipped the leash as soon as the front door closed behind them. Baby continued to stick close to Tex, not exploring the house or otherwise even looking like she was curious about where they were. She had eyes only for Tex.

After sitting at the kitchen table for about thirty minutes, and some general conversation, Caroline called it a night. She kissed Tex on the forehead and lovingly ran her hand over her husband's head before she left the room. Baby lifted her head and watched Caroline leave the room, but she didn't otherwise move from her spot at Tex's feet.

The men watched as Caroline disappeared from view, and they waited another couple of minutes. Finally Wolf spoke.

"Talk to me. What's going on? I know you. You wouldn't drive across the country on a whim. What's this girl to you?"

"Wolf, I've never met her, but she's in trouble."

"Don't get me wrong. I hate to see women hurting or in trouble myself, but it sounds like you're in deep with this woman you don't even know. It's odd."

"I said I've never met her," Tex repeated, "not that I don't know her. I've been talking to this woman for the last six months. She's in trouble and I have to help her."

"Okay, tell me what the team can do."

Tex smiled. He missed being a part of the teams. He remembered the instant loyalty and how no one ever questioned another when it was obvious they knew something was off or that it felt right.

"Honestly? I don't know. I'm operating on a hunch at this point. I don't even know if Melody is even *in* Anaheim."

"You know it's only a short trip up there if you need us. I'll let the Commander know that we might need to bug out for a few days if you need us."

"Thanks, Wolf, I appreciate it."

"Speaking of the Commander, he wasn't thrilled you sicced Julie Lytle on him."

Tex grinned. "Hey, I heard she wanted to talk to Cookie. I figured it'd be good for both of them if she was able to move on from what happened in Mexico."

"You know the Commander and her are together now don't you?" Wolf asked.

Tex simply raised his eyebrows at Wolf.

"Of course you do. Jesus, Tex. I shouldn't be surprised at who you know and how you have an uncanny ability to know what people need before they know they need it, but I still always am."

"Seriously," Tex commented, "I didn't know they'd end up together, but if anyone needed some luck in their life, it was Julie. And if Hurt is happy, more power to him. And I fully intend to call in my marker from the Commander if Melody needs it."

"Of course. I know he won't hesitate to do whatever it is to help you out. You know every one of us on the team owes you. Big." Knowing if he continued along that vein, Tex wouldn't appreciate it, Wolf changed the subject. "You taking the dog with you? You can leave her here if you want to."

"Thanks, but I'll keep her with me."

Baby looked up as if she could tell the men were talking about her and whined. Tex put his hand down and placed it on Baby's head.

"Okay, go on and get some sleep then. Just to give you a head's up, Caroline's invited the entire clan over for breakfast tomorrow. I know you're anxious to get on the road, but I'd appreciate it if you stuck around for a bit. They all want to meet you face-to-face."

Tex sighed in mock aggravation. Truth of the matter was, he was looking forward to meeting all the women as well. "I guess I can spare a few hours."

Wolf laughed as he stood up. "See you in the morning then. I think Ice bought enough food for you to live in the basement for months, but if there's something you need that's not down there, help yourself up here. I'll go out and get your bag."

"Appreciate it." And Tex did. His leg hurt and he needed to get off it for a while. "There's a bag of dog food out there too. Baby'll need it in the morning."

Wolf lifted a hand as he went out the door, not stopping, but acknowledging Tex's words.

"Need to go out once more, Baby?" Tex asked the dog at his feet. When Baby didn't move, but instead lay down with a sigh, Tex took that as a negative on the trip outside. "Then let's go catch some sleep. It's gonna be insane around here in the morning. Those women are crazy." His words were mocking, but the tone was affectionate.

Tex painfully pushed up from the chair at the table and made his way to the basement door. As he started down the stairs, Baby was right by his side. Tex stumbled once, but because Baby was there, pushing all her weight into his good leg, she righted his balance and he didn't fall. "Thanks, girl."

After Wolf brought his bag down the stairs, and Tex had visited the bathroom, he removed his prosthetic and massaged his stump with the lotion he always carried. It hurt more than usual because of the time spent immobile on the trip cross country.

Baby jumped up into the bed next to him. She turned in what seemed like ten circles before she finally deemed her "nest" complete. She sighed once and put her head on Tex's leg. He leaned down and patted her on the head. "Good girl."

Hoping against hope, Tex leaned over and grabbed his laptop off the bedside table where he'd placed it before taking off his prosthetic. He flipped it open and turned it on, waiting for Wolf's Wi-Fi to connect.

Tex logged into the chat room he and Melody had been using and waited, hoping she'd logged back on. He'd been checking every night, just in case. After a few minutes he sighed, disappointed. She hadn't . . . at least she hadn't joined back up with the same username she'd used in the past. If she was on with a different name, Tex had no idea what it was and no one sent him a private message either. Tex turned off the laptop and put it back on the table. He lay back on the bed and stared at the ceiling.

He had no idea where Melody was or what she was going through, but he hoped wherever it was, she was safe. She needed to stay that way until Tex could get to her. There was no doubt in his mind that he *would* get to her. He had to. There was no other option.

CHAPTER 3

*T*ex smiled as he drove away from Wolf's house. The last three
hours had been crazy, but he wouldn't have missed it for the
world. He hadn't forgotten Melody or why he was in California, but
meeting the women had been better than he could have imagined.

As soon as he stepped foot in the kitchen he had to get through the
women crying all over him. Fiona had grabbed onto him first and simply
sobbed. Tex felt as if he had the most connection with her. He'd talked to
her for three days in a row, every four hours, while Cookie and the team
had done their best to get back into the country from a mission. Even
though Fiona had been hallucinating, she remembered every word of
every conversation they'd had.

She whispered in his ear as Tex held her, "Thank you for holding on to
me when Hunter wasn't here to do it."

Tex had given her a big squeeze and whispered back, "Anytime you
need me, I'm here."

The other women had all taken their turn and hugged him tightly. Tex
had a hand in their men being able to find them all and rescue them from
horrible situations. Jessyka had even whispered to him before letting him
pull away, "Thank you for convincing the guys they needed those tracker
thingies too."

After Jess had been lured away by an ex who'd kidnapped Benny, she'd
railed at the SEALs for not protecting themselves, and she'd been right.

The only reason she'd been taken by her ex was because she'd been protecting Benny. While the SEALs had Tex make tracking devices for their women, they hadn't bothered with the same for themselves.

The men had just shook their heads at the women's emotional reactions to meeting Tex. Breakfast had been full of laughter and reminiscing of the good times in their lives. Baby had been slipped way too many pieces of bacon and sausage, but never left Tex's side for more than a moment.

Finally, Tex knew it was time to go. As much as he wanted to soak in the happiness that oozed from every pore of his friends' bodies, he couldn't get Melody out of his mind. She was out there . . . somewhere. She had no one. No friends like this to have her back. No military buddies to help her out. She was scared, she'd said it herself. And Tex hated that.

So as much as he loved being around Caroline and the other women, he had to go. Baby stood up as soon as he had and pranced to the door. It looked like she was just as ready to go as he was.

Now Tex's mind was going a mile a minute. He didn't really have a plan, except to head to Anaheim and see what he could find. He'd check the hotels and see if Melody had checked in. Of course that would assume she used her real name, Melody Grace, but that was unlikely. He had a photo of her Amy had given him that he could show hotel clerks, but again, they saw so many tourists that they'd probably not be able to recognize Melody from a photo. Tex would probably have to keep relying on his computer skills to narrow down her location, but he felt better knowing he was at least hopefully in the same city as she was.

After a couple of hours of driving through the city traffic, Tex pulled into a hotel only blocks from the large amusement park. Everywhere he looked he was reminded where he was. There were Disney characters everywhere. It verified his belief that when Melody had asked him about his favorite character, it was because it was an easy topic of conversation.

Tex checked in, making sure to get a room on the bottom floor so it'd be easier to walk Baby. He brought his bag in, as well as Baby's food and toys. He didn't bother with the dog bed, knowing Baby would just jump up on the mattress next to him to sleep. Tex put a bowl of water on the floor and smiled as Baby helped herself.

He sat at the table in the corner of the room by the window and plugged in his laptop. Tex was going to start with the closed caption companies and see what he could narrow down.

After thirty minutes of research and searching, he sat back in the chair. He was close. Very close. He felt it in his bones. It was easy enough to find the company Melody worked for. Just that day Melody had translated a graduation back in Indiana. Apparently the way it worked was whoever hired the service would hook up via Skype. Melody would watch the event, in this case, a graduation, and she would type out whatever was being said. Then whomever was at the graduation who needed the service would use an app and watch her typed words scroll across their smartphone screen as they sat in the audience.

It really was amazing, and it was something Tex had never really thought about before. No wonder Mel could type so fast when they were talking. He'd always wondered, but never thought to ask.

Since Melody had been online that day translating the graduation ceremony back in Indiana, Tex could trace the Wi-Fi signal back to one of two places in Anaheim. Goosebumps broke out over his skin. He was close. He absently rubbed his left thigh, trying to rub out the phantom pain that was always present. With this bit of news, it looked like a good time to head out for a cup of coffee. If Melody felt safe enough to use the internet once today, he hoped she would again.

* * *

MELODY SAT against the wall of her hotel room, behind the bed, with her knees drawn up in front of her. She held her cell phone clenched in one hand and had her head resting on her knees. It was time to move on, but she'd been in California for so long now that she really didn't want to go. If Melody was honest with herself, all she wanted to do was go home.

But whoever was stalking her had found her again, and was even more relentless than before. Melody thought she was being smart by switching hotel rooms every week and using a different hot-spot for her Internet connection, but whoever was stalking her was apparently smarter than she'd given him credit for. Melody had no idea how he was finding her, but she was tired of it all. She missed Amy. She missed Baby. She missed her parents. She missed Pennsylvania.

Melody stared at the letter that sat in the middle of the floor where she'd dropped it after reading it. The front desk clerk had given it to her as she came in that day, and Melody knew she really wouldn't like what was in it. Once she'd closed the door to the hotel room, Melody had reluctantly opened the note. She'd never forget the words.

No matter where you go, I'll find you. We're the same, you and I, why can't you see that?

Melody had no idea what it meant. This note was just as creepy as all the others. But there was no postmark on it. Whoever had sent it to her, had walked into the hotel and handed it to the clerk. That meant he was here. That also meant Melody had to go. Now.

Melody put her head back down on her knees. She was out of ideas. Well, she had one more idea, but she had to gather up the courage to follow up on it. She squeezed the phone in her hand harder. She'd bought a bunch of disposable phones to use to call her family and Amy. She'd seen enough shows on television to know they were untraceable. It obviously didn't matter now though. He'd found her anyway.

Melody picked up her head once again, held the phone up and looked at it. She'd memorized the phone number Tex had given her. She never had any intentions of calling him, but she'd memorized it anyway.

She was so tempted. Melody thought back to their conversations. Tex was a good guy. He oozed good guy through every pore in his body. He was an honest-to-God-hero and Melody needed a hero, but she didn't want to drag him down, and she knew she would. He'd get so embroiled in her situation and he'd want to "fix" it, but Melody had no idea how he could.

But she was tired and scared. She had money, thanks to her closed caption jobs and with Amy's help, to move on, but to where? To another hotel in another city where the same pattern would play out? She was as far away from Pennsylvania as she could be, but somehow whoever was stalking her had still found out where she was.

Melody absently opened the text app on the phone and slowly, number by number, pushed in the number she'd memorized. Then, without thinking, she typed out the first thing she thought of.

Putting the phone down on the floor without hitting send, Melody put her head on her knees again. Her dyed brown hair fell in waves around her head and spilled down her legs. She mentally argued with herself. *What would it hurt to send the text? It's not like Tex knows where I am. I miss him. I miss talking to him. He's kept me sane this last year. He made me feel normal.*

But what if he's mad I deleted my account on the chat site? What if he doesn't answer back? But what if he does? I need to feel connected to someone for just a little bit. I need to feel not so alone. He's a SEAL. He can help me.

Without thinking more about it, Melody picked up the phone and hit send. The two words she'd written seemed garish on the small screen, but summed up all her riotous emotions so well. Would Tex respond? Would he care? Melody put her head back on her knees and closed her eyes, afraid to hope, afraid to move, afraid to stay.

* * *

TEX SAT at the table in the little café across from the bookstore watching and waiting. Baby lay at his feet, her eyes seemingly also focused on the store across the street. It was as if she somehow knew Melody was nearby.

Tex was nervous, and he never got nervous. He was always known as the stoic one. The one who never broke a sweat before or during a mission. But Tex wasn't stoic now. He knew he was cutting it close. Melody deleting her account, the silence, the working so many jobs in a short period of time. She was getting ready to run and he needed to catch up with her before she did. He hoped like hell she'd be working another job today. She'd done an excellent job of keeping her exact whereabouts hidden, but Tex knew if he could find her, so could a stalker.

The thought of somebody terrorizing someone as sweet as Melody cut through Tex like a knife. There weren't a lot of truly "nice" people in this world, and from what he knew of Melody, she was one of them. Her family and friends couldn't think of one bad thing to say about her. Hell, even her dog was pining for her. It pissed him off that someone would dare to terrorize somebody as sweet as Melody.

If he was honest with himself, Tex was a little freaked about how much he cared about this woman. A woman he'd never actually met. It was frankly a little crazy. Melody had told him she was twenty-seven, and in all honesty, that was probably younger than what he was really looking for in a woman. He was thirty-five, a very ancient thirty-five, but it wasn't like he was actually looking to start something with her . . . or was he?

Tex leaned forward and pulled out his wallet and took out the picture Amy had given him. It was of Amy and Melody. They had their arms around each other and were smiling at the camera. The women were wearing shorts and T-shirts and Amy had told him it was taken at a barbeque she had at her house not too long before Melody disappeared.

Tex ran his fingers over Melody's face. He hadn't really thought much about what Mel would actually look like. He'd liked her for her wit and her sarcasm. Tex enjoyed talking to her and knew no matter what she looked like, he would still enjoy talking to her. But as it turned out, Melody was cute. Her hair was blond, shoulder length, and curly. She was neither short nor tall. Tex didn't think she'd ever be slender like a model; Melody was what Tex thought of as "luscious." Shaking his head, Tex put the picture back into his wallet for safe keeping.

He was nervous and confused. No woman had ever made him feel what Melody did. She soothed him, supported him, and wasn't afraid to call him on his bullshit. Tex had opened up more to her than anyone. She knew *him*, and that was scary as hell. She knew how he really felt about losing his leg. How he felt about the prosthetic. About being a SEAL. About his friends. She knew it all. A part of Tex was also hurt that Melody had cut him off so completely. They'd shared so much, and the fact that she could cut him out of her life so easily, was a blow.

Baby's head came up at Tex's feet as his phone vibrated and pinged with an incoming text message. The dog looked at him with her ears perked forward. Tex leaned down and smoothed his hand over her head. "It's probably Caroline or one of the girls wanting to make sure I arrived all right," he reassured the dog.

I'm scared

That's all the text said. Just those two words. Tex didn't recognize the number, but he immediately knew who it was. He sat up straight in his chair and quickly typed out a response. His heart was suddenly beating as quickly as if he'd just run a five mile race.

I know you are, Mel. Where are you?

Tex waited with bated breath for her response. He hoped like hell she'd text him back. He didn't know where her head was at, but if Melody admitted she was scared after almost two weeks of not talking to him at all, Tex knew it wasn't good. She was obviously skittish and Tex knew she could bolt at any time.

Nowhere

Cut the crap. Tell me where you are

Tex knew he had to get through to her. She was depressed and scared, not a good combination.

CA

WHERE exactly?

Anaheim

Keep going

What does it matter?

It matters to me. What hotel? What room?

What, are u going to come and get me?

Hotel? Room?

Holiday Inn Express. 305

Stay there. Don't move. Don't open the door to anyone. It's going to be OK

Tex didn't wait for her response. He knifed up out of the chair and grabbed Baby's leash. "Ready to go see mama, girl?" Baby whined in response, as if she knew exactly what was going on and where they were going.

Tex thanked God Melody had reached out to him. Tex headed to the garage where he'd parked his truck. He was going to get his girl. She wasn't alone anymore.

CHAPTER 4

$\mathcal{M}$elody put the phone down and rested her head on her knees once again and closed her eyes. Stay put. She could do that. She could *so* do that. She didn't have the strength to go anywhere anyway. She was done. She had no idea what Tex had planned, but somehow she felt better knowing someone, other than her stalker, knew where she was.

She thought back to an online conversation she'd had with Tex not too long ago. She'd finally gotten up the courage to ask if he wanted to exchange pictures. She'd never forget his words. *I don't need a picture to know you're beautiful.*

Melody had laughed out loud then asked him what he meant, that she could weigh eight hundred pounds and be a shut-in for all he knew. He'd told her that her friendship and unconditional support meant everything to him and that he knew she had a beautiful soul. His words made her smile for days afterwards.

But now Melody wished she knew what Tex looked like. She'd asked once and all he'd say was that he was a "washed up retired Navy guy who was missing half a leg." Melody didn't care if he was scarred, short, balding, or fat from eating too many doughnuts every day. He was her lifeline in this crazy new world she lived in. Melody knew he thought the loss of his leg was a deterrent for people getting close to him, but in her eyes, it made him who he was. And he was supportive, sensitive, and caring. Those things trumped physical looks in Melody's eyes any day.

But she couldn't help but picture Tex in her head as tall, dark, and handsome. He'd be taller than her, which wasn't hard since she was only five seven. He'd be big enough to envelop her in his arms and let her feel surrounded by his heat. She hadn't felt safe in so long, that alone would be heaven. He'd be muscular and strong, with bulging muscles, but not too bulky. His hair would be short, but still a bit too long to be military short, and his broad shoulders would be wide enough to . . . Melody stopped her thoughts with a jerk.

Whatever. All that stuff was crap. She didn't care if he didn't look like a man on the cover of a romance novel. She just needed *him*. His words and his strength. Melody had looked after herself for a long time now, and had done a pretty damn good job of it too. But it'd be nice to have some help.

Melody remembered that Tex's SEAL friends lived in California. Maybe he'd call them and they would offer to help. That had to be it. She assumed Tex would text her back to let her know what he had planned. He'd said for her not to open her door. Melody laughed a bitter little laugh. Tex didn't have to tell her. She wasn't opening the door for anyone. She didn't feel safe sitting in the floor curled into a little ball, but it was better than wandering outside or opening the door for someone who may or may not be a stalker bent on hurting her. She knew that for a fact.

Melody closed her eyes and concentrated on breathing. Nothing else, just breathing in and out. She could forget . . . for just a moment . . . that someone wanted her dead and she was alone in the world.

* * *

TEX IGNORED the dirty look he received from the front desk clerk as he walked as quickly as possible through the lobby to the elevator. He preferred the stairs, but his leg was still sore and he didn't want to push it any more than he already had. Tex knew he had to give it a rest soon, but until he made sure Melody was safe, he wasn't going to take the time.

Baby was silent at his side. Tex could tell she was tense, but she hadn't made a noise. Thank God the hotel was pet friendly, even if the clerk wasn't. The elevator opened at the third floor and Tex got out and followed the sign and headed down the hall toward room 305.

He paused outside the door and quickly sent Melody a text.

In a moment there will be a knock at your door. It's fine. Look through the peephole first.

Tex took a deep breath and reached down and picked Baby up. He knocked on the door with one hand and held the dog up so that her face was level with the peephole in the door. He could've just texted her and said he was there and to let him in, but wasn't sure she'd believe him. Tex knew of no other way to get Melody to trust him, to open the door, other than to show her Baby, her beloved dog. Of course it was also something a stalker might do, but Tex was hoping Mel would be so surprised and excited to see her dog, that she'd let him in. He'd remind her it wasn't smart after he was inside with her.

He waited, holding his breath, and suddenly the door was open.

The woman standing in front of Tex took his breath away. She seemed tired, and stressed, but other than the change in hair color, she looked just as she did in the photo Amy had given him. Tex had spent some time admiring Melody's photo, but he never would've imagined how cute she was in person.

Melody was about average height for a woman. She came up to about his chin. She had long brown hair that currently looked like it could use a good wash. She was wearing a pair of ragged jeans that probably should've been replaced a few years ago, but they looked well-worn and comfortable. She was wearing a simple T-shirt that showed nothing and everything at the same time. She was curvy. Tex didn't know sizes, he only knew what he liked, and he definitely liked what he was looking at. He hadn't really been able to see her curves in the picture of her standing next to Amy, but he approved.

Melody looked stressed, but healthy. He'd seen way too many women since he'd been in California that thought sexy meant starving yourself. Hell, he saw way too many women on his many missions that were scary underweight and would kill for the chance to eat enough to have the curves Melody had.

Her breasts strained against the shirt she was wearing and her hips flared out from her waist in a way that made Tex want to grab them and hold her against him. He would've stood there admiring her longer, but Baby was struggling to get out of his arms and he didn't want to drop her.

Tex set Baby on the ground and the dog leaped for Melody. Actually leaped. If Tex had any doubt in his mind that this *was* Melody, the dog had just obliterated them.

Mindful of the danger he swore he could actually feel in the air, Tex gently scooted the reunion out of the hallway and into Melody's room. He watched as dog and mistress jubilantly greeted each other after being apart for so long. Melody ended up sitting on the floor with the fifty pound coonhound in her lap frantically whining and licking the tears that coursed down her face.

"Baby! Oh my God, Baby. I can't believe you're here! I missed you so much."

Melody's words were halting and as heartfelt as any Tex had ever heard. He waited patiently, leaning up against the door, for Melody to notice him. It was the first time he'd ever been upstaged by a dog, but he loved every second of it.

Melody hugged her dog and buried her head in her scruff. She hadn't ever expected to see Baby again. The hardest part about leaving Pennsylvania had been leaving her dog. Melody had seen her on an online ad the shelter back home had run. Baby had been emaciated and covered in sores and fleas and ticks. Her sad eyes had sucked Melody in the first time she'd seen them looking at her through her computer screen.

Melody had dropped everything and gone to the shelter that afternoon. The employees told her that the dog had most likely been abused and was scared to death of people. She was set to be euthanized the next day, but the volunteers had wanted to try one more time to get her adopted. Melody had gone into the area where the dog pens were and almost cried when she'd seen Baby for the first time. She'd been huddled against the back wall of her enclosure and shivered uncontrollably. Melody had been allowed to go into the pen with her. It had taken thirty minutes, but Melody had patiently sat on the floor and talked to the dog. She murmured nonsense for every second of those thirty minutes.

Baby had eventually climbed into Melody's lap, all thirty-five underweight pounds of her, and shivered while Melody petted and cooed to her. Melody had taken her home that night and eventually Baby had come out of her shell. Melody knew she'd never be the most social dog, but they loved each other unconditionally.

The stalker had threatened to kill Baby though, which was why Melody left her behind in Pennsylvania. The note had said, *I hate animals. I'll cut off its head and leave it on a stick in your yard if you don't get rid of it.*

Melody believed it. She'd woken up the next morning to find a headless squirrel on her front porch stuck into a flower pot on a skewer. It was a warning Melody took to heart. She'd arranged to take Baby to Amy's house the next day and had left Pennsylvania within the week, after dropping off her beloved dog with her best friend.

Melody looked up through her tears at the man standing inside her hotel room. He hadn't said a word throughout her reunion with Baby. For a second she was scared. Yes, he'd brought her Baby, but it could be the stalker. She was a day late and a dollar short in her thinking, of course. He might have used her dog to gain entry to her room. She was an idiot. Just as Melody started panicking, the man moved.

He leaned over and pulled up the left leg of his jeans, just enough that Melody could see the shiny metal of a prosthetic device.

"Tex," Melody breathed, hardly believing he was here. *Here.* Tex was here. She stood up, awkwardly, not knowing what to say.

"Come here, Mel."

Melody sighed in relief. She took a step toward Tex and suddenly she was in his arms. She wrapped her arms around the man, not exactly a stranger, but not exactly someone she knew, and cried.

She cried in relief for not being alone. She cried because he'd brought her Baby. She cried for being so scared for so long. Melody didn't feel Tex moving her backwards, but somehow she found herself sitting in Tex's lap while he settled into the arm chair in the corner of the room.

"Shhhh, Mel. It's okay. I'm here. You're safe."

Not wanting to think about how awkward this should be, but somehow wasn't, and not wanting to think about anything else either, Melody buried her head in Tex's chest and held on to him even tighter.

Tex tightened his hold on the woman in his lap. His thoughts swung wildly from arousal, to sympathy, to joy that he was finally seeing, and holding the woman he'd slowly gotten to know over the past months. He'd be a liar if he hadn't thought about her in his arms at least once over the last half a year, but the reality was so much better.

Feeling the moment Melody got herself together, Tex waited. As much as he wanted to demand she tell him everything and scold her for not getting in touch with him sooner, he couldn't do it. He'd wait for her to be ready.

Melody took a deep breath. She had to get herself together. She picked her head up and looked around for Baby. She was sitting right at Tex's feet, just looking at the two of them. When she saw Melody looking at her, she leaned forward and put her head on the arm of the chair as her tail wagged rhythmically behind her. Melody reached out and petted the dog. "God, I missed you, Baby."

Baby whined and licked Melody's hand.

"That's enough, girl. Go lie down. I gotta talk to your mama." Tex's voice was affectionate, but stern at the same time.

Melody watched in amazement as her dog did what Tex told her to.

"How'd you get her to do that? I couldn't ever train her to do anything. Stubborn hound."

"Mel, look at me."

Tex's voice was low and rumbly and it made goosebumps rise up and down Melody's arms. He was . . . more than she expected. She'd told herself that she wouldn't care if he wasn't good looking, but lord. Seeing him in the flesh was overwhelming. He wasn't good looking . . . he was *good looking*. Melody couldn't feel an ounce of fat on him. Tex's thighs under her butt were rock hard. The chest she'd been lying against for the last ten minutes was also muscular and Melody would bet every dime she had that he had at least a six pack under his shirt. His dark hair was short at least she thought so, but it was his eyes that really struck her. They were a deep brown, and they looked at her as if she was the most important thing in the world. Tex didn't fidget. He didn't move. Melody knew he was looking right at her, waiting for her to meet his eyes.

She looked up. Yup. Those piercing eyes were focused on her.

"My name is John Keegan, but everyone calls me Tex. I'm thirty-five years old. I'm medically retired from the Navy. I was a Navy SEAL. My leg was injured in my last mission and they had to take half of it off. I have a prosthetic now. My stump isn't pretty. I've never had a pet, never really thought about it, but having spent the last four days or so with Baby, I'm a convert. I've been out of my mind with worry for you, Mel. I met Amy and her family. I drove three days straight across the country to get to you. I swear to you, I might not be whole anymore, but I'm your friend. I'm here to help you. We'll figure this out so you can get back to your life so you don't have to run or be scared anymore."

Melody knew her lip was quivering. She tried to hold her tears back. She'd cried way too much in the last day or so.

She followed his example, her voice low. "My name is Melody Grace. I'm twenty-seven. I eat too much crap and need to lose too many pounds to count. I'm a closed caption reporter, and I'm good at it. I can type one hundred words a minute with only a three percent error rate. In my spare time, when I was lonely, I used to surf the Internet for someone to talk to. I met someone a few months ago that I really liked." Melody looked down and felt Tex's hand at her chin, nudging it upward.

"Go on, Mel," Tex whispered.

"I have a dog, a stubborn dog that I love with all my heart. And I'm scared. I could use some help."

Tex leaned forward and Melody's heart rate increased. He kissed her on the forehead and brought his other hand up from her back to her face. He framed her face and kept his eyes locked on hers.

"You're not alone anymore, Mel. You reached out for me all those months ago, and I won't let you pull back. We'll figure this out and make you safe. Make Baby safe. Just don't cut me off like that again. Please. You have no idea what it did to me when I saw you'd deleted your account."

"I won't." The words were said with barely any audible tone to them, but Tex heard them anyway.

"How long has it been since you've gotten any sleep?"

"I don't know. What day is it?"

Tex swore. "Okay. I'll deal with that in a second. What happened today?"

"What do you mean?"

"What happened today to make you break your silence and text me? I know it had to be something. You haven't contacted me once via text . . . until today. What happened?"

Melody fidgeted. God, Tex was way too smart. She gestured toward the letter lying in the middle of the floor behind them. "He found me and hand delivered a note."

"Hand delivered?"

"Yeah, there wasn't a post mark and the front desk clerk gave it to me."

Tex's mind immediately kicked into gear. If the stalker knew where she was, they had to move quickly. Without tensing, he moved his hand and put it on the back of her neck and stroked her nape with his thumb. He didn't want to startle her, but he figured Melody was smart enough to know she wasn't in a good situation and needed to get out of there. Hell, she'd gotten in touch with him, she definitely knew she wasn't safe.

"Mel, you know I'm here to help you, right?" Tex waited for her to nod then continued. "You've done a hell of a job staying ahead of whoever this is." At her look of disbelief, Tex continued, "Seriously. You've done everything right. I have more resources available to me than the average person. That's why I was able to find you so quickly. But it's more than obvious that whoever this is isn't going to stop. I need to know if you'll let me help you. If you'll let me make some decisions for you. I need to make a plan, but I can't if I know you're going to fight me on every decision I make."

Melody looked at the man in front of her. Could she give up control to him? She wasn't the type of woman to let others do things for her. She didn't like to take handouts. Hell, she didn't even want to take out student loans when she went to college and had paid them back as soon as she could after she graduated. Could she let this man, this virtual stranger, take over?

"I . . ." She paused, then tried again. "I want to. I'm tired of running, of hiding. But I'm not that good at letting others help me."

"I know, Mel. Believe me, I know this. That's why I asked. But I'm begging you to trust me. Let me figure out who's doing this. Let me help you get back to your life."

When Tex put it that way, how could she refuse? Melody nodded wordlessly.

"Thank you. I swear to you, you won't regret it. Now, we need to pack you up and get out of here. We'll head down to Riverton and spend a few days with Wolf. Then we'll head back to Pennsylvania."

"No!"

Tex just quirked an eyebrow at her.

"It's just . . . go back to Pennsylvania? That's where it started. My friends . . . my family..."

"I know, Mel, but this needs to end. We need to be in a place where it *can* end. If that's where your stalker is from, it'll be easier to draw him out and finish it."

Melody nodded. "It makes sense, but—"

"I'll be there with you, Mel. I'm not going anywhere."

"But—"

"No buts."

"Would you let me finish?" Melody sighed in exasperation, smiling to let Tex know she wasn't really pissed, but that she was also serious.

"Sorry. I have a tendency to take over. Make sure you tell me when I'm doing it too often."

"I will. What I was *going* to say is that you must have a life. You can't just come back to Pennsylvania and spend all your time there. What if nothing happens? What if he waits until you're gone again?"

"You done?" Tex asked, completely serious. "Get it all out now. Then I'll respond."

"You're annoying. How did I not know you're this annoying while we were chatting all those months?"

Tex smiled at Melody this time and tightened the hold on the back of her neck for a moment before resuming his slow sweep of his thumb against the sensitive skin. "Because I'm charming and charismatic?"

Melody just shook her head. She loved the feel of his hand on her neck, ignoring the way her nipples peaked at the sensual feel of his thumb rubbing against her hairline, she got herself together and continued, getting it all out as he requested.

"What if he hurts Baby, or Amy, or someone else I care about? What if you get tired of being there and start to resent me? What if *you* get hurt? What if it never ends? I don't think I can live like this for the rest of my life."

Tex waited a beat after Melody had finished talking, making sure she was really done. His heart ached for her. He hadn't really understood how stalking could affect people, but seeing Mel now, scared and hurting, he was starting to get it.

"Mel, I'm retired. That means I get paid every month to do nothing if I want to. I have the means and the time to come home with you for as long as it takes. But it's not going to take forever. We need to move this back to where it started so it can end. Whoever this is won't like that you came home. Won't like that you came back home with *me*. Your friends will be safe, because you'll tell them everything. They'll be vigilant. I have connections. We'll set up security for anyone you want. We won't let Baby out of our sight."

"But what are you going to do?"

Tex sighed. He didn't like what he thought it would take. "We need to egg him on, Mel. We can't fight an invisible enemy. He needs to make a mistake."

"You want to make me bait." Melody watched as Tex grimaced.

"Want to? Fuck no. What I *want* is for you to be safe. I want you to be able to live where you want without having to worry about some asshole hurting you, your dog, or even your friends. I want to keep you as far away from whoever is doing this as possible. If I could, I'd lock you away so he couldn't ever find you. But that obviously hasn't worked so far, and I'd prefer to be able to take a walk down the street with you on my arm without having to worry about someone shooting either one of us. In order to get to that point, unfortunately, we have to go back to where it started. I need more information in order to figure this out. It pisses me off, and I guarantee I will hate every second of putting you in danger, but I have a gut feeling this is the only way to make it end." Tex paused for a moment, looking Mel straight in the eyes as he did it.

Melody's impression of Tex increased. It was obvious he didn't like having to put her in danger, but he wasn't hiding the truth from her.

Finally he continued, "Yeah, I fucking hate it, but hear this now, Mel, I'll be right there. He's not going to hurt you. And this *will* end. You won't have to live like this for the rest of your life. I'm going to pull every marker, and do whatever it takes to make you safe. Swear to God."

"Okay."

"Okay?"

"Yeah, okay. I know I can't keep running. I hate it. I was already contemplating going home even before I contacted you. I hate being away from my family and Amy. I hate being scared. I'd rather face this asshole face-to-face than deal with his notes scaring me to death."

Tex couldn't resist. He leaned toward her, bringing her head into him with the hand at the back of her neck. He put his forehead against hers. "You're one tough cookie, Melody Grace." Then Tex kissed her. It was light and brief. Lighter and briefer than he wanted it to be, but he didn't want to confuse Mel any more than she probably was. She had to be feeling gratitude toward him, but Tex didn't want that. He wanted more.

Putting her back from him and trying to ignore how good she felt in his lap, Tex moved his hands to her hips. "Okay, let's get going. I'll get the letter, you get your stuff, and we'll head back to my hotel and pick up Baby's and my things. Then we'll get to Wolf's house and figure out our next steps."

Melody slowly stood up and realized as Tex steadied her before sliding his hands away from her hips, how much she enjoyed his hands on her. She felt his touch to the marrow of her bones. It'd been so long since she'd been touched, and Tex's hands just felt right. Melody got herself together and headed over to pick up her bags that she'd packed earlier in preparation for fleeing the hotel and California.

She watched as Tex picked up the letter on the floor with a washcloth. Melody knew he was trying to preserve any fingerprints that might, by some miracle, still be on the paper. His jaw clenched as he read the words on the page, but he didn't say anything.

Melody looked over at Baby. She sat calmly by the door, her eyes moving from Melody to Tex. Melody knew she should probably be offended or hurt that her dog was looking to Tex as much as she looked to her, but Melody couldn't find it in her. Tex had brought Baby to her. He'd cared enough to drive across the country to find her. He was going to help her figure out who the hell hated her so much that he'd threaten to hurt her and the people she loved.

Melody couldn't wait to get out of this hotel room and out of Anaheim. As much as she was scared to be going home, she was also looking forward to it. It was time to get back to her life, her real life.

CHAPTER 5

*T*ex looked over at Melody. She was sitting in the passenger seat in his truck and Baby was sitting between them, her head resting on Mel's lap. Mel had her head against the headrest of the truck and her fingers were idly running over Baby's head. Baby had her eyes closed and every now and then Tex could hear a soft snore coming from the dog.

He hadn't lied to Melody. He'd never been around dogs much in his life, but Baby was awesome. She was sensitive, low-maintenance, and surprisingly protective. He liked that.

Keeping his voice low, he told Melody, "I need to tell you about my friends before we get there. It's likely they'll be overly exuberant."

Without opening her eyes, Tex heard Mel's response. "Overly exuberant? What's that code for?"

"It's code for the women were happy to see me yesterday, but they'll be absolutely thrilled to see me with *you*. They think I'm too much of a hermit and probably see me as Quasimodo. They'll probably push us together and assume we're sleeping together. Caroline will probably put us both in the basement together for the night."

"Wow. Uh. Okay."

"And the men know about you. Well, they know what I knew yesterday. They'll be concerned about you and will probably act overbearing and alpha. But I've got your back. Just go with it and know that I'll do what's best for *you*, no matter what *they* want to do."

Tex looked over Mel and saw she'd turned her head and was looking at him. He couldn't read what she was thinking, but he continued, "They're very 'hands on,' Mel. The men'll touch you, not sexually, but they'll put their hands on you. Your back, your head, your neck. The women'll hug you. A lot. They'll also probably pry a bit too much for just meeting you, but it's what they do. If you don't want that, tell me now and I'll tell them to back off. If it becomes too much, let me know and again, I'll tell them to lay off. They're touchy. They can't help it."

"Will you tell me more about them? How they met each other? What they're like? What you had to do with helping them?"

"Their stories aren't pretty, Mel."

"But they ended up together, right?"

"Yeah, they're together."

"Then their stories are beautiful."

Tex took his hand off the steering wheel and brought it to Mel's face. He ran his knuckles down her cheek once, then turned his attention back to the road.

"Wolf met Caroline when the plane they were on was hijacked. He left on a mission and the bad guys found her and stole her again. I helped Wolf find where they'd taken her. Abe and Alabama's story is a bit more tame, but essentially she saved his life in a fire, they got together, Abe did something dumb and Alabama took off. I tried to help find her, but it's a lot easier to hide when you don't use any kind of electronics. Then there was Fiona."

Tex's voice cracked. Fiona's story was the most personal to him. He felt Baby turn in between them and she reached up and licked his face once. Tex laughed and gently shoved Baby's face away from him. "Ew, girl . . ."

Melody laughed, leaned over and hugged Baby and tugged her back into her lap.

"I told you some of this online, but anyway, the team went into Mexico to rescue a Senator's daughter who'd been kidnapped, and they unexpectedly found Fiona there too. She was doing okay, but after they got home and the guys were on a mission, she had a flashback and ran. I found her because she used Cookie's credit card, and I talked to her every day, every four hours, until Cookie could get home and get to her."

His voice trailed off and this time it was Mel who reached over to offer comfort. She put her hand on his thigh, but didn't say anything.

"Then Mozart and Summer. Mozart met her when he went up to Big Bear. She was working at the motel where he was staying. The person Mozart had been tracking abducted her and tortured her with the intent to kill her. Luckily, I was able to trace the cell phone of another young lady he'd kidnapped that night as well. They got there in time to save both women. I heard Elizabeth, the other woman who was rescued with Summer, wasn't dealing well with what had happened to her and moved to Texas. I need to make a point to see what I can find out about her... how she's doing.

"Anyway, Dude and Cheyenne have a similar story. Dude is an expert with explosives. He met Cheyenne when he was called to a grocery store to diffuse a bomb some bad guys strapped to her. Of course he defused it, but then relatives of the bad guys took Cheyenne and tried to kill her and an apartment building full of people."

Tex took a deep breath and finished quickly. "Last there's Benny and Jessyka. She had a horrible ex who the guys took care of, but in order to get revenge he attacked Benny and lured Jessyka into his clutches. Even with her limp, she managed to save Benny's life. It would've been tough to find Benny without Jess leading me right to him."

"Leading you to him?"

Tex sighed. He knew this was coming. "This is going to sound bad, especially with what you're going through. But hear me out. Okay?"

"Ooo-kay."

Tex could hear the trepidation in her voice, but he continued on. It was going to come out sooner or later, so he might as well get it out in the open.

"My friends asked me to track their women. I made some GPS devices and sent them to the guys. They put them in earrings, their women's watches. Shoes. Clothes. I don't blame them one bit. Each one of them had been taken from them. None of us wanted it to happen again."

There was silence in the cab of the truck for a while. Tex let Mel think through what he said.

Finally she spoke. "It's not the same."

"What?"

"It's not the same. Your friends are doing it out of love. It's not the same."

Tex silently sighed in relief. He didn't think Melody would've freaked out, but he wasn't a hundred percent sure. "You're right, Mel. It's not. I'm the only one who receives the signals. The guys have the ability, but they trust me to keep the data. We've only needed to use it once, with Jessyka. She only let herself get taken because she knew Benny wasn't tracked and she was. She knew I'd know something was wrong."

"Can I have one?"

"What?" Tex couldn't believe he'd heard her right.

In a lower voice than she'd used before, Melody asked again, a little hesitantly, "Can you put one on me? I don't know what this guy wants. What if he takes me? You can find me if I have one of your tracking things right? You'll come and get me?"

Tex couldn't stand it. The tremble in her voice, the uncertainty, the vulnerability. He pulled the truck over to the side of the road and put it in park. Tex turned sideways in the seat and reached his hand out to Melody. He put it on the side of her head and held her eyes.

"I'd love to tell you that it'll never happen, Mel. But, unfortunately, I know more than anyone, that it can. I'll do everything possible to keep you safe, but sometimes it's not enough. So yes, if you want, I'll give you a tracker so if your stalker kidnaps you, I can find you. Whatever happens, don't you give up. If he finds you and takes you from me, do not egg this asshole on. Don't give him a reason to hurt or kill you. No matter what happens, we can get through it. Just remember that I'll be coming after you and I'll track you down. And I will, Mel. I will find you, you just have to give me the time to do it. Okay?"

Melody nodded. She knew asking to be tracked was weak, but she felt weak at the moment. Just him saying the words made her feel better. Made her feel more secure knowing someone, other than her stalker, would know where she was at all times. Someone she trusted. And she trusted Tex. She'd gotten to know him over the last six months they'd talked online. Hell, she knew him better than some of the people she'd grown up and went to school with. She knew him and, more importantly, she trusted him.

"Thank you for being honest with me. I know he's going to find me and it's just a matter of time before he catches up with me. Thank you for not pretending he won't. I swear, I won't give up. If he gets me, I'll hang on and wait for you to get to me."

Not addressing her pessimistic attitude, knowing there was a distinct possibility that she *could* get taken by her stalker, Tex said instead, "You're welcome. You okay? You need to stop? You hungry?"

Melody shook her head. "I'm okay. Even though they'll intimidate the hell out of me, I'm looking forward to meeting your friends."

"Don't feel intimidated, Mel. They're just like you. The women are strong and kick-ass and don't take any crap from their men. And my friends, they'll take one look at you and you'll be firmly in their 'you must be protected' camp."

"I'm not strong, Tex."

"The hell you aren't."

"I think I'm glad you see me that way."

"You'll see yourself that way too. Promise."

"Okay."

"Okay." Tex pulled Melody closer to him, ignoring the grunt of disapproval coming from Baby who was being mushed between them, and kissed her cheek. He pulled back and nodded at Mel. "Strong and kick-ass, Mel."

Tex then put the truck back in drive and pulled back onto the highway.

* * *

"Breathe."

Melody tried, she did, but she was really nervous about meeting Tex's friends. The women all sounded awesome, and the men just plain freaked her out. She wasn't really ready for this, but she knew these people were as close to family as Tex had and she wanted to make a good impression.

"I'm okay."

"They're going to love you."

Melody could only nod as Tex got out of the truck and walked around to her side. He helped her out and Baby jumped down after her. Melody held the leash tightly as Tex reached for her hand. Melody jumped at the chance to grab hold.

They walked up to the house and the door opened as they reached it. A large man stood there and Melody could hear the voices of many others behind him. He stepped forward and mostly closed the door behind him.

"Tex. Melody. Glad you made it back so soon."

"Wolf." Tex gave him a chin lift. "Are they all in there?"

"Every last one."

Tex smiled at that. Of course everyone was here. "It okay if we stay here tonight?"

"Hell, Tex, as if Caroline would let you stay anywhere else." Wolf turned to Melody and held out his hand. "Melody, I'm Wolf. It's great to meet you. I'm glad Tex found you, but I had no doubt that he would. He's that good. Please know you're welcome to stay here as long as you want."

Melody took Wolf's hand in hers and shook it. "Thanks, but I go where Tex goes."

Wolf nodded as if he expected the answer. "I'm gonna say this quickly because if I know my wife, she'll be out here before not too much longer. You have my protection, Melody. You have my team's protection. Whatever you need, you've got it. Tex is a good man, he'll keep you safe, but if you need us, if Tex needs us, we're there. Understand?"

Melody could only nod. No words would come out. Yesterday she'd been alone. Today she had a whole team of bad-ass SEALs at her back. It was hard to wrap her mind around.

At her side, Baby growled low. Melody realized Wolf still held her hand in his. She quickly dropped it and Baby moved in front of her, pushing Wolf back.

"Nice guard dog you got there."

"She's not a guard dog."

"Maybe not for anyone else, but she did the same thing when Tex was here before and Ice rushed him to give him a hug."

Melody turned to Tex. "Really?"

"Yeah, really."

Melody crouched down in front of Baby and whispered, "Good girl."

The men above her just laughed.

"Come on, Mel, let's get this over with."

Wolf laughed at the mock resignation in Tex's voice.

Tex held out a hand to Mel and helped her up. He put his arm around her waist and they followed Wolf into the house.

Melody could tell Tex was tired, because he was limping more than she'd noticed since meeting him. She remembered him telling her in one of their online conversations that when he overdid it, his limp would become more pronounced.

Before she could say anything, they entered a living room full of people.

"Tex is here!" One woman shouted and stood up quickly, and everyone in the room followed suit.

"Easy, Baby," Melody heard Tex say beside her. She looked down to see the scruff on the back of her dog's neck standing on end.

"You have to be Melody," another woman said a tad more calmly. "I'm Summer. I'm sure Tex has probably told you about all of us, but instead of using all their *real* names, he's probably only used their nicknames." She rolled her eyes and Melody smirked.

"Okay, so you met Wolf at the door." She pointed to each of the other men in the room and introduced them in succession. "Abe, Mozart, Dude, Benny, and Cookie."

"Wow, Summer, I'm impressed you know our nicknames," Cookie joked with her.

"Shut up, Hunter. Of course I know your nicknames. It's not like you guys will stop using them."

Melody just watched the by-play between everyone with amusement. She knew if she spent more time with this group of people she'd probably love them. They reminded her of her and Amy. A little goofy, a lot sarcastic, and funny to boot.

"Hi," Melody said shyly.

"Come sit over here by us. We can't wait to get to know you better!"

Melody looked away from Summer, and turned to Tex. Before she could say anything, Tex leaned down to her to whisper into her ear. "It's okay, Mel. I'll be in the other room with the guys if you need me."

Melody nodded. "Okay."

Before she knew it, she was sitting in the middle of the six other women, Baby at her feet, laughing at the stories they shared about their men. Through the stories the women told, Melody could hear the love that came through. These women adored their men, and it was one hundred percent reciprocal.

"So Melody, tell us about Tex." It was Fiona that asked.

"What about him?"

"How'd you guys meet?"

"Well, I just met him face-to-face today."

"Wow! That's kinda cool! We just met him in person this morning. Well, Caroline had met him before, but not the rest of us," Jessyka shared. "Isn't he the *best*?"

Melody smiled at the affection in Jessyka's voice. "Yeah, he is."

"So? Deets woman!" Caroline demanded teasingly.

"We met online. I was bored and went into a chat room one night. He messaged me, and we started talking." Melody stopped, and got serious, remembering all that the women had been through. "He was so worried about you guys. Fiona, I interrupted him when he was trying to help you and he was so concerned about you." Melody turned to Jessyka. "He was pissed at you, Jess, but so proud that you'd risked yourself for Benny. You're all so lucky to have him." She stopped before she burst into tears. She normally wasn't quick to cry, but the stress over the last few months was catching up with her with a vengeance.

Fiona got out of her chair and came over to kneel in front of Melody and put her hands on her knees. "We love Tex. He means more to us than you'll ever know. We don't take him for granted and we're so thrilled he's here. We've been wanting to meet him forever. Take good care of him for us."

"I . . . we . . . we aren't together like that."

"If the look in either of your eyes is any indication, you will be soon."

Melody didn't know what to say. She just looked at Fiona, then around at the other women. They all had something in common. They were with hardcore SEALs that would give their lives for their women. Melody wanted that. She hadn't admitted it to herself until now, but she wanted it.

They all turned as the men came into the room. Melody could see furrowed lines in Tex's forehead and his pronounced limp made it obvious he was in pain.

Ignoring everyone else around her, Melody stood up and went straight to Tex. Baby trailed after her, close on her heels. Thinking quickly, not wanting to embarrass him in front of everyone, Melody said to him, but loud enough for everyone to hear, "I'm tired, Tex."

Tex knew what she'd done, knew she was lying so he could get off his feet, but didn't call her on it. He wouldn't mind getting more one-on-one time with Mel, and he knew the girls could talk all night if given half a chance. Melody's words were the impetus to clear the room. Slowly everyone came over to say their good-byes to both Tex and Melody and Caroline and Wolf.

Cheyenne gave her a quick hug and stepped aside for her man. Dude put his hand under Melody's chin and lifted her head until she had no choice but to look him in the eyes.

"You might not know this, but you managed to hook up with the right man. Tex will do what it takes to make sure you're safe. He can do some amazing shit on the computer. We've all relied on him, the government relies on him, and I know for a fact there are several top-secret military groups out there who rely on him. But most importantly, you can trust him, Melody. We've got his, and your, back, but when push comes to shove, trust Tex."

Melody could only nod as she gazed up at the intense man in front of her. His words were more of a command than anything else and Mel almost felt compelled to agree with him. If it wasn't for Cheyenne standing next to him with a hand on his arm and smiling huge, she probably would've been worried. He had a way about him that Mel didn't get from the others. More...take-charge. That wasn't exactly the word she was looking for, but before she could think too much about it, Dude leaned down and gave her a brief kiss on the cheek before stepping back so the others could approach her and say their good-byes as well.

Melody got a hug from everyone before they left, along with more reassurances that she'd be safe with Tex. She was basically passed from one person to the next until there were only four of them left. Tex had been right. His friends were touchy, but Melody liked it. They were affectionate and it was obvious they cared about Tex.

"I've got the room all set up for you guys. Melody, I got Baby's food from the car and it's downstairs for you to feed her in the morning. Your bags are also down in the basement. If there's anything you need, just either let us know or help yourself. Tex, you know the drill."

Tex nodded at Wolf. "Thanks, man. Appreciate it."

"See you in the morning."

Tex turned and headed for the basement door. Baby, once again, put herself at his side as they began to head down the stairs. He had to let go of Mel and he limped down the stairs. Tex quickly tried to think about how this would work. He knew the bed was only a queen. It should be big enough for them, but he didn't know what Mel would think about it. He'd told her in the car that Caroline would probably put them in the basement room together. But most people would probably see this as very odd . . . them just meeting today and tonight sleeping in the same bed, but Tex felt as if he knew Melody a hundred times better than most of the women he'd slept with in the past.

More importantly was the issue of his prosthesis. He didn't want her to see his stump, but there was no way he could sleep in it. His leg was on fire. He needed to rub it down and give it a break from the confines of the prosthetic.

"If it's okay, I'll go first in the bathroom," Tex tried to be nonchalant.

"No problem." Melody watched as Tex limped into the small room. She couldn't quite read his mood. Hell, she didn't really know him, no wonder she couldn't read him. They did really well talking to each other on the computer, but in person it was different.

Melody looked around. There was a bed in the middle of the room with a dresser against a wall. Around a corner there was a small kitchenette that held a small refrigerator and a sink. There was a coffee maker on the counter and a little two-seater table with chairs tucked underneath.

She knew she should probably be asking Caroline if there was another room she could stay in. Sleeping in the same bed with Tex after only meeting him a few hours ago was insane. But it'd been so long since she'd felt safe, Melody couldn't bring herself to care. She knew Tex. Knew he was a kick-ass SEAL and that he could hurt her a million different ways, but she also knew he was insecure. He'd go out of his way to make her feel comfortable and he'd never ever hurt her. Maybe she was being naïve believing that, but after meeting Wolf and the other SEALs who obviously respected and admired Tex, and after hearing from the women he'd had a hand in saving, she knew she was safe, and that there was nowhere she'd rather be, than right by his side.

She turned toward the bathroom door and tilted her head. What was going through Tex's head? Baby jumped up on the bed and turned in circles at the foot. Melody smiled. It was obvious she'd been here before.

Melody looked back as the bathroom door opened behind her. Tex limped out wearing a tattered T-shirt and a pair of cut-off sweatpants which hung low on his hips. Melody gulped. She remembered thinking she wouldn't care if Tex had turned out to be overweight, and she wouldn't have, but he was gorgeous. Any woman who would turn him down because of his leg was obviously certifiably insane.

"It's all yours. Take your time."

Melody looked critically at Tex. Thinking about his personality and what she knew of him, something seemed off. She thought about it a bit more and it came to her.

"You don't have to be embarrassed about your leg with me."

Tex froze and turned to Melody, but didn't say anything.

"Seriously. I remember you told me how your leg would hurt when you wore your prosthetic all day. You told me how you had to massage it for it to feel better. I know about the phantom pains, Tex. You're in pain, I can see it. Please don't be embarrassed around me."

"It's not pretty, Mel."

"I didn't expect it would be."

Tex looked at Mel and struggled with himself. He didn't want to show her his leg. It was the last thing he wanted to do. He wanted to impress her, and he didn't think seeing his scarred leg would. He hated feeling like this, it went against everything he was, but the feeling was there and wouldn't leave.

"Trust me. I'm putting my life in your hands. Trust me not to let you down here," Melody whispered, not moving. When Tex nodded, she said, trying to be no-nonsense about it, "Okay, take off those pants and get on the bed. But don't take it off yet. I want to see how it works."

"Now who's bossy?"

Tex smiled as he said it, but Melody could see it didn't reach his eyes. She didn't push it, but turned to go into the bathroom, giving Tex some time to get comfortable without her around watching him. She hurried through her nightly routine, glad Wolf had the foresight to bring her bag downstairs, and went back into the bedroom. She'd changed into a long T-shirt and a pair of boxer shorts.

Tex had turned the lights down and he was sitting on the bed propped up by the pillows behind him. He'd removed his sweatpants and was in a pair of boxer shorts. Melody walked over to the bed and climbed on.

"Jesus, Tex, I know you're nervous as hell and you really *really* don't want to share this with me, but you are sex on a fucking stick. Seriously."

"Mel—"

"No, Tex. Look at you." Melody ran her eyes over the man lying next to her. "I'm so not in your league at all. I wish I had x-ray vision because I bet you have a six-pack under that shirt. Your arms are muscular as all hell and your legs? Damn. I'll never see another pair of boxers and not be able to recall this moment right here. You've been concerned all this time about how a woman would react when she sees your leg? I can tell you right now that they wouldn't even care. They'd be too busy looking at the rest of you because it is fiiiiine."

Tex burst out laughing. He'd been afraid Mel would be disgusted by his leg. He should've known better. Her words gave him back some of the self-esteem that had slowly eroded over the years since he'd been injured. "Mel, look at me."

Melody waved her hand at him, refusing to look away from his body. "Sorry, busy at the moment." She said it with a smile, still checking him out.

Tex grasped Mel's chin in his hand and gently turned her head toward him. "Thank you, Mel. And you're wrong, You're definitely in my league."

"I'm not, and it's fine."

Tex tightened the hold he had on her face when she tried to turn away. "No, look at me. You want to know what I thought the first time I saw you standing in that hotel room?"

"Not particularly."

Tex ignored her and continued. "I thought to myself that it was no wonder someone has become obsessed with you. A horrible thought, but true none-the-less."

Melody looked at Tex in bewilderment, her brows wrinkling in confusion.

"Yeah, you're beautiful."

"I'm not."

"Okay, to me you're not just beautiful, you're gorgeous. Your body is perfect."

"You haven't seen me, Tex. I'm far from gorgeous."

"You're wrong. I see you. You said you'll never see a pair of boxers the same way again? The same goes for me. You're lush. Men love that. They *want* that. The entertainment world tries to shove stick-figured women down our throats as the ideal woman, but they couldn't be further from the truth. Your curves are to die for. I know you probably don't feel that way, women never understand these things. But Mel, honestly, we don't want skin and bones, and muscular looks good on television and in magazines, but it feels so much better to have soft skin surrounding us than hard angles and muscles. We like soft, Mel. *I* like soft."

Melody knew she was breathing too hard, but she couldn't take her eyes away from Tex. His words slid over her like a warm blanket just taken from a dryer.

"If after you see me, all of me, you're still interested, Mel, I'm yours. I like you. I've gotten to know you over the last six months and I like what I've gotten to know. Seeing you? Feeling the chemistry between us? Fucking perfect. Yeah. I want you."

"It's only been a day," Melody whispered uncertainly, not really believing her own words.

"It hasn't only been a day and you know it. We started this six months ago. I'm not the kind of guy who chats with a woman every day for six months, Mel. Maybe a day or two, but not six months. We might have *seen* each other for the first time today, but I've known you for half a year. You think I would've come after you if it wasn't more?"

"Maybe. You're a SEAL, Tex. It's what you do."

"Bullshit. Yeah, I might have once rescued people for a living, but I'm retired now. I haven't suddenly dropped everything to go traipsing off around the country looking for random missing people. But the second *you* canceled your account online, I was trying to figure out how to find and get to you."

Tex dropped his hand from Melody's face and gestured to his leg with his chin as if to change the subject and tell her to get on with it.

Without a word, but with Tex's words tumbling around in her brain, Mel turned her attention to his leg. She said briskly, trying to hide how much his words confused, excited, and aroused her all at the same time, "Okay, show me how this thing works."

"I have what's known as a transfemoral amputation, meaning an amputation above the knee. The prosthetic is held in place by suction, so I don't need any other type of suspension to keep it in place. It fits snugly onto what's left of my leg and the airtight seal keeps it from slipping out."

"How do you break the seal to get it off?"

"The type of liner I have is a seal-in liner. It creates a strong, airtight seal which allows a good fit and it comes with a button that if you push it, it breaks the seal."

Melody couldn't prevent the little giggle that escaped and the inappropriate comment which spewed from her mouth. "You have a magic button."

Tex grinned at her. Jesus, she was cute. He couldn't stop the innuendo from coming out of his mouth if his life depended on it. "Yeah, Mel, now we both have a magic button." She blushed, as he knew she would, and he laughed, but sobered quickly, knowing what she was about to see. "It's not pretty, Mel. But if you're gonna do it, get it over with."

Melody reached out and pressed the button that Tex had shown her. The suction on the device was broken and it popped right off into her hands.

Working quickly, so as not to prolong any embarrassment he might have over what she was doing, Melody lifted the prosthetic leg and leaned over and placed it on the floor behind her. She turned back around to see Tex pulling the sleeve off his stump that served as the liner for the prosthetic.

He was right, the skin around his leg wasn't pretty. It was red and swollen and Melody winced in sympathy.

"Jeez, Tex. That looks like it's really painful. Do you have any lotion or something?"

"Yeah, I'm supposed to use it every night, but I haven't really taken it off much in the last week."

"Where is it?"

Without a word, Tex leaned over to the nightstand and grabbed a small bottle that Melody had missed. He'd obviously gotten it ready to go while she'd been in the bathroom.

Melody took it out of his hand and rubbed a large dollop of the eucalyptus smelling lotion between her hands then leaned over his leg.

Tex grabbed her wrist before she could touch him. "You don't have to do this. I can do it."

"I want to. Please."

Tex sat back and closed his eyes and braced.

CHAPTER 6

*M*elody refused to let the tears gathering in her eyes fall. She watched as Tex leaned back and closed his eyes. She looked back at what was left of his leg. Where his leg had been removed were scars crisscrossing it and it looked beyond painful. She rubbed her hands together warming the lotion before she put her hands on Tex's leg.

She massaged and rubbed the stump, making sure to rub the creamy soothing lotion into all parts of his leg. She moved her way up to his thigh, trying to rub out the sore muscles. Finally, she sat back and climbed off the bed.

She went into the bathroom and washed her hands, then came back into the room. Tex had gotten under the covers. Melody turned off the light on the side of the bed and climbed into the other side. She lay on her back for a moment. She knew Tex would be a gentleman and wouldn't make the first move.

She turned on her side and scooted over to Tex's side. She put one arm over his chest and laid her head on his shoulder as if she did it every night.

"Thank you," Melody whispered.

Tex shifted until one arm could curl around Mel's shoulder and whispered back, "No, thank *you.*"

Melody lay in bed for a long while, listening to Tex's breathing slow, then even out in the cadence of sleep. Once she knew he was asleep, she finally let the tears fall. She wept silently for the brave soldier Tex had been and for what he now was going through. From their many online conversations she knew he was still very sensitive about his disability and hated to bring attention to it. She also knew how painful it still was.

Finally the tears eased and Melody snuggled further into Tex's side. She sighed in bliss when his arm tightened around her for a moment and he murmured sleepily, not really awake, but not really asleep.

"Sleep, Mel."

"Okay," she whispered back. She closed her eyes and within moments was out. It was the first time in a long time she felt safe as she slept.

The next morning, Melody stirred when she heard Caroline call out from the vicinity of the stairs, "Good morning!"

She looked down and saw that she and Tex had thrown the covers off of themselves during the night, probably because their shared body heat made the blankets unnecessary, and Tex's stump was exposed. Melody saw the look of panic on his face at the thought of Caroline seeing him without his prosthetic. Without thinking, just wanting to protect Tex, Melody reached down to grab the blanket and pulled it up to their waists just as Caroline poked her head around the corner of the room.

"Morning, you two! I figured you'd want to get an early start this morning so I'm your wakeup call. I'll have breakfast ready for you when you get upstairs. Don't dawdle." Then she disappeared from view and Melody heard her heading back up the stairs.

Without looking at Tex, Melody went to scoot out of bed when she felt Tex's hand on her arm. She gestured at the bathroom, "I'm just going to—"

Her words were cut off when Tex pulled on her arm until she was lying back on the bed with him looming over her. "Why'd you do that?"

Knowing what he meant, Melody answered honestly, "Because I know it makes you uncomfortable for anyone to see your leg." Melody fidgeted as Tex continued to look down at her. "Should I—"

"Hush."

When Tex didn't say anything else, but continued to look down at her, Melody tried again. "Tex, I—"

"You didn't flinch. I watched and last night, you saw my leg and you didn't even flinch. You massaged it, you worked the kinks out of my thigh, you kept Ice from seeing it. You, looking like you do, draping yourself over my chest last night, being sweetly shy. I told you if you could stomach what you saw, that I'd be yours if you wanted me. Well, I'm telling you Mel, I'm yours."

Melody tried again. "Tex—"

He interrupted her again. "I haven't trusted anyone other than my doctors to see my leg since it happened. Not even the guys. No one. Just you."

"Would you stop interrupting me!" Melody huffed out irritably, but secretly pleased Tex had allowed her to see his leg when he hadn't even shown it to his friends.

Tex grinned down at her and acknowledged, not very apologetically, "Sorry."

"I have no idea why you're self-conscious about your leg. Yeah, you hurt it. Yeah, you limp a bit. Yeah, it looks painful. But you, Tex, you're amazing. You're more than your leg. I like you. I liked you before we met. I didn't talk to anyone else while I was hiding out. Only you. I hated to leave you waiting for me in that chat room. All that had *nothing* to do with your leg. It's *you*. Your friends won't care about your leg. They won't pity you, they won't think bad about you. They love you. You're confusing as hell. One minute I want to smack you, and the next I want to kiss you. You say stuff I don't get. And I don't know what it means when you say you're mine."

Still smiling, thinking her outburst was adorable, Tex told her, "It means whatever you want it to mean, Mel. We have a long drive ahead of us. We have to figure out who's stalking you. You need to get your life figured out. But I hope somewhere in there we can make time to get to know each other even better in real life instead of only on the computer. Somewhere along the line I hope you can decide if you *want* me to be yours."

"Okay, Tex." Melody knew she'd say anything to get away and have a second to think about what he'd just told her.

Seeing the confusion on her face and having pity on her, Tex told her, "Okay, Mel. Go on, get ready to go. I'll shower after you."

"Do you need help with—"

As usual, Tex cut her off and said with only a hint of sarcasm, "I've got it. I've been doing it on my own for a while now."

"But I'm here. I can help you. I *want* to help you."

"Not today. Last night was hard enough for me. Let me get used to it."

Melody shook her head. "All right, but if you're going to be mine, you have to let me help you sooner or later."

67

"Deal."

"Seriously you have to . . . wait . . . what?"

"I'm going to kiss you before I let you up to shower."

Melody's brain stuttered to a halt. He changed topics so quickly she was having a hard time keeping up, but a kiss? She'd been dreaming about him kissing her, *really* kissing her, since she'd met him standing in her hotel room. Hell, before that. She'd never admit, even under torture, that she'd gone to sleep more than once dreaming of the wonderful man she'd been chatting with online.

"Did you hear me, Mel?"

"Uh huh."

Tex grinned. "Fuck, you're cute when you're befuddled." Then he leaned down and took her mouth with his own. He supposed he should've kept it light and sweet, but he didn't feel light and sweet. He felt raw and exposed, and the chemistry they'd been dancing around for the last day exploded when his lips touched hers.

Melody slanted her head to improve the angle of their kiss. Her hands came up to grasp at his sides. Tex drove his tongue into Melody's mouth and stroked. He licked over her lips then plunged back inside. He mimicked what it might be like when they made love, because he knew they'd eventually end up doing more than just sleeping when they shared a bed.

Tex almost lost it when Melody captured his tongue and sucked on it, closing her lips around it and caressing it with her own tongue in the process. He lifted his head and stared down at Melody.

"Fuck, woman."

Melody smiled up at him and licked her lips. She flattened her hands at his waist and ran them up and down slowly. "That was . . . yeah . . . uh . . . wow."

Tex's mouth quirked into a grin. "Yeah. Wow. Thank you for looking out for me."

"You're welcome."

Rolling over and sitting up, Tex said, "Now, go shower. I'll take Baby out while you get ready."

Melody laughed. She'd forgotten all about her dog, who was still curled into a ball at the foot of the bed, watching them. "Okay, Tex. What-ever you say." She got up off the bed, snooter kissed Baby, and walked into the bathroom, managing not to look back at the sexy-as-hell man sitting on the bed.

CHAPTER 7

"Wanna play a game?" Melody asked Tex. It was the day after they'd left California and she was bored. The first day was exciting, just because it was different. When she'd fled Pennsylvania, she'd rented a car with cash she'd pulled out of her bank account and driven across the country, but somehow this was different. She wasn't as scared and since Tex had done most of the driving so far, she could watch the ever-changing countryside as it went by.

They'd stopped somewhere in eastern New Mexico the first night of their trip. Melody thought it would be awkward when they stopped, but Tex made it easier than she thought it could be.

He asked her to stay in the car while he checked in. He'd told her that while it might be a bit awkward to stay in the same room, he didn't want to leave her alone, even if she was just next door. Melody agreed without reservation, after all, they'd spent the night before in each other's arms and they weren't strangers. Besides that, she felt safe with Tex. She didn't want to be in a room by herself. She wanted to be with Tex.

Tex had gotten a room with two queen beds, not wanting to push Mel into anything she wasn't ready for, but when push came to shove, Melody had asked if she could sleep in the same bed as him. He'd agreed and after she'd once again massaged his leg and stump, they'd settled into each other arms.

Just as she'd been drifting off to sleep, Tex said in a low voice, "I hate traveling." Melody was instantly awake.

"Why?"

"Because without my prosthetic, I'm vulnerable. If something happens in the middle of the night, I can't jump up and deal with it like I used to be able to. Whether it's a knock on the door, someone trying to break in, a fire, or whatever. I'm stuck in bed until I can get my leg on. I hate it."

Melody wasn't sure what to say. She hadn't thought about it, but now that he put the images in her head, they wouldn't leave. "You're the least vulnerable man I've ever met." She put every ounce of conviction into her voice as she could.

"You don't have to—"

Melody interrupted him. "I'm not." She felt movement under her cheek and lifted her head to see he was laughing.

"You don't even know what I was going to say."

"Don't care. Whatever it was, was going to be crap. You could probably break someone in half if they broke in here. You could hop to the door and down the hall and outrun any fire that dared to try to burn you. If someone knocked, you could have your leg strapped on before they got any words out. In fact . . ." Melody pushed herself up even more and peered down at Tex in the dark room. "I bet you've practiced getting your leg on as fast as you can . . . haven't you?"

When he grinned sheepishly up at her, Melody smiled back and brought her hands up to tickle his sides. "How long? What's your fastest time?"

She let out a girly shriek when he flipped her over and trapped her hands in one of his above her head.

"There I was, getting all touchy feely with you and you had to go and ruin it." His words were said with a smile and a twinkle in his eye, but Melody still immediately felt bad.

"Seriously, Tex, I'm sorry you feel that way, but if I had my pick between all your friends and you, as to who would be with me in this hotel room right now, I'd still pick you. *You* make me feel safe. Two legs, one arm, no legs, no arms. I'd still pick you."

Without a word, Tex leaned down and kissed Melody deeply and with all the emotion he couldn't figure out how to put into words. Her trust meant the world to him. Since his surgery, he'd always felt somehow less than his other SEAL friends. Two sentences was all it took to bring back his self-esteem.

Not letting the kiss morph into anything more, it still seemed too soon, Tex turned again until they'd resumed their earlier positions. Throughout everything, Baby hadn't moved, she just slept, snoring softly, at the end of the bed in a super-ball.

When they'd settled down, and just as Melody was slipping back into sleep, she heard Tex whisper, "Twenty three seconds."

Melody merely smiled, turned her head and kissed his chest, and laid her cheek back down without a word. She'd known in her gut he'd practiced putting his prosthetic on.

Now it was four hours into another long driving day and Melody was bored.

"What kind of game did you have in mind?" Tex asked, briefly looking over at Melody.

"Well, it's not a game per se, but more of an information sharing thing. I'll tell you something interesting about me, and then you do the same."

Expecting an argument, Melody was surprised when Tex agreed immediately. "Sure. You go first."

Melody looked down at Baby who was sleeping between them in the truck. She'd been an excellent traveling companion. Melody had never traveled for as many hours on the road as this with her before, but it didn't really surprise her. Baby had always been reticent and quiet and eager to please. Melody supposed that had to do with whatever she went through before she ended up in the shelter. Melody ran her hand down her dog's head and back. Baby didn't move, but groaned in her sleep. Melody smiled.

"Growing up, I was a cat person. My parents had cats and I always knew when I grew up I was going to have a household full of cats too."

"What happened?"

"I got busy, didn't think it was fair to have a pet when I was busy all the time. Then I saw Baby's picture in an online ad the shelter had run and they'd said she would be euthanized the next day if she didn't get adopted. Something about her face tugged at my heartstrings and I went right down to the shelter."

"She was lucky."

"No," Melody countered, "I'm the lucky one. Baby is the best dog I could've asked for. It killed me to leave her behind when I left Pennsylvania, but I knew it'd be even worse if my stalker got a hold of her and killed her. I don't know what I'd do without her."

After a comfortable silence, Melody prodded Tex, "Your turn."

"I almost didn't message you that first night."

"Really? Why did you change your mind?"

"Well, there was someone calling herself Busty Betty who I messaged first. She didn't answer."

"So I was your second choice?" Melody looked over at Tex and saw he was trying to hide a grin. She smacked him in the arm. "You jerk. You're lying aren't you?"

Tex lost his battle with hiding his smile and laughed out loud. "Yeah, I was honest about almost not messaging you, but something told me it'd be worth my while."

"And was it?"

"Hell yeah. Best fucking decision I've made in my entire life." Tex glanced over at Mel so she'd know he was completely serious.

"I'm glad you did."

"Me too. Okay, your turn again."

"My second toe is longer than my big toe."

Tex laughed out loud. He hadn't realized how little he laughed until Mel came into his life. "I'll have to check that out for myself." He thought for a moment, then continued the game. "I can't stand bananas."

"Bananas?"

"Yeah, weird huh? I don't know if it's the consistency of the fruit or something. I just can't choke it down."

"What about banana flavored candy?" Mel asked curiously.

"Nope."

"That's weird."

"Hey!"

Melody chuckled. "Sorry, but it is." She continued on with the game. "My secret obsession is watching COPS."

"Please tell me you're kidding."

Giggling, Melody admitted, "Nope. Love it. People can be such idiots, and I especially love it when the police officers laugh at the criminals."

"I have an admission," Tex told her.

"Yeah?"

"I've never seen an episode of COPS."

"Oh my God! We are so finding one tonight when we get to the hotel."

Tex looked over at Mel and smiled. She was really funny. He knew he enjoyed talking to her online, but he had no idea she'd be just as quirky in person.

The rest of the day's drive passed quickly. They went back and forth in sharing more information about themselves and their lives. She'd laughed harder over the last four hours than she had in the last year.

They'd stopped a few times to eat and to let Baby stretch her legs and by the time they pulled up to the hotel that night, Melody felt as if she'd known Tex her entire life. It was dark when they parked in front of the hotel and Melody was exhausted. It was amazing how tiring it could be to sit in a car all day. She noticed Tex rubbing his thigh.

"You want me to go in and get the room?" Melody didn't want to make Tex feel bad, but she wanted to offer.

"No. I'd prefer to take care of it myself. To make sure you're safe here in the truck as I go in and rent us a room, but my leg is killing me and it fucking pisses me off that it'd probably be better if you went in and took care of it for us. I don't think we're in any danger here, as no one has been following us and we're in the middle of nowhere, but I still hate it. You don't mind?"

Ignoring his frustration, Melody calmly told him, "I wouldn't have asked if I did." Melody was surprised Tex actually relented, especially knowing how important it was to him to take care of her and to be in charge.

Tex leaned over and pulled out his wallet and handed her two one hundred dollar bills without a word.

Knowing better than to argue, but planning on paying him back one way or another, Melody took the money. "I'll be right back." Rubbing Baby on her head, she told her, "Be good, girl. I'll be right back." Baby licked her hand then immediately turned and put her head on Tex's leg. Melody smiled, shook her head, and closed the truck door.

She came out five minutes later and opened the truck door. "Head around back. There's a door back there we can use. Our room is on the first floor, on account of Baby."

Tex started the truck and followed her directions. The parking lot was mostly empty when Tex parked. They each got out, Melody holding Baby's leash while Tex carried their bags.

Melody used the swipe card to get them into the building and led the way to their room. She opened the door and Baby pranced into the room as if she didn't have a care in the world.

Melody unclipped Baby's leash and turned to Tex. "I'll take the bags. You go on and get changed. I'll get Baby some water."

Tex put his bag on the floor and handed Mel's bag to her. "I feel like I'm breaking some alpha man code here."

"What do you mean?"

Tex ran a hand through his hair then answered. "I should be the one telling *you* to go and relax. I should be taking care of Baby . . . I haven't done a good job of taking care of you so far."

"Bull," Melody told him, putting her hand on his arm. "I'm not eighteen years old. I've been taking care of myself and Baby for a while now. And you are doing more for me right now than you'll ever know. You came for me and you found me. I was scared out of my head, I'm still terrified my stalker is going to pop up behind us and attack me. But with you here . . . I feel like I have a fighting chance. I know you're hurting, and I hate that. So me letting you get changed and get off your feet . . . well, off your foot. . . isn't going to mean you have to turn in your man-card. Okay?"

Tex took a faltering step to her and tagged her behind the neck. He drew her to him and put his lips against her forehead. "Thanks."

Putting her hands on Tex's waist, Melody leaned into him and asked, "For what?"

"For being a great traveling companion, for trusting me, for letting me take you home, for knowing I'd kill to lay on that bed and get off this leg."

Not knowing what to say, Melody simply said, "You're welcome."

Tex lifted his head, looked her in the eyes, then leaned down. He kissed her once, hard, running his tongue over her bottom lip, but not giving her time to deepen the kiss. He pulled back. "Go see if you can find an episode of COPS. I'll be right out."

Melody watched Tex as he turned and entered the bathroom. She stood there for another moment, until she heard the water in the sink come on. She shook her head, kicked off her shoes, and walked over to the dresser. She put her bag on top and dug through it until she found a clean T-shirt to sleep in and another pair of boxers. She dug in another small bag and got Baby's bowl out and filled it at the sink with water. She put it on the floor and went back over to the television and turned it on. She stood in front of it flipping through the channels.

When Tex walked out of the bathroom she was still standing there. "I can't find it," Melody told Tex in a mock devastated voice.

"It's okay. I'm not sure we'd be able to stay awake to watch anyway."

"Don't think you're getting out of it. I'm making it my mission in life to introduce you to the best show on TV today."

Tex shook his head at her. "God, you're cute. Go on. Your turn in the bathroom."

"Don't touch that leg. I'll take care of it when I get out."

"Okay."

"I mean it, Tex."

Tex grinned. She read him so easily. "All right. I'll wait."

"Thanks. Get comfortable, I'll be right out."

Tex looked behind him at the king size bed. He hadn't told her what kind of room to get, but she'd chosen a room with only one bed. He didn't want to read into that, but he couldn't help it. He pulled back the covers and climbed in, propping the pillows up behind him. Placing the lotion on the bed next to his hip, he put his head back and closed his eyes. He felt Baby jump up on the bed. She padded up to him, lay down next to him and nudged his hand.

Without opening his eyes, Tex ran his hand from the top of Baby's head, to her tailbone, then he did it again. Then again. The soothing motion must have relaxed the dog because he felt her practically melt into the bed next to him.

When Melody walked out into the bedroom not too much later, she smiled at the man and dog on the bed. Both were fast asleep and were snoring quietly.

Melody didn't want to wake Tex, but knew he had to get his leg off. She walked over to the other side of the bed, and carefully broke the suction on his prosthetic. It popped off and Melody heard Tex's voice above her head.

"Sorry I fell asleep."

"It's fine. I got this. Close your eyes." She watched as he did just that. Feeling gooey inside that this alpha ex-SEAL was trusting her to do what he needed done, she got back to work. Melody peeled off the liner and reached for the lotion. Melody worked it into his stump, making sure to not put too much pressure on the sore spots, but pressing hard enough on his overused muscles to try to ease some of his aches.

When she finished, she wiped her hands on the sheet, figuring the staff would wash the sheets before the next guests stayed anyway. Before moving away from Tex, she leaned down and placed a soft kiss right on his stump. She sat up and looked up. Tex's eyes were open and he was staring at her in wonder.

Without another word, Melody walked around the bed and climbed in on the other side. She didn't have the heart to move Baby, so she spooned her dog and faced Tex. He'd turned to watch her progress as she walked around the bed and he was now on his side facing her. They both smoothed their hands over the dog between them, and when their hands nudged each other, Tex grasped Melody's fingers with his own.

As if they were in church, Tex kept his voice low and reverent. "No one has taken care of me like you just did since I was a little kid." He cleared his throat and continued, "I don't know what you see in me, Mel, but it feels good."

"You're a good man, Tex. You're sexy as hell and if we both weren't exhausted I might be tempted to show you just how sexy I think you are."

Tex grinned sleepily at her. "I'll be damned if I try to convince you otherwise."

"Good. 'Cause you wouldn't be able to."

"You always sleep with Baby?"

Allowing him to change the subject, Melody snorted. "Not hardly. She had a nice fluffy dog bed that she used to sleep in at the side of my bed."

"Looks like that's changed."

"Yeah."

They looked down at the dog's side, which was moving up and down under their clasped hands.

"She's a great dog."

"Yeah," Melody repeated.

"I'll look after her too, Mel."

Melody looked over at Tex in surprise. "But—"

"No buts. She means something to you so she means something to me. I'm not going to let him kill her if I can help it."

Tears filled Melody's eyes, and she pulled Tex's hand up to her mouth, kissed the back of it, then brought their hands back to Baby's side. "Thank you," was all she could get out, and her voice hitched anyway.

"As much as I love your dog, she better not get used to sleeping between us. I'm not into doggy voyeurism."

Melody shut her eyes and chuckled. She opened her eyes again and found Tex still watching her intently.

"Get some sleep, Mel. One more long day on the road before we get back to Pennsylvania. We'll have to figure out what's going on and what our next step is. But I'll tell you this, as soon as things calm down, and we have a minute to ourselves where we aren't exhausted or trying to figure out what a crazy person will do next, I plan on showing you how much you're starting to mean to me."

Melody bit her lip and nodded. She couldn't wait.

CHAPTER 8

*M*elody turned off the engine to the truck and gripped the steering wheel tightly. She and Tex had talked that morning and decided to push through and go all the way to Pennsylvania. About halfway through the trip, Melody had convinced Tex to let her drive. Once again, he wasn't happy about it, but his leg was hurting more and more and he'd reached a point where it was too painful for him to drive. He'd given her a million instructions and had only shut up when she'd snapped that she wasn't an idiot and had been driving since she was sixteen.

To his credit, he hadn't resisted when Melody had insisted he allow her to drive. After his lecture, and her snarky response, he'd only nodded and when they'd stopped to let Baby take a break, he handed her his keys, kissed her, and headed for the passenger side of the truck.

Melody had tried to push down how nervous she was to be back at her apartment complex. The last time she'd been home she'd been scared out of her mind and Melody wasn't sure she'd ever see it again.

On one hand, she was glad to be back at her place, but on the other, she was scared. She trusted Tex, but was still terrified to be back in her hometown where everything had started.

"Hey, look at me."

Melody jumped when Tex put his hand on her shoulder, and she turned her head toward him. She could just make him out in the dim light of the parking lot.

"It's going to be all right, Mel. I'm going to take care of this for you."

Melody nodded jerkily.

"Stay there, I'm coming around." Tex got out of the truck and went around the front, not breaking eye contact with Melody as he walked around to her side. He opened the door and as Melody stepped out, he crowded her against the side of the truck.

Tex put his hands on the seat behind her and leaned in. He sighed as Mel put her arms around his waist and held on to him. He could feel Baby nudging his arm, but he ignored the dog for the moment.

He rested his chin on Melody's shoulder and turned so he could whisper into her ear. "I know you're scared, but I'm so proud of you for staying strong. You aren't alone anymore. I'm here."

He felt her breath hitch once, before she locked it down again. He buried his nose into the space between her neck and shoulder and wrapped his arms around her, pulling her into his embrace.

They stood there in the parking lot for a few minutes before Tex finally pulled back. He brought his hands up and framed her face. "I mean it." His words were simple and heartfelt.

"I know. I feel like I've dragged you into this, whatever *this* is."

"Mel, you didn't drag me into anything. I brought myself into it. And if I didn't want to be here, I wouldn't be."

Melody licked her lips and finally, after a moment, whispered, "Okay."

Tex leaned toward her and kissed her on the lips. "Now, give me your keys and you and Baby stay here for a moment while I go and check your apartment out. I'll be right back and we can go inside and get some sleep. Tomorrow you can call Amy and we'll start figuring out what's going on. Hop back in and lock the doors and if you see anything that is out of the ordinary, or that scares you, lean on the horn and call me."

"Do you think he knows I'm here? Am I in danger? Are *you* in danger?"

Tex put his forehead against Melody's and put his hands on her waist and squeezed. "Calm, Mel. No, I don't think you're in danger. There's no way in hell I'd leave you sitting out here by yourself if I did. It's just a precaution. I have no idea if he knows you're back in town yet, but I won't be gone longer than a couple of minutes. You haven't been home in months, and I just want to make sure all's well with your place before we go sauntering in there."

Tex didn't mention that he wanted to make sure the stalker hadn't broken in and destroyed everything in her apartment. It was a possibility and he wanted to spare Mel that. He honestly didn't think the stalker knew they were back in town yet, so she should be safe enough while he checked things out. Tex drew back and put his hands on either side of her jaw and looked her in the eyes. "I wouldn't deliberately put you in danger, Mel. Okay?"

Melody sighed and then nodded. She reached into the truck for her purse. Baby, thrilled she could reach Melody's face, licked at her until Melody laughed and pushed her away. "Move, Baby, I gotta get my purse so we can go inside." As if she understood, Baby sat on her haunches and watched as her mistress pawed through her bag and pulled out the key ring she hadn't used in at least half a year. She turned and dropped it into Tex's outstretched hand.

"Be careful." At Tex's raised eyebrows Melody blushed, but refused to look away from him. "I know you were a SEAL and you could probably just look at someone and scare the hell out of them, but we don't know what this person is capable of."

"I will. Promise." Tex didn't waste time reassuring her, he just kissed her on the forehead and said, "Climb back in and shut and lock the door. I'll be back before you know it."

Melody did as Tex requested and watched as he strode confidently across the parking lot and disappeared into the hallway that led to her apartment. Baby whined next to her, and Melody pulled her into her lap, both to comfort the dog and herself. Baby had always been affectionate, but now that they'd been separated for so long, she was even more so. The dog nuzzled into Melody and rested her muzzle on Melody's shoulder. The two sat in the truck and waited for Tex to reappear.

Tex looked around Mel's apartment carefully. It was quiet and dark. It smelled normal, well as normal as a place that had been closed up for several months could be. It was a bit musty and stale. Flipping the light switch next to the front door, Tex tensed as if waiting for someone to pop out of the darkness. All was quiet.

The door opened up into a small hallway which led into a living area. There was a dark brown leather sofa sitting in the middle of the room with a brown and black coffee table in front of it. A large flat screen television was mounted on the wall across from the couch. A brown and black bookshelf sat against another wall. It was filled with books and had pictures scattered amongst the shelves. There was a small dining area that had a table that could seat four people and the kitchen was off to the side.

Tex took a step inside the room and looked into the kitchen. There was a stainless steel refrigerator and dishwasher and a four burner electric stove. The fridge held a few pictures, he assumed were drawn by Amy's kids. The cabinets were maple in color and the counters were granite.

Tex headed to the hallway opposite the kitchen off of the living area. There were four doors, three of which were standing open. Tex opened the door that was shut and saw that it was a linen closet. He moved down the hall and looked into a guest bedroom that held a double size bed and a dresser. The door across the hall from it was a bathroom.

Still vigilant, Tex headed for what had to be Mel's bedroom. He stopped in the doorway and took in her personal space. The bed was a queen size captain's bed. There were drawers underneath and two columns of cabinets and drawers lining each side of the bed. There was a television sitting on a stand opposite the bed. Other than that, the room was empty of other furniture. A large rectangle rug was sitting on the area between the bed and the TV. He looked down and smiled for the first time. Baby's dog bed was sitting next to the bed, just as Melody had claimed.

He turned and peeked into the small bathroom off to the side. It was functional and clean. All looked good in her apartment. For the first time, feeling relieved he hadn't found anything unusual or that would frighten Mel, Tex looked around her room with the eyes of a man, rather than with the eyes of a SEAL.

The room was comfortable and womanly. He could imagine Mel sleeping there. Hell he could imagine both of them sleeping . . . and loving there. He felt himself grow hard just imagining it. It was almost ridiculous how easy he was aroused just thinking about Melody. One part of his brain told him it was crazy, that he just met her. But the other part argued that it was right, that they knew each other very well after their long online talks.

Before he was injured, Tex was always the one to take the first step in any relationship, whether that relationship was long-term or a one night stand, but with Mel, he didn't want to mess anything up. He'd lost his confidence after being rejected one too many times by women who didn't want to get involved with a crippled veteran. Even his status as an ex-SEAL wasn't enough to entice them.

Tex halted his thoughts in their tracks. Melody was sitting unguarded in the parking lot, probably worried about him. He hadn't lied to her saying he thought she'd be safe while he went inside, but he still needed to stop daydreaming and get her inside where it was safer. He willed his erection to subside as he headed back to the parking lot and the woman who was quickly becoming the most important thing in his life.

Melody sat up straighter in her seat as she saw Tex coming toward her. He didn't look worried, just focused on getting back to her. Baby lifted her head as if she knew Tex was coming, and turned in his direction. Her tail started wagging, but she didn't climb off of Melody's lap.

Tex came over to the driver's side of his truck and opened the door after she unlocked it. He didn't make her wait or ask. "Everything looks fine. Let's get you guys inside."

Melody nodded and clipped Baby's leash on before she stepped out of the truck.

Tex opened the back door and got out their bags. He reached for Melody's free hand and was relieved when she grasped it tightly in hers as they walked to her apartment.

He pushed open the door when they reached it and Baby bounced in. Melody laughed and pulled her back long enough to unclip her leash.

"She's happy to be home," Tex commented unnecessarily.

"Yeah." Melody looked around her apartment and sighed. "Me too."

"Come here." Tex grabbed Melody's hand and shut the door with his foot. He walked them both over to the couch and he sat down and arranged her on his lap.

Melody had tried to be strong, but being back in her apartment, back where she'd been so scared, back where she didn't think she'd ever live again, she finally broke down. She could feel Tex soothing his hand down her back and over her head. After a few minutes she tried to control herself. She lifted tear stained eyes to Tex. "Jeez, Sorry. I swear I never cry. I'm not normally like this."

"Nothing to be sorry for, Mel. I'm surprised it took this long."

"It's just that, I was scared to come back here, and now I'm not as freaked since you're here, but I didn't think I'd ever *get* to come back."

"We'll get your life back."

"I hope so."

"We will."

"Okay, Tex."

"Come on, I'm exhausted. I know you are too. Let's get some sleep. Things'll look better in the morning."

Tex held Melody steady as she stood up and he kept a hand on her back as they walked down the hall to her bedroom. Tex steered Mel into the bathroom.

"Get ready for bed, I'll grab our bags and let Baby out one last time."

"But your leg—"

Tex put a finger against her lips and cut off her words. "You've taken care of me enough, Mel, let me take care of *you* tonight." When it looked like she was still going to protest he simply said, "Please."

He watched as Mel looked into his eyes for a moment, then gripped his wrist and nodded. She pursed her lips and kissed the finger he had held against her. "Okay, I'll be here waiting for you."

Tex smiled down at her. She was completely transparent. She didn't play games with him. She simply told him she wanted him to stay in her bedroom with her. "I'll be back as soon as I can."

Melody nodded and turned for the bathroom. Tex looked down at her dog. "Come on, Baby, want to go outside once more before calling it a night?" Baby's tongue was hanging out of her mouth and it looked she was grinning up at him. He chuckled as he left the room and headed for the front door.

When he came back into her bedroom about ten minutes later, he saw that Melody had changed the sheets on the bed, the old ones sitting in a lump in the corner of the room. Mel was sound asleep, curled into a tight ball as if protecting herself. Something shifted inside Tex. He'd do anything to keep this woman safe, but it went beyond that. It wasn't just that he wanted to keep her safe. He wanted to end everyday by seeing her in their bed. He wanted to wake up next to her, he wanted to listen to her laugh and talk to Baby in the cute sing-song voice she sometimes used.

Somehow Tex knew Mel was it for him. When he'd made the decision to track her down and drive cross country to find her and bring her home, he'd known. He could've called Wolf and his team to go and get her. He could've just shrugged and decided she'd deleted her online account in that chat room because she was blowing him off. But somehow he'd known. She was special.

Feeling emotional, Tex turned to the bathroom so he could get ready for bed. He came out minutes later and sat on the side of the bed she'd obviously left for him. Tex looked over at Baby, who was snoring at the end of the mattress. Knowing he should probably make the dog get up and get into her dog bed on the floor, he just smiled, shook his head and turned his attention to his leg. He removed his prosthetic and quickly rubbed some lotion into his stump.

He didn't do as good of a job as he knew Mel would've, but suddenly it was vital to him that he hold her in his arms. He propped his prosthetic leg up against the drawers next to the mattress and laid back. He turned to Mel, who was sleeping with her back to him, and he curled into her. He'd never spooned a woman before, but with Mel it felt right. Tex put his right arm around her and snuggled into her.

They were both wearing T-shirts and boxers, but Tex could feel Mel's body heat seep into his body.

"Are you all right?" Mel murmured sleepily.

"Shhhh, everything's fine. Go back to sleep."

"Did you rub your leg down?"

"Yes, sweetheart. I'm good. Sleep. I've got you." Tex whispered the words into her ear and smiled as he felt her snuggle back against him as if settling in for the long haul.

"Mmm-hummm."

Tex smiled and closed his eyes. The trust Mel put in him seemed to magically erase all the doubts he'd had about himself since he'd retired from the Navy. He knew she had no idea what she did for him, but Tex did. Holding her in his arms, knowing even half-asleep she worried about him and cared about him, was a feeling he'd never felt before in his life. He'd do anything to keep her safe. Absolutely anything. Protecting Melody, and Baby, was the only thing he'd be focused on for the foreseeable future. *She* was his future. Tex fell asleep holding Mel in his arms, excited about his future for the first time in a long time.

CHAPTER 9

"Yes, it's really me, Amy." Melody reassured her friend for what seemed like the hundredth time.

"Are you back for good?"

"I don't know. I hope so." Melody didn't want to lie to her friend. She knew she wouldn't have been able to get away with prevaricating if she'd been standing in front of her friend. Amy knew her way too well and could take one look at her and know when she was lying or leaving something out. They'd known each other too long to get away with not being honest with one another.

"Are you there alone?"

"No, Tex is here with me."

"Tex, huh?"

Melody could hear the teasing in Amy's voice. "Yeah, Tex." Looking over at Tex, Melody knew their conversation sounded like they were in junior high school, but she could only smile. Tex was sitting on the couch next to her petting Baby while she spoke to Amy. "And he's sitting right here staring at me wondering what the hell we're talking about." She smiled and looked back down at her dog, sleeping so peacefully between them.

"I like him, Melody. I mean, I wasn't sure when he first called me, but he brought you home, I think I might love him."

"Me too." As soon as the words left her mouth, Melody knew they were true. She looked back up at Tex in a panic, wondering if he'd over-heard Amy's words and understood what she'd said in response.

"Everything all right?" Tex whispered the words and leaned toward her, looking concerned.

Melody covered the mouthpiece and quickly told Tex, "Yeah, I'm good."

Tex nodded and leaned back into the couch again and continued watching her and petting Baby.

"We need to talk, woman," Amy said sternly.

"I know, I can't wait to see you, Cindy, and Becky."

"They can't wait to see you either."

"But I don't want to put them in danger, Ames."

Melody heard her friend sigh. "I know. Me either. Will you call me later so we can set up when we can get together? I really need to see you. I've missed you."

"I will. I need to talk to Tex so we can figure out where we're going from here."

"Okay. I'm glad you're back. I have a feeling Tex will figure this all out."

"I hope so. Okay, Love you, Amy. I'll talk to you later."

"Bye."

"Bye." Melody clicked the phone off and sat back against the couch.

"You guys are really close." Tex's words were matter of fact.

"Yeah. One of the hardest things about leaving was not being able to talk to Amy. Yeah, I missed my parents, but it's not the same as not being able to talk to my best friend."

"You ready to talk this through so we can see if we can't figure it out?"

"No, but yes."

Tex chuckled and gave Baby one last pat on the head and stood up. He held out his hand to Mel. "Come on. Let's sit at the table. I need to use my computer to see what I can find and to write everything down."

Melody grasped Tex's hand and let him lead her to her table. He pulled out the chair at the end of the table and when she was seated, took the chair next to her on the side of the table. He pulled over one of his laptops and fired it up.

"How about we start with how you were able to stay away and how you organized it all. Somehow this guy found you while you were in Cali-fornia, and we have to figure out how."

"Wouldn't it be easier to talk about who I think it might be first?"

"Not really. We'll get to a list of suspects in a bit. First, I just want you to talk. Tell me what you did while you were running. Don't filter what you tell me, let me figure that out."

What Tex said made sense. "Well, I left without really thinking everything through. I didn't have enough money to run indefinitely, but I knew I shouldn't use credit cards because they can be tracked somehow. I went to the bank and pulled a couple thousand dollars out of my account so I'd have the cash. I didn't know how smart my stalker was, but I figured using my cell phone and credit cards could lead someone right to me if they knew computers." She stopped when she saw Tex smirk at her.

"Yeah, like I have to tell *you* that."

"Keep going."

"I rented a car. I figured I'd use it until I decided where I was going and what I was going to do. So I'd been gone for about five days when I called Amy to help me. I knew I'd run out of cash eventually, so I filled out a Power of Attorney for her so she could go to the bank and pull money for me. She'd take out cash and mail it to me. I'd give her the address of a hotel, and then as soon as I got the letter with the cash in it, I'd switch hotels. I bought those throwaway phones that you can get at the store with the pre-set minutes. That way the stalker couldn't track me down that way.

"My job is actually really easy to do from anywhere. I work with a system called CART. It stands for Communication Access Realtime Translation. Basically I listen in to an event via Skype and I type what I'm hearing. My typed words are then broadcast to anyone at the actual venue on an app. They can read the words as they watch. There's a little time lag, but not too much. Since all I need is an Internet connection, that allowed me to keep working, even when I was on the run. I kept paying my rent in the hopes that I'd be able to come home eventually. Amy helped by picking up my mail and paying the bills that came through."

"Sounds like you couldn't have done this without Amy," Tex noted with no inflection in his voice.

"Don't," Melody warned in a low voice.

"Don't what?"

"Amy's not involved in this."

"I didn't say she was."

"Bullshit. I can tell what you're thinking. You're thinking that she knew exactly where I was. She had access to my apartment, but she wouldn't do this to me."

"I thought you weren't going to think about it while you told me what you did, Mel?" When she seemed ready to lose it, Tex quickly tried to calm her down. "For what it's worth, I don't think she's your stalker."

"You don't? Then why that look on your face?"

"Because as much as it sucks, we have to consider everyone, no matter how much it hurts. But remember, I met her Mel. She kept Baby for you. The stalker said he wanted to hurt Baby. Amy had the perfect opportunity to tell you that she ran away, got hit by a car, got sick . . . anything. But she didn't."

Melody looked down at Baby who was sleeping next to her chair. "Okay, sorry. I just . . . she's my best friend. I trust her implicitly."

Tex put his hand over Melody's. "I know you do. I didn't mean to imply she was involved, but that doesn't mean someone else you thought you could trust isn't involved or isn't actually your stalker."

Melody took a deep breath. "Okay, That makes sense. I just . . . I trust Amy as much as I trust you."

Tex picked up Mel's hand and kissed the palm, never losing eye contact. "Thank you for that. Continue?"

Melody curled her fingers in, as if holding in the kiss Tex had placed on her hand and did as he asked. "So yeah, I'd switch hotels every week or so. I'd rent a car when I needed to change cities, paying with cash, of course, then return the car once I was in a place where I could use public transportation. I would use the Internet in local coffee shops or fast food restaurants."

"Was the note you showed me in California the first one you'd received since you left Pennsylvania?"

Melody looked down at her hands. She'd been clenching them as she spoke. "No. I'd received one when I was in Florida. It said much the same thing as the one you saw."

"So whoever this is, he somehow was able to track you to at least Florida and California. Okay, let's talk about your life here."

"Here?"

"Yeah, here in Pennsylvania. Did you date before you left?"

Melody fidgeted in her seat, then suddenly got up to go into the kitchen. "Can I get you anything? A coffee refill?" She turned around to see if Tex wanted anything and shrieked in surprise when he was standing right in front of her. Jesus, he could move quietly.

Tex hated putting Mel through his questions, but he had to find out as much as he could so they could catch this guy. He put his finger under her chin. "You know I'm not doing this to pry, don't you Mel?"

She immediately dropped her head to his chest and sighed. "Yeah, I know. It's just . . . it's hard. I don't like to think that anyone I know would do this to me. It's just so horrible and evil . . . and to think that someone I might have dated, or who I know, who I talked to every day and had no idea he wanted to hurt me and kill my dog and my friends and family, is stalking me? It sucks."

"It does suck. I'm sorry."

"I'm also embarrassed for you to hear about how boring my life was."

"What?"

Melody lifted her head so she could see Tex. "Tex, you were a SEAL. You did exciting things all the time. You *lived* your life. Me? I'm boring as hell. I hung out in this small town. Excitement in my life was heading up to Pittsburgh to go shopping. It's embarrassing."

"Mel, it's not embarrassing. Those exciting things you think I did? They sucked. Every last one of them. I killed people, I hunted people, I rescued people who'd been starved, beaten, or raped . . . hell sometimes all three. Sometimes we weren't able to save them. We had to recover their bodies. There were times when I would've given anything for a so-called boring life as you call it."

"Tex . . ."

"So anything you tell me isn't embarrassing. One, it's about you and I want to know everything about you, and two . . ." His voice dropped and his fingers clenched at her sides. "I like the thought of you living here, safe, without anything like the shit I've seen and experienced touching you. I yearn for you to be able to call going up to the city as exciting again. Help me figure this out so you can get back to that as soon as possible."

"Okay. But I need to be doing something while I talk to you. This is stressing me out."

Tex kissed her on the forehead and looked down at her. "No problem."

"Why do you do that?"

"Do what?"

"Kiss me on the forehead? I like it, but sometimes it makes me feel like I'm eight years old."

"Because if I kiss you like I really wanted to, we wouldn't make it out of your apartment today, or maybe not even tomorrow. And the sooner we can figure out who this asshole is in your life, the sooner I can take you to bed and not have to worry about who might be watching or waiting for us to make a mistake."

"Oh."

"Yeah, oh. I'm controlling myself here, Mel, but trust me when I say there's nothing more I want than to take your mouth, to lift you up on this counter, which is at just the right height, and make you come on my mouth, and my dick, over and over again."

Melody could just stare at Tex for a moment. She could feel herself grow slick at his words. Never before in her life had a guy talked to her like that, but with Tex, she liked it. No, she loved it. She could picture how they'd look, and it turned her on.

Tex leaned forward and kissed her on the forehead again. "God, if you could see the look on your face. I'm going to go back to the table and write down everything you tell me. You stay here and . . . do something. After we talk we'll head out and make sure we're seen around town. Then you can call Amy and arrange to meet her somewhere. Then we'll come back here."

"And after that?"

"We'll see, Mel. I refuse to rush you."

"I think I want to be rushed."

"Fuck." The word was low and heartfelt, but Tex let go of Melody and backed away to the table. Tex leaned down and ran his hand over Baby's head before he sat back down. He put his hands on the keyboard and refused to look back up at Mel. He was holding on to his control by his fingernails. Knowing that apparently Mel wanted him as much as he wanted her? Torture. Pure torture.

"I didn't date much, but I had the occasional date here and there. I went to high school in this town, so I know a lot of people. I shop here, I bank here. I dated here."

"Give me the names, Mel."

Melody fiddled with the cup of coffee she held in her hands. Her stomach was churning so she didn't want to drink it. "Lee Davis. He was the last guy I dated. We were together for about three months."

"Why'd you break up?"

"He was kinda a jerk."

"In what way?" Tex's voice was hard.

Melody looked up in surprise. "Just little things. He'd always make me pay when we went out to dinner, saying it was because I made more money than him. He'd flirt with the waitress in front of me. Many times he didn't bother to call me back when I'd leave him a message . . . just in general he was a jerk."

"Why'd you date him in the first place? I can't imagine you'd put up with that."

Melody smiled at Tex from across the kitchen. His earlier words still flitted through her brain. "I think I was lonely. But you're right, as soon as he started doing those things, and stopped trying to impress me, I dumped him."

"Was he upset about it?"

Melody put the cup on the counter and leaned back against it, putting her weight on her hands. "No. I saw him with Diane the next week."

"Diane?"

"Yeah, she was two years behind me in school. She works at the bank."

"All right, who else?"

"Are we going to do this for every man I've ever dated?"

"If we have to."

"Damn. Okay. Let's see. Adam Grant. We dated for two months. I wouldn't sleep with him, so he dumped me. Jamie Wilde. We didn't last beyond the first date. I left him at the table, he had the worst manners I'd ever seen. Burping, being crass, he even slapped the waitress on the butt as she walked away from the table. I told him I had to use the restroom and I left."

Melody ignored Tex's chuckle and continued, watching as Tex frantically typed on his keyboard as she talked.

"Chris Myles, M-y-l-e-s. He was my longest relationship. We were together for around seven months. We were practically living together. He'd spend the night at my place or I'd spend the night at his. We were going to move in together, and I knew he was planning on asking me to marry him, but at the last minute I couldn't do it. I broke up with him."

Melody took a deep breath, remembering the fight that had ensued the night she told Chris she thought they should break up.

"Was he mad?"

"Yeah. He was mad." That was the understatement of the year.

"What about you? Were you okay?"

"Yeah. That was why I knew I had to break it off. The thought of not being with him didn't devastate me. The thought of actually living with Chris and being with him day in and day out held no appeal to me. I liked him, but it seemed as if I felt of him more as a friend than anything else. He didn't feel the same way."

"Honestly, do you think it could be him?"

Melody turned toward Tex. His jaw was tight, but he'd kept his voice low and controlled. "I don't know. Before today, I would've said no. But you said I had to suspect everyone, so I suppose, but it'd surprise me. He got married about a year and a half after we broke up. He lives in the area, but he's got three kids and the last time I saw him, he seemed genuinely happy with his wife and his life."

"All right. Anyone else?"

"I don't like this, Tex. Hell, I like you. I don't want to talk about past boyfriends with you. It doesn't feel right."

"I'm not liking it either, Mel. The thought of anyone's hands on you, other than mine, makes me want to do something illegal. But if we can be us, if we can be together, we have to figure out who's stalking you and stop it."

"I know." Mel closed her eyes and kept them closed as she finished reciting the names of the guys she dated. "Terry Neal, Larry Page, Don Ramper . . . I dated them in college. Robert Pletcher was my high school boyfriend. I don't think I've talked to any of them in years. I can't imagine any of them wanting to stalk me. Hell, they probably don't even remember me."

"They remember you, Mel. I can fucking promise you that. Change of plans. I've got all their names down and into my search program. In a few hours I'll have their driving history, credit reports, arrest record, former addresses, current addresses, jobs, salaries, and everything else that might be relevant."

Mel opened her eyes and looked at Tex. "That doesn't sound legal."

He didn't look up, but continued fiddling with his computer. "It's not, but I didn't think you'd mind if it gives us more information than we have right now."

"I don't . . . but I don't want you getting in trouble for helping me."

Tex did look up at that. Without breaking eye contact with Mel, he shut his laptop and stood by the table. "As I said, change of plans. I consider myself a reasonable man, but I find after listening to you talk about other men who may or may not have touched you, had you, had what I want so badly I'm about to lose my mind, that I'm not so reasonable after all. I need you, Mel. I want you under me. I want to wipe away the memory of any other man who's ever had what I want desperately. We need to get out of here and in public where I can't bend you over the couch or drag you into your room and make love to you all afternoon."

"Do you want to know why none of the men I've been with have made me want to be with them forever?"

"Mel, you need to stop talking about other men," Tex warned in a low voice. "I'm hanging on by a thread here."

Melody continued as if Tex hadn't interrupted her. "I had to make all the decisions in our relationships. Where we'd go to eat. Whether or not Chris and I would move in together. Who would pay for dinner. It went on and on. It was as if the men I dated knew I was a strong business woman and they figured I'd want to make all the decisions about our dating life. What they didn't realize was that it's tiring. I want someone who can take charge of some things every now and then. I'm not talking about a Dominant/submissive relationship, not that I think that sort of thing is bad, but I'm thinking of things like, deciding where we'd go eat dinner, taking charge with paying for things . . . I know I'm not saying this very well, but I've never had even one man who I've been interested in, make me quake where I stand and make me wet just by telling me he wants me . . . until now."

Melody stared at Tex, wondering if she'd been too honest. It was her experience that men liked strong take charge women. Would Tex be turned off by what she'd just said? She watched as Tex took a step toward her. Then another. Then he was in front of her.

Tex reached out and grabbed Mel by the waist and hauled her to him. "I gave you a chance, but you just kept pushing. Now hop up and put your legs around my waist." His words were guttural. Melody didn't hesitate. As soon as her legs curled around him, he turned and headed down the hall toward her bedroom.

CHAPTER 10

Melody didn't say a word, just watched the muscle in Tex's jaw tick as he carried her into her bedroom. They had a hundred things they should be doing, but she couldn't think of a single one right at that moment. All she could think of was Tex's body moving under hers as he walked.

Tex walked into the bedroom and shut the door behind him, ignoring Baby's whimpers as she was blocked out of the room.

"I can feel your heat against me, Mel. That's so fucking hot." Tex leaned over and put Mel on the bed on her back then leaned over her. "I wish I could promise that I'll make love to you for hours, but the reality is, I'm about to blow just feeling the hint of your wetness and heat against me. It's been a long time for me, but you aren't just an itch I want to scratch. I hope you know that going into this."

Melody nodded, her mouth too dry to comment.

"This first time is, unfortunately, going to be fast for me. But I swear, I'll take care of you. I won't leave you wanting. I'm glad you don't mind when a guy makes decisions, because I'm way too used to doing it to back off now. I don't want or need a submissive, but I'm probably going to piss you off sometimes with my take-charge attitude. I'll apologize now, but know that I don't ask you to do things because I'm a dick. I ask you to do things because I think they're in your, or our, best interest. I'm bossy. I'm a former SEAL and I've never wanted a woman in my life more than I want you this moment."

"God, Tex—"

"Take your shirt off."

Without hesitation, Melody brought her arms to the hem of her shirt and tugged it upward. Tex didn't back off, so she had to wiggle and maneuver herself to get it over her head. When she had it off, she watched as Tex ran his eyes from the top of her head down to her waist and back up, stopping at her bra covered chest.

"I'm not skinny . . ."

"You're not, and I fucking love it," Tex said without hesitation. He moved one hand and shifted his balance to his other hand. He covered her stomach with his hand and pressed down. "Fuck. Soft and womanly. A perfect balance to my hardness. When I take you, you'll cushion my thrusts with your body. I can pound into you without feeling like I'm hurting you. I'll tell you a secret . . . when you're on top of me, riding me, there will be nothing sexier than the sight of your tits bouncing up and down each time I hit bottom. And when I'm thrusting into you? Watching your body jiggle and move each time I pound in? Fucking heaven."

"Oh my God, Tex."

Tex's hand moved up and covered one of her breasts and squeezed, just a shade lighter than what would've been painful. "Show me your nipples."

Melody thought she was going to have a heart attack. Her heart was beating wildly and she'd never been more turned on in her life. She brought both hands up to her bra and pulled the cups down until her breasts popped up and over the material. The underwire of the bra pushed her mounds up. Melody looked down and gasped. Her nipples were tight and puckered, as if they were reaching for Tex.

"Tell me to stop now, Mel. If you don't want this. If you don't want what's happening between us, tell me now."

Melody looked up at Tex, expecting to see him looking at her body, but instead he was looking her in the eyes. His pupils were dilated and huge in his eyes. While she watched him, he took his hand off her breast and up to her face. He drew one finger down her cheek and lifted her chin with it. Melody felt him lean down and whisper against her lips. "I need you. I've waited for you my entire life. If we do this, I'm not letting you go."

The words came out without thought, but they felt right. They felt perfect.

"Don't stop."

As soon as the words were out of her mouth, Tex's lips were on hers. He wasn't gentle, but instead he plunged his tongue into her mouth and devoured her. Melody gave as good as she got. Their tongues swirled around each other and plunged in and out of each other's mouths. They both used their teeth to nip and play.

Tex pulled back. "Fuck, Mel." He moved, shifted up and looked down at her breasts. Her nipples were still pulled taut. He leaned down and pulled one of them into his mouth. There were no preliminaries, he didn't tease his way down, he just pulled her nipple into his mouth and sucked, hard.

"Tex. God!" Melody's voice was thin and high pitched. She brought her hand up to the back of his head as he rhythmically sucked against her. Just as she didn't think she could handle anymore, he moved to her other breast. Melody writhed under Tex and lifted her hips in search of something.

Tex released her nipple with a pop. "What do you need, Mel?"

"You. I need you."

Tex stood up abruptly and watched as Mel squirmed on the bed. She was so beautiful, he couldn't wait another second. He ripped the shirt off his body and quickly undid his pants. He reached into his back pocket and grabbed the condom that had been in his wallet forever, then shoved his pants down his legs and off without a thought about his prosthetic. He was as hard as he'd ever been in his life, and he quickly rolled the condom down his length, praying it hadn't expired.

"Yes, Tex. Help me." Melody was fumbling with the clasp at her back, while her hips were still thrusting up toward him.

Standing naked, but not feeling self-conscious for the first time since he'd had his surgery, Tex undid the button on Mel's pants and helped her remove them. Finally they were both naked.

"Since I know the second I get inside you I'm going to lose control, you're going to have to come at least twice before I get in there. I want this to be as good for you as I know it's going to be for me. Maybe in the future I'll let you choose how you want it, but not now. You said you like when a man takes charge? Well, I'm taking charge. Put your hands over your head and keep them there."

Melody tore her eyes away from Tex's body. He was built, everywhere.

She couldn't wait to explore him, but apparently now wasn't the time. She'd never had sex like this before, but if the way her body was reacting was any indication, she'd never forget it and would want more just like it . . . at least from Tex.

"Spread your legs."

Tex watched as Melody immediately complied. He ran his hands up her inner thighs and groaned when he found the slickness that covered them. "Oh yeah, you're so fucking wet, Mel. For me. All for me."

He heard her voice above him, but he was too focused on his prize to hear what she said. He leaned in and nuzzled the crease where her inner thigh stopped. "You smell like . . . I have no idea what, but I've never smelled anything like it. It's perfect. You're perfect." He shifted and licked her once from bottom to top. "Oh my God, Mel. I love this. I hope you're comfortable because I'm going to be here for a while."

Melody moaned as Tex gripped her legs and widened them even further. She closed her eyes as he settled in, resting his weight on his elbows next to her hips. His tongue was amazing. He swirled, licked, and sucked every inch of her. Melody hadn't ever really paid that much attention to her sex before. It was just . . . there. The men she'd slept with hadn't bothered either. They might've fingered her a bit or licked her a few times, but none of them had spent the time worshiping her as Tex was.

She stiffened suddenly as Tex took her clit in his mouth and sucked at the same time he flicked his tongue against her. "Tex! I'm coming!" Instead of lightening up, Tex increased his efforts, thrust a finger inside her and drew out her orgasm as she bucked against his face and hand.

Finally he lifted his head, but didn't let go of her. Melody looked down and saw him licking his lips. She blushed.

"Blushing, Mel? Seriously? Jesus, woman. You just get better and better."

"Aren't you going to—"

"Told you two orgasms, Mel. That was only one."

"Tex . . ." Melody could hear the whining in her voice.

"Turn over."

"What?"

Tex eased back onto his legs. "Turn. Over."

Looking at him, seeing the lust, but also the deeper emotion, Melody turned over, trusting Tex explicitly. She wasn't sure what to do with her legs, but Tex helped her. He tapped her calves and told her to shift. She shifted upward until her legs were folded under her.

"Put your arms over your head again."

Melody did as Tex asked. She felt way too vulnerable on her knees bent over in front of Tex. Her ass had to look huge like this. Her breathing increased and she lifted her head. "I don't think I like this."

"Shhhhh, Mel." Tex ran both hands down her back, soothing her. "It's okay. I'm not going to hurt you. Trust me."

Melody nodded and put her head back down, deciding if she could trust him with her life, she could certainly trust him with this.

"You have no idea how beautiful you look like this. Your skin is soft and you're completely open to me." Tex inched closer, spreading Mel's legs further apart in the process. He heard Mel whimper, and hurried to reassure her. "Easy, Mel. Fucking beautiful." He ran his hand over her sex, spreading her wetness over his palm. He then took his hand and smoothed it over her ass, watching as her juices glistened in the light. He did it again, and again. When Mel started shaking, he soothed her once again.

"Easy. I'll get you there."

Tex couldn't believe he was here. Couldn't believe he was here with Melody. He hadn't planned it, but he couldn't imagine his life without her in it now.

Spreading the cheeks of her ass he leaned down and licked her sex. Pulling back, he used his fingers to explore her intimately. Tex pushed a finger inside her and curled it to rub against the sensitive spongy wall inside. Mel jerked and moaned. Tex put a hand in the small of her back and pressed. "Easy, Mel. Hold on for me. Don't let go yet."

"I'm going to . . ."

"No. Hold it, Mel. Don't come."

He could see Melody hold her breath, then he heard as it came out in a rush. She did it again. Her butt clenched and her toes curled against him. She was doing everything she could to hold off . . . for him. Tex hadn't ever been so hard in his life. He wanted to plunge inside her more than he wanted his next breath, but he'd been honest with her earlier. He knew the second he pushed inside her tight sheathe, he'd be a goner.

"That's it, Mel . . . It's going to feel so good when you finally let go. But not yet . . . hang in there just a little longer."

"Tex, please . . . your hands feel too good. I need you."

"I can feel you clenching against me. You're gonna be so tight. You want me in there don't you?" His question was rhetorical, because he could feel how much she wanted him.

When her entire body was shaking, Tex said the words she'd been waiting for. "Now, Mel. Come for me *now*."

She did, and it was beautiful. Every muscle in her body tensed and shook. She threw her head back and moaned long and low. Her fingers gripped the pillowcase by her head as she shivered. "Please, Tex, now. Come inside. I want to feel you."

Tex turned Melody until she was on her back again. He took her ankles in his hands and bent her knees up until she was fully open. He eased forward until his cock nudged her sex. Thank God he'd had the foresight to put the condom on before they started playing. He was so hard he didn't have to worry about guiding himself in. It was as if his dick knew right where it wanted to go.

They both groaned as Tex finally eased himself inside her. He pushed in until he was in as far as he could go. Placing Mel's legs over his shoulders he leaned down and braced himself on his hands.

"I changed my mind about two, Mel. Reach down and touch yourself. I want one more out of you."

Melody hadn't yet recovered from the most intense orgasm she'd ever had, but she followed Tex's command anyway. She took one hand and snaked it between their bodies until she could reach where they were connected. She groaned as Tex pulled his hips back to give her some room. She couldn't help but move her hand lower and circle his length as he pulled out. She tightened her grip as he pushed back in, loving the groan that escaped his mouth.

"Touch yourself, Mel, not me. I'm holding on by a thread here as it is."

"But I like touching you."

"And I like you touching me. But I'm serious, hands off. I want to feel you squeezing my cock when you orgasm again, but I'm not going to be much help here. Touch yourself. Make yourself come and take me with you."

Since he put it that way . . . Mel moved her hand and ran her fingertip around her clit. She immediately arched her back. "I'm so sensitive."

"Yeah, you are." Tex looked down at Mel. She was so beautiful, and she was his. He moved his hips rhythmically. In and out. In and out. He watched as her breasts jiggled and he felt remorse for just a moment that he hadn't had time to worship them. Later. He'd spend time with them later.

He sped up his thrusts. He could feel the tingle in his balls, warning him his release was imminent. "Faster, Mel. I'm close. You're too tight and too wet. I can't hold off. Come on. Let me feel you squeeze me." He leaned down to take one quick taste of her nipples before he lost all control. He sucked one into his mouth and took it between his teeth. He pressed down with just enough pressure to be a bit uncomfortable, but not enough to cause her true pain. It was apparently enough.

Tex felt her inner muscles clamp down on his cock as she exploded once again. She bucked up into him as she orgasmed. He groaned and pushed his way in and out of her body, through her muscles that were still flexing and squeezing against him.

"Oh yeah. Fuck, Mel. Yes." Tex thrust one more time and held himself still as he emptied himself into the condom. He couldn't help but thrust one more time, then two. Finally when he couldn't hold himself up anymore, he collapsed down practically on top of Mel, partially off to her side.

It was many moments before Tex could bring himself to move. He propped himself up on an elbow, careful not to dislodge himself from her. He knew he had to pull out and get rid of the condom, he just didn't want to leave her yet. He brought up a hand and pushed Mel's hair out of her face. It had gotten stuck in the sweat that now covered her brow.

"You all right?"

"No."

Tex's lips quirked up into a smile. "No? Anything I can do to help?"

"Just let me lie here. You've killed me."

"But what a way to go, huh?"

Melody opened one eye and looked right into Tex's face. He was within an inch of hers and he was smiling. "Yeah. What a way to go."

"Is your leg okay?"

The smile on Tex's face faded and he got serious. "You're amazing. Seriously. You just had three orgasms and you did everything I wanted you to, and practically the first words out of your mouth are to ask if *I'm* all right?"

"Yeah. Are you?"

"Yeah, Mel. I'm perfect. You know what? For the first time since that fucking bomb blew up, my leg doesn't hurt. Not even a twinge."

Melody closed her eyes and pulled Tex down to her. "Now I know what to do when it hurts again. It's a new treatment for the phantom pains."

Tex laughed and pulled out of Mel with a groan and pulled off the condom and tied it off.

"The not-so-sexy part of sex," Melody commented wryly. "Just put it on the floor, we'll deal with it in a while."

Tex did as she suggested, then turned back and gathered her into his arms. "Your practicality is one of the things I like about you the most. That and your perfect body."

"Hush. I'm basking."

"Basking?"

"Yes, now shhhh."

Tex just shook his head and shushed. They had things to do. He knew Amy would be chomping at the bit to see her friend, but they had time to relax for a bit longer.

CHAPTER 11

*T*ex watched as Amy and Mel cried in each other's arms. After they'd gotten out of bed and cleaned up in the shower, which involved both of them orgasming again, they'd spent some time outside with Baby, then left to try to meet up with Amy. They hadn't gotten two steps away from the apartment when Baby had started howling relentlessly.

Tex looked over at Mel who had an astonished look on her face.

"I take it she's never done that before?"

"No, never."

Tex had calmly opened the apartment door and snapped his fingers. Baby immediately stopped howling and sat on the floor by the couch watching Tex with her tail swishing back and forth on the floor.

"All right, Baby, you can come with us this time."

As if she could understand English, Baby trotted over to the door and waited patiently for Melody to clip on her leash.

They walked out the door again and after Tex re-locked the door headed to Tex's truck. They'd stopped at the bank where Mel had pulled out some cash. She'd spoken for a while to Diane, the woman she knew from high school, as well as another woman who came into the bank while they were there.

When they'd left, Mel had explained the other woman was Heather

Wallace. Melody met her in college and while they weren't close friends, Heather seemed very happy to have seen her again.

Mel had used Tex's phone to call Amy and they'd agreed to meet at a fast food restaurant down the street. Now Tex watched as the two best friends were reunited.

"I'm so glad you're okay! I missed you so much!"

"I know, I missed you too, Ames."

Amy reared back out of Melody's arms and smacked her on the arm. "Don't do that shit again."

"He said he was going to hurt you. And Becks. And Cindy. And Baby. And my parents. I couldn't let that happen. I never would've forgiven myself if he hurt you."

"Hashtag best friends."

"Hashtag separated at birth."

Tex watched as the women smiled at each other. He couldn't resist butting in. They were so damn cute together. He'd never thought the things women did with each other as funny before, but now that he'd gotten to know his friends' women better and watching Mel and Amy together, he found that he liked it. "Hashtag you guys are too cute."

"No. You don't get to hashtag," Amy said immediately and seriously, glaring at Tex, not releasing Melody.

"It's ours," Melody tried to explain to Tex gently. "We started it our senior year in high school. It was our 'thing.' Twitter had just started and we were using it and saying it before it was even popular and people knew what it meant. It drove other people crazy, but it was just between us. As typical teenagers we drove our teachers and parents nuts with it. I think there were some days we didn't say anything that didn't start with 'hashtag.' We loved it. Most people hated it."

Amy and Melody looked at each other and smiled, obviously remembering good times.

"Okay ladies. No more hashtagging from me." Tex reassured them. "Come on though, let's get out of the main thoroughfare and you guys can continue your reunion." He steered them out of the middle of the parking lot and away from the prying eyes of anyone who might be in the restaurant or driving by.

He watched as the women talked about Amy's kids and how they were doing. Amy caught Melody up with the local gossip. Amy spent some time loving on Baby, who was very happy to see her. Finally, after thirty minutes or so, they'd gotten most of the basic information out of the way.

Amy kept her arm through Melody's and turned to Tex. "Now what? What can I do to help?"

"No, Amy," Melody told her seriously. "I don't want you involved."

"It's too late, Mels, I'm already involved. This asshole threatened me and my family. He doesn't get to do that and get away with it."

"Amy is right," Tex broke in. "At the very least, I need to talk to her to get her opinion on who might be doing this. She'll have a different viewpoint than you and could really help."

"I'm okay with that, Tex, but I'm not sure about anything else."

"Mel, I told you before, and I'll say it again. I wouldn't do *anything* that would put you or your friends in jeopardy. I honestly think this has to be someone here in your hometown. Face it, it's not like you're a world traveler or anything."

Amy giggled and tried to stifle it when Melody glared at her.

Melody sighed. "Okay, but . . ."

"No buts."

"God, you can be annoying," Melody huffed out.

"Shut it, Mels. He's not annoying," Amy told her. "He's hashtag cute hashtag protective."

"Hashtag you might be my best friend but I can still kick your butt."

"Okay ladies," Tex said laughing, "Amy, we'll be in touch. I'm thinking we need to show ourselves around town some more, get whomever it is to see us together and hopefully make him emotional enough to make a mistake."

"Keep her safe." Amy's voice was dead serious and aimed at Tex. "I could handle not seeing her for the last few months simply because I knew she was out there somewhere . . . alive. I *can't* handle it if she's dead."

"She will *not* get dead." Tex's response was just as serious as Amy's. He endured her intense look and inwardly sighed in relief when she nodded.

Amy turned back to Melody and put her hands on her hips. "Hashtag I think you have a lot to tell me, Mels."

"I love you, Ames. Watch your back." Melody hugged her friend.

"Love you back. You too."

Tex watched as Amy walked over to her car on the other side of the parking lot and got in.

"Come on, Mel, We have a date downtown to go shopping."

"Shopping?"

"Yup, what better place to be seen then downtown, the hub of the town? Since we have Baby we can't go to the mall, we'll do that maybe tomorrow. But for now we'll see who else you know that we can run into. I want this done."

"Me too."

"All right then, let's go. The sooner we get this over with the sooner we can go back to your place."

Tex helped Mel into his truck and walked around and got in. They parked downtown and they all got out. Melody held onto Baby's leash and they wandered around. Tex was amazed at how many people Mel actually knew. It seemed like every time they turned around, someone else was welcoming her home. They'd decided to tell people she had been gone because of work, and since no one really knew much about what a closed caption reporter did, it was easy to be vague in the explanation.

Tex paid close attention to both the people they met and Baby as they walked and talked with people. He tried to catalog people's responses. They met up with several people who seemed genuinely pleased to see Melody, and others who were pretty fake in their response to her.

Baby only growled once, at Lee Davis. Lee was the last guy Mel had dated before the stalker started leaving her notes and threatening her. Tex remembered Mel had told him he'd been a jerk, but he was now dating the girl who worked at the bank ... Diane.

Mel hadn't moved to shake his hand or hug him or anything, but that hadn't stopped him. He'd gone to embrace Melody, but Baby got between them and growled. Lee had quickly stepped back and ended their conversation not much longer after that.

The other person who Baby and Tex didn't like was Robert Pletcher. He'd been Mel's high school boyfriend and Tex hated him on sight. Tex just knew this was the man who'd taken Mel's virginity. He shouldn't have cared, it was a long time ago and he had no right to be pissed about it, or jealous, because he didn't even know Melody back then. But he still felt it. He clenched his teeth when Robert kissed her on the cheek.

Tex couldn't stop his actions, he stepped up to Mel and put his hand on the small of her back. He leaned down and whispered in her ear, loud enough for Robert to hear him. "Baby and I will be right over there." Tex pointed at a bench not too far away. "Take your time visiting with your old friend." Then he put one hand on her cheek and turned her head to face him. He swooped down and kissed her. Not quick, and not softly. Pulling back he brushed his knuckles over her cheek and grabbed Baby's leash and headed for the bench.

When he got there he sat down, crossed his arms, and watched as Mel spoke with Robert. Baby jumped up on the bench next to him and sat as if she was human. Tex put his hand on her back and stroked while they waited for Mel.

Within five minutes she finished her conversation with Robert and walked toward them, smiling. She sat down next to Tex and put her hand on his thigh. She leaned over and patted Baby on the head and sat back.

"You wanna explain that?" Melody asked Tex.

"Do you *need* me to explain it?"

She smiled. "I don't think so. Tex, you have nothing to be worried about where Robert's concerned."

"It's not that I'm concerned, Mel. I don't think you're suddenly going to dump me and declare your everlasting love for that schmuck. I just don't like knowing that you and he . . ."

Melody stretched up and kissed Tex quiet. "It was forever ago. And it wasn't even good."

"Doesn't matter. We could be eighty years old and I still wouldn't like it."

Melody giggled. "Come on. Can we go home now? I didn't get to explore earlier." Just as the words were out of her mouth Tex was up and walking quickly toward his truck, Mel's hand held tightly in his own.

"We'll stop and pick up dinner on the way back to your place." Looking down at Baby as they walked Tex apologized. "Sorry, Baby, you're going to be on your own again tonight. Gotta spend some quality time with my girl."

CHAPTER 12

*M*elody stretched and winced. She was sore in places she'd never been sore before. Well, at least without spending hours in the gym. Tex had been amazing last night. He'd let her play to her heart's content, then spent just as much time returning the favor.

She turned over only to find an empty bed next to her. The sheets were cold, but Melody could see the imprint of Tex's head in the pillow next to her. Looking at the clock, Melody saw it was seven in the morning. She was usually up before now, but Tex had tired her out last night. She stumbled into the bathroom, grabbing her T-shirt and boxers off the floor where Tex had thrown them last night.

After her morning routine, she padded out into her living room and stopped dead. Tex was there. He was currently doing pushups and Baby was keeping him company. She was trying to lick his face every time he pushed himself up. Melody had no idea how long Tex had been at it, but since he hadn't noticed her yet, she leaned against the doorjamb to watch.

Even though Baby looked like she was being annoying, Tex tolerated her interference in his workout regime with extreme patience. It was amazing to see him doing one legged pushups. Oh, he was using his prosthetic to balance himself, but Melody could see that all of his weight was on his good foot.

Tex turned over after a few more pushups and started doing sit-ups. Baby obviously thought this was a fun new game, because she stood over him and tried to climb into his lap every time he laid back on the ground. Finally he gave up and mock growled and grabbed Baby around her body and fell backward with the dog in his arms. Baby wiggled out of his grasp, but came right back at him.

Melody watched as man and dog roughhoused on the floor. Both looked like they were having the time of their lives. Melody realized she hadn't been this happy in a long time. She'd spent the last six months being scared and worried and she always woke up tense, wondering what the day would bring.

Tex had brought her some peace. She knew she wasn't out of the woods yet, but whatever happened, Tex would be there to help her figure it out. She didn't want to think about what would happen if her stalker didn't make a move. Or once he was hopefully caught. She lived here in Pennsylvania and Tex lived in Virginia. He was staying with her right now, but that wouldn't be forever.

Melody shook her head, refusing to think about the future. She'd just thought about how happy she was, she didn't want to ruin it.

Baby must have seen her movement because she struggled out of Tex's hold and leaped over to Melody.

She laughed, kneeled on the ground and greeted her. Baby really was a good dog. Even though she'd been locked out of the bedroom last night, she didn't hold any grudges toward her or Tex.

"Good morning, beautiful," Tex said above her. He'd gotten up and walked over to where she and Baby were.

"Help me up." Melody held out her hand to Tex. He immediately grabbed it and lifted her off the ground as if she weighed nothing. He didn't just help her up, but pulled her right into his arms.

"Good morning, beautiful," he repeated.

"Good morning, Tex." Melody blushed at the intense look Tex was giving her.

"I have no idea how you can blush after what we did last night, but I love that you do."

"Did you sleep okay?"

"Mel, I've never slept better in my entire life, and certainly not since my surgery. Holding you in my arms, listening to you breathe, knowing you were exhausted from the orgasms I'd given you . . . fucking perfect." Tex leaned down and kissed Mel long and hard. He pulled back and watched as Mel chewed on the corner of her bottom lip. "What is it? What aren't you saying? Come on, Mel, don't hold back."

107

"You weren't there this morning when I got up."

"You have nothing to worry about, swear to God. Mel, I was a SEAL. I'm used to getting by on a lot less hours sleep than you. I work out every morning. Even though I'm retired, I haven't broken the habit. As it was, I laid in bed for twenty minutes just listening to you breathe and feeling you against me. I probably would've stayed there if I didn't hear Baby outside the door."

"It's just . . ." Mel paused, knowing what she was going to say would sound needy, and not really wanting to seem that way to Tex, especially since they hadn't been together very long.

"Come here." Tex took Mel's hand and led her to the couch. As was his usual, he sat down and pulled her into his lap. "Now, go on, tell me what's going on in that brain of yours. I know this is new, but you weren't afraid to tell me what you were thinking when we were talking to each over the computer, don't be afraid now that we're face-to-face."

"Will you wake me up when you leave in the morning?" At the frown on Tex's face, Melody hurried to complete her thought. "It's just that . . . I want to start my morning with you. And I can't do that if you're not there. Oh, I get that you have things to do, you aren't tied to my bed, but if I can't wake up with you, I'd like to know when you get up." Mel took a deep breath and continued, not looking Tex in the eyes. "It's happened before. One of the guys I dated in college left in the middle of the night and never came back. I guess he wanted to break up with me and didn't know how to tell me. I'm a little sensitive about it now."

"What a fucker. Mel, I'm not going anywhere. You heard me when I said you were mine didn't you? That if you wanted me, I was yours? I wasn't kidding. Besides, you need your sleep. I don't want to wake you up."

"I'm not talking about you shaking me and making me get up and do twenty pushups before you go and save the world, run a marathon or whatever." Melody smiled at Tex. "But just kiss me or something. I can sleep anywhere, I won't have any problem falling back asleep. It'll make me feel better knowing you haven't packed up to get out of here and that I could say good morning when you got up."

"All right," Tex agreed immediately, understanding her angst about waking up to an empty bed. "But believe me when I say I'm not fucking going anywhere. We need to have a conversation about what comes next, but until things have been resolved here, I'm not sure we're ready to have it. But rest assured, I'm not going anywhere."

Melody smiled at Tex. "Okay."

"Okay. Now, I don't think I've said a proper good morning yet. Kiss me, Mel. Like you mean it."

"I always mean it," Melody said the words with a smile as she leaned into Tex. She licked a path up the side of his neck. "Mmmmmm, salty."

"Mel . . ." Tex warned, feeling himself growing hard under her.

"Can't help it. You're just so sexy and masculine, and you're here with *me*. It's all so unbelievable."

Tex didn't answer, just took her head in one of his hands and brought her face to his. He kissed her long and hard. If he had to kiss her to make her believe it, he would . . . gladly.

When Melody came back to herself, she was on her back on the couch with Tex on top of her. One hand was under her shirt at her braless breast, and the other was holding her knee up, so his erection was notched between her legs in just the right spot.

"Good morning, Mel," Tex whispered huskily, while rubbing the back of her knee with his thumb on his left hand and her nipple with the fingers on his right.

"Did you get your workout done?" Melody asked breathlessly, arching her back slightly, pushing her breast further into his hand.

"No, but I can think of another way to burn some calories."

Thirty minutes later Melody lay on top of Tex on the couch. Clothes had been thrown every which way and they were both mostly naked. Tex had stripped her of her clothes and had made her do all the work since he claimed he'd already worked out. Melody had never been with a lover who was as vocal as Tex was. He'd complimented her throughout their lovemaking, commenting on her body, the way it moved, the way it felt, the way it made *him* feel. Nothing seemed to embarrass him or turn him off. At one point, Melody had reached behind her to try to cup Tex's balls and her fingers had slipped and she'd accidently prodded him in the back-side. Instead of tensing up, Tex had moaned and gripped her hips harder and exclaimed, "Oh yeah, Mel, that feels amazing." Of course *she* had blushed and immediately moved her fingers to her intended target, but Tex had just smiled under her and winked.

As much as Melody wanted to go back to bed, she knew they had things to do today. Tex had to check his programs and see what information he could glean from them about the men she'd dated in the past and she had a job today. There was an assembly she had to translate for and she had to read the materials the company had sent for her to review beforehand. She'd taken too many days off driving cross-country and needed to get back in the swing of things.

Feeling Tex's hard body underneath her move slightly, Melody turned her head. He was laughing. "What's funny?"

Tex didn't answer out loud, but instead used his chin to gesture off to the left. Melody turned her head to see Baby sitting nearby. Her head was cocked and her tail was swishing back and forth along the floor. Melody dropped her forehead on Tex's chest and groaned. "Oh my God, we've corrupted my dog."

"So much for doggy voyeurism being out." Tex only laughed harder when Mel groaned against his chest again. "Come on, Mel, shower, by yourself, or we'll never get anything done. Breakfast first and we'll take a look at the results of my searches. Then we'll head out. We need to hit a grocery store and see if we can be seen around town some more."

Melody raised her head and propped herself up on Tex's chest. She looked at him for a moment before saying softly, "Thank you."

"Don't thank me," Tex scolded immediately. "There's nowhere I'd rather be than here with you. I don't care if you had three stalkers, an escaped murderer was at your door, and Baby was rabid and attacking. This is what I've waited my whole life for." When Mel's eyes teared up, Tex sat up, holding tight to her so she didn't fall. He kissed her eyes, one at a time. "Don't cry, Mel. This is the start of our beautiful life together."

Tex urged Mel to stand up, and when she did, he turned sideways on the couch and buried his head in her stomach, holding her to him. He felt her hands in his hair and on his head. He inhaled deeply, then tilted his head back to look up at her. "You smell amazing." Tex's hands gripped her backside and kneaded. "You smell like us."

"Tex."

Tex took one hand and cupped her sex, then brought that hand up and smeared her wetness on her belly. Without taking his eyes from hers he said seriously, "A beautiful life, Mel. I'm going to do whatever it takes to give that to you . . . to us. Now, as much as I want to spend all day naked with you, we've got things to do."

Tex caressed her belly one more time, then turned her and smacked her lightly on the ass. "Go shower, woman."

Melody giggled and took a step toward the hallway and her bedroom. She looked behind her at Tex still sitting on her couch. Baby had walked up to him and he had one hand on her head and the other was on his knee. His eyes were glued to her though. Melody put a bit of a sway in her step as she continued toward the shower. She heard him groan behind her and she smiled. Somehow Tex had made coming home fun . . . when it should've been nothing but terrifying.

Melody knew some people would claim they were moving way too fast. That having Tex basically living with her was crazy, that she only knew him for around a week, but she knew that wasn't true. She'd known Tex for over six months. Yes, she'd just met him in person, but the groundwork of friendship had been laid for months now. They'd danced around the sexual tension they felt while they were talking online, but had never done anything about it.

She had no idea where they were going or what her crazy stalker would do now that she was home, but Melody hoped like hell in the end, when the dust was all settled, she could find a future with Tex.

CHAPTER 13

*M*elody sat at her kitchen table with her head in her hands as Tex continued to type as he spoke with her.

"Nothing really stands out on the guys whose names you gave me. Your high school boyfriend, Robert, is married like you said he was, but it also looks like he's had a couple of affairs as well, so he's not as devoted to his family as he might make it appear. All of the men you told me about have debt, but Lee is in to it to his eyeballs. It's a good thing you ditched him when you did, Mel. He has three credit cards that are maxed out and it looks like he has a couple of speeding tickets that haven't been paid yet either. Not only that, but the cops have been called to his house at least twice for domestic violence issues."

"Bastard," Melody said with feeling. "Poor Diane. I know I've been gone, and I don't really know her that well, but no one should have to live with that crap. I hope she dumps his ass."

"Yeah, it looks like she's been hospitalized twice in the past at Saint Albin's hospital."

"Saint Albin's?"

"Yeah."

"That's a mental hospital."

"Yup."

"Is she okay?"

Tex sighed. "I can find out exactly why she was there and what her diagnosis was if I dig, but it looks like she was hospitalized before she started dating Lee."

"Well, he can't be good for her, that's for sure," Melody sympathized.

"Can I send this stuff to Wolf and his team to look over?"

Melody looked at Tex in surprise. "You're asking me?"

"Yeah. While I'm good, sometimes it helps to have another set of eyes. And I'm a bit too close to this whole situation to be completely unbiased. So I'd like to get your permission to show this stuff to my friends."

"Then, yeah, you can show it to them. I'm not sure what good it'll do, but it can't hurt."

"Thanks, Mel. You're right. It can't hurt." Tex immediately began tapping out a message on his keyboard. "I'll encrypt it before I send it so it can't be traced back to me, and so the information stays secure. Once I'm done here we need to go to the police station. We should've done it before now, but I got distracted . . ."

Tex looked up at Melody with a look so hot, she thought she'd melt in her seat.

Tex continued his thought, "I'm assuming you went to them before you headed out on the road?"

"Yeah, there wasn't anything they could do. They took the notes I'd received and made a report, but otherwise they told me just to be careful."

"That's what I thought. Well, we'll bring them the note you got in California, just to get it logged, and to let them know you're back in town. They might not be able to do much, but if anything *does* happen, at least they'll have a head's up."

Melody shuddered at the thought of her stalker catching up with her. "Do you think he's going to do something? I think I'd rather he just did it and got it over with rather than having this drag on and on."

Tex stopped typing and turned to Mel. "I don't know. My gut says he's not going to be happy I'm here with you. I'm guessing it's going to escalate things, and probably quickly. But I could be wrong. It could be he'll just hunker down and try to wait me out. But if that happens, we're good Mel, because I'm not going anywhere. He'll have a hell of a long 'hunker' if that's his plan."

Melody couldn't say anything. The intense look in Tex's eyes floored her, and made her yearn to reach for all the promises she could see in his eyes. Eventually, he looked down at his laptop and broke the sexual tension between them.

"Okay, I've sent the email. Let me get the note and we'll get out of here. If Baby will let us, we'll leave her here today and head to the police station first. Then we'll go to the mall and walk around. If there's any other places you usually hung out at before you left town, we'll stop there too. We'll call to meet up with Amy again today as well, if you want. I know you want to see her kids, but it's probably best at this point to leave that for later. But Mel, I know how much Amy means to you, if you want to see Becky and Cindy, I'll figure it out."

"I'd love to see Amy again today, but yeah, it's probably best if we left the kids out of it for now." Switching the topic, because it hurt to think of Amy's kids and not being able to see them, Melody said, "Let me talk to Baby. I'll see if I can't get her to agree to stay here for the day."

Before Melody moved to have a heart to heart with her dog, Tex pulled her across the short expanse separating them with a hand on the back of her neck. "You're so fucking cute. Tell Baby that if she stays here, I'll bring her home a nice juicy bone." Then he kissed her roughly, nipping her bottom lip as he pulled away.

Melody smiled at Tex, and put her hand on his cheek briefly. She got up and went over to sit on the couch with Baby. The dog jumped up next to her mistress and immediately demanded pets. "Okay, Baby, here's the deal. I need you to stay home today." Baby started whining before Melody could finish. She knew it was weird that she was talking to her dog as if she could understand her, but Melody figured that deep down, maybe Baby could recognize the emotions and feelings behind what she was saying. So while she wouldn't understand the words, per se, she could tell that something important was being said.

"I know, I know, I've missed you too, but we've been together for like six days straight now. I have to do some things today and you can't go with us. I don't want to have to leave you in the car. It's not safe or healthy for you. So if you stay here today, and be good, Tex said he'll bring you back a nice juicy surprise. You'd like that wouldn't you?" Baby tilted her head up and licked Melody's face and she giggled.

"Okay, Tex, we're all set." Melody said the words semi-loudly, turning her head only to screech in surprise when she saw Tex resting his elbows on the back of the couch right next to her.

"Jesus, Tex, stop sneaking up on me like that!"

"I wasn't sneaking, Mel. I was right there. Baby knew I was here, you were just concentrating too hard on her to notice me."

"No, Tex, even with that fake leg, you walk like a Native American in the forest hunting rabbits. You're completely silent and it's almost eerie."

"Habit, Mel. Habit."

Melody sighed. "I know, you can take the man out of the SEALs, but you can't take the SEAL out of the man."

"Hey, I like that!" Tex told her standing up and running his hand over Mel's hair. "Come on, let's get going."

Melody kissed the top of Baby's head and gave her one last pat. "I'm ready." She grabbed her purse off the counter as they headed out of the apartment.

Baby whined once as they were about to leave, but Tex merely turned around and said sharply, "Baby, stay."

The dog huffed once, then turned and trotted to the couch and climbed on. She settled onto the cushions, resting her head on the back of the couch so she could see them leave.

"She's good at the guilt trip thing," Melody commented unnecessarily.

Tex just chuckled and put his hand at the small of Melody's back to lead her out of the apartment. He locked the door behind them and thankfully Baby was silent as they headed to the parking lot.

Melody looked up at Tex and said, as they walked to his truck, "How do you get her to obey you so well? She's a hound, she doesn't obey anyone."

He didn't answer and Mel looked at him in confusion. His face had gotten hard and he moved his hand from her back, to grip her elbow. "Looks like the cops will come to us today, Mel."

"Huh?" Melody turned to look in the direction Tex was facing and gasped. His truck had been vandalized. All four tires were flat and both headlights had been smashed and broken. "Oh Tex, your truck."

"It's only a machine. It can be fixed."

As they walked closer to the truck, Melody could see the words that had been spray-painted on the truck. She ignored Tex as he called the police to report it and concentrated instead on the ugly words, the hate, sprayed on Tex's truck.

Bitch. Whore. You'll pay.

Melody realized that Tex hadn't taken his hand off of her elbow and she curled her arm through his and pressed up against his side. She looked around, as if expecting someone to spring from the bushes and attack them.

Tex put his arm around her, but after he hung up with the cops, turned his cell phone around and started clicking pictures of his truck and the area around it. Without looking at her, Tex tried to reassure Mel. "This is actually a good thing. I know it doesn't seem like it, but it is. It means that after only a day, we've gotten to him. He's emotional and pissed. He's seen me with you and he can't stand it. The more emotional he gets, the more mistakes he'll make."

"But your truck."

With her words, Tex lowered his phone and turned Mel in his arms so she was plastered against him. "It's only a truck. I couldn't give a flying fuck about it. Honestly. I'll rent a car today so we'll have transportation."

"We can use my car. It's parked over at Amy's."

"No, I'll rent something. Call it a man thing, or a SEAL thing, or even a boyfriend thing, but I'd prefer to stick close to you until this is done. Let me drive you around, Mel."

"Fine. It doesn't make sense for you to spend money on a car when I have a perfectly good one at our disposal, but whatever."

Tex continued as if they didn't have a side conversation about renting a stupid car. "I'm pissed at myself though. I should've already set up security cameras around your apartment. If I had, I'd have more to go on, but if he's done this now, already, he'll do it again. I'm going to catch him, Mel. I swear to God."

"I'm scared."

"I know, and I hate that. But, Mel, look at me." Tex tipped Mel's face up so she had no choice but to look at him. "I've just found you after all these months. I'm not going to let anything happen to you. Whoever is doing this is emotional and uncontrolled. That's much better than methodical and calculated. He'll make a mistake and this'll be over. Trust me."

"I do. You know I do. But I still hate this."

"I know. I'm not that fond of it myself. But we'll deal with it . . . together." They both looked up when they heard sirens coming their way. "I'm going to send the pictures to Wolf, we'll deal with the cops, I'll call a tow truck, then we'll do what we were going to do today before this."

Melody nodded. She tried to control the shaking of her body, and snuggled into Tex as he held her tighter to him. She could do this. She'd been dealing with it alone, just because she had Tex here now to help her didn't mean she wasn't the strong woman that had been on her own for months. She had to suck it up and really analyze everyone around her. She had to help Tex figure this out, not sit back like a pathetic woman who needed protecting.

* * *

MELODY SAT on a bench in the city park with Amy. She'd called and Amy had agreed to meet them there. Cindy and Becky were still in school and her husband was at work. Amy left work early and came straight to the park after hanging up with Melody.

Tex had stayed with Melody until Amy had arrived. Then he'd kissed her on the forehead and said, "Visit as long as you want. I'll be over there." He'd pointed to a bench about a hundred feet away and left her alone with Amy.

"How are you holding up?" Amy asked Melody, holding on to her hand tightly.

"I'm okay."

"Hashtag seriously? Mels, this is me. I know you better than that."

Melody sighed. She loved Amy, but sometimes hated that she couldn't lie worth a darn with her. "I'm scared out of my mind. Tex tells me not to worry, but I can't help it."

Amy looked down at their clenched hands and bit her lip. Then she looked up at Melody and squeezed her hand. "I love you like the sister I never had, Mels. And I know you enough to know what I'm going to say is most likely going to piss you off, but I'm saying it for your own good."

"Fuck," Melody said under her breath.

"How much do you really know about Tex? I mean, you started talking to him online and now he's living in your house and if I read you right, you're sleeping with him. I had him checked out with my connections at work, but what if *he's* your stalker? What if he's the one doing this to you? He found you in California right after you received that note. It looks bad and I wouldn't be a good friend if I didn't bring it up."

Melody stiffened on the seat and wanted to wrench her hands away from her best friend and storm away from her. But she knew Amy loved her and was looking out for her as best she could. Hell, if their roles were reversed, she knew she'd probably think the same thing. Tex had even thought *Amy* could be the stalker. It was an interesting coincidence that Amy also suspected Tex.

Melody looked up at Tex who was sitting across the way and saw he hadn't taken his eyes off of them. He was staring intently at her, always conscious about what she was feeling. She took a deep breath.

"It's not him, Ames." When Amy opened her mouth to interrupt, Melody continued quickly. "Please, let me explain how I know. Okay?" Waiting for Amy to nod, Melody squeezed her hand when she did.

"I was in some hellhole in Mississippi the first time Tex messaged me online. I'd been on the run for a few weeks and was tired and scared. The stalker had already found me in Florida and I was running. Tex messaged me and said he liked my username. He didn't say anything sexual, and he made me laugh for the first time since I'd received the first note. He didn't put any pressure on me, didn't make me feel as if he wanted anything from me. I wasn't going to talk to him again, but when he messaged me again, I couldn't help but respond. He was just as funny, and non-threatening. Amy, I chatted online with him for months, and not *once* did he overstep any bounds. He never asked me where I was, he never asked me for my picture, he never tried to sext me. Six months, Amy. *Six.* How many guys do you know that would do that?"

When Amy stayed silent, Melody continued, "Exactly. He talked to me about his life. He told me about his fears. He told me about how he felt about losing part of his leg. Not one guy I've met in my entire life has opened up to me like that before."

"That doesn't mean he didn't do it to gain your trust, Mels."

Melody knew Amy was just trying to play devil's advocate, but she was getting frustrated with her. She'd have to prove it to her. "He's not like that, Amy. He wants to protect me. He shields me from anything that might be painful. This morning when he saw his truck, the first thing he did was put his arm around me and pull me to his side. His eyes shifted back and forth to search out any threat that might be lingering. He doesn't want to hurt me, Ames. He's the best thing that's ever happened to me. Watch."

Without warning Amy about what she was going to do, she leaned over and grabbed her calf and yelled, "Ow!" Before Amy could move and before Melody could even look up, Tex was there.

"What's wrong, Mel? Move your hands, let me see." Tex was there, he had her calf in his hand and was massaging it. "Did it cramp up on you? Damn, we did too much today didn't we? We should get you home."

Melody put her hand on top of Tex's head. "I'm okay, Tex. Really. Just a little cramp. It feels better. I'm not ready to go yet."

Tex looked up at Melody, then looked over at Amy. Putting his hand on Mel's face he said seriously, "I don't want you upset. You've got enough going on, if you need to put off whatever conversation you've been having that's made you uncomfortable, you need to do that."

Amy smiled and cut into their talk and laid it out for him. "It's okay, Tex. I told Mels that maybe you were her stalker. She didn't like that."

Melody turned to look at her friend. She didn't think Amy would've come right out and told Tex she thought he was a suspect.

Not removing his hand from Melody's face, Tex turned to Amy. "I insinuated the same thing about you. She didn't take that any better than I bet she took you suggesting that I might be. Amy, I'm not her stalker. I give you my word as a Navy SEAL and as the man who cares about your friend a great deal."

"Good enough for me," Amy said immediately.

"Give us another twenty minutes or so?" Melody asked Tex softly.

"Of course." Tex stood up and kissed Mel on the forehead, which made her smile, remembering what he'd said about why he kissed her there and not on the lips. He did it all the time and she loved it.

As Tex walked back to the bench he'd been sitting on before Melody had faked a leg cramp, Amy commented in a breathless voice, "Hashtag holy shit."

"Hastag told you."

"Yes you did. Now, serious stuff . . . how is he in bed?"

"Amy!"

"Mels! Spill it!"

Melody squirmed in her seat, but admitted softly. "Amazing. Seriously Ames, I've never experienced anything like it before in my life."

"Does his leg make it weird?"

"His leg?"

Amy looked at her friend as if she were dense. "Yeah, Mels, his leg. You know, he's missing half of it? Is it weird? Does it look gross?"

Melody got mad at her friend for the first time in a long time. "Amy, what the hell? Seriously? His leg is fucking beautiful. You know why? Because it's a part of him. Because losing that leg means he's still here to be with me today. And the answer is no, it's not weird. He made me come twice last night before he even thought about satisfying himself. You think in the middle of that I could even spare a thought about what his fucking leg looks like or that I'd even *care*?"

"Uh, Mels—"

"And besides, his leg is fucking sexy as hell. You wouldn't think it was, but I've already had a fantasy or two about rubbing up against it as I make myself come. And trust me, Tex is the *least* disabled man I've ever met in my life. He might have a bionic leg, but Ames, his mouth, his fingers, and his cock more than make up for *any* disability you or anyone else thinks he might have."

"Mels, seriously—"

"No. That's what's wrong with this world today. People see someone with a limp or a prosthetic and they think something's wrong with them. There's not one fucking thing wrong with him. Not to mention he's a hero. He was a fucking SEAL, Ames. You think missing half his leg would ever slow him down? Hell, given half a chance he'd probably take his prosthetic off and beat the hell out of my stalker with it."

Melody was breathing hard, full of emotion and pissed off at her friend. She didn't mind talking about how great the sex was with Tex, but she'd be damned if she let anyone, including her best friend in the world, talk smack about him.

"Hashtag he's standing right behind you," Amy whispered, smiling at Melody.

Melody whipped her head around and saw Tex standing stock still about four feet from the bench she and Amy were sitting on. He was watching her with an intense look in his eyes. Melody had no idea what to say. She hadn't told her friend anything she didn't mean, but it was embarrassing none-the-less.

"Amy," Tex started without taking his eyes off of Melody. "Your friend is the best thing that has ever happened to me. I know most women feel the way you do about my prosthetic, but I've never had anyone stand up for me the way Mel just did. So while I don't mind if you want to girl-talk about our sex life, I don't like seeing Mel upset." He finally turned to look at Amy. "So if you want to know about my leg, in the future please ask *me*. You want to see it? I won't like it, but we can have a show and tell anytime you want. But I'd appreciate if you keep your thoughts about how weird it might be to have sex with me to yourself, simply because it upsets Mel."

"I didn't mean anything by it, Tex. I'm sorry," Amy told him in a small voice.

Tex nodded and turned back to Mel. "You about ready to go?"

"Can you give me a second?" Melody didn't think he was going to do it, but finally he nodded and stepped back about ten feet and turned his back to the bench. Melody figured he could probably still hear them, but she didn't want to push it.

"Mels, I'm sorry, I didn't mean . . ."

"No, I know you didn't, I overreacted," Melody tried to tell her friend.

"No, you didn't. You defended him and rightly so. I was being a bigot and stereotyping him. If George had a disability like that and you said something rude to me as I did to you, I would've done the same thing."

Amy dropped her voice to a whisper, "I love my husband, and it's obvious you love Tex. I'm thrilled to death for you that you have someone you feel that passionately about. Now, go back to your apartment and have some wild and crazy sex. The next time we meet up you can tell me all about it, hashtag without me being a bitch about his leg."

"I love you, Ames."

"I love you too, Mels. Now go. I have a feeling Tex is gonna catch this asshole sooner rather than later and you'll have your whole life to look forward to."

Melody smiled at Amy and hugged her once they stood up.

Tex came over as Amy was walking away and took Mel's hand in his own. "Ready to head home?"

"Yeah, about what I said . . ."

"Just so you know, I have a feeling Baby isn't going to get to sleep in our bed anytime soon. We don't want to corrupt her beyond all repair."

Melody smiled and teased Tex back as they walked to the rental car. "Yeah? You haven't changed your mind about the doggy voyeurism huh?"

Tex hooked one arm around Melody's neck and put another hand at her back and dipped her backward, ignoring her girly screech. "Frankly, as soon as I get a whiff of your arousal I forget everything else. Baby, where we are, the damn stalker . . . all I think about is tasting you, seeing you orgasm, and getting inside you. I'd apologize, but I know as soon as my lips hit yours, you're just as lost as I am."

"Tex. Jesus. Stop. Seriously. Let me up."

Tex leaned down and nuzzled her ear, still holding her practically upside down. "Are you wet for me, Mel?"

"You know I am."

Tex brought Mel upright and shook his head. "No games. I love it. Come on, let's get home. I have plans for you."

Mel gladly took Tex's hand and followed along beside and behind him. All thoughts of the stalker, someone that might be watching or following them, were gone from her head. All she could think about was what Tex might do to her, and what she wanted to do to him. She couldn't wait.

CHAPTER 14

"*I* hate this!" Melody complained, holding her head in her hands at her table. Baby whined next to her, sensing her mistress' distress. Melody felt as if she was suffocating. The last two weeks had been idyllic in one sense. She loved having Tex living with her. He was an easy person to share a space with. He wasn't perfect, but the things he did that were a little annoying, were way overshadowed by the many ways he helped make life easier around the apartment. He cleaned up after himself, he didn't leave little black hairs in the bathroom sink after he shaved, he cooked, he cleaned, hell, he even walked Baby when Melody couldn't bring herself to get out of bed.

It wasn't him. It was everything else. She didn't have a minute to herself. If Tex wasn't with her, he left her with Amy with strict instructions not to move until he came back to get her. He'd made good on his promise and had produced a tracking device that she now wore everywhere she went.

Melody fingered the small gold earring in her left ear. It looked so dainty and pretty, but Tex had shown her the software and how it showed her location on a map. Despite knowing how it would look to others, it made her feel better. She remembered weeks ago how she'd told him that it would make her feel better knowing he could find her in case the stalker decided to kidnap her.

"I know, Mel. I wish like hell I could do more."

Melody sighed. "You're doing everything you can, Tex. I'm very thankful for all of it."

"But you still feel smothered."

"Yeah."

"Would it help if I told you it was for your own good?"

"No."

"I didn't think so. You have a job today right?"

Not understanding where Tex was going with the question, Melody answered anyway. "Yeah, in about two hours. Why?"

Tex ran his hand though his hair and looked at Mel. "I thought maybe you could go to the library to do your thing today."

Melody could feel her heart start to beat faster. "Where will you be?"

"I've got some things I need to take care of today. You know I'm retired, but I . . . help other military teams out and they need me today."

Melody eyed Tex. "You know I'd never tell anyone anything about what you might say or do in my presence."

"I know, that's not what this is about. I don't give a flying fuck if you hear what I do or not. I think you know by now I don't exactly work by-the-book, but I trust you, Mel. I'd rather you stay here, inside, where I know where you are, where you're safe, but I also know you need some space. The library, in public, is the safest place I can think of to give you the space you're craving."

"Thank you. I'd love to go there to do my gig today."

"But you don't take that earring off, you keep your phone close at hand, if anything out of the ordinary happens, I expect you to call me right away."

"I will, Tex. Don't worry. I will."

Tex walked over to the table and sat in the chair next to Melody. He took her hands in his and kissed them. "How are you holding up really?"

"I hate it. How come we can't figure out who's doing this? I mean is he really that smart? You've seen the letters he won't stop sending. Hell, even Amy got one the other day, and that scares me more than anything. I don't understand what he means by, *"You'll pay."* Pay for what?"

Melody thought about the letter she received just that morning. It'd been taped onto her door. Tex had found it when he walked Baby.

YOU'RE A BITCH. *You'll always be a bitch. You might have others fooled, but I know you. You don't deserve anything you have in your life. You're going to pay*

123

for what you did. You better continue to keep that dog on a short leash. If you think that crippled excuse for a man will save you, you're delusional on top of everything else. Prepare to pay.

MELODY SHIVERED. "He continues to threaten everyone I love, including you, and I don't know how much more of this I can take, Tex. I just want it to end!"

Tex felt as if his heart stopped beating for a second, then it started again with a thud. He had no idea if Mel realized what she'd just said or not, but he knew her words would be forever engrained on his brain.

"We're closing in on him, Mel. He's getting more careless. We found a fingerprint on the last note. You know they only arrive in the middle of the night, so I'm fairly sure you'll be okay in the library today. But I swear to God, I'm doing everything in my power to make sure he doesn't touch one hair on your head."

Tex waited for her to nod. When she did, he leaned closer to her. "And, Mel, this might not be the time or the place, but I can't keep it in anymore. I love you. I love everything about you. I love how you scrunch your nose in your sleep. I love how you talk to Baby as if she can understand you. I love how you put everyone's well-being before your own. I love how you matter-of-factly help me with my leg every night. You don't make a big deal out of it because to you, it's *not* a big deal. I love how you can type a million words a minute and you don't think it's amazing. I love how you know everyone in this town and you say hello to each and every one of them. I love how you turn the other way when you know I'm doing something that isn't quite legal. Basically, I love everything about you. When this is over, if you still want me, I'm moving up here. I couldn't give a rat's ass where I live, as long as it's with you."

Tex's words seemed to echo in the room. Melody could only look at him in wonder. She didn't think she'd ever hear those words from him, and he'd done so much more than just say the words. "I love you, Tex."

"I know."

Melody smirked. "You're a jerk."

"Come here." Tex tugged Mel out of her chair and pulled her into his lap. She straddled him and ground down against his erection. "I know we don't have time for this right now, but tonight, I'm going to show you just how much I love every inch of this body." Tex ran his hands up and under her shirt at her back and stroked the sensitive skin at the small of her back.

"Only if you'll let me do the same."

"Fuck yeah." Tex leaned forward and kissed her on the forehead.

Melody smirked. She loved it when he did that. It was a secret communication between the two of them now. Each time he did it, she knew he really wanted to throw her down on the nearest flat surface and have his way with her.

"All right. I'll take Baby with me today. You go to the library. Sit out in the common area where the people are. Don't go in the back to the private rooms. You'll be able to concentrate enough out there?" At her nod, he continued. "Okay, I'll drop you off and come back three hours later. I know three hours isn't enough, Mel. I know you wish you could do what you want, when you want, and where you want. I swear we'll get there, but for now, please, for me, take every precaution you can."

"I will, Tex. I swear."

"Okay, let's get this show on the road."

* * *

MELODY CONCENTRATED on the last announcement being made at the meeting she was listening to over the Internet and typed what she was hearing. The voices from the other patrons in the library had faded the moment she'd put in the headphones and started concentrating on typing.

When Melody had arrived at the library she'd said hello to Meredith, the librarian, a woman she'd known her entire life and had settled down at a table to read the latest romance book by her favorite author. She hadn't had time to get through it yet because when she and Tex were home, most of the time he'd interrupted her . . . not that Melody was complaining. She read for a while then fired up her computer to get to work.

Melody looked up and saw Diane, from the bank, sitting next to her. Melody held up her finger, in the universal symbol for "hang on," as she finished up the presentation. She signed off the closed caption app and popped the headphones out of her ears.

"Hey, Diane."

"Hey, Melody. How are you?"

"I'm good." Melody wasn't quite comfortable talking to Diane, other than the usual pleasantries, because she didn't really know her. There was also that whole dating an ex of hers thing as well. Melody thought back to the information Tex had learned about Lee and felt some of her unease about the woman fade. She felt bad Diane had to live with him. No one deserved to be abused.

"That seems really interesting. I've never seen anyone type so fast before in all my life."

"Yeah, well, I'm actually typing in shorthand, it gets translated and fed back to the people who have the app."

Diane seemed really impressed. "Well, it's really cool. I'm sure the deaf people really are thankful."

"It feels good to be able to help people." Melody said, looking down at her watch and ignoring the less-than-politically-correct statement from Diane. "Well, look, I gotta get going. My boyfriend will be here in a bit to pick me up."

"Yeah, I've seen him around. He's hot." Diane didn't seem to notice Melody's unease at the turn in conversation.

"Look, I don't mean to be rude, but aren't you seeing Lee? I'm not that comfortable with you talking about Tex that way."

"Oh, I'm sorry. I didn't mean anything by it. Anyway, I just wanted to let you know that I admire you. Seriously. You're doing great things for people and you seem to have a great life."

"Thanks, Diane." Melody looked up and thankfully saw Tex sitting in his truck outside. They'd recently gotten his truck back from the shop. They'd cleaned the paint off and replaced all the tires. She'd missed being able to sit right next to Tex as he drove the rental car and being able to have Baby between them when she was allowed to accompany them.

Melody stood up and gathered her laptop and book. "He's here. I'll see you around."

"Maybe we can get together for lunch or something sometime?"

Diane seemed eager to be friends, that was obvious. Melody knew what kind of jerk Lee could be. She'd been lonely before too. "Sure. I'll call and we'll set it up."

Diane smiled widely. "Cool! See you around!"

Melody waved at Diane as she walked to the front door. Diane waved back and turned to head into the romance section of the library.

Melody smiled as she walked up to the truck. Baby was sitting in her usual seat in the front. Tex hopped out as she got to the truck to open her door, as he usually did. Melody had tried to tell him not to bother getting out, that she could open her own door and get into the vehicle on her own, but he'd just smiled and ignored her. Just as Melody reached Tex, they heard her name being called from a few spaces away.

Both Tex and Melody turned to see Robert Pletcher stalking their way.

"What the fuck, Melody?"

Melody took a step backward and bumped into the side of the truck. She heard Baby growling from inside.

"Watch it, Robert," Tex warned, putting one arm out and pushing Mel behind him a bit.

"Who the hell are you and how do you know my name?"

"We've met. When Mel first came back to town."

"Oh yeah, I remember now. You're the possessive fucker who couldn't keep your hands off her in the middle of town. I have no idea what she sees in you, some crippled asshole who's pretending he's infatuated with her. She's not that good of a lay, I'm sure you've figured that out on your own by now."

The words had barely left his mouth when Tex had him on the ground, his knee at his throat and Robert's arms locked against his sides by Tex's hands. "Calm the fuck down, man."

Robert struggled in Tex's hold, but it was obvious he wasn't going anywhere until Tex let him go.

"Care to explain what your problem is, buddy?"

"My problem?" Robert looked up at Melody who hadn't moved away from where she had plastered herself against the side of the truck. "Melody, what the fuck did I do to you? You think it's funny to ruin my marriage?" His voice came out as a croak because of the knee in his throat, but it obviously wasn't completely cutting off his air since he could speak.

"I don't know what you're talking about, Robert. I haven't seen you in ages besides when I got back into town."

"Don't give me that shit. I saw the note you gave Sheri. You told her all about Brooke. Brooke didn't mean shit. She was just a way to get off. Sheri's had three kids and hasn't lost the weight. The sex isn't all that great anymore. I needed more. That's *all* it was with Brooke. But now Sheri wants a divorce and it's all your fault!"

"Enough talking, asshole." Tex put more pressure on Robert's throat to shut him up. "First of all, Melody didn't write you any damn note. She has way too much class for that. She's moved on and doesn't give a shit about you and where you're sticking your dick. Secondly, cheating on your wife is an asshole thing to do. If the sex wasn't good it was your damn fault for not taking care of your woman and making her feel sexy and desired. So who else knew about your affair? It's obvious someone else knew and informed your wife."

"Melody signed the damn note, asswipe," Robert squeaked out.

Tex heard Melody gasp behind him. Dammit.

"And I'm telling you she didn't write it. Are you a handwriting expert? You've never thought that anyone could've signed Melody's name to it? It's all a moot issue anyway. You're missing the point. The point is that if you're sneaking around behind your wife, it's only a matter of time before she finds out. Looks to me you're getting what's coming to you."

Melody watched as Tex leaned down and whispered something in Robert's ear. She couldn't hear what he said, but Robert went still under Tex's body. Tex stood up with more grace than people with two uninjured legs probably would, and seemingly unconcerned about what Robert might do in retaliation, turned his back to him. Robert lay still on the ground, making no move to come after either Melody or Tex.

"Come on, Mel, let's go home." Tex opened the door of the car and urged Mel to climb in. She did and Baby whined next to her.

Tex got in behind her and started the engine. Robert had finally gotten up off the ground and was stalking away from the truck without a second glance.

"What'd you say to him?"

Tex thought about lying or just flat out not telling her, but she needed to know the person he really was. "I just let him know that as a former Navy SEAL I know twenty ways to kill a person that won't leave a mark. And furthermore, I know people who owe me favors who wouldn't hesitate for a second to get rid of his body where no one would ever find it."

"You did not." Melody's voice was low and shocked.

"I did." Tex glanced over at Mel and quickly looked straight ahead again. "I won't apologize for it, Mel. He was an asshole. And I wanted him to know that he couldn't accuse you of shit like that and get away with it. You might not get this, but I hope to hell you're starting to, but that shit won't fly with me. *No one* insults you and gets away with it. He knows you're off limits now."

"What if he's the stalker?"

"Then he knows that I'll protect you with my life. But I honestly don't think he is. If he was, he wouldn't have pulled something so stupid in public. He'd wait and send another fucking letter or something. But if he *is* your stalker, I hope to God he got the point and he'll stop it. But, Mel, I don't think it's him because it's obvious whoever has been after you, wrote that note to his wife and signed your name." When Melody didn't say anything after his announcement he looked over at her. She looked devastated.

"So now he's trying to get everyone to hate me. Is this ever going to end?"

Tex glanced at Mel again as he pulled out of the parking space and headed for her apartment. "Yes, it's fucking going to end. I'm done with this shit." Tex hated to see Mel trembling. She was clutching her hands together in her lap. Baby whimpered and put her head in Melody's lap, as if she understood the stress her mistress was under. Taking one hand off the steering wheel he put it on the back of Mel's head.

"I just don't understand how someone could hate me so much and want to hurt me, my friends, and everyone I love. Why Tex? What did I do?"

"You didn't do anything Mel. It's *him*. *He's* the one who's fucked up. I'm going to find him. I'm done dicking around."

Melody didn't lift her head. She was at her breaking point. "Maybe I should just go."

Tex's hand flexed on the steering wheel, and he willed the hand on the back of her head not to clench, but he stayed silent. This wasn't the time or the place for this conversation, but they'd be having it . . . soon.

CHAPTER 15

*M*elody went through the motions once they'd arrived home. What had been a good day, she'd felt free for the first time in months, had turned into just another nightmare that was her life. She wasn't close friends with Robert, but they'd parted on good terms and she'd never had any issues with him.

The stalker was making it so she never wanted to leave her apartment. Melody had been completely serious when she'd suggested to Tex that she leave again. She couldn't keep going through this. Melody had no idea what Tex really thought about it because he hadn't responded to her suggestion and he'd been quiet since they'd arrived home.

He took care of Baby and had even made her a quick dinner. He'd kept their conversation light and if she was honest with herself, it was freaking her out. Melody was deathly afraid he was going to decide she was too much trouble. It's what, she was ashamed to admit, she'd think about doing if the situation was reversed.

"Go get ready for bed, Mel. I'll be there in a bit."

Melody didn't argue. She padded down the hall to their room and for the first time in a long time, put on a T-shirt and boxers to sleep in. She hadn't been bothering to wear anything to bed because Tex always stripped whatever she'd been wearing off of her the second he came to her.

A while later, Melody watched as Tex padded into the room, Baby at his heels. He went into the bathroom and Baby jumped up on the bed. Melody smiled as her dog turned in about twenty circles, pawing at the covers until they were exactly how her little doggie mind deemed as perfect.

It was obvious Tex wasn't planning on making love to her since he'd let Baby in. Even after all the sex they'd had all over the apartment, he still wasn't comfortable doing it with Baby lying on the bed with them.

Tex came out of the bathroom with a pair of boxers on and sat on the side of the bed. He leaned over and expertly removed his leg. He pushed the covers back and got under the covers.

"Tex . . . your leg."

"Forget about my leg tonight. It'll be fine without being massaged for one night. Come here, I want to talk to you, but I want to do it when you're in my arms."

"You can talk from there."

"Screw that." Tex moved and pulled Mel into his arms. She fought him for a moment before finally sighing and melting into him. Tex put one of his hands on the back of her head and the other he curled over her waist and held her to him.

He held her to him for a couple of minutes, hating they weren't skin to skin, but understanding why she felt vulnerable tonight and why she'd put on the T-shirt armor.

"Seven months ago when I messaged you, I had no idea it would change my life. But that's what you've done, Mel. You've changed my life. I was only half living before I met you. You forced me out of my own little world, full of self-pity, sitting at home in front of my computers, and forced me to pay attention to what was going on around me.

"If you want to get out of here, go into hiding, no problem. But I'm coming with you. I've got the skills and connections to keep us hidden forever. We can keep on the move, never staying in one place for long, staying safe. But if we do it, you can't keep in touch with Amy or her kids. It would put all of us in danger. Same with your parents. Eventually you'll outlive them, but you can't come back for their funeral. It'd be too dangerous." Tex let his words sink in.

"You're being manipulative, Tex."

He smiled against her head. He knew she was smart and would know what he was doing. "I know, but I'm also being honest." After another pause, Tex continued. "Or you can let me do my thing. I've been waiting for this asshole to make a move, but that's over. I'm done fucking around with this guy. I've got some tricks up my sleeve. I can end this. But I'm serious. If you want to go, we'll go."

"Just like that?"

"Just like that."

"You know I don't really want to leave."

"I know."

"A part of me wants to run. Run so far that I don't have to deal with any of this. I have no idea how someone became so obsessed with me that he wants to make me completely miserable. But I want a life with you, Tex. I want to wake up morning after morning to you kissing me and saying you're going to work out. I want to rescue more dogs and give them all a better life. I want to see Cindy and Becky grow up and become amazing women. I want to get drunk with Amy and not have to worry about some psycho spiking my drink or trying to hurt us because of some perceived slight. And every pore in my body wants you, Tex. I want you to bury yourself so far inside of me that I can't think about anything other than you. That I can't feel anything other than you. That I can't remember anyone's hands on me except for yours."

"I can give you all of that, Mel. Fuck. *Please* let me give that to you."

"I'm yours, Tex. I'll go where you want me to go, I'll do what you want me to do."

Tex rolled until Mel was under him. "I want you to be safe and I'm going to make it so. But one thing's for sure."

"What's that?"

"You and Amy will never be able to get drunk in a bar and not have to worry about someone spiking your drink. Two gorgeous women drunk and sexy as fuck? Yeah, not happening. But I'll promise you this. I'll let you get drunk with your friend . . . as long as I'm there to keep watch."

"Deal."

Melody smiled up at Tex. "You always make me feel better."

"Good. Take off your shirt."

"But Baby . . ."

"I think we've already corrupted her, Mel. There's no way I'll let Baby keep me from loving you. She'll just have to get used to it."

"Doggy voyeur after all?"

"Guess so. Shirt off."

Melody shimmied under Tex and managed to get her shirt over her head. Tex had come to bed with only his boxers on, so he was already shirtless.

"I love your body. You're soft in all the right places." He cupped her right breast with his hand. "And you're hard in all the other right places." His thumb ran over her nipple, flicking it until it stood up as if begging for his touch.

"I love you, Mel. If push comes to shove I'd give my life for yours."

"No, don't say that!" Melody exclaimed in horror.

"It's true."

"Please, don't. I know you're used to protecting people and you're prepared to give your life for your country and all that. But I wouldn't be able to live if you got yourself killed saving my life. Don't you get it?" Melody grabbed Tex's head in her hands and willed him to understand. "You might think that sacrificing yourself is the ultimate act of love, but it isn't. I don't want to live if you can't too. How would you feel if I told you I'd die for you?"

Tex leaned down, dislodging her hands from his face and kissed her hard. "I'm not going to die, and you aren't either. We'll both make a pact right here and now that neither of us will do something stupid if push comes to shove. Trust me to know how and when to make a move without getting either one of us killed. Okay?"

"Okay."

"Now, lay back. I'm going to take my time tonight. I know you started on the pill after you got back home. I'd love nothing more than to come inside you tonight without the damn condom between us, but you know I'll use one every day for the rest of my life if it's the only way I can be inside you."

"I want you, just you, in me. I didn't know how to bring it up."

"Consider it brought up, discussed, and agreed upon."

Melody smiled at Tex. She shivered in anticipation. "I can't wait to feel you in me."

"And I can't wait to feel both of our juices coating my cock. You're going to be hot and wet and after I come inside you, you'll be filled up to the rim."

"Uh, that's kinda gross, Tex."

"No, it's not, it's beautiful. I plan on painting both our bodies with our essence. You'll love it as much as I will. I swear."

"I love anything you do to me, Tex."

"I love you, Mel."

"I love you too."

"Now, put your hands above your head and don't move them. It's time for me to play."

Melody smiled and did as she was told. She felt Baby move, but soon didn't think about anything but Tex. His hands, his mouth, his body. And he was right. After they'd made love, and after he'd come inside her, it *was* beautiful. Their combined juices he massaged into both their bodies was sexy as hell. She'd never forget this night. She never felt closer to anyone before, and it'd be forever burned into her brain.

CHAPTER 16

*M*elody held tight to Baby's leash as she walked her around the yard of the apartment complex. The stalker was escalating. That morning when Tex had gone out to his truck, he'd found a stuffed dog tied to his bumper by a noose around its neck. Even the cops were alarmed by the note that had been attached to it.

Roses are red, *Violets are blue. Baby will be dead, and so will you.*

As far as poetry goes, it was awful, but the meaning behind it was clear. Before the notes had just been vague grumblings about how someone didn't like her, but they'd moved into threats.

Melody sighed, remembering the dead cat that had been sitting on Tex's truck the morning before. The stalker was escalating and quickly. Tex had been right, his being around was obviously more than the stalker could deal with.

There were other things that had happened too. The electricity in Melody's apartment had been cut off. When she'd called about it, she'd been told she hadn't paid her bill. It had taken an hour on the phone with several different customer service agents, and finally a supervisor, to set it straight. Somehow her automatic payments had stopped going through. Melody had managed to give them her credit card to pay for all the missed payments and they'd been appeased, but both she and Tex knew this was just another thing the stalker had somehow done.

Two days ago Tex had convinced Amy to leave town for a week to go on vacation. She and George had taken the girls and they'd headed to Virginia Beach. Tex had set it all up for them. Amy had called Melody completely freaked out because she'd received a box of roses that morning, but when she opened the box, every bloom had been cut off the stem. Then her husband had said his boss, Sam, had received a phone call accusing him of sexual harassment on the job, and the last straw had been when Becky and Cindy had come home from school, each with a package addressed to them that had been sent to the school. The principal had examined the packages before they'd been given to the children, and hadn't seen anything to be worried about. But Amy had taken one look at the note that had accompanied the box of toys and candy and called Melody and Tex.

The note in the kids' boxes were identical and said merely:

KIDS ARE SO INNOCENT, *it's so sad when something tragic happens to them. Here's to hoping you never have to experience that.*

AFTER CALLING the police and getting all of the incidents documented, Tex had pulled out his laptop and suddenly Amy and her family had an all-inclusive trip to the beach planned, and paid for, by Tex. It was apparent how shaken up Amy was, because with only a token argument about the cost, she'd agreed to go.

Melody hated this. She was no long merely scared, she was pissed. No one had the right to do this to her. It'd be one thing if she was a terrible person and had been a bitch to people left and right, but she had no idea why someone thought she deserved this and wanted to see her hurt . . . or dead. It made no sense. Tex had grilled her night after night about why someone might have it in for her and Melody honestly had no idea why.

She'd told Tex every single thing she'd ever done in her life in the hopes that something would pan out and would make sense, but Melody knew that nothing she'd said had uncovered any leads. She now had absolutely no secrets from Tex. It was certainly one way to accelerate a relationship.

Tex knew about the two suckers she'd shoplifted from the local gas station when she was seven. He knew about the three cigarettes she'd smoked at a party in high school and how she'd puked for two hours when she'd gotten home. He knew what Halloween costumes she'd worn for the last ten years, he knew the names of her contacts at her job, and even more intimate details about her relationships with the men she'd dated.

The fact was, she had no idea what she'd been missing until Tex made love with her. Sometimes he let her lay there and allowed him do what he wanted to her, sometimes he made her do all the work, both on him and on herself. He worshiped her body and made her believe she was beautiful. She'd never thought she was ugly, but Tex had made her see she was beautiful no matter what her size was. He'd spent hours convincing her. She had no issues anymore walking around the house naked, sleeping naked, or even showering with Tex any chance she got. Basically, Tex had awakened her sensuous side and every time they made love, somehow Tex made her fall in love with him even more.

So here she was, walking Baby and wondering what was next. What the hell could the stalker do next? Would he pop out of a bush with a gun? Would he get a sniper rifle and come after her from afar? A car crash? Tamper with her brakes? There were a million things Melody could think of, none of them good. Tex had let her go outside and walk Baby by herself with a promise she'd come right back inside and she'd never be out of sight of the window to her apartment. Even now Melody knew Tex was watching her from the kitchen. He'd been on the phone when she'd left, talking to someone named "Ghost" and trying to call in some marker or another to try to end the hell they'd been going through.

Melody was so lost in her thoughts, and the routine of walking her dog, that she didn't realize Baby was straining to get something in the grass. Melody had tried to train Baby to leave things alone when she was walking her, but as a hound, it was almost impossible.

Melody pulled back on Baby's leash just before she could snatch up whatever was in the grass. "Forget it, Baby, I feed you, you don't need to eat random crap you find in the yard." She shortened the leash by wrapping it around her hand and took a step closer to whatever it was, trying to see what the hell had Baby so worked up.

137

She took one look and stepped back quickly. She stared in horror, not believing what she was seeing and spun around to run back upstairs. Baby ran after her as she jogged, thinking they were playing.

"Tex! Tex!" Melody burst into the apartment and looked around.

Tex met her at the door, obviously having seen her quick retreat from the dog walking area through the window. "What? What's wrong? Are you okay?" He examined her from head to toe to try to see if she was hurt.

"Outside . . . Baby . . ."

"Slow down, Mel." Tex took her by the shoulders and hauled her into his arms. He kept his eyes on her face, but ran his hands up and down her back, trying to soothe her. "Tell me what happened."

"I was walking Baby and not paying attention . . . she . . . she tried to get something in the grass. I pulled her away in time . . . I'm pretty sure . . . but Tex . . . it looked like a steak. An uneaten freaking steak. That *cannot* be a coincidence! Steaks don't just appear in thin air. Not in the pet walking area."

Tex's jaw ticked as he clenched it. "Okay, I'll call the cops again. You stay up here with Baby. Do we need to take her to the vet? You're sure she didn't get any of it?"

Melody sighed. She was so thankful Tex was here to take care of this for her, and that he was worried about her dog. "Yeah, I pulled her away as soon as I noticed her smelling near there. I think she's fine. But what if there's more?"

"I'm going down. I'll look around. Make sure so no one else's dog eats anything."

They looked at each other, remembering the threat from that morning. The steak was most likely poisoned, and meant for Baby.

"My God." Melody's words were whispered and tortured.

Tex didn't know anything he could say to make this any better. When he'd seen the stuffed dog with the noose around it tied to the bumper of his truck he'd been furious. This had gone on way too long. Mel wasn't sleeping well. She'd had a nightmare last night and all he could do was hold her and let her cry when he'd shaken her awake.

"I'll be right back," Tex told her gently.

Melody just nodded. She felt Tex kiss the top of her head and she moved to the couch when he closed and locked the front door behind him. Baby crawled into Melody's lap and rested her head on her shoulder. They stayed like that until Tex came back into the apartment an hour later.

Tex took one look at the woman he loved sitting so still and sad on the couch and immediately went to join her. Sitting next to her, he enveloped her, and Baby into his arms, and the three of them sat there, soaking up as much love and compassion from each other as they could.

CHAPTER 17

Two days later, Melody sat at the table typing what was being said at a luncheon for a company in Wyoming. It was an awards ceremony and they'd hired the closed caption company to translate for their three hearing-impaired employees. Melody had long ago learned not to really listen to the meaning of the words she heard, but only for the word itself. It made the work go faster and it was definitely less boring that way.

She refused to let her stalker interfere with her job. It was the only normal thing she had in her life at the moment, and it actually helped her not think about how scared and pissed she was for a few hours each day.

Tex had kissed her on the top of the head and told her he was going to take Baby for a walk and that he'd be back in a bit. After the cops had arrived and said the steak that was found in the yard downstairs had indeed been poisoned, Tex wouldn't let Melody walk Baby by herself anymore. He took the dog to different areas in the neighborhood and made sure he kept her on a short leash, just in case anything else had been left around.

As usual, Tex locked Melody into the apartment and warned her to be safe and not open the door to anyone, even someone she knew. Melody merely nodded, reassuring him she'd do as he said.

Twenty minutes later, she typed quickly, smiling when she heard Tex's key in the lock. She was thankful the ceremony she was translating for was almost over, Tex had promised they'd break in the kitchen counter after he got back from walking Baby. They hadn't yet made love there, they kept getting distracted and even though they'd discussed it and teased each other, it hadn't happened yet.

Melody turned to throw a quick smile at Tex as he entered the apartment. She stumbled over the words she was typing as what she was seeing slowly sunk in. Tex entered the apartment first, followed by Diane. Diane was holding a gun against his side and she had Baby's leash in her hand. She'd twisted it around her hand over and over until Baby's front feet weren't touching the ground and she was coughing against the pressure being put on her throat from the collar around her neck being pulled taut.

Tex's jaw was flexing and he was pissed. Melody had thought she'd seen Tex upset before, but it was nothing like what she was looking at right now. She was looking at Tex the killer, the Navy SEAL. It should've scared her, but instead it calmed her. He'd know what to do. The fact that he hadn't already disarmed Diane said volumes about the threat he thought she posed.

While Melody didn't like what she was seeing, a part of her was relieved it was finally coming to an end. One way or another, this stalking shit was going to end. Here. Today.

Melody's fingers continued typing automatically until Diane barked out, "Stop fucking typing, bitch!"

Melody lifted her hands off the keyboard immediately. She reached up and took the headphones out of her ears. She could hear the speaker continuing to talk, and she knew the people viewing the closed caption would be confused when the words coming across their apps didn't match the ceremony and then just stopped in mid-phrase, but it was obvious Diane was deadly serious.

"Go sit on the couch." Diane gestured to the leather couch with her head, not taking the gun off of Tex. She turned to him now. "Don't get any ideas soldier boy. Go sit at the table."

Melody's mind raced. Diane was separating them, making sure Tex didn't get close to her. Baby whined and Melody looked at her. She was standing on her hind feet trying to take the pressure off of her neck, but Diane wasn't giving her any extra room to breathe.

"Please, my dog. Diane, let her go."

"Shut up, Melody. I'll do whatever the hell I want. I've been telling you for months what was coming, but you're still acting all surprised. How fucking cute. It's too bad you didn't just let your precious *Baby* eat the meat and avoid this, but you didn't, so fucking deal."

Melody inhaled. They'd thought her stalker was a guy. All along they'd been searching for a man. Melody had no idea if Tex had even thought it could've been a woman or not, Amy notwithstanding, but it was a moot point now.

"Why, Diane? Why? I don't even really know you. Why would you do this to me? I thought we were friends."

Ignoring her, Diane waved the gun at Tex again. "Take off your fake leg, asshole."

Tex didn't move and Diane sneered at him. "Yeah, I know all about you, *John*." Tex's real name sounded obscene coming from Diane's lips. She'd obviously done her research. Melody had no idea how she'd found out anything about Tex. That freaked her out more than anything else.

"Take off the fucking leg or I'll kill the dog right now." She wrenched the leash she held in her hand and Melody flinched as Baby yelped in pain.

Tex's eyes didn't leave Diane's, but Melody could see that every muscle in his body was taut. He leaned over and lifted his pant leg until he could reach his prosthetic. "Let go of the dog." Even his voice was low and tight, and incredibly controlled.

He waited until Diane put some slack on the leash and Baby could be heard wheezing again, to pop off the suction on his leg.

Melody had no idea what to do. She was completely out of her league. She remembered what seemed like a long time ago telling Tex that even without his leg he was just as lethal as any other SEAL. She hoped like hell he believed it now. All three of their lives were depending on it...on him.

Once his leg was off, Diane ordered, "Scoot it over here to me." Tex shoved it and it clattered toward Diane and came to rest about three feet in front of her. Moving the gun so it was now pointed at Melody, she walked to Tex's leg and kicked it even further away from him, ensuring he couldn't simply fall forward and grab it. "Now sit your ass back down."

Tex did as she asked. Melody knew as long as Diane had the gun pointed at her and had Baby's leash pulled tight, Tex would bide his time.

Diane walked to the couch and leaned over, keeping the gun trained on Melody the entire time. "Stand up." Melody did and watched as Diane leaned over and shoved Baby's leash under the leg of the couch, effectively trapping the dog on a very short lead. Melody didn't like the awkward way Baby had to hold her head, but at least she was on all four legs and could breathe. Diane stood back up and gestured for Melody to sit back down.

Melody tried again to engage Diane. "Why are you doing this? Please, talk to me."

Diane rolled her eyes. "Oh sure, *now* you want to talk to me. You never did before, did you? You and Amy, best friends, queens of the school. Talking in your little hashtag language. You thought you were so fucking funny. Well, you weren't."

"This is because of high school?" Melody couldn't believe it. She tried to keep her voice calm. "That was years ago!"

"I don't care!" Diane shrieked the words, obviously losing it. "I looked up to you. I wanted to be your friend, and you completely dissed me in front of the entire school! You made a fool out of me!"

Trying to calm her down, Melody said in a low voice. "I'm sorry, Diane. Really, I'm so sorry."

"For what Melody? You have no idea do you? You're just saying that. You don't mean it. If you mean it, you tell me for what."

Thinking back to the conversation she'd had with Tex about how Diane had spent some time in at the mental hospital, Melody regretted not having him look into it more. She was obviously unstable and whatever had set her off had probably been festering for a while, but more importantly, Diane had decided to stalk her after having a mental break of some sort. That was the only logical explanation Melody could think of for why Diane was standing in her apartment ready to kill her for some imagined slight while they were in high school.

Melody frantically tried to search her mind for anything that could've set Diane off. She honestly had no idea. "Diane, look. I know Amy and I were a little crazy back in high school. We should've been nicer to people, I know that, but whatever I did to you, I was young. I didn't know any better."

Diane's voice lost its shrill tone, but the flat even cadence was somehow more frightening. "I saw you and Amy joking in the cafeteria one day. You'd been nice to me. I dropped my books in the hall once and you helped me pick them up. I thought you were different from everyone else. I thought we were friends. I heard you and Amy talking in that fucking way you had. I walked up and tried to join in. I said, 'Hashtag you look pretty today' and you know what you said?" Diane waited and then laughed bitterly. "You have no idea do you? You ruined my life and you have no clue. You said loud enough for everyone to hear, 'Hashtag Amy do you hear anything? Hashtag annoying underclassman alert.' And everyone around you laughed hysterically. From that day on no one would talk to me. For two and a half years everyone remembered what queen Melody had said. You ruined my life.

"So I decided to ruin yours in return. It took a while, but I did it. I followed you for years, Melody. I studied you. I had to wait until you got back from college, but once you did, I did what I could to learn everything about you. I wrote that letter to Robert. Now he hates you, as he should. I fucked with Amy. I saw my chance when you broke up with Lee. I got him. I won. He likes *me*, not you. You should hear him talk about what a lousy fuck you were."

Melody tried not to hyperventilate. Diane *was* crazy. She'd built up everything bad that had happened in high school and her life and blamed her. It made no sense. Knowing nothing she was saying was true, Melody tried to placate Diane. "I never slept with him."

"The hell you didn't!" Diane's voice was loud and shrill again. "He told me all about it. How you couldn't take his cock down your throat like I can! How you didn't like to take it up the ass, but I do that for him. *Me*! I do everything you wouldn't and he loves *me* now. I used to think you were so smart. I have no idea why I was so jealous of you. God. It was so easy to make you run. All I had to do was threaten your precious *dog*." Diane kicked at Baby, and the dog yelped as Diane's foot made contact with her back leg.

"Please, Diane. Not Baby. Please don't. She didn't do anything." Melody could feel the tears on her cheeks, but couldn't do anything about making them stop. Watching Baby do her best to escape the cruelty Diane inflicted on her was heart wrenching. Melody had rescued Baby from the shelter and a life where she was probably abused just like Diane was doing to her. She couldn't bear it if they got out of this alive and Baby reverted back to her skittish demeanor.

"Shut *up*," Diane hissed. "Fuck. Still so damn stupid. It was so fucking easy to track you. You thought you were so smart hiding in Florida, then running to California. You think I wouldn't figure out you'd have Amy helping you? The second she came into the bank with that Power of Attorney I knew. I kept my eye on her. After she'd take money out of your account, she'd put it the mail, in her own fucking mailbox. She's as 'hashtag stupid' as you."

Melody flinched, but Diane continued.

"It was so damn easy to rattle you. I called in sick and flew across the country to leave you that note. I knew exactly where you were. You weren't hiding. You're a joke."

"So what now?" Tex's voice was hard and flat from the corner of the room, effectively bringing Diane's attention back to him.

Diane whipped her head around to stare at him. "What now? Now she's going to see what it's like to feel humiliated. She's going to regret dissing me that day. And when I'm done here, I'm going to do the same thing to Amy. She's just as guilty as Melody."

"Amy's gone. You can't hurt her."

"Whatever, soldier boy. I found Melody, I can find Amy. But you know what? I think I'll start with you instead."

"No! Diane!" Melody stood up at the couch and Diane immediately swung the gun her way.

"Sit down, Mel," Tex told her in a stern voice. "Diane—"

"Aren't you just the concerned boyfriend?" Diane interrupted Tex in a sing-song voice. "No, Melody, don't sit. Go into your bedroom and find something to tie your boyfriend up with. I'll give you twenty seconds. If you don't find anything, I'm going to shoot him in the other leg."

"What?"

"One. Two."

Melody whirled and ran down the hall to her room. Fuck. Diane was bat shit crazy and Melody had no idea what to do. She looked around frantically, hearing Diane counting from the other room. She whipped open her lingerie drawer and pulled out couple pairs of panty hose.

"Eleven. Twelve."

Melody wrenched open the drawer next to the bed and pulled out the bondage ropes she'd bought recently. She'd meant to get them out and let Tex play with her, but it was too late now.

"Fifteen. Sixteen."

"I'm coming! Don't shoot him!"

Melody stumbled back into the living room and could feel a bead of sweat roll down her face. "I'm here!"

"Tie his ass up. And if you don't make it tight, I'll gut your dog and you can watch her bleed and die right now."

Melody looked and saw that Diane had obviously gone into the kitchen and grabbed one of her steak knives. She held a knife in one hand and the gun in the other. Melody knew Diane would kill Baby in a heartbeat. She dared a look at her dog. Baby was intently watching Diane and growling softly. At least she wasn't cowed by her, but Melody didn't have any time to think about Baby, she quickly walked over to Tex and kneeled at his side.

"I'm so sorry," she whispered dejectedly, dropping the items she'd collected from her room on the floor.

Tex didn't say a word, but kept his eyes trained on Diane. Melody took the pantyhose and wrapped his wrists together behind the chair. He sat tense and motionless as she maneuvered his limbs. She then took the rope and tied his hands to the slats on the chair. She wound the rope around his waist and down to his leg. She tied his good ankle to the chair leg. She wanted to keep the bindings loose, but didn't want to risk Baby's life.

"Now back the hell away from him and sit back on the couch, bitch."

Melody did as Diane asked with a pit in her stomach. She had no idea how they'd get out of this. Now that Tex was tied up, she had no clue what to do. He was supposed to be the one to save them. He'd promised.

Diane laughed a crazy laugh that made the hair on the back of Melody's neck stand up. She'd completely lost it and Melody was at a loss as to what she could do to get them all out of this in one piece.

Melody wanted to try to keep Diane's attention on her. Tex was way too vulnerable right now. "So what? Are you going to shoot me? How is that going to humiliate me? Are you going to kill me, Diane? Do you think you'll get away with that? If you shoot me you'll have to shoot Tex. And the second you pull the trigger someone will call the cops. I'm sorry. I'm truly sorry for anything I did when I was a teenager. Please."

"Oh I don't have to use the gun . . . yet. Besides, yeah, someone will call the cops, but I'll be long gone when they get here." Diane walked over to Tex. She was smart enough to keep the gun trained on Melody the entire time.

"I have no idea what she sees in you. You're pathetic. Look at you. One fucking leg. Disgusting. I'm sure it's all scarred up too. You must have a big dick, but I'm sure she doesn't satisfy you. Jesus, she's cold. Robert's told me all about it."

Diane took the steak knife she'd been holding and held it to Tex's face. "Diane . . ."

She sliced down Tex's cheek, leaving a thin red line of blood in its wake. "Every time you say a fucking word, he gets cut." The words were said nonchalantly, as if she was commenting on the weather.

Melody swallowed the bile that rose in her throat. She couldn't just sit here and let this crazy woman hurt Tex. But she had no idea what to do.

"Remember when your electricity was turned off? Yeah, that was me.

146

It's so easy to fuck with you, bitch. Seriously. You had your payments being directly taken out of your account. All it took was two clicks of my mouse and . . . whoops . . . those auto payments stopped."

"You did that?"

"Ah ah ah," Diane chided and she took the knife and ran it down the length of Tex's arm. Once more, blood welled up from the slice. This time Melody heard Tex draw in a quick breath, but he otherwise didn't move and kept his eyes on Diane the entire time.

Melody leaned over and put her head in her hands. She couldn't watch. There was no way.

"New rule." Melody heard Diane's words, but didn't raise her head. "Every five seconds you aren't watching, I cut him."

Melody's head came up quickly at that.

"Too late bitch, five seconds is up." Diane took the now bloody knife and put it against Tex's throat. She pressed in and laughed as she made a downward cutting motion.

Melody cried silently. She could see that each cut she made was deeper and longer. At least she hadn't cut horizontally across Tex's throat, but cutting him vertically was just as bad. The blood oozed from his neck and was absorbed into the collar of his T-shirt, turning it obscenely red in moments.

"It's too late for sorry-ass apologizes, Melody. I don't want to hear your fucking sorries."

Diane stepped away from Tex, obviously having tired of messing with him. Melody risked a look at him and could see that all of his attention was focused on Diane. It was as if he didn't even feel the cuts of the knife into his skin.

"I don't want to hear your fucking apologies, but I *do* want to hear you beg. *Beg* me to spare your pathetic crippled boyfriend's life. *Beg* me to save your dog's life."

Melody didn't waste any time, if Diane wanted her to beg, she'd beg. It wasn't a matter of pride, it was a matter of getting out of the situation alive. "Please, Diane. Don't do this. I'll do whatever you want. Please. I'm begging you. Don't hurt him anymore. Let Baby go. She's innocent in all of this."

"I changed my mind."

Melody's head hurt. She knew Diane was just playing with her. She might have been cutting Tex, but she was torturing *her*, and they all knew it.

"You have a choice. You want him to walk out of here? Well, he won't be walking will he? More like hopping!" Diane laughed like a loon. Melody kept her mouth shut, waiting to hear what horrible choice she wanted her to make.

"Choose. You or him."

"What? I don't understand."

Diane took a step toward Melody and raised the gun and aimed it at her head. She took another step. Then another. Then one more until she was right next to Melody and the gun was resting against Melody's forehead, right where Tex liked to kiss her. "You get to pick. I figure no matter your choice, it'll ruin your life. So fucking choose. Do I shoot you? Or him?"

Melody looked up at Diane in horror. Was she serious? Of course she was serious. She had a gun to her head and Melody could see the evil behind her eyes. There was no compassion there...at all. Nothing that showed Melody any of them would be getting out of the apartment alive. Diane was going to kill them all, no matter what game she was playing now.

"Me, she chooses me." They were the first words Tex had said since Melody had tied him up.

Diane raised the gun she'd been holding at Melody's head and pointed it at Tex. Before Melody could say anything, Diane pulled the trigger. The sound was obscenely loud and Baby yelped then went back to her low growling. The smell of gunpowder permeated the air around them.

"No!" Melody leaped off the couch, but quickly fell back down when Diane swiped the bloody steak knife over her arm, leaving a long gash. Melody kept her eyes on the kitchen table and was relieved to see Tex still sitting upright. Diane had missed. Thank God. Hopefully the sound of the gun going off would prompt one of her neighbors to call the police as she'd warned Diane earlier.

"Shut. The. Fuck. Up. Crip. This is not your choice. It's hers."

Melody held her bleeding right arm with her left hand and stared at the hole in the wall behind Tex. The next shot could take away the man she loved. All he was, all the good he'd done in the world, all the people who relied on him to help them...all of it would be wiped away by a mentally-ill woman with a crazy grudge.

"Now, Melody. I believe you have a choice to make. Would you rather I blow *his* brains out . . . and you can live. Or I can shoot you in the head, and *he* can live. Choose."

"Diane, you wanted me to beg, and I'm begging. Please, don't do this."

"Too fucking late. *Choose!*"

"Don't do it, Mel." Tex's voice sounded weird.

Melody couldn't tell if it was from fury or a deeper emotion. She looked over at him. Jesus. He seemed to be covered in blood. It was running down his face and his neck and there was even blood dropping on the floor from the gash in his arm. Melody didn't want either of them to die, but she didn't see any way out of what was about to happen. Tex was tied to the chair, *she'd* fucking tied him there, and Diane had a gun pointed at her head. Melody knew Diane would most likely kill Tex after she shot her, but maybe, just maybe her sacrifice would give Tex time to do…something, and he'd be able to get away.

"I love you." Melody mouthed the words to Tex and she watched as his face hardened in fury. Not at her, but at the situation. Beneath the fury, Melody thought she saw a hint of despair. If these were going to be her last moments, she wanted to be looking at Tex when she died. Tex. The man who'd driven across the country to find her. The man who promised he'd always be there for her. The man who she knew would die in her stead in a heartbeat. Melody tore her eyes away from him, suddenly deciding she didn't want to be looking at Tex when a bullet tore through her brain. It was better he didn't watch her life leave her body.

"Me. Kill me, but leave Tex alone."

Diane threw her head back and cackled. When she had herself back under control, she looked Melody straight in the eye and said in a completely normal voice, "It will be my pleasure."

Melody squeezed her eyes shut and lowered her head and waited. She hoped it wouldn't hurt. When push came to shove it seemed she wasn't as brave as she'd always hoped she'd be when it came to her mortality.

Several things seemed to happen at once. Melody heard the knife Diane was holding clatter to the ground. Baby made a sound Melody had never heard come out of her before and Diane cried out.

Suddenly she was knocked over sideways. Melody's eyes popped open but she couldn't see anything because she found herself underneath Tex. He'd leaped from the chair he'd been strapped to and tackled her off the couch. He'd obviously somehow been able to get out of the bindings she'd used on him.

Melody heard a shot and Tex was off of her before she could get her bearings. A loud shriek and a thud echoed through the apartment. The wailing of police sirens getting closer broke through the sudden silence in the apartment. The sound eerily monotonous and still sounding way too far away.

"Mel, I need you to get up and go to the door. Let the cops in. Don't look over here. You hear me? Do *not* look over here," Tex ordered in a low commanding voice, no hint of the loving man she'd come to know over the last few weeks.

"How'd you get out of the rope?"

"I'm a SEAL, Mel. It wasn't hard. I've been trained how to hold my body while being restrained to minimize the effect of the bindings. I'm assuming the cops were your doing? I don't think they would've gotten here so quickly if someone called them after hearing that first shot."

Melody sat up on the floor and leaned her back against the front of the couch, not looking toward Tex. She couldn't seem to get any air in her lungs. She was breathing way too fast and her heart felt like it was going to beat out of her chest. "Yeah, I typed in a quick message to the people at the ceremony I was translating for. I didn't know if it would work or not."

"You're fucking amazing, Mel. It obviously worked. Are you okay? You didn't get hit? How badly is your arm bleeding?" Tex's questions came at her quick and stoic.

Melody did a quick mental scan of her body. Her arm hurt, but she didn't have any other holes in her body that she could tell, so she was pretty sure she wasn't shot. "I don't think so. Of course, I have so much adrenaline going through my body right now I can't be positive, but I don't see any blood other than on my arm, so I think I'm good. Oh my God! What about you? I need to get you bandaged up."

"I'm good. Go on now. Do as I told you. Go to the door and don't look over here. Let the cops in."

"Tex, you're not okay, she cut you." Melody suddenly remembered. "Wait. What happened? Where's Baby?" she breathed.

"Mel, don't," Tex warned sternly.

But it was too late. Melody whipped her head around to where Diane had been standing next to the couch, on the other side from where Tex had thrown her when he'd yanked her off the couch and to the floor, and inhaled. Tex was lying on top of an unconscious Diane, holding both her hands in his, keeping her captive in case she came to before the police showed up. Melody had no idea what Tex had done to knock her unconscious, but it was obvious he wasn't going to give her a chance to get up and threaten them again anytime soon.

Melody looked to his side and couldn't believe what she was seeing.

Baby was lying next to Tex bleeding from her mouth and her haunch. Her eyes were open, but staring straight ahead sightlessly.

"Oh God. No. Baby." Melody scrambled up and crab walked on her hands and knees over to kneel at Baby's side. She raised tear drenched eyes to Tex. "What happened?"

"Baby saved our lives. She gnawed through her leash and attacked Diane. Just as she was about to pull the trigger and put a bullet in your brain, Baby leaped over and bit her on the thigh. Diane turned and shot her to try to get her to let go. I'd already worked through the knots you made, Diane didn't notice because she was too fucking busy torturing you, and Baby's distraction gave me enough time to get to you and then to Diane and disarm her. I'm so sorry, Mel."

"Nooooo. Tex, she can't have killed Baby. She was only trying to protect us." Melody wiped the tears away from her face with one hand and put her head down next to Baby's muzzle. "Oh God, Baby, please. Don't die. Don't. God. I never wanted this to happen to you." Melody put her hand high on her dog's leg where the blood was slowly oozing out. She looked up at Tex. "Look at the blood on her mouth. She got Diane good didn't she?" The words came out as hiccupped sobs, but Tex understood her anyway.

"Yeah, Mel. She got her good. She saved you. She loved you so much. I knew that the first time I met her. When Amy told me you had a dog I knew I had to bring her to you. Somehow I knew you needed her and she'd be important in this whole damn mess."

Melody sobbed harder and put both hands over the hole in Baby's haunch. The dog didn't even flinch as Melody pushed down to try to stop the bleeding. She had no idea if it was futile or not, but she had to do something. She couldn't sit there and watch the life bleed out of her precious dog.

Melody couldn't see what she was doing through the tears coursing down her face, but she babbled on as she watched the red well-up between her fingers as she tried to staunch the scary amount of blood oozing from the coonhound. "Baby never liked Diane. I never thought anything about it. I just thought she was still scared like she was in the shelter when I got her. But there was one time I clearly remember when we saw Diane on the street. She came up to me and Baby growled. I just backed up and laughed it off. I tried to tell Diane it was just because Baby was a shelter dog and scared, and she'd laughed it off. I should've listened. I should've remembered and told you about it, Tex. I'm so sorry, Baby. I should've listened to you."

Tex couldn't stand it anymore. He leaned up and took off his belt. He lashed Diane's hands together tightly and made sure the gun was kicked across the room. Knowing Mel needed him and Diane was out for the count at the moment, he awkwardly shuffled over to her, grimacing at the phantom pains shooting through his leg at the movement. He ignored them and came up beside Baby and Mel.

He put his hands on Mel's shoulders and tried to tug her into his arms.

Mel jerked away from his touch, not losing her grip on Baby. "No! Tex, no. Baby's not dead. She can't be dead. Call a vet or something. Please. We have to try. I can't let her go."

"Mel."

"God, Tex please. I can't lose her. Not like this. I love her, I need her."

Tex couldn't stand the anguish in Mel's voice. He pulled out his cell phone and swiped the screen, leaving a bloody smear across it, which he ignored. He punched in a number and quickly spoke into it.

"Yeah, I need your help. We're good. It's over, but I need a veterinarian, the best you can get a hold of. Baby was shot. Yeah, by the fucking stalker. Bad. Okay. 'Preciate it." Tex stuffed the phone back into his pocket and told Melody, "Wolf's taking care of it."

He watched as she nodded jerkily, but Tex wasn't sure she really heard him.

"Keep the pressure on her leg, but talk to her, Mel. Like you do. She'll hear you. Tell her to hang on."

Tex's heart broke as he watched the woman he loved speak to Baby through her sobs.

"Baby? You're the bravest dog I've ever met. I have no idea what you went through before I found you, but you have to hang on. You did it. You protected me and Tex. You saved our lives. I know you were probably just paying me back for saving yours, but I still need you. There are other bad people in this world and we need you.

"I swear you can sleep on our bed every night. We won't shut you out again. It's obvious you don't care if we make love with you there, so if you don't care, we won't either. I love it when you scrunch the blankets over and over until they're just right in whatever mysterious way you decide. I promise you can come with us wherever we go. Just please, don't leave me. I love you so much, Baby. I never knew how much. Please don't die. Not like this. I need you."

Melody looked down at the blood that was still slowly seeping through her fingers and onto the floor. Baby's eyes hadn't closed, but she wasn't blinking either. It was the most horrific thing she'd ever witnessed in her life. The tears fell harder. She turned to look at Tex. She could see he was as affected as she was at the sight of Baby motionless on the floor.

"What am I gonna do without her?"

A loud knock came on the door. "Police. Open the door."

Tex got up without a word and hopped to the door. Melody watched, absently noticing how even though he was hopping on one leg, he was steady and confident. All the practice he'd obviously done without his prosthetic had paid off. He was as confident hopping around the room as he was walking.

Tex held his hands up as the police stormed in with their guns drawn. Melody turned back to her beloved dog, not caring what the cops did. She wasn't going to move her hands from the hole in Baby's haunch until the vet got there. Melody couldn't tell if Baby was breathing or not, her hands were shaking too much and the tears prevented her from being able to see clearly. Ignoring the commotion behind her she leaned down to Baby again. She'd continue to talk to her until the vet arrived. Tex said Wolf would take care of it. She trusted him. "Hold on, Baby. Help's coming. Don't die. I love you."

CHAPTER 18

*M*elody sat in the circle of Tex's arms and looked around in wonderment. Her little apartment was overflowing with people. She wasn't sure exactly how it had happened, but all of Tex's friends were there as well as four of their women. Caroline couldn't come because she was in the middle of a huge research project and Alabama had a final exam at school that she couldn't miss. Both had sent their profuse apologizes for not being able to be there.

Melody wiped the tears from her eyes. It felt like she'd been crying forever, but she couldn't seem to make herself stop. She'd had one hit after another and now she found herself crying at the slightest provocation.

"I still don't understand what you're all doing here," she said, voice breaking once more.

"We're here because you needed us, Melody," Wolf told her. He was leaning against the wall as if he was overseeing the group. "All it took was a phone call and Commander Hurt helped get us on the next military flight out here. Tex might live on the other side of the country, but he's always been there for us, it's the least we can do for him to be here when you guys needed us.

"Thank you for getting Dr. Gaiser to come for Baby. We appreciate all he tried to do for her."

"You don't have to thank me, Melody. I'm just so sorry he couldn't save that leg."

"It's okay, Wolf. Baby's alive. That's all that matters. And you know what? I've seen lots of dogs get along just fine on three legs."

Tex ran his fingers through Melody's hair. "Besides, we're a matching set now. Me and Baby."

Everyone in the room laughed. Melody closed her eyes. She was exhausted. After being seen in the emergency room for the cut on her arm, and after Tex had been patched up as well— he'd required some stitches, but refused to be admitted to the hospital—she'd spent the last day at the emergency vet with Baby.

Dr. Gaiser had managed to save Baby's life, but the bullet had cut through her femoral artery, and he hadn't been able to save her leg. The first time Baby had woken up and licked Melody's fingers had been completely overwhelming. The doctor had finally kicked her out, telling her to go home and get some sleep. Baby would be coming home sooner rather than later and Melody and Tex would have their hands full keeping her from chewing on her stitches and helping her get used to her new reality.

"So this woman, Diane, was holding a grudge from when you guys were in high school together?" Summer's voice was incredulous.

"Apparently. I had no idea. But it wasn't just that. She had some sort of mental disorder. The specialists who'd treated her in the past recommended she stay on medication for the rest of her life, but after a couple of years she thought she was better and stopped taking them. That's when it really started. She saw me, and how happy I was with my life and suddenly I was the cause of all the bad things she'd had happened to her in her life. And well . . . you know the rest."

Amy, who'd rushed back to Pennsylvania from Virginia after hearing what had happened, and had also come over to the apartment, chimed in as well. "Seriously, the bitch used me to find out where Mels was. I can't believe it was her. I hardly even remember her from high school, but apparently she remembered us."

Melody blinked and tried to keep her eyes open. She knew it was rude, but she was exhausted. She'd been stressed for what seemed like forever and having the stalker off her back and knowing Baby would be okay, was making her feel lethargic and she knew she was crashing. Worse were Diane's words that kept echoing through her brain. *Choose, you or him.* It was a horrible decision to have to make. Melody knew Tex wasn't happy

155

about her choice, and that he'd want to talk to her about it, but she was just so tired.

She vaguely heard voices around her and put her arms around Tex as he picked her up and carried her somewhere. She didn't care where, as long she didn't have to open her eyes or talk to anyone. She felt herself being laid down and she gripped Tex's neck tighter. "Don't go."

"I'll be right back, Mel."

"Mmmm."

Tex walked out of the bedroom and into the living room. "Thanks for coming, everyone. I appreciate it more than you'll know." Everyone nodded, but looked worried. They'd seen how tired Melody was, and how emotionally fragile she seemed.

"How's she really doing?" Dude asked.

Tex took a deep breath. "She's fine. She's tough. I was worried there for a while when we didn't know if Baby was going to make it, but she rallied."

"Is Diane going to make an insanity plea?" It was Mozart that asked.

"Probably, but I have no idea, and I don't care. Mel will testify if she has to, but we'll just wait and see what happens. I know she just wants to move on with her life, with *our* life."

"Tex, we want you guys to move to California. We want you near us."

Tex shook his head at Cheyenne. "I love that you want us there, but, no. We'll be staying here. This is her hometown. Her friends are here, her family is here. She loves this place. I'll be moving up here to Pennsylvania as soon as Mel's ready."

"She's ready now, Tex," Amy said with certainty.

Tex smiled at Amy. "You bringing Becky and Cindy over tomorrow?"

"Yeah, just let me know when she's up and ready. She's had a tough few days. I don't want to rush her."

"Speaking of a tough few days, we're going to get out of your hair," Abe told Tex and came over to shake his hand. "If you need anything, just let us know. We'll probably be heading out in the morning. You don't need all of us here."

"Thanks, Abe. It means a lot to me that you guys came all the way out here."

"SEALs don't leave SEALs behind," Wolf said with a smile, remembering when he'd gotten together with Caroline how much those words had meant to him and his team.

Tex smiled at the SEAL motto. He might not be active duty anymore, but the words rang just as true today as they always had. He put his hand on Wolf's shoulder. "Thanks."

The men slowly left the apartment with their women and Tex watched them go. He felt lucky to have such good friends.

The last to leave was Amy. Tex knew she'd planned it that way and he waited for her to say what she had to say.

"Mels is my best friend. Neither of us had a sister and we became close when we were in grade school. We've been through a lot, and we've always been there for each other. When I got married I knew we were entering a new phase in our lives. I figured we'd grow apart, but Mels wouldn't let that happen. She browbeat me into going out when I was tired, and she forced me to come over and spend some one-on-one time with her. I love her as if she truly is my sister."

She took a breath and cleared her throat then continued, "When she came to me and told me someone was stalking her, it tore my heart in two. I didn't know what to do for her. The reality was that I couldn't do anything. When she called me and said she wasn't coming back because of the stalker, I cried for two days straight. She was hurting and scared and I couldn't help her. Thank you, Tex. Thank you for seeing something interesting in her stupid chat room handle. Thank you for making the effort to go and find her when she deleted her account. I know her. She would've just kept running if she thought I was in danger and me and my family would've never seen her again. You've given me back my sister and I can't ever repay you."

"I didn't do it for payment, Amy."

"I know, but you're gonna get it in one form or another anyway. My kids see Melody as their Aunt. That means you're now their Uncle. You've suddenly become a part of my crazy family. I hope you can handle it."

"I can handle it." Tex smiled, liking the thought of being an Uncle.

"Good. Now, what are your intentions toward my friend?"

Tex chuckled. "I love her. If it was up to me, we'd fly to Vegas tomorrow and get married, but I have a feeling the two of you have probably planned her wedding down to the minute detail."

Amy just smiled at him.

"Can I make a request?" Tex asked Amy seriously.

"You can, don't know if I can accommodate it, we've planned her wedding down to the color of the napkins on the tables after all," Amy quipped.

"I want Baby standing up with us."

157

"Done."

They smiled at each other and finally Amy told him, "Okay, enough mushy crap. I'm glad that you're okay. I don't know what went down with Diane yet, but eventually Mels will tell me, but I can tell it gutted her in a way that her physical injuries didn't. Give me a hug, and then get back in there with my best friend. Be forewarned, I expect a girl's night out soon, so be prepared."

"No problem." Tex grabbed Amy's wrist and hauled her to him in a bear hug. "Thanks for being such a good friend, Amy." He felt her nod against him then she pulled away.

Tex watched until she got in her car and pulled out of the parking lot, then he closed the door and headed for Mel, without caring about the mess in the rest of the apartment. There would be time to deal with that later, now he needed to hold Mel in his arms and rejoice they were all still alive.

CHAPTER 19

 elody snuggled into Tex's arms and sighed. She loved waking up with Tex. She vaguely remembered the night before, and was embarrassed she'd slept through all his friends leaving. She opened her eyes to see Tex staring at her.

"You're still here."

"I didn't want to leave you this morning."

Melody smiled. She'd gotten used to him getting up before her, kissing her awake, then heading out to take care of Baby and to workout. Melody was true to her word and had always fallen right back asleep after he'd left.

"I didn't dream it, did I? Baby's going to be okay?"

"Yeah, Mel. She's going to be just fine. We'll go and see her today and see when Dr. Gaiser thinks she can come home."

"Good. I can't wait to bring her home. I miss her."

"Me too. Mel, we need to talk about what happened." When Melody turned her head away from him, he put his finger under her chin and gently turned her head back to him. "I love you, but you made the wrong choice."

Melody knew immediately what he was talking about. "No, I—"

"You did. I told you once and I'll tell you again, I'd die for you. You mean everything to me. I've known my entire life that I could die on a mission. I was ready for that. We went through training in the Navy on how to withstand torture. You, Mel, *you* are the most important mission of my life. I swear to fucking God I can't live without you. If she'd shot you and you'd died, I wouldn't have been able to go on without you."

"Tex—"

"No. You are the most important thing. You always come first. I don't care what the situation is. First in line, first to eat, first to come, first in everything." Tex's voice hitched and he cleared his throat, forcing back the tears that threatened. He was a big tough Navy SEAL. SEALs didn't cry. "When you said you loved me and you turned and told that bitch that you chose yourself, my heart literally stopped. I can't live without you, Mel. I can't."

"Don't you get it, Tex?" Melody said earnestly, hoping like hell he was hearing her. "Everything you just said I felt in my own heart as I tried to decide what I was supposed to do. I can't live without *you*. I couldn't have lived with myself if I'd told her to kill you. I couldn't. It was an impossible situation, a fucked up impossible situation. Please don't hold it against me. Please?"

Tex hauled Mel into his arms as she sniffed. He rested his cheek on her hair and gritted his teeth, feeling more emotional than he could ever remember being in his life. Jesus, they'd come so close to losing each other. Baby truly was their hero. Tex had been about ready to strike out at Diane, but he might not have made it before she got off a shot. Diane had been standing so close to Melody that it was likely she would've killed her before he could've reached Diane to disarm her.

Tex could feel Melody pulling back and trying to control herself. He pulled back and wiped the tears off her face as she reached up and put her hand on the back of his neck. Tex put thoughts of Diane and how close they'd all come to dying out of this mind. Mel was alive and in his arms. That was all that mattered.

"It was nice of your friends to come all the way out here."

"They're your friends too, Mel."

"I guess. I'm still getting used to it. It's just been me and Amy for so long, and when I was on the run, it was only me."

Tex rolled until she was underneath him. "I'll tell you this now, Mel. You're now a part of a big crazy family that includes six SEAL members and their women. Wait . . . sorry, that's seven team members . . . I heard Commander Hurt recently got serious with the woman the team went down to Mexico to rescue." At her look of confusion, Tex brushed it off. "I'm sure you'll get the whole long story from the girls later. Anyway, you'll also probably be adopted by the other SEAL and Delta Force teams I help out as well. They'll all drive you crazy before long, I have no doubt." He watched as she smiled. Tex took a deep breath and said what had been in the back of his mind for longer than Melody would ever realize. "I have something to ask you."

"Okay."

"Will you marry me?"

"What?"

"Will you marry me?"

"Oh my God, that's what I thought you said. I thought you were going to ask me something like what I wanted for breakfast."

Tex just smiled and stared down at the woman he loved.

"Yes, John Keegan, I'll marry you."

"Thank fuck."

Melody giggled. "I'm not sure that's the appropriate response."

"Do you care?"

"No."

"I'll get to work today in getting my stuff moved up here. I hope you aren't too attached to this apartment. We really need a bigger place, one with a yard so we can let Baby out and not have to walk her on a leash."

"Uh, Tex—"

"And you'll need to make sure you contact your boss to make sure she's okay with what happened the other day."

"Tex, wait. You're moving up here?"

"Yeah, Mel. You agreed to marry me, Of course I'm moving up here."

"There's no of course about it, Tex. We both have portable jobs, we could go wherever we wanted."

"We could live anywhere, but *this* is your home. I would never take you from Amy, and your parents, and from here. You ran long enough. I'm more than happy to come up here and live with you."

"I love you, Tex."

"I love you too."

"No, I *love* you."

Tex chuckled. "If I remember, we never did get to break-in that counter. It'd be a shame to move out of here before we lived out that little fantasy of ours."

"I think I'm hungry. Care to meet me in the kitchen?"

Tex leaned down and kissed Mel deeply. "We were made for each other, Mel. You make me feel more of a man than I ever have before. Thank you. Thank you for loving me, for letting me love you back."

"You're welcome. Now, come on, I'm hungry."

The look in her eye was so carnal, Tex could feel the blood pump into his erection.

He couldn't resist. He leaned down and kissed her, holding nothing back. Melody gave as good as she got. She plunged her tongue into his mouth and countered his thrusts with her own. Tex's hand made its way up her belly, under her shirt, until he reached her nipple. As he squeezed the taut nipple she broke her mouth away from his and gasped, throwing her head back.

"Tex."

"That's it, Mel. That's it." Tex could feel her legs trembling against him. He paused long enough to pull her shirt up and off her head until she was bare from the waist up. He'd never get tired of her. "You're beautiful. And mine." He lowered his head until he had one nipple in his mouth. He used his hand to plump up the other breast and to tease that peak until it pebbled.

Tex loved feeling Melody writhe and arch up to him. He took hold of the bud he had between his teeth, and watching her eyes, pulled upward. When she gasped, he let go and watched as she brought her hand up to his face.

"I need you, Tex. Now. Take me."

"We have a date with a kitchen counter. Go on. When I walk in there I want to see you on the counter, naked, legs apart waiting for me. You'll eat soon enough, but I think it's my turn to go first."

Melody smiled as she climbed out of bed and headed for the door. She made her way down the hall to the kitchen. After removing her boxers, she thought about her life. She had everything she'd ever wanted. Friends, family, and now a man who would not only stand next to her, but in front of her when she needed it and behind her when it suited him. He was perfect. She couldn't wait to become Melody Keegan.

Melody sent up a silent prayer of thanks to Diane. In a sick way, it if wasn't for her delusions, Melody never would've met Tex. Everything happened for a reason, sometimes you just had to wait around for a while to figure out what those reasons were.

As Melody hopped up on the counter and leaned back on her hands, waiting for her fiancé, she grinned. Life was good.

EPILOGUE

"Come on, Baby, come 'ere girl!" Melody called to her dog and watched with a smile as the dog ran toward her. She only had three legs, but she'd never let it slow her down. From the first day Dr. Gaiser had put her upright in the animal hospital, she'd hopped along like she'd been doing it her entire life. Melody had, of course, cried with joy.

The only difference Melody could see with her dog was that she now never let her mistress out of her sight. Baby would follow Melody around their house, not caring what she was doing, if Melody got up, Baby went after her.

"You ready to go, Mel?"

Melody nodded up at Tex. They'd come to the park to let Baby get some exercise, the vet had said it was important that she not just sit around, but that she exercise her leg and make sure she used her muscles more since they were compensating for the loss of her back leg.

"Let's go home. The girls will be calling in thirty minutes."

The Skype phone calls had started the week after their incident. All the girls would get together out in California and call to talk. Soon it had turned into a free-for-all because the men wanted to be there too. One night the call lasted for three hours. Everyone had laughed and told stories all night long.

Afterwards, when Melody was in bed with Tex, trying to recover after a long love-making session which involved the bondage ropes Melody finally convinced Tex to use on her, she'd commented on the close friendship everyone had.

"Being in the military makes men have a special bond. Combat makes that bond stronger. Being a Navy SEAL means that connection is unbreakable. Those men have been through hell and back, and so have their women. Because of their experiences, they know they have a group of people that will always have their back, no matter what. And Mel, you're a part of that too. I know we don't live out there with them, but they feel it just the same."

"I know, Tex. I feel it. I didn't understand when we were talking online all those months ago. I told you that your friends were taking advantage of you because they didn't come out and visit you. But I get it now. They weren't. Your bond is just as strong from thousands of miles away then if you were right there with them. You're a part of that team. You know it. They know it. The women know it."

"Yup."

"I love you."

"I love you too."

"I have a question for you, and you can say no."

"What is it, Mel?"

"Do you think all your friends will be able to fly to Vegas this month?"

"Why?"

"I want us to get married now."

Tex went up on an elbow over Melody in the bed and put his hand on her cheek. "Why?"

"I want to be connected to you so badly. I just . . . I need that. I don't want to wait."

"But your dream wedding. You and Amy have been planning this for your entire life."

"Here's the thing, Tex. When Diane had that gun aimed at me and was about to shoot, all I could think about was how much I was sorry I wasn't yours . . . officially. I honestly don't give a damn about a white dress and all that shit. All I want is to belong to you. And for you to belong to me. I already talked to Amy. We can still have the reception. We'll do that here for all my friends and family, but I want to have the ceremony itself with *your* family. I want to bring Baby and find a chapel in Las Vegas that won't mind if she's there. I want everyone to come and stand up with us. Amy and George will be there with their girls too. My parents said they'd fly out there for the actual ceremony as well. It feels right."

Tex dipped his head and kissed Melody's forehead. "God, I love you so fucking much. When I think about how close we came to never meeting . . ."

"I know."

"I'll call Wolf in the morning and see when they can get free. We'll drive out there with Baby, but take the time to sightsee along the way without rushing. We'll have the best damn Vegas wedding ever. But know this, you belong to me and I belong to you no matter when or if we get married."

"Damn straight."

Tex smiled. She was so damn cute. "I'm feeling awfully awake now, Mel."

She grinned up at him. "Oh?"

"Yeah. Turn over."

"Bossy."

"Yup, you said it yourself. You can take the man out of the SEALs, but you can't take the SEAL out of the man. Turn. Over."

Melody did as Tex asked, knowing that whatever he had planned meant hours of enjoyment for her. He always took care of her. He was completely serious when he'd told her that she came first in all things.

* * *

ON THE OTHER side of the country six Navy SEALs and their women were settling down into their beds for the night. Each couple had been through hell and come out on the other side. Each man had claimed their woman as theirs, and each woman had claimed her man right back. Some people would look at them and wonder how in the hell their marriages and relationships could survive the stress and uncertainty that came with being an elite fighting machine. But if they were asked each one would say it was because of love. They'd seen what life could be without the other and had made promises, spoken and unspoken, that they'd always be together.

And if the women got together when the men left on missions and cried and got drunk, no one told their SEALs, and the SEALs pretended it didn't happen. But ultimately it was the friendship they all had with one another that helped make the separations feel shorter and their love stronger.

IN TEX'S OFFICE, two computers stayed on all day and all night. Seven red dots blinked on a map, six dots in California and one in Pennsylvania. Seven Navy SEALs and women slept easier at night because of those blinking red dots. Some wouldn't understand, but those people hadn't been in their shoes.

* * *

LOOK for the last book in the SEAL of Protection Series, *Protecting the Future*, available now. See what all your favorite couples are up to two years in the future.

PROTECTING THE FUTURE

SEAL OF PROTECTION, BOOK 8

Wolf and his fellow SEAL team members have saved many lives, and been in even more harrowing situations, but their latest mission might prove the most difficult of all. Charged with rescuing American soldier, Sergeant Penelope Turner, from the clutches of ISIS, the men infiltrate the refugee camp where she's believed to be held. The conditions are horrific, the search nearly impossible, but Penelope herself could prove the key to their success…if the SEALs can interpret her clues.

An unforgiving desert, perilous mountain terrain, a rising body count and insurgents on the hunt…all of this and more stands between the SEALs completing their mission and returning home to their women, left to bravely deal with fears of their own stateside.

Sometimes a mission is more than one team can handle. With a little help from newfound friends, the SEALS won't stop until they've won the day. Failure is not an option.

** Protecting the Future is the 8th and final book in the Seal of Protection Series. Each book is a stand-alone, with no cliffhanger endings.

To sign up for Susan's Newsletter go to:
http://bit.ly/SusanStokerNewsletter

❀ Created with Vellum

Guide to the SEALs:
    Matthew "Wolf" Steel – Caroline Martin Steel

Christopher "Abe" Powers – Alabama Ford Smith Powers
    Adopted Daughters: Brinique & Davisa

Hunter "Cookie" Knox – Fiona Storme Knox

Sam "Mozart" Reed – Summer James Pack Reed
    Daughter: April

Faulkner "Dude" Cooper – Cheyenne Nicole Cotton Cooper
    Unborn Daughter: As yet unnamed

Kason "Benny" Sawyer – Jessyka Allen Sawyer
    Daughter: Sara
    Son: John

John "Tex" Keegan – Melody Grace Keegan
    Adopted Iraqi Daughter: Akilah

Patrick Hurt – Julie Lytle

PROLOGUE

*O*ur top story tonight is the kidnapping of four service members by the terrorist group ISIS in Syria. A new video has surfaced showing who is believed to be Sergeant Penelope Turner, once again declaring her allegiance to Allah and warning the United States and Great Britain that if they don't pull all troops out of the Middle East, the wrath of Allah will be brought down upon all Americans and Brits.

Sergeant Turner, along with three other Army personnel, was kidnapped about a month ago while she was on a humanitarian mission in Turkey. The refugee camps on the Syrian border have swelled to hundreds of thousands of people trying to escape the unrest in Syria. There's no running water and not a lot of food. The conditions are primitive, at best. The Turkish forces are doing all they can to deal with the influx of people, but it's simply not enough. The President authorized American troops to go in and assist with the situation. Turner and the other soldiers were kidnapped while patrolling a particularly dangerous section of the camp. Unfortunately, the men who were taken along with Turner were found two days later; they'd been strung up on crosses and burned alive.

There had been no word of Turner's fate until two weeks ago when the first video surfaced. She was wearing a veil, and while not much of her could be seen, officials say she sounded good and looked like she hadn't been heavily tortured.

Her fate is still unknown, and as of now, the government has no idea where she's being held. They continue to reassure her family that they are doing all they *can to find and rescue her. Stay tuned for an interview with Penelope's brother, Cade Turner, a firefighter from San Antonio, Texas.*

CHAPTER 1

*C*aroline lay in bed with one arm slung over her husband's chest and idly ran her fingers over his nipple. They were both content and sated after making love for the second time that night.

"Do you think they'll ever find her?"

"Who, darlin'?"

"Penelope. That woman who was kidnapped in the Middle East."

Matthew "Wolf" Steel shifted under his wife and kissed her forehead lightly. "Probably not." He felt Caroline sigh as she turned her head into his chest and nuzzled farther into him.

"I can't help but imagine myself in her place," Caroline said sadly.

"Ice, I can't—"

"No, I know. It's not the same thing really at all, but every time they've shown that video of her and how she's probably being forced to say all those horrible things, all I can think of is that her tone doesn't match the look in her eyes."

"What do you mean?" Wolf asked, genuinely curious.

"She sounds meek and serious, but I swear, Matthew, her eyes look pissed. As if she's just waiting for her chance to turn around and kill all those men who are keeping her captive. And I see it because I know just how she feels. When I was kidnapped and that jerk was filming me, I was saying one thing, but deep inside felt something way different. And I was doing everything I could to send a message to you, and whoever else might watch that video, through my eyes. I know, it was stupid to think you could actually read what I wanted to say in my eyes, but inside I was thinking about how much I loved you. I was trying to tell you where I was, and I was pleading for you to come and find me. I could be wrong, but it's obvious, at least to me, that Penelope Turner is trying to say many of the same things."

Wolf turned until Caroline was on her back and he loomed over her. He braced himself up on an elbow and brushed a strand of her dark hair behind her ear with his other hand. She grabbed his biceps and looked up at him with such love, he still had to pinch himself sometimes to make sure it was real.

Three years had passed since he'd made her his wife, and every day since then he thanked his lucky stars they'd found each other. She made him happier than he'd ever been in his life.

"Yeah, I saw it back then as I watched you on tape, and I see it in Sergeant Turner now."

Caroline bit her lip, then asked, "Do you think they're…hurting her?"

Wolf kept his voice low and tried to sound reassuring. "It's hard to say. They're certainly keeping her for a reason, probably because she's small, blonde, and a woman. They want to force the world to pay more attention to them and take them seriously."

"You mean the bombing of that wedding last month didn't do it?" Caroline's tone showed her irritation.

Wolf shook his head, amazed that he could fall in love with his wife more every time she opened her mouth. He loved that she didn't take things at face value, that she felt deeply and wasn't afraid to speak her mind. "Unfortunately, no. They need something bigger than that. And kidnapping a group of Americans isn't big, not like on the scale that 9/11 was, but if they keep the U.S. distracted—and putting a beautiful, petite woman on television and making her say anti-American and anti-British things is distracting—perhaps they can work their way up to another grand gesture."

"I love you, Matthew."

Wolf smiled down at Caroline, not surprised at her change in subject. "I love you too, Ice."

"I'm also very proud of you."

"Thank you, baby. You've done some pretty awesome things yourself in your research too."

"I wasn't done," Caroline pouted, gripping Matthew's arms tighter.

"Sorry," Wolf chuckled. "Go ahead."

"I'm proud of you, but if you ever get kidnapped by those assholes, I'm gonna have to gather the girls, and Tex, and knock some heads."

"I'm not gonna get kidnapped. I hate to say it, but those soldiers didn't follow proper protocol. I'm not sure what happened, but they obviously separated from their unit in that refugee camp and didn't have backup. I don't know if they were lured away from the rest of their unit, if they simply didn't think they were in danger, or even if they were ordered to patrol without proper procedure being followed, but you know the team and I are always very careful, Ice. We'd never willingly expose ourselves to danger."

"Okay, I'm just saying."

Wolf smiled, leaned over, and kissed Caroline. "What time is this thing tomorrow?"

Caroline smiled hugely and Wolf eased down next to her onto the mattress again, letting Caroline snuggle into his chest once more. He never got tired of her affectionate nature, and the way she would immediately throw a leg over his, and how she'd curl into his side the second he lay down.

"Well, it's supposed to start at two, but I'm sure the others will trickle in as they can get there. Jess is always late, but I can't blame her. It has to suck trying to get two babies out and ready and gather up all the stuff she needs to bring with her. I swear, I've never seen so much baby stuff as she and Kason have!"

Wolf chuckled. "Yeah, and where did she get all that baby stuff?" He felt Caroline smile.

"Okay, me and the girls might have gone overboard two years ago, but Sara was the first baby born to any of us and we wanted to make sure Jess and Kason had everything they needed. Besides, it's still getting plenty of use with John."

"I think they certainly have everything they need, and then some," Wolf said with a short laugh.

Caroline poked him. "Hush."

They were silent for a moment, then Caroline asked softly, "Are you sorry we don't have kids?"

"No." Wolf's answer was immediate and sincere. "I've never felt the urge to have kids like a lot of men have, and as I've told you before, I like having you to myself. If that makes me selfish, so be it."

"You don't get asked by the others when you're having kids?"

"Nope. They know where I stand. And Ice, they're our friends, they couldn't give a shit if we have them or not, as long as we're happy."

"It's just that…"

Wolf squeezed Caroline. "I know. We've been over this. Screw society. I know many people don't think we're normal if we don't have kids. That we should be popping them out by now. But there's no rule book that says we have to have children if we don't want them. Besides, you're kept busy with everyone else's kids. I know you babysit every chance you get."

"I love them, but I also love being able to give them back."

Wolf smiled and kissed the top of Caroline's head. "Go to sleep, baby. You have to work in the morning, I've got PT, and then we have to survive the craziness that will be Brinique and Davisa's adoption party. I have a feeling you girls went overboard."

Caroline didn't answer, but Wolf felt her smile against him. Yup. They totally went overboard.

"Love you, Matthew."

"Love you too, Ice."

CHAPTER 2

*A*labama Powers stood next to her friend, Summer Reed. Summer held her sleeping daughter, April, in her arms and they watched Brinique and Davisa screeching and jumping in the playhouse they'd rented for the party.

"They seem to be doing good," Summer said quietly.

"Yeah. For the most part they are," Alabama said easily. "Brinique sometimes still cries at night and Davisa has the occasional nightmare, but they've eased up a lot over the last few months."

"You've done an awesome thing, Alabama."

Alabama shrugged. "I've always wanted children, but growing up the way I did, I knew there were tons of kids out there who needed to be out of horrible home situations. Adoption is really the only way I want to have children."

"I love that Christopher didn't even blink when you told him you wanted to adopt."

Alabama smiled and looked over at her husband. He was standing by the bounce house watching his girls with a protective stance she knew would never really fade. "He didn't. I brought up fostering to him first, and he was a hundred percent in from the get-go. I know I've told you this already, but the very first call we got for placement was for Brinique and Davisa. Their mom was a drug addict and they were left to fend for themselves most of the time."

Alabama turned to Summer, getting worked up in her annoyance, repeating a story that Summer had heard many times. "When Child Protective Services showed up at their house for the first time, Brinique was only four and she was wearing a T-shirt of her mom's because she didn't have any clothes of her own. She stood over a naked Davisa and screeched, not letting the male officer get anywhere close to her." Alabama shuddered. "I can't stand to think about why, at *four*, Brinique felt she had to protect her three-year-old sister from a man."

Summer laid her hand on Alabama's shoulder. "Easy, girl. You've got them now. They're safe."

Alabama smiled at Summer and stated fiercely, "Yes, they are. And they're gonna stay that way."

The two women looked down at Davisa, who'd wandered over to where they were standing. She put her hand on Alabama's pants and tugged lightly. Alabama immediately kneeled down so she was eye level to her little girl. "Yes, sweetie?"

"Can I hold the baby?"

Alabama looked up at Summer, who smiled. "Of course. Come on, let's go sit over here."

The trio moved to a ring of chairs that had been set up. Alabama helped her daughter sit in one and Summer gently put April in Davisa's arms. "Hold on tight. I know she's only six months old, but she's heavy."

The women watched as the five-year-old carefully held the baby. Davisa didn't say anything for the longest time, she simply studied the infant carefully. Finally, she looked up in wonder. "She's so pale."

Summer supposed compared to Davisa, who had beautiful, warm chocolate-brown skin, April *was* very pale.

"Do you think my mommy would've wanted me if I was pale too?"

Alabama immediately kneeled down next to the little girl who was officially declared "hers" just that morning by the judge. Before she could speak, Abe was there.

He scooped up the little girl and the baby all together and sat in the chair and held the duo in his lap. Brinique had followed her dad over to the women and scooted up next to the chair as well. Summer stood back and watched one of her best friends in the world and her husband's teammate have a beautiful moment with their new daughters, feeling as if her heart would burst.

Abe put one arm around Brinique standing at his side and held his daughter to him, being careful not to jostle baby April. "Your birth mother didn't deserve you. And I'm not saying that to be mean, it's the truth. She had two of the most beautiful daughters on the planet, who she didn't take care of. She was selfish and only wanted to do what *she* wanted to do. Children are precious and parents have a responsibility to them to make sure they're fed, safe, and loved."

Abe looked his children in the eyes as he spoke. "You had a rough start to life, but you know what? You're a Powers now. You're mine. You're Alabama's, and you belong to every one of the men and women here today. We're one big family. You'll never be hungry again. You'll never be neglected again." He looked at Brinique. "You'll never have to worry about scary men coming into our house and hurting you or your sister. We love you. You're ours. Forever. I wouldn't care if your skin was purple or green or that it's darker than mine. It's what's inside that skin that I care about."

"What's inside our skin?" Davisa asked softly.

Without hesitation, Abe answered. "Your heart. Your blood. Your mind. You. *You* are inside your skin. And that's why I love you. And that's why Alabama loves you. And that's why everyone here loves you. Got it?"

"You won't send us back?" Brinique asked.

"No. You aren't ever going back."

"Even when we're bad?"

Alabama leaned in and touched Brinique's arm, picking up where her husband left off. "Baby, you'll never be bad. You might misbehave. You might do something that isn't right, but those are simply bad decisions. They don't make you a bad person. And the bottom line is that you're not going back. The judge today gave you to us forever. Your last name is now Powers. Just like mine. Just like Christopher's." She smiled at her daughter. "You're stuck with us now."

Brinique smiled hugely, showing off her crooked teeth. "I like being stuck with you guys."

"We like it too."

Davisa spoke up. "Does that mean we can call you Mommy and Daddy now?"

Alabama heard Summer sniff loudly from behind her, but she didn't look away from Davisa. This was perhaps one of the proudest moments in her life, no way was she missing a second of it. "You can call us whatever you're most comfortable with. Dad. Mom. Mommy. Daddy. Alabama. Abe. Christopher...whatever you want. But nothing would make me happier than having you call me your mom or mommy."

Davisa nodded solemnly and looked down at the baby in her lap. "Okay. Mommy?"

"Yes, sweetheart?"

"I think the baby just pooped."

Alabama laughed, loving how she'd just had one of the most emotional conversations she'd ever had in her life, and Davisa could move on without blinking.

"How about I take her then?" Summer asked from behind them.

Davisa nodded and Summer leaned in and gathered April in her arms.

"Can we go play some more?"

"Of course, but be careful," Abe warned, helping Davisa off his lap.

"Okay, Daddy, we will," Brinique said brightly, before she and her sister ran off toward the bounce house again.

"Come here," Abe said to Alabama, pulling her into his lap.

Alabama settled in and sighed.

"You okay?"

She nodded. "Yeah, I know we've talked to them about what it means to be a foster kid and how we were working toward adopting them, but I didn't realize they still had doubts."

"Baby, hell, you had doubts when we met and you were an adult. They'll adjust. We just need to keep telling them that we love them for who they are. We need to make them feel safe…they'll be fine."

"I love you, Christopher."

"Love you too…now, when can we have cake?"

Alabama laughed and got off of her husband's lap. "Why are you always hungry?"

"Because my wife is insatiable and I need to keep my energy up to satisfy her?"

Alabama playfully slugged Christopher on the arm. "Whatever. Go watch your kids while I get the table ready."

Abe leaned over and picked her up until her feet dangled off the ground. "This has been one of the happiest days of my life. Besides the day you forgave me for being an ass, and our wedding, of course."

Alabama put her arms around his neck and kissed him, hard. "Me too. Now put me down. I have work to do."

* * *

CHEYENNE WADDLED over to where Summer was sitting with Fiona.

Faulkner "Dude" Cooper, her very protective and attentive husband, had dropped her off before going to park the car.

"Hey, ladies."

"Hey, Cheyenne, you look ready to pop!"

"Don't I know it! Can you believe I have three more weeks to go?"

"It's crazy. Every time we hang out I'm ready to bend down and catch that baby before it can hit the ground," Summer teased.

"Hush. Don't say that around Faulkner. He's already super-protective. If he heard that, he wouldn't let me go anywhere. As it was, I had to beg to be able to come today."

"Beg?" Fiona asked with a raised eyebrow.

"Hush," Cheyenne said while blushing.

Fiona didn't hush. "Oh, I'm sure *that* was a hardship."

Cheyenne had shared with all the other women her husband's penchant to be dominant in the bedroom. But they all knew it worked well for the couple. "Yeah, well, I might have turned the tables on him a bit. He's…reluctant to go too far with me these days, so I use it to my advantage as much as I can."

Fiona laughed. "You are so in trouble once you have this baby and he can have his way with you again."

Cheyenne smiled widely. "I know. I can't wait."

"You okay? Need anything?" Faulkner had come up behind them while Cheyenne was getting settled into the chair.

"No, I'm good, hon. Thanks for dropping me off."

"Like I'd make you walk all the way from the parking lot. This place is packed. It's like Abe and Alabama invited the entire base!"

There were indeed lots and lots of people at the park. Kids were running everywhere and the happiness could almost be felt in the air.

"Yeah, well, those two precious girls deserve a huge party after everything they've been through," Cheyenne commented.

"Agreed. I'm going to go and find the guys. Are you sure you don't need anything?" Dude asked.

"I'm good. Fiona and Summer will take care of me."

Dude leaned down and kissed Cheyenne, a bit longer and more inappropriately than the surroundings and company would merit, but Fiona and Summer were used to it. When he wandered off looking for his teammates, Summer adjusted April in her arms and sighed. "It seems like I'm always blushing when I'm around the two of you."

Cheyenne laughed. "Me too."

"How's April doing?" Fiona asked, leaning over and peering down at the still sleeping infant. "Is she sleeping better?"

"Yeah, she can go almost all night now, thank God. When we first brought her home, every time she moved Sam was up checking on her. As much as I'll miss the times when he brings her to me and watches fascinated as I breastfeed her, I'm looking forward to sleeping through the night again."

"I can't believe you agreed to name her April."

Summer sighed. "I know. Sam loves my name, even though I sometimes think it's ridiculous, but he was so proud of himself for thinking up the name April. I mean, I know her birthday is in April, but it still seems silly."

"It's not silly," Mozart said from behind them. All three women jumped in surprise.

"Jeez, Sam, don't sneak up on us!"

"I didn't sneak, I walked up just like everyone else does."

"No, you sneak. You SEALs think you're walking normally, but it's ingrained in you to be quiet and silent when you move. One of these days I'm putting a bell on you."

Mozart only smiled. "As I said, April's name isn't silly. It's beautiful, just like her mom. Now you and her have something in common. You were named after when you were born. I love it, and I love you."

Summer tilted her head up and was rewarded with a kiss from her husband.

"Can I get you anything?"

"No, I'm good. Thanks. Can you see if you can find Jess and Kason though? I know those two babies of hers are probably slowing them down. I want to make sure she gets to rest when she gets here," Summer commented.

"Will do. I'll send them over as soon as I track them down. Love you."

"Love you too, Sam."

The women watched as Sam "Mozart" Reed walked away.

"He's as good looking from the back as he is from the front," Fiona commented dryly.

Everyone laughed.

"How are you healing? Are you really all good now?" Fiona asked. "April certainly did a number on your body."

"Yeah, having that many stitches down there wasn't fun, but I'm good.

This will be our only baby though. I'm almost forty and while I love her, Sam doesn't want to put my body through that again, and I can't say I disagree. I also want to be able to raise her and then kick her out to go to college when she's eighteen so Sam and I can enjoy our retirement...you know?"

"Yeah, makes sense," Cheyenne agreed immediately. "Faulkner and I want lots of babies after this one, but I know I might change my mind once she's actually here. But I'm also not even thirty yet, so I have lots of time to decide to have more, or to dissuade Faulkner."

"Yo! How about some help here?"

Fiona immediately got up and waved off Cheyenne and Summer. "I got this. Stay put." She hurried over to the duo. Jessyka was loaded down with one-year-old John in her arms and a bag over her right shoulder. Kason was walking next to her with their daughter in his arms and another, bigger bag over *his* shoulder.

Fiona went straight for Sara, the two-year-old, who was thankfully sleeping in her dad's arms.

Jess was used to her friends wanting to get their hands on her kids rather than being more practical and helping her with what seemed like the ten bags she was always carrying. It didn't bother her, she was happy they all shared her love for her kids. "I finally got her out of the house after two temper tantrums because she first wanted to wear her princess dress...the dress she wore at your wedding, Cheyenne," Jess said as they arrived at the little group, "and then because she wanted to wear her plastic play-dress-up shoes instead of her sandals. She's going to make me gray before my time."

"She's a little angel, how can you say that?"

Kason dropped the bag on the ground next to an empty chair. "You got this, babe?"

Jess leaned up and wrapped her free arm around Kason. "I got this. Go on, go have fun with your friends. Be good."

Benny shook his head and rolled his eyes at his wife. "I'll be back to check on you in a bit. Don't let her sleep too long, she needs to run off some of her energy if we want to sleep at all tonight." He leaned in close to Jess, "I have plans for later, and I don't want to be interrupted by a toddler who can't sleep because she's too excited."

Jess blushed, glancing at her friends to see if they'd heard her husband's words. Seeing they were cooing over her kids, but smiling, she realized they'd heard every word her husband had said. Knowing they were happy for her, she nevertheless whispered back at Kason, trying to keep her friends from hearing *everything*, "Don't worry, I'll make sure she's up in a bit. I like it when you have plans. Love you."

Kason kissed Jess hard, then stepped back. "Love you too."

Jessyka settled down into an empty chair and watched as Kason sauntered away toward his teammates, and then smiled as her three friends settled into the chairs beside her.

Soon, Caroline and Alabama wandered over to join the little group. They pulled up chairs and sat in a semi-circle, watching the kids play in the bounce house and the other equipment in the park.

"I freaking love this," Fiona announced.

"What?"

"This. Us. Being here. Holding babies. Watching the kids play. Watching our husbands talk about who knows what manly shit they're talking about. We are six lucky women, that's for sure."

Everyone nodded.

"Five and a half kids, six husbands, six friends."

"Five and a half?" Caroline questioned.

Fiona gestured toward Cheyenne's protruding belly. "Yeah, I'm counting Cheyenne's baby as a half until she's born. Until Cheyenne has to change diapers, it's only a half."

Cheyenne laughed at her friend. "You know what's missing?"

"What?" Fiona asked.

"Tex and Melody."

"True. We should totally Skype them while we're here," Caroline proclaimed.

"Oh, hell yeah. That'll be awesome. I haven't seen her and Akilah in too long!" Fiona chimed in.

"How's Akilah doing?" Cheyenne asked.

"Last I heard from Melody, she was great. She had the amputation, and Tex is teaching her the ropes on how to take care of her stump and how the prosthetic works," Caroline told the group.

"Does she miss Iraq?"

"I don't think so. Tex and Melody have done a great job in making sure they cook her familiar foods, and they've even found a support group there in Pittsburgh so she can talk to and be friends with other girls displaced from Iraq."

"Did they ever find her parents?" Alabama asked.

Caroline shook her head sadly. "Akilah says they were killed, and Tex doesn't think she's lying about it. She was lucky the United Nations doctor over in Baghdad felt sorry for her and pulled strings to get her seen back here in the States. Contacting Tex and letting him know her story was the best thing that ever happened to her."

"How's she doing in school?" Summer asked.

"Melody says she's still struggling with English a bit, but she gets better every day. It's hard enough being twelve years old, but to be twelve in a new country, learning the language, *and* dealing with a major injury and how to get about in daily life with only one arm…well, Melody is amazed at how well she's doing."

"We are *so* Skyping them today!" Alabama announced resolutely.

After chatting for a bit longer, Sara finally woke up and Fiona put her down and all the women watched the little two-year-old toddle off to play with a group of kids in a big sandbox nearby. Jess waved at one of the other mothers from the base, who motioned that she'd watch the little girl.

The group sat around talking about feeding, toddlers, childbirth and other random topics until one by one their husbands came over. Wolf and Mozart pulled up chairs next to their wives, Dude stood behind Cheyenne and rubbed her shoulders. Benny and Cookie sat on the ground next to their wives, and Abe scooped Alabama out of her chair and sat in it, with his wife on his lap. Brinique and Davisa wandered back over, finally tired from running around, and sat next to their new mom and dad.

"Thank you all for coming out today," Alabama told everyone. "It means more than you'll ever know. I'm proud of us. I have two children who I helped take out of a horrible situation, much as I had growing up. Jess, you and Kason got right to work and started popping out babies right after you were married. The house you guys bought out in the countryside is beautiful, and after Kason finishes fixing it up, it's going to be even better. Fiona, you've come a long way from where you were after Hunter found you."

"Well, I've had a lot of therapy," Fiona said honestly. "And a lot of help from my friends."

Everyone nodded in agreement and Alabama continued. "Cheyenne, you're the most beautiful pregnant woman I've ever seen. And I swear if you didn't tell me the doctor had most definitely said there was only one baby in there, I'd think you were having triplets."

"Shut your mouth, evil woman," Cheyenne teased. They all laughed at the gleam in Faulkner's eyes.

"Looks like Faulkner wouldn't mind, though."

"Yeah, well, *he* doesn't have to squeeze them out his—"

Alabama interrupted Cheyenne, gesturing toward Brinique and Davisa in warning as she did. "And Summer, I'm so proud of you for getting that HR Director job. I know you weren't sure you wanted to get back into the field, but the small-company thing is working for you. And April is beautiful as well."

Alabama took a deep breath and turned to Caroline. "And Caroline. What would all of us have done without you? Seriously. You're our leader. You took us in and cared for us from the get-go."

"Well, except for warning me off Faulkner," Cheyenne said with a laugh.

"You and Matthew might not have any kids, but why do I feel sometimes as if we're *all* your kids? You're there when we have questions and worries. You've looked after John when he was colicky and Jess didn't know what to do anymore. You babysit Brinique and Davisa whenever I ask, without question. You make sure Tex, Melody, and Akilah are always included and invited when we do things. You're the glue that holds us all together when our men go off to save the world. I love you more than I can ever say. Thank you for being you, and for being our friend."

Wolf, Abe, Cookie, Mozart, Dude, and Benny all rolled their eyes at each other good naturedly when their wives all started crying. They might be tough-as-nails women who wouldn't let them get away with any crap, but with the pregnancy hormones and general happiness they all felt at the moment, it seemed as if they could all cry at the drop of a hat.

"I thought Mommy was happy?" Davisa said in confusion in a too-loud whisper to Christopher.

Everyone laughed at the five-year-old's innocent statement and wiped their eyes.

"We are happy, baby. But sometimes people cry happy tears," Alabama tried to explain.

"Grownups are weird," Brinique explained to her sister. "Can we go play some more?"

Abe palmed his daughter's head. "Yes. Be careful though."

"We will. Come on, Davisa, race you to the monkey bars!"

The two girls ran away from the group shrieking with laughter.

"This is one of the best days of my life," Cheyenne declared. "Friends, kids, and the love of my life by my side. What else could we ask for?"

Everyone agreed wholeheartedly.

Each of the twelve people in the close-knit group would remember this day and the joy and love surrounding it in the upcoming weeks, needing the memories to keep them going.

CHAPTER 3

Sergeant Penelope Turner was once again seen on a videotape provided by ISIS. Turner has been missing for six weeks now. This video was the longest one of the kidnapped American soldier to date. She is seen sitting in what seems to be a tent and reading from a long-winded, rambling letter that extols Allah and claims, among other things, that there will be more killing and deaths if the Americans don't stop sending soldiers to the Middle East.

She reads the letter in a monotone voice, and doesn't look up at the camera at all. She only looks up after a voice is heard reprimanding her in the background. Analysts have concluded that Turner looks like she has lost some weight, but she is still remarkably healthy, all things considered.

There has been no word from the President about what, if any, rescue attempts are in the works for this brave American soldier. Her family continues to push for information and for the government to make some sort of gesture to gain her freedom. The official response is that the United States does not negotiate with terrorists.

More information at the ten o'clock hour.

* * *

CHEYENNE SAT on the couch with Faulkner and held his hand firmly.

"We're leaving in the morning."

"But—"

Dude hauled Cheyenne into his arms and held her as tightly as he could with her enormous belly hampering his efforts. "I don't want to go. Dammit, I don't want to go. I even asked Commander Hurt if I could sit this one out, and was denied."

"Really?"

Dude nodded. "Yeah. Which means every single one of us is needed for this mission. I won't lie to you, baby. I have a bad feeling about it. I don't know if it's because I have to leave you here, about to have my baby, or if it's because of the mission itself. But mark my words. *Nothing* is going to keep me from getting back here to you and our little one. Nothing. Got it?"

Cheyenne nodded and sniffed. She'd always tried to be brave when Faulkner had to leave, but this time was different. They'd practiced breathing techniques together, he'd gone to every doctor appointment with her. He hadn't missed one step of her pregnancy. The thought of her husband missing the actual birth of their daughter made her feel empty inside.

"Words, Shy."

She smiled at that. He hadn't changed in the two years since they'd met. He was still as bossy as ever. "Yeah. I got it."

"Your only job is to stay safe. Keep our daughter safe. You've got all the girls here to keep you busy. If, God forbid, I miss the birth of our daughter, make sure you get someone to film it for me."

"What?" They hadn't talked about that at all. "I'm not filming it. Gross!"

"Shy, I've waited my entire life for this moment. To watch my child being born is not gross, it's fucking beautiful."

"But, Faulkner—"

"Please."

Well shit. He'd said please. *She* was usually the one begging, not him. She nodded reluctantly. "Okay, but we are not breaking out the video of my cooter to show off to anyone else. Ever."

Dude only smiled. Double shit. He sobered and said in a gruff tone, "And if your so-called family dares to show their faces at the hospital or try to insinuate they should be allowed to see my daughter, sic Caroline on them."

Cheyenne smiled, remembering the last time Faulkner had "sicced" Caroline on her mom and sister. They'd shown up at *Aces Bar and Grill* while they were eating, and Caroline had headed them off before they'd even gotten close to their table. Cheyenne didn't know exactly why they'd come to see her, Caroline wouldn't really tell her, but they'd probably wanted something from her.

Caroline had gone off on her family. Cheyenne hadn't even *heard* of some of the insults she'd hurled at them. Faulkner had kept his eyes on the trio, but hadn't moved while Caroline was giving them hell. It wasn't like him to not take the opportunity to tell her family how much he didn't respect or like them, but he'd told her later that Caroline had been doing such a great job at dressing them down, he didn't feel the need to join in.

Cheyenne answered Faulkner, "I will, although I don't think they'll show up. I think they finally got the hint when you returned their Christmas card unopened with the words, 'You don't exist for Cheyenne anymore,' scrawled on the back."

Dude leaned down and buried his face in his wife's hair and rested his hand on her swollen belly, not addressing her comment about the stupid Christmas card, but instead saying what was foremost on his mind. "I love you, Shy. And I love our daughter. I don't know what I'd do without you in my life. You take me as I am. You're my match in every way. I'm dying inside thinking I might not be around for one of the most important days in our lives."

Cheyenne held on to Faulkner, knowing she had to reassure him. "Even if you don't get back for her birth, this is only the start of this child's life. Even if you miss the big events, you'll be there in the middle of the night when she needs changing. You'll be there when she has a nightmare. You'll chase the boogeyman out of the closet for her. You'll take her for ice cream and let her cry on your shoulder when she falls down. You'll teach her to ride a bicycle. You'll be there giving the evil eye to her first date. You'll be there for her everyday life. Missing events here and there doesn't matter. It's being there for the everyday, boring things that she'll remember most and that are important. Yeah?"

"Fuck, I love you."

Cheyenne smiled. "I love you too. Should we talk about names again?" She hated to bring it up, as they usually ended up arguing about it, but if Faulkner had a feeling he might not make it home for her birth, they'd better talk about it now.

"No, I don't want to jinx it. If we decide now, I *know* I won't make it home in time."

Cheyenne smiled at him in exasperation. "But if you don't make it home, I'll have to name her without you. I don't want you to be disappointed."

"We've talked about this enough, Shy, you know what I like and what I don't. *If* I don't get back, I trust you to give our daughter a name she won't get made fun of for the rest of her life and that she won't want to change as soon as she's old enough to think for herself. Now, if we're done with this conversation, I need to show my daughter who her daddy is one more time."

"Jeez, Faulkner, I swear you're hornier now when I'm as big as a house than you were when we first got married."

"I can't help it. You're just so fucking beautiful with my child inside you, I can't get enough."

Cheyenne let Faulkner help her off the couch—lord knew she had trouble getting out of it on her own nowadays—and lead her into their bedroom. There, he proceeded to strip her out of her nightgown and he spent the next few hours worshiping her body and showing her in every way he could how much she meant to him. He loved her as if it might be the last time he'd ever get to love her.

* * *

"You've got your tracking thing, right?" Jessyka asked Kason nervously for the third time that night after they'd put the kids to bed.

"I've got it. Don't worry."

"I can't not worry. Every time you step out of the house, I worry."

"I know, and that's one of the four hundred and thirty-three reasons why I love you."

"Only four hundred and thirty-three?"

"Come here, Jess." Benny hauled his wife into his arms. "We get called away on missions a lot. Why are you so worried?"

"I don't know. I just have a feeling this time is different."

Benny didn't say anything, because he had the same feeling. He changed the subject. "Are you all set with John and Sara? Will you be able to do your volunteering thing at the youth center without me to help with them?"

"Yeah, Caroline said we could come and stay there for a few nights and Fiona said the same thing. I can go and volunteer while they're looking after the kids."

"I hate that you don't feel comfortable being out here in our house when I'm not here."

Jess tried to explain. "It's not that I don't feel comfortable, but you do a lot, and you don't even realize it, I don't think. With John and Sara being so close in age, and John just now starting to walk and Sara needing lots of attention, it's just easier for me to have help."

Seeing the dismayed look on her husband's face, Jess hurried to reassure him. "I'm not saying this to make you feel guilty. Single parents do it by themselves all the time, and I have a newfound respect for all the men and women out in the world who are raising their kids on their own. Caroline and Fiona have offered to be that help. That's all."

"Okay, Jess. I'll let it go. I'll be back as soon as I can and I'll work even harder to get the house finished up so you'll feel more comfortable here. Maybe we can look into getting some help around the house. A nanny or something. I don't want you to lose yourself either. I know how important volunteering at the youth center is. It's your way of helping kids like Tabitha."

Jess sighed as she thought of the young girl she'd loved, but ultimately couldn't help.

"Yeah, I can't help but think that if Tabitha had had some sort of safe place to go after school, maybe she wouldn't have felt so isolated and maybe she would've spoken up about the abuse she was going through."

"I'm proud of you, Jess. You could be bitter or depressed over what happened to Tabitha, but you aren't. You turned the experience around and used it to fuel your desire to help other teenagers."

"You're the best husband ever, Kason. Don't forget it." Jess smiled at him. She loved him so much and had no idea what she'd done to get so lucky to have him in her life, but she wasn't going to look a gift horse in the mouth. She wasn't letting him go. Ever.

"I won't, but if you feel like showing me how great I am before I go...I wouldn't be opposed."

Jess giggled and stepped back from him and pointed over his shoulder. "What is *that*?"

When he turned to look, Jessyka smiled and hurried out of the room toward their bedroom as fast as her body would take her. She threw her words over her shoulder as she made her way down the hall. "Ha! Made you look! First one in the bedroom gets to be on top!"

"Why, you little sneak!" Benny said with no heat. He came after her, but made sure to let Jess stay in front of him. He liked her on top as much as she liked being there. Her limp, a result of one leg being shorter than the other, didn't really slow her down, but they both knew if he really wanted to, he could overtake her in a second. Watching his wife's sexy ass sway as she fast-walked down the hall to their bedroom never failed to make him smile.

Later that night, Benny knew he'd never forget the look on Jess's face as she rode him. Her head thrown back, her long black hair brushing against his thighs, and the smile on her face. It was pure gold, and she was all his.

* * *

MOZART SAT in the rocking chair holding his six-month-old daughter and looking down at her in awe. She was the most amazing thing he'd ever seen. He wasn't a sappy man. He'd lived a hard life and never expected to have a wife, never mind a daughter. One of his favorite things ever was watching as April breastfed from Summer. His girls. They were so beautiful it made his heart hurt.

April had woken up a bit ago. She was doing better at sleeping through the night, but still had times where she'd wake up, and he'd fetched her and brought her to Summer. Summer had only been half awake and Mozart had helped April latch on to his wife's nipple and he'd held his daughter to his wife's breast as she nursed. Summer had smiled tiredly at him, and palmed his face when April had finished.

"Thank you, Sam. I love you."

"Shhh, you're welcome. I love you too. Go back to sleep. I'll be back."

Now he was sitting in April's room. His daughter had fallen back to sleep a while ago, but he was enjoying breathing in her baby scent and holding her in his arms. She was growing up so fast and he could suddenly envision her as a teenager, not wanting her dad to hug her. In the back of his mind, Mozart tried to tamp down the worry he had about the mission they were about to go on. Even though they'd been on many missions similar to this one, somehow he knew this one would be different.

Summer found Sam in their baby's room, rocking her and watching her sleep. "You didn't come back," she said softly, not wanting to disturb her daughter.

Mozart looked up at his beautiful wife. Her blonde hair was in disarray around her face and her blue eyes were sleepy. She'd thrown on one of his shirts that he'd inevitably left on the floor and was holding it closed around her body with her arms crossed in front of her. His heart felt as if it was going to burst with love for her. He'd come so close to losing her two years ago, and there wasn't a day that went by that he didn't thank God the team had gotten to her in time.

"Hey. Sorry. Can you believe we've had her in our lives for six months already? You never know what you're missing until you have it in the first place."

"Like you."

"What?"

"Like you. I never knew I was missing you, until I *had* you."

"Come here, Sunshine."

Summer padded over to her husband and kneeled on the carpet next to the chair. She palmed his scarred cheek and ran her thumb over his lips. "Even if we'd never had April, my life would've been completely full. April isn't a culmination of our love. I love you, Sam Reed."

"You'll never know how glad I am that you stood up for me that day up at Big Bear. By some miracle you don't see my flaws, and I'm not only talking about the scar on my cheek. I love you too, Sunshine. You and April are the most important things in my life. I'll move heaven and earth to always come home to you."

"I know you will. Come to bed, hon."

Mozart nodded and stood up, careful not to jostle his little girl. He lay her gently in her crib and kissed her on the top of her head, her fuzzy hair soft against his lips. He put his hand on her back, amazed at how tiny she still was. He could cover her entire back with the palm of one hand. "Rest easy, Angel. Daddy loves you."

Summer took Sam's hand and led him back to their bedroom. She stripped him of his flannel pants and took her time showing him just how much he was loved.

Later, when they were dozing off—Summer after having come several times, and Mozart after finally allowing himself to release inside the love of his life—he heard her say softly and groggily in his ear, "Rest easy, Sam. I love you."

* * *

COOKIE SAT across from Fiona at the table as they ate. "Are you sure you're going to be okay while I'm gone?"

Fiona smiled at Hunter, not getting irritated with him, knowing he asked out of love. "For the tenth time, yes, hon, I'll be fine. I haven't had a flashback in a couple of months now."

"I know, but—"

"I understand that you get nervous every time you leave because of what happened two years ago when you were on that mission, but I *swear* I've got the tracker on, and I'll call Caroline or Tex if I start to feel weird. I'm not going to run off like I did before. I'm much better now. You've made sure of that."

Cookie pushed his mostly empty plate away and put his elbows on the table and leaned toward Fiona. "I just worry about you."

"I know, and I love you for it. You worry about me just like I worry about you. You about done?"

Cookie nodded and watched as Fiona took his plate to the sink. He stood up and opened the dishwasher and took the dishes after Fiona rinsed them, placing them into the machine. They worked in tandem, without words, just as they had many nights before.

The kitchen was clean and the dishes were done. "Want to take a bath?"

Fiona looked at her husband. Something was off about him, but she wasn't sure what. "Sure. You going to join me?"

He shook his head. "Not tonight. I just want to pamper you."

Fiona nodded.

"Okay, give me a few minutes, and I'll go get it started for you."

"I can do it."

"I know, but I want to."

"All right. I'll find a book to read and join you in a few."

Fiona watched Hunter walk down the hall to their bedroom. She cocked her head, trying to figure out what his deal was. He was usually protective of her, especially before he left for a mission, but this was new. He'd drawn her a bath before, but tonight it somehow felt different. In the past he'd make love to her as if it would be the last time they'd ever be together, *then* give her the lecture about being safe and asking if she'd be okay. He didn't usually delay going to bed with a bath for her first.

Fiona grabbed a romance novel off the shelf, one of her favorites, and headed to their bedroom. She could hear the water running into the tub, but didn't expect the candles when she entered their large bathroom. Hunter had lit as many as he could find, not caring that they were all different scents and the smell would probably give them both a headache later. It was simply beautiful.

He didn't say much, but watched as she stripped out of her clothes and climbed into the tub.

"Is the temperature okay?"

"Scalding hot...so it's perfect."

Hunter smiled at her. "Okay, I'll be back in twenty minutes or so to check on you."

Fiona nodded and again worried as she watched him leave. Something was bothering him and she had to get him to fess up before the night was over.

After her bath, and after Hunter had dried every inch of her skin, and after he'd bent her over their mattress and had taken her from behind—quite thoroughly and satisfyingly—and after they'd snuggled down into the soft pillowy mattress, Fiona asked the question that had been nagging at her all night.

"What's up, Hunter?"

"What do you mean?"

"I mean, you've never been quite so...caring—before you've left before."

He was silent so long, Fiona wondered if he was going to answer her at all...indeed if he was still awake.

"I know I'm not supposed to admit it, but this one worries me."

Trying not to tense up, Fiona asked him why.

"You know I can't tell you where I'm going, but I could be gone for a while. I'm worried about you. I'm worried about the other women. I'm worried about their kids. I'm just worried in general."

A little alarmed, as it wasn't like Hunter to be this concerned about anything—he usually had a kick-butt-and-take-no-prisoners attitude—Fiona tried to reassure him. "I can't ask you not to be worried. Hell, if you told me not to be concerned about *you*, I'd laugh in your face. But I'll be okay. The girls will be okay. Everyone will be just fine. We look after each other when you guys are gone, just as you all have each other's backs when you're on a mission. Trust in us to keep on keepin' on while you're all gone. No matter what, this is our family. We might not have any kids, but I'd do anything for John, Sara, Brinique, Davisa, April and the as-of-yet-unnamed baby Cooper."

"Just promise me...*promise me*, if I don't come home, you'll take care of yourself. I can't stand to think of you as lost and alone and broken as you were when I found you two years ago when you'd run north."

Wanting to comment on the "not coming home" part, and break out in tears, Fiona held them back. She needed to be a rock for Hunter. He needed her to be strong. "I promise."

Cookie nodded because he couldn't say anything through the knot in his throat, and wrapped his arms around Fiona as tightly as he thought she could stand. He hitched one leg over her hip and surrounded himself in her scent and her body. If this was the last time he'd be able to hold her, as his gut was screaming at him it possibly could be, he wanted to imprint himself onto her.

He felt the second Fiona fell asleep in his arms. They'd both ignored the tears that leaked out of her eyes as they held each other. Cookie didn't sleep even a minute. He wanted to cherish every last second with the love of his life in his arms.

* * *

ALABAMA AND CHRISTOPHER sat on the couch next to each other, each with a little girl on their lap, explaining that Daddy was leaving on another trip. Over the last year and a half that Brinique and Davisa been living with them, they'd slowly understood more and more about what it was Daddy did.

"When will you be back?" Brinique asked tearfully.

"I'm not sure, pumpkin," Abe told his daughter, wiping away the tears that made streaks down her little face. "But I *will* be back."

"My other daddy left and never came back," Davisa said matter-of-factly. Alabama knew she'd never known who her real father was, her birth mother probably never knew either, but Davisa had most likely heard the woman complaining that the man had left without a backward glance anyway.

"He might have left, but I'll do everything in my power to get back," Christopher promised. "Do you think I'd leave three such beautiful women forever? Not if I can help it. I love you all too much. No matter what happens in your life, you need to know that your mom and I love you very much. We *picked* you. A lot of other mommies and daddies don't get a choice in their children. We had a choice and we choose you guys. Don't ever forget it."

Brinique sat up straight in Christopher's lap. "Yeah. You picked us. Out of all the little boys and girls who needed a home. You picked *us*."

Abe nodded and repeated the words Brinique obviously wanted to hear. "That's right, little one. We chose you. So even though I'm leaving, I'm not leaving because of anything you did. It's my job. It's what I do."

"Mommy said you're one of the good guys. You go out into the world and put the bad people in jail."

Abe looked over at Alabama and winked. "Well, yeah, sorta, but that's the basics."

"Where's the world?"

"What do you mean, sweetie?"

"You go out into the world...where's the world?"

"Ah." Abe shifted in his seat, snuggling Brinique closer to his chest as he did. "The world is anywhere other than where we are right now." He tried to keep it simple for his six-year-old.

"So, will you be in another state?"

Alabama knew this was getting trickier now. She knew Abe couldn't tell anyone where they were going, not even his precocious little girl. She stepped in. "We don't know where Daddy will be, but Uncle Hunter and all your other uncles will take care of him for us until he can get back home."

"But Super Tex will know where you are, right? Mommy, you said Uncle Tex always knows where everyone is 'cos he's tacking them and that makes him kinda like a super hero...right?"

Alabama tried not to wince. Obviously Davisa was smarter than the average five-year-old. She remembered every single thing she was told. "*Tracking*, not tacking, and yes, Uncle Tex will know."

"Okay then. As long as Daddy doesn't get lost and can find his way back home, it's good. Will you read us a story tonight, Daddy?"

Alabama wished she could turn off her worry as easily as her daughters seemed to be able to. She and Christopher helped the girls get ready for bed and tucked them in. They still slept in the same room, feeling more comfortable being together, even after a year and a half away from their horrible birth mother. Christopher read a bedtime story and the girls were out before he'd reached page six.

They both kissed their cheeks and Abe whispered what he told them every night whether they were asleep or awake. "The sooner you go to sleep, the sooner a new day will come." They stood in the doorway for a long moment.

"They're beautiful kids, Alabama. I'm so proud of you for taking the initiative and pushing me to accept the foster placement. I can't even imagine our life without them in it, and I don't want to."

"Does it bother you when they call us Mom and Dad in public and people look twice?"

"Because we're white and they're black? Fuck no. Let people say whatever they want. Those girls are *mine*."

God, Alabama loved this man.

Abe eased the girls' door closed, leaving it open a crack so they could hear either of them if they needed them in the night, and they went across the hall to their bedroom. They'd had to be creative and careful whenever they'd made love in the past year. Neither wanted their kids walking in on something they shouldn't be seeing.

Abe made easy, sweet love to Alabama, making sure they were both quiet as they climaxed. He pulled Alabama on top of him and felt her relax, boneless, into him. He knew they had to get up and put something on, just in case the girls came wandering into their room, but at the moment he didn't want to move. The feel of Alabama's smooth skin against his was as close as he'd get to heaven here on earth.

"I'm going to miss you." Alabama's voice was muted and heartfelt.

"I'm going to miss you too."

Alabama knew she couldn't demand Christopher promise to come back to her, but she wanted to.

"Do me a favor?"

"Anything," Alabama told her husband honestly.

"Don't accept any more foster placements until I get back."

Alabama pushed herself up on Christopher's chest until she could just see him in the low light of the room. "What?"

"I know you. You'll get anxious, and you'll worry while I'm gone. I know you deal with stress better if you're busy. So I figure if asked, you'd gladly take on another child in need. When we take in another foster, I want to be here. I want to help him or her acclimate. And I can't do that if you're here by yourself."

Alabama relaxed into Christopher. For a second she'd thought he didn't want to adopt any more kids. Yes, they'd talked about it, and agreed they both wanted a large family of adopted kids, but she'd jumped to conclusions. She loved him all the more for wanting to be a part of every potential foster they had. "Okay, I can do that."

"If something happens to me—"

"No. Nothing will happen to you," Alabama butted in.

Abe continued as if she hadn't interrupted. "If something happens to me, I still want you to have the large family you've always dreamed about. Don't let it stop you."

Alabama's breath hitched in her chest. "I won't," she got out, and buried her face in the space between his shoulder and his face. She felt Christopher's hand wrap around the back of her neck.

"I worry about you from the moment I get up in the morning to the second I fall asleep. I might be away on a mission, and I might be a hundred percent focused on that mission, but you're always there, in the back of my mind. I know you're here, with our kids, waiting on me, and it makes me more determined than ever to get back to you. I know there's always a risk that one day that stubbornness on my part might not be enough, and I want you to reach for your dreams, whether I'm standing next to you cheering you on or not. Okay?"

"Okay," Alabama told him through her watery tears, not able to rebut his comments. They were beautiful and heartbreaking all at the same time.

"Sleep now, sweetheart. The sooner you sleep, the sooner I'll be home."

* * *

CAROLINE STOOD at the door of the house looking out into the dark yard. Matthew stood behind her with his arms around her waist, holding her against his chest. They stood without talking for a long while. Finally, Caroline broke the silence.

"You're being sent in to try to rescue that girl, aren't you?"

Wolf didn't answer, and Caroline sighed. She turned in her husband's embrace and looped her arms around his neck as she gazed up at him. He looked down at her with such love and patience, she almost couldn't stand it.

"I know, you can't tell me, but in my gut I know that's where you guys are going. Don't worry, I won't say anything to the others, but can I just say one thing before I drop it?" Caroline knew Matthew was uncomfortable with the conversation, but he'd never admit it.

"Of course, Ice. Say whatever you need."

"You'll get her out. You'll find her, kill those assholes, and get her home. I *know* it."

At that, she saw Matthew's lips quirk upward. "You do, huh?"

"Yeah. You guys wouldn't rest until I was home and safe, and you didn't really even know me then either. This woman has *got* to be tough as hell. If she's been held for as long as the TV reporters say she has, she has to be."

"Ice—" Wolf began, but Caroline talked over him.

"I'm over what happened to me, we've talked about it, and I spoke to that therapist last year when I started having those nightmares, but there's something about this woman that gets to me. I heard her brother's interview with that talk-show host the other night. She joined the Army Reserves because she wanted to serve her country on a larger scale than being a firefighter did. Her brother says she's an excellent firefighter. She's worked her butt off and all the guys respect the hell out of her. She can make it through this, she's just waiting for some help. And who better to help her than you? And Hunter, Christopher, Sam, Faulkner, and Kason? You guys have all helped your women get out of shitty situations, so I know this will be no different. But please, do me a favor, Matthew."

"What's that, Ice?"

Caroline noticed he was careful to neither confirm nor deny where the team was going.

"This Penelope Turner is someone's sister. She's someone's daughter and friend. She's just like me. Or Fiona, or any of the others. I know I don't have to tell you to do whatever you have to in order to get her out of there…because I know you will. She's suffered enough and she needs to come home."

Wolf leaned down and gathered his wife to his chest. Fuck, he loved this woman. She could be railing at him to be careful, or crying because she was upset. Instead she'd already taken an unknown woman under her wing as if she was a part of her posse. She had more love inside her than any other woman he'd ever known.

"Okay, Ice." It was as close as he'd ever come to breaking his top-secret government clearance.

He felt Caroline nod against his chest. She obviously knew he was uneasy with his words because she immediately changed the subject.

"All right then. Come on. You're leaving in the morning. It's time for you to make love to your wife."

Wolf grinned. "Yes, ma'am."

* * *

ON THE OTHER side of the country, Melody woke and saw that Tex hadn't joined her in their bed yet. She yawned and swung her feet over the side of the mattress, disturbing Baby in the process. But the dog didn't move other than to lift her head, sigh, and plop it down to go back to sleep.

Grinning at her lazy dog, but thankful she was still around to *be* lazy, Melody grabbed her ratty robe that was more comfortable than anything she'd ever worn, and sauntered out into the hall to find her husband.

Looking into the living room but not seeing him, and ignoring the mess that inevitably came from having an almost-teenager in the house, Melody went down into the basement to Tex's safe-room office. He'd set it up because of the extra security his computers warranted, and also, in his words, just in case they needed it for protection.

She pushed open the door Tex had left ajar, knowing she'd probably miss him in their bed and come looking for him. Melody saw her husband sitting at his desk fiddling with the mouse. She came up behind him and buried her face in his neck, giving him a chance to blacken the screen if there was something on there he didn't want her to see.

She'd learned over the last year and a half to let him have the privacy he needed. She didn't want to know half the stuff he did. She was better off *not* knowing.

"Everything okay?"

"Hummmm."

Okaaaay, that meant no. "The team?"

"They leave in the morning for a mission."

Melody waited.

"It's not going to be good."

Melody wasn't sure what to say. Tex helped lots of Special Forces teams across the country. She figured he meant the SEAL team from California since he didn't specify which team...since she was closest to them. Wolf and his team, and their wives and children, meant the world to them both, and hearing that the guys would be headed out on a mission that was "not going to be good" was very bad indeed.

"What can I do?"

Tex turned in his chair, grabbed Melody and pulled her so she had no choice but to straddle him. Her legs bent at the knees and fit into the spaces by his hips on the chair. He pulled her into him until they were groin to groin and chest to chest. He slowly undid the knot of the belt on the robe and pulled it open. He knew she'd be naked underneath. She liked to sleep that way as much as he enjoyed finding her that way when he joined her in bed.

He slipped his hands around her waist and buried his face in her cleavage. Tex felt Melody's hand clasp the back of his head as she held him to her.

"I love you. I love that you don't ask questions, but the first thing you say is 'what can I do?' I love that you miss me enough when I don't come to bed that you come looking for me. I love that you didn't even flinch when I said I wanted to adopt a handicapped, pre-adolescent girl from Iraq that I'd never even met. Most of all, I just love you. Every last inch of you. And to answer your question, there's nothing we can really do. Just wait and pray. You might call the girls a bit more, and if you feel up for it, you might even take a trip out there."

"Can you come too? I know they'd love to see you."

Tex shook his head. "I'd love to see them, but I need to be here. Watching. Waiting. I want to be here with my computers and servers in case they need me. And I have a bad feeling they *will* need me."

"Oh, Tex. You aren't Superman, no matter what Alabama's daughters call you."

"I know, but the hair on the back of my neck is sticking up and I'm certain they're gonna need my help where they're going."

Melody studied her husband. They'd taken a very long vacation after an ex-classmate, Diane, had been arrested for stalking her. They'd driven out with Baby to Las Vegas and gotten married, just as they'd planned. Diane had managed to kill herself in prison while awaiting trial, something Melody knew she should've been upset about, but couldn't bring herself to be.

"I expect you to tell me what you need from me until they're home. If you need me to bring your food down here, I will. If you need me to leave you alone, I will. If you need a quick fuck, I'm your girl. Just don't block me out. You have a tendency to get a bit single-minded when you're working, and because these are your friends, I'm worried you won't take care of yourself. You need to stand up and walk around every hour. Don't forget to take off your prosthetic every now and then. In fact, I'll send Akilah down to remind you, and you two can clean and massage your stumps together, and—"

Tex cut Melody off by pulling her face to his and kissing the stuffing out of her. "Thank you for taking care of me. If I get too absorbed, I give you permission to get in my face."

"All I'm asking is, don't be a stranger. You know Baby misses you when you get too deep into your work."

Tex smiled. "God forbid the dog misses me."

Melody smiled back. "Okay, I miss you too."

Tex ran his hand down Melody's chest, not missing how her nipples tightened at his touch. "I've got a while before the mission starts...have any ideas on how we can pass the time?"

Melody smirked and pushed into Tex's hand, encouraging him to continue his caresses. "I might have an idea or two. I'm not sure we've tested this particular chair before, have we? Think it can hold up if I take you right here?"

"Now's a great time to try it and see."

* * *

COMMANDER HURT STUDIED the orders from the President. He wasn't happy about the mission. He hated having to send his SEALs into an unknown situation. Oh, it happened a lot, but this time the situation wasn't just unknown, it was unstable, full of hate, and they were being set up to fail. Trying to find an American woman, dressed in a burka, in the middle of a refugee camp, filled with other women wearing similar outfits, would be next to impossible. Not to mention the disease and unsanitary conditions that were running rampant in the crowded, filthy, treacherous camp.

Four hundred thousand people in a camp in the middle of the hot desert—scared, worried and unstable—was a recipe for disaster. The only redeeming factor for the mission was that it was under JSOC command. Joint Special Operations Command was in charge and the mission would involve another SEAL team based out of Norfolk, an Army Ranger team, the Army Night Stalkers would pilot the helos, and, if needed, a Delta Force unit was on standby.

The President's constituents weren't happy that Penelope had been kidnapped and was being used as a pawn in ISIS's deadly game. The world had seen way too many videos of the torture the terrorists put their captives through, and it would be a huge public relations nightmare if Sergeant Penelope Turner ended up in one of those gruesome videos. She was now the country's sister, daughter, friend, and the face of this horrible new war.

Her family, most especially her brother, had been pushing hard and gaining the support of many influential politicians to go in and find his sister. Homeland Security had received enough credible reports that the woman was being held in the refugee camp for the President to authorize a rescue attempt.

"Are you all right, Patrick?"

He turned and held out his arm and sighed when his wife, Julie, snuggled into his side. He felt one arm snake around his belly and the other around his back.

"Yeah, I'm okay."

"I don't think you are. Is it my SEALs?"

Patrick smiled at Julie's terminology. She knew he commanded several different SEAL teams, but she always referred to Cookie and the rest of the men as "hers" since they'd rescued her from Mexico.

Over the years, she'd remained friendly with all their women. She helped Jessyka match up some of the teenagers in the after-school program with prom dresses. Summer had gotten Julie's store included in her company's annual donation campaign, and Julie and Cheyenne emailed each other all the time.

Patrick knew her relationship with Fiona took a lot of hard work to cultivate. She didn't push, but went out of her way to make sure Fiona knew she was thinking about her and to try to be friendly. Just as Patrick had predicted, Julie and his men's wives weren't best friends, but they did seem to enjoy each other's company when they met up at company get-togethers.

"You know I can't say much, but yes, your SEALs are leaving for a mission in the morning."

"Should I call Fiona and see how she's doing? Maybe we should invite her over, make sure she's okay. I can take some time off from the store. My employees know what they're doing, and now that I've hired some of the teenagers to take my place at the front, I'm really just in the way when I'm there anyway. Maybe I can—"

Patrick leaned down and kissed Julie quiet. When he felt her melt into him, he pulled away. "I'm sure she'd love to hear from you, sweetheart." When Julie nodded and moved her hand lower until it brushed against his quickly hardening shaft, Patrick smiled down at her.

"Come to bed. I can tell you're tense, let me help you lose some of that tension."

"I love you, Julie. I'll be there in a little bit."

"Okay, but don't take too long or I'll have to take matters into my own hands," Julie teased.

Patrick leaned down, kissed his wife once again and set her away from him. "Feel free to get yourself off, but know that when I get there I'll be making you come at least twice before I get my turn…so you might want to pace yourself."

Julie blushed and backed away, smiling. Patrick watched until she disappeared around the door to his home office, and he turned his attention back to the file in front of him, distracted with thoughts of his wife now, but still concerned for his men.

The commander in him hoped like hell it wouldn't be a futile mission that would end in the deaths of one, or more, of the finest men he'd ever known. He certainly didn't want Sergeant. Turner to die at the hands of terrorists, but he especially didn't want to have to tell any of the women and children of his own men, who he'd come to know and respect, that their husband, or father, wouldn't be coming home ever again.

Finally, with a small sigh and a quick prayer, Patrick locked the file back into the small office safe and tried to shake off the uneasy feeling he'd had since first seeing the orders. He had a wife to satisfy. He'd take the time to concentrate on her, and on how much he loved her, before having to delve back into the dangerous world of the SEALs the next day. He needed Julie's brand of relaxation.

CHAPTER 4

$\mathcal{W}$olf gazed around the tent at his men. It'd been a tough forty-eight hours. They'd flown to the Middle East, done a HALO—a high-altitude, low-opening parachute drop—to get into Turkey undetected. They'd thought about jumping into Syria instead, but finally decided they'd be stealthier if they came in from the Turkish side and tried to blend in with the other aid workers.

They'd made the landing without issue and headed to the refugee camp near the city of Cizre, Turkey. It was exactly as described by their commander and as the intelligence had reported. It smelled horrible, and sickness was rampant all around them. They hadn't even been there that long and they'd already witnessed two mothers crying hysterically while clutching their dead babies. None of the team knew what the infants had died from, but ultimately it didn't matter. Dehydration, disease, starvation...seeing the dead babies reminded them all a bit too much of their families back home.

"What's the plan for today?" Abe asked.

Wolf laid out the aerial photographs of the camp they'd received back in California. "The best way to do this is a grid search, but we all know, if Turner is here, they're moving her around. They probably don't spend the night in the same spot twice or at least more than a couple nights. So a grid search won't do us much good. We'll have to cover a lot of ground in this shithole every day so we'll need to break up into teams. We can cover more area in groups of two than if we patrolled together, and we'll blend in better. But remember, that's how we think ISIS got ahold of Turner and the others...they were separated from the rest of the patrol. And we all know ISIS would love to get ahold of a SEAL, so stay on your toes. Everyone has their radios, right?"

The men all nodded, so Wolf continued, "Okay, Benny, you're with me. Dude and Abe, you're together, and Cookie and Mozart. Benny and I will take the left side." Wolf pointed out the area on his map. "Dude, you and Abe take the middle, and Cookie and Mozart, you're on the right. Cover as much ground as you can, be observant, but not obvious. Turner is small, five foot two. She's got light-blonde hair, so if it's not completely covered up, she'll stick out like a sore thumb around here."

"What if they *do* have it covered up?" Benny asked seriously.

"Then we're fucked," Wolf said succinctly. "If she's covered from head to toe in robes, or if they've got her in a burka, there's no way we'll be able to spot her. But be on the guard for groups of young men looking suspicious. Hell, look around. Most people are concerned about food and water; if you see any group of men looking fit and healthy, that's suspicious. Also, the men are armed. Perhaps blatantly so. Abe, got any other ideas?"

"The American and British troops in the area haven't been much help. Intel from Commander Hurt says no one really knows where the soldiers were when they were taken and there's been no sign of Sergeant Turner since she and the others were snatched," Abe said. He took a deep breath, then continued, "I think we should take the first day or so to get the lay of the land, walk around and see what we can find out. But if we don't immediately spot her, we should use the interpreters. Fall into the role of aid worker more deeply. See if we can't find out from the refugees who they're afraid of. The Syrians aren't stupid. If they aren't in ISIS, they probably know who they should keep away from. Since none of us know Turkish, we'll have to rely on the interpreters."

Wolf nodded. "Good. Whatever you do, don't start a war in the middle of the camp. Our objective is to identify the target, and steal her away. We don't want to start a firefight, otherwise a lot of innocent people could die, and the last thing either government wants is an incident. It's a snatch-and-grab if we can swing it."

"What if she's injured or if she's been abused?" Dude asked calmly. Although they could all see he was anything but calm.

"We take her however we can. If she freaks out, knock her out. If she can't walk, carry her. If she's scared of us, do what you can to reassure her. Whatever you do, get the fuck out as soon as you can. Got it?"

All five men nodded at Wolf. They'd all thought the mission was going to be hell, but now that they were here in person, and could see the living conditions of everyone around them, they were sure of it.

"We'll set out first thing in the morning. I know none of us have gotten much sleep in the last two days. Sleep tonight and hopefully we'll be out of this dump sooner rather than later."

The men settled down on their sleeping mats, each lost in their own thoughts about their wife, kids, and what they might find, *if* they find, America's Darling, Sergeant Penelope Turner.

* * *

THE NEXT MORNING the men were up and ready before the sun came up. They headed out in pairs, ready for anything. Meeting back at the tent they'd been assigned by the aid workers that night, each pair of men reported what they'd observed.

"The west side of the camp looks to be the older side. The shelters are more established and the people there seem more settled," Cookie told the group. I think it looks promising for the general area where Turner could be held. There wasn't a lot of love for us as we walked around and when Mozart asked some of the other aid workers about that area, they said they rarely ventured too far into that side because they didn't feel safe."

Wolf nodded. "Makes sense. We were on the other side and there were a lot of women and children over there."

"That could be a good place to hide her," Dude commented, trying to play Devil's Advocate.

"Yeah, but most of the men we saw were either very old or very young. It doesn't seem to be a hotbed of ISIS activity. At least not at first glance," Wolf cautioned.

"So it sounds like we can stick to the west and middle tomorrow then," Abe said. "The center of camp seems to be a mix of families, single people, and kids."

"Did anyone see anything that screamed 'terrorist camp' or did you get a glimpse of anyone that could be our target?" Wolf asked the group.

The men all shook their heads. "Not really. The robes and veils make this op almost impossible," Cookie grumbled.

"We have to find her. I can't bear to think of her in this shithole at the hands of those assholes," Dude said, running a hand through his hair.

"We'll do our best." Wolf's words were heartfelt, but they all knew they weren't enough. They had to find this woman. "We'll head out first thing in the morning. After tomorrow, we'll take shifts and walk through the nights as well."

"I'll take the first night shift," Dude volunteered. Wolf looked at his friend critically, knowing Dude wasn't sleeping well because he was worried about Cheyenne and the pregnancy. He nodded. "That's fine. I'll work it with you to start."

* * *

SERGEANT PENELOPE TURNER was pissed off. She figured she probably should be scared or freaked-out, but honestly? She was just plain angry. As far as being kidnapped and held by terrorists went, she'd been lucky. They'd beaten the shit out of her the first couple of days they'd had her, but after the first video had gone viral, they'd realized she was more valuable as a propaganda tool than anything else.

They'd asked if she was a virgin, and Penelope had thought long and hard about which would be the best way to answer, and finally she'd admitted that she was not. She hadn't been raped...yet, but figured the men were saving that as a torture technique for later if they needed it.

She'd been forced to read long soliloquies about ISIS's complaints with the West and America, and honestly Penelope had no heartburn over reading whatever they wanted her to. She'd read *War and Peace* if they asked her to. It wasn't as if she really believed what she was reading, and figured America in general would probably understand she was being forced to say the things she was.

But she *did* care about her fellow soldiers. She hadn't seen her friends since they'd been kidnapped. Penelope had no idea how long she'd been in the company of the terrorist group, but thought it'd been around two months.

Thomas Black and Henry White were hilarious. Thomas was from Maine and had red hair and freckles. He frequently joked that he was a down-home "ginger from the north." Henry was from Mississippi and had the darkest skin Penelope had ever seen on anyone before. They'd been teased by the other soldiers, since Thomas's last name was Black and Henry's last name was White, and they were complete opposites of their names. But the men were close friends. They'd bonded the first time they met and had done everything together since they'd arrived in the Middle East. They made an oddly striking pair, but friendship knew no color in the Army. The third man, Robert Wilson, Penelope didn't know very well, but he'd been friendly enough to her and she worried about him just as much as Thomas and Henry.

She figured they were all probably dead, and that pissed her off even more. These ISIS assholes didn't have the right to kill anyone, not when *they* were the ones terrorizing the poor people all around them and kidnapping innocent soldiers like her and her friends who were just trying to help the refugees.

Penelope had volunteered to come over to Turkey to help people and provide some much needed help at the camps. Her Reserve unit, stationed out of Fort Hood, Texas, had sent a company of soldiers, around one hundred and twenty people, to help provide security at the camp. From the second they'd landed, it'd been obvious the major in charge of the troops at the refugee camp wasn't a very good leader. Even though the captains and lieutenants tried to explain how dangerous the security patrols could be, they were still ordered to scout in small groups which could be easily overwhelmed.

She, White, Black, and Wilson had been ordered to patrol the west side of the camp one day, and when she'd protested, claiming it was too dangerous to send them in alone, she'd been reprimanded publically and told to suck it up.

She knew it was because she was a woman and actually had the guts to speak up. If she'd been a man, maybe they would've taken her more seriously. But they'd been sent off with the proverbial pat on the head and look what had happened. Penelope was fucking right and she'd been stuck in this hellhole for who knew how long.

Penelope had wanted to escape long before now, but the assholes who'd kidnapped her weren't actually as idiotic as she'd hoped, or as they'd seemed at first. They moved her almost every night to a different tent. They only allowed her outside whatever tent they were keeping her in if she was covered from head to toe in the flowing robes and garments the women in the region wore.

Penelope knew her blonde hair would give her away if she dared take off the covering. She'd thought about it more than once, simply whipping the material off her head and running screaming through the camp, but she'd seen how the men around her were. She'd either be shot dead immediately, or she'd suffer horribly and wish she was dead long before they were done with her. So far, she hadn't been raped, tortured, burned alive, or had her head cut off, and she took all of that as a win.

So she was in limbo. Waiting for something to happen.

One good thing—Penelope always tried to find good in every situation —was that the everyday thugs in the camp were scared of ISIS. She didn't have to worry about them on top of everything else she worried about.

So she waited. Day in and day out, pretending to be meek and scared, while silently seething inside and on the lookout for something, anything, that would get her out of there. If she made it home, and could hug her brother, she'd never step foot outside Texas again.

The sounds of the camp faded around her. They never really quieted all the way, but they did settle down as night fell. Penelope figured most people were scared to walk around when the sun dipped below the horizon, as well they should be.

The door to the tent opened and Penelope quickly looked down, trying not to make eye contact with whoever it was who'd entered her tent. She'd learned the hard way that looking one of the terrorists in the eye only set them off.

"Up," he grunted.

Some of her guards spoke excellent English, while others knew only the basic words. She thought about trying to send some message on the videos she was forced to record, but knew there were too many people around her and involved with ISIS who knew English. The video would never make it out and they'd probably kill her for daring to defy them. It made more sense to bide her time and pray she'd get the chance to escape or that someone would come to free her.

She stood up at the guard's request. He shoved the robe at her that she'd been forced to wear every time they moved. "Put it on."

Penelope sighed. Looked like it was moving time. She hated the robe with a passion. It was hot, and stunk like pee, sweat, and who knew what the hell else. But shit, *she* stunk; she couldn't really ask for a shower in the middle of the desert.

Moving tents meant uncertainty. She'd been at the same tent now for three nights, an eternity in her world. Penelope held her breath and slipped the foul garment over her head, doing what her captor demanded, and hoped like hell this would end...preferably sooner rather than later, and preferably with her going home, rather than with her head rolling around on the sand after being chopped off.

CHAPTER 5

*I*t's been two months since American Penelope Turner was kidnapped by ISIS operatives. She was participating in a humanitarian mission at the Cizre, Turkey, refugee camp. Thousands of Syrians have been streaming over the border, on the run from the multiple terrorist groups and the ethnic cleansing in Syria.

Sergeant Turner was snatched while on a routine patrol of the camp, along with three other men. You might remember Thomas Black and Henry White were beheaded and nailed to a cross, and Robert Wilson was set on fire while still alive.

There have been conflicting reports of where Turner might be held captive, but sources say the U.S. Government has been looking into rescue attempts. All efforts to get more information on this possibility have been ignored or deflected by the White House Director of Communication.

Penelope's brother has been leading the charge to get troops to head into Syria to look for his sister. There is an online petition with over one hundred thousand signatures gathered so far, addressed to the President, to try to urge him to do something to rescue his sister.

The video of Cade Turner being interviewed by our affiliate station in San Antonio, Texas, has gone viral. His impassioned statement of, "Fine, don't negotiate with the terrorists, just go in and get her the BLEEP out," has resonated with Americans throughout the country. There have been T-shirts, bumper stickers, and even posters made with Cade's statement. America wants Penelope Turner home.

There has been no video of Sergeant Turner since the last one released two weeks ago.

* * *

CAROLINE CUDDLED John in her lap as Brinique and Davisa tried to entertain Sara. Watching the five and six-year-old interact with two-year-old Sara was endearing and entertaining as hell.

"How you holding up, Jess?" Alabama asked her friend.

"I'm okay, thanks. Caroline, I appreciate you letting me stay with you for a few days."

"No problem. You know I love having you guys here."

"Do you think they're all right?"

They all knew who Jess was asking about.

"Yes. I'm sure they're fine," Caroline tried to soothe.

"It's just...Kason was more worried than usual about this mission."

"Christopher was too. Should we be concerned?" Alabama's voice was muted so her daughters couldn't hear her.

Caroline wanted to tell her friends what she suspected, but kept it to herself, as she knew Matthew would want her to. "No. Our men are professionals. They know what they're doing. They'd be irritated if we sat at home and cried all the time about them. They've been gone before and we were fine. This is the same thing."

The other two women nodded, but didn't look appeased.

"We should get out of the house and have some fun today," Caroline told them decidedly.

"I need to go and check on the bar. Fiona's working today. We could go and visit her."

"Perfect!" Caroline exclaimed. "I'm so happy for you. You totally deserved to be named manager after Mr. Davis retired."

"He said if it worked out, he'd consider selling it to me as well," Jessyka told her friends.

"Oh my God. That's awesome!" Alabama got up and hugged Jess. "When were you going to tell us? Does anyone else know?"

"Well, Fiona knows. She would have to, since she's the assistant manager."

"Good for you. Let's see if we can't get these kids packed up in under an hour. Lord, I had no idea it took so long to get out of the house with kids in tow," Alabama mock grumbled.

"It takes even longer when they're *this* age," Jess said, motioning to her two. "I've gotten to the point where whatever Sara wants to wear, I let her. It's easier than arguing with her about it. And believe me, you never win when arguing with a two-year-old!"

They all laughed and stood to get ready to go.

An hour later the group made their way inside *Aces*. It was early enough that most of the patrons were eating a late lunch and the alcohol hadn't started to flow yet. Caroline knew Alabama wouldn't bring her daughters into the bar if there was the slightest chance anything inappropriate would be going on.

"Feeeeeeeee!" Sara screeched, toddling her way into the room and looking for her favorite babysitter.

Fiona stuck her head out the office door down the long hall and laughed as Sara waddled her way to her with her arms outstretched. She snatched the little girl up before she could fall and swung her around in a circle before sitting her on her hip. "Hey, pretty girl. What brings you and your mommy and brother here today?"

"Twip!"

"A trip, huh?" Fiona laughed and looked at Jess, who was limping down the hall toward her.

"Caroline decided we all needed some air, so here we are."

"Well, I'm glad to see you. I need a break too. My eyes are crossing from looking at numbers."

"I told them about the bar," Jess told her friend.

"Good. It's about time. They were happy for you, weren't they?"

Jess smiled. "Yeah. Come on, take a break with us. I'm sure Alabama has Brinique and Davisa settled in with some ice cream and I'm afraid if I leave John with Caroline for too long, she'll steal him from me."

The two women laughed at Jess's long-standing joke as they went back into the main room and joined their friends.

After sitting for a while and laughing at the antics of the kids, and commenting on how good of a baby John was, Jess excused herself and headed for the bathroom.

Caroline handed John off to Fiona and headed after Jess, wanting to make sure she was all right. She found her kneeling in front of one the toilets, having thrown up the delicious snack they'd just eaten.

"Are you all right?"

"Shit, Caroline. I'm so screwed."

"What? Are you sick? Do you need to go to the doctor?"

Jess snorted and leaned back on her heels and wiped her mouth. "No, I'm not sick in the sense you're talking about."

Caroline seemed to suddenly understand. "Oh lord. You're pregnant again?"

"Yeah, I think so. I haven't taken a test or anything, and I only started feeling nauseous yesterday and today. But I recognize the signs. I feel like I'm the only person on the planet who gets afternoon sickness instead of morning sickness."

Caroline giggled, she couldn't help it, and laughed outright when Jess glared up at her from her crouching position on the floor. "Come on, let me help you up." Caroline reached out a hand, relieved when Jess accepted it. Between the two of them, they got Jess off the floor. "I've never met anyone as fertile as you and Kason."

"I know, it's ridiculous. We said we were gonna wait and put a bit more time between John and a new brother or sister."

"What happened?"

Jess gave Caroline an evil look and held it even as Caroline laughed at her. "Oh, yeah. Our men are horny devils, aren't they?"

"He promised to use condoms because he knows birth control pills make me feel bloated and they wreak havoc with my moods," Jess grumbled. "But then you had to be all noble and offer to babysit John and Sara for an entire weekend. We were really careful the first night, but as the weekend went on, we got more and more lazy...and here I am."

Caroline gave Jessyka a big hug. "Well, congrats, woman."

"I still need to take a test to find out for certain, but I'm pretty sure. I recognize this feeling." Jess put a hand on her still-rounded stomach from the baby weight she hadn't been able to lose after having John. "As much as it freaks me out, I have to say I'm pretty happy. I'd give Kason a million babies if I could."

"A million is a bit much, you dork. If you want to set up a doctor's appointment, you know I'll either babysit for you or hold your hand when you go."

"I wish Kason was here."

"I know you do. But you'll get through this just fine. It's what we Navy SEAL wives do. We keep on keepin' on while our men are off saving the world. Just think about how you want to let Kason know when he gets home that he's going to be a father...again."

Jess stood up, washed her hands and swished some water around her mouth. "You're right. We're strong, capable women who don't need a man to be by our side all the time."

"Damn straight. You don't think I'll be able to keep this from the others, do you?"

Jess smiled at Caroline. "You mean you haven't already mind-melded with them to let them know? I'm disappointed in you."

"Hey, I can keep a secret."

"Uh-huh."

"Seriously."

Jess smiled at her friend. "Caroline, I don't care if you tell them. Tell the world. I'm so happy with my life right now, it almost seems unfair to everyone else."

Caroline smiled at Jess. "I'll try to control myself and let you tell the others, but you better start with Alabama and Fiona, who are waiting out at the table for us."

They joined arms and headed out to the bar to tell their friends there'd be another little Sawyer arriving in about seven months.

CHAPTER 6

he SEALs exasperated sighs demonstrated their annoyance with the situation. They'd been at the godforsaken refugee camp for seven days now and hadn't had one glimpse of Penelope Turner or anyone who could possibly be her. Of course, trying to find anyone in the huge tent city was like trying to find a needle in a haystack. They'd uncovered a lot of crooked and criminal shit, but had to ignore it all and focus on their mission.

Wolf knew the long frustrating search was taking its toll on the team. Dude wanted to hurry up and find Penelope not only so they could get her out of the situation, but also so he could get back to Cheyenne. They hadn't had any updates from home, and they were all hoping she hadn't gone into premature labor and had his daughter yet.

Abe was wondering how Brinique and Davisa were doing, and worried about Alabama taking on too much. Benny was in much the same frame of mind and was worrying about Jessyka overdoing things with their two young kids and trying to keep *Aces* up and running.

They all were completely focused on the mission, but couldn't help but worry about their women and children back home.

And in the forefront of all their minds was Penelope Turner. The refugee camp was hell on earth. It was male-dominated, dirty, miserably hot, and the threat of violence hung over the camp like a bomb that was slowly ticking down, every second bringing it closer to detonation. It was obvious all hell could break loose at any moment. It was as if everyone was holding their breath, but they knew they couldn't hold it forever. The thought of Penelope or any vulnerable woman being in the middle of his hellhole, turned all their stomachs.

There were what Wolf called "roving gangs" prowling the camp, especially at night. They were looking for the vulnerable and the weak. The gangs would steal what little food they could find, and if they were in the mood, would rape any female they came across. No one was safe, from the littlest girls to the oldest grandmothers.

The team had no idea if Penelope was safe or if she was suffering the same fate as many of the other females in the camp. There had been no word of another video surfacing, so it was all speculation as to whether she was still alive or even at the camp at all.

Two days ago, another SEAL team had arrived to join in the search for the missing sergeant, and Wolf was damn glad. They could use all the help they could get. The other team was based out of Virginia and had been recommended by Tex to join the mission. Wolf's team had worked with them once before and knew they were extremely competent. Wolf didn't know all the members on the team personally, but was impressed with what he'd seen in the past and thus far out in the desert.

The teams had split up further and combed the refugee camp looking for Penelope. The place was huge, and their job was made tougher because of the burka most of the women wore. Wolf knew many of the women now wore the head-to-toe coverings to try to protect themselves from the men stalking the camp for victims rather than for any religious ideology.

They were on the lookout for a group of men with a lone woman, who would most likely be covered from head to toe in a robe, and she'd be short, at least compared to them. That was about all they had. It would be unusual for a single woman to be with a group of men, as in the Muslim culture, the men tended to hang out with other men and the women banded together as well. The women would do chores around their chosen tent, while the men would gather, talk, and try to find food for their families or groups.

One of the SEALs on the other team, Rocco, spoke Turkish, thank God. Today's plan was to see what information they could glean from some of the men they'd befriended in their guise as aid workers. Wolf knew most of the groups of Syrians they'd made contact with had a pretty good idea they weren't who they said they were, but so far, their luck had held and they hadn't had any trouble. But they all knew that luck would probably run out sooner rather than later.

If ISIS had any idea there were two groups of elite Navy SEALs in the camp looking for them and Penelope, they'd most likely either kill her and run, or take her with them when they left and probably kill her later, in a very horrific and public way in retaliation. For the moment, the terrorists were feeling safe in the anonymity of the huge refugee camp.

Both SEAL teams knew their time was running out to find Penelope and bring her home alive.

Ace and Gumby, two of the men from the Virginia team, and Cookie and Dude were currently out searching the camp. They'd taken the night shift. The groups had night-vision goggles, but they'd be very obvious if they wore them around the camp, so they'd decided not to use them. But the time was quickly coming where they were going to be needed. They hadn't made any headway thus far and all of the men were becoming frustrated with their lack of success.

The groups radioed back to the others their locations and if they found anything suspicious. One of the men at the tent they'd started calling the Command Tent, or CT, would take notes and mark on a large aerial photo what regions of the camp had been searched and what areas the guys deemed to have suspicious activity and should be rechecked, either another night, or the next day when there was light.

The radio crackled. Abe and a Vietnamese man called Ho Chi Minh, from the other SEAL team, were manning the radios while the other men got some much-needed sleep.

"Rover one to CT." Gumby's voice was quiet and toneless. It was the tone they all used when talking on the radios so as not to bring attention to themselves. The thugs in the camp would kill to get their hands on a high-tech set of radios such as the teams had.

"This is CT. Go ahead."

"Found a ripped piece of pink cloth at coordinates, LG3777633131."

"The same kind as before?" Ho Chi Mien asked.

"Roger."

Abe got up and shook Wolf awake. This was the second piece of pink cloth the teams had found, and there was no way it was a coincidence. First of all, there wasn't a lot of material around that was pink, and second, it was highly unlikely there would be random scraps of pink material floating around the refugee camp. It had to be a fucking clue.

They were running on empty and any kind of anomaly, no matter how small, was cause for celebration and worth a second look.

"Wolf," Abe said softly, not touching the man, letting his voice wake him up. "Gumby found a clue."

"I'm up. What is it?" Wolf asked, rolling to his feet, immediately awake. The ability to be asleep one second and completely awake the next was a life-saving skill they'd all gained over the years on the team. And while it might fade when they were home for a while, they could all pick it up without missing a beat while on a mission.

"Pink cloth." Abe didn't have to say anything else.

"Coordinates?"

The men walked over to the table where Ho Chi Mien was marking Gumby's find on the map.

"Looks like it's in the same general area as the other one."

Abe looked at Wolf. "She's fucking leaving us breadcrumbs."

"Don't get your hopes up, it might not be her," Wolf warned, although it was obvious he was more than pleased with the development.

"Yeah, maybe not. But it's more than we had an hour ago."

Wolf nodded and studied the map.

"Your men are meeting up with Gumby and Ace. They'll see what else they can find at the location," Ho Chi Mien stated softly.

Wolf nodded. "Good. Anything is better than what we've got so far at this point. We'll send in the teams tomorrow to search in the daylight. I know Rocco was up late tonight talking with some men, but we need him to go out there and see what the people around the area know."

"No problem," Ho Chi Mien stated immediately. "This has become personal."

"For us too," Abe agreed.

"All we can think of is our women back home," the Asian man continued. "What if this was our girlfriend, or daughter, or sister? I can't blame her brother for putting up as big of a raucous as he has."

"What did we miss?" Wolf asked, obviously not knowing what Ho Chi Mien was talking about in regards to the missing soldier's brother.

"Last I heard, there was an online petition to the President with over two hundred thousand signatures, to go in and do something to rescue her."

Wolf chuckled flatly. "Well, here we are. Doing something."

"Yeah. The guy's been on every news channel giving interviews and telling the world about his sister. They seem to be really close; it's irritating that we can't find her for him."

Abe shook his head at the other SEAL's words. Irritating. Yeah, that about summed it up. "Okay, so let's say this *is* our target. We're still no closer to finding her than we were before."

"Yeah, but now we know what we're looking for, at least somewhat. We know she's leaving clues, and we can try to see if there's a pattern. I'd bet everything I own, these guys are moving her around in fucking circles, using the same hidey-holes. If we can find enough clues to sense their pattern, we can find the missing sergeant," Wolf told his friend and teammate.

Abe nodded. "It's a long shot, but it's all we've got right now."

* * *

PENELOPE SIGHED IN FRUSTRATION. She was hot, tired, and bored. It felt somewhat messed up to say she was bored, but she was. She did nothing all day. She'd started trying to keep her strength up by doing pushups and sit-ups during the day, but she knew she was weakening, and it both irritated and scared her. Without her strength, the ability to escape at a moment's notice was lessened immensely.

Her captors would usually bring her something to eat in the morning, a stale crust of bread, or some sort of mystery-meat stew, and while she wanted to refuse it, she knew she couldn't. The water was disgusting, but again, she needed the liquid. She was on the verge of dehydration as it was, refusing to drink what they brought would be tantamount to suicide.

Her captors were ramping up to something, but Penelope didn't know what. She had no idea if anyone was looking for her, but knowing her brother as she did, she hoped someone was. Just as she'd do for him, Cade wouldn't stop until she was found, dead or alive.

They were extremely close. They weren't too far apart in age and Penelope could remember tagging along after Cade when they were kids...and he'd let her. They even played games together when they were young, just the two of them. One of the games she remembered most vividly was a game they called, "War." There was a field near their house and they'd go hide in the bushes, lying on their bellies and pretending there were bad guys out in the field looking for them. Cade hadn't seemed to care she was a girl, or his younger sister.

As they got older, the games stopped, but Cade's support and love for her never ceased. He was the reason she'd made it as far in the fire service as she had. He was the reason her fellow firefighters supported and trusted her to have their backs. It was Cade's unending and unflagging encouragement she'd received in the past that made her continue to hold on in the hellacious situation she currently found herself in, and the reason she knew he was doing what he could to find her.

So she'd started trying to leave parts of herself behind any chance she could get. Penelope had taken off her panties, they were beyond disgusting at this point anyway, and ripped the seams out. Once upon a time they were her favorite pair. Stupid to bring such a girly pair of underwear on an Army mission in the first place, but she'd always tried to keep her feminine side alive and well, even if it was under her uniform. She might work in a male-dominated profession—well, two of them—but she'd be damned if she lost her femininity altogether. She'd hidden the material under the robes her captors were constantly making her wear, and since, so far, they hadn't had any interest in raping her, the material had gone unnoticed.

Penelope had been leaving little pieces behind, like breadcrumbs. She'd always loved the fairytale Hansel and Gretel growing up. She only hoped they weren't being swept away as she left them, as had happened in the story.

She had no idea who might be looking for her, if anyone, but she hoped with all her heart they were smart and observant. All the places she'd been taken looked the same to her, but it was after she'd been leaving the pieces of cloth for a while, and had been moved again, that she noticed one of her breadcrumbs that she'd left in the past.

The bastards were using the same tents to hold her in. Moving her all the time, yes, but to the same tents over and over again. It gave her hope someone would notice and find her. She only had to wait. But Penelope had no idea how much time she had and hoped it wouldn't run out before someone cottoned on to the trail she was leaving.

"Up. Come."

The words were loud and heavily accented. Penelope jumped a foot. Dammit, she'd been so far inside her head, she hadn't heard the man enter her tent. That shit would get her killed. She stood up and took the robe the man shoved at her. She put it on quickly and winced as the man grabbed her arm and he led her outside.

He force-marched her toward a group of men who were talking excitedly and seemed almost giddy with anticipation. Oh shit, was this it? Was it her time to die? Were they taking her to chop off her head? Death didn't scare her, but knowing they'd record it and show it to the world—and her brother—scared the shit out of her. She didn't want Cade's last glimpse of her to be her head rolling off her neck and onto the ground.

No one said anything as they surrounded her, and the entire group meandered through the refugee camp. Penelope tried to keep track of where they were and where they were headed, but it was impossible. The group finally stopped in front of a large truck and Penelope was shoved into the back and the men all clambered in behind her.

The truck was a deuce and a half...a large truck that looked like it had an eighteen-wheeler type of cab, and a huge sorta pickup type of bed. The back was covered with a large tarp, not unlike what the tents were made out of, and there were two benches. It looked like a military vehicle that had been jerry-rigged to hold a large amount of people. Men were sitting along the benches, and there was a blindfolded man wearing some sort of uniform, arms bound behind his back, kneeling in the back of the truck against the cab.

There were six men already in the truck when their little group climbed aboard, each of the six were holding AK-47 assault rifles. No one spoke to her, but they did talk with each other. Penelope had no idea what was being said, but she had a very bad feeling about what was about to happen.

She looked at the blindfolded man and hoped like hell they'd both make it out alive.

CHAPTER 7

*A*nother video of kidnapped American Penelope Turner has surfaced. ISIS posted it on their webpage sometime last night. In the video, an Australian soldier is shown being led to an unknown location and being forced to lean over a large boulder. He was blindfolded and had his arms tied behind his back.

The Australian government says the man is Thomas Bauer, a lieutenant in the Australian Army. He was apparently taken two days ago from the same refugee camp where Turner and the other murdered Americans had been working. As a result of the multiple kidnappings and murders, most countries have ceased humanitarian efforts in the region and are quietly pulling out their troops.

In the video, Bauer isn't given a chance to say anything, but is beheaded after a man in a mask reads a manifesto of some sort in Arabic. Immediately after the murder, a woman, believed to be Penelope Turner, reads a long letter, presumably written by the terrorists, denouncing Australia's partnership with the West, specifically the United States, and warning there will be more kidnappings and beheadings to come, all in the name of Allah.

Several Islamic religious groups in the Washington DC area have converged in a peaceful march to show the world, and the U.S., that their religion does not preach hate and to show they are not in support of what ISIS is doing in the name of their God.

Cade Turner, the brother of the kidnapped Sergeant Turner, will be on an hour-long special broadcast tonight to discuss the latest development and what it might mean for his sister.

* * *

CAROLINE SAT TRANSFIXED, staring at the television. She'd been trying to follow the case of the missing American soldier, but every time she saw or heard anything, it made her stomach hurt. She knew, deep in her gut, the guys were over there trying to find her. She felt horrible for the woman's brother. He was on all the talk and news shows. She hoped like hell Matthew and the team could bring her home, but Caroline was selfish. She wanted her man home, where he was safe.

She couldn't talk about what she thought was going on or where she figured the men were with the other women, so as not to worry them, and it was eating her up inside.

The phone rang, scaring the bejeezus out of Caroline. She laughed a bit and muted the television and answered.

"Hello?"

"Hey, Caroline. It's Melody. How are you?"

"Melody! It's great to hear from you! I'm good. How are you and Tex and Akilah?"

"We're good. Tex actually found a therapist who speaks Arabic. I really think it's helped her."

"That's awesome. I totally need to take a trip out there to see you all. Hell, without any drama the last two years, I've missed talking to Tex."

"I'll tell him to call you more often." Melody paused, then asked, "How is everyone holding up? How are *you* holding up?"

"It's tough. I miss Matthew more than ever, and with Cheyenne being about to pop any day now, I know she's more stressed than she's ever been. Of course everyone is trying to hide it, and doing a crap job of it."

Melody laughed lightly. "If it makes you feel any better, Tex has been holed up in the basement with his computers for the last two weeks since they left."

Caroline sighed. "Actually, yeah, that does make me feel a lot better. I know Tex is there and they are...wherever they are...but knowing he's watching over the guys makes me feel better."

"And you."

"What?"

"He's watching over you and the others too."

"And I appreciate that. After everything that's happened to us in the past, it's good."

"What I'm saying is that Tex will know if Cheyenne goes to the hospital, so he can get word to the guys. When that baby starts coming, don't worry about taking the time to call Commander Hurt. Tex will take care of it."

"Thanks. Please tell Tex thanks too."

"You know I will."

"Melody, have you been watching the news?" Caroline knew she was treading on dangerous ground, but since Melody wasn't technically a SEAL wife—Tex was retired, after all—she didn't feel as if she was breaking the unspoken rules as badly as if she'd brought up her concerns with any of her friends there in California. Caroline wasn't a SEAL, so she wasn't under any obligation to keep any of her guesses as to where the men were or what they were doing to herself, but in order to spare her friends, they had enough on their minds, she decided to speak to Melody about it.

"Yeah. Anything specifically?"

"Penelope Turner."

"Ah."

Caroline waited for Melody to say something else.

"That's a sucky situation."

"Do you think they'll find her?"

"Yeah. If anyone can, they can."

And there it was. Additional confirmation that what Caroline had thought was true. She knew Tex most likely wasn't sharing details with Melody, he was as secretive as anyone she'd ever met, but Melody was smart. She could read between the lines just as well as Caroline could. The guys *were* in Turkey. They *were* looking for the missing soldier. And they *were* most likely in a lot of danger. Just the thought of ISIS getting hold of a SEAL made Caroline shudder in horror.

"I'm scared, Melody," she whispered, as if the very words spoken aloud would make something horrible happen.

"Me too. You keep it hidden well though. You're the glue that holds the girls together. They all rely on you, Caroline. You're their rock."

"I know," Caroline whispered. "I don't know if I'm worthy of it though."

"You are. You know how I know?"

"How?"

"Because you're scared out of your mind, but you aren't letting on. You're going to work, you're babysitting, you're going out with them to keep their mind off of their men. You're probably Cheyenne's new breathing coach since Dude isn't there…right?" Melody didn't wait for Caroline to respond. "That's *your* posse, and nothing is going to touch them as long as you're around." It wasn't a question.

"I *am* scared."

"Of course you are. I'd be worried about you if you weren't."

"Matthew is *my* rock. I depend on him. I lean on him. I'm good when he's not here because I know he'll be back and I can let some of my worries and responsibilities slide. He'll pick up the slack. But this time—"

"No, don't even say it."

"But—"

"No. I mean it, Caroline. You can't think that way. Ever. But here's what I know. *You're* the rock. You just think Matthew is because he's your match, but in reality, you are *his* rock. Remember back to when you were kidnapped. Jesus, Caroline, you were beaten, shot and left to die in the freaking ocean. But you didn't. You held on. For Matthew. Don't you think he'd move heaven and earth to come back to you?"

Caroline sobbed once, then ruthlessly controlled it. Melody was right. "You're right."

"Of course I am."

A short laugh escaped Caroline. "When are you coming to visit again?"

"Actually, that's why I called in the first place. Tex basically ordered me out of the house. I'd like to come visit and bring Akilah, if at all possible."

"Hell yeah. I'd love to see you guys. The basement apartment is always open for you."

"Thanks. I didn't think you'd say no. Tex already got us tickets."

They both laughed. "It'll be good to see you, Mel," Caroline said honestly. "I could use a distraction."

"That's me…one distraction, coming right up."

"Thanks. Send me the details and I'll be sure to be waiting at the airport for you. I'll also tell the girls. Maybe it'll give Cheyenne some incentive to hold that baby inside for a while longer, although I'm not sure Faulkner is gonna make it home in time."

"I don't know either, but you never know, they might get lucky."

CHAPTER 8

ell, we might just get lucky, Wolf thought to himself as he and Dude scoured the most likely area where Penelope was being held. After the Australian soldier had been killed, the SEAL teams had doubled their efforts to find any kind of clue Penelope might be leaving behind. The international forces that were at the camp were slowly pulling out, because the danger finally outweighed the benefits of being there. Their exit made the SEALs' existence at the camp shaky. Being the only western-looking soldiers there wasn't a good thing and made them stand out like sore thumbs.

ISIS was still using Penelope as their spokesperson, and it was effective as hell. Wolf knew the news channels all over the world would have no problem showing the petite, fragile-looking woman reading the manifestos the terrorists had written. It was a great way to get the word out to the world and to spread their hate.

The SEALs were *not* happy that she was obviously present at the last beheading, and hated how her voice had quavered while she'd read ISIS's hateful words right after the Australian soldier had been killed. She might be a soldier and trained for combat, but she was also a woman, and every man on the teams wanted to shield her from what she was obviously seeing and going through.

But while she had to be scared out of her mind, she was also holding on. She was smart. It'd taken Bubba, another Virginia SEAL team member, and Mozart two days to find all of her subtle clues. She was anchoring a piece of the pink cloth to the bottom outside edge of the tent she was most likely being held in. She probably reached under the tarp from the inside and secured it so it could be seen from the outside. It wasn't obvious; Bubba was the first to find the small clue, and Mozart wasn't sure at first it was even a clue at all.

But after Mozart found another attached to the back side of a tent not too far from the first, it was as obvious as if she'd stood up and screamed, 'Here I am!'"

It'd taken a week to determine any kind of pattern and to find as many clues as possible, but when all her pink so-called flags had been marked on the map, the pattern was clear. How many nights she was being kept at each tent was unknown and probably varied, but it looked as if they were simply rotating her to the same tents over and over again.

Both teams were on reconnaissance that night. They had to figure out which tent Sergeant Turner was being held in, and plan the best way to get her out. They would find her tonight, and tomorrow they'd get the fuck out of dodge.

There were five teams of two searching the camp, and two men back at the command tent waiting for information. Wolf and Dude slowly made their way toward their objective. Wolf thought there was a pretty good chance Penelope would be there because, after analyzing the probability and knowing where she'd been, and when, this tent hadn't been used in a couple of days. It was due.

Occasionally tripping over objects left in their path, the men heard snoring, groaning, moaning, and the occasional unmistakable sound of sex as they made their way through the dark passageways of the camp. They'd reached the end of the row of tents they were searching and the light of the morning sunrise was about to peek over the horizon.

The men stopped in their tracks at the sound of English somewhere nearby. They hadn't heard English being spoken by anyone outside their team since they'd arrived at the camp. They stopped to listen. The voice was faint and irritated and they could only hear part of what was being said.

"Motherfuckers. What's ... so goddamn long? I've left ... breadcrumbs for a fucking child to find... Are they incompetent or what?"

The mutterings continued, and Wolf and Dude smiled at each other. They were so thankful to hear what had to be Sergeant Penelope Turner's irritated voice, they didn't even care she'd been disparaging them. Hell, her feisty attitude was a welcome sound. It would hopefully be much easier to rescue her than if she was beaten down and terrified. They'd take a pissed-off soldier, ready to get the hell out, over a hysterical, crying woman any day of the week.

"Rover five to CT." Wolf's voice was low and barely audible as he spoke into his radio.

"This is CT."

"Target located."

"Repeat."

"Target. Fucking. Located," Wolf enunciated again into the radio, not able to keep the enthusiasm out of his voice this time.

"You're cutting out, but did I hear Target located? Confirm." Cookie's voice was also hushed, but Wolf could hear the excitement cutting through his no-nonsense words anyway.

"Affirmative."

"Copy that. Target located and location marked. Will notify other rovers. Out."

Wolf clipped the radio to his belt and motioned to Dude. They slunk back through the dark the way they'd come. They hated to leave Penelope, but they had a rescue to plan, they couldn't go by the seat of their pants on this one. No way would they risk losing her that way.

By this time tomorrow, they'd all be well on their way to the Special Forces base at Yuksekova, about two hundred miles east, and then on their way home. Halle-fucking-lujah.

* * *

PENELOPE SAT on the ground in the newest tent she'd been moved to, drew her knees up in front of her and clasped her hands around them. For what seemed like the millionth time, she pushed her hair out of her face. She'd literally kill someone for a shower. If they were standing between her and fresh, clean water—cold or hot didn't matter at this point—she'd use her bare hands to kill them to get at it. But a shower was so far outside what she could imagine happening, it wasn't even funny.

Her hair felt greasy and nasty and she had several snarls in it that she knew would take a miracle to get out without cutting off all her hair. Her hands were gray with dirt and her fingernails were torn and ragged and had dirt caked under them. She itched, and figured she probably had lice or some other nasty bug infestation. The hair on her legs and under her arms was long and she sometimes felt like a hairy beast. But she was alive. And she'd stay that way as long as she could and would endure bugs, dirt, and body hair that was way too long for her comfort for as long as it'd take to be rescued.

But it was the thirst that was the hardest thing to endure. The heat of the desert, along with the hot-as-hell tents she'd been holed up in, were finally starting to wear her body down. She wasn't even sweating anymore and the few times she'd broken down, she didn't even have enough extra water in her body for tears to fall from her eyes. Her muscles frequently cramped up from lack of water. Penelope knew her body would continue to slowly shut down if she didn't get more water. She'd been drinking questionable warm water for weeks now. She'd been really sick the first few weeks, but figured her body had acclimated to whatever organisms were swimming in the little water she did get. But it wasn't enough. It was *never* enough.

The night before, when she'd been moved, had been different. She hadn't seen any of the men who'd been in charge of her before, and the men who'd moved her had been way more "handsy" than anyone had been in the past. Penelope didn't think that boded well for her future.

She thought about her brother again. Cade wouldn't allow the government to forget about her, or give up, of that she had no doubt. Even if she was killed over here in the desert, Cade would make sure she was remembered. Hell, he'd probably lobby to get her name added to history books or something. Penelope knew she was tired when she didn't even smile at the thought.

When Cade had decided to be a firefighter, Penelope decided she'd be one too. He hadn't laughed, or tried to talk her out of it, he encouraged and bullied her until she'd made it. When she'd thought about going into the Reserves, again, he'd encouraged her and told her she'd be awesome at whatever she decided to do with her life. Cade made her a better human being and was the one person Penelope longed to see again. As one of her best friends, *he* was who she missed the most.

Penelope knew she wasn't the tallest woman in the world, and that most people underestimated her. She was strong. Well, she *used* to be strong, before she'd been underfed, confined, and not able to work out other than the occasional sit-ups and pushups. She wasn't looking her best at the moment; months with no shower would do that to a person. But she wasn't going to give up. Not until a bullet was entering her brain or a big-ass machete was cutting her head from her shoulders.

She remembered how the Australian soldier hadn't fought or cried. He'd been stoic, almost resigned to the fact he was going to die. Penelope had no idea if she'd be able to be as calm as he was when it was her turn to face death. She'd most likely fight like hell until her captors managed to kill her.

She'd taken up talking to herself, if nothing else, simply to hear the English language. "I'll never complain about someone talking too much again. I'd give anything to have a real conversation with someone. Forget the pigeon-English shit."

Penelope put her head down on her knees and tried to ignore the warmth of the tent she was in. As the sun rose high in the sky, so did the temperature. Because she couldn't sweat, she dreamed about the days when she came out of training or got through with working out, covered in sweat, and tilted up her water bottle to quench her thirst.

One day at a time. She had to make it through one day at a time. Someone would find her. They had to. She was slowly losing her mind.

CHAPTER 9

olf, Abe, Cookie, Mozart, Dude, Benny, and the six members of the other SEAL team, Rocco, Gumby, Ace, Ho Chi Mien, Bubba, and Rex, huddled around the map. Wolf explained the extraction plan for the third time, making sure everyone knew exactly where they were supposed to be and when.

The plan was for Rex and his team to cause a distraction near the area where Penelope was being held, but not close enough to cause suspicion. Wolf's team would move in, under the cover of darkness and ensuing chaos. Dude and Cookie would enter through the back of the tent and extract the sergeant. After they extracted her, Wolf and Benny would lead the way and Abe and Mozart would take up the rear.

They'd contacted the JSOC and the plan was for the Night Stalkers, the Army's elite helicopter crew, to swoop in on the other side of the camp and pick them up. They'd fly the two hundred miles east to the Special Forces base at Yuksekova, and there Penelope would be seen by a doctor. They'd all be flown to Ramstein Air Base in Germany, where she could be examined more thoroughly by the base's medical team, and then they'd all head home.

After Wolf's group was safely away with Penelope, the Virginia SEAL team would slip back to their command tent and hike north away from the camp, and be picked up by another Night Stalker team.

The entire operation should take no more than thirty minutes to extract Penelope, two hours to fly to the Special Forces Base, and they should be home within thirty six hours after that.

Of course, they'd all learned that the only sure thing in a mission was that something could go wrong, and the only easy day was yesterday, so they had a Plan B and a Plan C.

The first thing that was most obviously wrong before they even set out to rescue Sergeant Turner was that the batteries in their radios were dying. The hell of it was, they couldn't do anything about it. Batteries died. Period. It wasn't feasible to carry a pocket full of replacement batteries on a mission, and anyway, the ones in the radios were rechargeable. They'd each brought an extra pack, but with the increased usage of the electronics at the camp during their patrols and searches, those had also been exhausted.

Without any electricity they hadn't been able to charge them back up, and even if they'd known they'd be out of pocket for as long as they had been, there wouldn't have been anything they could've done to prevent the batteries from dying. Rex had given Dude one of their radios, since their batteries were a week newer than Wolf's team, but they were seriously screwed if something major happened. They'd be cut off from all communications with each other *and* the Joint Special Operations Command.

After the debrief, Wolf and the rest of his team were sitting around, killing time, waiting for darkness to fall and for the camp to quiet down, when Benny brought up their trackers.

"I've learned the hard way, and just wanted to touch base before we do this tonight. God forbid those ISIS assholes get ahold of any of us. Everyone got your trackers?"

Everyone nodded, but Mozart suddenly looked guilty.

"What the fuck?" Wolf asked in a stifled, rough voice. "I thought we agreed on this."

"We did, but honestly, with getting April and Summer settled and saying goodbye that morning, I simply forgot to grab it on my way out," Mozart defended himself. "It's usually in my tactical bag, but I took it out when we went on that one training exercise. It was stupid, I know."

Abe sighed. "Okay, it's not the end of the world. I'll stick to Mozart. Tex will have known we only had five trackers between the six of us from the moment we left. We got this."

The guys had given in reluctantly to their women's request to wear a tracker while they were on missions. After Benny had been kidnapped, and the fact that Tex's inability to track him led to Jess sacrificing herself and letting herself get taken as well, simply because she knew the tracker *she* was wearing would lead Tex right to Benny, they'd agreed to wear the GPS devices. The men had balked at first, saying their missions were highly classified, but Caroline had run roughshod over any and all of their arguments, correctly stating that Tex had the same security clearance as the rest of the team and he'd be the only one who would see where they were. She'd had a point, and eventually the guys agreed the extra security and peace of mind the trackers would give them, and their women, was worth it.

It wasn't the first time one of the guys had forgotten the small GPS tracking device, but this was the first time any of them thought it might just be a necessity.

ISIS didn't follow any rules of engagement. They were a ruthless gang of thugs who used the excuse of religion to torture and kill anyone they felt would further their cause. Not only would the team be up against a dangerous group of men, they'd be trying to snatch a prized possession right out from under the terrorists' noses. The probability was high they'd get separated in the chaos of the rescue and the trackers would've made everyone feel better about that possibility.

Wanting to lighten the mood, and change the subject away from his faux pas, Mozart asked, "Dude, what names are you guys considering for your little girl?"

"Honestly? I don't give a fuck. As long as she's alive and kicking, I couldn't care less."

"Really? So if Cheyenne names her Bertha, you're good with it?"

"Yup. She's gonna be my little cupcake no matter what name Cheyenne gives her." A few years ago, all the men would've given Dude no end of shit for his statement, but now, with families of their own? They got it. Dude continued, "I love egging Shy on though, so I've messed with her head so much, she doesn't know what she wants anymore."

"Not sure that's cool, honestly," Benny said. "Names are important, and if you've confused Cheyenne about what you want to name the baby versus what she wants to name her, that can be really stressful. I should know. Jess and I went back and forth and finally decided to give our kids as normal as names as possible. John and Sara are strong names and ones they won't be made fun of for."

"Like you were?" Wolf asked.

"Yeah. There weren't too many Kasons around when I was growing up, hell, even now, and it made my life hell."

"Shy knows I'm teasing her, Benny," Dude said seriously. "I wouldn't do one thing to cause Cheyenne more stress than she's already under. We laugh about it together. We see who can come up with the most ridiculous name. But we've had some serious conversations about it too. Any stress Shy has about naming our baby, she's bringing about on her own. Believe me, I've threatened to paddle her ass if she didn't stop vacillating back and forth, but she swears she wants to *see* our daughter before she picks a name. That she wants to make sure the name she has in her head matches what she sees when she looks at her face for the first time."

The men were quiet. They all knew Dude, knew he liked control, and knew any paddling he gave his wife would end in both their pleasure. They understood he'd never do anything purposely to hurt Cheyenne, just as any of them wouldn't hurt their wives.

"Sorry, man, I know you wouldn't hurt her. It's just—"

Dude cut Benny off. "It's cool. I get it. I just hope like fuck this can be done so I can be with her when it's time."

The men nodded. They all hoped so too, although before tonight, they hadn't expected it to happen.

"Speaking of names," Cookie started with a grin, "you told your woman how you got your nickname yet, Benny?"

"Hell no," Benny immediately responded. "One, Jess would probably laugh her head off and I'd never hear the end of it, and two, there's no way in hell I ever want her knowing a prostitute somewhere in the depths of Africa gave that nickname to me."

The guys laughed quietly.

"This sounds like a good story," Rex said when the laughter had died down.

Abe didn't give Benny a chance to deflect the unasked question. "We were chilling out at a bar after a mission in Africa. A prostitute came up to our table to try to score for the night. She asked our man here if he was looking for a good time. Benny, thinking he was being witty, said, 'Been there, done that, got the T-shirt.' It was noisy in the bar and the prostitute didn't understand English that well and thought he was telling her his name. So she said, 'Ten Dollars for you, Benny Dunhat with the T-shirt.' It stuck."

Now it was the Virginia team's turn to laugh uproariously.

"Fucking classic," Rex said, and nodded approvingly.

239

"Assholes," Benny said putting his hands behind his head and trying to relax back into his bedroll. "If Jess finds out, I'm holding you all responsible. I like the way she tries to convince me to tell her the story."

His teammates all laughed, but Benny knew if they'd kept their mouths shut for the last two years, he was good. They might make fun of him, but Benny knew it was all good-natured teasing. He didn't really care if Jess knew how he'd gotten his nickname, of course she and the other women knew prostitutes existed, but the more the girls asked, the more it became an ongoing inside joke with the guys. They all knew it drove the women nuts not to know the origin of Benny's nickname, and that made it all the more fun to keep it from them.

The tent quieted down, except for the regular noises of the camp settling in for the night around them. Rex's team had talked together quietly for a while, but now the men were slowly getting into battle mode. It was almost time.

* * *

PENELOPE SAT against one side of the tent thinking about what she wanted to eat first, after she drank a gallon of cold, clean water, when she got back to the States. A double-meat hamburger from *Whataburger*. No, that lava desert thing from *Chili's*. Hell, she didn't care. As long as it was big and she could eat until she felt like she would burst. That was what was most important.

She was in the middle of dreaming about food when she heard something. A bang sounded off to the east of her tent. It wasn't terribly loud, but it was enough to get her attention.

She heard two men speaking frantically in Arabic outside her tent, but no one entered. A little while later, Penelope heard a noise she'd dreamed about, but had started to think she'd never really hear.

The sound of the thick canvas material that made up the walls of her prison tearing. It could've been a terrorist or other bad guy coming to get her, but she didn't think so. They'd simply barge in the flap in the front, not try to be stealthy in the back. It had to be the cavalry.

Penelope turned to the sound and saw a black shape entering the tent from a large slice made in the back side of the tent.

"It's about fucking time," she said slowly and with extreme emotion, standing up and facing the shape, being cautious because there was still a *chance* it could be someone in the camp there to cause trouble.

Dude stood up inside the tent and looked at Sergeant Penelope Turner. She looked exactly like their intel said she'd look, albeit a little worse for the wear. Her blonde hair hung lanky around her shoulders and she looked as if she'd lost at least twenty pounds she couldn't spare. She wasn't very tall; the five-foot-two description was probably right on.

She stood in front of him, waiting for him to say something, more thankful than she could ever express he was there.

"United States Navy SEAL, Sergeant. We're here to take you home," Dude said in a muted tone.

"Awesome. I don't care if you're the President of the United States, as long as you're here to get me the fuck out of here."

Dude almost smiled. The team had a long discussion about the condition in which they might find this woman when they entered the tent. He'd been ready for anything, including resistance, but was more than happy to see she wasn't broken. Hell, she didn't even look bent.

"Any chance you have a weapon for me?"

Dude frowned down at her. "Can you handle it?" At her immediate scowl, he clarified, "I meant, you probably haven't eaten a whole lot. We have a ways to go to get to the extraction point. We don't exactly need you dropping it or losing control of it if we run into trouble." He watched as she thought through his words and his respect for her grew.

"Fuck. Yeah, you're probably right. I feel shaky as hell and I'm not sure how far I can go on my own steam. Got any water?" Penelope was frustrated that the SEAL thought she couldn't handle a pistol, but knew deep down he was probably right to be cautious. The last thing she wanted was to be a liability and somehow screw up her own rescue.

"We've got to get out of here, but as soon as we can find a safe spot and we're a good distance away, I'll make sure you get some water."

Penelope nodded. It was what she'd expected, and she'd prefer to get the hell out of there right now, rather than to take a drink and possibly get caught, but she was extremely thirsty and couldn't help the question from coming out anyway. She gestured to the slice in the tent. "Are you leading, or am I?"

Dude allowed his smile to come out this time. Damn, she was feisty. She reminded him a lot of his Shy. He gestured for her to go first. "I've got a man right outside, don't trip over him."

The look she gave him clearly told him to fuck off. He smiled again and watched as she carefully parted the material and took her first step toward freedom.

* * *

THE TRIP THROUGH THE QUIET, dark camp was surprisingly anticlimactic. Wolf and Benny led the way, making sure to notify Cookie and Dude of any detours they needed to make, while Mozart and Abe had their backs, making sure they weren't followed or harassed as they made their way through the camp.

Rex's SEAL team had done their job well. They didn't encounter anyone suspicious and made good time toward the extraction point.

Penelope followed Dude as best she could. He'd stopped about ten minutes after they'd left the tent and given her a canteen of water. Penelope wanted to guzzle it down and then pour another over her head, but she controlled her urges and took only a few sips. The last thing she wanted to do was get sick in the middle of her rescue. She handed it back to the SEAL who had entered her tent and felt a warmth in her belly at the look of approval in his eyes. It had been so long since anyone had looked at her with respect, it felt good. She shrugged it off and did what she usually did, said something snarky, simply to get through the moment without crying. "If you're done eyeballin' me, how 'bout we get out of this fucking desert?"

But instead of pissing him off, which was what her comebacks usually did, he merely smiled and nodded at her, then at the SEAL behind her, and set off again.

Just when Penelope didn't think she could take another step, they stopped and the SEAL in front of her gestured for her to crouch down. She couldn't see much; it was darker than ever with no moon to help illuminate their path. She'd made her way through the camp with one hand on the SEAL's back or tucked into his vest. She kneeled down and strained to see something, anything.

"In about three minutes, an MH-60 Blackhawk is gonna scream in here from the north. Keep your eyes closed as it comes in so you don't get any sand in them, and whatever you do, don't let go of my vest. Got it?"

"How will *you* be able to see?" Penelope had never been one to blindly follow orders, even back home at the firehouse.

"I've got night-vision goggles on, they'll shield my eyes from the blowing sand and dirt. You're gonna have to run. Can you do that? And be honest."

Penelope tried to look up at the man, but dammit, it was still too dark to clearly see him. She thought about it. Could she run? The walk across

242

the camp had almost done her in. But run to freedom? Hell yeah, she could do it. "Yes." She didn't elaborate.

"All right. If for any reason you think you can't make it to the chopper, pull down hard on my vest. I'll get your ass there. We aren't leaving this fucking desert without you, Sergeant. No way in hell."

Penelope felt the tears gather in her eyes. Crap. No. She couldn't break down. Not now. Not when she was so close to freedom. "Thank you." She paused, then asked, "What was your name again?"

"Dude. And that's Cookie behind you. I don't know if you'll remember or not, but Wolf and Benny cleared the way ahead of us as we went through camp, and Mozart and Abe brought up the rear. We'll all pile in the chopper with you, so once we get there, scoot your ass in as far as you can. You know the MH-60?"

"Yeah," Penelope told him, impressed with his professionalism and his abilities so far. "Holds ten comfortably in the back. Pilot, copilot, gunner, and crew chief in the front."

"You know the MH-60." This time it wasn't a question.

Penelope smiled, loving when she could surprise people. It happened all the time because people judged her based on her size and her looks. It was nice, for the first time in a long few months, to be treated as if she was an equal.

"Brace." Dude's voice was quiet, and Penelope braced. Within seconds she heard the hum of the rotors of the chopper. Before she'd joined the military, she'd only been familiar with single-rotor helicopters that were mostly used by hospitals and ambulance services. Because of the single rotor, they made the stereotypical whap-whap-whap sound. The MH-60 was a more powerful and bigger chopper and thus had several blades on the rotor. She'd never heard anything so wonderful before in her life as that helicopter hovering overhead in the dark night.

The chopper was flying low and with no lights. It entered the clearing and lowered until it was hovering inches from the ground.

"Let's go. Now!" Dude said.

Penelope felt him stand up as she'd already grabbed on to his vest and her eyes popped open. They were running toward the huge machine before she could think. She tripped once, but her grip on the SEAL's vest kept her from face-planting into the unforgiving desert floor. She got her feet under her and continued running as if the hounds of hell were at her heels. She felt a hand on her back and didn't have to look back to know it was the other SEAL who had been by her side throughout their journey out of the camp.

They arrived at the open bay door on the right side of the chopper and a man, most likely the crew chief, was there with his hand outstretched, ready to help them in.

Penelope let go of the vest she was holding and Dude leaped into the cargo area. He immediately turned to help her up. She threw both hands upward and felt the men already in the helicopter grab hold of her hands and there was a hand on her butt that boosted her up at the same time. She immediately moved away from the open door when her hands were let go, scrabbling back on her hands and knees.

She watched as five more dark shapes leaped onboard the helicopter with only minimal help from Dude. The crew chief went back up to his seat on the right side of the chopper and Penelope felt the machine rising into the air about two seconds after the last SEAL leaped into the cargo area.

With the seven of them in the space, it suddenly seemed smaller than when she'd first been hauled aboard. There wasn't time to strap into any seats so Penelope crab-walked backwards until she felt her spine hit something solid. She braced herself and held on as the helicopter raced off into the black night.

CHAPTER 10

"Cade, your sister has been missing for over three months now. Do you think you'll ever see her again?"

"Yes, absolutely."

"How can you be sure?"

"How can anyone be sure of anything? My sister is a fighter, but more than that, she's smart. You've seen her on those videos, everyone in America has seen her. She does exactly what she's told to do, and it's kept her alive this long. Those BLEEP are keeping her alive to use her. She's pretty, and they're using her as a propaganda tool. All she needs is for the government to send someone in to get her. Knowing her, she'll probably complain to their faces about how long it took them to find her and get her out."

"The government has said time and time again that they don't negotiate with terrorists, do you really think they're going to spend possibly millions of dollars, and risk countless lives, to send a team in to rescue her?"

"First of all, there aren't any negotiations needed. They can go in and steal her back. Second of all, I can't believe you're putting a price on my sister's head. She's an American soldier. She put her life on the line when she was sent over there in the first place. The United States government sent her there, they can damn well go and get her back."

"What will be the first words you say to your sister if you see her again?"

"When I see her, I'll tell her I love her and that I never gave up trying to find her."

The reporter faced the camera for the first time and said to the viewing audience, "In case you missed it before, here's the last tape that has been released of Sergeant Turner reading a message from the ISIS terrorists..."

* * *

FIONA SAT with Melody and they watched as Akilah played with little Sara. Jessyka was glad to let Fiona babysit her toddler for a while. It was a good break for both mother and daughter. Akilah didn't speak perfect English yet, but neither did the two-year-old, so they actually entertained each other very easily.

"I'm so proud of you and Tex for adopting Akilah."

"*I'm* glad Tex was able to make arrangements so quickly so we *could* adopt her."

"Does it ever bother you that Tex can...make things happen...so easily?"

Melody knew what Fiona was asking. "You know what? I trust Tex explicitly. He's too damn honest to do anything for himself, or us, illegally."

Fiona laughed, catching the "or us" that Melody threw in there. "Well, I know you know this, but Tex holds a special place in my heart. I'd do anything for him and I'm thrilled knowing you guys found each other."

"*He* found *me*, you mean," Melody corrected.

"Yeah, that's what I meant. We've always said Tex could find anyone, and of course we were right." Fiona noticed that Melody's gaze was on her daughter. She looked over and saw that Akilah was watching the television with rapt attention. She looked at the screen and saw the last video of the poor American soldier that had been made public had just finished playing.

"What is it, Akilah?" Melody asked softly.

Akilah just shrugged and went back to playing with Sara. Melody and Fiona looked at each other again.

"Is she really okay? I can't imagine what sorts of things she witnessed over in Iraq," Fiona asked in a low voice.

"I think so. Sometimes I'll catch her staring off into space, but she always smiles at me and says she's fine when I ask if she's all right."

"Do you think she misses it?"

"Sometimes, yeah. It'd be like us suddenly moving to Germany and not speaking German. We could acclimate, but sometimes we'd long for a *McDonald's* burger...you know?"

Fiona did understand, better than she figured Melody thought after spending all that time in Mexico when she'd been kidnapped. Surprisingly, having Julie living in the same town was cathartic. Having someone who Fiona could talk to about what they went through, and knowing that the other woman honestly understood where she was coming from and what she was feeling, was a relief. While she and Julie didn't hang out all the time, they'd come far enough in their relationship to actually call themselves friends and go out every now and then for lunch.

They visited for a while longer and finally Melody figured it was time to head back to Caroline's. They were all going to try to meet at *Aces* for dinner, and Melody knew Akilah would need a mental break before they headed out to meet in a big group like that. She was doing really well, but Melody didn't want to push it.

They were in Caroline's car that she let them borrow and on their way back to Caroline's house when Akilah asked from the backseat, "What was TV about?"

Melody looked up at the rearview mirror at her daughter, feeling lucky for the millionth time that she was in her and Tex's life. She tried to explain without getting into too much detail. Akilah was only twelve, but she'd seen enough that she sometimes acted thirty. Melody wanted to keep her as young as possible for as long as possible. "An American soldier was kidnapped by ISIS."

"She on video?

"Yes, people think that is her."

Akilah was silent for a while then said, bizarrely, "I speak Arabic."

"Yes, honey, I know you do."

"There was Arabic on TV."

Melody looked sharply at her daughter. "Yes, I saw some men in the background talking. You know what they were saying?"

Akilah didn't look happy. "Yes."

"Did you hear them?"

"No. Lips."

"You could read their lips? And they were speaking in Arabic?"

Akilah nodded, eyes wide.

"Was it something bad?"

"Yes."

"Do you need to tell Tex?"

Akilah looked out the window and thought about what to tell Melody. She might only be twelve years old, but she knew enough about her new father to know he was different from the other fathers in the special school she attended. She knew Tex was like her, missing a limb, but also because he talked to her one night about what it was he did. He'd been honest, and Akilah understood most of it. He used his computers to help people. He found people who were lost, he did research to help the American soldiers and the American government, and he could…she didn't know what the strange phrase meant when Tex had told her, but she remembered the phrase and figured it meant he could do special things other people couldn't. All because of his computer.

Pull strings. That's the funny American saying he'd used. If her new dad could pull these strings and help the poor American woman who was lost and who had a horrible accent when she'd been reading the few Arabic words on the letter, then she needed to tell him what she'd heard.

"Yes," Akilah said solemnly.

"Okay. We'll call him when we get to Caroline's house."

Akilah sat back and relaxed a little bit. She was very happy Melody treated her as if she was important. When she spoke, Melody listened, unlike back in her country, where many times women's opinions and thoughts were dismissed or ignored. It made her feel good inside, happy to be here in America with her new family. She wanted to help in any way she could.

CHAPTER 11

*S*omeone handed Penelope a set of headphones. She could hear the pilots talking to each other in muted voices, and every now and then one of the SEALs would say something to another. But she kept silent. She was so very thankful she was alive and away from the damn kidnappers. If she stopped to think for one second about what she'd just lived through, she knew she'd be a basket-case.

Penelope also didn't want to think right now about that poor Australian soldier, or Thomas, Henry, and Robert. She'd remember their lives, and deaths, at another time and another place; this wasn't it. While she was thankful to be away from the refugee camp, she'd overheard enough from the pilots and the SEALs to know they weren't completely out of danger.

While she'd been in the hands of ISIS, there wasn't one moment that went by that she didn't feel scared because she was a female in the midst of a male dominated society, and one that was definitely anti-woman.

She'd known at any time she could be raped, or passed around to each of the terrorists. God only knew why they'd left her alone all these months. She thought she remembered reading one time that blonde-haired women were somehow regarded suspiciously in the Muslim culture, but she could've been making that up. Whatever the reason, she was more thankful than she thought she could even express.

But right now, in this helicopter, surrounded by ten very masculine men...men who could easily hold her down and do whatever they wanted with her, she wasn't scared at all. First, these were American soldiers; second, they'd come to rescue her. Third, she could sense, at least with the SEALs, they oozed honor and protectiveness from their very bones. She was safe with them. Utterly and completely safe. Penelope was dehydrated and hungry, and had been beaten up more than once, but she was here and alive and, for the moment, safe. She'd take it.

Penelope was just starting to relax into a kind of half-asleep/half-awake state, when she heard one of the pilots swear through the headphones she was wearing.

"Fucking hell. Brace, brace, brace! Incoming!"

Those were the last words she remembered hearing before the chopper lurched after a large explosion and everything went black.

CHAPTER 12

"Hey, Tex. It's me. Please call me back as soon as you can. I know you're holed up in your cave, but this is important. Akilah needs to tell you what she saw on the news. She was watching a clip of that kidnapped woman soldier reading something, and she saw some men in the background speaking Arabic. Apparently she read their lips, and she won't tell me what they said, but she did admit that you needed to know. Please. Call me as soon as you can."

Melody hung up the phone and sighed. Short of doing something underhanded, like putting her tracker in a Dumpster and letting it get carried to the landfill, which would certainly get her husband's attention, she didn't know what to do. He was usually very protective of both her and Akilah, but with everything else that had been going on it was possible he'd lost track of time. Eventually he'd come out of his cave to shower, or eat, and he'd notice she'd left a message both on his cell phone and on their ancient house phone.

In the meantime, she did what she could to help out her friends. Jess was feeling frazzled with not only her two kids, but the "afternoon sickness," as she called it. Alabama was doing fine with Brinique and Davisa, but the two girls were feeling clingy since Christopher had left. Summer was good, glowing and fully recovered after April's birth, but she was struggling with being back at work and away from April all day after her maternity leave was up.

Melody knew Caroline was worried about Fiona. She hadn't been around much, because she'd been working so hard, and everyone always worried about her when their men were off on a mission. And finally there was Cheyenne. Caroline had tried to get her to sleep at her house, so if she needed to go have her baby in the middle of the night, Caroline would be there to help, but so far she'd refused, saying she was fine and didn't want to get in anyone's way.

Melody, as always, was impressed with Caroline. The woman took a lot on, but honestly seemed to thrive on it. She could work a full shift at the lab, then come home, babysit, give advice, and even host a dinner get-together for all the women and their kids...and still come out on the other side smiling.

She went into the kitchen to see Caroline teaching Akilah how to make cookies from scratch. Akilah was obsessed with cooking. Anytime she ate something she enjoyed, she'd ask how to make it and bug Melody until they made the dish together. Melody figured it was because growing up in Iraq, food could be scarce, so she had no problem sharing what she knew with her new daughter. All too soon, Akilah would be a teenager and probably have no time for her mother.

Caroline's phone rang when she was wrist-deep in the middle of mixing the cookie dough by hand, which she insisted was the only way to make sure all the ingredients got mixed together properly. She'd even claimed her chemistry background proved it was true.

"I'll get it," Melody said as she reached for the phone. "Hello?"

"Caroline?"

"No, this is Melody. Cheyenne?"

"Yeah...uh..."

"Are you all right?"

Melody heard her panting on the other end of the line, then she said, "Yeah, but it's time."

"It's time? Baby time? Are you sure?"

"Yeah. I'm sure."

Melody held her hand over the phone and screeched to Caroline, "It's time!" Then she moved her hand and got back to Cheyenne. "Where are you? Have you called an ambulance? We're coming to get you."

"I'm still at home, I haven't called an ambulance yet...I called Caroline. But—"

"Okay, then we're on our way. Do you have your suitcase there with you? We can't forget that."

"I was calling to tell Caroline, but I'm about to call the ambulance. Can you guys meet me at the hospital?"

"Yeah, of course, but why don't we just come get you? That baby isn't going to come in the next ten minutes... Wait...is she?"

"No, I don't think so...but...I'm bleeding. It's not right."

"Shit, okay, I'm hanging up now. Call 911 immediately and we'll meet you at the hospital. I'm sure it's fine. Don't panic. All right?"

"Okay. Melody?"

"Yeah, Cheyenne?"

"I'm scared."

"It's going to be fine. Now, shut up, hang up, and call 911."

"Okay, see you soon."

Melody clicked off the phone and saw that Caroline had already washed her hands and was impatiently waiting to hear what was going on.

Melody shoved the phone at Caroline and reached in her back pocket for her own. "That was obviously Cheyenne. She's having the baby now, but she's bleeding. Damn woman called *you* before calling 911. I swear, cops and doctors and nurses, and apparently 911 operators, are always the last to call for help when they need it. You call Alabama and Fiona. I'll call Jessyka and Summer. We need to get to the hospital. Pronto."

Caroline nodded and immediately dialed. Operation Baby Cooper was happening. Now.

CHAPTER 13

*P*enelope came back to consciousness suddenly. She'd always read about how people gradually came back into themselves after being knocked out, but that wasn't the case with her.

She could smell aviation fuel and smoke from a fire. She opened her eyes and saw destruction all around her. Jesus.

She remembered now, the helicopter she'd been in had obviously crashed, or been shot down, more likely.

She looked around and saw nothing but rocks and scrub bushes. They were obviously in the mountains, but she had no idea what mountains or in what country. But first things first. Penelope's EMT training kicked in. She painfully got up on her hands and knees and paused, taking stock of herself.

Nothing seemed broken, except maybe a rib or two. She could function with that, no problem. It hurt like hell, but in the scope of her current situation, it was negligible. She also had cuts, scrapes, and probably a hell of a lot of bruises. All in all, she was in remarkable shape for falling out of the sky while inside a metal box.

Penelope looked around and saw three men lying near her. She crawled over and vaguely noticed they were three of the SEALs who had helped her escape. Penelope couldn't remember their names, but at the moment it didn't matter. All three were out cold but, when she checked, thankfully they were breathing. Taking a quick look at them, Penelope thought one had a broken arm—it was lying above his head at a weird angle—and the other two looked relatively whole. She couldn't tell if they had any kind of internal bleeding or head wounds though.

She looked up when she heard a noise. It was Dude, the man who'd appeared in her tent prison as if an angel from God.

"You good?" he asked gruffly. He was carrying one of the men from the helicopter, who didn't look good at all.

Penelope nodded. "I'm good. What can I do to help?"

Dude eyed the small woman carefully. They were in a world of hurt, and were fucked if they didn't get their shit together. He might as well use her as much as she'd be able to help him. He ignored the tweaks in his injured ankle and told her solemnly, "Copilot is dead. Gunner and crew chief are in bad shape. My teammates are generally all right, but have various injuries. The pilots did a hell of a job getting the bird down without killing us all. But we're fucked if we don't get the hell out of here." Dude waited for Penelope to nod, and continued. "I'll get everyone out here, but I need your help in triaging them. Can you do that?"

"Yes. I'm an EMT back home in Texas. I'll do my best."

"Thank you." The two words were short and heartfelt.

Penelope nodded and turned back to the men who were in front of her. She looked around and saw a red bag with a white cross on it. At one time, she would've questioned how it was right where she needed it to be at exactly the right moment, but after seeing more than one miracle as a firefighter and EMT, now she took them in stride. She made her way over to the first-aid kit and dragged it back to the SEALs. She saw one of the men's eyes were open and he was watching her intently.

"Hi, remember me? I'm Penelope and I'm going to help you." She fell into emergency medical technician mode automatically. This was something she was familiar with. "Are you all right? Does anything hurt?"

She watched the man take stock of himself. He moved his legs slowly, then each arm, and finally he rotated his head back and forth. "I think I'm in one piece. Everything hurts, but nothing's broken. Sit rep?"

Penelope sighed in relief. Thank God he was alive. One man's condition known, seven to go. She answered the SEAL. "From what I'm guessing, RPG took down the chopper. One dead, seven unknown."

"I'm Cookie. I wasn't sure if you remembered who I was."

"I didn't, and I can't promise to remember you later either, but thank you. Can you help me?" Penelope gestured to the man with the obviously broken arm who hadn't woken up yet.

"What do you need?"

"We need to set his arm. It's gonna hurt like hell and I'm not sure I can hold him if he wakes up in the middle of it."

"Fuck. Wolf is not going to be happy about this."

"Wolf?"

"Yeah, this is Wolf, our team leader. And the man there," Cookie gestured to the other motionless man, "is Benny."

Penelope nodded and the two got to work. Cookie was also trained in first aid, probably more than she was since he was a SEAL, and they quickly were able to set Wolf's arm against his side, keeping it immobile. He was just coming around when Dude came back to them with the pilot. He had a large wound on his head and was bleeding profusely.

"Pilot's in bad shape. I'm not sure we can move any of the Night Stalkers." His words were directed at Cookie.

Cookie nodded. "Let me help you get the others and we'll go to Plan D."

The two men left to go back toward the wrecked hunk of metal that used to be an MH-60 helicopter and Penelope turned to Benny. Cookie and Dude returned quickly, each carrying another one of the men from the helicopter crew.

"Mozart's coming around in the chopper. He's got a large gash on his upper arm, but is otherwise whole. Where's Abe?"

"Shit. He's the only one unaccounted for."

Penelope suddenly felt weighed down with guilt. She sat back on her heels and looked at the six men lying broken on the ground in front of her. Damn.

"This is not your fucking fault."

Penelope turned and looked at the man with the broken arm, Wolf, who'd spoken. "How do you know what I was thinking?" she asked in surprise.

"It's written all over your face, sweetheart."

"I don't think you're allowed to call me sweetheart."

Wolf laughed. Actually laughed. "Sorry, when you're about as big as a bug and as cute as a button, don't think I can call you anything *but* sweetheart, regardless of your rank and obvious competence as a soldier."

"Are you fucking kidding me? That's the most sexist thing I've heard since I've been in this country, and that's saying something," Penelope groused at Wolf.

He laughed again upon seeing her glare. "Sorry. Help me sit up." Now *that* actually sounded like a command.

Penelope helped ease him to a sitting position. "That arm's gonna hurt like hell. We gave you some morphine, but not a lot. Cookie didn't think you should be loopy when we try to outrun insurgents in the fucking mountains...his words, not mine."

Wolf nodded. "How're they?" It was as if his earlier words hadn't been spoken. Penelope was much more comfortable with this no-nonsense, sticking to the details conversation.

"Copilot's dead. I haven't gotten to the other three men. I can't see anything wrong with...Benny, I think the others called him, and they're off looking for Abe. Dude is limping a bit, but he's acting impervious to pain, so it's probably not too bad. Mozart seems to be okay and will probably drag his carcass over here soon; again, their words, not mine."

Wolf scooted toward the unconscious Army pilots as Penelope did the same. They worked in silence, Wolf helping her bandage where he could and offering suggestions. They heard noises in the shrubs behind them and before Penelope could think, Wolf had turned and aimed a pistol in the direction of the footsteps.

"Easy, Wolf, it's us," Penelope heard, right before three SEALs emerged from the dense underbrush.

The man they'd called Abe was walking...sort of. There was blood on the bottom of his pants and it was obvious, if not for the help from his teammates, he wouldn't be mobile at all.

"Fuck, Abe, what'd you go and do?"

Dude answered for him. "We pulled a nice-sized chunk of metal out of his thigh. We field dressed it, but it's gonna need stitches when we get to where we're going."

They set Abe down on the ground next to Benny, who was finally coming around. Upon further examination, Benny was all right. He had a raging headache but no open head wound, which, unfortunately, meant he probably had a concussion. Mozart walked into their midst, wobbling a bit but upright and mobile. It was something, at least.

"Plan D discussion," Wolf said in a quiet, serious voice. "Sergeant Turner, listen up, you're a part of this team now too."

Penelope nodded, glad they weren't going to try to shove her off to the side while they made all the decisions. She had a sudden *need* to know what was going on. She'd been kept in the dark about everything for the last few months. It felt good to be included.

"Abe's out with that leg, and that means he'll need two of us to help him. I've got a broken arm, Benny has a concussion. Mozart is moving, but that arm is gonna be about as useless as mine. Tiger here is favoring her right side, so I'm assuming she's got some sort of broken or cracked ribs."

"Wait, what? Tiger?" Penelope wasn't sure she liked that nickname, although it was a hell of a lot better than what the guys back at the firehouse called her.

"Fierce as a fucking tiger," Wolf said without even a smile. He continued as if she hadn't interrupted him. "So that leaves us with Dude and Cookie relatively unscathed, but you guys will need to help Abe." He looked sadly at the Night Stalkers. "We can't take them with us."

The men were silent for a moment, then Benny said, "Our trackers. We've got five of them. If we leave one on each of them, Tex can track 'em."

"What's the radio situation?" Abe asked.

Cookie shook his head in response. "No radios. They're dead. I agree with Benny. We can't take them with us, but we can't leave them at the mercy of the insurgents either," he said.

"What?" Penelope felt like a broken record. "The radios are dead? And trackers? What trackers?"

"No time to fully explain, but in a nutshell, five of us have GPS trackers on us that are being monitored by the best fucking hacker I've ever met in my life. He's got our back at all times, including while we're on missions," Mozart told her.

"That's not legal is it?"

"Who the fuck cares? Right now it's all these guys have. It's their only chance to get out of this fucking country with their heads attached," Benny said somewhat bitterly.

Penelope winced. Dammit. He was right. "But the copilot? He's already dead—"

Wolf didn't let her finish. "A SEAL doesn't leave a SEAL behind, ever. He might be dead, and there's a chance the insurgents will ignore his body and leave him alone, but if they decide to take him somewhere and desecrate his body for one of their fucking videos, he'll hopefully be able to be found before that can happen. We'll leave the trackers with the others as well. If the insurgents get their hands on them there's a possibility they could be separated, so each of them having a tracker will make it easier for the cavalry to find them."

Penelope gulped. Okay, she got it. These men were loyal to the core, and it didn't matter that the Night Stalkers were Army, not Navy. They'd come to get her out, and had refused to leave her behind as well. Just the type of soldiers she wanted to be around. "Right."

Cookie walked to Wolf, Abe, and Benny, and collected their trackers. While he was busy planting them on the other men, Penelope asked. "Why only five when there are six of you?"

It was Mozart who answered without hesitating. "Because I was the dumbass who forgot it. You can bet my wife will kick my ass when I get home. Believe me, I'm kicking my own ass right about now."

Penelope watched as Cookie spoke to each of the injured men, obviously explaining what was going on. His face was serious and grim when he returned.

"Okay, here's the deal. The pilot said the RPG came from the southeast. We're too far from Yuksekova to get to the base on foot. We're in the middle of the Hakkari Daglari mountain range, which separates Iraq and Turkey. Our best bet at this point is to find a good place to hunker down and wait them out. We need to take the high ground if we're gonna have any chance of surviving an onslaught by ISIS or Al Qaeda. Tex will know where we went down and will most likely get with JSOC. They should send in Delta Force or even Rex's SEAL team. We don't have a lot of time, but Benny and I will move the injured Night Stalkers to safer ground, and then the seven of us will bug out of here. We'll head up into the mountains where there's a large cave system."

"But aren't the caves where the insurgents generally hole up?" Penelope asked uncertainly.

Cookie merely shrugged and nodded.

"How are we gonna avoid them?"

"Luck."

Penelope growled. She definitely didn't like the answers she was getting. "Wouldn't it be better to stay here with the pilots and let your friend do his thing? If anyone comes we can fight them off defensively here."

Wolf didn't get angry over her disagreement, but his words were impatient, as if he knew they were running out of time. "Cookie, Benny, go ahead and move the others. We'll prepare what we can while you're gone." He turned to Penelope to answer her question. "We can't defend this position. Look around, we're in a hole. We need to get up high to have a good vantage point. We're sitting ducks here. We still have Dude's tracker, Tex will know something's up, and will be able to find us."

"But..." Penelope looked at the men Dude and Cookie were currently helping take a more defensive position. "Do they know about how hard it is to defend this position?"

Wolf nodded grimly.

Holy freaking shit. Penelope swallowed hard once. Then twice. By agreeing to stay, by not demanding to go with them, the men were basically signing their death warrants. But if they insisted on going with them, they were *all* in grave danger.

Wolf's voice was subdued and gentle, if not sad at the same time. "The gunner has two broken legs. The crew chief hasn't regained consciousness and is bleeding out of his ears and nose. The pilot broke both ankles and both wrists in the crash. With our injuries we can't carry them. They know the odds, Tiger. I'm just thankful we can leave the trackers with them. It'll give them a better shot than if they didn't have them."

Penelope abruptly turned away and started to gather as much gear as she could find, and that she thought they'd need. She knew she'd see those men's faces and hear their voices in her dreams for years to come. She made a vow to herself, to make sure every American knew what a huge sacrifice they'd made and how brave they'd been in the face of certain death.

She felt a hand on her forearm and looked up. It was Dude.

"Tex will find them. He'll get them home to their families. He'll find them, and the cavalry will find *us*."

Penelope nodded, knowing if she opened her mouth she'd embarrass herself by bursting into tears. There was only so much a girl could take, and she'd about reached the end of her rope.

Cookie, Dude, Wolf, Mozart, and Penelope gathered as much as they could easily carry, being sure to take as much ammo and as many firearms as possible. Penelope didn't say a word as Dude handed her a KA-BAR knife and a loaded pistol. She nodded at him in thanks, remembering their conversation from back in the tent, and they got ready to leave. She wasn't in any better shape than she was when she'd been rescued from the tent city, but the game had changed. She was a vital part of the team now, and as one of the least wounded amongst them, she had to carry her weight.

Wolf led the way, with Dude and Cookie supporting Abe on either side, following him. Benny was next, then Mozart, and finally Penelope.

She was aware of the significance of being last in the line. It was her responsibility to have their sixes, their asses. It wasn't something she took lightly. She'd pull her weight with these men or die trying. Her brother hadn't browbeat and nagged her into passing the firefighter certification test for nothing. She was a Turner, she wouldn't let them down.

As they headed up into the mountains, Penelope took one more look back before they went over a rise. She could see the black smoke rising up from the wreckage of the chopper, a beacon for any and all insurgents in the area. She couldn't see the pilot and the other men, but knew they were there in the shadows, waiting to fight, and possibly die.

The thought was too much. She allowed the tears to fall as she walked, knowing the SEALs in front of her were too preoccupied to notice.

CHAPTER 14

*I*n world news today, a source at the White House has confirmed the
crash of an MH-60 helicopter in the Hakkari Daglari mountain
range, between Turkey and Iraq. There's no word of injuries or how many were
onboard, but speculation is that the occupants were either on their way to attempt
to rescue kidnapped American soldier, Penelope Turner, or were returning after
an attempt. No word on if the rescue was attempted or if it was successful, and
there is no information on casualties from the crash. Stay tuned for an update on
the ten o'clock news.

* * *

MELODY LOOKED down at the vibrating phone in her hand. Thank
freaking God. "Hello?"

"Cheyenne is having the baby?"

Melody wasn't surprised Tex knew they were all at the hospital and
the only reason—well, the only good reason—was because Cheyenne
was in labor. "Yeah, she was bleeding when her water broke and we
convinced her to call 911. She finally did and we're all here waiting
now."

"I got your message. I'm sorry I didn't answer when you called. I
promise I'm trying to get better at making sure I keep my phone with me
and on," Tex apologized.

"I know you are. Is...everything okay?" Melody had seen the news, there wasn't any way to avoid it.

"Is Akilah there? I don't have a lot of time."

Well shit. If he wasn't answering her, everything wasn't all right. She didn't protest, or ask any more questions. "Yeah, she's here, hang on...okay?"

"Of course. Mel?"

Melody paused mid-turn toward her daughter. "Yeah, Tex?"

"I love you. I love you more than I've ever loved anyone or anything in my life. You know that, right?"

Man oh man oh man. Something was terribly wrong. Thinking back to the newscast about the crashed helicopter, Melody's mouth got dry and she felt as if she was going to throw up. She wasn't going to ask though. There was no way she'd be able to keep something like that from her friends, so she didn't want to know. Besides, Cheyenne was about to have a baby. This was no time to bring any heartache or worries into the mix.

"I love you too, Tex. To Vegas and back." It was their saying. Ever since they'd driven across the country twice, the second time to get married, it had become their thing.

"Get Akilah for me. Stay safe. Love you."

"I will. Love you too. Hang on." Melody turned and gestured to Akilah, who'd had her eyes on her probably the entire time she'd been speaking to Tex. She held out the phone to the twelve-year-old. "It's Tex," she said in a soft voice. "Tell him what you saw on the TV."

Akilah took the phone and nodded and walked out to the main reception room and outside the hospital doors. "Hello?"

"Hi, sweetie. Mel says you heard something?"

"Read words on television in Arabic."

Tex had gotten used to reading between the lines when it came to Akilah's broken English. She'd gotten much better over the last few months, but especially over the phone, he had to help her find the right words. "You were watching the news and someone was speaking Arabic and you could tell what they said by reading their lips?"

"Yes."

"What did they say?"

"Lady was reading letter in English. Man in black standing behind. Turned and talk to other man."

"Okay, go on."

"Said wanted to take more Americans."

"Take? Like the female soldier?"

"Yes. Said now was good time. Lots of soldiers in camp."

This wasn't huge news to Tex, he knew the government was well aware ISIS wanted to kidnap and torture as many English speaking soldiers as possible, but he was still impressed with his daughter. "Anything else?"

"No."

"Thank you, Akilah. You are amazing."

"I help?"

"You helped a lot."

Akilah smiled. She enjoyed feeling useful. Tex and Melody always made sure they told her how proud they were of her and how happy they were she was with them. "Miss you."

"Oh, sweetie, I miss you too. Tell Mel to get you guys home soon. Yeah?"

"Okay."

"Take care of Melody for me. I love you."

"I will. Love you too."

Tex smiled broadly on the other side of the country. He thought that was the first time Akilah had said the words. He didn't want to make a big deal out of it though, it might embarrass her and she'd be reluctant to say them again in the future. "I'll talk to you later. If you hear or read anything else on the news, call me right away."

"Yes."

"Okay, talk to you later."

"Bye."

"Bye, Akilah."

Tex hung up the phone and turned back to the bank of computer screens in front of him. He'd known the helicopter had crashed the second it'd gone down. The program that tracked his friends was up and he'd watched as the red dots suddenly stopped moving well before they'd reached the Special Forces base at Yuksekova. When there were four dots which stayed put and one which started up the mountains, Tex knew they were in trouble. Splitting up wasn't standard operating procedure. He'd immediately reached out to his contacts and given them the coordinates of where those four dots were.

He'd been informed that JSOC was putting together a Delta Force team at that very moment to head into the mountains to get his friends. Tex's information would cut their search time dramatically, but he was glad to hear they were already aware something had gone wrong and were heading out on the rescue mission.

What they'd find when they got there was anyone's guess. Tex had no idea who the four motionless trackers were attached to and he could only hope he wouldn't have to be telling his wife, or the women he'd come to love as sisters, that some of their men wouldn't be coming home alive.

CHAPTER 15

*P*enelope had been good for the first hour of walking, adrenaline and nervousness propelling her on, but slowly, as they settled into the hike, her strength had waned. Lack of exercise, lack of proper nutrition, lack of enough good clean water, and some cracked ribs, it was all taking its toll.

But she felt better knowing she wasn't the only one. Apparently Abe wasn't light, and Cookie and Dude were having a hard time helping him get over the boulders and hills that were between them and the dubious safety of a hole in the side of a mountain. Abe was helping as much as he could, but the shrapnel in his thigh had done a number on him, and even with his help, it was slow going. Penelope had no idea how Wolf and the rest of the guys were going to decide *which* cave was the best for them, but she had no doubt that they'd find the perfect place.

One foot in front of the other was her mantra. She'd be damned if *she'd* be the reason they were held up. She felt guilty enough as it was for putting these men in this position in the first place. Oh, intellectually she knew that *she* hadn't done it, but there was no getting around the fact that they were all here, tromping through the mountains in Turkey, injured and most likely being hunted by insurgents, because they were sent to rescue her.

Penelope wiped away the sweat from her brow, thankful she'd gotten enough liquid in her to be *able* to sweat, for what seemed the millionth time and trudged on. She finally saw Dude and Cookie ease Abe to the ground and sighed in relief. Thank freaking God. She honestly had no idea how much longer she could've continued.

"We'll stop here for the night. We can't stay here for good, but we've gone far enough. We all need the break. Abe, we'll get your leg properly sewed up and stuff you full of antibiotics. Mozart, same for you. Tiger, if you need those ribs wrapped, we'll do that as well."

"What about you, Wolf? How's the arm?" Penelope dared to ask, irritated when every single man grinned at her. "What? What's so fucking funny?" She was tired, hungry, thirsty, and her ribs hurt like hell. The last thing she appreciated were six hot guys laughing at her.

Mozart cleared his throat and was the first to speak. "Nothing's funny, Tiger. I suppose it's just that you remind us of our women. They're kind of like you. Spunky and motherly all at the same time."

Penelope looked at them in horror. "I'm not motherly."

Everyone but Benny was able to hold back their laughter. Benny snorted in disbelief and he mocked her in a remarkably good imitation. "How's the arm, Wolf?"

"Shut up. Just because I'm a decent human being doesn't mean I'm motherly. Admit it, you all wanted to know as well."

"Well, yeah, but you were the one who said it," Abe joked through his pain.

Penelope rolled her eyes. "Fine. I hope his arm falls off, and your head, and your leg," she groused, looking at Wolf, Benny, and Abe respectively.

"Come on, we need to work to get this area ready for us to spend the night. It's not ideal, but it'll have to do," Wolf said, interrupting the light joking.

Cookie and Dude got to work putting together a makeshift bunk for each of them while at the same time concealing them as much as possible.

Penelope sat next to Abe and did her best to clean, sew, and bandage his leg. The wound was jagged and deep, and her stitches wouldn't win any awards by the Cosmetology Center of America, but she didn't think Abe cared. More important than her sewing skills, she hoped the antibiotic cream and the antibiotics he'd swallowed would stave off any infection.

Since everyone was exhausted, they settled down fairly quickly after coming up with a rotation for who would stay up first on watch. They decided to schedule the watch in pairs, to make sure no one fell asleep. The last thing they needed was an insurgent sneaking up on the camp because someone was too tired and injured to stay awake. Penelope insisted on taking a turn as well, and she was relieved when Wolf didn't fight her on it and let her join one of the pairs on their shift.

The MRE she'd had for dinner was one of the best things Penelope remembered eating in all of her life. Oh, it wasn't gourmet food by any stretch of the imagination, but having been deprived of real calories and a somewhat balanced meal for so long, it was heaven. She could only eat about half of everything because her stomach had shrunk so much during her captivity, but she swore she could feel her body literally absorbing the nutrients as she ate. She'd been given a canteen of her own, filled with the most beautiful, tasting water she'd ever had the privilege of drinking. Yeah, it had a metallic taste from the purification tablets that had been used to make sure it was safe, but Penelope wasn't going to complain.

Finally, after they'd been quiet for a while, Wolf asked what she'd been expecting him to bring up for most of the day.

"So, Tiger...can you tell us what the hell happened? How did those bastards get their hands on you and the others?"

Penelope sighed. She didn't hesitate to tell the SEALs what happened. She'd waited a long time to tell someone, anyone, that she honestly didn't think it was their fault they were captured, that they weren't idiots who were running around the most dangerous section of the refugee camp as if they were at Disneyworld. "We were ordered to patrol the west side of the camp and look for trouble."

"By yourself? What idiot ordered that?" Dude asked immediately. After spending time in the camp looking for her, they obviously knew about the west side.

"Yeah. By ourselves. I protested the assignment as much as I could, but the major was new. New to the unit and new to combat. Granted, this wasn't really combat, but he had no idea how dangerous that side of the camp had gotten. The rest of us who had been there a while knew, and had been simply avoiding patrols over there. There really was no use. The thugs and terrorists had that side well and truly controlled, but the major decided that *he* knew best and our disagreeing was simply a matter of us being difficult. So we went."

Penelope shrugged and continued, "Thomas was the first to sense danger. We all knew we were closely watched while we patrolled, but he noticed that the same men watching us that day, had been following us the day before. While we'd been walking, they'd surrounded us, boxing us in. They had about twenty men to our four. We were sitting ducks. They beat the shit out of us and took our weapons. They dragged me off separately from the guys." Penelope tried to keep her voice emotionless and asked the question she already knew the answer to. "They're dead, aren't they?"

"Yeah," Dude confirmed.

Penelope didn't want to know any details, dead was dead, and continued on. "So they beat me up for a few days, then decided to throw me in front of the camera reading that asinine shit they called a manifesto or some such fucking thing. I did whatever they wanted and didn't put up a fight."

"Did they rape you?"

Cookie's words were pissed off and urgent...and to the point. Penelope figured there was some story there, but didn't ask and wasn't offended by the question. Hell, she was pretty surprised she hadn't been violated herself. "No. And before you ask, I'm not lying. They asked if I was a virgin, and I said no, which is the truth, by the way. I didn't want them trying to use me as a prize for some warped ideology they had. Of course, the suicide bomber is supposed to get the seventy-two virgins when they're *dead*, but I didn't want to risk someone trying to claim their virgin before they died."

"You know that's a myth right? Muslims don't really believe that," Cookie told her matter-of-factly.

"I know, but I had no idea what *these* guys thought. We all know the sun rises in the east and sets in the west, but if someone is brainwashed enough they can swear in front of a judge that it's the opposite."

The men nodded in understanding.

"Were you held at the camp the entire time?" It was Mozart who asked.

"Yeah, I'm pretty sure. It was hard to tell because in the beginning, I was pretty out of it from the beatings, but after they stopped that shit, I don't think they moved me much."

"The pink material was genius, by the way," Wolf told her.

Penelope half laughed. "Well, I don't know about genius, but I figured it couldn't hurt. I never thought my fancy underwear would be strewn across a refugee camp when I put it on all those months ago. When they mummified me up every time I went outside the tent, I knew no one would be able to tell it was me, and that any clue I could drop would help someone find me if they were looking."

"How'd you know we'd be looking?"

"Well, I didn't, not for sure. But I know my brother. Cade wouldn't let me disappear without a trace."

"You'll be glad to know you're correct. He's been all over the news back home. Making petitions, organizing rallies, sending letters to the President, basically being a pest of the highest order," Benny told her.

"Great, I bet he even dragged out my stupid college graduation picture, didn't he?"

Wolf smiled. "Yeah, if it's the picture of you and him standing next to each other with his elbow resting on your head and you laughing hysterically."

Penelope laughed. "That's the one. I hate that picture, but he loves it. And the rest of it certainly sounds like him, and while I was being held captive, I counted on it. He's worked his ass off to get where he is today. He's one of the best firefighters San Antonio has ever seen."

"But you're not biased or anything," Benny joked.

"I'm not biased," Penelope said in a dead-even voice. "Yes, I'm related to him, but I've seen him in action," Penelope insisted and tried to explain. "Once, we arrived at a building fully engulfed in flames on the top three floors, but someone said there might be a child trapped inside. I know it's his job, but none of the other firefighters there would go in. Cade didn't even hesitate, but plunged right into the house and found her and brought her out alive."

"Sounds impulsive and risky to me," Dude commented dryly.

"From the outside looking in, it probably does, but he doesn't do anything impulsively. Not even close. Cade knows fire. He knows how it behaves, and how it works. He's studied it and he has this weird sense for it. He told me afterwards that he could tell by the way it looked he knew he had time to get in, find the girl and get out. He's the least-impulsive man I've ever known in my life." Penelope knew her words were passionate, but she'd defend her brother to anyone, anytime. He was *that* good at what he did.

"Got anyone waiting for you back home?" Abe asked.

"Besides my family and fellow firefighters at Station 7 where I work? Nope. Between firefighting and the Army Reserves, I don't have a lot of extra time to date. Although after this, I think I'll be retiring from the Reserves. I'll be happy never to step foot outside Texas again."

Everyone chuckled lightly.

"What about you guys? I think you're all married, right? That's unusual for a SEAL team, isn't it?"

Wolf answered for the group. "Maybe. Being married to a SEAL isn't exactly a walk in the park. Our wives can't know where we're going or how long we'll be gone. Most can't handle the stress."

"But your wives can?" Penelope asked, genuinely curious.

"Yeah. Our wives can," Dude said firmly.

"That's great, really. Kids?"

"Yup. Abe's got two adopted daughters. They plucked them right out from under their worthless mother's nose and never looked back. Mozart has a six-month-old girl; Benny has two, a two-year-old daughter and a one-year-old son; and my wife is pregnant." Dude paused and laughed, but in a way Penelope could tell he wasn't amused. "Well, she was when I left. I was hoping to get home in time to see my daughter being born, but doesn't look like that's gonna happen now."

Penelope didn't know what to say. Sorry didn't seem to cut it, and besides, she wasn't the one who'd shot down their helicopter. Finally she said, somewhat lamely to her own ears, "They sound great."

"Yeah. They are great," Mozart agreed quietly.

The conversation seemed to dry up after that. Each lost in their own thoughts. Thinking about their loved ones and wondering when they'd get to see them again.

CHAPTER 16

iona paced the waiting room at the hospital. Because Faulkner wasn't available, Caroline was allowed to be in the delivery room with Cheyenne. They'd been there most of the day because no one wanted to take a chance on leaving and missing the birth of Cheyenne's baby. But after being cooped up all day, Jess had taken John and Sara out to get some fresh air, and Alabama had finally relented and taken Davisa and Brinique out to get something to eat. That left Summer with her infant daughter, Melody and Akilah, and Fiona...and Fiona couldn't sit still any longer.

Caroline had been periodically coming out with updates. Apparently the bleeding Cheyenne had at home when her water broke wasn't exactly serious, though the doctors were keeping their eye on it. But the women hadn't heard from Caroline in a while and Fiona was about to burst.

Just when Fiona didn't think she'd be able to stand it for a second longer, Caroline appeared in the doorway. She was as pale as the white tiles on the floor under their feet.

"Oh my God, is the baby okay? Cheyenne? What's wrong?" Fiona fretted, rushing over and grabbing Caroline's hands.

"The baby is perfect. Eight pounds, nine ounces—no wonder Shy looked like she was having triplets. Good lung sounds and all ten toes and fingers. Cutest little baby I've ever seen...including Jess's kids."

"Then what? What's wrong?" Fiona questioned.

"It's Cheyenne. She's bleeding and the doctors were having a hard time getting it stopped. They made me leave, but I heard the nurse tell the doctor she thought it was a postpartum hemorrhage."

Summer sucked in a sharp breath. "Oh my God, a hemorrhage? That doesn't sound good. Did they get it stopped?"

"I don't know. They kicked me out." Caroline took a deep breath, and when it came out, it was a sob. "She was s-s-so happy that the baby was fine, she'd b-b-been so worried. She held her in her arms and looked up at me and said she didn't feel so good. Then she went limp and just kinda faded away. I had to grab the baby so she didn't tumble out of Cheyenne's arms."

"Oh, Caroline, come 'ere." Fiona gathered Caroline in her arms and felt Melody crowd up against her back. Summer came up beside them and put one arm around Caroline's shoulders and held baby April in the other. The four women stood in the busy waiting room in each other's arms, trying to take strength and comfort from one another. Fiona could feel Caroline shuddering against her and felt so helpless to do anything for her or for their friend.

Caroline finally got herself together and pulled back. "We were so worried about the baby, we didn't even *think* about anything happening to Cheyenne. She's too young for this."

"I don't think age has anything to do with it," Summer said gently. "Should we call the others?"

"I think Jess and Alabama will be back soon anyway, let's not freak them out until we have more information," Fiona said, not knowing if it was the right decision or not. "Maybe by the time they get back, the doctors will have come out here and told us she'll be fine."

"Come on, let's sit. There's nothing we can do but wait," Melody cajoled, and they all wandered over to a group of chairs in the corner of the room.

Twenty minutes later, Jessyka returned with her toddlers and ten minutes after that, Alabama came over with Davisa and Brinique in tow. It was a somber group that waited to hear from the doctor. They should've been thrilled beyond belief about the healthy newborn baby, but instead they were hoping they wouldn't have to get a Red Cross message to Commander Hurt and try to get Faulkner home to bury his wife.

Another hour passed before the group heard anything else about Cheyenne, and by that time everyone was more than ready to hear some news. The kids were restless and their grumpiness was making everyone edgy.

A nurse finally came into the waiting room and asked for Cheyenne's family. All six women got up and when the nurse saw how many of them there were, she led them all into a more private conference room. She stood looking at the large group of women and children as if she didn't know where to start.

"For God's sake, just tell us," Caroline pleaded, not able to stand the suspense any longer. "How's Cheyenne? When can we see her?"

"As you all know, there were...complications. Cheyenne was bleeding so heavily that she had to be transferred to the operating room."

"Oh. My. God," Melody whispered, saying out loud what everyone in the room was thinking. "Is she still alive?"

Everyone's eyes were glued to the harried-looking nurse sent into the lion's den, so to speak, to notify the family of the patient's condition.

"I understand her husband is in the service and is out of the country on a mission?" At the nods all around her, she said gravely, "I recommend he be contacted as soon as possible. He needs to get home. Now."

The waiting room was silent for a beat until Caroline's soft inhale and her devastated words as she repeated Melody's question. "Is Cheyenne still alive?"

CHAPTER 17

*D*ude woke up suddenly and lurched forward, choking back a cry. "Holy shit," he whispered into the chilly night air.

"You all right, Dude?" Wolf asked from beside him.

Dude ran his hand down his face and tried to clear the all too real images from his brain, and noticed his hand was shaking. His hand was fucking *shaking*. He was the unflappable one. The one who took things in stride. The Dom who was always in control. But at the moment he felt anything but strong. "No," he answered his friend.

"Wanna talk?"

No, Dude didn't want to talk, but he did anyway, thinking maybe it'd help him get back on track. "I dreamed Cheyenne had the baby."

"That's good, right?" Wolf asked, propping himself up on his uninjured elbow and keeping his voice quiet so he wouldn't disturb the others.

"Yeah, but right after she was born, Cheyenne looked up at me, said she loved me and to make sure the baby knew how much she was loved by her mom, then closed her eyes and fucking died. Right there in front of me. I could hear our baby crying in the background and everything."

"It was just a dream, Dude. You're stressed about not being able to be there," Wolf said, trying to soothe his friend.

"Yeah, a dream. But it seemed too fucking real."

Wolf didn't know what to say to that. They both had seen some crazy shit in their lives, things some people would say were impossible. Because of that, they both knew that maybe Dude's dream wasn't so much a dream as it was foreshadowing. Finally, he told Dude in an earnest voice, "I'm doing everything I can to get us home."

"I know." Dude rubbed his hand down his face once more, feeling the beard that had grown in the weeks they'd been gone. Changing the subject, he asked, "How far north should we go?" Dude knew as well as Wolf that they needed to gain higher ground and find a good place to dig in and defend themselves. If push came to shove and they got into a fire-fight, they'd eventually lose, simply because they didn't have enough ammunition to outlast the insurgents. Their best bet was to hunker down and stay undetected long enough for Tex, and the government, to send in another chopper to get them the hell out of dodge.

"How far north?" Wolf repeated. "As far as we can. It's unlikely we can stay under their radar forever, especially since they could have thermal imaging and there are seven of us. If it was only one or two of us we could probably stay undetected, but we can't leave Benny and Abe alone, and I can't do much with this broken arm, so we have to stick together."

"As if we'd break up," Dude snorted.

Wolf smiled grimly. They both knew there was no way in hell they'd ever leave any of the others behind. They were too close to do that, and besides, they'd been trained way too well.

"What do you make of Tiger?" Dude asked. "Think she's telling the truth about not being violated?"

"Yeah, I do," Wolf said immediately, turning to look at the woman sleeping on the ground a bit away from them. They could hear her slightly snoring, but she was clearly out, sleeping the sleep of a woman who knows she's safe for the moment. "She's one tough cookie. I think she'd be more leery around us if she'd been raped."

"I agree to a point, but I also think she'd keep going until she fell over just so she wouldn't look weak in our eyes," Dude pointed out. "I've seen women like this before. They don't want to look weak in any way, so they'll lie and hide their pain, feelings, or thoughts, no matter how many times they're asked if they're okay."

Wolf knew Dude was talking about his experience as a Dominant, and he had a good point, but somehow Wolf knew in his gut, he was wrong this time. "Turner isn't the kind of soldier, or woman, to keep her thoughts inside. If she was upset, she wouldn't be afraid to let us know. Yesterday when she was hungry, she asked for something to eat. You told me yourself the first thing she did when you showed up in her tent, was ask for something to drink."

Dude nodded. "True."

Wolf continued, "She reminds me a lot of Caroline. She'll fight to the death to survive and to get respect. I think that's why she's so successful as a firefighter."

"Yeah."

"If you guys are done talking about me, can we get a move on or what?"

Dude and Wolf looked up in surprise, seeing Penelope was awake and leaning up on an elbow watching them.

"Yeah, as soon as we get the others up, we can finalize the plan for the day." Wolf didn't bother to apologize for talking about her. He smiled a bit at the scowl that moved across her face.

"Great," Penelope muttered and sat up, holding her ribs and groaning. She ignored her pain, as it was manageable, and moved over to Abe who was waking up as well. "How's the leg feel? Can I look at it?"

"Knock yourself out, Tiger." Abe's spoke quietly and if Penelope hadn't spent a lot of time taking care of injured people, she would've been fooled by his nonchalant tone of voice. He was in pain. A lot of it. She eased his ripped pants to the side and unwound the bandages she'd put on earlier. Penelope grimaced at the look of the wound.

"Fuck," Cookie said from behind her in a hushed voice.

Abe didn't pick his head up off the ground. "It's infected, isn't it?" he asked evenly.

"Yeah," Cookie agreed.

Penelope interrupted their monosyllable conversation. "Well, us swearing at it isn't going to magically make it any better. Cookie, think you can get me some more of those alcohol pads? And what kind of painkillers do we have? He needs something if we're going to get his ass up this mountain and to a safer place."

"Yes, ma'am," Cookie said with a smile on his face. There wasn't anything to smile about, but Penelope was so darn cute and feisty, he couldn't help it.

"I think—" Abe started, but Penelope interrupted him.

"No."

"No what?" Abe asked in confusion.

"No to whatever you were going to say. It was going to be bullshit," Penelope told him without rancor, still concentrating on his leg.

Benny laughed from the sitting position he'd pulled himself into when he'd woken up. "She's got you pegged, Abe."

"Fuck off," Abe told his teammate and closed his eyes, but didn't resume saying whatever it was that had been on his mind.

Penelope smiled, enjoying the camaraderie of the men; it reminded her of the guys she worked with back in San Antonio. Taco and Driftwood were the comedians of the group, always ready with a quick comeback and joke. Chief was a lot like Wolf, in charge of them all, but also their friend too. Squirrel and Crash were like brothers to her, and of course Cade, otherwise known as Sledge, *was* her brother. Moose was quiet and introspective, but never missed anything going on around him. She missed them all fiercely, and would do whatever she could to get back to them and to hear their ribbing and joking around the station.

It was Wolf who handed her the alcohol pads from the first-aid kit. Penelope set to work trying to clean Abe's wound without hurting him too much, while Cookie injected more painkillers and antibiotics into his veins.

"Okay, we're going to continue to head up today, much as we did yesterday. We'll stop more often to drink and to check everyone's wounds. We need to be as close to one hundred percent as we can get if we're gonna make it out of here. Benny, you need to let us know if you continue to be dizzy or if you get nauseous. Dude, wrap your ankle up tight, but don't overdo it. When we stop, you need to put it up to try to keep the swelling down. Abe, talk to us about that leg. I don't want it falling off somewhere along the trail." The others chuckled at that, and Wolf continued, "Tiger, we'll wrap your ribs before we set out, but unfortunately there's not too much we can do about them. If you need something for the pain, let us know. You'll need to drink more than us as well, you have a lot of catching up to do. Also, make sure you continuously snack as the day goes on as well. You might be smaller than us, but you need the calories and energy."

Penelope nodded. Wolf was right, and he wasn't telling her anything she didn't already know she needed to do if she was going to be able to continue on and carry her own weight. Even though this was her rescue, she'd do whatever it took to not be a burden.

"I'll monitor my arm. It hurts, but it's not unbearable. You guys set it perfectly," Wolf complimented, looking at Penelope and Cookie. "We need to find a good hidey-hole today. If those bastards do have thermals, we'll need to be able to get far enough back and out of sight of anyone that might be scanning the area. But at the same time, we need to be able to get out and to a rescue chopper at a moment's notice. Everyone keep your eyes open."

At the nods all around, the group got ready to head out. The day was going to be tough, but as every SEAL knew, the only easy day was yesterday.

CHAPTER 18

$\mathcal{J}$ess and Summer sat with their babies, and the others stood around the small conference room, waiting for the nurse to continue telling them what was going on with Cheyenne. Akilah was once again a lifesaver, taking over the entertainment of Sara.

"Cheyenne was transferred to the operating room as a precaution. Basically PPH is a condition where the uterus doesn't contract properly after giving birth. We gave her some painkillers and hand-delivered the placenta. Usually once the placenta is out, the uterus will start to contract on its own, and the bleeding will stop," the nurse explained slowly and carefully, looking at each woman to make sure they understood.

When everyone nodded, she continued. "We gave her some medicine to try to assist the uterus to contract, and thus stop the bleeding on its own, with no luck. The bleeding slowed, but didn't stop. Finally after a blood transfusion, and more specialized drugs, the bleeding stopped. We didn't have to do a hysterectomy, which was the next step if we couldn't get the bleeding stopped with these other measures."

"Oh my God, a hysterectomy," Jessyka breathed, putting a hand on her own still-flat stomach as if she could protect the baby growing there from the word.

"Yeah, but we didn't need to go that far. Cheyenne is fine for now. She's sleeping off the painkillers. I recommend getting her husband home as soon as possible because when she woke up, she was asking for him. She had a really close call today, and honestly, she's not completely out of the woods yet. She'll continue to get fluids and drugs to make sure her uterus stays contracted. She's going to need to stay here probably tonight and tomorrow night. After that, the doctor will take a look and see what she thinks about letting her go home. But once home, she'll need to take it easy and get lots of sleep, fluids, and good nutritious food. No fast food and no junk food for at least a couple of weeks. She'll need to rest and not overdo anything. It's been my experience that new moms want to get back into their normal routine as soon as possible, but that's not in her best interest. The doctor will prescribe some prenatal vitamins as well to make sure her folic acid and iron intake are high."

"Will she be able to breastfeed?" Summer asked.

"Of course. Nothing else about the care of her daughter will change." When everyone nodded in relief, the nurse continued. "If anyone has any other questions, don't hesitate to ask the nurse on duty on her floor. She's going to be in ICU tonight, and most likely in the morning she'll be moved to a regular floor. Only one of you will be able to see her tonight, but once she's completely awake and out of the woods, and she's moved to a regular room, you'll all be able to visit her...but I recommend not all at the same time."

This time the women in the room laughed lightly, relieved that it sounded like Cheyenne was going to be all right.

"Can we see baby?" Akilah asked.

The nurse turned to her and agreed. "Yes, but again, maybe take turns? There are a lot of you here."

"We will," Caroline reassured the friendly nurse. "Thank you for taking the time to talk to us and reassure us about Cheyenne. I'm not sure we can get her husband, or any of our husbands home right now, but we'll take care of her until he *can* get home. We'll take turns staying with her and browbeating her to take it easy. It's what we do best."

"You're more than welcome. And it's very nice to see that she's got such great friends. And by the way, thank you all for your husbands' service to our country. While they might be the ones doing the actual fighting, I know spouses also make a lot of sacrifices. So thank you."

The women all nodded their heads and watched as the nurse left the room. It was always nice to be included in the thanks, even if, as the nurse said, they weren't the ones out on the front lines.

"Caroline, you and Akilah and Melody go first to see Baby Cooper," Fiona said decisively. "We'll wait until you get back."

"Are you sure?" Caroline asked, looking around at the group of women in the room.

"Of course," Jessyka enthused. "We'll wait."

"Hey, Caroline, what did Cheyenne name the baby?" Alabama asked quietly.

"I don't know," Caroline answered. "She didn't have time before she passed out. The doctor had just put the baby in her arms and she was counting her fingers and toes when it happened."

Alabama laughed a little. "Figures. We'll just have to keep calling her Baby Cooper until Cheyenne can wake up and tell the doctor what to put on the birth certificate."

"Taylor!" Davisa said in the silence of the room.

"What, honey? Alabama asked her daughter.

"Taylor. It's the baby's name."

Alabama tried to let her new daughter down easily so she wasn't disappointed. "Davisa, that's a great name, but Cheyenne and Faulkner probably have a name in mind already."

"Taylor," the five-year-old insisted again stubbornly.

"We'll see," Alabama said, trying to head off a tantrum. All the other mothers in the room laughed, recognizing the avoidance technique.

"Okay, we'll be back. Alabama, Jess, and Summer, you guys need to get your kids home and to bed. We'll be quick and you can take your turn. Fiona and I will stay the night and the rest of you can come back tomorrow," Caroline said, trying to organize the group.

"I stay too," Akilah insisted.

Caroline looked at Melody, who was looking at her daughter, deciding whether or not they should stay. Finally she nodded. "Yeah, we'll stay with you guys too."

"Okay, it's a plan. We'll hurry and you guys can see the new baby and get out of here."

Everyone agreed and the trio headed out of the conference room and continued toward the viewing room where the babies were kept while waiting to go home with their new moms and dads.

When they were on their way, Caroline asked Melody quietly, "Are you going to call Tex? I can call the commander if you take care of Tex."

Melody nodded. "Yeah, I'll do it as soon as we see Cheyenne's baby."

They both knew Tex would do what he could to get word to the team about Cheyenne's condition and the birth of Faulkner's daughter. Melody remembered the news story about the crashed helicopter, and decided once again to keep it to herself. This was no time to bring it up, and besides, it might not be at all relevant anyway.

CHAPTER 19

*P*enelope looked around the cave with a critical eye. It wasn't huge, but it was big enough for all seven of them to fit inside comfortably. Cookie and Mozart had been mostly carrying Abe by the time they'd come up on the hole in the side of the mountain. Wolf was the one who spotted the cave first.

It was about halfway up a steep, rocky incline and the opening was only partly visible from where they'd been hiking. Cookie, Mozart, and Wolf had headed up the uneven terrain to check it out. They'd returned thirty minutes later with the news that they thought it would work.

Penelope felt bad for Cookie and Mozart, as they ended up making *three* trips up the mountainside, helping their teammates hoof it to their new hidey-hole.

There were some scrub bushes growing alongside the opening, giving them a place to take care of personal business. There was no clear or easy way to continue up the side of the mountain if they needed to make a quick exit, but there were a lot more of the scrub bushes that could give some cover if they needed it.

Penelope didn't want to ask, but she couldn't help it. She was never one to hold back when she had questions, so she didn't even try. "What now?"

"What now?" Mozart repeated.

284

"Yeah, what now? We're sitting tight in this hole in a rock, but for how long? What's the plan?"

"The plan is to wait," Wolf answered calmly.

"Wait?" Penelope asked incredulously. "For what?"

"Tex."

Penelope massaged her temples. "Who the fuck is Tex? That's like the third time you've mentioned him. And you should all know, I'm not good at waiting."

None of the men tensed up, none of them looked upset in any way. It was Cookie who answered, but not in the way Penelope would've thought. "About two and a half years or so ago, we were in Mexico on a rescue mission. We were sent in to rescue a young woman who'd been kidnapped. When we got there, we found another woman who had also been kidnapped, but no one was looking for her. We ended up all getting out of the country without any injuries."

He paused, and that gave Penelope enough time to ask, "I don't under-stand what—"

"Listen, Tiger," Wolf scolded.

Penelope shut her mouth and nodded, holding back her frustration at the cryptic answer to her question.

"Fiona seemed to be all right on the outside. She was brave and stoic, much as you are, Penelope. She'd been drugged and fought the addiction and came through the other side. I didn't follow my instincts and thought she was good. We left on a mission and Fee had a flashback. She thought she was back in Mexico and she ran. Ran from phantom kidnappers who only existed in her mind. I was out of the country and couldn't get back home for at least a day and a half. In the meantime, she was out there, alone, freaked-out, and suffering."

Cookie took a deep breath, then continued, "Tex found her. He tracked her down and kept her safe until I could get home. I trust Tex with my life, with my wife's life, with my teammates' lives and with their women's lives. Tex will find us. I'd stake everything I own, including my life, on it."

"You *are* staking your life on it," Penelope murmured, still not one hundred percent sure they should put all their proverbial eggs into Tex's basket.

"Tiger, each of us sitting here today owes everything to Tex. He's been responsible in some way for helping each of us save the lives of our wives.

I can guarantee that right this moment he's doing everything he can to bring us home," Benny said seriously.

Penelope looked at the SEAL who so far had been the quietest as he continued speaking.

"We don't ask, he doesn't tell, but we all know what he does isn't quite legal, but none of us give a fuck. He knows people. He used to be a SEAL himself, but he works with the CIA, FBI, Delta Force, the Rangers, and I wouldn't be surprised if he didn't personally know some fucking terrorist over here in Iraq who owes him a favor. If he has to, Tex will mobilize every single one of them to get us the fuck out of here. You just have to have faith."

"It's not in me to trust," Penelope said honestly, "but I trust *you* guys. You got me out of that hellhole I was being held in. If you say I should trust this Tex person, I will."

"Good," Benny nodded in satisfaction.

"But..."

All six men groaned and Penelope couldn't help but smile. They were all such...guys, it wasn't funny. "Do we have a plan for what we're gonna do if the insurgents find us before Tex gets the cavalry here?"

"Yeah. Stay alive."

Penelope growled in frustration at Abe's response. She shook her head. "Never mind. Jesus."

Wolf spoke up again. "We've all got ammo and weapons, Tiger. We'll fight whoever dares show their face near this hole. We aren't just gonna sit here and let someone kill us."

"What if they use an RPG?" Penelope asked, voicing one of her greatest fears.

"They might."

Penelope wasn't reassured by Wolf's comment, but he continued before she could say anything.

"But it's a chance we're going to have to take. We'll hang low until we absolutely have to engage them in battle. If luck is with us, the worst they have is grenades."

"Shit," Penelope whispered, horrified, imagining one of the insidious little devices being lobbed into the cave and blowing up, killing them all.

"Fuck," Dude said under his breath. "Way to freak her out, Wolf."

"Look," Wolf cautioned, "There's no guarantee we'll come out of this alive, but if you follow our lead, we'll get you out, we *have* had experience in this shit."

Penelope thought about it and decided to let it go. Wolf was right. She was grilling them over something they couldn't possibly predict. They were trained SEALs. When put into a dangerous situation, they acted, just as she did when she was thrust into a situation inside a burning building. If they were civilians inside a burning building, would she want them asking as many questions as she had been of these men? No. It would just piss her off. She'd tell them to trust her and follow her lead.

She took a deep breath and said, "You're right. I'll do whatever you tell me to do if the shit hits the fan. Promise."

Wolf nodded in relief. "Good."

An uneasy silence fell over the group as they all waited for something...anything...to happen.

* * *

TEX CONCENTRATED on the computer screen in front of him. He'd worked with Keane "Ghost" Bryson on a mission in the past. The Delta Force soldier was damn good at his job and had actually saved Tex's life. They hadn't talked in person after that mission, but they had kept in touch periodically over the years electronically.

Commander Hurt already had intel that the helicopter had crashed, but hadn't known where. Tex passed along the coordinates and knew the SEAL team that was already in the country was being mobilized, but Tex had a gut feeling his friends were going to need additional backup.

It seemed obvious that Wolf and his team had left four trackers with four people who were either injured or dead, and had kept the last one for themselves. There was no way they'd split up otherwise. Tex watched as the single red dot made its way north, away from the others. The question was, who was with each of the trackers.

If Wolf needed additional backup, that's exactly what he was going to do his best to send to them. The SEALs couldn't have crashed in a worse place. They'd landed smack-dab in the middle of Insurgent Central. It was as if they'd been plunked down on top of a hornets' nest...and slowly but surely the hornets were swarming out of that nest looking for what had disturbed them.

But that's where Ghost and his Delta Force team came in. Tex contacted Ghost as soon as he hung up with the commander. He'd listened to Tex's concerns and immediately got in touch with *his* commander. The government typically didn't work that quickly, but

Ghost and his Delta Force team obviously had a lot of pull and within a few hours, the Deltas were on their way to the Middle East.

Tex kept his eyes on the screen. On the left side there were four motionless blinking red dots and one lone red dot getting further and further away from the others. On the right side of the screen was a satellite picture. A surprisingly crisp and clear picture. Tex had hacked into the government's top-secret satellites and was looking at a live feed over the mountains of Turkey. He looked on, helpless, as shadowy figures moved closer and closer to the four unmoving dots hidden on the hillside.

He held his breath in frustration, knowing all he could do was watch.

CHAPTER 20

*I*t's been two days since reports of a helicopter crashing in the mountains between Turkey and Iraq. There hasn't been any confirmation of who was onboard that helicopter or of any casualties as a result of the crash. The President has been close-lipped about the incident and, unusually, there have been no leaked reports of any kind.

No terrorist group has claimed responsibility for the crash yet, and even ISIS has been silent.

You might remember that Sergeant Penelope Turner was kidnapped by ISIS terrorists and has been seen fairly regularly in propaganda videos. News of Sergeant Turner's fate is still unknown as of now, but there's speculation of a connection between the helicopter crash and Sergeant Turner.

Stay tuned for our report at ten, where we delve deeper into the life of a Navy SEAL and what goes into preparing for a rescue attempt. We will be interviewing a retired member of SEAL Team Six, which, as you know, was one of the main forces behind the mission that finally killed Osama Bin Laden in 2011.

* * *

CHEYENNE LOOKED up at one of her best friends as she held her new baby in her arms and said, "I dreamed I was lying in bed and I looked up at Faulkner, told him I loved him and to make sure our baby knew how much I loved her. Then I closed my eyes and died."

Jessyka sat next to Cheyenne's bed and squeezed her free hand tightly. "But you're here now."

Cheyenne nodded, but didn't say anything for a long while. She simply looked down at her daughter lovingly.

Jess finally broke the silence. "So...are you going to put us out of our misery and tell us what you named your beautiful daughter?"

Jess was horrified to see tears rise in Cheyenne's eyes and roll down her face.

"Oh my God, what is it? What'd I say?" Jess asked frantically, concerned she'd said something to upset her friend.

Cheyenne looked up at Jess again. "It's s-stupid. I just...I just thought I'd be sitting here with Faulkner. That we'd greet our baby together, we'd fill out her birth certificate together."

Jess leaned over and held Cheyenne as best she could with the baby between them. She whispered in her ear as she held her friend, "Seriously, I *know*. But he'll be home soon and you'll have a ton of other memories to make together. It sucks that he's not here, but think about how you now get to hand her to him when he *does* get home and introduce him to his daughter for the first time. It's not the same, but it'll be special in its own way."

Jess felt Cheyenne nod against her and sniff once. She pulled back and reached over for a tissue. She wiped Cheyenne's tears from her face and then handed it over so she could blow her nose. Once her friend had gotten control over her emotions, Jess asked again, "So...you gonna tell me her name, or keep it a secret forever and make me call your daughter 'girl' for the rest of her life?"

Cheyenne smiled, as she knew Jess had planned for her to. "Taylor Caroline Cooper."

Jess looked startled for a moment, then beamed. "Holy crap. Davisa told me that's what you were going to call her, but I didn't believe her. Have you told Caroline yet?"

"That kid is smart, and no, I haven't told Caroline yet."

"Promise I can be there when you do."

Cheyenne laughed softly. "Promise."

Jess hugged her friend one more time, then stood up. "Okay, I have to get back to my monsters now, but we'll all be back this afternoon to take both of you to Caroline's house."

"Oh, but I thought—"

"Nope," Jess interrupted. "I know you thought you were going home, but you aren't. The doctor said you needed to take it easy and we all know if we let you go home, you won't. And until Faulkner is back, we're going to make sure you follow the doc's instructions to a tee."

"I won't—"

Jess interrupted again, "Yes, you would. But now you won't."

Cheyenne sighed in mock agitation and huffed, "Fine."

"Fine." Jess smiled. "So as I was saying, we'll be back this afternoon to bring you home to Caroline's. Be good and I'll see you in a bit. I've called the nurse and she's gonna come and get Taylor. You need some rest before we spring you from here."

"Okay. Thanks, Jess."

"No thanks necessary. You scared the hell out of us. We're just glad you're all right, and we're planning on making sure you stay that way."

"You're acting as bossy as Faulkner."

"Ha, as if," Jess snorted. "That man has cornered the market on bossy… and you love it."

"I do. Any word?"

Jess knew what Cheyenne meant. "No. Nothing."

"Did you ask Melody?"

Jess shook her head. "No. I don't really want to pressure her about it. I don't want her to feel like she's a middle-man between us and what Tex knows."

Cheyenne nodded. "Yeah, it's not fair of us to ask, is it?"

"Not really, but I'm sure she'd tell us if she knew anything."

"Hummmm." Cheyenne didn't agree or disagree with Jess. She'd only seen Melody once since she'd woken up in the hospital, but the worried lines around her mouth and the smile that didn't seem to be as honest as usual made her think Melody knew more than she was saying. But she let it go. "Thanks for everything. I'll see you later."

Jess nodded and left, smiling at the nurse who was arriving to take little Taylor back to the nursery.

* * *

MELODY SAT in the room Caroline and Wolf had set up like a little apartment in the basement of their house with her back against the wall and her knees bent up with her arms around them. There was a perfectly good bed and chair she could've sat on, but for some reason she felt more comfortable curled up where she was. Melody held the phone up to her ear, fingers white against the plastic.

"You haven't heard from them?" she asked Tex, voice wobbling.

"No."

Melody knew Tex was deliberately being vague, but his vagueness wasn't reassuring her at all. "Do you think they're alive?"

"Yes."

"How do you know if you haven't heard from them?"

"Mel," Tex's voice was quiet and reassuring, "they might be your friends' husbands, and you might know them as those kids' fathers who go ga-ga over every little move they make, but I know them as lethal, bad-ass Navy SEALs."

Melody could read between Tex's words. "Right."

"I love you, baby. Don't worry about this. Well, as much as possible. I honestly don't know what's going on, but rest assured I'm doing everything in my power to get them home. Okay?"

"Okay, Tex."

"Now, how's my girl?"

Melody smiled, loving how much Tex loved Akilah. "She's good. I've been helping her with her prosthetic every night, even though she really doesn't need my help much anymore. She's been great with Jess's kids and little Sara has really taken to her."

"Yeah?"

"Yeah."

Tex was silent a moment, then said, "I've been thinking about it. We talked about it before Akilah came into our lives, but we haven't had a chance since then. But I want a baby with you, Melody. I want a daughter with your blonde hair, your beautiful eyes and features running around. I'd love to give Akilah a little sister of her own."

When Melody didn't say anything, Tex asked worriedly, "Mel?" Then he heard a sniff. Oh shit. "Mel? I'm sorry, I didn't mean to make you cry."

"Did you mean it?"

"Every last word."

"I want that too," Melody breathed, wiping away the tears from her face.

"Thank fuck," Tex said under his breath. "When are you coming home?"

"Cheyenne comes home from the hospital today. We were going to go and stay with Jess to help her with John and Sara. I didn't really have a date in mind, but now I want to come home tomorrow."

Tex chuckled. "There's no rush, Mel. You need to go off the pill, and it could take a while for you to get pregnant anyway."

"I know, but that doesn't mean that I don't want to enjoy the process."

"Jesus, Mel. Seriously…you can't do this to me."

Melody giggled. "Okay, sorry. How about this. I'll stay for another week. That'll give you time to hopefully get the guys home, we'll be able to help Jess and spend time with the rest of the girls."

"Sounds good."

"Okay, but Tex…"

"Yeah, baby?"

"Think Amy will look after Akilah for a weekend when we get home? I'd like to give the baby-making thing my best shot, and that's easier if our daughter isn't in the next room."

"I'll call her as soon as we hang up, but consider it done. Amy's your best friend, she'd do anything for you. Fuck, I love you, Mel."

Melody smiled and hugged her knees harder. "And I love you too. Kiss Baby for me."

"I will. She's been whining at the front door every night. She obviously misses you." Tex's voice turned serious. "Stay strong, Mel. Those men are coming home sooner rather than later if I have anything to say about it."

"I know. You're Super Tex. You'll do your thing."

"Text me to let me know what you're up to."

"I will. Love you, Tex."

"Love you to Vegas and back. Stay safe."

"Bye."

"Bye."

Melody clicked off the phone and put her head on her knees. So many emotions were coursing through her brain, she didn't know which to process first. Worry for her friends, satisfaction that Akilah was settling in, happiness that Cheyenne was going to be okay and had a healthy new baby, love for her husband, *lust* for her husband, and a deep-seated contentment that Tex wanted a baby with her.

She sighed and finally stood up. It was time to go get Cheyenne and her newborn and get them settled.

CHAPTER 21

$\mathcal{T}$he echo of a gunshot startled Penelope and she sat upright in confusion. Looking around, she saw Dude and Cookie lying on their stomachs at the front of the cave. Mozart and Benny were nowhere to be seen. Wolf was standing at the side of the cave, his pistol in his hand by his side. Every now and then he'd lean and peek out, then bring his head back inside.

Abe lay still and quiet behind her. He hadn't gotten any better, no matter how many antibiotics they'd pumped into him. His leg needed more attention than they could give him in the field. Penelope worried that if they didn't get him real medical care, at the very least, he could lose his leg, at worst…his life.

More shots rang out and Penelope flinched again, but forced herself to crawl over to Wolf's side. "What's up?" she whispered, feeling stupid for trying to be quiet, but not able to help herself. They were hiding, it seemed like the right thing to do, but there was no way anyone would be able to hear her with the distance the gunshots were from their location.

"Gunshots." Wolf's answer was short and succinct.

"No shit, Sherlock," was Penelope's irritated response. When no one laughed, she got serious. "Are they shooting at us?"

"No."

Penelope sighed. Getting information out of these men was like pulling teeth. She lay on her stomach, ignoring the twinges from her ribs, and crawled over to Dude and Cookie. She peered out of the cave and saw nothing. "Who are they shooting at?"

"Don't know."

"Is that good or bad?" Penelope asked.

"Could go either way," Dude told her.

"So what're we doing?"

"Waiting," Cookie answered.

"Waiting sucks," Penelope murmured, backing away from the front of the cave and heading back over to Abe. She wanted to take another look at his leg. She'd clean it again, hopefully that would help in some way.

* * *

GHOST HELD up his hand to signal his team to stop. They'd HALO'd into the country and made their way toward the coordinates Tex had sent to them. Ghost respected the hell out of Tex. He was someone who Ghost was happy to know. He was a man who knew how to get things done. And if Tex wanted a favor, Ghost and the rest of his team were more than happy to grant it. Lord knew he'd helped them out more than once.

Fletch and Coach fanned out to his right and Hollywood and Beatle came up on his left flank. Ghost knew Blade and Truck were protecting their rear. He crouched down and waited for the insurgents to show themselves. None of them figured they'd be able to march right up to where Tex said there should be at least four men without running into trouble. Soon enough, that trouble made itself known.

The warning came through his earpiece just as the first gunshot rang out through the mountainside. The Delta Force team quickly made their way toward the firefight, adrenaline coursing through their blood, ready for a fight.

The sound of gunfire was sporadic and loud as it echoed through the hills. Instead of rushing in with guns blazing, Ghost and his team operated like the apparition their leader was named for. Four terrorists were dead before they'd even comprehended someone was behind them. Ghost motioned for Fletch and Beatle to make their way west, and he, Coach, and Blade made their way east. Truck and Hollywood quietly headed up toward where they hoped they'd find the missing SEALs.

The operatives made short work of the remaining terrorists in the area, knowing full well more were probably on their way as they headed up to meet their teammates.

"Five to one," Ghost heard in his ear.

"One, this is five, go ahead," he responded.

"All clear to approach."

"Clear." Ghost knew the other men heard the exchange and they carefully made their way up to where the SEALs were supposed to be. They arrived to find four men, not six, and no kidnapped Army sergeant to be seen.

They were surprised to realize it was the Night Stalker crew of the helicopter. The copilot and the gunner were deceased. The pilot and crew chief were alive, but in bad shape. They'd been the ones shooting back at the terrorists and defending their position.

Ghost crouched down next to the pilot and watched as Truck checked him over and started first aid on him. He looked over to the crew chief and watched as Beatle did what he could to make that man comfortable. "Sit rep?" he asked the pilot.

"Eleven on board. RPG came out of nowhere and we went down. Copilot was killed in the crash."

"Status of the others?"

"Honestly, I'm not sure," the pilot told Ghost in a dim, pained voice. "I was mostly out of it. They spoke to us before they left, but not what their plan was. Some of them were injured."

"The female?"

"Safe, Sir."

Something loosened inside Ghost knowing that Sergeant Turner had apparently been rescued, but he didn't let on. "They left you here?" His words were obviously not as toneless and emotionless as he wanted them to be when the pilot hurried to reassure him.

"Yes, but not like you might be thinking. They told me about the trackers they were leaving with us and made sure we knew the odds. We encouraged them to go. If they tried to take us with them, all of our chances would have been shit."

Ghost nodded. He didn't want to think badly of the SEALs. Thank God they were operating all on the same page. "Did they say where they were going?"

"Nothing other than up. They wanted to take a defensible position against the insurgents and figured their best chance would be up in one of the caves. They also hoped their moving would lead the terrorists away from us."

Ghost nodded, knowing it was what he would've done if he was in their position too. He thought quickly about their next plan of action. He wasn't going to leave these men here, not if he could help it.

He stood and headed off to the side and motioned for his men to follow. They gathered together out of hearing of the injured Night Stalkers.

He did what he always did, laid out their options so they could decide as a team their next steps. "One, we leave the Night Stalkers here and head up to find the SEALs and our sergeant. Two, we take the Night Stalkers with us and head up to find the SEALs and our sergeant. Three, we call in for a helo to pick up the Night Stalkers and after they're up and away, we continue north to the SEALs and our sergeant. Four, we split up and three of us stay here with the Night Stalkers, and the rest of us head north. When we find the SEALs, we head back down here then call for pickup."

Ghost's men answered immediately with exactly the option he figured they would.

"Three," Hollywood said.

"Three," Beatle confirmed.

"Three," Blade also agreed.

The others chimed in with their agreement as well and everyone chose option three, without hesitation. There was no way they'd leave their comrades behind for the terrorists to get their hands on. Delta Force teams were under the umbrella of the U.S. Army, but all Special Forces teams were all brothers at heart.

The SEAL team planting mysterious trackers on the injured Army crew saved at least two men's lives. Ghost knew he'd be having a conversation with Tex about the trackers, and what the fuck an elite Navy SEAL team was doing wearing them on a top-secret mission. It was obviously not sanctioned by anyone at JSOC or the Navy, but at the moment he was damn glad for them.

Ghost nodded at his team, knowing they'd made the right decision, and reached for his radio. The right decision wasn't necessarily the safest decision, but they'd deal with any fallout as it came.

Two hours and two skirmishes with insurgents later, an MH-60 came screaming over the nearest hill toward them. If Ghost hadn't been used to it, it would've scared the shit out of him. Fletch and Coach grabbed the two deceased men, and Hollywood and Truck helped the two injured men into the helicopter. They'd barely handed the soldiers into the arms of the men waiting inside the chopper when it took off back the way it came. The entire rescue operation took about two-point-five minutes.

When the sound of the helicopter faded into the mountains, Ghost looked at his team. "Playtime's over. Let's go get our soldier back."

The others nodded, faces determined. It wouldn't matter how many terrorists got in their way. It was time to bring Sergeant Penelope Turner home.

CHAPTER 22

R eports have come in about the helicopter crash we reported on last night in the mountains between Turkey and Iraq. A confidential source has reported to us that there were four men brought to Ramstein Air Base in Germany, two deceased and two injured. We have not been able to confirm their identities, but our source says they were in the helicopter when it crashed. There's no word on whether any of the four people were female. We will continue to try to get more information and to see if Sergeant Penelope Turner was among the wounded or deceased who were aboard the helicopter when it went down. Tune in later tonight.

* * *

CAROLINE STOOD in front of the small television in her and Matthew's bedroom and gasped after hearing the newscaster's latest story. It didn't say a lot, but it said enough. Helicopter crash. Two men dead, two men hurt, not a lot of information. Of course, there were six on Wolf's team, but the news could've gotten their information wrong.

She could feel her heart beating way too hard, but no tears would come. She stood staring at the TV, even though there was a silly ad on. Caroline wasn't seeing it, she was lost in her own worry and fear for her husband and her friends' husbands.

"Hey, Caroline, where can I find… Caroline?" Melody's words tapered off when she saw her friend standing in the middle of her bedroom, arms around her waist, whimpering softly. Melody went to her and put one arm around her, and put a hand lightly on Caroline's cheek and turned her face so she could see it clearly. "What is it, Caroline?" Melody whispered.

She watched as Caroline blinked once, then twice, before literally pulling herself together in front of Melody's eyes. "What? Um…"

Melody let go of Caroline's face, but turned to the TV as the news came back on. Suddenly realizing what might have been wrong, Melody asked carefully, "Did they have a report on the helicopter crash in the Middle East?"

At her words, Caroline turned suddenly and looked her in the eyes. "Yes."

"What'd they say?" Melody said softly.

"Two injured, two dead. They brought them to Ramstein Air Base in Germany."

"Any other information?"

"No."

Melody paused. "I don't have any information, Caroline, but for what it's worth, Tex thinks they're coming home."

Both women knew they were skirting the edge of what they promised they'd never do, speculate about their men's missions, but realizing they each knew more than they'd admitted up until now was a relief.

"It's worth a lot," Caroline told her. They hugged each other tightly and didn't let go until they heard a knock on the door. It was Akilah.

"Did you find paper plates?"

Caroline pulled back and looked at Melody questioningly.

Melody shrugged. "I came up to ask if you had any and where they might be. We thought it'd be better to serve everyone on the paper plates so we wouldn't have to do dishes later."

"Good thinking. And yes, I have some. I'll come down and show you where they are."

Melody nodded and she and Caroline linked elbows and headed out of the room and downstairs. Everyone was coming over to Caroline's and would be there in about an hour. They were serving all finger foods and celebrating Cheyenne's continued improvement and her new daughter. Cheyenne promised she'd reveal the name of her daughter that night as well.

She'd been as cagey as Kason was with his nickname and refused to tell them what she'd named her baby, saying she wanted to wait until they were all together. Caroline had rolled her eyes, but honestly didn't care. Cheyenne was alive and healthy, so she'd wait until she was ready to tell them all.

Caroline was thankful for Melody's help with the get-together. Seven adults, two kids, one near-teenager, two toddlers and a newborn were a bit daunting, even for Caroline.

Melody, Caroline, and Akilah worked alongside each other to put together various appetizers, a veggie tray, deviled eggs, and little peanut butter sandwiches for the kids. Cheyenne sat in the nearby family room, dozing before everyone arrived.

Finally when the food and drinks were almost ready, the other women started arriving. After all the greetings and cooing over Cheyenne's baby was done, everyone scattered around Caroline's living room. It was a tight fit, but they'd pushed the coffee table out of the way and brought up two chairs from the basement.

Cheyenne was in the big, fluffy armchair, holding her sleeping daughter in her arms. Jess, Summer, and Fiona were sitting on the large dark-brown leather couch, Alabama was in the other armchair, and Caroline and Melody were flitting back and forth to the kitchen, refilling drinks and bringing in more food for everyone when they ran out. They finally settled on the floor in front of the couch. Akilah was sitting next to Sara in front of all of them, playing with her quietly. John had finally crashed after running rampant throughout the house on his wobbly one-year-old legs. And even Brinique and Davisa had settled down and seemed content to be playing with some ancient dolls Caroline had unearthed from somewhere.

The room was full of love and contentment and Caroline was over-joyed to be a part of it. She thanked her lucky stars, as well as fate, every day that she'd been seated next to Matthew on that flight so long ago.

"All right, Cheyenne. Spill," Alabama griped good-naturedly at their friend. "I swear if you think you're gonna pull a Benny with us we might have to use drastic tickling measures to get it out of you. What is your beauty's name?"

Cheyenne didn't hesitate and smiled broadly as she announced, "Taylor Caroline Cooper."

Everyone oohed and ahhed and got up to step closer to Cheyenne and Taylor to congratulate her...again. Everyone except for Caroline.

Davisa watched as Caroline slipped out of the room and into the kitchen. She was confused. She thought her new mom's friend would've been happy to have the new baby named after her. She gave the doll she'd been playing with to Brinique, and followed Caroline.

She found her in the kitchen. Caroline was leaning against the counter with tears coursing down her face. "You aren't happy?" Davisa asked.

Caroline jerked in surprise, not having heard anyone come in after her. She turned and looked at Alabama's daughter. Her brow was furrowed and she looked terribly concerned...for her. Caroline wiped the tears from her face and tried to get control of herself. "I'm happy."

"Why are you crying then?"

"Sometimes people cry when they're happy, Davisa. I was surprised Cheyenne gave her daughter my name."

"They decided on that name a long time ago."

"What?" Caroline asked in surprise.

"Yeah, I heard her and Uncle Dude talking one night when they were looking after me and Brinique. They were laughing and giggling about first names, but Caroline was the first name they agreed on for her middle name."

Caroline could feel the tears welling up again. Well shit. Davisa continued.

"Uncle Dude's favorite name out of all of the names they talked about was Taylor, so I thought that was what Cheyenne would pick."

"You're a smart little girl. Did you know that?" Caroline asked, once again wiping away her tears.

"Yeah. I know."

Caroline smiled. "Come on, let's go back in and see little Taylor Caroline...shall we?"

"Okay, but I don't like babies. I'll wait until she's older then we can play Barbies together."

Caroline didn't have the heart to tell Davisa that by the time Taylor was old enough to want to play with Barbies, Davisa would probably be too old and would've moved on to other things. She took her hand and they walked back into the family room. She saw Cheyenne look up in concern and Caroline went right to her, letting go of Davisa's hand and watching her go back over to her sister and the pile of Barbie dolls.

Cheyenne grabbed Caroline's hand as she got close and Caroline sat down at the edge of the chair.

"Taylor is beautiful. I've never been so honored in all my life."

"Faulkner and I talked about it a lot. He has the utmost respect for

Matthew, both as a man and as his team leader. If this baby was a boy, he would've had the middle name Matthew, but we figured we could just as easily honor the two of you by giving her your name as the middle name. It was the easiest part of naming this child, to tell you the truth."

Caroline felt her lip quivering again, and waited until the need to burst into noisy, messy tears passed before speaking. "I don't know how we all got so lucky, but thank God we all found each other." There was so much more she wanted to say, but Taylor chose that moment to wake up and she let out a screech. That in turn woke up April, who added her cries to the commotion.

The women and children spent another few hours together, laughing and smiling with each other. Finally, when the kids started getting grumpy and sleepy, everyone packed up to go to their own homes.

Melody was leaving with Jessyka to help her out for a few days before heading home to Virginia. Alabama got her girls ready to go, including the entire box of Barbies that Caroline said they could use until they decided they wanted to play with something else. Fiona helped Summer gather up her things, and finally Caroline and Cheyenne were left alone.

The house was quiet again at last.

"As much as I love everyone, I have to admit I love the peace and quiet that is left when they're all gone."

Cheyenne chuckled softly, making sure not to wake up Taylor, who was sleeping peacefully in a portable crib next to her chair. "Yeah, I have a feeling I'll be one of the people you'll be glad to see the back of in a few months when Taylor gets a bit older and more demanding."

The two friends smiled at each other. "You ready for bed?" Caroline asked.

Cheyenne smothered a yawn. "Yeah, I think so. Is it sad that I'm excited about going to bed every night?"

"No, you've had a tough few days. Give your body time to heal. Don't be so hard on yourself."

"Have I thanked you for everything you've done for me, Caroline?"

"Yes, but you know I'd do anything for you."

"Well, you being there when Faulkner couldn't meant the world to me, and him. He'd say the same thing if he was here."

"They'll be home soon, I feel it."

"I hope so."

"Believe it." Caroline helped Cheyenne up and out of the chair and lifted Taylor into her arms as they headed down the stairs to the basement. "You've got the walkie-talkie so you can call me in the night if you need help, right?" Caroline asked bossily.

"Yes, ma'am."

Caroline sighed. "You won't call me, will you?"

"No. But I'll be fine. Swear."

"Okay, but please know I'm here if you need me."

"I do know it. And appreciate it."

Caroline put Taylor into her crib next to the bed and watched as the baby shifted and then settled into a deep sleep again. She leaned over and hugged Cheyenne. "Thank you for honoring me as you did. I love you, woman."

Cheyenne hugged Caroline back. "Love you too."

Caroline left her friend and headed up the stairs. She closed the basement door and made sure all the doors to the house were locked. She checked the kitchen and started the dishwasher. They didn't have many things to wash, only some platters and cups, but Caroline wanted to get the washing out of the way before she went to bed.

She turned off the lights, except for one in the kitchen, in case Cheyenne needed something in the middle of the night, and finally headed upstairs to her and Matthew's bedroom. She got ready for bed and slipped on a T-shirt of Matthew's. She crawled under the covers and pulled the pillow Matthew usually used into her body and cuddled it close. It didn't smell like him anymore, he'd been gone too long.

After everything that had happened that day, Caroline finally let go enough to let herself cry. And it wasn't a dainty cry. It was a gut-wrenching, I-miss-my-man, hope-he-is-safe-and-uninjured-and will-be-home-soon cry.

Caroline fell asleep with tears on her face and Matthew's face imprinted on her mind.

CHAPTER 23

*W*olf and his teammates stayed alert throughout the night and into the next morning. They heard gunshots every now and then, but hadn't seen any people. Wolf and Cookie looked at each other as they heard the telltale sound of an MH-60. They waited and watched, but never caught sight of it.

They knew Penelope hadn't even heard it, or if she did, she never commented on it. The chopper was there one minute and gone the next. Wolf hoped like hell they'd gotten there in time to rescue the Night Stalkers. He didn't regret his decision to leave them, but it still ate at him like an ulcer. They weren't used to leaving anyone behind, so the thought that perhaps, just perhaps, Tex had come through and gotten a rescue put into place to come retrieve their fellow military comrades, felt good.

Now the question was…who was coming for them, and when? And Wolf had no doubt someone *was* coming for them. No doubts whatsoever.

"Wolf, ten o'clock." Cookie's voice was low and urgent.

Wolf looked to where Cookie indicated and saw movement. He took out his binoculars and scanned the area below them. "I see them. Also nine, three, and twelve." The insurgents were moving methodically and swiftly up the mountain toward their hiding place. It wouldn't be too long before they'd be right where the SEALs had been a few days ago when they'd spotted the small cave. The insurgents would have to realize it was an excellent hiding place, and a good place to dig in for an assault.

"Keep eyes on them," Wolf ordered, knowing he really didn't even need to ask Cookie to do so, he'd make sure he knew where every bad guy was to the second.

Wolf scooted backwards awkwardly with one good arm without standing up, not wanting to give their position away prematurely. When he was far enough from the mouth of the cave to move freely, he stood and went over to where Penelope was sitting with Abe.

The thought of his friend being so sick made Wolf's heart hurt, but he put it aside. They had other things to worry about. Abe didn't have a chance if they didn't get out of here alive. And as much as he wanted to be the one helping Abe, he needed Sergeant Turner's help. She wasn't a SEAL, but she *was* a trained soldier.

Wolf looked at Abe and found that at the moment, he was either sleeping or unconscious. He turned to Penelope and saw her eyes boring into his. He laid it out for her. "It's showtime, Tiger. We've got insurgents coming, and coming fast."

"Where do you need me?"

Wolf inwardly smiled. God, this woman was amazing. Every time she opened her mouth, she reminded him of his Ice...and made him all the more determined to get back to her. "What I'm gonna ask you to do will probably piss you off, but I'm not saying it to purposely irritate you." Wolf continued quickly, "I need you to reload for us. I've only got one good arm and can't do it quickly myself. "

Wolf watched as Penelope cocked her head and considered his words. His respect for her went up a notch. He saw the moment she reached a decision about her words.

"That makes sense. You guys are better trained for this and probably better shots. I'll do my best to keep up with you. How much ammo do we have?"

Wolf closed his eyes briefly, more thankful than he could ever say that Penelope was the way she was. This entire rescue mission could have gone completely the other direction if she was a different kind of person. Wolf's thoughts went to Cookie and the stories he'd told them about when he'd tromped through the Mexican jungle with Fiona and the senator's daughter, Julie. Thank God Penelope was more like Fiona than the spoiled, not-prepared-for-any-kind-of-adversity Julie.

Julie had more than made up for her bitchiness though. She'd gone out of her way to apologize not only to Cookie and Fiona, but also to the rest of the team. Wolf never thought he'd be thinking about Julie as a strong woman who simply didn't deal with adversity well, but that's where he was. He brought himself back to the present; he didn't have time to be thinking about the commander's wife and the history between her and the team right now.

He opened his eyes and answered, "Probably not enough, but we'll fight as long as we can. We're trained to make every bullet count. I'm hoping we can knock out the first wave, then make our escape before the next one comes."

"Okay. Help me move Abe back a bit more?" Penelope asked, turning away from Wolf. She had to turn away because she knew if Wolf could see her face, he'd realize how incredibly scared and freaked-out she was. There was no time to give in to it though.

This was it. Do-or-die time.

Wolf came over and helped as best he could with his wounded arm to get Abe settled as far back from the mouth of the cave as possible. They stacked a few of the packs the SEALs had carried from the plane in front of his body to give another layer of protection from any stray bullets that might make their way into their hidey-hole. They worked in silence as Cookie and Benny continued to monitor the movements of the insurgents as they came toward their hiding spot.

"Wolf," Cookie cautioned.

Wolf made his way back to the mouth of the small opening and ungracefully laid himself out next to his teammate, careful to keep his arm as still as possible. Penelope lay on the ground and crawled her way over behind the men. She settled herself between the two of them, so she could reach their empty weapons with ease. It would also be a simple matter of leaning one way or the other to reach the weapons that Benny and Dude had as they stood at the edges of the cave.

"Where's Mozart?" Penelope murmured quickly before things got crazy.

"Recon," Wolf responded curtly, which really told her nothing, but Penelope didn't ask anything else as the first shot rang out in the quiet mountainside.

Penelope startled so badly at that first gunshot, she would've laughed at herself if she had it in her. She ducked down and turned her attention to the men around her. She needed to make sure she was an asset instead of a liability. The last thing she wanted to do was to be a burden on these men. She'd do what she could to help them.

Penelope had no idea how long the firefight lasted. She concentrated on reloading the pistols that were handed back to her when they were empty. She noticed that Cookie had a sniper rifle, thank goodness. It would've been a very different fight without it, a much closer and more personal fight. As it was, the insurgents obviously knew where they were now hiding, but the sniper rifle kept them away from the entrance.

Finally the gunshots tapered off and then stopped altogether.

"Everyone all right?" Wolf asked quietly into the silence.

"Clear."

"Clear."

"Clear."

"I'm good."

The three SEALs and Penelope answered affirmatively.

"Ammo situation?"

The SEALs examined their leftover ammo and the result wasn't good. They each had about three clips for their pistols and Cookie had about twenty more shots with his rifle. Mozart's ammo was still unknown, but Wolf guessed it was probably about the same.

"We've got about an hour, I'm guessing, before the next wave hits. Some of them were bound to have retreated as soon as bullets started flying to get backup and to report our position to the others. We either move up, or try to get past them going down as they're going up."

There was silence for a moment until Benny responded. "I say up. I might be the one with the head injury, but it'll be much easier for a helo to swoop in and snatch us up, the higher we are."

Wolf nodded in immediate agreement. "Let's get the lead out."

"What about Mozart?" Penelope asked, happy to not be a sitting duck in their cave anymore.

"He'll meet up with us," Cookie said with complete confidence.

They packed the bags and had a short discussion about the safest way to get Abe out of the cave and up the mountain. As they were discussing it, he came to. Penelope thought he'd volunteer to be left behind, but she had never hung out with SEALs before. It was obvious he knew his teammates would never, ever leave him behind, so he didn't even suggest it. "I'll help as much as I can. Give me a pistol. If the shit hits the fan, I can at least shoot as you all carry my ass."

Wolf laughed. Penelope couldn't believe anyone could actually laugh about what Abe said, the picture in her mind was anything but funny, but she was finding out that these SEALs were a lot like the guys back home at the firehouse. When they were the most juiced-up on adrenaline and in the midst of danger, they seemed to get more and more crude. It was actually reassuring.

"With our luck, you'd shoot *us* in the ass, Abe."

When the group was ready, Cookie and Dude took Abe by the arms and helped him stand up. He was shaky, and couldn't put any weight on his injured leg, but he was upright. Cookie stuck his shoulder in Abe's armpit and wrapped his arm around Abe's back. Abe wrapped his arm around Cookie's waist and they hobbled toward the entrance to the cave.

Penelope couldn't have stopped the words from coming out of her mouth if her life depended on it. "You two look like you're ready for the world championship three-legged race at the county fair down in Texas." She was relieved that Cookie and Abe both laughed, rather than getting irritated at her inappropriate humor.

"Oh hell yeah, we're *so* entering one of those when we get home, aren't we, Abe?" Cookie said with a smile.

Abe's voice was a bit lower and had less strength, but he responded with, "Yeah, when we get home."

"Okay, Benny will head out first. We'll give him a ten-minute head start. Our radios aren't working for shit, so we'll wait, and if he doesn't come back and tell us otherwise, Tiger, you and Dude will be next, followed by Frick and Frack, and I'll bring up the rear. Stay low when you get to the top and wait for us to get up there. If something happens, dig in and we'll rendezvous as soon as we can. Got it?"

As everyone agreed, Benny slipped out and disappeared around the side of their hidey-hole. Penelope waited, holding her breath. Ten minutes passed slower than molasses in January. Penelope grimaced at herself. Why she was thinking about corny clichés, she had no idea.

Finally, Wolf gestured at her and Dude. She took a deep breath and headed out behind Dude, sticking as close to him as she'd done when they'd left the tent at the refugee camp.

The first part was the most difficult. Penelope slipped several times, scraping her hands as she caught herself. She had no idea how in the hell Cookie was going to get a semi-conscious Abe up the hill, but she figured if anyone could, it'd be the SEALs. They seemed to be able to do anything, at least from what she'd seen so far.

She made sure to stay behind the small scrub bushes as they passed them, just in case any of the insurgents were still watching. The thought of being shot in the back not a pleasant one.

She'd reached the top of the ridge and looked around, not seeing Benny or Mozart, when she felt an arm wrap around her from behind. A hand covered her mouth and she was pulled into a large, hard body.

She immediately flailed, trying to get away, but she was a beat too slow.

Another arm came around her waist and held her in a grip so tight she had no prayer of moving. The arm around her compressed against her chest, and her cracked ribs. It hurt. Penelope panicked. No, hell no. She hadn't survived all she had to be kidnapped again. She frantically struggled in the tight grip holding her still, to no avail. She felt herself being half dragged and half carried backwards, and there was nothing she could do about it.

Just as Penelope was about to fall into complete despair, she heard Mozart's voice. She looked up and saw six and a half feet of pissed-off Navy SEAL. He had a pistol aimed somewhere above her head. His words were stifled and deadly. "Let her go, asshole, and I might let you live."

Penelope held her breath as the man behind her didn't move.

CHAPTER 24

There's still no news of kidnapped U.S. Army Sergeant Penelope Turner. She was kidnapped almost four months ago by ISIS and it's been a while since any video of her has surfaced. We continue to follow this story.

In other news, a new reality show premieres tonight featuring men competing to become the ultimate Alaskan. Stay tuned for an interview with one of the contestants.

* * *

Caroline turned off the television in disgust. How anyone could watch that reality show drivel was beyond her. It wasn't as if it was actually real. The only reality show she'd ever been remotely interested in was some sort of dating show set in Australia…at least the man had seemed down-to-earth. She didn't remember how it turned out, but she thought she remembered some sort of scandal, but in the end the man found an actual real love.

Her thoughts were interrupted by the ringing of her cell phone. She headed over to the kitchen counter where she'd left it and picked it up. She recognized the prefix of the Naval base, but not the number itself.

"Hello?"

"Hello, is this Caroline Steel?"

"Yes, who is this?"

"This is Commander Hurt."

"Oh, sorry, Patrick. I didn't recognize your voice." Caroline stiffened suddenly. Oh shit. Why was Wolf's commander calling her? "Is everything all right? Is Julie okay? The guys?"

Ignoring her question, Hurt said solemnly, "I wanted you to hear it from me, rather than the Casualty Assistance Officers who will be showing up at your door within the hour."

Caroline felt her knees give out and she slid to the floor with her back against the kitchen cabinets. She couldn't get any words out.

"Wolf and his team are considered Missing in Action."

Caroline's breath came out in a whoosh. "What?" she whispered.

"MIA. We haven't heard from them since the other SEAL team they were working with reported that they'd completed their mission. They should've been home by now, but we haven't heard anything from them." Patrick knew he was misleading Caroline a bit, but didn't want to tell her everything he knew...not yet. Tex had given him coordinates of where he thought they were, but until their location had been verified by the Delta Force team, the government was declaring them MIA. The trackers weren't common knowledge and Patrick wasn't going to let that detail slip to Command.

Caroline took in a deep breath. "They're not dead?"

The commander's voice lowered. "We don't know. As of now, they're missing."

Caroline nodded to herself. Okay, this she could deal with. "Then they're just out of pocket. They're not dead. They'll figure it out and get in touch when they can."

"Caroline—"

The commander's tone was sympathetic and a bit pitying, but Caroline didn't let it deter her. "With all due respect, Patrick," she interrupted the senior military official she'd known for a long time, "I appreciate you giving me a head's up. I do. But I'd hope that, as long as you've known Matthew and his team, you'd know that they're tough as hell. Until I see and touch Matthew's cold body for myself, I'll never, ever believe he's dead. Call me naïve, call me idiotic, but I know deep in my heart that they're good at what they do. If there's any way possible they'll be able to make it back home, they will. Even if the odds are a hundred to one. Or a thousand to one. There's still a chance. So if you'll excuse me, I need to start Operation Girl Time and get my posse together. I'm assuming the others will have visitors as well?"

"Yes." The commander's voice held so much respect in that one word, it made Caroline want to weep.

"Okay, then I need to deal with the Navy Officers about to descend on my door, then make some calls to my girls." Her voice softened, sounding uncertain. "You'll keep me informed?"

"Yes ma'am. I'll be sure to call you personally the second I hear anything."

"Thank you. I'll make sure you get an invite to the huge party we're gonna have when our men are home. Deal?"

"Deal. Let me know if you need anything. And I mean *anything*, Caroline. It's the least I can do."

"Just tell me the truth. And keep me informed. That's all I need."

"You got it. Caroline?"

"Yeah?"

"Julie asked if you thought it'd be okay if she came over too. I said I'd talk to you about it. She doesn't want to overstep, but she's worried about all of you."

Caroline swallowed hard. She and the rest of the women hadn't been very nice to Julie when they'd first figured out who she was. Knowing she was the woman who Fiona had spent time with down in Mexico, and who'd been so horrible to her, was a surprising blow to them all. But slowly, Julie had proven that she had changed, and they'd all decided if Fiona could forgive her, so could they.

Besides that, she was now married to Commander Hurt. They saw her all the time and were genuinely thrilled with how happy their husbands' commander was with her. "Yeah, I think we'd like that."

"Thanks. I'll let her know and send her over in a bit."

"Sounds good. I'll talk to you later then? You'll let me know the second you hear something?"

"Of course I will. Bye, Caroline."

Caroline clicked off the phone and laid her head on her knees briefly before stiffening her spine. She had shit to do, there was no time to cry. Hell, there was no reason *to* cry. Every word she'd told the commander came from her gut. Matthew was alive. Everyone was. She had to believe it.

* * *

LATER THAT NIGHT, Caroline once again sat in her living room with a full

313

house. She'd been able to catch all of her friends on the phone before they'd had their visits with the officers from the base, except for Fiona. She'd been out running errands, and had missed both her call and the visit from the base...thankfully.

Alabama had finally gotten ahold of Fiona and told her to drop what she was doing and get her butt over to Caroline's house. She was the last to arrive. Even Julie had made it there before Fiona, and had been just as shocked and upset as the others, but now they sat around talking about what might be happening with their men.

"Caroline, what do you really think is going on?"

Caroline thought hard about Fiona's question, trying to decide what to tell them. She caught Melody's eyes from across the room and her slight nod. She took a deep breath.

"We've never been the type of Navy SEAL wives to question our men, or even to speculate about where they might be when they've been sent on a mission. I don't feel comfortable doing it now, but with what's going on, I feel like I need to."

She looked around at her friends and knew she had their utmost attention. Most of the kids were sleeping. Sara and John were downstairs in the basement, April and Taylor were snoring in their mother's arms, and Akilah was upstairs with Brinique and Davisa, entertaining them as they played with their dolls. It was just the eight of them. Six women who were worried and stressed about the loves of their lives, and Melody and Julie, who were just as worried that their friends' men wouldn't come home again.

"I'm pretty sure they went over to the Middle East to try to rescue that kidnapped American soldier." Caroline ignored their gasps and continued on quickly, "Matthew didn't tell me, but I kinda guessed, and asked enough leading questions that he actually answered to figure out I was right."

"The helicopter crash?" Summer surmised quietly.

Caroline nodded. "Yeah, I think so."

"But the news reports say there were only four men aboard, and that they were brought to Germany," Cheyenne said.

"Yeah, it doesn't make sense. The only thing I can think of is that chopper was on the way to get them out when it crashed. And Patrick said they were missing, not dead. So I think maybe they've found the woman, and they're just not able to communicate with anyone for some reason. Maybe they're just hunkered down waiting for the right time to come out." Caroline tried to reason what was going on out loud.

"How can they be missing if they have their trackers on? Couldn't Tex just tell the commander where they are?" Jessyka asked the group.

Everyone looked at Melody and Julie. They both looked uncertain.

"Let's leave Melody and Julie out of this," Caroline told everyone as she pulled out her phone. "It's not fair to put them in the middle. I should've thought of it before, but I'll call Tex and we'll see what, if anything, he can tell us."

Julie piped up before Caroline could get ahold of Tex. "I don't know."

"What?" Summer asked.

"I don't know anything about your husbands. Patrick and I don't talk about his work. I know what he does is extremely sensitive and he could get in big trouble if he told me anything, so I never ask him about it and he never tells me. I would tell you if I knew even the smallest detail. I swear."

"Thanks for that," Alabama said softly. "We appreciate it."

Caroline nodded at Julie and dialed her cell and put it on the coffee table. All eight women hunkered down around it and waited for Tex to answer.

Finally on the fifth ring, he did. "What's up, Caroline?"

"Where are the guys?"

Tex was silent for a moment before he asked, "Why do you ask?"

"Cut the shit, Tex," Fiona said more harshly than she'd ever spoken to Tex before. "I'm sure you already know we were all visited by the base Casualty Assistance Officers today. They've declared Hunter and the others MIA. But we want to know how they can be missing if they have their trackers on?"

Tex cleared his throat. "You know I can't talk about this, Fee. Even though I'm not active duty anymore, I've still got my government clearance since I work for them, but it's not cool that you're putting me in this position."

"And you know I wouldn't do it if I wasn't completely freaked-out that I'm gonna lose the best man I've ever known, the love of my life, and the lives of the bravest fucking men I've ever met. We're at our wits end here, Tex. God, please. Can't you tell us anything?" Fiona's voice started out hard and unrelenting, but at the end of her impassioned plea, she was near tears.

"Fuck," Tex said. He sighed deeply, obviously effected by Fiona's tone of voice, then said, "Only five of them brought their trackers with them. I can only assume someone forgot it. I doubt whoever it was would deliberately not bring it with him."

"Do you know who forgot it?" Jess asked.

"Yes, but I'm not going to tell you, it doesn't matter," Tex told her.

"So they really are missing then?" Cheyenne's voice was low and strained.

"Sort of."

"Sort of?" Caroline snapped. "Jesus, Tex. You're killing us here. Just spit it out...and in regular English, not any of that coded crap you're so good at."

Tex ignored the snark in Caroline's words, knowing she was stressed-out beyond what most women would be able to handle. She, and all of the women, were actually accepting this very well, all things considered. "They're missing, but I believe I know their general whereabouts. I'm hoping there will be information soon."

There was a lot Tex wanted to tell the women. That there was still a tracker working and he was pretty sure it was with the group. That he'd been in communication with the Delta Force commander and knew they rescued the helicopter crew and were on the trail of Wolf and his men. He hoped the women would trust him to do what was best for their men.

Silence filled the room for a moment before Summer spoke up. "Thank you, Tex. Seriously. I know you told us way more than you should've, but it means everything to us."

"Yeah...Mel?"

Melody spoke up for the first time. "I'm here."

"You still coming home tomorrow?"

Everyone in the room could practically feel the longing in Tex's voice. Sometimes they forgot he was more than just the person who looked over them and kept them safe. He was a father, a husband, and a man who very obviously was feeling the pain of his friends being missing and wanted his wife by his side.

"Yeah. We leave around noon and land around eight your time."

"I'll be at the airport waiting."

"Okay, Tex."

"You ladies need anything else?" Tex asked, obviously asking the other women in the room.

"No, we're as good as we can be at the moment," Alabama told him honestly.

"Okay. For what it's worth, I have a feeling we'll be hearing good news soon," Tex said in a cautiously optimistic tone.

"From your lips to God's ears," Caroline said fervently.

"I'll talk to you guys later." His voice dropped. "See you tomorrow, Mel."

Everyone said their goodbyes and Caroline clicked off the phone. The women stared at each other for a moment before Caroline announced, "Sleepover time. Nobody's going anywhere until our men are found. You too, Julie. You're here, so you're staying. We need all the support we can get."

No one disagreed. They found comfort in being with each other. No one cared that they'd be cramped and things would be crazy with all the bodies in the house. It was better than going home to their empty, lonely homes that would remind them of their missing husbands.

Julie didn't complain, thankful that she'd finally broken through the "acquaintance barrier" that had seemed to stand between her and the other women. Over the couple of years she'd been with Patrick, she'd heard story after story about all of these women and how amazing they were. The fact that Caroline had asked her to stay meant the world. She'd stay with them and support them until their men came home...or through the horror if they never came home at all.

CHAPTER 25

*P*enelope held her breath and didn't move a muscle. If she could've moved, she still would've stayed right where she was. It wasn't fun looking down the barrel of a gun, even if she knew it wasn't aimed at her. Her attention stayed on the man standing behind her, holding her immobile in his grasp.

"I said, let her the fuck go. Right now." Mozart's voice communicated he was about five seconds away from losing his shit, or blowing someone's head off.

"How about you drop *your* gun, and stop pointing it at my teammate instead?"

Penelope held her breath. Oh jeez. This was quickly turning into a major clusterfuck. There was another man dressed in desert camouflage now holding a gun at *Mozart's* head. She didn't think he was an insurgent, not only because she'd only seen them in whatever raggedy clothes they happened to have, not a uniform, but also because the man had spoken perfect English with only a slight southern twang. But the bottom line was that she had no idea who he was. It would've been humorous if she'd been watching it on television back home, safe in her apartment in San Antonio. But being in the middle of it herself was absolutely *not* funny at all. She couldn't hold back her snarky words, but unfortunately, or fortunately, they came out all garbled because the man behind her still had his hand over her mouth.

Her meaning must've come through, if not her words, because the second man who'd appeared out of nowhere said, "Captain Keane Bryson, Delta Force."

Mozart lowered his pistol immediately and turned to the man. "About fucking time."

They grinned at each other in a weird manly way, as if they hadn't just been about to kill each other two seconds earlier.

Penelope squirmed in the hold of the man behind her again and he finally dropped his arms. She turned to glare at him, shoving against his chest with both arms, annoyed because he didn't even have to step back a foot at her push, before turning back to Mozart and the man who called himself Keane Bryson and saying in a snarky voice, "I don't know how you found us, or what the hell your plan is, but can we *please* get on with it and get the fuck out of here? If you didn't notice, we're not exactly at the Officer's Club on base."

The new guy ignored her and turned to Mozart. "She's got a mouth on her, didn't expect that."

Mozart shrugged and agreed, "She does, but she's one hell of a soldier."

Penelope was ready to throw up her hands in exasperation at the conversation, but at Mozart's words, she could only stare at him dumb-founded. He, a Navy SEAL, thought *she* was a hell of a soldier? Well, okay then.

Mozart held out his hand to the man. "Mozart. Glad you're here. We could use the help. We've got a man down, and the rest of us aren't at a hundred percent."

"Sit rep," the captain requested, now all business.

Before Mozart could respond, Wolf appeared out of the brush. He had his finger on the trigger of his pistol and looked ready to use it before seeing Mozart's signal for friend. Following up behind Wolf was the rest of his team. Penelope was glad to see Abe was still conscious…barely. She went over to Cookie and took some of Abe's weight on herself. She was so much shorter than them she couldn't do much, but she figured every little bit would help.

They all watched as five more men materialized out of the desert landscape. Penelope thought it almost looked like a showdown at the O.K. Corral. Six men lined up on one side, seven on the other.

Wolf gestured toward each of the men on his team. "I'm Wolf, this is Mozart, Benny, and Dude. Abe is the one who looks like he's about to pass out and Cookie is holding him up. You've apparently met Tiger, otherwise known as Sergeant Penelope Turner, formerly a guest of ISIS."

The Army Delta Force men each nodded at the SEALs and their captain introduced them. "I'm Ghost, and this is Fletch, Coach, Hollywood, Beatle, Blade, and Truck."

The testosterone was thick enough on the ridge to choke a horse, but Penelope didn't care. All she cared about was that the odds of them getting out of Turkey, or Iraq, or wherever the hell they were, were just raised about a thousand percent. She would've kissed the Special Forces men if she thought it would've been appropriate at that moment.

Wolf, apparently done with the pleasantries, got down to business. "First, we left four men down near the crash site of the MH-60. Any chance you took care of that?"

"Taken care of," Ghost said matter-of-factly. He didn't elaborate, and Penelope really would've liked to have known more about how they were doing and what was going on with them, but obviously now wasn't the time.

Wolf nodded at Ghost. "Obliged." He continued with the sit rep, "We repelled the first round of insurgents, but expect another any moment. We holed up down there," he gestured back the way they came, "but they obviously found us. We're down to a few clips per person. Abe has a leg wound that needs more medical attention than we've got. My arm is busted. Mozart has an arm wound, but it doesn't seem to be too bad. Benny had a concussion and some bleeding and Dude's ankle isn't a hundred percent."

"And Tiger?" Ghost's words were no-nonsense and clipped.

"Dehydration, hungry, bent ribs, and tough as fucking hell."

Ghost nodded in approval. "Good to know the odds are in our favor."

Penelope gawked at the huge man. Was he high? Wolf had just run through enough issues to make any general cringe, and the dangerous looking man standing in front of her acted as if Wolf had told him they had heat-seeking missiles hidden in their packs. She'd never understand these Special Forces guys. Give her a fireman any day of the week. The ones she worked with might be a bit redneck and a lot country, but at least they weren't fucking crazy.

"Okay, we'll pair up, one of my men with one of yours. They'll hook your guys up with additional ammo. Truck and Blade will take Abe. Sergeant Turner, you stick with me and Wolf. You'll be home before you know it."

Penelope nodded and stepped away from Abe as the two Delta Force men, Blade and Truck, came forward to take him under their shoulders. Cookie nodded at them with respect and gratitude, and the other men got down to business shifting their loads and distributing ammunition.

Penelope was hunkered down between Wolf and Ghost when the first gunshot rang out through the air.

She flinched and ducked, remembering the firefight that they'd lived through not too long ago.

"Easy, sergeant. We've got this," Ghost reassured her with a hand on her shoulder.

Penelope nodded and waited. Surprisingly, Wolf and Ghost didn't even pull out their weapons, but spoke to each other about the plans for extraction as their men shot at insurgents around them.

"You call it in?" Wolf asked Ghost.

"Yeah, an MH-47 is en route."

"Probably best to wait until we take care of this first."

"Yeah, it'll be over before the Chinook gets here."

"From here?"

"Incirlik then Ramstein."

Wolf nodded in approval. "Good. Any chance you can relay a message back home? Our radios are out. Dead batteries."

"Of course."

Wolf leaned toward Ghost and Penelope heard him speaking in what had to be code, because she didn't understand a word of what was said. She was beginning to get irritated and her head reeled, not only from the extremely loud firefight around them, but from confusion as to what was going on and probably a bit of lack of water and food as well.

"Can one of you please translate what the hell is going on?" she demanded, still feeling snarky. Her world was changing too fast for her to keep up and it was extremely confusing and scary.

Ghost laughed, not meanly. "As soon as our boys take care of the assholes, a big-ass helicopter will come and pick us all up. We'll fly to Incirlik U.S. Air Base east of here on the Mediterranean Sea. From there, you'll probably be packed up and shipped off to Ramstein Air Base in Germany. There, you and Wolf's men will get medical attention, then you'll all be headed home."

"Home?" The word soaked into Penelope's psyche like a parasite burrowing in for the long haul.

"Home," Ghost confirmed.

Penelope turned to Wolf with a smile. "Can you tell your guys to hurry the hell up then, we have a chopper to catch."

Wolf smiled down at the petite woman between them. She didn't come to their chin, was dirty and actually pretty disgusting-smelling and looking, but her strong personality and quirkiness came through loud and clear. She might be down, but she sure as hell wasn't out.

"Yes, ma'am," Wolf told her, laughing.

"That's sergeant, not ma'am. I'm not an officer," Penelope told Wolf haughtily, but smiled so he knew she was teasing him.

Wolf didn't answer, but Penelope knew he heard her.

And Ghost was right, it wasn't too much longer before the last gunshot rang out over the mountains. It was almost too quiet. "Is it over?" Penelope whispered into the sudden silence.

"Almost."

CHAPTER 26

*S*tay tuned for a breaking news story out of Germany on the evening
news.

* * *

CAROLINE LAY on her couch with her cell phone in her hand and stared up
at the ceiling. Alabama was upstairs in her bed with Brinique and Davisa.
Fiona was sleeping in one of the armchairs next to her, and Summer was
in the other chair. They'd made a cradle out of a dresser drawer for April,
and she was sleeping soundly next to her mother.

Cheyenne and Julie were downstairs in the basement apartment with
Taylor, and Jess was in the guestroom with both Sara and John. They
were certainly crowded, but not one of the women wanted to be
anywhere else.

The kids were resilient and thought it was fun to have a sleepover.
Caroline and Fiona had taken Melody and Akilah to the airport the day
before. It was always sad to say goodbye to her. Even though she lived on
the other side of the country, Melody was still very much a part of their
group.

Caroline fingered the cell phone impatiently. She hadn't slept well at
all, she had a feeling something was happening. She had no factual basis
for the feeling, but it was there nonetheless.

Having the Navy say that Matthew and the other men were "missing," was tough. It was one thing to say goodbye to Matthew every time he left for a mission and not know where he was going or when he'd be back, but she and the other women knew that *someone* knew where they were and what they were doing. But this time, not even the U.S. Navy knew their whereabouts, and that was what freaked her out the most.

Was he hurt? Was anyone else hurt? Caroline refused to believe Matthew was dead. Absolutely refused. As she'd told Commander Hurt, she'd have to see and touch his dead body to believe it...something many SEAL wives never got to do.

Even though Caroline was hoping and praying her phone would ring, she was startled when it actually did vibrate in her grasp. The number came up as "unavailable," but Caroline didn't hesitate to swing her legs over the side of the couch and head into the kitchen and the side door of the house. She didn't want to wake anyone up, but she had a good feeling in her gut about the call.

Caroline eased the door shut behind her and clicked the phone to answer it before the person on the other end hung up.

"Hello?"

"Ice, it's me."

"Oh thank God! Are you all right? Is everyone else okay?" She could hear the smile in Matthew's voice as he answered her.

"That's my Ice, always worrying about others. We're good."

"Does the commander know where you are? He said you were MIA."

Wolf laughed outright. Caroline had been a Navy spouse for a couple of years now, but she still sometimes was very naïve about how things worked. "Of course he knows, Baby."

"Okay. Can I ask when you guys will be home?"

"I don't know for sure, but I promise it'll be soon."

"Good. Matthew?"

"Yeah, Ice?"

"Can I tell the others?"

"Of course. I told the guys I'd call you. Make sure the others know they'll call as soon as they can, but we've got meetings and stuff we gotta do at the moment."

"I know, I'll tell them. You really are okay?"

Wolf heard the break in his wife's voice and actually felt tears well up in his own eyes. He was a bad-ass SEAL, but nothing could bring him to his knees faster than his Caroline. "We're all going to be fine."

There was a huge difference in Caroline's mind, but she didn't push it. Right now, *going* to be fine was just as good as fine. "Okay, we'll see you at the base?"

"Probably not. We have to debrief with Hurt and others before we'll be allowed to come home. It'll probably be a couple of days, but I'll text when I'm on my way."

"Okay. Matthew?"

Wolf grinned again. "Yes, Ice?"

"Did you win?"

He knew exactly what she meant and he was proud as fuck that he was able to say, "Yeah, baby. We won."

"Thank God. I love you."

"I love you too."

"I knew you'd find your way home."

"Always. I've got you to come home to. How could I not?"

"Okay, I'm sure you have shit to do." Caroline's voice was back to its usual take-charge tone. "I've got six adults, two toddlers, two babies and two little girls who are going to be getting up any moment now, and will be hungry. Travel safe and I'll see you soon, honey." She could've gone into detail about baby Taylor and Cheyenne's hospital scare and about Jess being pregnant again, but decided her husband had enough on his plate at the moment. Faulkner and the others would learn soon enough all that happened while they were gone. They'd call their wives as soon as they could. It was enough for now that they weren't lost anymore and would be home soon.

"Yes, you will. Stay safe until I get home."

"I will. Love you, bye."

"Bye, Ice."

Caroline clicked off the phone and dropped her head and sighed in relief. Thank God.

CHAPTER 27

*P*enelope grimaced at the image staring back at her in the mirror on the base. She and the six SEALs had arrived at the Air Base in Germany without incident. The trip out of the mountains of Turkey had been somewhat anticlimactic. The huge Chinook helicopter swooped down they'd all jumped in, and they'd taken off. And that was that.

They'd landed at Incirlik Air Base in Turkey and Penelope watched as Ghost and his men walked away from the helicopter without a look back. She'd called out, "Ghost!"

The large man had stopped and turned to her.

Penelope had been at a loss for words. What did you say to the man who helped save your life? "Thank you." The words were inadequate, but she hadn't had time to come up with anything else.

Ghost hadn't said a word, but dipped his head in acknowledgement.

Penelope looked behind him and saw that all six of the other Delta Force men had stopped as well. Maybe they'd been waiting for their leader, but whatever the reason, every single man, one by one, had raised their hand and saluted her. She'd barely seen them through the water filling her eyes.

"I'm not an officer, you can't salute me," she'd managed to get out.

Penelope thought it was the man called Coach who'd replied, "We salute those we respect. And woman, *you* we respect."

Holy. Shit. She'd watched as the group of men turned and continued on their way. That was the last she'd seen of the Special Forces team. They'd disappeared into a building on the base and hadn't resurfaced. Penelope had no idea where they'd gone, or what was next on their agenda, but she'd always remember them.

She ran her hand over her short hair. She'd decided that it all needed to come off after her first shower. It was so snarled and disgusting, it was easier to simply cut it short and start over. Penelope had never been the kind of woman to overly worry about her looks. After it was done, she even thought it might be easier to keep it short as a firefighter. Less upkeep and she'd have to worry about it less under her helmet as she worked.

She'd had a long conversation with her brother Cade the first night she'd been in Germany. They'd both cried and Cade had told her all he'd been doing to make sure the government didn't forget about her. She'd also had to meet with the Army lawyers and psychologists. That part wasn't as fun.

Overall, she was exhausted, and feeling a bit claustrophobic. She couldn't go anywhere without someone being right at her side. She didn't want to talk to anyone at the moment, but she also didn't want to be alone. It was ridiculous. She wanted to feel safe, and the one place she'd know she was safe was with the SEALs who'd managed to find her and smuggle her out of the hellhole she'd been in.

Penelope threw on a T-shirt and a pair of Army sweats. She peered out of the barracks room where she'd been housed and didn't see anyone in the hall. Someone had been with her from the second they'd landed through her doctor visit and her brief session with an Army psychologist. It was late, so it was no wonder no one was around, but she kinda expected someone to still be hovering nearby. She tiptoed down the hall as if she was a teenager sneaking out in the middle of the night to meet her boyfriend.

She eased out of the building and made her way across the quiet base, nodding at the security sentry she saw along her way. She'd been introduced to the private when she'd been shown the barracks, and Penelope was glad he recognized her now and didn't ask her any questions about where she might be going. She headed toward the infirmary. She greeted the nurse on duty on the floor she knew Abe was on. She signed in, and headed down to his room.

Penelope knew she was probably given more leeway because of her situation. She'd found out that the American press had dubbed her the Army Princess...which annoyed her to no end. She much preferred Tiger.

She eased open the door to Abe's room and slipped in.

"It's late."

Penelope knew she probably wouldn't be able to sneak in on Abe, but she was still startled at his words. "Yeah."

"Couldn't sleep?"

"Nope."

"Me either."

"How's the leg?"

"Still attached."

Penelope sighed. It was like pulling teeth. "But it's okay?"

"It will be."

"Good."

They were both silent for a moment, until Abe asked, "What's up, Tiger?"

Penelope didn't even try to prevaricate. "Can I sleep here?"

"Yes." Abe's answer was immediate and, Penelope could tell, heartfelt.

She didn't say anything else, but grabbed two blankets that were on the end of Abe's bed. She laid one on the ground under the window on the far side of Abe's bed, away from the door, lay down, and pulled the other blanket over her. She rested her head on her elbow and sighed in contentment.

She heard Abe moving above her and a pillow suddenly landed on the floor next to her head.

"Take it. I don't need it."

Penelope said, "Thanks," in a soft voice. Nothing else was said between the two military veterans.

Abe listened as the brave Army sergeant fell into sleep and started snoring softly. He didn't like that she was on the floor, but didn't push the issue. She didn't know it, but her actions went a long way toward giving him back his pride. By choosing him over all of his teammates, and putting him between her and the door, and unconsciously letting him protect her, she made him feel better about being unconscious for part of her dangerous rescue.

* * *

PENELOPE WAS glad none of the SEALs mentioned or gave her shit about sleeping in Abe's room the night before. She'd woken up to quiet conversation and all five of Abe's teammates in the room. She'd forgotten about her hair, and went to brush it away from her face, realizing at the last second that there was no hair there to push out of the way.

She excused herself and used the small restroom off of Abe's room. She finger-brushed her teeth—she'd never take brushing her teeth for granted again—and splashed water on her face. She drank a huge cup of water, then straightened her clothes and stepped back into the room.

"So, when are we heading home?" Penelope asked brightly, hoping the answer would be "today."

"I think you're out of here tonight."

"Awesome," Penelope breathed, hardly able to believe it. She'd been dreaming of seeing Cade again, and stepping foot on her home soil and it looked like it would finally be happening. Then she thought about what Wolf had said. "Wait, *I'm* out of here tonight? What about you guys?"

"We're headed out this morning," Cookie told her.

"We're not going together?" Penelope asked, confused.

"Tiger, you're headed back to Fort Hood in Texas. We're going back to Coronado out in California."

"Oh." Penelope felt stupid. Of course they were. They were Navy, she was Army. Their families were out in California. It still seemed odd, even though she hadn't know these men for long. They'd been through a lot. They'd saved her. It was weird. "Do your wives know you're coming home?"

"Yeah," Wolf answered for all of them.

Penelope suddenly remembered more about their families. "Dude, did your wife have your baby?"

Dude's jaw tightened and he nodded. "Yeah, a healthy baby girl. She was born a couple of days ago."

"I'm sorry you missed it," Penelope told him honestly. "If I hadn't—"

Dude strode over to the small woman who they'd rescued and put a finger over her mouth to shush her. "I might have missed her birth, but she'll be there when I get back. I wouldn't have been anywhere else for the world. And you know what? The day my daughter was born was the same day we pulled you out of that tent. I'd say it was more than worth it."

Penelope stepped away from Dude's touch, and tried to smile at him. God. These men. She knew they were taken, but they were everything she'd ever wanted in a man. They were a bit chauvinistic, a bit heavy-handed, but they weren't afraid to give credit where it was due and she could tell they loved their families with every fiber of their beings. She wanted that. She wanted it more than she'd ever admit to anyone.

"Well, thank you. Thanks to all of you. Seriously. And you know what? From now on, during the Army-Navy football game...I'm rooting for Navy in tribute to you guys."

Everyone laughed, as she'd hoped they would. She needed the tone to be lightened, and it had been.

"Is it allowed for us to keep in touch? I mean, I know what you guys do is pretty hush-hush, so I didn't know if we could openly communicate with each other or if it'd be frowned on." Penelope watched as the men gave each other indescribable looks. She continued, "Oh, okay, I understand, I was just—"

"Yeah, we'll keep in touch," Wolf interrupted her.

"But, if you'll get in trouble—"

"We'll keep in touch," Wolf repeated, resolutely.

"Okay. I'd like that," Penelope stated, then hurried on. "I have to go...I have an appointment this morning...or something." She knew she couldn't stay there and shoot the shit with these amazing men any longer. She had to make the break. "I'm glad you're all going to be okay...get home to your families." She nodded at each of them and turned and left the room, knowing if she stayed any longer, or if any of them tried to shake her hand or, God forbid, hug her, she'd lose it.

After she left, Benny was the first to speak. "That's one hell of a woman."

"Agreed," Wolf said then changed the subject. "You guys ready to get the hell out of here?"

"Oh fuck yeah," Abe said with enough gusto for all of them.

"Wheels up in two hours. Our women are waiting for us."

CHAPTER 28

As we told you last night, U.S. Army Sergeant Penelope Turner has been rescued from the Middle East. She'd been kidnapped approximately four months ago by ISIS. The three men she'd been taken with were beheaded and burnt and the videotape of their deaths was distributed by ISIS. Turner had been seen on several taped videos extolling the ideology of ISIS and denouncing the Western World's governments.

Late this past weekend, a plane touched down at Fort Hood, Texas, with Sergeant Turner, her hair cut short, and flanked by several high-ranking Army officials. She waved from the plane and was hustled into a waiting SUV before being whisked off, most likely to debriefing. She spent a few nights at Ramstein Air Base in Germany before flying back to the States.

There has been no word on her rescue or rescuers, but we are hoping to get more details soon. While the Army Princess, as she has been dubbed by the press, has not accepted any interviews, we will be talking to Cade Turner, Penelope's brother, next week when he sits down for an exclusive interview. Stay tuned for more details, and let us be the first to say welcome home, Sergeant Turner!

* * *

CAROLINE SAT ALONE in her house and waited impatiently for Matthew to get home. After speaking with him on the phone the other morning, she'd gone back into her house and was happy to let all the others know their men were on the way home.

As usual, they were all gracious and they all understood that it wasn't feasible for all of the guys to call home immediately and talk to them right at that moment. It sucked, but sometimes their job came first, even over family. They all knew they'd call as soon as they could. It was enough for that moment to know they were all safe and on their way home.

Caroline also spoke with Commander Hurt that morning, and he was happy to let her know Matthew was safe and they were going to be on their way home soon. Caroline didn't mention that Matthew had already called her, but she figured he was probably well aware of it.

Julie had pulled her aside before she'd left and let her know that the commander had told Dude about his new daughter. Caroline didn't think Cheyenne would be upset. She knew the guys would've figured she'd had the baby by now.

Caroline and the other women had been texting each other to try to find out when their guys would land, but no one had heard from any of them yet, telling them they were in California, but they all had a feeling it would be soon. Caroline couldn't keep still and she couldn't wait for Matthew to come through the front door.

She was rinsing the plate she'd used for dinner when she heard a key in the squeaky lock from the other side of the house. She spun and for some reason, couldn't get her feet to move. She heard the front door open, then shut, and then heavy footsteps sounded on the wooden floor. Caroline held her breath and then Matthew finally appeared in the doorway to their kitchen. The relief she felt was similar to when she'd seen Matthew appear in her safe house after their plane had been taken over by terrorists.

Caroline drank him in, Matthew looked tired, one arm was in a sling, but he was standing in front of her, and in one piece. She'd take it. She took a step, then another, then another, and then she was in his arms. He'd obviously dropped his bag by the front door, because his good arm wrapped around her and held her tight enough that her feet left the ground. Neither of them said a word, but no words were necessary.

Matthew walked them both over to the couch and sat, never letting go of Caroline. She buried her face in his neck and inhaled, loving his scent, and realizing just how much she missed it when he was gone. She giggled, realizing Matthew had put his nose in her hair and had been inhaling her scent as much as she'd been his.

Finally Caroline pulled back and framed his face with her hands. "I missed you."

"I missed you too, Ice."

"Everyone's really okay?"

"Everyone's really okay."

"Including Sergeant Turner?"

Wolf smiled at his wife. He loved her caring nature. She'd never even met the woman, yet she was full of compassion and concern for her. "From what I've seen on the news, she's fine."

Caroline waited a beat, looking into Matthew's eyes, and knowing she'd pushed him past his comfort point when it came to what he could and couldn't say about his job, let it go. He couldn't exactly admit he knew first-hand how Penelope was doing. She put her head back on Matthew's chest.

"I wouldn't be surprised if we received a Christmas card from Texas in the future, though," he mused, grinning.

Matthew's words surprised her, and she smiled but didn't lift her head. She was about done talking. Time to show her man how happy she was that he was home.

Caroline brought one hand up to his chest and slowly started undoing his button-up shirt. She slipped her hand under the shirt and played with the skin she'd uncovered. She felt her nipples tighten as she played, just as she felt Matthew get hard under her. She licked his neck and bit down on his earlobe.

"I love you, Matthew," she murmured into his ear. "I missed you. I need you."

As ever a man of few words, Wolf stood up easily, still holding Caroline against his side. "Far be it from me to refuse my wife something she needs," he said easily, striding to their bedroom, not letting go and leaving Caroline to stumble alongside him as she tried to keep up with his large strides.

He laid her down on their bed and crawled on his knees over her as she settled. He put his good hand next to her shoulders and straddled her thighs. He leaned down and touched his forehead to hers. "No matter where I go, no matter what I do, *this* is why I do it. To come home to this. To you. I love you, Caroline Martin Steel. You are my home, my everything. I'd fight through the deepest jungles, the driest deserts, and the widest oceans to end my journey right here in your arms."

Wolf leaned down and kissed away the tears leaking out of her eyes.

"Less talk and more action please, kind sir," Caroline teased, running her hands up Matthew's chest, pushing his shirt up as she went.

"Yes, ma'am."

No words were spoken for a long while as the SEAL team leader and his wife reaffirmed their love.

* * *

ALABAMA SAT with Davisa and Brinique and absently watched as they played with their Barbie dolls. They'd been uncharacteristically energetic throughout the day, and Alabama figured it was because they'd somehow sensed Christopher was coming home.

"You're pretty, Mom," Brinique told her out of the blue.

Alabama smiled, realizing again how bright her daughters were. "Thank you, Sweetie. I appreciate it."

Brinique smiled, and kept her eyes on her mom. "Is Daddy coming home today?"

Alabama nodded. "I think so. I'm not sure when, but yeah, I think he'll be home tonight." She had explained to her daughters how Christopher had been hurt, but thought she'd better bring it up again. "You guys remember how I told you Daddy had been hurt while he was away fighting the bad guys, right?"

Both girls nodded solemnly.

"So you have to be careful when he gets here. You can't run into him because he's going to be on crutches. Go easy on him and be careful of his hurt leg. Okay?"

Davisa got up off the floor and went over to Alabama and crawled into her lap. She looked up with her big brown eyes and asked, "We will, Mommy, promise. We'll be really careful."

Alabama hugged her. "I know you will, hon." She squeezed her daughter, and they both looked up when they heard a noise at their front door.

"Daddy!" Brinique screeched, springing up from the floor with an ease only a six-year-old could know and racing toward the front of the house.

Davisa squirmed off of Alabama's lap and hurried after her sister. Alabama quickly followed and held her breath at the first glimpse of her husband after a very long and stressful mission. He was standing with both arms around his girls, with a pair of crutches balanced precariously under his armpits. He looked a bit pale to Alabama, but otherwise unscathed. He was wearing khaki pants and a button-up shirt. There was a faint tan line on his face where a beard had recently been scraped off, but it was the pain lines around his eyes that made her go to him.

She moved to his side and grabbed one of the crutches, propping it up against the wall. She put her shoulder under him and wrapped her arm around his back. Looking up, she murmured, "Welcome home, Christopher."

Abe looked down at the three females in his life and felt his heart expand. God, he'd almost fucked this up a few years ago. He'd almost let this...perfection...slip through his fingers. He thanked God every single day for getting a second chance, that Alabama had *given* him a second chance. Abe lowered his head and brushed his lips across his wife's, relishing the taste and feel of her under him. "Thanks. It's good to be home."

"Daddy, Daddy, we got Barbies!" Davisa shrieked. "Aunt Caroline found them in a box and said we could play with them for as long as we wanted!" She continued, "And Aunt Jess has been throwing up *every day*, and Aunt Cheyenne named her baby Taylor just like I said, and—"

Brinique interrupted her sister. "It's *my* turn to talk. Daddy, I can write the entire alphabet and I'm in charge of brushing my own teeth now, and Akilah taught me how to say 'I love you' in Iraqi and we miiiiissed you."

Abe smiled down at his girls. He'd missed their nonstop chatter more than he'd realized until right this moment.

"Come on, girls, let's let Daddy come in and sit, shall we?" Alabama asked rhetorically, already moving the reunion party farther into the house. She got Christopher settled on the couch, helping him prop his leg onto an ottoman, and they spent the next hour catching each other up with their lives.

Finally the time came for Brinique and Davisa to go to bed. Abe read them two stories and kissed them each on the forehead. "The sooner you go to sleep, the sooner a new day will come." The familiar words seemed to soothe the girls and Abe could hear them snoring before he shut the door behind him.

Abe knew the hardest conversation was still to come. He knew when he sat, he'd be down for the night, so he hobbled into the bathroom to take care of business and then made his way into the bedroom. Alabama was already changed into one of his T-shirts for bed. She put one hand on his face as she went to the bathroom. "I'll be out in a moment. Get comfortable."

Abe nodded and watched with gratitude as his wife went into the bathroom. He quickly stripped off his clothes until he was nude. He needed the closeness being skin to skin with Alabama would bring tonight.

He lay on the bed and didn't bother pulling the covers up and over his legs. He knew Alabama would need to see for herself his injury and make sure he was all right. He didn't begrudge her that in the least.

Alabama came out of the bathroom and over to their bed. Without a word, she sat on the side next to Christopher's injured leg and brushed her fingertips over the still-healing wound, which was covered in a thick bandage.

Abe didn't say anything, he simply let his wife reassure herself that he was there, and was all right. He'd been injured before, but not like this. He hated to seem weak in front of Alabama, but he knew she needed this.

Finally, after another few minutes, Alabama leaned down and kissed the skin above and below the bandage, then she stood up, removed the shirt she was wearing, and climbed into bed. She didn't bother crossing over to the other side, she carefully crawled over him by straddling his knees and moving to his other side. She pulled the covers out from under him and pulled the sheet over them both.

Abe wrapped an arm under her shoulders and sighed in pure contentment as Alabama lay her head on his shoulder and wrapped her free arm over his belly.

"Welcome home, Christopher," she said softly, running her fingers over and around his belly button.

"Thank you. It's good to be home."

"The girls missed you. *I* missed you."

"I missed you too."

"You're really all right?"

"Yeah. To be honest, I missed most of the exciting stuff 'cos I was either high on the pain killers the guys kept forcing into me or passed out, but I'm good. The team took care of me and I'm here and in one piece." Abe didn't censor his words too much. He always wanted to be honest with Alabama, as much as he could be while not worrying her further or breaking his top-secret clearance with the government.

He inhaled as Alabama's hand lowered. When she circled him and squeezed, he stopped breathing. "Alabama..."

"I figured you needed a proper welcome home. I'm not hurting your leg, am I?"

"Fuck no. This would never hurt me."

Alabama chuckled and shifted in his grasp. She felt Christopher hold his breath as she moved down his body and kneeled next to his hip. She glanced up at him as her hands fondled his now hardening shaft. "Well, let me know if I *do* hurt you…" And she lowered her head, doing what she'd dreamed of the many nights that her husband had been gone. She'd always loved taking him in her mouth. He was the only man she'd gone down on, and she loved that she could make him lose his tightly held control when she did this for him.

Fifteen minutes later, Alabama snuggled up next to Christopher again, listening as his breathing settled into a normal pattern again. She smiled against him.

"Jesus, woman. You're gonna kill me."

"But what a way to go, huh?"

"Yeah. I love you."

"I love you too."

"The only thing on my mind while I was out there, lying wounded and not knowing how things would turn out, was you. You're everything to me. *Everything.* I love you," Abe told Alabama, his words quiet in the dark room.

"Christopher—"

"No, I know you know, but I want you to *know* that you've burrowed yourself so far into my heart that you'll always be there."

"Seriously, Christopher—"

Abe didn't give her a chance to finish. "Now…" He tightened his hold on her shoulders and urged her to roll onto him. "Come up here and let me show you how much you mean to me."

Alabama felt her insides moisten as she straddled Christopher's stomach. "I don't want to hurt you."

"As much as I hate to admit it, I'm not up for making love yet, but," he put his hands on her ass and pulled her forward, "I *am* up for this. Let me taste you, babe. Let me *show* you how much you're loved."

Alabama didn't say anything else, she simply did as she was told. She held on to their headboard as Christopher did indeed show her how much he loved her and how much he'd missed her.

* * *

FIONA SAT OUTSIDE on her front porch, not wanting to miss Hunter when he pulled up. She knew he'd be coming home soon, and as much as she wanted to know the exact time, there was something about the anticipation coursing through her belly that made this moment unlike anything she'd ever experienced before.

She hadn't been able to eat anything earlier because of her excitement, but she could now hear her belly growling. There was no question of whether or not she'd leave her post to grab something. She wasn't leaving until Hunter was in her arms.

The light was leaving the sky when Fiona finally heard the sound she'd been waiting for. She stood up and watched as Hunter's truck came rumbling down the street. She stepped off the porch and waited on the grass next to the steps until he stopped the vehicle. Then she was there as he turned the engine off and reached for the door handle. She took a step backward to allow Hunter to open the door, but didn't give him a chance to get out.

Fiona threw her arms around Hunter's waist and held on as tightly as she could.

Cookie swallowed the lump in his throat. It would never get old to be welcomed as honestly and joyfully as Fiona always welcomed him home. He put his arms around her shoulders, waiting for her to get her initial rush of tears out of the way. She always cried when she first saw him.

Finally she pulled her head back and looked up at him. Fuck, he was the luckiest man alive. She was beautiful with her eyes wet with tears and the small smile on her face.

"Welcome home, Hunter."

"Thank you, Fee." He waited, then smiled when she didn't say anything else and didn't move. "You gonna let me get out or are we going to stay out here all night?"

She smiled but didn't move. He smiled back. So be it. He put his hands under her arms and hauled her up and onto him until she was straddling him on the seat. It was a tight fit because of the steering wheel next to his arm, but she didn't seem to care. She wrapped her arms around him and buried her face in his neck.

Cookie shifted his weight and turned with one hand on the small of Fiona's back she was resting against the steering wheel. He leaned over and shut the door to the truck, then reached down and pulled the level that shifted the seat until it was as far back as it could go. Finally Fiona pulled back and smiled down at him.

"Are we going somewhere?"

"No, but you didn't seem to be in any hurry to go inside, and I'm content holding you in my arms no matter where we are, so right here is as good a place as any to make love to my wife."

"Hunter!" Fiona groused without heat. "We can't make love out here."

"Why not?"

"Well…because. We're outside. It's still light."

"It won't be light for long." Cookie put both hands on her jaw and looked into her eyes. "I love you, Fee. You're a sight for sore eyes."

Fiona stopped complaining; hell, she was happy right where she was. She moved her hips forward and nudged against his hard shaft. She'd missed him, but she'd also missed his body. She never thought she'd become as comfortable with her sexuality as she was after all she'd been through, but she believed deep down it was because she trusted Hunter explicitly. He took things slowly with her and made sure she was comfortable with anything they did together. He'd even gone to the clinic and stayed with her every second as she'd had blood drawn and been examined for any sexually transmitted diseases. By some miracle, she'd escaped any physical long-term effects of her time south of the border. And mentally, she was as whole as she was because of the man sitting in front of her.

"I love you too, Hunter. Is everything okay? Is that girl all right?"

Cookie gave Fiona a weird look. He hadn't told her anything about the mission, but obviously she knew, had figured out, some of what they'd done and where they'd been. Knowing she never would've brought up the issue if it hadn't been for her own history, Cookie told her what he could, while still retaining the confidentiality of the mission. "Yeah, she's amazing, actually. She reminded me a lot of you. No complaints and she did what she had to do."

Fiona sighed in relief. God, she was happy to have Hunter home. She reached down and worked on releasing him from the confines of his pants. "You're right. It's getting dark, we're on private property, and our neighbors aren't close enough to see us. I need you."

Cookie smiled and leaned back in the seat as far as he could, giving his wife room to work. "I need you too," he groaned when Fee finally pulled him free of his pants. He looked down to watch her stroking him.

She looked up and licked her lips seductively. "Help me get out of my pants?"

Cookie leaned over, without breaking eye contact and rummaged into the side pocket of his duffle bag sitting on the seat next to him until he found his KA-BAR knife. He flicked it open and reached for the waistband of her yoga pants. "These aren't your favorites, are they?" he asked.

"No. But even if they were, I wouldn't care. Do it." Cutting her clothes off wasn't exactly the help she'd been expecting, but she'd take it if it meant getting her husband inside her quicker.

Cookie took his time and ran the knife down the cotton of her pants, easily slicing through them. She wasn't wearing any underwear, which made him even harder in her grip than he was before.

"Lift up," he demanded.

Fiona came up on her knees and Cookie pulled at her ruined clothes until he could see to the heart of her.

"Fucking beautiful," Cookie murmured, closing his knife and blindly throwing it toward his bag on the seat, not taking his eyes off of Fiona. He brought his hand down and found her soaking-wet folds. With the other hand, he shoved up her shirt and palmed her naked breast, feeling her nipple peak at his touch.

"This is gonna be fast, Fee. It's been too long since I've been inside you."

"Oh yeah, do it. I'm ready," she breathed, panting.

Cookie brushed her hand away from him and ordered, "Hold on to me." When she put both hands on his shoulders, he took himself in his hand and palmed his wife's ass. "Lift up and scoot forward."

Fiona did as he asked and after he'd notched himself where he most wanted to be, he let go and took both her ass cheeks in his hands.

Fiona didn't wait for Hunter to make the next move, she dropped down onto him and ground her pelvis forward, seating him as far inside her as he could go.

"Jesus, fuck," Cookie groaned.

"God, yes," Fiona said at the same time. She tangled her fingers into his too-long hair, remotely taking note that he needed a haircut, and slowly lifted her hips before slamming down. She did it again, and then again before Hunter took over their rhythm.

He moved his hands from her ass to the sides of her hips and gripped her hard enough to leave marks. Neither cared. It was a tight fit, and they couldn't move more than a few inches, but it was enough.

When Cookie felt himself getting close to losing it, and realized Fiona wasn't quite there yet, he ordered, "Take yourself there, Fee. Do it."

He watched as she straightened her spine and sat up on his lap. She moved one of her hands down to where they were joined and used their fluids to coat her fingers before touching herself. She moaned and threw her head back as she continued to quickly flick against her bundle of nerves.

Cookie could tell she was getting close by the way her body gripped him rhythmically. "That's it, Fee. That's it. You're so beautiful. I'm the luckiest bastard in the world. Fuck me, Beautiful. Take me."

At his last words, he felt Fiona grind down on him and hunch into his chest. Her muscles sucked him in and squeezed him so hard he groaned. He lost it and couldn't help his hips from thrusting up once, then again as he emptied himself inside the most beautiful woman he'd ever known, inside and out.

Neither moved, enjoying the closeness and intimacy between them after being apart for so long.

"I love you, Fee," Cookie told his wife, shoving one hand up and under her shirt to rest on her back. The other moved to her ass, holding her to him.

"I love you too. More than I think I'll ever be able to put into words."

* * *

SUMMER WOKE UP SLOWLY, wondering what had disturbed her. She didn't hear April fussing on the baby monitor next to their bed, so wasn't sure what was going on for a moment.

"Hi, Sunshine."

The words were hushed and spoken right next to her. Summer looked up into the eyes of her husband. "Sam," she breathed, trying to clear her sleep-muzzled head. "You're home."

"I'm home," he said simply.

Summer scooted up until her back rested against the headboard. She reached out and hauled Sam into her arms, loving how great it felt to have him home again. She realized he was wearing only a pair of sweats, and no shirt when she felt the crisp hairs of his chest against her cheek. She pulled back and looked up. "How long have you been home?"

"About ten minutes. I looked in on April, then came in here, took off my shirt and I've been sitting here watching you sleep for the last five minutes or so."

"I meant to be awake when you got here, but April has been fussy and waking up more often at night."

"Probably because she feels your stress. She'll sleep better now that I'm home," Mozart said with a bit of arrogance.

Summer would've called him on it, but he was most likely right.

"It looks like I got here just in time though," Mozart said, looking down at Summer's chest.

She looked down and blushed, even though it wasn't the first time her breasts had leaked in front of her husband.

"I'll go get April, settle in," he told her, standing up.

Summer saw the bandage on his arm for the first time. "Sam, your arm! Are you okay?"

"It's nothing. Swear. I'll let you examine it tomorrow."

Satisfied he was telling the truth, Summer nodded. "Okay. Now, go get our daughter before I flood the place."

Sam left the room and returned with April cradled in his arms. Summer moved over and picked up the nursing pillow. Sam put April on it and flicked open the buttons to the shirt Summer was wearing. He parted the material and held up her breast as Summer guided April to her chest.

Mozart settled down deeper into the pillows next to his wife and watched his daughter nurse. It wasn't something he ever thought he'd be interested in watching, but he couldn't get enough of it now. It was amazing to see Summer nurturing his daughter in front of his eyes. April's lips suckled and pursed as she nursed. Her little fist clenched against her mom's upper breast as she fed.

Mozart looked up into Summer's eyes. She was watching him, not April. "You like this," she stated.

Mozart could only nod.

She smiled at him. God, she loved this man. "Switch sides?" she asked, and watched as he turned April and readjusted the pillow. He again held her breast up while Summer guided April's mouth to her breast. Sam's head was right next to his daughter's now and he stroked her head as she fed. When she was full, April's mouth fell away from Summer's nipple.

Mozart ran a finger over the tip of Summer's breast and wiped away a stray drop of milk. "Fucking beautiful," he muttered, before reaching for April. He brought his infant up to his shoulder and stood. "I'll burp her and put her back down. I'll be back. Don't move."

When Summer went to pull her shirt back together, Sam stopped her. "I said, don't move. Not an inch." Summer smiled up at her husband and put her hands back at her sides. "Okay, honey. Hurry back."

Sam was back within five minutes. Without a word, he stripped his sweats off and climbed into bed next to her, completely naked. It was obvious he was happy to see her.

He pulled the shirt she'd been wearing the rest of the way off her shoulders and eased Summer down flat on the bed.

Mozart nuzzled his wife's breasts, loving the sweet smell of milk that lingered after April had fed. He wasn't interested in the milk she could produce, but he *was* interested in how sensitive her breasts were. He pinched both nipples gently, watching as a bit of milk came out of each breast. She squirmed under him, and Mozart smiled. Oh yeah, he loved how sensitive she was.

"I love you, Summer. You're the most beautiful person I've ever seen in my life."

"You're just horny."

Mozart didn't get upset, just smiled wider at his wife. "That too, but that's not why I think you're the most beautiful woman I've ever seen. It's because you just are."

"Yeah, I smell a little funky, and I manage to ruin half the clothes I wear because I can't stop lactating. I've got stretch marks all—"

Her words were cut off when Mozart put his hand over her mouth lightly. "You have stretch marks because you were carrying my child. I don't care how many clothes you ruin, I'll buy you more. You have no idea how amazing it is to watch April suckle from your breast. I understand why some people have kinky baby/mommy fantasies now."

Summer laughed and Mozart continued.

"You carried my child for nine months and you now nourish her. That's a miracle. You are *my* miracle. I know we might not ever have another child because we're concerned about your age, but it doesn't matter. I have you and I have April. I can die a lucky man."

Mozart moved his hand from Summer's mouth and hovered over her, loving how she immediately spread her legs to give him room. He settled himself and reached down to ease himself inside her already wet folds. He kept one hand on her right breast, kneading and caressing her, ignoring the liquid that oozed out and down her side onto the sheet below them.

They were both lost in the moment of being together again after a long, terrifying separation. "You're the love of my life. I adore you, Summer."

Summer arched into Sam's arms, not feeling one iota of embarrassment about her body and what Sam was doing to it. Everything they did was natural and loving. "I love you too, Sam Reed. Always and forever."

"Always and forever," Mozart repeated, making love to his wife as if it was the first time all over again.

* * *

DUDE STRODE INTO HIS HOUSE, dropping his bag on the floor without a thought. He needed to see Cheyenne. After hearing all she'd been though and realizing how close he'd come to almost losing her, all he wanted to do was hold her in his arms.

"Shy!" he bellowed, trying to find her.

"For God's sake, Faulkner, hush! I just got her down!" Cheyenne scolded as she popped her head out of their bedroom.

Dude felt his breath stutter and his heart literally stop beating for a moment. Seeing Cheyenne upright and healthy looking brought it home to him that she really was all right. He'd half imagined he'd find her in bed, pale and sickly. He should've known. His Shy wouldn't let anything keep her down for long.

He headed for her, and she must've seen something in his eyes, because she backed away from him as he entered their bedroom. She backed up until her knees hit their bed and she sat down hard.

Dude didn't stop, but came at her until he was over her with his hands on the mattress at her hips. He leaned over and took her mouth without a word. Loving that she immediately submitted to his kiss, Dude felt himself grow hard against her.

It was still way too soon to take her the way he really wanted and needed to, though. She'd had his baby not a week earlier, and had been through hell in the process. Dude breathed through his nose and tried to calm himself down. There'd be time later to tie her to their bed and make her explode over and over before burying himself in her heat.

He pulled back. "We aren't having any more babies." It wasn't what he thought he was going to say, but as soon as he said it, it felt right. There was no way he was going to risk her life again. No fucking way.

"Faulkner, I'm fine." Cheyenne put her hand on her husband's chest and stroked him, trying to ease his worries.

"Don't care. No more babies."

Cheyenne decided to let it go for now. After seeing Taylor, she knew she wanted more. She'd just have to give Faulkner time to get to know and love Taylor. He'd want a son, she knew it. They'd just have to keep trying until that happened.

"Do you want to meet your daughter?" Cheyenne asked Faulkner gently.

He blinked. It was obvious he'd been so intent on seeing her and making sure she was all right, he hadn't even remembered he *had* a daughter.

"Christ. Yeah," he whispered.

"Help me up," Cheyenne told him.

He did and she kept hold of his hand and led him over to the crib in the corner of their room. Taylor was sleeping soundly. Cheyenne watched as Faulkner leaned over the crib to look more closely at the baby.

"Can I pick her up?" he asked in an awed whisper.

Cheyenne held back the laugh that threatened. "Of course," she told him. "Just be sure to support her head."

Dude reached for his daughter and put one hand under her head and the other under her back. His hands were so big just one covered her entire back and most of her butt as well. He lifted her up and cradled her to his chest. He looked around and brought her over to their bed.

He gently put her down and started unsnapping her onesie. He knew Cheyenne was watching him carefully, but he didn't let it deter him. He pulled one arm, then the other out of her clothes and eased the material down her little body and off. He un-taped her tiny diaper and moved it to the side.

Dude couldn't believe how small and perfect the little human was, lying on the bed where she was conceived. He leaned down and nuzzled her little foot. Then he ran his pinkie, which still looked huge, up her leg to her waist. He marveled at her still-healing belly button.

"An outie," he breathed, looking at Cheyenne for the first time.

She smiled and simply nodded.

Dude turned his attention back to his daughter. He put his finger in her palm and felt his heart clench when she immediately clutched it tightly. He looked over her face. Her button nose, the little patch of dark hair on her head, her tiny perfect ears. Her lips pursed and she squirmed a bit as he watched.

Cheyenne appeared next to him and handed him a soft, fuzzy blanket. "Better wrap her up so she doesn't get cold. You don't want to wake her up."

Dude held the blanket and looked down at his daughter. He wasn't sure how to swaddle her. "Help me?" he asked Cheyenne.

He watched as his wife made quick work of wrapping up their daughter until she resembled a small burrito. She held her out to him. Dude took her and looked down at the little miracle resting in the crook of his arms.

Cheyenne sat next to him on the bed and said, "Faulkner Cooper, meet your daughter, Taylor Caroline Cooper."

Cheyenne never thought she'd ever see her big, bad, dominant, over-bearing, controlling SEAL of a husband cry, but sitting next to him, watching as the tears fell from his eyes and landed on the blanket holding their daughter, was a moment she knew she'd never forget, and would hold dear for the rest of her life.

* * *

JESS LEANED against Kason's car at the Naval base. She'd had the balls to call Commander Hurt and demand to know when her husband would be home. He must've felt some remorse about the entire situation and how they'd all been declared MIA, because he told her they should be heading home by early evening.

Jessyka had taken a taxi to the base to wait for him. She didn't have the patience to wait at home. She wanted to see him as soon as possible, and if that meant she took her ass to him, then so be it. It wasn't the most practical thing she'd ever done in her life, but she didn't care.

She'd taken Sara and John out to eat first. They'd stuffed themselves with chicken fingers then played on the playground at the fast-food place. Then she'd taken them to the park on the Naval base and let them run around even longer.

She'd even forgone their usual nap, not caring they had reached their limit and were grumpy as hell. After the taxi had driven around the parking lot until they'd found Benny's car, Jess had strapped their sleepy bodies into their car seats she'd brought with her, turned on a kids' movie on their tablets, and they were now sleeping the sleep of full and extremely tired toddlers.

Benny walked quickly toward his car, wanting nothing more than to get home to Jess and the kids. He wasn't paying attention, something that could get him killed if he'd been on a mission, but in the middle of a public parking lot at the base, he wasn't too concerned. He'd reached into his pocket to fish out his keys when he heard a feminine voice say, "Hey."

He looked up and gawked. What the hell was Jess doing here?

He didn't care. He surged forward and snatched his wife up in his arms, twirling her around and around, loving her laugh ringing through the parking lot. He lowered her until her feet hit the ground.

"Where're the kids?"

She gestured to the car behind them with her head. Benny turned and looked, seeing his son and daughter sleeping soundly in the back seat, the slight breeze ruffling their hair from the open windows. He turned back to Jess and lowered his head.

She met him halfway and they made out in the parking lot as if they were back in high school. Finally, when Benny felt Jess's hand move over the front of his jeans, he knew he had to pull back. It seemed that Jess was the horn dog in their relationship, and he loved it.

"It's great to see you, Jess. It's *so* good to see you."

"Are you all right?" Jessyka asked, fingering the bandage on the back of his head.

"Yeah, you know how hard my head is." Jess smiled at him. "You should've waited at home. I'm sure it was a pain in the butt to lug those two all the way out here."

"I couldn't wait. I wanted to see you as soon as possible. The extra twenty minutes it would've taken you to get home would've been twenty more minutes I'd've had to wait to see you." She cleared her throat before continuing. "And I have something I wanted to tell you."

Benny stiffened. It was never good when a woman said she wanted to talk. To be fair, Jess hadn't exactly said those words, but that's what he heard. "What is it? Is everyone okay? The girls? Oh shit, the other kids?"

Jess soothed Kason by running her hands down his shirt. "Everyone's fine. It's nothing like that." She watched as he let out the breath he'd obviously been holding.

"Then what is it? What was so important that it couldn't wait until I got home?"

"I'm pregnant." Jess didn't mince words.

"What?"

"Pregnant. It looks like you have the most determined sperm in the history of mankind. Of course, I'm not really surprised, considering they belong to you, but still. We were going to wait, but I guess that plan is shot to hell."

"You're pregnant?"

"Yeah, that's what I've been telling you." Now Jess started to get nervous. Kason hadn't said much. Maybe he was upset?

"Fuck, woman. I love you so much it's not even funny!"

Jess smiled even as Kason was kissing her again. He obviously wasn't upset.

Benny pulled back from his wife, and looked her in the eyes. "I love you. I love that I've knocked you up again. I know it's hard on you to have so many young kids in the house, and I'd already decided to hire a nanny to help you out, but you should know, I plan on keeping you pregnant as much as I can. I want as many kids as you'll let me get away with. I want a huge family, full of laughter, smiles, drama, tears, toys, shit on the floor, arguments over who gets to use the bathroom, and general mayhem. I know I can't bring Tabitha back, and I can't ever take away that hurt, but I love that your womb was made for my sperm."

Jess rolled her eyes. Kason could be such a dork, but at the same time sweet too. "As long as it's safe, and we have healthy kids, I'm not adverse to a big family. But Kason, don't think I'll be like that huge family on television where the mom is having kids into her sixties or whatever."

"Deal." Benny smiled huge and leaned in to Jess to whisper in her ear. "And I love how horny you get when you're pregnant. Bonus for me."

"Kason!" Jess scolded even as he brought her to him again.

"I'm going to take you home, put our kids to bed, then fuck you until you can't walk."

Jess simply shook her head. She loved this man. He was her everything.

* * *

JULIE SNUGGLED up next to Patrick on the couch. "Is Penelope all right?"

Patrick tightened his arm around his wife. He knew she'd need to know about the kidnapped sergeant, and she'd been very patient and hadn't asked. He carefully worded his answer so as not to break his security clearance.

Hell, who was he kidding? He'd already broken it, he just hoped not to smash it into smithereens.

"She's good, Julie."

"Did she..." Julie stopped and cleared her throat and tried again. "Did she handle the rescue all right?"

Patrick's heart about broke at the question. He knew Julie still had feelings of guilt over how she'd acted when *she'd* been rescued by the team. She's mostly worked through them, but it wasn't surprising that this mission brought her insecurities back to the surface. He nodded, then pushed Julie until she was lying on her back on the couch and he moved up so he was hovering over her.

"She was scared, but she was fine. The guys took care of her. But, Julie, it's going to affect her. No one can go through what she...and you...went through and not be affected. You've talked about this with Dr. Hancock, everyone deals with things differently."

Julie bit her lip and looked away from him. Patrick put his hand on her cheek and pulled her lip away from her teeth. "Look at me, honey."

When she lifted her eyes to him, he continued. "I love you. You can be all take-no-prisoners one minute, and the next you're sitting in a room full of teenagers trying on prom dresses, giggling and laughing. Let it go. You're here. You're mine, and I'm not letting you go."

She nodded up at him. "Okay, Patrick. Thank you. I try not to compare myself...but sometimes it's hard."

"I know, but you were with the girls this week and it was all good."

"Yeah, it was. I finally feel like they've truly forgiven me. I was happy to be there for them and that I could help out when they were so worried."

"Good. Now...there's something else I wanted to talk to you about..."

"Yeah? Is everything all right?" Julie looked into Patrick's eyes worriedly.

"Everything is fine...except we haven't been able to spend much one-on-one time together recently. But after this mission, the guys have been given a mandatory two-week convalescence leave. And although I command two other SEAL teams, I've also been granted those two weeks as well..." His voice trailed off as the smile crept across Julie's face.

"Really?" she breathed. "Two whole weeks?"

"Yup. Think you can take the time off from the store?"

"Hell yeah. I own the thing, I'm sure I can manage to sneak away. Oh, Patrick, I'm so excited to spend time with you!"

"We'd better get some sleep," Patrick told her with a smirk.

"What? Why?"

"Because tomorrow we're going to be busy packing and doing last-minutes errands. I'm sure you'll have instructions for your staff."

"Packing? For what?"

"We're headed to Hawaii the day after tomorrow."

Patrick smiled and sat up as Julie screeched and wiggled out from under him on the couch. "Oh my God! Are you serious? I've always wanted to go to Hawaii!"

"I know."

It was as if he hadn't spoken. "I have a million things to do! I need to—"

Julie's words were cut off before she could get going. Patrick swung her over his shoulder and strode for their bedroom door. He knew if he let her get all worked up now, she wouldn't get to sleep for hours...and he had plans.

"Patrick, let me down! I have to—"

"What you have to do is let me love you. Let me show you how much you mean to me. We'll get a good night's sleep...after...and then tomorrow you can worry about packing." He dumped her gently on their bed and caged her down with his body and arms.

"I love you, Julie Hurt. I know you worry about the team, and their women, but I want to give you ten days of worry-free vacation time. Just you and me."

Julie put both her hands on Patrick's face. "I love you. Thank you for seeing the good in me, even when I wasn't sure it was really there. I'd be more than willing to stay here in our house, in our bed, with you for ten days, but Hawaii? You're so getting lucky, mister."

Patrick smiled down at his wife. "I'm counting on it, Babe." He leaned down and kissed his wife, and neither came up for air for a good long while.

* * *

MELODY THREW her head back and tried to get some much-needed air into her lungs. She gripped Tex's sides, knowing she was probably leaving marks on his skin, but not caring. Every time he thrust his hips forward, he rubbed against the bundle of nerves at the top of her mound to make her cry out.

When he scooted forward and pulled her ass farther up onto his lap, Melody's eyes popped open and she looked up. Tex had an intense look on his face as he looked down to where they were joined. He moved one hand and put his thumb over her clit and rubbed her hard as he continued to shift his hips back and forth.

"If you aren't already pregnant, you will be after tonight, I can feel it. Take my seed, Mel. Take it."

Melody couldn't have stopped the words from flowing out of her mouth if her life had depended on it. She and Tex had always had a healthy sex life, but now that there was the possibility she could get pregnant, Tex seemed to be even more vigorous. "Yeah, I want it. Give it to me, Tex. Give me your baby."

"Oh fuck, Mel. I love you so much." Tex's words were torn from his throat as he planted himself inside her as far as he could go and frantically rubbed her most sensitive spot. "Come with me, Mel. Squeeze me dry."

That was it; that was all it took. Mel's back bowed and felt herself squeeze Tex as she exploded in orgasm. She shuddered and shook, and it wasn't until much later that she realized Tex hadn't pulled out or otherwise moved.

She could feel that he wasn't hard anymore, but he hadn't made any move to change position. Melody stretched and arched her back, throwing her arms over her head, enjoying the look of lust in her husband's eyes as he took in her body below him. "Usually we're snuggling by now," Melody said lightly, keeping her arms above her head.

"I want to keep my sperm inside you as long as possible," Tex said in a low voice.

Melody laughed, and felt Tex slip out of her.

"Oh man, you weren't supposed to laugh, Mel."

She couldn't help it—that made her giggle more. Her laughter stopped when she felt Tex's finger entering her and swirling in their combined juices. "You don't think you're pushing it all back in, do you?" she managed to ask semi-seriously, eyeing Tex as he didn't take his gaze from her sex.

"No. Okay…maybe."

Melody smiled again. Sometimes he acted so far from the bad-ass SEAL he used to be, she couldn't even imagine him on a mission. She had no doubt he was as lethal as any SEAL could be, she'd seen him in action when Diane had threatened her life, but it was times like this she treasured the most. "Come here, Tex. Snuggle with me."

Tex scooted backward and let Mel's legs drop. He immediately turned her onto her side and spooned her from behind. One hand went under her head, and the other went to cup her sex gently. They lay like that for quite a while and Melody even dozed a bit before Tex finally spoke.

"All my life I've been told how smart and talented I am. I joined the

Navy and was told how strong I was. I earned a spot on a SEAL team and gave my life over to them and was told I was a team player and valuable as a SEAL. When I was injured, people still told me that I could use my computer skills to help others. It hurt that I couldn't be out in the field, but I did the best I could to help anyone and everyone I could. I enjoyed it. But I have to tell you, Mel, I've never been happier in my entire life than I've been lying next to you here in my bed. My ring on your finger, my come coating your insides, and hopefully my baby growing in your belly. I love you. I'll protect you and Akilah and any children we might have with my life. *You* are what I've waited my entire life for. *You* are why I lost my leg. *You* are my reason for being here. You make me happy just the way you are."

Melody knew there was nothing she could say that would sum up how happy she was, and how much she loved her husband. She settled for the completely understated statement of, "I love you too, Tex."

CHAPTER 29

*P*enelope Turner, the so-called Army Princess, stood at attention in her dress uniform and watched as two coffins were lowered into the ground at Arlington National Cemetery. Lieutenant James D. Love and Sergeant Richard S. Hess were being laid to rest in a private ceremony. She watched as two men she never had a chance to get to know were buried and thanked for their service to their country.

Deep down, Penelope couldn't shake the survivor's guilt she continued to feel.

She'd met with therapists and had some long talks with her brother, but she still couldn't get rid of the feeling that if it wasn't for her, these two brave men would still be alive today, laughing and joking with their friends and family. She vowed to find some sort of therapy group back home in San Antonio. She wanted to find others who might have gone through something similar to what she did…she probably wouldn't be able to find anyone who'd been kidnapped by a terrorist group and held for four months, but there had to be others out there who'd been held against their will and had some of the bad feelings churning inside them as she did.

Penelope looked over at the family members who'd gathered to pay their respects. She only knew what she'd read in the newspapers, but she assumed the gathering included their parents, grandparents, sisters, brothers, sisters-in-law, brothers-in-law, and even an aunt and uncle or two. Neither man was married, not that it made Penelope feel any better.

She watched as the family members left and the cemetery workers continued their work to bury the coffins in the ground. She stood and watched as the dirt was tamped down. She stood still even as a light rain began to fall.

Cade, as well as all the other firefighters had offered to come with her today, but she'd declined. It meant the world to her that Moose, Crash, Squirrel, Chief, Taco, and Driftwood had even offered. They weren't the touchy-feely kind of men, and knowing they cared enough about her as a member of their team was enough to make her break into tears.

Penelope sighed once, continuing to mourn the life of Lieutenant Love, who'd copiloted the plane that had gotten her out of the shithole that was the refugee camp and her temporary prison. She thought about Sergeant Hess. She'd never spoken to him, but he'd been the one to grasp her hand and help her onboard the MH-60. She'd looked into his eyes and seen nothing but confidence that they'd get the hell out of there in one piece.

She turned to leave—and stopped abruptly.

Standing behind her in a single-file line, at attention, were seven men, all in their Navy dress white uniforms. They wore no medals, no ribbons, only their name badges. They stood there, supporting her, and supporting the two dead Army soldiers behind her.

Refusing to cry, Penelope walked slowly over to the men standing so stoically and still. Knowing she was probably making a fool out of herself, she started with the first man. His name tag read, "Keegan." She'd never met him, but supposed this was probably the elusive, Tex. Before she could chicken out, she stepped up to him and wrapped her arms around him, hugging him tightly for a moment, before letting go and stepping back. "Thank you for finding us, Tex," she said softly, watching as the man nodded in return, but didn't say anything.

She moved to the next man in line. His nametag said, "Cooper," but she knew him as Dude, the man who'd first freed her from her prison. He was ready for her, and hugged her back when she wrapped her arms around him. "Thank you," Penelope said softly.

Then it was Benny's turn. His nametag read "Sawyer." She hugged him, and again, simply said, "Thank you."

Penelope moved down the line of men, hugging each one in turn. "Reed", otherwise known to her as Mozart; "Knox" who was Cookie; and

"Powers" who was Abe. To him, she said "Thank you," but added, "You looked like shit the last time I saw you, glad to see you clean up well."

Ignoring his chuckle, Penelope moved to the last man in line. Wolf. The man in charge. The man who'd taken responsibility of this group and had moved heaven and earth to get her the hell out of Turkey and away from ISIS. The man she knew she'd never forget as long as she lived.

She wrapped her arms around him and felt him hug her back so hard, he lifted her off the ground in his embrace. "Thank you, Wolf. Thank you for not giving up on me." She wasn't expecting his response.

He eased her back to the ground, but didn't let go of her. "Thank *you*, Tiger, for being the kind of woman, and soldier, who could hold on until we could get there. Go live your life in peace. You've earned every second of happiness you can get. You've got seven big brothers in us now. We'll be watching out for you. Wherever you go, whatever you do, if you need us, all you have to do is ask."

Penelope felt Wolf move his hands down her back and rest on her ass for a moment before he let her go. It surprised her, but she figured it was an accident. The seven men saluted her, then left, fading back into the trees. She watched as they disappeared, not bothering to wipe away the tears that fell from her eyes and dripped down her face.

She turned to walk back to her car. She was spending the night in Washington DC, the President was awarding her with the Bronze Star the next day in a very public and televised event. She wasn't very excited about it, knowing there were others way braver than she'd been who would never be recognized publically and couldn't even tell anyone they'd been over there with her. But she'd take the reward on behalf of Lieutenant Love and Sergeants Hess, Black, White, and Wilson, and even that poor Australian soldier who had been killed in front of her eyes. Penelope thought about the Delta Force soldiers as well, they'd never get any recognition, other than her undying thanks and devotion.

The war with ISIS wasn't going to end anytime soon, but Penelope was done fighting it. She'd met with her commander and they'd agreed she was done with the military. She had a few more commitments she had to the government, but for all intents and purposes, she was free to be a full-time firefighter for the rest of her life. Her honorable discharge papers would be waiting for her when she got home.

She put her hands in her back pockets as she wandered down the too-long row of tombstones. Feeling something strange, she pulled her hand out and stared down at the small black object in her hand.

What the hell?

She unwrapped the folded piece of paper and found a small pendent in the shape of a Maltese Cross. The paper it had been wrapped in said, *Our men rescued us, and since they rescued you too, you're now one of us. Wear this and you'll never be lost again.*

Penelope thought about it and finally smiled for the first time that day. It sounded like it was a gift from the wives of the SEALs who had rescued her. Not only that, but apparently it was also a tracker like the men, and their women, wore. Wolf had slipped it into her pocket.

A tracker.

His words suddenly made sense and her smile grew. They'd be watching over her. It felt good. Right. She felt better for the first time in a long time. If she ever needed anyone at her back again, she not only had her firefighting buddies, but she had an entire SEAL team, and apparently their wives, as well.

Feeling stronger than she had in a long time, Sergeant Penelope Turner took a deep breath and straightened her shoulders. She'd make it through today. Then tomorrow. Then the next day. Then the next day after that. No problem. Piece of cake.

The End

Author's Note: This is the end of the SEAL of Protection Series, but as you can probably imagine it's not the end of the road for some of your most loved characters. The Delta Force team you were introduced to in this story gets their own series, starting in Feb 2016, and of course you'll see Penelope and her firefighting teammates in a future series as well. And if you couldn't tell, Tex will continue to be the behind-the-scenes lifesaver in future books. That man knows everyone!

THANK you for your love and interest in my SEAL team. I never dreamed you'd fall as much in love with them as I did as I was writing them. In the meantime, check out the Badge of Honor series, featuring law enforcement/firefighter heroes, and of course, Tex makes an appearance as well.

THE FIRST BOOK in the Delta Force Heroes Series is NOW available. Find out more about Ghost in *Rescuing Rayne*. For an exclusive peek at Ghost's story, scroll to the end of the book for the first two chapters!

RESCUING Rayne

As a flight attendant, Rayne Jackson is used to cancellations, but she never dreamed her latest would lead to a whirlwind tour of London with a handsome stranger...or a life-altering night in his bed. One evening is all the enigmatic man can give her, and Rayne greedily takes it, despite suspecting it will never be enough.

Heading home after another extreme mission, Keane "Ghost" Bryson hadn't planned to seduce someone during his layover, but Rayne is too sweet to resist. Being a Delta Force member means lying to protect his identity, which is unfortunate, considering Rayne seems made for Ghost, right down to the tattoo on her back. For the first time in his life, regret fills him as he slips away the following morning.

Both are shocked when, months later, they meet again—under the worst possible circumstances. Seems fate has given them a second chance...if they can survive the terrorist situation they're in. If Rayne can forgive Ghost his lies. And if Ghost can trust Rayne to be strong enough to endure the secrets and uncertainty that come with loving a Delta Force soldier.

** Rescuing Rayne is the 1st book in the *Delta Force Heroes* Series. Each book is a stand-alone, with no cliffhanger endings.

To sign up for Susan's Newsletter go to:
http://bit.ly/SusanStokerNewsletter

PROTECTING KIERA

SEAL OF PROTECTION, BOOK 9

CHAPTER 1

*K*iera Hamilton stood in a corner of *My Sister's Closet*, the secondhand clothing store owned by her friend, Julie Hurt, and sipped the lukewarm champagne she'd been nursing for most of the night.

She'd only agreed to attend the shindig because Julie had let it slip that Cooper would be there.

Cooper Nelson. The man was six feet, two inches of perfection, and way out of her league. Not only that, he was too young for her. There were a million other reasons why it was stupid for Kiera to have a school-girl crush on the man, but it hadn't prevented her from going out of her way to attend the small party.

Kiera had met Julie when her first-grade class had toured the Navy base. Julie had been there visiting her husband, and when one of the children in the class had wet his pants, she'd come to the rescue. Her car had been full of clothes she'd just picked up from the cleaners to take to her store to sell, and she just happened to have a couple pairs of little boy pants. They'd hit it off, and now spent most of their free time together.

Kiera knew all about Julie's past...how she was the daughter of a senator who'd been kidnapped a few years ago. Julie had been upfront about how awful she'd been to her rescuers during that ordeal, and how she now felt like she'd finally found the person she was meant to be.

She owned and operated the small boutique, selling used designer clothes. She also donated a healthy amount of her inventory to homeless women who needed nice outfits to interview in, lower-income girls who needed dresses to wear to high school dances, and lately, she'd even begun selling men's clothing, as well as donating Armani and other designer suits to down-on-their-luck men who needed to make a good impression.

"Are you having a good time?"

Kiera startled and almost dropped the flute of champagne, but managed to keep hold of it. She turned with a smile to Julie. "Of course. You must be thrilled at the turnout tonight."

Julie's smile was huge as she nodded. "Sometimes I have to pinch myself at how well things have worked out. Not only did I find the man of my dreams, but I've actually been able to make a difference in many people's lives. It feels good."

Kiera beamed at her friend. Tonight's celebration came about because a young woman who Julie had given a professional outfit to a few years ago was interviewed by a local television station in Los Angeles, and the story had subsequently gone national. The woman's story, unfortunately, wasn't unusual. She'd escaped an abusive relationship, had gotten into drugs and was living on the streets. She'd cleaned herself up enough to get into a homeless shelter, but couldn't find a job.

Julie had met her in her first year of business, during one of her trips to the shelter to talk to the women who ran it. She'd invited Rebecca, the woman looking for a job, to her shop to pick out an outfit free of charge. To make a long story short, Rebecca had gotten the job she'd interviewed for and now, two short years later, had made her way up to an executive manager position.

The party tonight was more to celebrate Rebecca's success than anything else, but the influx of donations, both monetary and clothing, was a boon to rejoice in as well.

Kiera looked around, noting there were quite a few of Riverton's elite at the party. The mayor was there with his wife and she recognized the Chief of Police as well. As her gaze swung around the room, she stopped on Cooper and sighed. She had it so bad for him.

Cooper had been under Julie's husband's command as a Navy SEAL, but was injured while on a mission and had retired. An explosion had gone off too close to where he'd been standing, and while he'd gotten away with all his limbs, he'd lost hearing in his right ear, and almost seventy percent in his left.

Kiera worked with deaf children at the Riverton School for the Deaf, and had seen Cooper when he'd shown up to volunteer with the children. The first time she'd seen him standing in the hallway of the school, she'd been surprised at the immediate attraction she'd had toward him. She wasn't the kind of woman who fell in lust at first sight, but Cooper just did something for her. He was tall, which she loved. Even though she'd spent her life looking up at people, there was just something about a man towering over her that turned her on. It made her feel more feminine, protected...something.

He had russet-colored eyes that were a shade lighter than his dark brown hair, which was badly in need of a trim. He'd been wearing jeans that molded to his muscular thighs and a short-sleeve polo shirt had shown off his bulging biceps. All in all, he was beautiful and intimidating at the same time.

She was just Kiera. Not a super soldier or really anyone extraordinary. Like a lot of women, she had extra pounds on her slight frame that she couldn't seem to get rid of...not that she'd really tried. After a bad experience with extreme dieting in college, Kiera had decided to try to live a life of moderation, not deprivation. She ate and drank what she wanted, tried to stay fairly active without being a crazy workout freak, and as a result, was content with her body.

But looking at Cooper that day, she'd suddenly wished she spent more time at the gym and hadn't eaten the sleeve of Girl Scout cookies the night before. Amazingly, however, he hadn't seemed bothered by her weight. He'd smiled at her, shook her hand and, unless she was completely misinterpreting the look in his eyes, seemed to be attracted to her.

Since that first meeting, Kiera had spoken to Cooper every time he'd visited the school. They'd laughed together and she'd thought they were hitting it off. She'd believed their attraction was mutual, but he hadn't done anything about it. She figured that maybe he was reluctant because she worked at the school where he was volunteering, so when Julie said Cooper had promised to come to the party that night, Kiera had jumped at the chance to attend.

But she might as well've stayed home, doing what she usually did on Saturday nights...namely, sitting on her couch either reading or watching TV. Cooper was at the party, but it almost seemed as if he was avoiding her, staying on the far side of the store. Kiera had watched him, and he seemed out of sorts and irritated, not talking to anyone, merely giving chin lifts to the other SEALs who were attending.

Kiera had pretty good self-esteem, she liked her job, loved working with children, and even though she was short, liked her body most days. And she generally didn't mind the fact that she was an introvert, preferring to sit at home by herself than go out and hang with friends. But standing in a corner, watching the groups of women laughing together, how the attached men doted on their wives without them seeming to notice, and as Julie's husband, Patrick, kept glancing over at his wife and smiling, made Cooper's standoffish manner—after she'd thought they were friends—all the more frustrating and depressing.

She was brought out of her musings by Julie's hand on her arm. She'd almost forgotten the other woman was standing next to her and they'd been having a discussion about how she'd gotten together with her husband. "You've totally made a difference in Riverton. You should be proud of yourself."

Kiera's gaze swung behind the other woman and she said, "Speaking of the man of your dreams," She got the words out right before Patrick came up behind Julie and put his arm around her waist.

"It's good to see you, Kiera," he said after kissing his wife on the temple.

"You too. All good on base?"

"Can't complain. You talked to Coop tonight?"

Kiera wasn't surprised he'd brought him up. He'd told her, in confidence, that Cooper was having a hard time adjusting to civilian life. He'd planned on being in the Navy for as long as they'd have him...but losing most of his hearing made that time end about twenty years before he was ready.

"No. Our paths haven't crossed," Kiera told him honestly, not mentioning that it wasn't for lack of effort on her part.

"Damn stubborn sailor," Patrick murmured under his breath.

Kiera's eyes flicked over to the corner Cooper had been occupying almost without her thinking about it. He was still there, frowning and looking extremely tense. She knew Julie was talking, but Kiera barely heard her. Something about Cooper's body language was bugging her. She tilted her head and kept her eyes on him for a long moment.

"...right?" Julie nudged her arm to get her attention.

"I'm sorry...what?" Kiera asked, looking back at Julie apologetically.

"I was just saying that Patrick talked to his secretary and he—"

"Admin assistant," Patrick interrupted.

"What?" Julie asked.

"Admin assistant. Not secretary. I don't think Cutter would enjoy being called a secretary."

Julie rolled her eyes at her husband and smiled at Kiera. "Sorry... Patrick's admin assistant," she brought her hands up and used them to make air quotes around the words, "said he'd gladly arrange another visit if you wanted. He loved hanging out with the kids."

"I don't know, we were quite the intrusion," Kiera said reluctantly. And they had been. Taking kids who couldn't hear on any field trip was never easy, but a trip to a working base with men in uniform and all their toys had been especially interesting with her group. The fourteen kids in her class could hardly contain their excitement, signing in their limited vocabulary and loving the attention they'd received from the sailors.

"Never an intrusion," Patrick said with a smile. "Kids are a gift." His hand moved to Julie's belly and he pulled her back against him, caressing her all the while.

"Oh my God, are you pregnant?" Kiera blurted, eyes wide.

Julie smiled and tilted her head up to Patrick. Her hand came to cover his on her stomach and she nodded.

"Congrats, that's so great!" Kiera gushed.

"Thanks. We're pretty happy," Julie told her friend.

"As well you should be. When are you due?"

"Six months or so. I'm only about twelve weeks along."

"Seriously, that's awesome."

"Yeah. We think so too. Anyway, Coop's been coming to the school, right?" Patrick asked.

Kiera nodded. "I saw him several times last week. We even had lunch one day."

"What's his problem then?" Patrick mused, more to himself than either of the women standing with him. "He's standing over there acting like an asshole. I'm going to tell him to get his head out of his ass or go home."

Patrick shifted behind Julie as if to do exactly that when it finally hit Kiera what was up with Cooper.

"No, don't. Let me talk to him."

Both Patrick and Julie's eyes came to her. "Something I need to know?" Patrick asked in a commanding voice.

Kiera shook her head quickly. "It's just...I think I know why he's been so out of sorts tonight."

"Want to share?" Patrick asked.

Kiera bit her lip in indecision.

"Never mind," Julie's husband said. "I suppose it's not important. If you can get through to him, I'd be grateful. But, Kiera..."

She looked up at the tall, forceful man. She'd more than once had the thought that Julie was a lucky woman after talking with Patrick. He was everything she'd always wanted in a man...and hadn't been able to find. Strong, sure of himself, gentlemanly, and protective.

When she met his gaze, Patrick continued, "If he's not polite to you, let me know. He might not be under my command anymore, but no man disrespects a woman when I'm around. I'll be watching."

Kiera swallowed hard. She knew Julie and Patrick, but they weren't people she would exactly call best friends. But hearing Patrick say he'd have her back felt good. Really good. It had been a long time since anyone had done what Julie's husband was offering...even if she didn't think it was necessary.

"I'll be fine," Kiera reassured Patrick. "Cooper wouldn't do anything like that."

Patrick shrugged. "Maybe the Coop I used to know. But ever since he was injured, I'm not sure."

Kiera started to get upset. Even though Cooper had been ignoring her all night, she didn't think he'd be disrespectful to her face, and still wanted to defend him. "Maybe you don't know him as well as you think you do," Kiera fired back, an angry flush to her cheeks. It was a juvenile come-back, as the man knew Cooper way better than she did, but she couldn't stand there and say nothing.

Patrick didn't respond for a long moment before his lips twitched as if he was suppressing a smile. "Let me know if I can help in any way."

"I will," Kiera forced herself to say. She didn't want to piss off the commander, but jeez. "I'll talk to you later, Julie."

"Later, Kiera," the other woman responded.

Kiera put her champagne glass down on a tray sitting nearby and headed across the room toward Cooper. She couldn't believe it had taken her so long to figure out what his issue was. Now that she had, she kicked herself for not acting sooner.

CHAPTER 2

*C*ooper Nelson stood against the wall of the small boutique that belonged to his former commander's wife and stared blankly at the people milling about around him. His head felt like it was going to explode. He glanced down at his watch to see how much longer he had to suffer before he could politely bow out.

He genuinely wanted to be there; he was happy for Julie and Patrick, but the ringing in his ears was excruciating. It was almost ironic that while he'd lost most of his hearing, at the moment he wished he'd lost all of it.

Cooper hadn't thought much about the party and how it would affect him. He'd just gotten in his car and showed up, as he would've before he was injured. But the longer he was there, and the more people filled the small space, he quickly realized that the buzz of voices and low music playing was amplified by his hearing aid. He'd tried turning the volume on the device down, but as a result he'd been unable to hear what anyone said to him when they spoke, so he'd turned it back up. And the fact that the noise was only registering on one side of his head made him feel off kilter, and even a little sick to his stomach.

He'd arrived at the get-together excited to see Julie's friend again, but his excitement had quickly waned when he realized how hard it was to hear, and now he just wanted to go home and hide in his blissfully silent apartment.

Just as he'd decided that it was time to leave, whether or not it was rude, he felt a hand on his arm. Looking down, Cooper saw the reason he was at the party at all standing next to him, her brow furrowed in concern.

Kiera Hamilton.

He'd been fascinated by the woman since the first day he'd met her. Patrick had recommended/ordered he volunteer at a deaf school near the base, and Cooper hadn't been happy about it. He'd felt as if his commander was pushing his disability down his throat and it had pissed him off. He'd gone, but had sworn to himself that he was just doing it the one time to placate Patrick.

The moment Cooper had seen Kiera, he'd been smitten.

Smitten. It was such a silly word for how she made him feel. It didn't matter that she was ten years older than him or that she was way out of his league. The second he saw her signing with a child in the middle of the lunchroom, he'd wanted to get to know her.

He'd seen a lot of dark things in his twenty-seven years, things no human should ever witness, let alone participate in. He'd known it going in. Had known being a Navy SEAL wasn't all glorious Hollywood-style hostage rescues, but the reality had been much harsher than even he could've imagined. Body parts strewn across the sand after a bomb exploded, hostages who had been abused so badly they were mere shells of who they used to be, blood, guts, gore, and the worst of humanity.

He didn't remember much about the explosion that had stolen his hearing...only recalled the horrible pain in his ears and the blood pouring out of them as if a faucet had been turned on high.

But seeing Kiera's smile as they were introduced had almost made everything he'd seen and done disappear. She was his reward, she just didn't know it yet.

So when Patrick had not-so-subtly told him that Kiera was going to be at his wife's party that night, Cooper had jumped at the chance to talk to her outside of her work. To discuss something other than learning sign language, how his hearing aid was working out, and what he thought about the school lunches he'd been eating with the children.

But his fantasies of chatting with her in a neutral setting disappeared like smoke when Cooper realized that he'd never be able to hear her in the noisy room, and when the pain in his head started.

"Come on," Kiera demanded.

Cooper didn't actually hear the words, but instead read her lips. She surprised the hell out of him when she reached down and intertwined her fingers with his and tugged. Without protest—Kiera could hold his hand anywhere, anytime—Cooper docilely followed behind her.

If his former teammates could see him now, they'd get a kick out of the situation. The woman clutching his hand wouldn't be able to budge him if he didn't want to go with her, but he did. Cooper had no idea where she was taking him, but it didn't matter. He'd follow her to the ends of the earth. The view of her ass in her skirt was merely a bonus. Even though it felt as if there were hundreds of gnomes pounding inside his head with little hammers, he smiled.

As the diminutive woman led them toward the front door of the boutique, Cooper placed the glass of champagne he hadn't been drinking on a table they passed. He noted absently that Kiera waved off at least three people, not stopping to chat, not even to be polite. He appreciated it. He needed fresh air. Badly. Before the nausea swirling deep in his belly got the better of him. He didn't think Julie would appreciate him hurling all over the floor of her shop.

Catching Patrick's eye, Cooper lifted his chin in a goodbye of sorts. In return, the other man flashed him the hand signal for "be careful."

Kiera didn't give him a chance to respond, but Cooper understood Patrick's warning. Kiera was friends with his wife. If he fucked with her, he'd fuck with his former commander. But Cooper had no intention of fucking with Kiera...not in the sense Patrick was warning him about.

Cooper had the quick thought that the hand signals the teams used to talk to each other when they couldn't speak were an awful lot like sign language, but before he could dwell on that more, they were outside the small shop.

The immediate silence of the night was blissful. Even the slight ringing in his left ear was tolerable. Kiera didn't stop, but continued as if she had a specific destination in mind, and Cooper didn't say a word.

She led them past the independently owned businesses that lined the street to Julie's store until they reached a small square. It reminded him of the ones in the rural towns he'd grown up around in the Midwest, all it was missing was a large courthouse. There was a building in the middle of the area—Cooper had no idea what was inside—and around it was green lawn, a fountain off to one side, and a multitude of benches. It was a cozy place where shoppers could come to rest, employees could eat their lunch, or parents could bring their kids to be out in the fresh air instead of cooped up inside.

Kiera led him to a bench and stopped. She pointed down at it and signed the word for sit. Cooper's lips twitched but he did as she ordered.

When they were both seated, she frowned up at him and said slowly, giving him a chance to read her lips in case his ears were still ringing, "When you're in a small, enclosed area with lots of people, you should turn off your hearing aid. All it's gonna do is give you a headache."

She was right.

"You're right." He tried to monitor how loud he was speaking, but couldn't. There were times he knew he was talking way too loud and others when whoever he was speaking to had to ask him to repeat whatever it was he'd said, as he was almost whispering and didn't know it, but Kiera didn't give him any clues if his voice was at an appropriate level or not. She just responded.

"I know."

Cooper couldn't hold back his grin anymore. "How'd you know?"

"That you were in pain?"

He nodded.

"Besides the fact your brows were permanently drawn down, you kept tilting your head to the left as if that would block the sound, you fiddled with your ear several times and you were squinting?"

Cooper's grin left his face. Damn. He'd thought he'd hidden his discomfort better than that. "Yeah, besides that."

Kiera put her hand over his on his leg. The warmth of her touch almost scorched him. He froze, not wanting to move even an inch if it'd mean her removing her hand from his.

"For one, I've seen the kids in my class with partial hearing act exactly the same way you were when the noise is too loud. It took me a bit, as I'm used to watching in the classroom for signs someone's hearing aid is bothering them, not at a party like the one tonight. And secondly, you were being rude. Not talking to anyone. Not even saying hello to me."

"I'm sorry, I—"

"No, don't apologize. I wouldn't talk to anyone either if my ears were ringing and a jackhammer was going off in my brain." She smiled when she said it, and Cooper could see the sincerity in her eyes.

"How do you know what it feels like?"

"I don't. Not really. But I've talked to enough of my students and heard them describe the feeling that I've learned to recognize it. It took me longer with you though."

When she didn't continue, Cooper asked, "Why?"

A slight blush moved up her neck and into her cheeks, giving her a rosy glow. She pulled her hand away from his and clasped them together in her lap. She looked away from him and shrugged.

Cooper put one finger under her chin and gently pulled her back to face him. "Why?" he repeated.

"My feelings were hurt that you didn't seem to want to talk to me," Kiera blurted, then pressed her lips together.

"I'm sorry."

"No, it's fine. It's silly really. I just…I usually stay at home on the weekends. I'm an introvert at heart, and after a week of being with the kids and talking with the other teachers and parents, I'm exhausted. But when Julie told me you were going to be at her party, I thought maybe we could talk away from school." She shrugged, not taking her eyes from his. "Then I got there and you wouldn't even look at me. It hurt. But I understand now. It's not a big deal."

Cooper's stomach tightened, but not from nausea this time. Kiera had wanted to talk to him. She came to the party because he was going to be there. He felt just like he had when he was ten years old and Renee Vanderswart said he could walk her to her bus after school one day. Giddy. Excited.

He put his hand over hers in her lap. "The only reason I was there was because Patrick said you'd be there."

Cooper saw her blue eyes light up. "Really?"

"Yeah," he confirmed. "But by the time I got there, it was already crowded. The second I walked in the store, my hearing aid started buzzing. I knew I wouldn't be able to have a decent conversation with you, and I was too stubborn and embarrassed to take the stupid thing out and fiddle with it. So I thought I'd stay long enough to be polite and then take off. I'd already decided to explain when I saw you at school in a few days."

"I understand."

"I don't think you do," Cooper countered.

She tilted her head and wrinkled her brow.

"Kiera, I wanted to impress you. But I knew I wouldn't be able to hear myself speak, and I couldn't tell if I was yelling or whispering. Not to mention, I wouldn't be able to hear what you were saying. I'm getting better at reading lips, but I still have a long way to go. And since I'm being honest, I still can't tell if I'm talking too loud or soft, but I can hear you pretty well at the moment, so there's that."

"You're doing fine," she reassured him.

Cooper squeezed her hands. "The point is, I want you to see me as a man, Kiera. Not as a wounded ex-sailor. Not as a student."

She stared at him for a long moment, and Cooper could feel his heart beating hard in his chest. It was ridiculous. He'd stared down the scope on a rifle for hours waiting for the right moment to take his shot and hadn't felt this kind of adrenaline rush.

Kiera took a deep breath, but didn't look away from him. In many ways, she was eons braver than he'd ever been.

"I'm old enough to be your mother."

Cooper stared at her for a beat, then threw his head back and laughed. When he got himself under control, he looked back down at Kiera and chuckled anew. She was glaring up at him with squinty eyes. He ran a fingertip between her eyebrows. "The only way you'd be able to be my mother is if you were sexually active in elementary school, sweetheart."

"You're missing the point," she huffed, trying to pull her hands out from under his. "And how do you know how old I am anyway?"

Cooper got serious. "I'm not missing the point, and I asked Patrick."

She gaped up at him. "You asked Patrick?"

"Yup. He asked his wife, who told him, and he told me. You're thirty-seven. Have been working at the Riverton School for the Deaf for ten years. Your mom is deaf and that's how you learned to sign. You've never been married and haven't dated seriously in at least five years. You met Julie when you took your kids to the base for a tour. She had an extra pair of pants for one of your students when he had an accident."

Kiera gaped up at him.

Cooper smiled, loving having the upper hand. Loving the dance. He'd been pussyfooting around her for long enough. It was time he stopped and let her know how he felt. "Yeah, I asked, Kiera. I wanted to know everything about you."

"Why?"

"You have to ask?"

She dropped her eyes for the first time and the blush returned.

"I want to get to know you. I want to know what you like to eat, about your childhood. I want to meet your parents, but hopefully you can teach me to be more fluent in sign language before we do. I want to be able to talk to your mom and have her tell me stories about what you were like when you were a kid. I want to know what your home looks like, if you can cook, and what you like to watch on TV."

She bit her lip and took a deep breath.

Cooper forced himself to continue. "I want all that stuff, but I know you could do so much better than me. I've seen stuff that would make you reel in horror. Things I don't ever want to think or talk about again. Most of the time I'm uncouth and say the wrong thing. I don't have patience for stupid people and I'm not sure I want to have children. I don't have a college degree and I'm disabled. I'm afraid I won't be able to protect a woman like I should, since I can't hear what's going on around me, and that sucks."

"Cooper—" Kiera began, but he interrupted her, wanting to get it all out.

"I don't give a shit about the ten years between us. I'm twenty-seven, but some days I feel eighty-seven. It's not about the number, it's about this feeling inside me that is screaming you're the reason that bomb didn't rip me to pieces. It should've, Kiera. I was standing right there. I know I sound insane, but I think everything happens for a reason, and the reason I lost my hearing was so I could meet you. All I'm asking for is a chance. Give me a chance to show you I'm not an asshole...well, not to *you*. I swear if you let me into your life, I'll do everything in my power to make your next forty years better than the first."

Cooper stopped talking and could see emotions swirling through Kiera's eyes. He held his breath, waiting for her response.

CHAPTER 3

*K*iera stared up at Cooper in disbelief. There was so much in what he'd said...she didn't know where to start.

He'd asked about her. Her. Not only asked, but probed.

But one thing stuck out above everything else. "You're not disabled."

He snorted. "I hate to be the one to break this to you, but I am."

Kiera shook her head vehemently. "Gandhi once said, 'Strength does not come from physical capacity. It comes from an indomitable will.' My other favorite quote is by Oscar Pistorius. He's the South African Olympic sprinter who had both legs amputated below the knee when he was a baby."

"I know who he is," Cooper said with a smile. "Wasn't he also convicted of killing his girlfriend?"

"Yes, but that's beside the point. Actually, it probably makes my point more. I bet if he saw himself as disabled he wouldn't have been able to kill anyone. *Anyway*, I was going to tell you something he once said. 'You're not disabled by the disabilities you have, you are able by the abilities you have.'"

"I'm not sure my abilities are things polite society wants or needs," Cooper said dryly.

Kiera moved one of her hands to his leg and said softly, "I teach the children in my classes that they can be whatever they want. They can do whatever they want. They might need to make adjustments to accommodate them, but just because there's never been a deaf opera singer doesn't mean there never will be."

"I bet if I Googled it, I'd find one," Cooper told her.

"You're missing my point," Kiera huffed, sitting back in frustration.

"I'm not, I'm just teasing. I promise to work on my attitude about my loss of hearing, but you'll need to give me some time. I was a SEAL, sweetheart. One of the most feared and respected men in the military. Now I'm out of a job and struggling to figure out what to do with the rest of my life. I can't do many of the things I took for granted and it's…hard."

Kiera had more respect for Cooper at that moment than she did for most other people. He didn't shy away from the fact that he was floundering after retiring from the Navy. She decided to move on and commented on some of the other things he'd said earlier.

"First of all, you're more…male…than most men I've ever met. You being able to hear or not has no bearing on that whatsoever."

His lips didn't move, but the lines around his eyes deepened with her words…as if he was smiling with his eyes. She continued, hoping she'd convinced him on that particular point.

"I don't care if you say the wrong thing at the wrong time. I'm too old to care what others think about me or my friends. Stupid people are one of my pet peeves. And I love kids and being around them all day, but I also love going home to my quiet apartment, putting my feet up, and drinking a glass of wine. I'm not sure at this point in my life I want kids either."

It was the first time she'd said the words out loud and they were somehow freeing. "Society thinks women who don't want to procreate are somehow wacked in the head. But I enjoy my life. I *like* being able to go on vacation wherever and whenever I want. I don't care about your lack of a degree; you're smart, have common sense, and I'd rather be around you than a lot of so-called educated people I know. You don't have to protect me. I've been taking care of myself for a really long time. And if there is something you need to know that you can't hear, I don't mind passing along the intel."

They stared at each other for a long moment.

"Does that mean you're okay with our age difference?" Cooper asked quietly. So softly Kiera could barely hear him.

"Not really," she said honestly. When his brows wrinkled in frustration or disbelief, she wasn't sure which, she hurried to explain. "I'm afraid if we do get together you'll decide in a few years that you've wasted your late twenties. That you'll think you've missed out. I'll be in my late forties when you're still in your thirties. I'll be hitting menopause when you're—"

Cooper stopped her rambling with a hand over her mouth. When she stopped speaking, he moved his hand until his fingertips rested against the back of her neck and his thumb brushed the apple of her cheek.

"If you give me a shot, and we end up together, I'll never, ever, regret a second of our time with each other. I haven't been a monk, but any desire I might've had to take random women home with me died the second that bomb exploded. I didn't have anyone to talk to, to sit by my side as I recuperated...and I realized how much time I'd wasted. I don't want a meaningless hookup. I want a committed relationship with a woman who wants to spend her life with me. Give me a chance, Kiera. A chance to show you that I'm not a fuckup. That I can be the kind of man who'll treat you like you were meant to be treated."

"Promise me one thing," Kiera said.

"Anything."

"That if you change your mind, if the difference in our ages does start to bother you, you do want kids, or if you want more than the boring life of sitting around and watching TV on a Saturday night, you'll tell me. Don't cheat on me, hit me, or do something else so *I* have to break up with *you*."

"I promise," he said immediately. "But I'll tell you right now, it's never gonna happen. First, I'd be an idiot to cheat on you. I know for a fact that we're gonna be combustible in bed together. Sitting here holding your hand has me more excited and aroused than I've ever been before. I have no doubt you're gonna blow my mind if we ever make love. And after the last few years on the teams, I can't think of anything better than hanging out with you every night doing nothing. I've had enough excitement to last me a lifetime. And there's no way in hell I'd ever hurt you. No way."

"But if—"

"No ifs, ands, or buts about it, sweetheart. But if it makes you feel better, yes, I promise I'll tell you straight up if I don't think things are working out between us, so we can both move on with no hard feelings."

Kiera sighed in relief, then nodded.

They stared at each other for a long moment before she asked, "How's your head?"

"Better."

She brought her hand up to his face and mirrored his hand placement, brushing her thumb against his cheek. "So...now what?"

"A kiss to seal the deal?"

Her lips twitched. "To *SEAL* the deal?"

He grinned. "Yeah."

"I'd like that."

Cooper's head moved toward hers and Kiera held her breath. If asked, she never would've guessed this was how the night would've ended, especially not after seeing Cooper standing in a corner, his shields up, rebuffing anyone who tried to come near him.

Kiera closed her eyes and the second their bodies made contact, she swore she saw stars. His lips brushed hers tentatively once, then with more confidence a second time. Kiera tightened her grip on his neck and pulled him into her, telling him without words how much she liked his touch.

When Cooper's tongue swiped along her bottom lip, she gasped, giving him the opening he'd obviously been waiting for. He used his hold on her to tilt her head to a better angle and he wasted no time delving inside her mouth.

He used his tongue as well as she imagined he handled a weapon—with pinpoint accuracy and confidence. He knew what he was doing... and Kiera could only hang on for the ride. He alternated between forceful thrusts, which mimicked what she so desperately wanted him to do to her body at a later date, and easy, soft caresses.

After several moments, he pulled back and nuzzled her nose with his own. Kiera opened her eyes and blinked up at him, licking her lips, tasting him on them. "So...now what?" she repeated.

Cooper smiled. "Now what? We date. Get to know each other. Flirt at your workplace. Steal kisses. You'll continue to teach me to sign and I'll treat you like you're the most important thing in my life."

"I have a feeling you're not going to have any issues picking up sign language, if the last couple of weeks have been any indication," Kiera told him. She'd been impressed with how quickly he'd been able to learn the basics, and knew with more time spent on it, he'd quickly become proficient.

Cooper leaned forward, kissed her once more—a closed-mouth kiss that still made her knees weak—and stood. "I have a good teacher. Come on, I'll walk you to your car."

With a smile, Kiera stood and they walked hand in hand to the parking lot.

* * *

THE NEXT MORNING, Cooper walked through the building he used to call his home at the Navy base. He nodded at some of the SEALs who were hanging around. He'd gotten to know some of them a lot better since his injury. He'd been afraid after he was medically retired that he'd never again have the kind of camaraderie he'd come to rely on from his team, but the men, and sometimes their wives, had been there throughout his recovery. They'd brought food, come to visit, and encouraged him to work out with them in the mornings.

A man with salt and pepper hair and a neatly trimmed mustache and beard, a former SEAL himself, sat at a desk outside Patrick Hurt's office and lifted his chin as Cooper came toward him.

"Hey, Coop. Lookin' good."

"Thanks, Cutter. How're things?"

"Can't complain," Slade "Cutter" Cutsinger responded. "Hurt's waiting for you."

Cooper only heard every other word the man said, but understood enough to get the gist. Patrick had invited him to the base for a meeting this morning. In the past, Cooper might've been upset with the man for continuing to want to butt into his life, but this morning, after kissing Kiera the night before and learning that she was open to going out with him, he was hard-pressed to be annoyed about anything.

He pushed open the door to his former commander's office and stopped in his tracks. He'd expected Patrick to be alone, but instead there was another man already sitting in one of the chairs in front of the large desk. Cooper didn't recognize him, but immediately knew he was either currently a Special Forces operative, or used to be. It wasn't something he could explain to someone who wasn't in their small circle. It just was.

His dark hair and brown eyes might lure some people into thinking he was a pretty boy, but they'd be wrong. Lethalness seemed to ooze from his pores even though he was simply sitting there.

Without thought, Cooper reached up to his left ear and pressed on his hearing aid. He felt it shift inside his ear canal, and he sighed in relief when he heard Hurt's chair squeal as the man stood.

"Thanks for coming, Coop," Hurt said.

Cooper concentrated on the other man's lips, and that, along with the amplification of his hearing aid, was able to help him understand him. It

378

was a relief. He instinctively wanted to be on top of his game with the stranger.

"No problem. What's up?"

"I'd like you to meet a friend of mine. John Keegan…otherwise known as Tex."

Cooper turned to the other man and held out his hand. "*The* Tex?"

"The one and only," Tex answered with a small smile on his face as he shook his hand.

"Wow. It's really good to meet you."

Tex smiled. "Same. I've heard good things about you too and when Hurt called and asked for my help, I decided to take a trip out here. It's been a while since I've seen my friends."

Cooper knew about Tex. Hurt had talked about him quite often. A former SEAL, Tex had lost his leg, and now helped the commander—and probably a lot of other top-secret teams—with missions. He was a computer genius, and even though Cooper didn't know most of what the man did, he knew enough to know the SEALs and US government were lucky to have him on their side.

"Is everything all right?" Cooper asked Hurt. "Why's Tex here?"

"As you probably know, Tex lives on the east coast with his wife, Melody. He assists me and many other commanders around the country in gathering intel. He knows a lot of military men, retired and active duty, SEALs and Delta Force operatives who were either injured on duty or who have had enough of the teams."

Cooper eyed Tex a little more closely as Hurt continued. His initial reaction to Tex, before he knew he was the infamous former SEAL, had been correct, it was nice to know he hadn't lost all of his intuitiveness after being injured and away from the teams.

"I asked him to come down and spend a few days talking with you. I know you've met with the Navy psychologists, but there's no one who knows what you're going through better than someone who has been in your shoes."

Tex interrupted Patrick at that point. "Look, I have no idea what you're going through with your hearing. I have to deal with my leg giving me fits now and then, but it's not the same as losing my hearing, sight, or something else. I'm not here to tell you how to deal with that. Hurt asked me to talk with you about my transition to civilian life."

Cooper blinked. That so wasn't what he'd thought the other man was going to say. He'd had lots of people tell him how he should deal with the loss of his hearing and what to do with the rest of his life. But no one understood what it was like to try to transition from constantly being on call for his country and flying off at a moment's notice, to sitting around an apartment with no one needing him and no chance of *getting* that call.

His first inclination was to tell Tex to fuck off, that he was transitioning just fine, thank you very much, but then he thought about Kiera. He wanted to be worthy of her, and he was afraid if he didn't get his head screwed on straight and figure out what he wanted to do, he'd lose her. Maybe this former SEAL could help him.

"I can't say that I'm thrilled with Hurt going behind my back, but I wouldn't mind having a beer or two with you. But not at a bar. I can't hear shit."

Tex chuckled. "Not a problem."

"Now, if we're done bonding, I need to get going."

"You get a job I don't know about, Coop?" Hurt asked, leaning forward in his chair.

Cooper smirked. "No, Dad. I'm volunteering at the deaf school you guilted me into going to a few weeks ago."

The look that spread across Hurt's face could only be described as smug. "Let me guess...Ms. Hamilton's classroom?"

"Fuck off," Cooper said without heat.

"Ms. Hamilton?" Tex queried.

"She's a teacher at the school. I thought it might do Coop some good to see how easily kids can adapt to a life without being able to hear."

"And it wasn't a bonus that Kiera was friends with Julie?" Cooper asked.

"You still owe me for sending her to you," Tex told the commander.

Hurt smiled and rolled his eyes. Then he turned back to Cooper and got serious. "Kiera is a wonderful person. She works hard and is a good friend to Julie. But more than that...I like you, Coop. And if you got together with a friend of my wife's, I'd see you more. And I'd like that too."

Coop didn't know exactly what to say to that. But it felt good. Damn good to know that his former commander was more than just a boss. He was a friend too.

"Now...get the hell out of my office so I can get some work done," Hurt said, ending the touchy-feely conversation. "And say hello to Kiera for me."

Cooper and Tex both stood. They gave chin lifts to Patrick and headed out of his office.

"Hey, Coop," Cutter called out.

Cooper didn't hear him and continued toward the door. Tex touched Cooper's arm and gestured toward the administrative assistant with his head.

Fighting the urge to apologize for not hearing the summons, Cooper turned to the older man and raised his eyebrows in question.

"Wolf and the rest of his team have challenged you and Tex to a duel… so to speak. They think you guys are going soft now that you're retired. Tonight. Eighteen hundred. On the beach."

Cooper's eyes gleamed. "You wanna join us, old man?" he asked.

Cutter smiled. "Fuck yeah."

"See you later," Cooper said

"Later," Cutter responded.

As he and Tex were walking to their cars in the parking lot, the other man commented, "To be honest, I don't know why Hurt asked me down here. Don't get me wrong, I'm thrilled to be able to hang out with my friends, but you seem like you're doing just fine."

Cooper shrugged. "Maybe. Maybe not. But I'd love to hear your story. I haven't heard the story of how you met your wife."

Tex smiled. "I pretty much cyber stalked her."

Shocked, Cooper stared at the man in disbelief.

Tex chuckled. "We met online. She was being stalked and ghosted on me. I tracked her down."

"And her stalker was caught?" Cooper asked.

Tex nodded.

"I can't wait to hear this story."

"And I'll tell it to you…over a couple beers."

"I'm looking forward to it." And for once, Cooper wasn't telling someone what he thought they wanted to hear. He meant it.

The two men pounded on each other's backs and climbed into their respective cars.

As curious as Cooper was to hear Tex's story, all thoughts of the other man and the upcoming competition on the beach fled. He was looking more forward to seeing Kiera again.

CHAPTER 4

$\mathcal{K}$iera smiled as Cooper knocked on the door to her classroom. She'd been informed by the principal that Cooper requested to volunteer with her class today. Even though he'd been at the school many times over the last couple months, he hadn't ever been in her room. She'd tried not to be hurt by that, but couldn't deny it had.

She'd just gotten her first graders settled down with their tablets when Cooper arrived. The students were watching videos of a book being read and signed at the same time. Getting the youngsters familiar with both the written word, a picture, and the sign for the word was imperative in their cognitive development. They typically learned slower than children who could hear, but she'd found that most were starved for knowledge and, once they got the hang of reading, were extremely quick to pick it up and correlate words with the correct signs.

She walked over to greet him and blushed as he stared at her lips as if he wanted to devour her right there in the doorway. "Hey."

"Hey. Is this a bad time?"

Kiera shook her head. "Not at all. I just got them settled with books. How come you haven't ever volunteered in my classroom before?"

"I'm not great with kids this young," Cooper admitted as he followed her into the room. "The older ones I can impress with my background, but little ones aren't as easily swayed."

"You'll be fine," Kiera told him, his insecurity somehow making him all the more appealing to her. "Wait here while I get their attention," she told Cooper, pointing to a spot at the front. When he nodded, she walked around the room, putting her hand on each child's shoulder and signing something to them.

When she had everyone's attention, she signed at the same time as she spoke. "Class, this is Cooper Nelson. He is here to read with you."

A little girl threw up her hand in question.

"Yes, Becca?"

The little girl's hands moved slowly, but she was obviously asking a question about Cooper as she gestured to him several times.

Kiera repeated her question for all the other children in the class. She found that sometimes the children had a hard time reading someone else's signs and it was good practice for everyone to see the same signs done several times.

"Becca asked if Mr. Nelson knows sign language. She also asked if he was deaf. He knows some sign language, but he just started learning, like all of you. Cooper can hear a little out of his left ear, but wears a hearing aid like some of you do. He is completely deaf in his right ear."

A little boy's hand went up, and Kiera pointed at him and said while signing, "Yes, Billy?"

Billy's hands moved as he asked his question.

Cooper put his hand on Kiera's arm and asked, "Can I answer?"

She smiled up at him and nodded.

Cooper kneeled on the ground and turned his head to the kids and pointed to his hearing aid. Then he signed, slowly, and imprecisely, "I was standing too close to a..." He paused and looked up at Kiera and shrugged.

Her heart melted. He was trying so hard, and getting on the same level as the kids was something a lot of people didn't realize made a huge difference. She quickly said and signed "explosion." He smiled at her and turned back to the children, who had been watching the two adults with wide eyes.

"Explosion," Cooper signed. "It made me lose my hearing."

Six children immediately raised their hands with questions. Kiera chuckled.

They spent the next twenty minutes playing question and answer. Cooper painstakingly tried to answer each question and Kiera helped him with the correct sign when he didn't know it, which was often.

Cooper answered questions about whether he had any scars, if he was married, if he had children, how old he was, what he did for a living and if the explosion had hurt. He'd answered them as honestly as he could and didn't laugh at some of the silly questions the kids asked.

The awe and adoration was clear to see on most of the children's faces. It wasn't often they'd seen a man like Cooper—a strong, tall, *masculine* man—make the effort to talk to them in their language. His obvious lack of expertise made him seem more approachable to them, as did his constant laughing at his ineptitude.

Just when Kiera was about to tell the children to get back to work, a little boy sitting in the back of the classroom slowly raised his hand. She hid her surprise. Frankie was small for his age and wasn't making much progress. He was very reluctant to sign and hadn't made any friends in the class since he'd been there. He frequently resorted to pushing the kids in his class when he couldn't understand them or when he wanted his way.

Kiera knew his attitude was a result of his tumultuous home life and starting in a new school and her heart hurt for him. Frankie's father was excited about the chance for his son to be in the special school. They'd moved down to Riverton from Los Angeles for a fresh start after a contentious divorce. His ex-wife was a drug addict who was deemed unfit to have custody of their son. Until recently, she'd been allowed to have supervised visitations with Frankie, but after slipping away from the court-ordered supervisor and taking Frankie to the mall to a drug drop, she'd had all parental rights stripped from her.

Kiera understood that the little boy was probably having issues dealing with all the upheaval in his life, but it had been two months since he'd started school and he wasn't getting any better. The fact that he'd engaged enough to raise his hand and ask a question was almost a miracle at this point.

She pointed at the skinny boy and signed, "Yes, Frankie?"

He mostly used the alphabet to spell out his question, but it was understandable, if not painful to wait for him to get through.

Kiera swallowed and flicked her eyes to Cooper before repeating the question for the rest of the class. "Frankie asked what his tough military friends thought of Cooper using his hands to speak in such a sissy way."

A few of the kids gasped and whipped their heads around to gaze at Frankie with wide eyes. Kiera hadn't realized that was what Frankie thought of sign language. It was as heartbreaking as it was shocking.

Bless Cooper, he didn't even blink at the question. He got up and went over to where Frankie was sitting. When he got there, he sat on his butt and awkwardly crossed his legs. Then he proceeded to blow Kiera's mind.

He used mostly finger spelling, as Frankie had, and not once did he look to Kiera for a sign. "My friends are jealous that I have my own secret language. Believe it or not, Frankie, my team had our own hand signals for stuff. This," he made a movement with his hands that Kiera didn't recognize, "meant danger. And this," he did it again, making another sign that clearly wasn't American Sign Language, "meant bad guy ahead. I don't know who told you that sign language was sissy, but it absolutely isn't. It's cool. The coolest thing I've ever tried to learn. I can talk to you, your classmates, or Ms. Hamilton, and people who aren't deaf can't understand me. It's like being an undercover spy right under people's noses. I love knowing a secret language, even if I'm not very good at it yet."

If Kiera hadn't been watching Frankie carefully, she would've missed it, but his eyes got big and she could literally see the knowledge that a big, strong man like Cooper thought sign language was cool sinking into his psyche.

She'd tried for months to get Frankie to show an ounce of interest in anything she did or said, to no avail. But with one painstakingly finger-spelled answer, Cooper had somehow bonded with the young boy in a way she'd rarely seen before.

Swallowing hard so she wouldn't burst into tears, Kiera waved her hand in the air to get the children's attention. She sighed, "Now that we have all met Cooper, time to get back to your lessons."

The kids all nodded and shuffled back to various places around the room with their tablets. There were beanbags strewn around the classroom, as well as small couches, and big fluffy rugs... more than enough choices for the children to settle in comfortably somewhere.

She looked over at Frankie and Cooper and caught the tail end of Cooper's question to the little boy. "...me sit with you while you read?"

Frankie nodded his head and Kiera watched in awe as Cooper and her troublemaker student shifted so they were sitting facing each other, knees touching, with the tablet off to their right. Frankie reached out and turned it on, activating the story he'd been reading before the interruption.

Over the next thirty minutes, Kiera watched from the corner of her eye as Frankie and Cooper went through one story, then another, then finally a third. She'd never seen the little boy as interested and engrossed in a lesson as he was during that half hour. He and Cooper signed each word as the narrator of the book instructed. They smiled at each other often and at one point, Frankie even reached out and corrected one of Cooper's signs.

It was time for lunch and Kiera corralled the children and got them lined up to head down to the lunchroom. There were several monitors who assisted the kids who needed it in getting their lunch trays and generally kept order in the large cafeteria. As they were waiting for a monitor to lead everyone down the hall, Kiera eavesdropped on the conversation between Frankie and Cooper.

"Will you come back?" Frankie finger spelled.

"Yes," Cooper signed.

"When?"

Cooper paused for a long moment then finally signed, "If you want me to, I'll be here every day."

Kiera gasped. He couldn't tell Frankie that. It would crush the little boy when he didn't actually show up every day. Before she could rush over and do damage control, Frankie surprised her.

"Don't say it if you don't mean it," the little boy spelled out.

Cooper placed one of his large hands on Frankie's thin shoulder and spelled out with his other hand. "I don't say things I don't mean. Do you want to learn a secret sign me and my military friends use?" Cooper asked in a mixture of letters and signs.

Frankie eagerly signed, "Yes."

"Okay, but it's super-secret and it's a man code. You can only greet other men this way. Okay?"

Frankie impatiently signed once again. "Yes."

"Watch carefully," Cooper signed, then lifted his chin in the way Kiera had seen him greet his friends in the past.

She used her hand to cover the smile on her face.

Frankie furrowed his little brow and tried to imitate Cooper.

"Pretty good, but instead of making it look like a nod, just lift your chin a little bit instead." Cooper demonstrated again.

Frankie mirrored him and this time, amazingly, he did it. The chin lift he gave Cooper was a mini-version of the badass "hey" Cooper gave his friends.

"That's it! You did it. Good job. Now remember...only manly men get that chin lift. It's our secret hello and goodbye code." He glanced over at

Kiera and winked, then turned back to Frankie. "I'll see you tomorrow Frankie, right?"

Frankie nodded and had a big smile on his face. The first time Kiera could remember the little boy ever doing so since he'd started school.

The line started to move, and Cooper stood up straight and looked down at Frankie. He gave him the chin lift and signed, "Goodbye."

Frankie returned the chin lift and sign, then walked proudly out of the room behind his classmates.

Kiera shut the door behind her students and walked directly to Cooper.

"I—"

She didn't let him get any other words out before standing on her tiptoes and putting both hands on either side of his face. She tugged his head toward hers and planted her lips on his. His arms immediately locked around her and he pulled her into him so they were touching from hips to chest.

He let her control the kiss for a moment, then took over. Devouring her mouth as if he hadn't seen her in years instead of the night before. They finally broke apart, but Cooper didn't let go of her. He kept her plastered to the front of his body as he asked, "What was that for?"

"You are a miracle worker," Kiera told him.

He chuckled. "Don't think Mother Theresa would agree with you on that one, sweetheart."

Kiera shook her head. "Seriously. I've been trying to get Frankie to respond to me with a tenth of the enthusiasm he showed you today...with no luck. And you spent thirty minutes with him and he's like a completely different child."

"All he needed was some attention," Cooper protested. "I didn't do anything special."

"No, that's not it," Kiera insisted.

"I know." Cooper's voice had dropped until it was barely audible, but Kiera didn't interrupt him. "Someone's been filling his head with shit about how a real man acts. I think seeing me, a former Special Forces operative using sign language, legitimized it somehow. All I had to do was show him that it's okay to talk with my hands. That it doesn't make him any less of a boy. I want ten minutes in a room with whoever has been filling his head with that shit. Probably his dad."

"It's not him," Kiera told him, running her fingernails lightly down the back of Cooper's neck where she'd rested her hands. "His dad loves him to pieces. He's a single dad who is working his ass off to get his son what he needs to succeed."

"Whoever it is should be shot," Cooper murmured, then lowered his head to the space between Kiera's neck and shoulder. He inhaled and nuzzled the skin there.

Kiera felt goosebumps move over her at the feel of his lips against her bare skin. She tugged lightly on his hair and he lifted his head to look at her.

"Are you really going to come every day like you told Frankie? You can't lie to these kids, Cooper. If you tell them something, you have to follow through."

"I wasn't lying. I really would like to stop by every day...if that's all right," he finished uncertainly.

"It's all right," Kiera reassured him immediately. "But I'm afraid you'll get bored."

"Kiera, I spent almost eight years of my life getting shot at, blowing shit up, and putting my life on the line for my country. Spending time with kids, helping them learn, helping myself learn, sounds like heaven."

Kiera swallowed hard. She didn't know any men, not one, who would say something like Cooper just had. "Okay."

"Okay." Cooper smiled at her, then pulled her hips harder into his own. She could feel his erection against her core and her inner muscles clenched. God. "You want to have dinner tonight?"

"Yes," she answered immediately. She wanted as much of Cooper's time as he'd give her. It didn't matter that it was a school night. It didn't matter that she wasn't playing hard to get. If Cooper wanted to spend time with her, she would grab on to that with both hands.

He smiled down at her. "I have to do a thing with the SEALs on the beach at six, but maybe I can pick you up afterwards?"

"What thing?"

Cooper rolled his eyes. "Me and two other retired SEALs were challenged by an active-duty team."

"Challenged how?" Kiera asked, tilting her head.

"Not to the death, if that's what you're thinking," Cooper grinned. "You should've seen your face. Just to a friendly physical competition on the beach. Sit-ups, running with the Zodiac, swimming, that sort of thing."

"Can I come watch?"

She saw some sort of emotion move through Cooper's eyes, but couldn't interpret it. She hurried to say, "If it's not allowed, that's okay, I just thought it might be fun to watch you in action."

"You'd like that?" he questioned.

"Seeing you and a bunch of other SEALs, hopefully in nothing but short shorts, running around on the beach flexing and trying to prove who's stronger and more badass? Hell yeah, I'd like that," Kiera told him with a smile.

His hands moved to her waist and he started to tickle her. Kiera screeched and tried to wiggle out of his grasp. "Cooper, stop! I'm extremely ticklish!" She couldn't stop giggling, and her hands pushing at his chest were ineffective to stop the intimate torture.

"You want to look at other men's bodies, Kiera?"

She giggled some more and said, "No, just yours!"

"But you said you wanted to check out my friends' asses."

"No, I didn't. I'll only look at your ass...swear!"

"Promise?"

Kiera couldn't stop giggling. Coopers fingers might've been tickling her, but she loved having his hands on her...and his playfulness. "I promise...please..."

"Please what?" Cooper asked, putting his arms back around her and yanking her into his rock-hard body once more.

Kiera looked up at him then and brought her arms up between them, signing as she said, "Please kiss me."

Cooper glanced at the door, and while Kiera appreciated his awareness of where they were and the fact anyone could come inside the classroom at any time, at the moment, she didn't care. She needed his lips on hers again.

Without a word, Cooper did as she asked. He kissed her as if his life depended on it. Slow and fast, deep and shallow. It wasn't just a kiss, he learned what she liked, that she moaned deep in her throat when he sucked on her tongue and dug her nails into his chest when he nibbled on her bottom lip.

Five minutes later, Cooper pulled back and looked down at her. He placed a hand on her forehead and ran it gently over her blonde hair, smoothing it down as he went. "Do you really want to come tonight?"

Kiera nodded.

"I'll pick you up at five-twenty?"

She nodded again.

"Means a lot to me, Kiera."

"What does?"

"That you want to be involved in my world. Not just be with me because I have a good body, or because I'm good with the kids in your class."

"Cooper, I wouldn't care if you were a world-class chess player...I'd want to be there to support you because you enjoy doing it. And while I won't deny that I can't wait to see your body tonight, that's not why I'm with you."

"Why *are* you?" he asked.

Kiera could see the insecurity in the badass man in front of her and it made him that much more real to her. "I've never been as attracted to anyone as I am to you. You're a good person. From the first time you walked into the school, I could tell that you were uncomfortable, but you didn't let it stop you from jumping in with both feet. You aren't afraid to admit that you don't understand something, and so far, you haven't been discouraged when learning a new language gets tough. You see me—not just the teacher, not just Julie's friend, but me. I'm not afraid to be myself around you, and even though I'm scared to death you're gonna take one look at my naked body and ask yourself what the hell you're doing with an almost-forty-year-old woman...I can't wait to make love with you."

"Damn," Cooper breathed.

"You asked," Kiera said with a smile.

"That I did. And for the record, the feeling is definitely mutual. You don't see only the SEAL when you look at me, at least I don't think you do. You see me. So I get what you're saying. And no worries, Kiera..." Cooper moved his hands until they were grasping the globes of her ass and pulled her into him until she was standing on her tiptoes. Their crotches were aligned, and Kiera could feel every inch of his hard cock against her. She shifted in his grasp and tried to get closer...to no avail.

"I'm going to love every inch of your body. Have no doubt." He leaned down and took her mouth in one more hard, intimate kiss before pulling back and putting a couple inches of space between their bodies.

"Wear comfortable clothes tonight. Jeans, blouse, flip-flops...after we kick the SEALs' asses, I'll shower and we'll go somewhere casual for dinner. Burgers all right?"

"Absolutely."

As if he couldn't help himself, Cooper leaned down and kissed Kiera once more then stepped away from her and dropped his hands. "See you tonight then."

Kiera nodded, then gave him a chin lift.

His lips quirked, and he said, "Sorry hon, that's reserved for us men." Then he winked and was gone.

Kiera sat at her desk to eat lunch and thought about Cooper. She'd known the man a few weeks now, ever since he'd begun volunteering at the school, but somehow over the last twenty-four hours he'd become not just a man she'd like to get to know better, but one she didn't think she could live without.

Smiling big, she finished her lunch and thought about what she was going to wear that night. Yeah, seeing Cooper and his friends rolling around the sand in minimal clothing certainly wasn't a hardship. Not at all.

CHAPTER 5

$\mathcal{K}$iera sat on a sand dune that overlooked a section of beach on Coronado Island. Cooper had picked her up right at five-twenty...but they'd still been ten minutes late to the beach. He'd taken one look at her in her skinny jeans, flip-flops, navy blue scoop-neck shirt that had a picture of a military man aiming a rifle and lying in a puddle of water with the words, *Stay Low, Go Fast. Kill First, Die Last. One Shot, One Kill. No Luck, All Skill*, and her blonde hair flowing freely around her shoulders instead of confined back in the bun she usually wore at the school, and he'd backed her against the front door and proceeded to ravish her.

It had taken his phone vibrating in his pocket with a text from a man named Cutter, warning him not to be late, to break them apart. He'd closed his eyes, rested his forehead against hers and said in a low, controlled voice, "You're gonna be the death of me."

Kiera had simply responded, "But what a way to go."

Now she was sitting on a giant pile of sand with four other women, watching as their men competed against each other down near the surf.

"I'll never get tired of this," Julie stated with a sigh.

One of the other women—she'd been introduced as Caroline—agreed. "Right? When Wolf told me he'd challenged Tex and two other former SEALs to a physical battle, there was no way I wasn't going to be here."

"I'm just thankful Fiona could watch our kids on such short notice," a Navy wife named Jessyka said.

"Anyone bring any popcorn?" the last woman in their group, who had been introduced as Cheyenne, asked.

Kiera had liked the other women immediately. They'd made her feel comfortable and not at all awkward, as she usually did when she met new people. Julie had mentioned all three of them at one point in past conversations, but this was the first time she was getting to spend any time with them.

"You know what...Tex is hot," Cheyenne observed.

Jessyka rolled her eyes. "You do remember that you're a married woman, right?" she asked her friend.

"Of course. Faulkner won't let me forget it, not that I would want to. But there's nothing wrong with looking. And I don't think I've ever seen so much of Tex before."

Kiera agreed wholeheartedly. She knew the other SEALs knew Cooper's new friend Tex, but wasn't exactly sure how he was connected to everyone. She let it go. The spectacle below them was definitely too drool-worthy to think about anything else at the moment. The men had stripped off their T-shirts and were currently wrestling with each other... she wasn't sure exactly what they were doing, but didn't really care either.

"I swear to God, every time I see Cutter, I send up a prayer that Benny will look just like him in a decade or so," Jessyka murmured, resting her chin on her hand as she gazed down at the men. "He's just so...manly looking."

"Manly looking?" Julie laughed. "As if the other guys aren't?"

"You know what I mean. He looks distinguished. His graying hair and beard, his broad shoulders...even the hint of gray in his chest hair is fucking hot."

"Is he dating anyone?" Julie asked. "Patrick tells me all about how awesome he's been since he's started working as his admin assistant, but he doesn't tell me about anyone's love life."

Caroline shrugged. "I don't think so, but Wolf is the same way. They'll gossip like girls with each other and in the office, but then he'll tell me that it's a man code thing and he can't share details. Sometimes I wish our men weren't so honorable."

Everyone chuckled but Kiera inhaled sharply when a foot came shooting toward Cooper's face.

"Relax," Cheyenne soothed, resting her hand on Kiera's arm. "Your man has this."

And he did. As soon as the foot moved toward him, Cooper had grabbed hold and wrenched it upward, throwing one of the SEALs to the sand on his back. The men all laughed and continued to try to beat the crap out of each other. At least that's what it looked like to her.

"Can anyone tell who's winning?" Cheyenne asked.

"Does it matter?" Jessyka asked.

Cheyenne laughed. "I guess not. I know that I'll reap the benefits of all that bottled-up testosterone tonight though."

Kiera giggled along with the other women and shifted in her seat. She'd love to be on the receiving end of Cooper's bottled-up hormones. The thought excited her. She liked the thought of her man being romantic as much as the next woman, but the image of Cooper ravishing her and taking what he wanted, how he wanted, and as hard as he wanted, was a huge turn-on.

They continued to watch as the men put each other through their paces. Like Cheyenne, Kiera couldn't tell who was winning and what exactly each competition was, but watching the men move was like seeing poetry in motion. They were all built, buff, and in extremely good shape. It was obvious the three retired SEALs had no problem keeping up with the active-duty guys. Even Tex, with his prosthetic leg, made the physical exertion look easy.

After about an hour, and a final dip in the ocean to rinse off the sand, the men all shook each other's hands. Five men headed up the sand dune toward their women, while the rest gave each other chin lifts and headed for the parking lot or the offices.

Kiera's lips twitched at seeing the chin lifts back and forth, it reminded her of little Frankie and how awesome Cooper had been with him. She met his eyes as he climbed the slight rise to get to them.

He came right up to her and took her head in his hands and kissed her. It didn't even seem awkward to have him stake his claim so publicly and carnally.

"Hey," she said when he finally pulled back.

Cooper shook his head and pointed to his ear, indicating he wasn't wearing his hearing aid.

Kiera hadn't seen him remove it, but it made sense. It probably wouldn't have been good to get sand under it, not to mention the sea water. Not knowing how he felt about signing in front of his friends, she hesitated. But she shouldn't have. As if he could read her mind, he half-signed, half-spelled, "You think I'd say all that stuff to Frankie then be embarrassed to sign in front of my friends?"

Kiera smiled back and quickly signed, "No, but I didn't want to do anything that might jeopardize my chance of getting some at a later date."

Cooper barked out a laugh and grinned from ear to ear.

"No fair, man," Wolf complained. "Want to let us in on the joke?"

Kiera looked to Cooper, who was still watching Wolf. She quickly signed, "Wolf wants to know what's funny."

"Nothing you need to know about," Cooper said out loud to his friend, still grinning. "You know, I never really thought twice about the nonverbal signals we always used on the teams, but it's amazing how similar some are to ASL, American Sign Language."

Kiera loved that he had no problem speaking with his friends, even without his hearing aid and without being able to hear their responses.

She barely heard the other men agreeing and mumbling about needing showers. She only had eyes for Cooper. Every moment she spent around him had her falling harder. All the weeks she'd gotten to know him during his time spent at the school had morphed her feelings from respect and admiration, to lust and longing. She couldn't say she loved him yet, but she knew it wouldn't take long. Not if he continued blowing her away with his awesomeness.

"I need a shower," he signed.

"Yes, you do," she returned.

His lips quirked. "Don't be shy. Tell me what you think."

"I will. Hope that isn't a problem."

"No. I love it. Come on. Let me shower, put my ear back in, and we'll go."

She loved how he'd phrased that...put my ear back in. It was casual and not at all self-conscious. It was perfect.

"How long have you known Cooper?" Cheyenne asked as the group headed down off the sand dune toward the offices and showers.

"About two months, I think," Kiera told her. She turned to Cooper and had a quick conversation with him, confirming the date before turning back to Cheyenne. "Yup, two months."

"It really is cool how you can talk to him like that," Julie said quietly.

Kiera shrugged. "ASL is a language. Just like Spanish, German, or any other. I think others view deaf people as handicapped, when in reality they're just bilingual."

"That's so true," Jessyka said, the awe clear in her tone. "I never really thought of it that way before."

"I'm going to see if I can start a training program to teach the SEALs under my command sign language. I know most of the guys have some sort of pigeon non verbal signs they already use, but I think it could be beneficial if everyone knew the same signals and language," Patrick informed the group.

"I'm in," Wolf said immediately.

"Me too," the large man next to Cheyenne agreed.

"I know all the guys on our team would be up for it," Jessyka's husband agreed.

"It might be a while, don't get too excited," the commander warned. "I need to find an acceptable teacher. It's not like I can bring in any ol' teacher off the street...no offense intended, Kiera."

She waved off his concern. "No, I get it. The things you guys do are top secret, and even though it's just words, you want to get someone who understands what it is you do and the situations you get into, so you can learn the most appropriate words. There's no need to necessarily learn things like apple or asparagus."

Cooper tapped her on the shoulder and signed, "What's he saying?"

Quickly, Kiera brought him up to speed on the conversation. Cooper didn't respond, but he got an introspective look on his face. She brought her hands up to ask him what he was thinking, but was interrupted by Cheyenne's screech.

"Faulkner! Put me down!"

Her husband had slung her over his shoulder and was striding toward the parking lot.

"See you tomorrow, Dude!" Wolf called out, chuckling.

Kiera could hear Cheyenne's giggles as she half-heartedly tried to wiggle out of her husband's grasp. She couldn't hear whatever it was the SEAL said to his wife, but it made Cheyenne go limp, and he swung her around until he was cradling her in his arms as he kept walking.

Kiera saw Cheyenne put one hand on his face and smile up at him before they got too far away to see specifics anymore. She remembered the other woman's comment about benefiting from her husband's testosterone and got turned on all over again.

They arrived at the door to the offices and Kiera felt a hand on her face and turned to Cooper. "Give me twenty minutes to shower?" he asked softly.

She nodded, and he kissed her briefly on the lips then disappeared into the offices with the rest of the men.

"I'm gonna head out and get the kids and meet Kason at home," Jessyka told them. "It was good to meet you, Kiera. Hopefully we'll see more of you around."

"Same. See ya," Kiera answered.

She sank onto a bench next to Julie to wait for Cooper.

"So…you and Coop? Officially?" Julie asked with a smile.

Kiera merely smiled. "Yup."

"Awesome," her friend breathed, nudging her with her shoulder.

"I have to say, he looks like he's doing really well," Caroline observed. "I mean, we're not best friends or anything, but Wolf told me he was having a hard time after he was injured. He didn't want to be around anyone and never went anywhere without his hearing aid. I'm so glad to see him relaxing a bit."

Kiera nodded. "Yeah, I've noticed the same change. When he first started volunteering at my school, he didn't say much to anyone and kinda kept to himself a lot. But the more he helped the kids, the more he seemed to realize that being deaf wasn't the end of the world."

"I saw you drag him out of my party," Julie noted. "You think that has anything to do with his new and improved attitude?"

"No. I have nothing to do with it," Kiera protested.

"I think you're wrong," Julie countered. "I'm not saying you're wrong that the kids and volunteering have helped him. Patrick wouldn't have highly suggested he do it if he didn't think it would help. But these guys… they're a lot more sensitive than they'd have the world believe. They get shot, no problem, they can suck it up and deal, looking forward to getting back on the front lines. But being injured enough that they can't do what they've spent the better part of their adult lives perfecting? It hits them harder than nonmilitary guys. Especially if they're single. They start thinking they aren't good enough. That no one will ever love them the way they are. The feelings escalate until they think all anyone can see is that disability. A scar. A limp. Their loss of hearing."

The women were silent for a long moment, then Julie went on after laughing nervously. "I'm not an expert, but I've been reading up on this and watching Patrick's men. I'm telling you, I can see a difference between the Cooper of a week ago and the man who was messing around with his friends on the beach tonight. I think you're one reason why he's suddenly come to grips with his loss of hearing, Kiera."

She knew she was blushing, but Kiera managed a shrug. "I'm not looking to be his hero."

"But apparently you are anyway," Caroline stated evenly. Then smiled. "Welcome to the weird and wacky world of loving a Navy SEAL. Retired or not, your man is every inch a SEAL."

Kiera smiled. "Do I get a pin or something for joining the club?"

"A pin for what?" Cooper asked as he strode out the door.

Kiera popped up from her seat and turned to him. He looked good. Really good. His hair was still damp from his shower and she could smell the soap on his skin. She shook her head. "Nothing. Girl talk."

"Sweet Jesus, I'm in trouble," he teased. "Girl talk with Caroline and Julie can't mean anything good."

"Shut it, buddy," Julie said as she stood.

"Be afraid, be very afraid," Caroline deadpanned.

Their men came out the door then and Wolf asked, "Afraid of what?"

Kiera shook her head. She couldn't help it. The guys were funny.

"Never mind. Ready to go?" Caroline asked her husband.

"If you are," Wolf responded.

"Babe, do you mind if we stop at the hospital on the way home? I'd like to visit a sailor who just arrived," Patrick asked after kissing Julie on the temple tenderly.

"Of course not," Julie said. "A SEAL?"

"Nope. Just a regular sailor. He apparently got really sick on the aircraft carrier he was on and had his appendix taken out onboard, but there were complications and they ended up flying him home. He could use some cheering up, as his family hasn't arrived yet."

"What are we waiting for?" Julie asked, pulling on Patrick's hand. "Let's go. See you later, Kiera!" she called out as she towed her husband toward the parking lot.

"Alone at last," Cooper said after the other two couples were out of sight.

"Got your ear back in?" Kiera asked.

Cooper nodded. "Yup. Although I'm not sure I'm up for a crowded restaurant. How do you feel about takeout?"

"Love it," Kiera agreed. "I'd much rather hang out with you in the peace and quiet of one of our apartments than yell over a nasty, germy table anyway."

Cooper laughed. "Me too. And I hadn't thought of restaurant tables as nasty and germy until now, thank you very much."

"Oh, believe me, they are. Most of the time no one even wipes them down between customers. They're petri dishes of nastiness just waiting for a victim to latch onto and cause havoc in their digestive system."

He leaned over and kissed the top of Kiera's head. "I love the way you think."

She looked up at him in confusion. "You love that I think about how germy and disgusting tables in restaurants are?"

"No. I love that I have no idea what's going to come out of your mouth. I love knowing that when I'm around you, I'm gonna laugh at some point during our time together. I love that you say what you're thinking. I love watching you sign with your students and that you can make them smile as easily as you do me."

Kiera stared up at Cooper, not sure how to respond. He might be ten years younger than her, but he was more mature than every man she'd dated. He never blew smoke up her ass and every word out of his mouth was sincere and made her fall for him even more.

"Come on," he said, obviously seeing how flustered she was. "Let's go find something to eat and then relax. I didn't really mean to start out our first date by ignoring you in favor of showing up my SEAL brethren."

"But I got to see you almost naked," Kiera blurted. "I'd say it was a good start."

Cooper barked out a laugh then ran his hand over her hair, smoothing it away from her face tenderly. "See? You're funny. Come on. I'm starved."

Kiera melted into Cooper's side when, instead of taking her hand, he put his arm around her shoulders and pulled her into him. She snaked her arm around his waist and they walked toward the parking lot together.

CHAPTER 6

*H*ours later, Cooper sat on Kiera's tan suede couch, relaxed and content. Kiera was leaning against the armrest, her legs resting over his lap, and had been sipping wine since they'd finished dinner.

The Green Mile was playing on the television, with subtitles of course, but neither of them were watching it. They'd started out the night on opposite sides of the sofa, but when she'd complained that her feet hurt, he'd offered to give her a foot massage and now, here they were.

Halfway through dinner, he'd asked if she wouldn't mind signing as she spoke with him, to give him practice. She'd agreed and they'd been talking nonstop since.

"What was it like growing up with a deaf parent?" Cooper asked.

Kiera shrugged. "Like any other kid, I expect. Since I don't have anything to compare it to, I couldn't really say."

"Were you teased?"

"Not really," Kiera said, then picked up her wine glass, took a sip, and placed it back on the table next to the couch so she could continue signing as she spoke. "When I was at school, I didn't sign. When I was at home, I signed and spoke, just like I'm doing now." She shrugged. "I never really thought much of it. Signing comes as naturally to me as someone who grew up speaking, say, Spanish in the home and English outside of it."

"I think you're amazing," Cooper told her, squeezing her leg. "I find it incredibly difficult to coordinate my hands with what I'm hearing and making it all work together."

"Give yourself a break, Cooper. You haven't been doing this very long. It takes practice. Just like being a SEAL does. You didn't learn how to do some of the stuff you did overnight."

He nodded. "You're right, I know you are. But I've never been a patient man."

The look of desire in her eyes made him swallow hard. As did her subtle shifting in her seat. He wanted her. Now. He wanted her naked and on her knees in front of him, sucking him off. Wanted her laid out on her couch, wet and ready for him. Hell, he wanted her any way he could get her. Up against a wall, over her kitchen table, in the shower, in her bed. The visions he had of them making love slammed into his brain and he immediately got hard. Kiera didn't miss it.

She shifted her legs until one brushed against his erection and they both inhaled sharply. Showing her maturity, which Cooper found refreshing as hell, she said, "Patience is overrated."

He grinned and shifted until he was crouched over her. At his movements, she'd lain back. Her hands gripped his biceps and she smiled up at him. "You're beautiful," he breathed as he gazed down at her.

Her nipples were hard little peaks under her T-shirt, he could feel the heat of her body against his inner thighs as he straddled her, and her blue eyes sparkled with interest.

When she didn't respond, he said what was on his mind. "I don't want to rush this. I think it's obvious that I want you." Cooper let his body weight rest on hers for a moment, letting her feel how hard he was, how turned on, before he flexed his muscles and crouched over her again.

Her hips pressed upward, trying to follow him, but she relaxed when it was obvious he wasn't going to give her the pressure she wanted.

"Cooper," she complained, but he didn't give her a chance to beg him. He couldn't. If she did, he'd probably give in.

"I've wanted you for two months, and I'm not going to jump you in the first twenty-four hours I find out my interest is returned. I was a Navy SEAL. I've got more fortitude than that."

"You have to know I want you back," Kiera said breathlessly, staring up at him as if he was the best thing since sliced bread.

"I hoped you did, but thank you for confirming, sweetheart. But I still don't want to rush this. I want to enjoy the experience."

"What experience?"

"Making you mine. I don't want to fall into any stereotypes you might have in your mind about how a younger man operates when he's entering a relationship. Yes, I want you. I want you every way I can get you. I can't *wait* to have you, but sex isn't why I want to be with you. I admire you more than I can say. The way you work with the kids in your class. The way you care, truly care about them. You might not want children, but I can see how much you love them. I want to get to know everything about you before I learn how your body trembles in the throes of an orgasm. I want to know what you're like in the morning before I learn how you taste after you come. I want to figure out what makes you happy and what makes you grumpy before I experience your hot, wet body squeezing my dick as you explode under me. The bottom line, sweetheart, is that as much as I want to shove your jeans down your legs and bury my face in your crotch, I want to get to know you as a woman first. Can I tell you a secret?"

Kiera swallowed hard before licking her lips and saying softly, "If it's going to blow my mind more than what you just said, I'm not sure I can handle it."

Cooper leaned down and kissed her forehead before straightening. "You can. I'm coming to realize you can handle just about anything. From the first day we met, I realized that you were my reward."

"What? I don't understand."

"I've lived my life from one day to the next. Not really thinking about the future, figuring I had my entire life to worry about that. Then after I was injured, I was struggling. I didn't want to leave my apartment, didn't want to interact with anyone because I was embarrassed that I had to ask them to repeat what they'd said to me so many times. I was bitter that I'd given so much to my country and didn't have much to show for it. Then I met you and I understood. You are my reward. My reward for all that I did. All that I sacrificed. You are the cosmos' gift to me for surviving that blast."

"Oh my God," Kiera whispered, shaking her head. "Cooper, no, that's not—"

"I didn't tell you that to freak you out."

"Major fail," she said dryly, blinking furiously to try to hold back the tears he could see pooling in her eyes.

"You're everything I ever wanted in a woman. Self-assured. Successful. Intelligent. You don't *need* me, but I'm hoping you *want* me."

"I do," she said immediately.

"All I'm saying is that from the first day I met you, I wanted you. And every day I've been near you since has only solidified that fact. Yes, I want to make love with you. I also want to fuck you. But I want to date you first. Get to know you. Have you get to know me. Is that all right?"

"Yes," Kiera answered immediately. "God, yes." She shifted under him. "But does that mean we can't…make out every now and then while we're getting to know each other?"

He chuckled. "No. We can make out. But don't think you can make me forget that I want to wait to…" He sat up on his knees, made a circle with one hand and, using the pointer finger on his other, pantomimed the crude and rude version of making love.

Kiera laughed and reached up to grab his hands. "What you just did is kinda the sign for anal sex."

Cooper immediately dropped his hands. Good Lord, the last thing he wanted to do was tell Kiera he wanted to fuck her in the ass on their first date.

But instead of being offended, she laughed at him. "If you could only see your face right now, Cooper. There are lots of dirty words I can teach you, but only if you promise not to show them to Frankie or anyone else."

Cooper knew his eyebrows had shot up in horror. "As if I would! He's seven!"

"I was only kidding. I know you wouldn't." She wrinkled her nose, which he thought was adorable, then said, "Okay then. I'll show you how to say 'fuck.' Make a peace sign with both hands." She demonstrated, holding up her hands.

Cooper mimicked her and waited with a grin on his face. If someone had told him right after he was injured that he'd be here, kneeling over the woman he longed to make his own, learning how to say fuck in sign language, he would've kicked their ass and told them to stop messing with his mind.

"Then turn one hand so the back is facing the floor, and with the back of your other hand facing the ceiling, knock them together…it kinda looks like two bunnies going at it."

Again, she demonstrated, and Cooper could feel the dumb smile on his face. He copied her movements and she nodded up at him. "That's it."

Without a word, Cooper leaned down and kissed her. Using nothing more than his lips, he tried to show her how much she already meant to him.

Kiera tried to pull him down so he was lying on her, but he stubbornly refused to budge. Finally, realizing he wasn't going to do what she wanted, she ran her fingernails lightly up and down his biceps and gave herself over to his kiss, letting him take control.

Cooper closed his eyes and concentrated on memorizing the taste and feel of Kiera's mouth under his. How a kiss could turn him on almost to the point he thought he'd come in his pants, he didn't know, but he'd never been happier in his life.

Pulling back, he gazed down at her and waited for her eyes to open. When they did, he said softly, "It's late. I need to go."

Pouting, Kiera asked, "So soon?"

"I've been here for hours," Cooper told her.

"So soon?" Kiera repeated with a small smile.

He sat up and pulled her upright next to him. "Thank you for a wonderful first date, sweetheart. Want to grab lunch tomorrow?"

"Yes."

Her answer was immediate and heartfelt. Even though he'd had a pretty good idea she was going to agree, he was still relieved. He'd dated enough to know that many times women played games, like thinking there needed to be three days between dates, or that agreeing to see a man too soon after a first date meant he would get bored and think she wasn't worth the chase. Where they got those ideas, he'd never know.

"I'll call you and we can figure it out. Okay?"

"Sounds good. Cooper?"

"Yeah?"

"Thank you."

"For what?"

"For being a good guy. For making me feel special. For being able to get past whatever shit went through your head after you were hurt to be the awesome guy you are today. For not getting dead while you were a SEAL. And for agreeing to volunteer at my school."

"You're welcome." There was a lot more he could've said, but he figured the simple answer said it all.

On his way home ten minutes later, Cooper couldn't hold back the grin. He realized that for the first time in a long time, he was happy. He was horny, but happy. Knowing he was in for long weeks of cold showers and masturbating while wishing he was with Kiera, he still grinned. It would be worth it. *She* would be worth it.

CHAPTER 7

"When are you coming back down?" Cooper asked Tex as he sat in his car outside the Riverton School for the Deaf. He'd learned that if he turned his hearing aid up all the way, he could use the phone without the teleprompter. Sometimes it was easier to go ahead and use the translation service, but when he spoke with his friends, and of course Kiera, he liked being able to talk to them directly rather than read their words on the screen.

He and the former SEAL had hit if off when he'd visited two months ago, and they'd kept in touch since then. They'd had a couple long conversations about how hard it was to acclimate into civilian after that of a Special Forces operative for so long. Tex had a lot of good tips that had made Cooper really think about his own life and finally come to terms with the shift it'd taken.

But for the last month, they'd been calling to simply shoot the shit. Cooper genuinely liked Tex and they'd made tentative plans for him to visit again. It felt good that Tex wanted to come out specifically to see him. He knew Tex was friends with Wolf and the other SEALs that worked with Commander Hurt, but to hear the other man specifically say he wanted to spend time with him, made Cooper feel as if Tex truly was a friend and wasn't just doing Hurt a favor. At some point Cooper wanted to return the favor and go to Virginia to meet Melody and their children, and to bring Kiera with him when he went.

He and Kiera had spent time almost every day together, and he'd never been happier. Tonight was Friday, and after work she was coming over to his place. Tonight was the night.

He'd wooed and courted her for two months. He'd learned a lot about her, just as she'd done with him. He'd learned that if she didn't have coffee first thing in the morning, he shouldn't try to talk to her about anything important. Just as she'd learned he was very much a morning person rather than a night owl.

They'd had a few disagreements—he wouldn't call them arguments— but they'd ended with better knowledge on both their sides of who the other was. All in all, Cooper was more than certain Kiera was the woman he wanted to spend the rest of his life with, and he hoped she felt the same.

Tonight, he wanted to make love with her. Wanted to show her how much he loved her. He knew she was ready, she'd been telling him with the way she clung to him when they made out, the way she begged him to keep going, and how she'd been pouting when he did pull away. He truly hadn't meant to be a tease, but last weekend, when she'd accused him of just that, he realized that the reason for wanting to wait had long been made moot. He knew her, just as she knew him. It was time to stop torturing them both.

Tex's voice brought him out of his daydreaming about Kiera and back to the present.

"Thought I'd come down next week...if that's all right."

"Hell yeah. It's more than all right. Will Melody and the kids be coming with you?"

"Not this time," Tex said with a hint of displeasure in his tone. "And neither she or the other wives are happy about it. Akilah has a thing at school that she doesn't want to miss."

"Are *you* okay missing it?" Cooper asked.

"Yeah. It's a play and Akilah has a tiny bit part. I've seen her do her lines several times and practiced with her. Not only that, but it's being performed two weekends in a row. I'm seeing her tonight, but Melody wants to go to every performance. There's only so much of that I can take," Tex said with a chuckle.

"How long can you stay?"

"Only a few days. Patrick said he'd put together a quick training session with Wolf's team for me, so I can make it tax deductible and my security company can pay for the trip."

"Awesome," Cooper told him. "Glad that'll work out."

"Me too. So I'll be there on Wednesday and will leave on Sunday. That work?"

"Of course. You want to come to the school and hang out for a couple of hours with me on Thursday? I told the principal I'd give presentations to the older classes about the Navy and being a SEAL."

"I don't know sign language," Tex admitted.

"No biggie. I can translate for you."

"Then yeah, it sounds like fun."

"Have you made arrangements for where you'll stay yet?"

"Nope. That was next on my agenda."

"You can stay at my place," Cooper told him. "I'm sure Wolf and the others would also have no problem with you staying with them."

"I appreciate the offer. You sure I won't be in your way?" Tex asked.

"Nope. I'm fairly certain I can stay with Kiera while you're here."

"That going well then?"

"Yeah. I've never met anyone like her. When I'm not with her, I'm thinking about being with her. And when I *am*, I can't imagine being anywhere else."

"Sounds like me and Melody. I'm happy for you, man," Tex told him.

"Thanks. So I'll see you Wednesday. You need a ride from the airport?" Cooper asked.

"Nope. I'll have Wolf pick me up. See you next week."

"Later."

"Bye."

Cooper clicked off the phone and immediately opened his car door. He'd been spending more and more time at the school and loved every minute of it. Not only did he get to see Kiera, he was able to spend time with Frankie and the other kids. He still rotated classrooms when he was there, but he always made sure to stop into her class before he left for the day.

Seeing Frankie's eyes light up when he saw him was almost as good as seeing Kiera's do the same. Almost.

Trying to keep his mind off the upcoming night, Cooper adjusted his dick in his pants and willed it to recede. The last thing he needed was to pop a woody in a classroom. That shit could get him banned for life…and for good reason. Taking deep breaths, he strode to the door of the school. He would stop by the main office and sign in, see where he could be the most useful, then see Kiera. It was going to be a great day.

* * *

KIERA COULDN'T BELIEVE what a difference Cooper had made in Frankie's educational and emotional advancement. Since the day he'd begun to volunteer in her classroom, Frankie had gone from being closed-off to the most popular kid in the class. All the other children wanted to sit by him, they vied to partner with him on assignments and he hadn't sat alone in the lunchroom since that day.

He'd also begun to excel in all aspects of the curriculum. His signing was one hundred percent improved, now that he was putting in the effort to learn it. He was reading on the same level as the rest of the kids in the class and his math skills, which were already pretty good, were out of this world. One of Kiera's favorite things about being a teacher was seeing a student make progress, and the progress Frankie was making was remarkable.

The little boy's situation at home was apparently much more stable now that he and his dad had settled in and his mother was out of his life. At the last parent-teacher conference, his father had admitted that his ex had tried to contact Frankie a few times by calling and hoping her son would answer the phone, but luckily the dad had intercepted the calls. Without the toxic influence of his mother, the little boy was blossoming and thriving.

But it wasn't just Frankie who was doing exceptionally well. Cooper himself had apparently gotten the sign language bug and was learning ASL at an amazing rate. He freely signed with the other teachers at the school now and very rarely had to ask Kiera to interpret, or for a sign anymore. He'd showed her an app he'd been using to help teach himself and it was amazing how well it had worked.

Cooper might not have a college degree, but he was smart, very smart, and Kiera felt extremely lucky to be with him. She'd questioned him a lot when they'd first started dating about if he really wanted to be with *her*, an older woman who wasn't exactly Miss America, and he'd reassured her over and over until, one night, he'd actually gotten pissed at her.

It wasn't exactly a fight, but he'd been so frustrated with her lack of self-esteem when it came to their relationship that he told her it was making him feel self-conscious. He'd said that if he didn't want to be with her, he wouldn't. But he was extremely happy for the first time in his life and being with her made him proud, and had made his transition to civilian life easier.

When she'd thought about it, Kiera had realized he was right. She needed to stop asking herself why Cooper was with her and just enjoy it. No one was pointing and laughing when they went out together. But the bottom line was that if it didn't matter between the two of them, to hell with what anyone else thought.

Once she got past her own hurdles with their ages, the last month had been idyllic...except for his stubborn refusal to have sex. Kiera was starting to get a complex. She'd all but begged him to make love with her the other night and he'd still refused. What guy did that?

It was confusing and frustrating, but it didn't make her want to break up with him. She just wanted to understand what was holding him back. When they'd first starting dating, she'd gotten it. She liked that Cooper wanted to go slow and really get to know each other before consummating their relationship. But now? She was ready. More than ready. She was going to have a serious talk with him tonight and see where his head was at.

The class was currently having their "talk circle." It was an informal time every day for each child to get to tell the others something they had done the night before or just share a story. It helped with their sign language and social skills.

Little Jenny typically told the class what she'd had for dinner the night before, Rebecca liked to talk about the new puppy her family had just gotten. The rest of the class members each had their own quirks and generally Kiera knew what they would talk about. But not Frankie.

The things he talked about ranged from the mundane to what his mother used to tell him. Kiera would never forget the day he'd opened up —she figured it was because Cooper had been there—about how his mom had told him he got sick and lost his hearing when he was a baby because God made a mistake in letting him be born in the first place and was punishing him.

Kiera had been appalled, and had done her best to reassure him that whatever his mom had said wasn't true. But it wasn't until one of the little girls in the class had innocently told him, "But if you weren't here then we couldn't be friends," that he'd seemed to loosen up. Thank God for the innocence of children.

Today in the talk circle, Frankie wanted to know more about Cooper's time on the SEAL team.

"Can you tell us more about when you had to use your secret signs with your friends?" he asked Cooper through signing. He'd been obsessed with the topic ever since Cooper had first mentioned it.

She and Cooper had talked about the boundaries of what the first-graders should hear about his military career and what they shouldn't, so Kiera had no doubt that Cooper wouldn't tell the children something that would scare them.

When he answered, he signed slowly and precisely so all the kids could understand him. She was so proud of how far he'd come in his signing ability and confidence.

"One time we were in the jungle and were watching the bad guys. We had to be very quiet so they didn't hear us."

"Like hide and seek?" Frankie interrupted.

"Exactly like that, bud," Cooper signed with a smile. "Anyway, I was lying near one of my buddies and saw a huge snake in the branches above his head. I knew he was scared to death of snakes, so I signaled to him that there was danger above his head. We had no signal for snake. He nodded and signaled back that he understood and was watching the bad guys. I shook my head and tried to tell him again, but he again misunderstood. Finally, I pointed over his head, then made a weird sign for snake, like this…" Cooper demonstrated, using an exaggerated hand movement that looked nothing like the ASL for snake, and all the kids laughed.

"That got through to my friend. He couldn't stand up because the bad guys would've seen him, he couldn't scream because again…bad guys."

"What did he do?" Frankie signed with a big smile on his face.

"He fainted," Cooper told the little boy and the rest of the kids. "He was so scared, he literally closed his eyes and passed out right there in the jungle in the middle of the job."

Everyone giggled. Kiera loved the sound. Her classroom was typically very quiet, unlike a room with hearing children. But when her kids laughed, it was one of the most joyous sounds she'd ever heard.

"Did the snake get him?" Frankie asked when he'd stopped laughing.

Cooper shook his head. "No. It didn't come anywhere near him. It just slithered away as if my friend wasn't worth his time. Want to know the best part of the story?"

"What?" Frankie impatiently signed.

"From that moment on, my friend's new nickname was Snake."

Once again, all the kids giggled.

Glancing at her watch and seeing it was time for recess, Kiera waved her hands and informed the kids it was time for break. They immediately stood and began to push their chairs back to their desks as they'd been taught. She watched as Frankie went up to Cooper and tugged on his shirt to get his attention.

When he had it, Frankie signed, "I love you."

Her heart melted.

Cooper crouched down on the balls of his feet and returned the sign, pulling Frankie into his arms for a hug.

Just when she thought she couldn't love the man any more, he blew her away with something like this.

Love. Yes, she loved him. Two months was fast, but deep in her heart, she knew Cooper was the real deal.

Frankie pulled away, smiled up at Cooper, then ran toward his cubby to grab his jacket before lining up behind the other kids.

It was her turn to watch the kids at recess; the teachers took turns so they could all get a break during the day. Kiera didn't have the time she wanted to tell, and show, Cooper how much she appreciated him, so she settled for a quick hug while the kids were busy with their jackets and lining up.

She stood on her tiptoes and tugged his head down to put her lips next to his left ear so he'd be sure to hear her. "You are amazing, Cooper Nelson. I can't wait to show you how amazing I think you are tonight."

He squeezed her hips and smiled down at her when she pulled back. "I'll meet you at your place when you get home, sweetheart."

"Okay."

Then he leaned down and put his own lips at her ear. And he blew her mind. "I'd like to change the nature of our relationship tonight…if you're receptive."

Kiera shivered at the promise she heard in his voice. Finally. "Oh, I'm receptive," she told him breathlessly. "*Very* receptive."

They stood there grinning at each other until a tug on her shirt got Kiera's attention. It was Jenny. "It's time for recess," she signed impatiently.

Cooper immediately let go of Kiera and stepped back, putting a respectable distance between them. "I'll see you later," he signed, then winked at her.

He walked to the front of the line of children, who were waiting patiently to be allowed to go outside. He said goodbye to each one, making sure to ruffle their hair or otherwise make them feel special. When he got to Frankie, Cooper lifted his chin in the way he'd taught the little boy the first day they'd met. When he got a chin lift in return, as well as an, "I think Ms. Kiera likes you," signed in return, he chuckled.

"I'm glad. Because I like her too," he told the little boy. Then he put his big hand on the boy's shoulder, gave it a squeeze and was gone.

Kiera took a deep breath and led her class outside to get some fresh air. As was her routine, she walked around the schoolyard as the kids played, rather than standing against the building. She figured it was better to be on the lookout and accessible in case any of the kids needed anything, rather than huddled near the school.

She took a deep breath, then another, and tried to remember what underwear she'd put on that morning. It looked like Cooper was finally making his move...and she couldn't be more thrilled.

CHAPTER 8

*K*iera was late getting home. It had been one thing after another at the end of the day. First, Frankie's dad had wanted a word with her when he came to pick up his son to make sure she was aware that his ex was apparently causing trouble. She was harassing him and threatening to have Frankie taken away for good if he didn't allow her to see him.

He'd contacted the police, both here in Riverton and up in Los Angeles where his ex lived, but he wanted to make sure the school knew to be vigilant when it came to his son.

Kiera reassured the man, letting him know how well Frankie had been doing, before another teacher asked for Kiera's opinion about a lesson plan. Then the principal had come in to shoot the shit.

So she'd been an hour and a half late in leaving for home. As she'd expected, Cooper was waiting when she pulled into the parking lot of her apartment. He was leaning against his car, knee bent, the toe of one boot resting on the concrete, his muscular arms crossed on his chest, sunglasses on, his dark hair shining in the late afternoon sun, and Kiera was aroused just by looking at him.

He oozed masculinity and she knew without a doubt that if the boogie man popped out from behind a bush, Cooper would do whatever it took to keep her safe. It was her certainty that he'd do anything for her that made him so attractive. His good looks were merely a bonus.

"Hey," Kiera said as she climbed out of her car from the parking space next to his. "Sorry I'm late."

Without a word, he straightened and stalked toward her. He put his hands on either side of her neck, tilted her neck up, and kissed her. It wasn't long, but it wasn't short either. She gazed up at him and swallowed hard. Cooper was always intense, but tonight he seemed even more so.

"The rest of your day go okay?" he asked softly.

Kiera nodded. "Yours?"

"Fine. You hungry?"

"I could eat," she told him.

Cooper stared down at her for a long moment before saying, "I've waited my whole life for you, Kiera. I didn't know it was you I was waiting for, but now that I've found you, I never want to let you go."

Her stomach doing summersaults, Kiera brought her hands up and rested them on his biceps. "I don't want you to let me go."

"I'll do stuff in the future that pisses you off, I know I will. I'll say stupid shit, and do things that seem insensitive. But I swear to God, I'll never purposely hurt you."

"I know you won't," Kiera said softly. And she did. As she'd gotten to know Cooper, she'd seen firsthand how careful he was with her.

"But I need to say this..."

He paused as if fortifying himself and Kiera tensed. She dug her fingernails into his arms unconsciously. She couldn't imagine what in the world he had to say that had him so nervous.

He looked her right in the eyes and said, "If you let me inside your body, I'm never letting you go. You need to understand that. Even if I piss you off and you tell me to fuck off, I won't. I'll fight with every molecule in my body to keep you. To make you forgive me. If you're not ready for that level of commitment, tell me now and I'll back off. We'll go inside, have dinner, make out like we've been doing and I'll go home. I do not take you giving me your body lightly, Kiera. If you give yourself to me, you're giving yourself to me. Mind, body, and soul. Be sure, sweetheart. Be absolutely certain you want me in your life before we go any further."

"I love you," Kiera blurted out—then closed her eyes in embarrassment.

She hadn't meant to just throw it out there like that. She had wanted to say it when they were in a romantic moment. Deciding that, now that it was out there, she'd go with it, her eyes opened and she started to say more, but she froze at the look on Cooper's face.

He was staring down at her in awe, but his jaw was ticking like it did when he was pissed about something. Losing her nerve, Kiera simply stared up at him.

Several moments passed, which seemed like an eternity to her, and finally he spoke. "I love you too, Kiera. So much, some days I don't think I can go five more minutes without talking to you, seeing you. So much that the thought of you leaving me makes my heart literally hurt."

She moved a hand to his chest, over his heart, and rubbed gently. "Then why do you look mad?"

"I'm not mad," he countered immediately. "Not in the least. I'm trying not to throw you over my shoulder, run to your apartment and break the door down so I can get you in bed faster."

Kiera smiled then, finally understanding why every muscle in his body seemed so tense. "Why don't you?"

At her words, if possible, his body hardened even more. "Because my woman has been working all day and is hungry. I need to feed her."

"Feed me after, Cooper," she told him, moving her hands up his chest to clasp around the back of his neck. She stood on tiptoes and plastered her body to his. "I've been waiting to have you naked in my bed, to have you inside me, for way too long. Make love with me, Cooper. Put out the fire inside me that no one else but you can douse. Please. For the love of God, I need you."

"And you're okay with what I said earlier? That once I sink into your hot little pussy, I'll never let you go?"

"I'm counting on it. I'm giving you my heart free and clear. I know you'll take care of it. Even if you piss me off in the future, I'm not going anywhere. Just as when I do the same to you, I know you'll never storm out of the house and leave me."

Without another word, Cooper moved one arm so it was around her waist and, keeping her plastered to his side, began to walk toward her apartment.

Kiera smiled, knowing she'd gladly let him lead her wherever he wanted to go.

He used her key to open her door and shut it with one foot once they were inside. He took the time to throw the deadbolt, but otherwise didn't pause. He walked them straight to her bedroom and didn't stop until they were both standing next to her bed.

"Strip," he said, not taking his eyes from hers.

Instead of getting irritated at his order, Kiera did as he asked. She first reached back and removed the barrette from her hair, shaking her head as the blonde locks fell around her shoulders. Loving the gasp that came from Cooper's mouth, she grinned.

"God. I haven't seen an inch of your naked skin yet and I'm so hard, I'm about ready to blow just by looking at your hair," Cooper mumbled.

Kiera didn't stop at his words, even though they made her weak in the knees. She toed off her shoes and then unbuttoned and unzipped her slacks. She pushed them over her hips until they pooled at her feet. Somehow taking her pants off first didn't seem as scary as whipping her shirt off over her head.

Cooper had no such hang-ups. The first thing to go was his shirt, he grabbed a fistful of material at the back of his neck and wrenched it up and over his head with one quick jerk.

Faltering at the hard expanse of his chest exposed in all its glory, Kiera paused to admire him.

"Don't stop," Cooper ordered in a hoarse tone.

Remembering what she'd been doing, and why, Kiera decided to get it over with quickly, like removing a Band-Aid. Crossing her hands at her waist, she gripped the material of her blouse and quickly brought it up and over her head.

She stood awkwardly in front of Cooper in nothing but her underwear. Her non-matching cotton underwear. Her panties were leopard print and her bra was white. They weren't anything fancy or seductive. She'd put them on that morning because they were comfortable, not with the thought she'd be wearing them in front of Cooper that night.

Blushing, and trying not to feel self-conscious, Kiera jerked when she felt Cooper's hands on her hips. He pulled her into his own nearly naked body and she shivered in delight when she felt his warm skin against hers.

"You are beautiful," he said reverently, using his thumbs to brush up and down on her sensitive skin.

"My underwear isn't fancy," Kiera said, biting her lip.

"It's you. And I love it. I love you," he said before dipping his head to kiss her.

They kissed for a long time. Surprisingly, with no urgency. Just long, slow swipes of their tongues, lazily caressing and exploring. Kiera could feel Cooper's erection against her stomach and it made her feel sexy and desired. More than anything he could've said, the evidence of his arousal reassured her.

They both pulled back after several moments and Kiera felt Cooper's hands move up her back. He stopped with his fingers on the clasp of her bra and asked, "Okay?"

Everything he did made her fall that much more in love with him. "Yes, please," she said.

Cooper made quick work of releasing the clasp of her bra, and then she stood in front of him in nothing but her panties.

His eyes went from her face to her chest, and Kiera could see his breathing speed up. He took a deep breath and slowly brought his hands up to her breasts. As if she were made of glass, he caressed her, moving his fingers lightly over each throbbing globe. She squirmed as his light touch tickled her.

"Harder, Cooper," she demanded, putting one of her own hands over his and pressing down with a firm touch. "I won't break."

Following her lead, Cooper used more pressure to caress her. Seeing he had the hang of it, Kiera dropped her hands to his hips and pushed her fingers under the waistband of his boxer briefs. She didn't push them down and off, simply enjoyed the intimacy of the moment.

Cooper caressed her breasts and took both nipples between his fingers and rolled them, making them peak even harder than they'd been. Moving slowly, as if asking permission without words, his head lowered. Kiera arched her back, giving him the permission he sought, and sighed in ecstasy when his lips closed around her nipple.

For several moments, he paid homage to her breasts. Licking, nipping, and even sucking on her. At one point, he sucked so hard on the inside curve of her right breast, Kiera wondered if it would leave a mark.

When he lifted his head, examined the mark he'd left, ran a fingertip over it and smiled, Kiera figured he knew what he was doing the entire time and that he'd purposely given her a hickey.

"Having fun?" she asked dryly.

"Loads," he told her.

Deciding it was time to move the show along, Kiera moved her palms down the outside of his thighs, pushing his underwear with them. She kept going until she was kneeling at his feet and his erection was bobbing in her face.

Taking hold of the almost angry-looking appendage, Kiera had a brief moment of worry that he wouldn't fit. He was big...probably not any more so than other six-foot-two man, but she'd never dated anyone his size.

"It'll fit," Cooper murmured, his hands fluttering around her as if he didn't know where he should put them. He settled on placing them on her shoulders and rubbing her collarbone with his thumbs.

Without a word, Kiera took hold of the base of his dick with one hand and braced herself on his thigh with the other. She lowered her head and licked from the bottom to the pulsing tip. He visibly twitched in her grasp, so she did it again.

A drop of precome appeared at the tip of the purple head and she licked it off.

He groaned and his hands tightened on her shoulders.

She licked him again, then without warning, lowered her mouth over him, taking as much of his length in her mouth as she could.

"Oh my God," Cooper swore. "Fuck, that feels good."

Concentrating on making him feel half as good as he made her feel on a daily basis, she wasn't prepared for him to suddenly hook her under her arms and haul her up so she was standing in front of him once again. She felt the wetness from her mouth and his excitement on her belly as he took several deep breaths.

"Why did you stop me?" Kiera asked somewhat shyly. "Was I not doing it right?"

"Not doing it right?" he asked, his eyebrows shooting up in disbelief. "If anything, you were doing it too right. The first time I come with you, I don't want it to be in your mouth. I want to be deep inside you, feeling your own orgasm squeezing my cock as I explode."

"Oh."

"Yeah, oh." Without another word, he stripped her of her undies and encouraged her to lie back on the mattress. He quickly joined her and knelt over her.

"I love your blonde curls," he said, his eyes glued between her legs.

"You don't want me to shave? It seems to be the current fashion."

"Absolutely not," he said quickly, running a hand through the coarse hair between her legs, spreading the wetness from her center up to her clit. "I love you just the way you are."

Kiera spread her legs, giving him access to where she wanted him most, and couldn't help the way her hips tilted up toward him when she felt his dick brush against her. Looking at the difference between her blonde hair and his dark, was the most erotic thing she'd ever seen.

Without a word, he held up a condom he had between his fingers and asked, "You want to do the honors?"

Kiera shook her head. "I've never done that for a man before. I don't want to mess it up."

"There's not much to mess up, sweetheart," Cooper said with a broad grin on his face. "But I understand. I'll teach you some other time. But you should know, now that you're mine, I would really like to feel nothing between us in the future. You gonna be okay with that?"

Kiera nodded. "Yeah. I'm on the pill. More to regulate my periods than for birth control. As long as we're careful and I don't get pregnant, I'd love to feel you inside me without a condom."

He closed his eyes as if her words alone were enough to send him over the edge, then opened them and said, "Just the thought of orgasming inside you and coating you with my come threatens my tightly held control. Spread your legs wider, sweetheart."

She did as he asked, watching as he quickly took care of covering himself. He gripped the base of his cock and shuffled forward on his knees. He ran his tip up and down her slit then said, "I want to lick and suck every inch of your beautiful pussy, but I'm holding on by a thread as it is. The second I taste you, I know I'll lose all control, so I'll have to save that for later. You ready for me, Kiera?"

"Yes. Make me yours, Cooper."

He groaned and pressed into her slightly, the tip of his cock disappearing between her folds as he said, "Fuck."

Kiera could feel her body clenching at his size, trying to keep him out.

"Relax, sweetheart," he murmured, using his thumb to gently caress the bundle of nerves between her thighs.

His touch on her clit made Kiera moan in delight and she opened her legs farther, wanting more of the pleasurable sensation. He pressed in as he continued to use his hand to distract her.

"Cooper," she said, not knowing if she was distressed or super turned on.

"I'm in, sweetheart. Breathe. Take a breath," he said tenderly.

She did as he suggested, and felt him deep inside her. She felt full, extremely full, and was more thankful than she could say for him giving her a moment to adjust to his size.

Kiera looked up at him and saw that he was crouched over her and wasn't moving a muscle.

"I'm sorry," she whispered.

"For what?" he asked.

She wasn't sure. It just felt like she needed to apologize.

"I know you aren't apologizing for being tight. Or because you obviously haven't had a man in quite a while. Or that you need a moment to adjust. Because if you are, I'm gonna be pissed."

Kiera's lips twitched. When he put it like that, it did sound stupid. She squirmed under him and they both inhaled at the movement.

"Fuck, you feel good," Cooper breathed. "How you doin'?"

"I'm okay. You can move," Kiera told him, not entirely sure she was telling the truth, but it wasn't like they could lie there motionless all night.

Cooper pulled back an inch, then pushed inside her again.

It felt good.

"That felt good," she told him.

He didn't respond, but smiled down at her. He did it again. And again. Each time pulling out farther before pushing back inside her wet heat slowly and carefully. Eventually his easy, careful thrusts weren't enough.

"More," Kiera said firmly. "I'm good now. I need more."

"Then you'll get it. I'll always give you what you need, sweetheart."

His words were sweet, but at the moment, she didn't want sweet. When he pulled out and thrust inside her the next time, Kiera pressed her own hips up, taking him hard.

"Are you sure?" Cooper asked.

"Yes. Fuck me. Please."

And he did. Time ceased to exist. Only Cooper did. He used his hands, cock, and body to make sure she was pleased. And she was.

After the first time she came, Kiera thought that was it, that Cooper would do what he needed in order to make himself come, but he didn't. He merely smiled down at her, brushed his hand over her forehead and hair, and told her that her exploding in his arms, under him, around him, was the most amazing thing he'd ever seen and felt. Then he proceeded to tell her he wanted to see and feel it again.

It wasn't until she'd come a third time that he finally lost control. He put both hands next to her shoulders on the mattress and took what he needed.

Kiera's gaze wandered from his face to where they were connected and back again. Watching him ramp up to the point of no return was sexy as fuck. When he did finally lose it, he pressed himself as far inside her as he could get and held very still. Kiera could feel him throbbing and wished that she could feel his hot come filling her.

His jaw tensed and his eyes closed in ecstasy as he came. Finally, when he'd emptied himself, his eyes opened and the look in them made Kiera inhale sharply.

"You're mine," he declared. "I'm never letting you go."

"Good. I don't want you to," Kiera fired back.

He smiled, then eased himself down onto her, being careful not to crush her. He rolled to his back and pulled her with him. They both groaned when his softening cock slipped out of her body.

"Do you need to take care of the condom?" she asked softly, running her fingers through the hair on his chest.

"In a minute. I'm enjoying this too much to move," he said in a sleepy voice.

"Me too."

"Close your eyes. Relax."

Kiera tried, but when her stomach growled, they both chuckled. "Guess I'm hungrier than I thought," she said sheepishly.

Cooper turned his head and looked her in the eyes. "I've never laughed during sex before."

"Uh, we're not actually having sex at the moment," she informed him.

His smile got wider. "You know what I mean."

She nodded. "Yeah."

"I like it."

"Me too."

Her stomach growled again.

Cooper shook his head in amusement. "Guess we're getting up."

"Look on the bright side," Kiera said. "We can get up, eat, then have the energy to come back here and do that some more."

"Yeah, I could have dessert after we eat. Good plan."

Kiera knew she was blushing, but nodded anyway.

He had pity on her and sat up, pulling her with him. "I'll take care of the condom. Put on my shirt. Nothing else. I'll meet you in the kitchen to help put something together."

"Bossy," Kiera complained without heat.

He leaned down and kissed her hard, then said, "I warned you what would happen if you let me into that hot body of yours."

"You said that I'd be yours, not that you'd turn into a grunting Neanderthal who wants me barefoot and naked in the kitchen."

"Same thing, baby, same thing," he teased. "Tell me you don't want to wear my shirt and I'll back off."

Kiera bit her lip. She totally wanted to wear his shirt. It would smell like him, come down to at least the middle of her thighs, so she'd be completely covered...and there was just something about wearing his clothes that got to her. She wrinkled her nose and refused to answer.

He merely laughed. "Go on, sweetheart. I'll meet you in the kitchen."

"Okay."

"One more thing," Cooper said.

Kiera turned toward him and raised an eyebrow in question.

"Thank you. Thank you for loving me. For trusting me. For letting me in. You won't regret it."

"I know I won't," Kiera told him decisively. Then she kissed him and climbed out of bed. Knowing she was putting on a show for him, she reached down and grabbed his shirt and pulled it over her head. Grinning at him over her shoulder, she walked toward the door of the bedroom, putting a bit of swagger in her step. "After we eat, we can bring the can of whipped cream back here and see what trouble we can get into."

Laughing at the growl that came out of his mouth, Kiera quickly left the room. She'd never been so happy in her life. She was sexually and emotionally satisfied and had a gorgeous former SEAL in her bedroom, soon to be next to her in the kitchen, helping to make them something for dinner. It was funny how life turned out.

CHAPTER 9

The rest of the weekend went much like Friday night. Lots of laughter, eating good food, and sex. Lots of sex. If someone had told Kiera she'd one day find a man who was ten years younger than her, couldn't keep his hands and mouth off her, and she'd have so much sex she'd be sore as a result...she would've laughed at them and told them they were insane.

But by the time Sunday had come around, Kiera was delightfully sore. Cooper was...enthusiastic...which she loved and encouraged. As a result, on Monday morning—he'd stayed all weekend and was still there when her alarm went off for work—realizing sex would be uncomfortable for her, he'd gone down on her and given her a morning orgasm that set the tone for the week.

She'd been sated and content in the knowledge her man genuinely enjoyed not only her body, but being with her.

Now, even after less than a week, they'd already settled into a routine. After she woke up, he made her breakfast while she was in the shower. He left at the same time she did in the morning, going back to his place to grab workout clothes and either meet up with Cutter, Patrick's admin assistant, or run along the beach by himself. He'd show up at the school a little before lunch and they'd spend a pleasant twenty minutes or so eating together before she'd go back to her classroom, and Cooper would wander off to spend time in some of the other classes. He'd always make an appearance in Kiera's class before leaving and meeting her back at her apartment when she got home.

They'd fix dinner together, which was awesomely fun, watch some television while she graded papers and made sure her lessons for the next day were in order, then go to bed. Most of the time it was a couple hours before they actually slept, as the time before was spent enjoying each other's bodies.

Kiera hadn't ever been with a man like Cooper. He was attentive, caring, sexy, and most of all, made sure she was happy. Happy with what they were eating for dinner, happy with what they were watching on television, happy with the temperature, and of course, happy while they were intimate.

It wasn't something she was used to, and she realized pretty quickly that she would need to make sure she didn't take advantage of Cooper's attentiveness and desire to please her. He was stubborn and could be bossy, but she truly loved being around him.

Seeing him at school was simply a bonus. Not many women got to hang out with their boyfriends in the middle of the workday.

"How's your day been?" Cooper asked as he took a bite of the sandwich he'd brought to eat for lunch. He'd also packed her a cup of leftover potato soup they'd made for dinner the night before.

"Good. I think Frankie has a girlfriend."

Cooper grinned. "Let me guess...Jenny?"

"Yup. He's obviously been paying attention to you, because today before morning recess, he held her jacket out for her to put her arms through. He's seen you do that for me several times now."

"And what'd Jenny do?"

"She signed thank you, then kissed him on the cheek."

Cooper's smile got bigger. "Hey, there's nothing wrong with trainin' 'em young."

Kiera rolled her eyes, but couldn't hold back the grin on her face. "True. Did you have fun with your friend this morning?"

"Fun might not be the word," Cooper told her. "We met up with Cutter and did suicides on the beach. Tex sure can move fast for a man with only one leg."

"Let me guess, you did your best to keep up with him."

"He can move fast, but not fast enough," Cooper joked.

Kiera chuckled. "You'll both probably need four ice bags tonight. You retired SEALs think you're supermen, but you pay the price after being all macho."

Cooper leaned toward her and put one hand behind her neck, pulling her closer until they were nose to nose. "Newsflash, sweetheart...we *are* supermen."

Kiera giggled and wrinkled her nose. "And oh so modest too."

Chuckling, Cooper kissed her on the nose and sat back. "I'll admit to a twinge or two, but I'm hoping maybe tonight I can get a back rub from my girlfriend."

"I don't know," Kiera said, lifting one eyebrow. "I bet she'll want something in return."

"Oh, I'll give her something all right," Cooper deadpanned.

A snort escaped Kiera before she could hold it back, and she put her hand over her mouth in mortification at the weird sound.

Cooper merely shook his head at her. "Goof."

"You wouldn't have me any other way," she returned. Expecting him to have another witty comeback, she was somewhat surprised when he didn't even smile.

"You're right, I wouldn't. I adore you, Kiera. Don't ever think I take you for granted, because I don't."

"I know. And the feeling's mutual," she told him.

They stared at each other for a long moment before Kiera broke the intense silence. "You about done?"

"Yeah. You mind if Tex and I pop into your class this afternoon once we give our presentation to the older grades?"

Kiera shook her head. "Absolutely not. The kids will love to see you." She'd mentioned to her principal that a friend of Cooper's would be in town and she'd suggested that maybe the two of them could give a short presentation to the older children about the Navy, what it meant to be a SEAL, and how much work it was.

He stood and crumpled his paper bag. He quickly disposed of it and came back to Kiera. She loved how he towered over her, it made her feel feminine, and the way he took her head in both of his hands only added to that feeling. "How about if we come right before recess again? Will that fit into your lesson plans?"

"I can switch some things around. I'll just move the talk circle to then and we'll do our math lesson later."

"Okay. If it's not a problem."

"It's not a problem," she confirmed.

Cooper leaned down and kissed her gently. He'd kissed her a lot of ways in the last week. Hard, soft, passionate, out of control, teasingly... but she loved the way he kissed her while in public. Easy and gently, with a little bit of tongue, and enough banked passion for her to know he *wished* he could take her right then and there, but was restraining himself.

She smiled up at him. "See you later."

"Yes, you will," he told her. He ran one hand over her hair in a gentle caress before turning and heading out of her classroom into the hall.

Kiera sagged back in her chair and blew out a breath. Whew, Cooper Nelson was lethal...and he was all hers.

Two hours later, Kiera made the "applause" sign along with her students. Cooper and Tex had mesmerized the kids. She'd interpreted for Tex, as he didn't know sign language, and had laughed as Cooper and the kids teased him for not knowing even the simplest signs. She appreciated him playing along. The pride her students felt in knowing something the big, strong military man didn't was obvious in their faces, giggles, and puffed-out chests.

She told the kids to get their jackets and to line up for recess and had a quick conversation with Cooper and Tex. "You guys were great. I appreciate you hamming up your lack of communication skills with the kids, Tex."

"No problem, darlin'. And I wasn't hamming it up. They definitely know more than me when it comes to ASL." He turned to Cooper. "And since when did you get so damn fluent?"

Cooper laughed. "Since I've been here every day for the last two months. And I've been studying at home. And I have the app. And Kiera practices with me, and—"

"Okay, okay, I get your point," Tex said. "I'm impressed."

"Me too, if I'm being honest," Cooper said.

"You know, That Frankie boy reminds me of a little girl I know. I'd love to get them together somehow," Tex said.

"Frankie could use some more friends," Kiera said. "Does she live around here?"

Tex shook his head. "No. She's the daughter of a Delta Force soldier I know who lives in Texas."

Kiera's brows drew down. "I'm not sure a friend would work out with her being so far away."

Tex smiled a somewhat secret smile. "You don't know Annie like I do," he said cryptically.

Looking at her watch, Kiera said, "I gotta go. It's my day to monitor recess. I need to get out there."

"Want some company?" Cooper asked.

"Yours? Absolutely. But I won't necessarily be able to talk much. I walk around the playground, making sure all is well with the kids."

"No problem. I won't get in your way. I might like to play with the kids myself. Tex, you in?"

"Oh yeah. Maybe we can interest some of the kids in a game of kick the can or something."

"Kick the can?" Kiera asked in disbelief. "Didn't that game go out of style in the eighties?"

Tex looked a little sheepish. "It's fun, don't knock it."

Kiera giggled. "Whatever. I'll see you guys outside."

Cooper, never letting a chance to kiss her go by, swooped down and touched his lips to her cheek quickly. Kiera caught him winking at Frankie after he did it. She simply smiled. She'd never complain about Cooper kissing her, she was just glad he kept it age-appropriate.

She led her students from the classroom and down the hall to the outside door. Once it was open, they all ran out as if the hounds of hell were after them. Kiera smiled. She remembered feeling exactly the same way when she was young.

The schoolyard was surrounded by a chain-link fence to protect the children. There were a few gates around the property, as the intent wasn't to lock the kids inside, but merely to keep them contained and safe while they were playing. Deaf children couldn't hear horns honking or other signs of nearby dangers.

Kiera began her walk around the area, smiling at a group of kids playing in the dirt, stopping to push a few students on the swings, and warning an older group of children to be careful as they tossed a basketball at each other.

She smiled at Tex and Cooper. They had collected a group of kids, both older and younger, and had split them into two teams. She had no idea what they were playing, but it looked like a mixture of keep away, soccer, and tag. Whatever rules they'd made up were a mystery to her, but since everyone seemed to be having a good time, and running off pent-up energy, it didn't really matter.

Something moved in the corner of her eye and Kiera swung her gaze from her extremely fit boyfriend to whatever it was that had caught her attention. She stared for a long moment, not understanding what she was seeing.

Even before her brain caught up to her eyes, she was moving. Frankie was on the far end of the playground and a woman she'd never seen before was inside the play area. She was average height and slender. Her hair was dark and stringy, hanging limply around her face. Her jaw was set and she looked pissed. Her jeans were tight, but the black T-shirt she was wearing was loose on her frame. She had her hand around Frankie's biceps and was forcing him to walk toward the open gate. A blue, older-model car was idling in the parking lot in the direction the woman was taking Frankie.

A kidnapping from school grounds was every teacher's nightmare— hell, it was every person's nightmare, no matter where it happened. And if she could stop it, or at least get a license plate, she would.

Kiera raced toward Frankie and the mystery woman. She caught up to them just as the woman reached the gate.

"Hey, what are you doing?" Kiera yelled, knowing it was a stupid question because it was obvious what the woman was doing.

She didn't answer, but pushed Frankie through the gap in the fence and started for the car. Kiera followed and got around the woman. She stood in front of her and asked again, "What are you doing?"

"I'm here to take my son to the dentist."

Kiera blinked. "What?" she blurted.

"Frankie is my son. He's coming with me," the lady said, a little more belligerently that time.

"Is this your mother?" Kiera signed to Frankie.

Instead of signing back, he simply nodded.

Okay then. All the things Frankie's dad said about his ex raced through Kiera's mind. She was a drug addict. She was refused custody of Frankie by the courts. She'd been trying to get ahold of Frankie, but his dad had run interference. This wasn't good.

Kiera quickly glanced back at the playground where she'd last seen Cooper. He was still there, oblivious to what was happening on the far end of the play area. She saw a couple of kids standing on the other side of the fence, staring at her in confusion. They obviously knew it was against the rules to leave the school through the fence. The staff at the school had hammered that home over and over again. All visitors had to come into the school through the main doors and check in. They had to leave the same way.

The woman steered Frankie around Kiera and toward the car once more.

Making a split-second decision, Kiera quickly shot off a quick sign to the children standing in the playground watching them. She wanted to scream out to Cooper and Tex, but didn't want to do anything that would put Frankie in even more danger than she instinctively felt he was already in. Without waiting to see what they'd do, she ran to catch up with the surprisingly fast woman and Frankie.

No one was allowed to take a child from the school that wasn't on an approved person list. They were supposed to go to the main office and check the child out...after the secretary made sure it was permitted. And it was certainly not okay for Frankie's mom to pick him up. Not even close.

She grabbed hold of Frankie's shoulder and tried to wrench his mom's grasp off his bicep, but the other woman held on, squeezing her son's arm even tighter, and punched out at Kiera with her free hand.

Kiera let go of Frankie to protect herself, and felt the air whoosh by her face as his mom's fist barely missed her. By the time she stepped back toward the duo, she'd already opened the back door and had shoved her son inside.

Not knowing what else she was supposed to do, Kiera ran around to the other side of the vehicle and breathed a sigh of relief when the door on the opposite side was unlocked. She slipped inside the car and slammed the door behind her.

What am I doing? This is insane. I should leave this to the cops. But I can't let her take Frankie. No way.

She sighed in relief when the man behind the wheel didn't immediately drive off. If she'd yelled for Cooper or his friend he most certainly would have. It might take longer for help to arrive as a result, but every second she could keep the two adults talking was another second Cooper had to get to her and Frankie.

"Get out," the woman snarled at Kiera.

She sat back and crossed her arms over her chest. "No."

"What the fuck?" the man in the driver's seat swore. "You didn't say nothin' about no other woman comin' with us, Twila."

"That's because she's not. Get out," Twila ordered again.

"No," Kiera repeated. "You need me to translate for Frankie." It was stupid, but it was the first thing she thought of.

"He's my son. I don't need you to tell him what I'm sayin'."

"You know sign language?" Kiera asked, already knowing the answer from what Frankie's dad had told her.

"No. But no son of mine is gonna do that sissy talking with his hands. He needs to learn how to read lips and say what he wants."

"We gotta get the fuck outta here," the man snarled.

"Then fucking drive," Twila told him with narrowed eyes.

"I'm not kidnappin' no fucking woman."

"But you'll kidnap a kid?" Kiera asked, knowing she should keep her mouth shut, but she was so appalled at what the man implied, it popped out without thought.

"It ain't kidnapping since it's her own fucking kid."

Kiera was glad Frankie couldn't hear. The man had an obvious love of the word fuck, and that wasn't something Frankie needed to pick up. Using her right hand, she reached over and grabbed Frankie's, giving him moral support as she continued to stall for time.

"Um, the courts would disagree," Kiera told him. "And Frankie isn't *your* kid, so it most definitely is kidnapping since you're driving."

"Just drive slow, we'll shove her ass out when we get to the main road," Twila said.

Kiera's hand tightened on Frankie's. She wasn't getting out of this car without him. No way. She signed the word "run" with her left hand, hoping Frankie saw it as she continued to engage Frankie's mom and the thug behind the wheel.

"Look, whatever you think you're going to do with Frankie isn't going to work, he—"

"What I'm going to do is make sure he learns how to talk, instead of grunting and using his hands to try to fucking talk. Then he's gonna learn how to read lips. It's much more manly than using his hands."

"Reading lips is extremely difficult," Kiera told Twila. "It can take years for someone to learn how to do that. Frankie needs to learn how to read first, and since he can't hear, he needs to associate the words on a page with something. It's not as easy as it seems." She'd had this argument with a few parents over the years but at the moment, she didn't really care if Twila believed her or not, she only needed to stall.

She noted that they were moving very slowly toward the school's exit. She'd prefer they were stationary while they had their talk, but she'd take slow. *Come on, Cooper. I need you.*

"On second thought, why don't we keep 'er?" the slimy man asked. "We owe money to Bud. Maybe he'd take her. High-class pussy that hasn't fucked every man on the block might appeal to him."

Kiera inhaled. "Are you seriously talking about trading me, a human being, for drugs?"

"No," Twila said immediately, and Kiera relaxed a fraction. But her next words had her gasping in shock. "He's talking about giving you to the leader of a gang so he can pimp you out in exchange for drugs." Twila turned her gaze to the man. "I think she'd probably be more trouble than it'd be worth."

"What about it?" the man asked her, catching her eyes in the rearview mirror. "You gonna be trouble?"

CHAPTER 10

*C*ooper laughed as Tex barely missed being hit by the small plastic ball. He had no idea what they were doing, but the kids were having a good time running around after the balls while he and Tex tried to keep them away from them. There weren't any official rules, but not getting hit by a ball seemed to be one. They were also trying to prevent the kids from getting from one end of the field to the other. It seemed to be a mixture of soccer and dodgeball.

All his attention was on the four balls being kicked and thrown around the small area and not on what was going on around him, but when he heard an urgent grunting, he whipped his head up and scanned the area.

There were four children running pell-mell toward their group playing with the balls. They were all vocalizing their urgency. They weren't screaming or talking, but the noises coming out of their mouths were definitely panicked.

"What the hell?" Tex asked, coming up beside him.

Cooper barely noticed, his attention was on the children's hands.

"They left by the gate."

"Teacher said to get help."

"Teacher signed kidnap."

"They got in a car."

"Help, help, help!"

The signs were being repeated over and over and Cooper almost didn't understand them, they were so frantic. But as soon as he realized what was happening, his eyes searched the playground for Kiera. The last time he'd seen her, she was walking on the far side of the play area near the fence.

"What color car?" Cooper signed as soon as the kids got to him.

"What's going on?" Tex asked urgently.

Without taking his eyes from the children giving him information, he explained, "They say a teacher and a kid were kidnapped. They got in a blue car outside the gate."

"Fuck," Tex swore.

Both men were on the move before anything else was said. Cooper ran backward and quickly signed to the children, "Get everyone inside. Find a teacher and call the police."

As soon as he saw the kids understood him, he turned and sprinted for where the kids had pointed they'd last seen the car.

He couldn't outrun a vehicle, but he had to see if he could catch up enough to read the license plate. He knew it was Kiera in the car. First, she was the only teacher on the playground, and second, if someone had tried to kidnap one of the children, he knew without a doubt she wouldn't just stand by and let it happen.

"Go," Tex said, falling behind. "My leg won't let me go as fast as you, I'm right behind you."

Cooper didn't bother to respond. He just ran faster. He leaped over the four-foot fence as if he was a world-class hurdler—and couldn't believe it when he saw an older-model navy-blue Mustang going only a couple miles an hour toward the exit.

What the hell was the driver doing? If he or she had just kidnapped a kid, and Kiera, they should be driving like a bat out of hell to escape.

Everything inside him became focused on the car. It was still there. It wasn't too late. If they got out of the parking lot, it would be almost impossible to find...at least quickly. And giving a kidnapper time to hurt Kiera wasn't something he was willing to do. His muscles responded without input from his brain, his SEAL training kicking in.

Seeing the direction the car was going, he ran diagonally across the lot, never taking his eyes off it. Cooper could see two people in the front and two in the backseat, one being a child. He could tell it was Kiera in the car, even from just the back of her head. He'd recognize her anywhere.

The adrenaline surged through his body. No fucking way was anyone going to take away the best thing that had ever happened to him.

Running through his options, Cooper shoved his hand in his pocket. Jackpot. Having his key ring and the tool on it would make entry into the kidnapper's vehicle easy, but everything else was a crap shoot. He knew Tex would be at his back as soon as he caught up. He had no idea how Kiera would react, but he had to think she'd do whatever she could to protect the child. He could take care of the two assholes in the front.

Time slowed as he approached the getaway car from the driver's side. As he got closer, Cooper could see it was Frankie in the backseat with Kiera. His teeth ground together.

No. Just no. No one was going to hurt that little boy. Not on his watch.

He gripped his keys tightly and timed his actions. He had to strike at the perfect time. Too soon and he'd lose the element of surprise and the driver would most likely take off. Too late and the car would turn onto the main road and be gone. No, he had to time this perfectly.

* * *

KIERA COULDN'T BELIEVE Frankie's mom and the thug were talking about selling her to a man so he could pimp her out. It was unbelievable. It was ridiculous. It was terrifying. "Am I going to be trouble?" she asked, repeating his question. "Yeah, you bet your ass I am. Look, Twila, you haven't done anything yet. You haven't even left the school premises. Just stop the car and let me and Frankie get out. We won't say anything."

"You think I believe that?" she asked.

"You should. I don't want to be sold so people can have sex with me, and I think your son would truly love a relationship with you that doesn't include being scared for his life. But you won't have that unless you let us out right now."

"Let's dump her ass," the man said. "She talks too much."

"I agree," Twila said, then turned in her seat and pointed at Kiera. "Get out."

"No," Kiera said. "I'm not leaving without Frankie."

Twila fiddled with something in her lap, and the next thing Kiera knew, she was looking down the barrel of a gun. "I said, get out."

Kiera had never even held a gun in her life, let alone looked down the ass end of one. "N-no." she stammered. "You don't want to shoot me in front of your son."

"Why not?" Twila asked, as if she didn't have a care in the world. "It might make him more of a man."

Kiera snorted. "You think making him watch his beloved teacher get shot right in front of him will make him more of a man? It'll probably make him a psychotic mess who will end up killing you when he's in his twenties for making his life a living hell."

"You're a little dramatic," Twila observed.

"And you're a little insane."

The two women glared at each other. Kiera heard Frankie making distressed noises in the back of his throat, but she refused to look away from the gun. If she only had a few more seconds left on this Earth, she wasn't going to be a coward.

Everything seemed to happen in slow motion after that.

The sound of breaking glass was loud in the small space of the car and Kiera flinched, thinking for a moment Twila had actually pulled the trigger.

The man driving swore and slammed on the brake. Since no one was wearing a seat belt, they all flew forward. Kiera saw an arm reach through the broken driver's side window and pull the man driving out through the small space. But before she could move, Twila had recovered and was reaching into the backseat toward Frankie.

Kiera reacted without thought. She threw herself in front of the little boy and grabbed the handle of his door. As it popped open, she pushed Frankie with all her strength. He flew sideways and she saw his little feet go flying in the air as he landed on his back and butt on the ground outside the vehicle.

She hoped he'd do as she'd told him earlier and run, but Kiera didn't have time to worry about him. Twila was pissed. And was acting like a woman possessed. She hit and clawed every inch of skin she could reach. Kiera turned her head to protect her eyes and did her best to keep Twila from hurting her.

Not able to see what was going on with the driver, only hearing grunts and the sounds of fists landing on bare skin, Kiera got up on her knees and began to fight back. It was awkward with the seat between them, but the thought of Twila overpowering her and getting her hands back on Frankie was enough to fuel Kiera's adrenaline.

After an especially hard punch to the side of her head, Kiera decided to reciprocate. She fisted her hand and swung it at Twila. When she made contact with the woman's face, it hurt, but she did it again, then again.

With each strike, Twila would grunt, but then she'd come right back at Kiera.

Kiera hurt. Her hand hurt where she'd been hitting the other woman. Her face and head ached where Twila had landed blows, and she was tiring. She loved that Cooper worked out, but it wasn't the top of her favorite things to do.

Just as she made the decision to back off and get out of the car and haul ass, which she should've done the second she pushed Frankie out, the front door next to Twila opened and a large arm reached into the car.

Twila was hauled out and away from Kiera, and she watched in relief as Tex easily manhandled the other woman into submission. He had one arm around her chest and the other around her neck. Even though she twisted, screamed, and fought against him, she wasn't going anywhere.

"You all right?" Tex asked.

Remembering Frankie for the first time, Kiera didn't answer him, but scooted toward the open side door and quickly stood. "Frankie!" she yelled frantically.

"He's fine," Tex told her. "Ran like the wind back toward the school. Smart kid."

Kiera breathed out a sigh of relief.

"Kiera," a voice said from next to her.

Whirling, and wincing at the pain it caused, she saw Cooper standing next to her. She'd never seen a more welcome sight in all her life. She threw herself at him and sighed in relief when she felt his arms close around her. She rested her cheek against his chest and clutched at the back of his T-shirt.

"Shhhhh, I got you," Cooper murmured. "You're safe."

Kiera was shaking so hard she knew she wouldn't be able to stand if Cooper wasn't holding her up.

"I hear sirens," Tex announced.

Kiera didn't even lift her head. Sirens meant the cops, hopefully. "Where's the driver?" she mumbled.

"Unconscious," Tex told her.

Kiera lifted her head, which felt as if it weighed nine hundred pounds, and looked up at Cooper. He had a trickle of blood coming out of his left ear. She brought a hand up to his face and gently pushed. He allowed it, and she saw he no longer had his hearing aid in. Taking a deep breath, she brought her other hand up between them and signed, "Are you okay? You're bleeding."

"So are you," Cooper said out loud. He traced a line down her cheek and she winced.

"You need to see a doctor about your ear. It's bleeding," Kiera insisted…as much as she could insist through signing.

"He got a lucky shot. As I pulled him out of the car, he punched me in the side of the head. My hearing aid took the brunt of the damage. I'm okay, sweetheart."

"Are you sure?"

"I'm sure."

"Okay." Kiera took him at his word. She wanted to know how he'd gotten in the car so easily, but it would have to wait. She was extremely grateful he'd shown up when he had. She'd hoped she could stall long enough that the students she'd signed to could get help, but she hadn't been positive. They'd been so close to the main road. So close to having Twila succeed. So close to disaster.

But her SEAL had protected her. He'd gotten there in time. Everything else could wait.

CHAPTER 11

"Frankie, it's your turn in the talk circle," Kiera said gently. "Do you have anything you want to share?"

It had been a week since Frankie's mom had tried to kidnap him, and today was the boy's first day back in school. Kiera herself had taken a few days off, but even though she still had bruises and deep scratches on her face from Twila's fingernails, Kiera refused to stay home.

She wanted to be with her kids. Not only the ones in her class, but all of them. Those who had run to get help, who gave her huge hugs in the hallways, and even the kids she didn't know but who'd made it a point to stop her and tell her they were glad she was all right.

She hadn't set out to be a hero, but when she'd seen Frankie being hauled away, she'd made the split-second decision to do everything she could to stop the abduction. Not only was it her obligation as a teacher at the school, but it was Frankie. She loved all the kids in her class, but he was special.

He'd reverted back to shades of the person he'd been when he'd first started attending the special school. But Kiera had confidence he'd bounce back quickly.

Without looking up, Frankie slowly signed, "I was scared when my mom came to take me away. But Ms. Kiera was suddenly right there with me. She didn't let me be taken." He looked up then. "I love you."

Kiera's eyes filled with tears and she smiled at the little boy. "Come here," she signed. He got up and came over to her. Kiera pulled him into her lap, put her arm around him, and signed to him, and the rest of the class.

"I love you all. You are special to me. I will always do everything I can to keep you safe."

Frankie turned in her arms and ran a little finger over the worst scratch on her face. It was scabbed over and bruised, but she didn't even feel his gentle touch. "You got hurt."

"So did you," Kiera said, touching his upper arm gently where she knew he had bruises from the tight grip his mom had on him.

Suddenly, he smiled. A smile so wide she was momentarily blinded. "We used our secret language."

Kiera grinned back at him. "Yes, we did."

"I like it."

"You like to sign?"

He nodded. "I can talk to people without anyone knowing what I am saying. Like you did when you told me to run. Like Cooper and his friends do."

Kiera wanted to laugh and rejoice in the resilience of children, but she needed to get a word of caution in before she did. "It's not nice to talk about people when they don't understand. You don't like it when people talk in front of you and you can't hear what they're saying, do you?"

Frankie shook his head.

"It's the same sort of thing, sweetie. Don't ever be a bully and make fun of people or purposely talk about them when they don't understand."

"But if we need to, like when my mommy stole me, it's okay?"

"Yes, in emergencies, it's okay."

"Okay," he signed, then squirmed to get off her lap.

"Anyone else want to share anything before recess?"

As if she'd said the magic word, all the kids leaped up from their spots on the floor and ran toward their cubbies.

Kiera laughed, knowing that would be their reaction. Remarkably, even though Frankie had been taken from the playground, the other children didn't seem to have any aversion or reluctance to go outside. The adults, however, were another matter.

The principal had made sure all of the gates were locked the very next day and was making plans for even more security. It had been a rude awakening for a school that hadn't ever had any violence directed toward it, but danger was always a threat and should be mitigated as much as possible. He apologized to Kiera for being reactive rather than proactive, but she'd told him he had nothing to be sorry for. No one could've predicted Frankie's mom would've done what she did.

Kiera felt an arm curl around her waist as she stood at her windows watching the kids run around outside. Frankie and the others might be okay with being on the playground, but she was having a harder time.

"Good afternoon, sweetheart," Cooper said into her ear.

Kiera relaxed back into him. "Hey, how'd your meeting with Patrick go?" She turned in his arms and rested her hands on his chest.

"Really good. He listened to my entire presentation, all twenty minutes of it, without a word. I was sweating bullets, thinking he was merely humoring me and he was about to tell me I wasn't qualified, or that it wasn't a good idea."

"And?" Kiera asked when he paused. "What did he say?"

"He said the job was mine as soon as I opened my mouth. Bastard made me go through my entire presentation for nothing."

Kiera grinned up at Cooper. "I'm proud of you."

"Thanks. But don't be proud yet. I haven't even started."

She shook her head. "You've come a really long way, Cooper. You told me yourself that you had no idea what to do when you retired. Now you're learning sign language, really quickly as a matter of fact, and you made your own job as a consultant to the SEALs teaching them that language. It's amazing."

He shrugged. "The longer I thought about it, the more I realized it was really important for the SEALs to all be on the same page when it came to our signals. I've seen Wolf and his team talk with each other via signals and didn't understand anything they were saying. The same with Tex. When we were playing with the kids that day, I was trying to signal him to go one way and he had no clue what I was trying to say. I know a lot of the teams stay together for a long time, but sometimes they don't. It would be so much easier if the signs everyone used were the same. Especially if we needed backup in the field."

"I love you," she told him.

"I love you too," he returned. "And I have a present for you." He loosened one hand from around her waist and moved it to one of his front pockets. "Hold out your hand."

She did. He placed a plastic device in her palm, and Kiera blinked down at it in confusion. "Uh...thanks...what is it?"

Cooper chuckled. "It's a glass popper."

She nodded in understanding. "Like the one you used?"

"Yup. It fits nicely on a key ring. You never know when having a little device to easily break a car window will come in handy."

"Thank God you had yours in your pocket when you came after us," Kiera mused, still looking down at the lifesaving device in her hand. "It wasn't like he was going to open the door and let you in." She told him something he knew.

Cooper didn't say anything but instead returned his hand to her lower back and pressed her into him. "Move in with me."

Kiera's gaze whipped up to his. "What?"

"Move in with me," he repeated. "We've been living together for the past week or so and dating for the last couple months."

"Are you asking because of what happened?" she asked gently. "Because that was a fluke thing."

"Yes and no," he told her. "When I realized that it was you in the back of that car, I swear my life flashed in front of my eyes in a way it never had before. I've been in tight spots in the past, but nothing had prepared me to come face to face with the reality of my life without you. I'm not an idiot, I know either one of us could be in a car accident and killed tomorrow. We could get sick, a crazed terrorist could blow up an airplane we just happened to be in, or we could die a hundred other ways. But I want to spend as much time with you as possible. I want to hear your laughter before I go to sleep each night and I want your beautiful blue eyes to be the first things I see when I wake up each morning. I think you more than proved you can take care of yourself last week. I just can't imagine not spending the rest of my life with you, and I want the rest of my life to start as soon as possible."

"Yes," Kiera said as soon as he finished speaking.

"Yes?"

"Yes," she repeated. "I'll move in with you. I love you. I've loved being with you every night and morning over the last week. I crave it."

They smiled at each other for a long moment before Cooper said, "I'm going to ask you to marry me, you know."

"Good. I'm going to say yes."

"Tex says he wants us to come to Virginia and visit him and Melody. And he promises that it'll be more laid back than his vacation down here was."

Kiera burst out laughing. She liked Tex. Not only did he help come to her rescue, he was funny and down to earth. And with the stories he told about his wife, she had a feeling she'd like her too. "I'm sure I can get a few days off. It's not like the principal is gonna deny me," she said with a grin.

"I love you, Kiera Hamilton. You scared ten years off my life last week."

"I think they were scared off of me too," she admitted. "Thank you for coming to my rescue. In case I haven't told you yet."

"Only eighty times," Cooper teased.

They heard the kids entering the hallway, coming in from recess.

"Looks like break time is over," Kiera said unnecessarily. "I'll see you at home?"

"Home. I like that," Cooper said. "Yeah, you'll see me at home."

He kissed her quickly before the kids came into the room, then pulled away. He greeted each child as they entered and headed for the door. Kiera watched as he turned in the doorway. He signed "I love you" to her, then turned to Frankie and gave him a small chin lift.

The little boy returned the gesture, grinning from ear to ear.

Kiera smiled, knowing Frankie would be okay. And so would she. Bruises would fade, as would the memories of the week before, but her love for the gentle, badass former SEAL, who by some miracle loved her, would last a lifetime.

* * *

MAKE sure you pick up Cutter's story...*Protecting Dakota*. Find out who the Silver Fox decides is his and how he protects her!

JOIN my Newsletter and find out about sales, free books, contests and new releases before anyone else!! Click HERE

Want to know when my books go on sale? Follow me on Bookbub HERE!

Would you like Susan's Book Protecting Caroline for FREE?
Click HERE

PROTECTING DAKOTA

SEAL OF PROTECTION, BOOK 10

A Note to the Reader

This is a special book to me for a couple of reasons.

It was a collaboration born over several glasses of wine at an author convention. The twelve of us decided we wanted to write books that were linked together, but still connected to our own series'. I loved the conception of a former commander who was tasked to covertly take down homegrown terrorists. I also loved that the books could be read in any order. I hope you'll check out the other books in the Sleeper SEAL series.

The other reason this book means a lot to me is because it's the last official book in the original SEAL of Protection Series. Protecting Caroline was my first indie published book, and it's only right that she kicks as much butt in this book as she did in her own.

BUT, this is not the end of the SEALs. You have been introduced to another team of SEALs in past books, but you'll get to meet Gumby, Rocco, Ace, Bubba, Rex, and Phantom once again here. Their series, SEAL of Protection: Legacy will debut soon.

And just because Wolf and the gang will be transitioned from an active SEAL team to a training role, doesn't mean that you won't see them again and get to catch up with their families.

Thank you for your support of my SEALs. Here's to many more missions, adventures, and love stories with the Legacy team!

Also…the A'Le'Inn is a real place. As is Rachel, Nevada, as is the Goldfield Motel. It's a fascinating part of the United States and I recommend that if you get a chance, you head out into the desert and check it out.

If you do, make sure to stop by Rachel and the A'Le'Inn and ask for Pat or Connie. They are also real people and have amazingly wonderful stories to tell. They're very nice people and they love to meet tourists! Stay a night in their trailer/motel and take in the stars. Oh, and if you see a geocacher or two, honk and wave…and be careful of the cows!

PROLOGUE

*R*etired Navy Commander Greg Lambert leaned forward to rake in the pile of chips his full house had netted him. Tonight, he would leave the weekly gathering not only with his pockets full, but his pride intact.

The scowls he earned from his poker buddies at his unusual good luck were an added bonus.

They'd become too accustomed to him coming up on the losing side of Five Card Stud. It was about time he taught them to never underestimate him.

Vice President Warren Angelo downed the rest of his bourbon and stubbed out his Cuban cigar. "Looks like Lady Luck is on your side tonight, Commander."

After he neatly stacked his chips in a row at the rail in front of him, Greg glanced around at his friends. It occurred to him right then, this weekly meeting wasn't so different from the joint sessions they used to have at the Pentagon during his last five years of service.

While the location was now the Secretary of State's basement, the gatherings still included top-ranking military brass, politicians, and the director of the CIA, who had been staring at him strangely all night long.

"It's about time the bitch smiled my way, don't you think? She usually just cleans out my pockets and gives you my money," Greg replied with a sharp laugh as his eyes roved over the spacious man cave with envy before they snagged on the wall clock.

It was well past midnight, their normal break-up time. He needed to get home, but what did he have to go home to? Four walls, and Karen's mean-as-hell Chihuahua who hated him.

Greg stood, scooted back his chair, and stretched his shoulders. The rest of his poker buddies quickly left, except for Vice President Angelo, Benedict Hughes with the CIA, and their host tonight, Percy Long, the Secretary of State.

Greg took the last swig of his bourbon, then set the glass on the table. When he took a step to leave, they moved to block his way to the door. "Something on your minds, gentlemen?" he asked, their cold, sober stares making the hair on the back of his neck stand up.

It wasn't a comfortable feeling, but one he was familiar with from his days as a Navy SEAL. That feeling usually didn't portend anything good was about to go down, but neither did the looks on these men's faces.

Warren cleared his throat and leaned against the mahogany bar with its leather trimmings. "There's been a significant amount of chatter lately." He glanced at Ben. "We're concerned."

Greg backed up a few steps, putting some distance between himself and the men. "Why are you telling me this? I've been out of the loop for a while now." Greg was retired, and bored stiff, but not stiff enough to tackle all that was wrong in the United States at the moment or fight the politics involved in fixing things.

Ben let out a harsh breath then gulped down his glass of water. He set the empty glass down on the bar with a sigh and met Greg's eyes. "We need your help, and we're not going to beat around the bush," he said, making Greg's short hairs stand taller.

Greg put his hands in his pockets, rattling the change in his right pocket and his car keys in the left while he waited for the hammer. Nothing in Washington, D.C. was plain and simple anymore. Not that it ever had been.

"Spit it out, Ben," he said, eyeballing the younger man. "I'm all ears."

"Things have changed in the US. Terrorists are everywhere now," he started, and Greg bit back a laugh at the understatement of the century.

He'd gotten out before the recent INCONUS attacks started, but he was still in service on 9/11 for the ultimate attack. The day that replaced Pearl Harbor as the day that would go down in infamy.

"That's not news, Ben," Greg said, his frustration mounting in his tone.

"What does that have to do with me, other than being a concerned citizen?"

"More cells are being identified every day," Ben replied, his five o'clock shadow standing in stark contrast to his now paler face. "The chatter about imminent threats, big jihad events that are in the works, is getting louder every day."

"You do understand that I'm no longer active service, right?" Greg shrugged. "I don't see how I can be of much help there."

"We want you to head a new division at the CIA," Warren interjected. "Ghost Ops, a sleeper cell of SEALs to help us combat the terrorist sleeper cells in the US...and whatever the hell else might pop up later."

Greg laughed. "And where do you think I'll find these SEALs to sign up? Most are deployed over—"

"We want *retired* SEALs like yourself. We've spent millions training these men, and letting them sit idle stateside while we fight this losing battle alone is just a waste." Ben huffed a breath. "I know they'd respect you when you ask them to join the contract team you'd be heading up. You'd have a much better chance of convincing them to help than we will."

"Most of those guys are like me, worn out to the bone or injured when they finally give up the teams. Otherwise, they'd still be active. SEALs don't just quit." *Unless their wives were taken by cancer and their kids were off at college, leaving them alone in a rambling house when they were supposed to be traveling together and enjoying life.*

"What kind of threats are you talking about?" Greg asked, wondering why he was even entertaining such a stupid idea.

"There are many. More every day. Too many for us to fight alone," Ben started, but Warren held up his palm.

"The president is taking a lot of heat. He has three and a half years left in his term, and taking out these threats was a campaign promise. He wants the cells identified and the terror threats eradicated quickly."

These two, and the president, sat behind desks all day. They'd never been in a field op before, so they had no idea the planning and training that took place before a team ever made it to the field. Training a team of broken-down SEALs to work together would take double that time, because each knew better than the rest how things should be done, so there was no "quick" about it.

"That's a tall order. I can't possibly get a team of twelve men on the same page in under a year. Even if I can find them." Why in the hell was he getting excited, then? "Most are probably out enjoying life on a beach somewhere." Exactly where he would be with Karen if she hadn't fucking died on him as soon as he'd retired four years ago.

"We don't want a *team*, Greg," Percy Long corrected, unfolding his arms as he stepped toward him. "This has to be done stealthily because we don't want to panic the public. If word got out about the severity of the threats, people wouldn't leave their homes. The press would pump it up until they created a frenzy. You know how that works."

"So, let me get this straight. You want individual SEALs, sleeper guys who agree to be called up for special ops, to perform solo missions?" Greg asked, his eyebrows lifting. "That's not usually how they work."

"Unusual times call for unusual methods, Greg. They have the skills to get it done quickly and quietly," Warren replied, and Greg couldn't argue. That's exactly the way SEALs operated—they did whatever it took to get the job done.

Ben approached him, placed his hand on his shoulder as if this was a tag-team effort, and Greg had no doubt that it was just that. "Every terrorist or wannabe terror organization has roots here now. Al Qaeda, the Muslim Brotherhood, Isis, or the Taliban—you name it. They're not here looking for asylum. They're actively recruiting followers and planning events to create a caliphate on our home turf. We can't let that happen, Greg, or the United States will never be the same."

"You'll be a CIA contractor, and can name your price," Warren inserted, and Greg's eyes swung to him. "You'll be on your own in the decision making. We need to have plausible deniability if anything goes wrong."

"Of course," Greg replied, shaking his head. If anything went south, they needed a fall guy, and that would be him in this scenario. Not much different from the dark ops his teams performed under his command when he was active duty.

God, why did this stupid idea suddenly sound so intriguing? Why did he think he might be able to make it work? And why in the hell did he suddenly think it was just what he needed to break out of the funk he'd been living in for four years?

"I can get you a list of potential hires, newly retired SEALs, and the president says *anything* else you need," Warren continued quickly. "All we need is your commitment."

The room went silent, and Greg looked deeply into each man's eyes as he pondered a decision. What the hell did he have to lose? If he didn't agree, he'd just die a slow, agonizing death in his recliner at home. At only forty-seven and still fit, that could be a lot of years spent in that chair.

"Get me the intel, the list, and the contract," he said, and a surge of adrenaline made his knees weak.

He was back in the game.

CHAPTER 1

"Hey, Wolf, how'd it go?" Slade "Cutter" Cutsinger asked the SEAL as he entered the office on the Naval base.

"I'd tell ya, Cutter, but then I'd have to kill you," Wolf joked as he smiled at Slade.

It was a long-running joke between the two men. Slade was a retired SEAL himself, now working as a contractor for the Navy. He worked directly under Patrick Hurt, Wolf's commander. Slade probably knew more about the mission Wolf and his team had been on than Wolf did himself.

"The commander's waiting in his office for a debrief," Slade told the other man with a chin lift, indicating the door to his right. "All good at home? Caroline okay?"

"She's good," Wolf told him. "Thanks for asking. And I should've said something before now, but I appreciate you checking on her during that last mission. She's used to them, as much as she *can* be used to her spouse leaving for who-knows-where for who-knows-how-long. She told me you helped make her and the others feel better about that mission. You know if you ever need anything, all you've got to do is ask."

"I do know, and it's appreciated," Slade told him.

He hadn't ever worked in the field with Wolf or the other guys on his team, but he respected the hell out of all of them. They were extremely successful on their missions, didn't take absurd chances, and most importantly to Slade, all took care of their families. And by "take care," Slade meant they realized how precious their women and children were and worked their asses off to make sure they knew it. They didn't sleep around on them. If they were running late on a mission, Wolf always made sure Slade checked up on their families. And they had tracking devices on their women, just in case.

Slade wasn't supposed to know about the trackers, but his friend, Tex, had let that little gem slip one night when they were shooting the shit on the phone. Slade had worked on a team with Tex before he'd been medically retired, and hadn't ever found another man for whom he had more respect. When he'd found out about Tex marrying, and then adopting a child from Iraq, he'd been almost as proud for the man as Tex probably was himself.

They'd been talking on the phone one night and Tex had told him that his wife, Melody, had given birth to a little girl named Hope, then he'd told Slade that he'd be damned if any of their enemies got their hands on his baby. With his wife's approval and encouragement, he'd had a bracelet made for his daughter to wear with a tiny tracking device. That's when he'd let the cat out of the bag about the women who belonged to Wolf's team also voluntarily wearing similar jewelry.

Slade had felt a little melancholy that he hadn't ever found a woman he cared about enough to want to protect like that...and who would let him. His ex, Cynthia—not Cindy; God forbid someone call her Cindy—didn't have much interest in anything he did and by the end of their four-year marriage, the feeling was definitely mutual.

All his life, he'd wanted to feel a special connection with a woman. For some reason, he had a feeling he'd just know when he met her. In his twenties, he hadn't been too anxious to find her because he'd been young and eager to make a difference in the Navy. In his thirties, he was ready to settle down, even though he was neck deep working on the SEAL teams. And now, in his late forties, he felt way too old to try to start a serious relationship. He figured he'd lost his chance.

So now he was a confirmed bachelor who kept tabs on the families of the SEALs that worked for Commander Hurt instead.

Mentally shrugging, Slade tried to concentrate on the paperwork in front of him. He missed the action of being on a SEAL team, but he was definitely too old to do the work of the younger men anymore. He gladly left it to them.

The phone next to him rang, and Slade answered. "Cutsinger. How may I help you?"

"I'm looking for Slade Cutsinger. Is this he?"

Slade didn't recognize the voice, but he definitely recognized the authority behind the words.

"Yes, Sir. I'm Cutsinger."

"This is retired Navy Commander Greg Lambert. Is this line secure?"

Slade was taken aback. He didn't remember ever working with a Greg Lambert, and he had a good memory. "No, Sir, it is not. If you need to talk to Commander Hurt, I recommend—"

"It's you I need," Greg interrupted. "I'm going to give you a phone number. I expect you to call me tonight from a secure line. I have a proposition for you."

"No disrespect, Sir, but I don't know you," Slade said, having trouble keeping his tone professional. He didn't mind taking orders, but usually he knew the person who was giving those orders.

"You don't, but we have a mutual friend who speaks highly of you."

When he didn't continue, Slade asked, "A mutual friend?"

"John Keegan."

Fuckin' A. Tex. What the hell had the man gotten him into now? "He's one of the best men I've ever met," Slade told Greg honestly.

"Ditto. Got a pen?"

"Yeah." Slade dutifully jotted down the number he was given.

"Needless to say, this is a highly sensitive matter. John assured me that you were discreet and would be extremely interested."

"At least he's half right," Slade mumbled, and ignored the chuckle on the other end of the line. "I'll call around nineteen hundred, if that's all right."

"I'll be waiting." And the former commander ended the call without another word.

Slade slowly hung up the phone on his end, lost in thought. He tried to quash the spark of interest that flared deep in his belly, but didn't quite succeed. Working as a contractor for the US Navy kept his toe dipped into the dangerous waters he used to swim in, but it wasn't the same. Somehow, he knew that whatever Lambert had to say to him tonight would change his life. Whether or not it was for the better remained to be seen.

* * *

"WHAT THE FUCK have you gotten me into now, Tex?" Slade asked as soon as his friend picked up the phone.

"Hello to you too, Cutter. How's the weather out there in California? Let me guess, you're sitting on the balcony of your apartment watching the ocean and wishing you weren't bored off your ass."

"Asshole," Slade said with a smile. Tex knew him too well. That's what happened when you worked side by side, getting shot at and saving each other's lives too many times to count. "I got a call from a former Commander Lambert today. He said you two talked about me."

"Not beating around the bush, I see," Tex said.

"I'm supposed to call him back in thirty on a secure line," Slade told his old teammate.

"Gotcha. Lambert is one of the good guys. Worked with him a few times. He has a new job, under the table, and wanted the names of some of the best of the best former SEALs I knew. You were at the top of that list."

"Under the table?" Slade asked. "Not sure I like the sound of that."

"Nothing we haven't been involved with before," Tex reassured him. "Hear him out."

"You been briefed on this job?"

"No. I know Lambert wanted to ask me to help out, but with Hope being so young and Akilah still settling in, I didn't want to do anything that would take me away from home," Tex told him.

Slade got that. If he had a wife and new baby, not to mention a recently adopted teenager, he wouldn't want to leave home either. Feeling restless, he got up and went into his apartment. "You have your hands full with all the teams you work with as well," Slade told his old friend.

"That I do. But I love it. I enjoy being involved in all aspects of our Armed Forces. But it's more than that. I do it to keep the men safe so they can get home to their families."

"It's more appreciated than you'll ever know," Slade told Tex.

As if uncomfortable with the turn in conversation, Tex replied, "That being said, even though I'm not the man for this job, you need anything, you better call. You know no one can find needles in haystacks better than me."

"I don't know, man. I hear there's a chick in Texas who's giving you a run for your money," Slade teased.

"I'll deny it if it comes up later, but that's no lie," Tex said immediately.

"Beth is amazing, and she's been able to hack into some places I wouldn't even have tried."

Glancing at his watch, and seeing his time was up, Slade reluctantly said, "Gotta run. Appreciate the head's up and the confirmation that this is on the up and up."

"Anytime. I wasn't kidding, Cutter," Tex said in a hard voice. "You need *anything*, you call. I don't know what Lambert has up his sleeve, but I'm guessing since he didn't brief me when he called, he wants whatever he's asking to be on the down-low...meaning you working alone since you're retired, but nothing is ever fucking solo when it comes to my teams."

"I'll see what he has to say and make the decision whether or not to bring in anyone else," Cutter told Tex. "But I hear you. I'll call if I need you."

"Good. Later."

"Later," Slade echoed and clicked off the phone. He put his personal cell down on the arm of the chair he was sitting in and took a deep breath. Inhaling the scent of salt and sea drifting through the open balcony door, he took a moment to try to calm his mind and body. The pesky feeling that his life was about to change was relentless.

Slade thought about his life. He liked it...for the most part. His ocean-side apartment was perfect for him. Not huge, not tiny. He'd saved up his money while he was active duty, and his retirement check wasn't anything to sneeze at. He had a fancy-ass 4K television in the living room behind him, good friends he worked with who he had drinks with every so often, and he could be in the ocean swimming in three minutes, if he was so inclined.

His family was good. His sister, Sabrina, was married with three kids, and his brother also had a wife and two kids. His siblings were both younger than he was, and lived on the other side of the country. He didn't see his nieces and nephews often, but when he did, it was as if no time at all had passed. He missed his parents, but he'd never had the kind of relationship with them where they'd communicated on a regular basis.

But Slade had to be honest with himself. He was lonely. He had a great apartment, a good job, but no one to share his life with. He'd tried online dating, *that* had been a disaster, and he was way too fucking old to pick up chicks at *Aces Bar and Grill*, the notorious hangout for current and former Navy SEALs. It had become less of a pick-up joint since it was now owned by Jessyka Sawyer, the wife of one of Wolf's teammates, but a bar would always be a bar and there would always be women trolling for a one-night stand or the chance to snag a military guy, and men hoping for a quick hook-up.

Without giving himself a chance to get any more morose than he already was, Slade picked up the secure cell phone he'd been issued by the Navy so he could talk to Commander Hurt and the SEALs under his command, and brought it back out to the balcony with him. He dialed the former Commander Lambert's number.

"Right on time," the commander said as a greeting. "Bodes well for our working relationship."

"I'm not sure I *want* a working relationship with you," Slade told him honestly.

"This line is secure, correct?" Greg asked.

Irritated that he'd think for a second he'd call on one that wasn't when the man had made it more than clear he wouldn't talk otherwise, Slade bit out, "Yes."

Greg chuckled. "Had to ask. No offense intended. You talk to John?"

"Just hung up with him," Slade confirmed.

"Figured. I'm just going to get right down to it, if you don't mind."

"I prefer it, actually," Slade said, his body tensing with whatever he was about to hear.

"I'm in charge of a new initiative, a secret one, to take down sleeper cells of terrorists around the country. The fuckers are getting the drop on us, and it needs to stop. I've been authorized to mobilize my own brand of sleeper cells...retired SEALs."

Slade wasn't sure he understood. "And?"

"And I want *you*, Cutter. I've read your file. I know your strengths and weaknesses. I've spoken with John and some of your other teammates. You're levelheaded and you gather all the intel before jumping into anything. You're determined and have a love for your country that isn't matched by many people. But more importantly, you've been successful on your own."

"I was *never* on my own," Slade protested. "Not once. Even if I went in to get a hostage, my team was at my back."

"I know that." Greg backed off a bit. "What I meant was that when the shit hit the fan, you didn't panic. You simply changed to Plan B...or C, D, or E. I need you."

Slade took a deep breath and let it out slowly. He was curious. Dammit. "Tell me more," he demanded grumpily.

"Six months ago, there was a bombing at LAX."

When the other man didn't elaborate, Slade prompted, "Yeah? I remember it. There was one bomber, he took a handful of hostages. The building was in the process of being evacuated, but the fucker blew himself up, along with all of the hostages, before everyone was out. Ansar al-Shari'a took responsibility."

"Correct. That's what was reported in the news," Greg said.

The hair on the back of Slade's neck stood on end. "That's what was reported on the news?" he repeated.

"Yes. Internet chatter has been extremely active. The bomber was a college kid. He'd been recruited online. The leader's name is Aziz Fourati. Government believes he's Tunisian, and based on the success of the LAX bombing, he's actively recruiting more soldiers. He wants to duplicate his success...on a national level."

"Jesus," Slade swore. "If we thought 9/11 was bad, if he's successful, he could cripple transportation in this country for months."

"Exactly. But that's not all."

"Fuck. What else?"

"He was there," Greg said flatly.

"Where?"

"At the bombing. He was one of the so-called hostages. Gave a speech and everything right before the kid pulled the trigger and blew everyone sky-high."

"How do you know?" Slade demanded.

"All security cameras at the airport were jammed right before everything went down. So there's no public video of anything that happened inside, but someone's been posting audio and video on the Dark Web of his speech on the Internet, and using it as a recruitment tool."

Slade knew there was more. "And? Jesus, spit it out."

"Besides Fourati, who slipped out right before the bomber let loose, there was one other survivor."

The words seemed to echo across the phone line. "What? *Who?*"

"Her name is Dakota James. She was supposed to be flying to a conference in Orlando that day."

"There wasn't ever anything in the newspaper," Slade protested. "How do you know for sure?"

"I've got copies of the propaganda videos Fourati has been sending to his minions. She's there, but her body wasn't one of those found when the pieces of that section of the airport were sorted. Lo and behold, she showed up at work the next week with a broken arm. Told her co-workers she'd fallen down a flight of stairs."

"So, what's the deal? What'd she say about the bombing?"

"That's just it," Greg told Slade. "She's in the wind."

"She's gone? What about her job?"

"Quit."

"Just like that?" Slade asked.

"Just like that," Greg confirmed.

"You think she's involved? That what you need me for?"

"No. We don't think she's involved, but we have nothing on Fourati. We have no photos, no videos that show his face. Nada. Zip. Zilch."

"But Dakota James saw him," Slade concluded.

"Exactly. We need her. Fourati has to be stopped before he can carry through with his plan. As far as we can tell, right now he only has a handful of men he's recruited, but the more he gets, the more his plan can snowball."

"You want me to find her."

"Yes. Find her. Get a description of Fourati, then track that asshole down and eliminate the threat."

Ah, there it was.

Slade had been waiting for confirmation that the former commander wanted him to kill for his country once again. The thought should've been repugnant. He'd left that part of his life behind. But then Slade remembered the pictures of the ruined section of the airport. Remembered the pictures and videos of the victims. A mother traveling with her three-month-old baby. The couple celebrating their fiftieth wedding anniversary by flying to Hawaii for a two-week vacation. The business men and women who were caught in the crosshairs of a terrorist.

The resolve to take down the asshole responsible solidified in his belly.

He opened his mouth to agree to take the job, when Greg spoke again. "There's one more thing…"

Ah, shit.

"Fourati has decided that Dakota James is his." Lambert's voice was matter-of-fact.

"What? How does he even know her?"

"Apparently, he saw her in the crowd at the airport, and whatever happened between them made him decide that he wants her for his own. This is why we think she ran."

"Fuckin' A," Slade swore. "She obviously didn't want to be a terrorist's plaything."

"Apparently not. From what we've been able to intercept and decode, he's on her trail."

"Where is she?" Slade demanded. The thought of the poor woman surviving a terrorist bombing, only to be on the run because said terrorist wanted her for his own, was too much for his psyche. His team had told him on more than one occasion that he had a knight-in-shining-armor complex, but Slade didn't care. He loved women. All kinds. Short, tall, fat, skinny, it didn't matter. When push came to shove on a mission, if it involved a woman, Slade was made point. He did whatever it took to protect the women and children.

"That's the thing. We don't know."

"What *do* you know?" he bit out impatiently. "From where I'm sitting, it's precious little. You know there was a woman, and her name, and that she quit her job, but that's about it."

Greg didn't even sound the least bit upset. "That's why we need you. Find Dakota. Get her to tell you what Fourati said before his soldier blew himself up. Figure out what that fucker looks like so we can find him, shut down his dot-com operation, and get one more terrorist off our streets. Yeah?"

"What backup do I have?" Slade asked, knowing he was going to say yes, but wanting as many details as he could get before he did.

"None," was Greg's answer. "Well, none officially. You can call me and I can get you information. But as far as the operation goes, you're on your own. This is an unsanctioned op. If you get caught, you're also on your own. The US government will not bail you out and, if asked, will deny any responsibility for anything."

Slade wasn't surprised in the least. He'd expected that. "Compensation?"

Greg named a figure that made Slade's eyebrows draw up in surprise. Apparently, the government wasn't fucking around.

"I'm in," Slade told him. He wasn't concerned about failing. He'd find Ms. James, get a description of Fourati, kill him, and continue on with his life. He was actually looking forward to the assignment. Not to kill someone, that wasn't something he ever enjoyed, but getting out into the field once more. Using his skills to eliminate a threat.

Once a SEAL, always a SEAL, apparently.

"Good. I've already arranged with Commander Hurt for you to take some time off. Starting tomorrow. There's a relatively new but vetted employee who will be transferred over to your job immediately. Even though he doesn't have your level of clearance, he can still help Hurt keep his head above water until you return. Your replacement has been briefed and your job is secure until you get back."

"Wow," Slade exclaimed. "I shouldn't be surprised, yet I still am. How'd you know I'd say yes?"

"John said you would. I trust him."

Slade mentally nodded. Yeah, he trusted Tex, too.

"Tomorrow at o-eight hundred, a folder will be delivered to your apartment with all the information I have on the terrorist group, Fourati, and, of course, Ms. James. Find her, get the intel, then stop Aziz Fourati once and for all."

"Is there a time limit?" Slade asked.

"Not per se. But time is always of the essence. As of right now, Fourati doesn't seem to have enough followers to be a viable threat. However, the more recruits he gets, the higher the possibility that someone will be able to take his place and carry out the threat if he's killed."

Slade understood that. So while Greg said there was no time limit, there was.

"Oh, and not only that, Fourati has said that he wants his new wife by his side before the new year hits."

"Fuck," Slade swore quietly. It was almost the end of November. That meant Fourati was getting impatient, and could have a lead on where Dakota was hiding. The urgency of the case just got ramped up. "I'll look for that folder," Slade informed him.

"Thank you, Cutter," Greg said, using Slade's SEAL nickname once again, proving he really did know a lot about him. "Your country will never know about this, but they're in your debt nevertheless."

"Is this the number I should contact you at if I have questions?" Slade asked. He knew the deal. He knew no one would ever know how many times he'd killed for the sake of national security. He'd long ago gotten over that.

"Yes. I'll be waiting for updates." And with that, Greg hung up.

Slade clicked off the phone and put his head back on the seat. A million things were racing through his brain. Details about the weapons he'd need, how best to take down Fourati without causing a panic, and how in the world he'd pull it all off on his own.

But the one thing that wouldn't let go, that he kept coming back to, was Dakota James. Where was she?

CHAPTER 2

"*H*ello, Mr. James. My name is Slade Cutsinger. May I speak with you for a moment?"

Slade waited patiently a respectable distance away from the door he was standing in front of. He'd received the information folder the morning after his phone call with the former commander and had read every word, twice.

It wasn't a lot of information to go off of—it was no wonder Greg had called him—but the picture of Dakota James had made his teeth clench and his hands curl into fists.

He'd never had as visceral a reaction to seeing someone before in his life as he'd had when he'd gazed into her green eyes. They seemed to grab him around the throat from the paper. She wasn't classically beautiful, her facial symmetry was a bit off for that, but it was the happiness and glee he saw in her eyes that made him want to know everything about her.

The picture was from the latest yearbook from Sunset Heights Elementary School where she was the principal...or *had been*. She was wearing a dark blue suit jacket with a white blouse underneath. She had earrings in the shape of apples in her ears, and her dark blonde hair was in a bun at her neck. Her makeup was minimal, but still, her eyes were her best feature and needed no enhancement.

Slade had stared at her picture for a full ten minutes, shock holding him immobile as he memorized her facial features. He wanted to see more of her. Wanted to see her body, see how tall she was when she was standing next to him, talk to her—was her voice low or high?—touch her. He'd had a sudden and unmistakable reaction to her photo. What would it be like to actually be in her presence?

Thinking about what Dakota had been through made him growl low in his throat, which shocked him back into awareness of where he was and what he was doing.

He wanted her. It wasn't rational, it wasn't normal by any stretch of the imagination, but there it was. Slade wanted to see her smile at him. Wanted to see her eyes twinkle with joy as she looked at him. Wanted to see her eating across a table from him, and most definitely wanted to see her green eyes open and look sleepily at him from the other side of his bed.

Slade had looked at hundreds of dossiers, seen hundreds of targets, and not once had any ever affected him like Dakota James. He would make her safe if it was the last thing he did.

Intel about Dakota's father had been included in the file he'd received from Lambert. He was in his upper seventies and living in a house just north of San Diego. Not sure if the man would give him any information about his daughter—he actually hoped he wouldn't, that he was being extremely cautious about Dakota's whereabouts—Slade had packed his saddlebags on his Harley just in case, and headed out.

Feeling as if time truly was running out for Dakota and she was in extreme danger, his only goal was to get to her as soon as he could. He couldn't explain the feeling, and if he tried, knew he'd sound insane, but Slade's intuition had served him well for his career on the teams. He wasn't going to ignore it now.

"What are you selling?" Dakota's dad barked from behind the screen. "I don't need no cookies, I'm fat enough, the election's over, and I don't need my lawn mowed."

"I'm a friend of Dakota's," Slade said.

"Bullshit," he responded immediately. "Dakota wouldn't have a friend like you. No way."

Offended, but also somewhat amused, Slade asked, "Why not?"

"You're too good lookin'," her dad said. "Her friends all wear fucking sweaters and khaki pants. And no way in hell they'd be ridin' a Harley like you've got parked in my driveway."

"My leather jacket gave it away, huh?" Slade asked, trying to keep a straight face. He respected this man. He said it like it was.

"Just a bit. Want to try again and tell me why you're here, askin' about my Dakota?"

"Your daughter's in danger and I'm probably the only person who can get her out of it."

The older man was silent for a long moment, but Slade stood still and let him look his fill. Finally, after what seemed like hours, but was in reality only a minute or so, Mr. James flipped up the little hook holding the screen door shut and said, "It's cold out there. Don't know what you're thinkin', ridin' around on a motorcycle. Come on in."

Letting out a relieved sigh, Slade followed the gray-haired man into the house and stood back as he closed and locked the front door. He shuffled slowly into a small living room toward a beat-up chocolate-brown recliner that had seen better days. The television was on and a show about female killers was playing. Dakota's father lowered the volume, but didn't turn it off, and gestured to the sofa nearby. "Go on. Sit. Don't got any refreshments to offer. I don't snack much and the Meals on Wheels lady hasn't come by yet. Thought you were her, honestly. You want to know where my Dakota is, don't ya?"

"Why do you say that?"

"Because I'm old, not stupid," was his response. "Look, you're not the first person to come knocking on my door asking if I know where my daughter is. I'll tell you the same thing I told them, I don't know where she is. And I wouldn't tell you even if I did."

"Who else has been here asking about her?" Slade questioned, his brows drawn down in concern.

The older man waved his hand in the air. "Government types, police types, people from work...you know, the usual."

Slade wasn't sure about that, but he let it go for now. "Mr. James, I—"

"Finnegan."

"I'm sorry, what?"

"My name's Finnegan. Finn."

"Right. Finn, I think you know that Dakota's in danger."

Slade sat still even though Finn narrowed his eyes and stared at him for a long moment before saying, "Why would I know that?"

Taking a chance that Dakota was close with her father, Slade laid it out for him...well, as much as he could. "You and I both know she's the only survivor of that bombing at LAX. She not only saw things she shouldn't have, she probably heard them too. If I was a terrorist who wanted to make sure my future plans went off without a hitch, I'd want to ensure all ends were tied up in a nice fancy bow."

The silence in the room was deafening.

Finally, Finn asked quietly, "Who did you say you were again?"

"My name is Slade Cutsinger. I'm a retired Navy SEAL. I know Dakota has to be scared. I don't blame her. And Finn, she has reason to be. I'm not bullshitting you about that. I can't tell you much, but I *can* say that Dakota has *nothing* to be worried about with me. My only goal is to help her put this behind her so she can move on with her life. Safely."

"You got ID?"

His lips twitched. Hell if he didn't like this old man. Slade slowly reached for his wallet. He slid out his driver's license and government ID, then leaned over to hand them to Finn.

After several moments of scrutiny, Finn returned them and reclined back into his chair. "See that box on the floor next to the television?"

Slade turned his head and nodded when he saw the beat-up old shoebox sitting under a stack of at least a week's worth of newspapers.

"Get it for me."

Doing as he was told, Slade retrieved it and handed it to Finn.

The old man fingered the top of the box lovingly as he said, "Dakota is all I have. My wife died ten years ago, and me and my girl have taken care of each other. She pays for someone to look in on me every day. Pays for the Meals on Wheels people to bring me lunch and dinner. She even makes sure my bills and mortgage are paid. She's a good girl, and doesn't deserve any of this. All she did was go about her daily business and get thrust into a situation neither of us understand."

"I know," Slade said softly.

"She's not here," Finn continued. "Not in San Diego or LA, and probably not even California. She was real shook up after that airport thing. Didn't say much about it, but told me enough that I put two and two together. Then something happened at her school, though she wouldn't tell me what. A couple of days later, her apartment complex burned to the ground. Newspapers said it was some idiot burning candles in an apartment, but I'm not sure what to believe."

"When was this?" Slade asked.

"September. She was so excited for the new school year, but said she had to quit. That someone was following her and she didn't want to endanger the kids at the school."

"You haven't heard from her at all?" Slade doubted that. Someone who obviously loved her dad enough to make sure he was taken care of wouldn't just completely cut off communication.

"She sends postcards," Finn told Slade as he ran his wrinkled palm over the box once more. "Not often, but sometimes."

"Can I see them?" Slade asked, wanting to grab the box out of the old man's lap and get to work finding Dakota.

"If you hurt her, I swear to God I'll kill you," Finn threatened.

"I'm not going to hurt her."

Dakota's dad continued as if he hadn't spoken. "I don't care who you are or where you hide. I'll find you and put a bullet through your heart. It doesn't matter if I go to jail for it either. I'm old, I'm gonna die soon anyway, but it'd be worth it to kill you if you dare do anything that will make my baby suffer more than she already has."

"I've spent my life fighting for the underdog. I've gone where I've been sent and seen and done things that no one should ever have to," Slade told Finn, looking him straight in the eyes. "But one look at a picture of your daughter, and I knew I'd do whatever it took to make her safe."

Finn held his gaze for a moment, then looked down. He cleared his throat twice, as if trying to compose himself, then held out the box. "They're not signed, but I know they're from Dakota."

Slade took the shoebox from Finn and sat back on the couch. He eased the top off and picked up the first postcard. It was from Australia and had a kangaroo on the front. He flipped it over and saw Finn's address written in a womanly script. As the man had said, it wasn't signed, but there was one word written. "Peace." The postmark was from Las Vegas.

He picked up another. It was a picture of the Statue of Liberty, and once again Finn's address was on the back in the same handwriting as the first. This one said "Love." It was appropriately postmarked from New York City.

Slade flipped through the rest; there weren't a lot, about ten or so. Each had a different postmark and only one word written on it.

"Do you think she's really traveling all over the country?" Slade looked down at the cards in his hand. "From New York to Florida to Seattle?"

"No," Finn said without any hesitation. "She's getting others to mail them for her."

"But she could be," Slade insisted.

"Me and my girl would watch TV when she came to visit," Finn said, gesturing to the television set older than Slade. "The ID Channel. Mystery, forensic, and murder shows. We used to talk about how people could get away with killing for years before they were caught, without even really trying. Not long after the airport thing, she was here and we were watching one of them murder shows. I could tell something was wrong, but didn't want to pry. She flat-out told me she might have to to lie low for a while. I told her she could stay with me, but she shook her head and said the last thing she was going to do was put her daddy in danger..."

Slade sat patiently, waiting for the older man to regain his composure.

Finally, he cleared his throat and said, "She told me she didn't know how safe it would be to call, and was leery of writing letters with any information in them that could lead anyone to her."

"Postcards," Slade said softly.

Finn nodded. "Postcards," he confirmed. "I don't know where she is, but she's gotten her hands on them postcards from all over. Then she has others mail them when they get home from wherever they're visiting when they meet her."

"And the messages on them? Do they mean anything?" Slade asked.

"It's not code, if that's what you're asking," Finn said. "It's just Dakota's way of letting me know she's fine. Love. Peace. Contentment. Happy. She's trying to reassure me she's okay. But she's *not* okay," Finn said. "Look at that last one. The one with the Grand Canyon on it."

Slade pulled it out and turned it over.

"Fucking ink ran. She was cryin' when she wrote it. My baby was cryin' and I can't do anything about it," Finn said bitterly.

"This one's postmarked Las Vegas," Slade mused. "There was another one from Vegas as well."

Finn simply shrugged. "Told her a father would instinctively know if his little girl was alive. What an idiot I was." The old man pinned Slade with a hard gaze. "I *don't* know if she's alive, if she's in pain, if whoever she thought was following her has caught up to her and is hurting her. She could be hungry, or cold, and I'm sitting here snug and happy in my house and can't do a damn thing about it."

"But I can," Slade said firmly.

"If she's in danger, don't bring her back here," Finn replied. "Just let her know her old man loves her and is thinkin' about her."

"I will, but I have a feeling she already knows." Slade put the items back in the box and ran his finger over the mark on the last postcard where one of Dakota's tears had fallen and smeared the ink. Simply touching the same piece of paper she had somehow made her all the more real to him. He'd fallen hard for the woman in the photograph, but seeing how much she loved her dad, and was loved in return, really struck home for him.

He returned the lid to the box and stood, placing it back by the television stand and replacing the newspapers on top.

Finn pushed himself up and out of the chair and the two men stood toe to toe. Slade was at least five or six inches taller, but Finn didn't let Slade's size intimidate him. "Remember what I said," he ordered gruffly.

"I'll remember," Slade told him. "But I'll say it again, you and your daughter have nothing to fear from me."

A knock sounded and Slade's head whipped around to stare at the front door.

"Meals on Wheels," Finn reminded him. "She's right on time."

Slade nodded, but kept close to Finn as he opened the door just in case. As he'd said, a woman wearing a company jacket stood on the other side. "Hello, Mr. James, it's good to see you today."

"You too, Eve," Finn said and unlocked the screen, letting the woman inside. "I'll be right in, give me a second to say goodbye to my guest."

"No problem. I'll just get this served up," Eve said as she breezed past them, obviously having been inside the house before.

Finn put his hand on Slade's leather-covered arm. "She means the world to me," he said seriously.

"I don't even know her, and I think she means the world to me too," Slade responded, dryly.

Finn laughed then. A dry, rough chuckle that sounded like it hurt. "That's my Dakota," he said, smiling.

Slade's lips curled up in response and he nodded at the man. He was about to leave when Finn said softly, "She's not going to trust you. You're going to have to prove that you've talked to me. That *I* trust you."

Finn had all his attention now. Slade's lips pressed together as he waited.

"Dakota loves Starbucks. Their peppermint mocha was always her preferred choice this time of year. And donuts. Glazed with that maple frosting shit on top. She won't eat no other kind. You bring those with you when you find her, and tell her I told you they were her favorites. The rest is up to you."

Knowing the old man was right, and that he did need a way to convince Dakota to at least hear him out before she ran, he nodded in appreciation. "Thanks. I'll remember. Can I ask something?"

"Sure."

"Why did you let me in? Tell me all that about Dakota?"

Finn looked at Slade for a long time before he said, "My daughter told me the bad guys might come here pretendin' to be good guys. She warned me not to trust anyone, no matter what they looked like." The old man paused. "Several have tried to get me to talk. Reporters pretending to be Dakota's friends, people sayin' they're government employees who just have her best interests at heart. Bah—liars, all of them. But you...you weren't lyin' to me."

Slade's lips twitched. His former team members would get a kick out of Finn's assessment of him, especially considering he was always the best liar of the bunch.

"Man ridin' around on a Harley, leather jacket, bags packed...you can't exactly kidnap a woman on a motorcycle. Besides...your eyes told me what I needed to know."

"My eyes?"

"Yeah. You took one look at my Dakota's picture and that was it for you." Finn nodded. "Love is a weird thing. When it hits you, it hits you. I knew the second I saw my late wife that I wanted to spend the rest of my life with her. Take care of my girl, Slade. I've worried about her since she was born. The one thing I want is to see her protected and taken care of when I'm gone. Oh, I know, she can take care of herself, but as self-sufficient as she is, she needs someone who will make sure she eats when she gets busy, give her a backrub when she's had a hard day, and will be there for her when she needs to talk."

Finn's words struck Slade hard. Yes. That's what he'd wanted all his life. To have a woman by his side and to be the one someone else leaned on.

"Am I wrong?"

"You're not wrong," Slade said "I'm not going to stand here and tell you that your daughter and I will get married and all your worries are over, but I *am* telling you that I'll do everything in my power to make her safe and allow her to return to her normal life. After that?" He shrugged. "It's up to her. But, if my reaction to her picture was any indication, I'm going to do what I can to convince her to let me be a part of her life."

"That's why I let you in. Why I told you what I did," Finn said, then stuck out his hand. "Good luck. Make my baby safe."

After a final handshake, Slade strode toward his Harley in the driveway, knowing Mr. James was watching him as he did so. He swung a leg over the leather seat and grabbed his helmet.

He began to buckle it when Finn said loudly from the doorway, "You got two of those? Because if you plan to have a passenger, I expect her head to be protected."

Slade grinned, despite the seriousness of the situation. Without a word, he twisted his body and unsnapped one of the saddlebags. He pulled out an identical helmet to the one he was wearing, except a size smaller, and held it up for Finn's inspection.

"Good," was all Finn said, before backing into his house and closing the door.

Slade stowed the extra helmet he'd bought specifically with the intention of having Dakota James on the back of his bike and turned to face the front. He backed out of the drive and headed for the highway. He'd call Tex as soon as he could and let him know he was on his way to Vegas, but first he needed to beat the LA traffic out of town. I-15 to the Nevada border was always a crapshoot this time of year. Starting his search in Las Vegas was a given, as there were two postcards with that postmark.

Whether or not Dakota was there wasn't quite as certain, but one thing was clear...Slade was more determined than ever to find her and keep her safe. Any woman who cared enough about her father to try to reassure him she was all right while on the run from terrorists was someone he wanted to know. But because it was *Dakota* who'd done it... she'd just blown away any doubts he'd had about her. He'd find her, make her safe, then hopefully convince her to give an old retired SEAL like him a chance.

CHAPTER 3

"*H*ave you ever seen an alien out here?"

Dakota James forced a smile and turned to face the tourist. She was working the afternoon shift at the Little A'Le'Inn in Rachel, Nevada, and got asked this exact same question at least once a day. But she really couldn't blame them. They *were*, after all, right outside Area 51 in the Nevada desert, and the small diner she worked at had gone out of its way to put every kitschy piece of alien crap on sale that it could find.

"Nope. Just lots of hungry tourists," she told the teenager, then shrugged in apology for the lame answer and hurried to bring a platter with three plates of hamburgers and fries to the group sitting at a small circular table in the middle of the room.

She smiled and left them hungrily tucking into the food she'd brought them.

Working as a waitress and sales clerk wasn't what she'd had in mind for a life plan when she'd gotten her master's degree in higher education, but life had a funny way of making sure you never got too big for your britches.

Wiping her hands on her apron, Dakota rang up a T-shirt with an alien head on it, a bumper sticker and mug with the A'Le'Inn logo, and an inflatable plastic green alien, then collected money from the pair standing at the register.

She'd been working at the small restaurant/bar for quite a while now and knew it was about time for her to move on. She was grateful that Pat and her daughter, Connie, had hired her. They'd obviously seen the desperation in her eyes when she'd shown up all those weeks ago.

Rachel, Nevada, population around fifty-four, wasn't exactly on the beaten path. People didn't accidentally end up there, and Dakota was no exception. She'd hidden out in Las Vegas for a week, but hadn't liked how dirty the city seemed. Not only that, she always felt as if she was being watched...and since there were so many people, she couldn't figure out if she was *really* being watched, or if it was only in her head.

So she'd left, deciding to make her way across the US, away from California and *him*. She'd stopped for gas just east of Vegas and started chatting with a happy-go-lucky group from Indiana. They'd said they were geocachers, and were headed to the ET Highway. Dakota had no idea what they were talking about, but she'd gotten a crash course soon enough.

Apparently geocaching was kind of like treasure hunting with a GPS. The players downloaded coordinates from a website and followed them to the "treasure." It could be a Tupperware container, film canister, or even a large ammo box. Sometimes there were toys inside, and others only enough room for a log book, which the players were required to sign.

The group was on its way to the ET Highway because there were literally thousands of geocaches alongside the ninety-eight-mile road. They'd talked about the black mailbox, Area 51, the town of Rachel, and the Little A'Le'Inn as if anyone who didn't see them once in their life was absolutely missing out.

So off she'd gone. Instead of heading out of Nevada along Interstate 15, she'd turned north on Route 93 to Highway 375—also known as the ET Highway.

It'd actually been fun. She'd stopped at the black mailbox, which was now painted white. Enjoyed the desert vistas, mooed at some random cows, and waved at clusters of people she now knew were geocachers who'd randomly stopped along the road searching for the elusive little containers.

Rachel certainly wasn't what she'd been expecting. She thought it would be a typical little town, with a gas station, hotel, and fast food restaurants...but it wasn't. It was literally a pit stop in the middle of nowhere. There were no businesses, other than the A'Le'Inn bar and restaurant. No other places to eat and, more importantly, no gas stations.

She'd planned on seeing what the fuss regarding Rachel was all about, then continuing north to Reno and eventually up into Idaho. Since she'd coasted into town on fumes, she was temporarily stuck. But the second she'd seen the tiny town, she'd decided it was actually a good place to lie low for a while.

Pat and Connie, the owners of the Little A'Le'Inn, had agreed to let her work as a waitress in the restaurant/bar and as a maid for the rooms they rented out—mostly to geocachers on their way through—in the trailers behind the bar. The pay wasn't huge, but it was enough to slowly increase her meager cash reserves before she headed off again.

She'd rented a small room from a local resident, but didn't stay there often. The owner was a smoker who didn't get out much. Dakota had slept in her car most nights, preferring that to being cooped up in a trailer home full of cigarette smoke. Pat caught her one morning and, after hearing why she was sleeping in her car, offered to let her stay in one of the motel's trailers when it wasn't booked.

Working at the motel/bar/restaurant also allowed her to see most of the people who came to town. It wasn't foolproof; if *he* walked in and found her, he wouldn't hesitate to hurt anyone who came to her aid. But the little town suited her. She much preferred the genuine caring nature of most of the people of Rachel to the city folks she'd come into contact with in Vegas.

She'd changed her name to Dallas, thinking it was close enough to her own that she might actually remember to answer to it. The work was monotonous, but the people she met kept the job from being absolutely horrible.

She'd also admitted to Connie that she'd run out of gas, and the other woman had volunteered to bring back enough to allow her to get to either Tonopah or Warm Springs. Dakota had taken her up on the offer, and felt good knowing she wasn't trapped in the small town. She could leave at any time.

Until now, she'd been enjoying working for cash; it kept her from using credit cards and being tracked through them. Though recently, she felt itchy and nervous. As if someone was watching her again. As much as she hated to just up and leave the quirky little town, it was looking like the time was coming when she'd need to do just that.

"Hey, Dallas, order up," George called from the back. He was the line cook who worked from one to seven. Pat or Connie usually had the morning shift, serving breakfast and early lunch, and after seven, tourists who stopped in could choose from pre-packaged snacks and drinks.

Dakota shook herself and smiled at the older man. Rachel, Nevada, might literally be in the middle of nowhere, but the people who lived and worked there were some of the friendliest she'd ever met. It was too bad she'd be leaving soon.

* * *

"Hey, Tex," Slade said when his old friend picked up the phone.

"'Bout time you called, Cutter," Tex complained. "I figured you were glued to the slot machines or something. Leaving a message telling me where you're going isn't the same as actually talking to me, you know."

"Yeah, well, I was a bit busy," Slade told him. He'd called two days ago when he'd reached Primm, the border town between California and Nevada. Tex hadn't answered, so he'd left a message about what he'd found out and where he was headed. He'd waited until now to call again because he'd wanted to have some concrete information to share, not simply conjecture.

"I did some checking while waiting for you to call back, and there's been a lot of chatter on the Net about picking up a certain package and preparing for a ceremony," Tex told him.

"Fuck," Slade murmured.

"You got any ideas where she might be?" Tex asked.

"I've been all over this city in the last couple of days. I've shown her picture to everyone, and I might have a lead."

"Yeah?"

"Yeah. You ever been out to Area 51?" Slade asked Tex.

"Nope. Is there anything out there other than desert?"

"Not much. But I'm at a gas station just northeast of Vegas and a clerk says she thinks she remembers someone matching Dakota's description asking about the infamous ET Highway a couple months ago. Said she remembered her because she specifically asked if they had any peppermint flavor for her coffee, and picked up a flier about the road on her way out. I could use your help checking traffic cams for any more recent signs of her in the city, in case this lead is bogus. I thought I'd check out Rachel, Nevada, midway point of the ET Highway, and see if she's been there."

"Already on it," Tex told him. "Started my search right after you left your message. So far, I haven't found anything from the last day and a half, but I'll keep on it. If I find she's been in Vegas recently, I'll let you know."

"Appreciate it."

"You be careful," Tex warned. "With the increased chatter, it certainly sounds as if Fourati has intel on where Dakota might be hiding and could be moving in."

"I will."

"Eyes on your six, Cutter," Tex told him. "If anything feels off, get the hell out of dodge. And don't hesitate to live up to that nickname of yours. Hear me? I'll cover your ass if it comes to it."

"Got it." Slade didn't like the fact that Tex was feeling nervous. If he thought Fourati had a lock on where Dakota was, and had sent some of his minions after her, he was probably right. And Tex telling him not to hesitate to slit someone's throat was telling.

It was Tex who had come up with the moniker during one of their first missions together. Slade had cut the throat of a terrorist who'd had no idea his position had been compromised. It wasn't the first person he'd killed that way, and certainly wasn't the last. Tex had congratulated him on the kill and that was that. The story Slade usually told people, however, was that he was called Cutter because of his last name. It was a bit more politically correct than airing his SEAL kills to polite society.

"I'll call when I can," Slade told Tex.

"You do that. Later."

"Later." Slade hung up and sighed in frustration. The fact that Fourati was one step behind him wasn't comforting, but at least he was *behind* him, and not *ahead* of him.

Slade slipped the phone back into his pocket and headed into the gas station. If he was going out into the desert, he wanted to top off his tank. He got great gas mileage with his Harley, but had no idea what he'd find when he hit Area 51 and wanted to be ready for anything.

An hour later, Slade turned onto the ET Highway and grimaced. He was suddenly very glad he'd let the gas station attendant talk him into the extra four gallons strapped to the seat behind him. The weather was chilly, but he knew he'd actually lucked out. It could be a lot worse, and he hoped the weather would hold out until he made it to Rachel and, if he was lucky, found Dakota.

The chatty gas station attendant had told him all about how Rachel was the only town along the ET Highway, and they didn't have any services there, only a bar, which seemed wrong to Slade, but nobody asked him. This long desert road wasn't the place to be driving drunk, that was for sure. Not only would it be extremely easy to drive right off the road, it was actually active grazing land for hundreds of cows. The attendant took great delight in telling him two gory stories about motorists who'd hit cows that were standing in the road, minding their own business in the middle of the night.

Taking a deep breath, Slade gave the Harley some throttle as he continued down the long stretch of highway. The faster he found Dakota and got her to safety, the better.

* * *

DAKOTA GRIMACED when the bell over the door to the bar tinkled. She was tired and ready to get out of there. She'd been playing bartender for a while now. Doug and Alex, two brothers who worked at the Tonopah Test Range, had come in at the tail end of the day and asked for a couple of beers. They'd said they didn't want any food as they'd grabbed sandwiches at home before heading up to the bar. That had been hours ago, and they weren't acting like they wanted to leave anytime soon.

It was Dakota's responsibility to make sure people got what they wanted to drink, paid, and to try to talk them out of driving if they were out-of-towners. She'd shot the shit with the brothers for a while, but she was bored, tired, and wanted nothing more than to head to the open room in one of the trailers for the night. Luckily, there had been a cancelation that day, which meant she got to sleep in a real bed.

The stress of constantly being on the lookout was getting to her. It was definitely time to head out and find a new place to settle for a while. One more populated than Rachel this time. She'd talk to Pat and Connie tomorrow and let them know she would be moving on.

She smiled in the direction of the doorway—and froze when she saw the man who'd just walked in. He was probably a couple years older than she was. His black hair was graying, but instead of making him look old, it only made him sexier. He had a short beard that was well trimmed and brought attention to his full lips. He had on a leather jacket and an old, worn pair of jeans with black boots. His nose looked like it'd been broken at least once and his cheeks were rosy from the cold, dry air.

He was tall, really tall, at least half a foot taller than her own five-eight. He wasn't skinny, but he wasn't fat either. He was...built. Muscular.

She should've been scared. He could easily overpower and hurt her, but somehow, she knew he wouldn't. How she knew that, Dakota had no idea, but for just a moment, the thought that she knew him flashed through her mind.

That was crazy. She'd never seen this man before in her life, she would've remembered if she had. But the spark of recognition was there, nevertheless.

The man lifted his chin at her in greeting, and Dakota's knees wobbled. How in the hell he could make her want him with a mere chin lift she had no idea, but suddenly, having a wild fling with a stranger sounded like the best idea she'd ever had. It had been a long time since she'd had any sexual feelings about anyone, especially in the last couple of months, but all her worries seemed to drain away simply by looking into his dark eyes.

"Welcome to the Little A'Le'Inn," she said automatically. Business was business, and she didn't want to be the reason the bar got a bad review online. "Grill's closed, but we've got snacks and liquid refreshments. Although if you're continuing on your way to Tonopah, I don't recommend drinking anything alcoholic. It'd be dangerous." Dakota smiled as she said the last, wanting to seem friendly instead of preachy. It would be an absolute shame for this man to come to any harm, that was for sure.

The man's eyes seemed to pierce right into her soul, as if with one look he knew all her secrets. The scariest thing was that it wasn't an altogether unpleasant thought. She'd never had someone she could lean on to help with troubles in her life. She'd been okay with that, modern woman and all, but in that moment, all she could think was that *this* man would keep her safe. He'd never let anyone do her harm.

Dakota turned her back on him, pretending to wipe off the counter to try to regain her equilibrium.

Out of the corner of her eye, she saw the man saunter into the dimly lit building and gaze around. She'd seen many reactions from tourists who'd wandered into the eclectic bar, but this man had absolutely no reaction whatsoever. It was…odd.

"Nice place," he said, and Dakota's toes curled in her sneakers. His voice was low and growly and she felt it all the way to her tummy. She had no idea why she was reacting to this man's obvious maleness, but she was.

"Yeah. The owners have worked hard to make it…unique."

"Slade," the man said, holding his hand out to her in greeting.

"Oh...uh...I'm Dallas," Dakota said shakily, almost forgetting her fake name, and tentatively put her hand in his own.

She was half afraid he'd crush hers with his brute strength, but he merely smiled and grasped her palm with a firm, but not bruising grip and said, "It's good to meet you."

Dakota gave him a half smile. "You too."

They stood still for a beat, each looking at the other without blinking, before Dakota reluctantly pulled her hand back. He let go without complaint, but she swore she could feel his touch long after they'd dropped their hands. He had calluses, which made her think about what his hands would feel like on her bare skin. Damn, she had to get it together.

"So, what's it gonna be?" Dakota asked.

"Just a Coke, I think," Slade said.

"What kind?"

"What kind of Coke?"

Dakota chuckled and shook her head in self-deprecation. "Sorry. Habit. I call all soda, 'Coke.' I use it generically. I can get you one," she finished quickly, knowing she was beat red with embarrassment.

"So if someone asks for a Coke, you ask what kind, and they say a Pepsi. Or Dr. Pepper, or something else?" Slade asked with a friendly smile. He leaned his forearms on the scratched wooden bar top in front of him.

For a moment, Dakota wished that it was summer and Slade was wearing a short-sleeved T-shirt. She'd pay just about any amount of money to see his biceps and forearms. She'd bet they were muscular as hell. When he tipped his head and raised his eyebrows as she continued to stare at him, she blushed even harder. "Sorry. Yeah, that's how it works. So you really do want a Coke, right?"

"Yes, please. If it's not too much trouble," Slade said with a smile.

"Of course not. It's my job," Dakota told him, glad to have a reason to go into the back room for a moment. There were a few cans under the bar, but she wanted to get him a cold drink from the refrigerator in the back.

She used the few moments alone to give herself a stern talk. *He's just passing through, Dakota. The last thing you need right now is to get involved with a guy, even if it's only for the night. No matter how sexy he is and how badly you want him. Get ahold of yourself.*

Satisfied that she had her head on straight, Dakota went back into the bar area with a smile on her face and held up the can. "Got it!" Instead of drooling over the fine specimen of a man who was sitting at the bar, she got busy grabbing a glass and filling it with ice. She poured the cola into the glass, concentrating so hard on what she was doing, she jumped when Doug pounded on the bar top down by the cash register.

"We're gonna get out of your hair, Dallas."

Dakota looked up and nodded, putting down the half-empty can because her hands were shaking too hard to finish. She glanced around and met Slade's concerned eyes.

"You okay?" he asked quietly.

Dakota nodded quickly and pushed the glass and can of soda over to him. "Here ya go. Excuse me."

He nodded and she took the few steps to the register. She made small talk with Doug and Alex while she rang up their drinks. After they left, the room seemed to shrink. Being alone with Slade made her extremely nervous for some reason. She tucked a stray piece of hair behind her ear and smiled awkwardly at him.

"You worked here long?" he asked.

Dakota shrugged. She'd learned to keep her answers vague. "Not really."

"It's a long way from civilization, isn't it?"

She shrugged again. "It is what it is. I've met some of the nicest people around. You on your way north or south?"

It was his turn to shrug. "I came up from Crystal Springs, but I'm not sure if I'm going to go back that way or carry on. Anything worth looking at if I go up to Tonopah?"

"Depends on what you like to look at," Dakota told him. "I've heard Goldfield is really interesting, with the history of being haunted and all, but there's not much out here in either direction, if I'm being honest."

"Hmmm. Any place to stay the night around here?" Slade asked.

Dakota swallowed hard. Damn. There went her bed for the night. But she smiled brightly and told him the truth. "You're in luck. There was a cancelation tonight so there's a room available. It's not fancy, you actually share a trailer with another couple, but they checked in about an hour ago and I think they're planning on being up early, so they won't be a bother. The middle is a common space, and the two bedrooms are on either side and have locking doors. It really is private."

Dakota knew she was babbling, but couldn't stop. "It's only forty-five bucks for the night, which is a really great deal. There's hot water and you can use the wi-fi here at the restaurant for free. Breakfast is included. Nothing gourmet, just cinnamon rolls and juice, but again, it's safer to stay than to try to make it all the way up to Tonopah in the dark."

Slade chuckled, and Dakota's womanly parts spasmed at the sound. Jesus, he was beautiful.

"I'll take it. How could I not after that wonderful sales pitch?"

"Sorry. People just tend to turn up their noses because it's a trailer and they have to share it, but I promise it's clean, safe, and totally worth the money."

Slade tipped his head back and chugged the rest of the Coke in the glass. He pulled out a five-dollar bill and slid it over to her. "Sounds good. I'm beat."

"Let me get your change."

Slade waved her off. "Keep it."

"Oh, okay, thanks. If you're ready, I can walk you over to your room."

He looked at his watch. "You're closing?"

Dakota nodded. "Yeah, we're not expecting anyone else tonight and it's dark. The locals know we close up around now."

"Don't want any aliens to wander in when the sun goes down, huh?" Slade joked.

Dakota chuckled even though she'd heard it before. "Yeah, something like that. If you want, I'll meet you outside in five minutes or so? I need to finish up in here." Actually, she needed to give herself another talking to, but he didn't need to know that.

"Sure. I'll be out by my bike."

Dakota nodded. Her eyes were glued to his ass as he walked out the door. He was definitely a fine specimen of a man. And it figured he'd have a motorcycle, just to amp up the sexiness. She'd never ridden on one, but once upon a time, before she'd gotten old enough to have given up on many of her dreams, she'd imagined what it would be like to sit behind a man, her arms wrapped around him, her chin on his shoulder as the wind blew in her hair and they flew down the highway.

Shaking her head in disgust at herself, she mumbled, "Get ahold of yourself. Jesus, you'd think you weren't on the run from a psycho crazy terrorist or something. You've got no time for mooning over a man. No matter how sexy he is or how much you want to know if his beard is soft or scratchy."

Satisfied with her pep talk, Dakota quickly washed the dirty glasses and locked the ancient cash register. There wasn't a bank in Rachel to take the cash to, and besides, most people paid by credit card anyway.

She hung up her apron and smoothed her hair, securing it back into a bun at the nape of her neck, and walked out the door.

Slade was leaning against his Harley with one ankle resting on the other. His arms were crossed on his chest and he was frowning. Dakota quickly turned and locked the door, making sure the closed sign was clearly visible to anyone who might pull up later. Taking a deep breath, she turned to Slade. "Everything okay?"

He shook his head. "There's no cell service."

"Yeah, sorry. Once upon a time the residents petitioned the big phone companies to put a tower out here, but it wasn't worth the money. And if you ask me, the government put the kibosh on that as well. It's in their best interest to keep things on the down low out here, if you know what I mean. Area 51 and all. If it's any consolation, once you get up to Warm Springs and past the big mountain up there, you'll be in range again. If you really need to get ahold of someone, I could ask Pat—she owns this place with her daughter—if she'll call someone for you. There are a few residents who have satellite phones out here."

Slade shook his head. "No, it's okay. I can wait. I was just hoping to get ahold of my friend and let him know I made it safely and that I'd be spending the night."

"Sorry," Dakota apologized again. "You could probably send him an email later if you wanted. I'll make sure you have the password for the wi-fi. Ready to see where you'll be staying?"

"Don't I need to pay for the room?" he asked.

She waved her hand. "Don't worry about it. You can pay Pat or Connie in the morning. They man the restaurant until I come on in the afternoon."

"Trusting," Slade observed.

Dakota smiled at that. "Yes, they are. Come on, it's around back."

He straightened and turned to grab the handlebars of his motorcycle. He pushed the bike as they walked silently around the front of the iconic restaurant, past the giant metal spaceship announcing to anyone who passed by that they'd reached the A'Le'Inn, to one of the trailers off to the side of the parking lot.

"Here it is. And I know it doesn't look like much, but I promise it's clean."

"I believe you," Slade told her, holding out his hand for the key Dakota had been playing with.

"Oh yeah, here ya go." She inhaled when her fingertips brushed Slade's palm. He was warm, and she was quickly getting chilly in the desert air. "Right, so there's the entrance, just turn to the right when you enter and that's your room. Sleep well."

"See you later," Slade said as he nodded at her.

"Yeah, okay," Dakota mumbled, knowing he wouldn't. She did her best to avoid the restaurant in the mornings, not wanting to interact with the people who stayed the night, and needing the time to herself. Connie let her use her computer in the mornings, and Dakota used the time to search the Internet for mentions of her name, and to try to see if she could figure out the name of the asshole who was following her. So far, she hadn't had any luck, but it didn't really matter. She knew she was in trouble; the guy had practically told her straight up she would be his. She shuddered at the memory.

Turning and heading for her car, which was behind Pat's trailer, Dakota mentally reminded herself once more to talk to the other woman soon. It was time to go.

* * *

THREE HOURS LATER, Slade walked silently past the trailers that were rented out to tourists and headed for where he'd last seen Dakota. She looked exactly like her picture, right down to the bun at the back of her head. At least she'd altered her name a bit; it wasn't much, but it was something. She hadn't tried to disguise herself at all.

But then again, why would she think anyone would follow her to Rachel, Nevada?

The town seemed like it was at the end of the world. Strangers stood out like sore thumbs and she knew exactly who was sleeping where each night. Slade had used the wi-fi to kill time and find out more information on the small town. He knew Dakota wasn't going anywhere, she didn't seem to be suspicious of him at all.

And if he wasn't mistaken, she'd been struck by the same thing he had when she'd lain eyes on him the first time. Slade recognized the look of interest and lust in her eyes, because he knew it was the same look on *his* face when he'd first seen her photo. And as he thought she would be, she was even more beautiful in person. She was curvy, and he estimated her to be around five-eight or nine; her head came to about his chin. Slade knew she'd fit against him perfectly.

She was funny and endearing when she got nervous. He could absolutely see her as an elementary school teacher and principal. It was the uncertainty and uneasiness behind her eyes that really struck him, though. He hated that she was scared, and wanted to hold her tightly and reassure her that he'd make sure Aziz Fourati didn't get anywhere near her. He needed to be smart, but didn't have the luxury of time to let her get comfortable with him. He needed to talk to her about her situation, get her to trust him, and get the hell out of Rachel, Nevada.

The bottom line was that Dakota James was no longer merely a face on a piece of paper. She was a flesh-and-blood woman, and Slade wanted her more than he wanted his next breath. But he wanted to keep her safe more than he wanted, or needed, to have her under him...for now.

He'd been planning to break out the bribe he'd picked up for her in Vegas when they'd been alone at the bar, but she'd seemed too uneasy around him. And he was afraid she'd bolt if he spooked her. So, he was biding his time, and he'd catch up with her in the morning.

Slade really wished he could get ahold of Tex and find out if he had any information about Fourati, and if he or his cronies were on their way to Rachel, but for now, he was winging it. He didn't trust email to be secure and decided he'd wait.

When enough time had passed, Slade had eased out of the plain and simple room in the trailer and was now looking for Dakota.

The wind blew in from the north and he shivered in the cool night air. Winter was definitely arriving in the valley, and Slade wouldn't be surprised if there was snow in the forecast. Peering around one of the trailers, he grinned. Bingo.

Tex had given him the details on Dakota's car...a two thousand and eight Subaru Impreza. Gray. And it was parked in front of him. She hadn't even taken off her California plates. Slade inwardly grimaced. She didn't have the first clue how to hide. It was both endearing and frightening at the same time. It was a good thing it was *him* there looking for her and not Fourati.

Slade walked silently up to the car and peered in, not expecting to see anything worth his time. He stopped short and stared through the window.

Dakota was wrapped up in a blanket in the driver's seat, only the top of her head and blonde hair showing. She was sleeping in her car.

She was *sleeping* in her fucking *car*.

Slade wanted to hit something. Wanted to bang on the glass and wake her up and read her the riot act. It was cold out there, but honestly that was the least of her worries. What if he'd been Fourati? Or a drunk resident who'd decided she was free game? Yeah, Dakota was tall, but she wouldn't be any match for a drunk, horny guy.

Swearing under his breath at the entire situation and hating himself for not confronting her earlier that evening, Slade turned around and headed back to his room. If he was going to watch over one Miss Dakota James, he needed warmer clothing.

She might not have asked for it, but starting right now, she had a protector. Seeing her sleeping, vulnerable, and probably cold, had ramped up his interest in her from warm to red hot. Dakota needed protecting, and he'd be the man to do so.

And when she no longer needed protecting, he'd still be the man in her life.

CHAPTER 4

*D*akota came awake slowly. The morning sky was just beginning to lighten and was casting a purplish hue over the valley. She shifted in her seat and grimaced. Every muscle in her body was stiff, and it was cold. Surprised her windshield wasn't iced over, she bent her neck to the left, then the right to stretch it out.

Something moved out of the corner of her eye and she glanced to the side—and squeaked in terror.

Sitting next to her, *right* next to her, inside her car, was the man from the night before.

Slade.

He was propped against the passenger door, his arms crossed over his chest, one leg bent at the knee and resting on the seat, and he was scowling. At her.

"What the heck?" Dakota breathed, and immediately reached for the door handle, her breaths coming out in quick pants, the cold air making it obvious how freaked she was.

"You're sleeping in your car," Slade said in a flat tone.

Dakota nodded and cursed under her breath. She didn't want to take her eyes from Slade's, but she couldn't find the stupid handle.

"I told you last night, but my name is Slade Cutsinger. I'm a retired Navy SEAL and I'm here to keep you safe."

"Uh huh," Dakota murmured, only partly listening. She found the handle, finally, and pulled, planning on getting the hell away from the huge man currently glaring at her.

"I talked to your dad the other day. I saw the postcards. It's how I found you."

Dakota froze with one foot on the hard dirt outside her vehicle and spun back around to face Slade. "He has nothing to do with this. Leave him alone," she whispered shakily.

"I know he doesn't," Slade reassured her. "The postcards were a good idea, by the way. Your dad was sure you were doing okay, as was your intention. Unfortunately, a few people you gave them to got lazy and instead of waiting until they got home, mailed them from Vegas."

"Darn," Dakota said. She figured she might as well listen to what Slade had to say. Since he knew about the postcards, he most likely *had* seen her dad. She might be stupid, but she wasn't getting scary vibes from Slade, so hopefully her dad was in his house secure in the knowledge his daughter was okay...even if she *was* on the run from a terrorist.

"I know all about the bombing in the airport, Dakota," Slade said softly, bringing her out of her musings.

Dakota's stomach cramped. He'd used her real name.

Of course he had. If he'd seen her dad, he had to know who she really was.

"I know you were the only survivor. I know that you saw Aziz Fourati, and I also know that you're the only one in the world right now who can identify him. He *also* knows this, and not only wants to make sure you keep that information to yourself, but wants you for his own. To be his wife."

Dakota shut her car door and shivered. Damn, it was cold. She tried to clear her foggy morning brain. She never functioned well before she'd had a cup of coffee. "His name is Aziz?"

She'd surprised him. Slade's eyebrows went up and he tilted his head as he asked, "You didn't know his name?"

"No. He never said it. What's his last name again?" She was trying really hard not to freak out. Oh, she was leaving today for sure, but she needed to know what Slade knew before she bolted. Information was power.

"Fourati."

"That sounds foreign," Dakota observed, proud of herself for how calm she sounded.

"It is. Best guess is that he's Tunisian."

"Tunisian?" she asked, really confused now.

"Yeah, Tunisian. The country between Algeria and Libya in Northern Africa."

"I know where Tunisia is," Dakota answered grumpily. "I just…" She paused for a moment, realizing that she should definitely not be talking to Slade about anything. She didn't know him. He could be one of Aziz Fourati's goons. She was happy to have a name for the guy who was making her life a living hell, but she needed to be smart…no matter how much her intuition was screaming that she could trust the man next to her.

Slade leaned over and grabbed something off the floor at his feet. It was a metal travel cup. He offered it to her without a word.

Dakota stared at the cup, then back at him. If he thought she was going to drink something he gave her, he was insane. "No thank you," she said politely.

"You don't know what it is," Slade said evenly.

"I don't know who *you* are," she returned a bit snarkily. "The only reason I'm still sitting in here right now is because it's cold outside, and there's nowhere for me to go. I'm sure if you wanted to, you could catch me in two-point-three seconds and slit my throat. Call me a glutton for punishment, but I'd like to get as much information as I can about why my life is in the crapper before I die."

"You don't swear."

"What?"

"You don't swear," he repeated patiently.

Dakota shrugged. "I'm an elementary school principal. Or I was. I can't exactly go around saying fuck, shit, and damn all the time."

"True. I like it."

"I can die happy," Dakota grumped.

His voice lowered further, if that was even possible, and as much as she hated it, goosebumps broke out on her arms at his tone. "I'm one of the good guys, Dakota," he told her. "The short story is that the government knows Fourati is behind the airport bombing and they want to make sure he's punished for what he did. But now he's gathering soldiers online. Trying to convert them to his cause. He wants to do it again, but on a grander scale this time."

"I'm aware," Dakota whispered, and she was. Aziz had bragged about his plans while she and the other hostages had huddled together, scared out of their minds in the airport.

"Then you know how important it is to stop him."

"I almost died that day." Dakota told him something he probably already knew.

He confirmed it by saying simply, "I know."

"You can't just show up out of the blue, tell me you've been looking for me, and expect me to trust you are who you say you are."

"Why not?"

"What do you mean, why not?" Dakota asked, confused.

He continued to hold the cup out to her, but said, "I told you that I'd been to see your dad. I saw the postcards. I *am* a retired Navy SEAL. I'm not Tunisian and couldn't pass for an Arabic terrorist on a good day. If I had cell reception, I'd call one of my best friends in the world and let him vouch for me. But that will have to wait until we're back in civilization. I'm one of the good guys, Dakota. Swear to God."

"That's what *a terrorist* would say," she informed him, not swayed in the least. "Besides, calling someone in order to vouch for your trustworthiness isn't going to make me believe them."

"Take the cup," Slade ordered gently.

Without thought, Dakota obeyed his urgent words. She reached out and took the stainless-steel travel mug from him. Her fingers brushed his, and she swore she could feel the heat from his fingers shoot up her arm.

But no, it wasn't his fingers that caused the heat, it was the mug. It was warm. She looked up in question.

"I stopped by the restaurant before coming here and asked Pat to warm up the contents for me." He looked sheepish for a moment before saying, "I'm sure it doesn't taste the best after two days, but your dad told me what you liked. He said you'd know I was telling the truth about talking to him if I brought this."

Dakota slowly and carefully turned the plastic lid—and immediately the smell of peppermint wafted up to her nose. She closed her eyes in ecstasy and brought the mug closer to her face. She inhaled the delicious scent of her absolute favorite coffee in the world, and thought about all the times she and her dad had shared a cup of coffee like this while sitting in his small living room. She fought the tears that sprang to her eyes.

"And this," Slade said softly, interrupting the memory.

Dakota opened her eyes and saw he was holding out a small white paper bag. She knew what was inside without having to look.

"A maple-iced donut," she said.

"That's right. Although I'm afraid it's probably a bit worse for wear after being in my saddlebag on the back of my bike."

Dakota reached out and snagged the bag from his fingertips, being careful not to touch him this time, and peered inside. Sure enough, the donut was mushed on one side and the maple icing was mostly stuck to the bag rather than on the pastry itself, but again, the memories that assailed her were almost overwhelming.

"You really did go see my dad."

"I did."

"And you *swear* you didn't hurt him?"

Slade made a weird sound and Dakota's gaze went to his. He looked pissed now. "No, I didn't hurt him," Slade growled. "I'm exactly who I've told you I am."

Dakota studied Slade for a long moment. The heat from the metal cup seeped into her palm, warming her cold hand. The paper from the bag crinkled as she shifted in her seat. Would a terrorist haul a cup of peppermint mocha coffee all the way from Vegas? Would he sit in a car next to her for who knows how long waiting for her to wake up without hurting her? Aziz certainly wouldn't. She was well aware of what *he* would do if he was in Slade's shoes.

Aziz Fourati wanted her. Dakota knew that without a doubt. But he wouldn't have his men treat her like this. Friendly. Respectful. Cautious. She knew exactly how they would treat her, *had* treated her that day back in the airport.

"You said that you couldn't pass for an Arabic terrorist on a good day," Dakota said softly.

"That's right," Slade agreed. "Once upon a time, I took pride in being able to move amongst people in the Middle East and blend in, but those days are over. This is the real me…graying beard and all." He gestured to his face as he said the last.

Dakota paused to take a small sip of the ambrosia she held in her hands and sighed as the peppermint flavor exploded on her tongue. The coffee was lukewarm, and a bit stale, but was still the best thing she'd tasted in a very long time. She looked up into Slade's eyes. She might be signing her death warrant by confiding in the man, but even in the short amount of time she'd spent with him…she trusted him. There was just something about him that she felt down in her soul. That he was meant to find her.

She'd never been very religious in her life, but she did believe in souls.

And reincarnation. Her parents had been soul mates; of that she was sure. She'd hoped to find the man meant to be hers in this lifetime, but had just about given up...until Slade had walked into the Little A'Le'Inn last night.

So far, Slade had been patient and protective of her...but more than that, she could see the honesty in his eyes. Aziz and his friends had cold, dead eyes. Slade's were a warm dark brown, and while she was well aware that he could probably kill her with his bare hands—he was a retired SEAL, after all—she knew he wouldn't.

When she didn't say anything else, Slade suggested, "How about we get out of the cold and grab something other than caffeine and sugar for you?"

"You came all the way out here because you wanted to know what Aziz looks like so you could catch him," Dakota said in confusion. "Why are you being so nice to me?"

"You're right, I did come all the way out here to find you and get more information on Fourati. But that's not the only reason. Sweetheart, you're shivering from cold, you have to be stiff from sitting here all night. I'm more concerned with taking care of *you* right now than getting information about Fourati."

Dakota licked her lips nervously, tasting the lingering peppermint that clung there, and asked, "Don't you need to report back to your superiors or whatever they're called and track him down? It's why you're here," she insisted again.

Slade immediately shook his head. "No. I won't lie, that's the original reason, yes. But the second I saw your picture in the mission folder, I knew I had to find you for a different reason."

He didn't elaborate, and Dakota asked, "Why?"

Slade's hand moved again. His fingers brushed her cheek, but then the heavy weight of his palm eased around and rested against the back of her neck. Dakota felt the goosebumps rise again and shoot all the way down both arms this time. With her hands full of the mug and paper bag, she couldn't do anything but lean on him when he put pressure on his hand and slowly tugged her forward.

His other hand went under her chin and he raised her head so she had no choice but to look him in the eye. She felt surrounded by him. His warmth. His caring. His passion.

"I'm not a young man, Dakota. I'm forty-eight years old. And not once in all that time have I been so affected by a photo as I was yours. I've seen hundreds of pictures of women who were in need of protection and rescue. Not one made me lose my breath and feel as if I was smacked on the back of the head. It was as if you reached out and snagged a piece of my heart. But that was nothing compared to seeing you in person. When I walked into the bar last night, I felt as if I had finally found what I've been looking for my entire life. You."

Holy crap. Was he serious? Did he really think that? Could he truly be the man she'd been looking for all *her* life? Dakota shook her head in weak denial. "That's not possible. You're just saying that to get me to tell you what I know."

"I don't give a shit what you know," Slade returned immediately. "I don't care if you never tell me what Fourati looks like. I'll just tell my boss you don't know anything."

"But you'll get in trouble," Dakota told him.

"I won't get in trouble because this isn't a government-sanctioned op. Besides, I'm retired. Dakota, I don't give a shit what the person who hired me thinks. The point is, *you* are my main concern. I found you, and so can Fourati. I'd be surprised if he and his goons weren't already on their way here. In fact, I'm fairly certain they *are* on their way here. It's only a matter of time…how much, I don't know. I believe I have a couple days lead on them, but can't be sure. But whatever happens, know that my main mission from this moment forward is keeping you safe. Not capturing Fourati."

Dakota had no idea how to respond. On one hand, she absolutely knew what Slade was talking about because from the second she'd lain eyes on him she'd felt…calm. As though she could finally take a deep breath and relax the hyper alertness she'd had for the last couple of months. He would stand between her and the rest of the world. But on the other hand, that was crazy talk. Insane. She didn't know the first thing about the man sitting next to her practically holding her in his embrace.

Luckily, he didn't give her a chance to say anything. He gently bent her head down, kissed the top, then straightened and said, "Come on. Let's get you inside and warmed up. Then we can discuss where we're going from here."

Feeling docile and mellow, Dakota simply nodded and sat back. It felt good for someone else to make the decisions for once. They looked at each other for a long moment, then Slade turned and opened his door. Shaking off her lassitude, Dakota followed suit after twisting to grab her backpack from the backseat. As soon as she was standing, Slade was there. He took the paper bag from her and tucked her hand into the crook of his arm, protecting her fingers from the chilly morning air.

"You have your car keys?"

"Why?"

"So we can lock it."

Dakota laughed. "Nobody is going to steal my car out here. The key's been in the ignition since I parked it. With my luck, I'd lose the stupid thing otherwise."

Slade shook his head as if exasperated, but didn't say anything else. He shut her car door and began to lead them to the trailer where he'd spent the night.

"I thought we were going to the restaurant?" Dakota asked as they approached.

"I figured you might want to shower to warm up first. And it's more private for us to talk in the trailer. The other occupants left already, like you said they probably would."

It was considerate of him. Dakota stopped suddenly, forcing him to as well.

It was considerate, but it was also conniving and potentially dangerous. The last thing she wanted to do was get naked with him nearby. She'd be vulnerable and—

"While you're showering, I'll head over to the restaurant. Give you some privacy."

"Thank you," she told him. Even though she didn't one hundred percent trust him, she still felt bad for thinking the worst.

Slade unlocked the door and led them inside. Dakota glanced into the bedroom and came to an abrupt stop.

Then she found herself staring at Slade's muscular back as he forced her backwards away from the bedroom, even as he was asking, "What? What did you see?"

"Nothing, I...the bed's still made."

As if realizing she wasn't in mortal danger, Slade slowly turned around and took a deep breath. "Yeah, and?"

"You made the bed before you left this morning?" she asked, knowing the answer before he said it.

"No. I didn't sleep there. I wanted to make sure you were safe last night, and when I saw you were sleeping in your car, I kept watch."

"You kept watch," Dakota said woodenly.

"Yeah."

"Over me."

"Yeah, Dakota. I wasn't going to fucking let you sleep in your car in the middle of nowhere when a fucking terrorist is after you. No fucking way."

She wasn't about to comment on the fact that he'd said "fuck" three times in two sentences. The precisely made bed in the other room did more for making her believe he was exactly who he said he was, a retired Navy SEAL, and that he was there to keep her safe, than anything he could've said.

Still holding the mug with both hands now, Dakota didn't even think. She leaned forward and rested her forehead against the cool leather of his jacket on his chest.

His arms immediately folded around her, resting on the small of her back, gathering her close. She couldn't hug him in return with her hands full, but it didn't seem to matter.

This time when he spoke, the anger was gone and all that was left was concern...for her. "You were going to sleep *here* before I showed up, weren't you?"

She nodded against him. "Pat and Connie let me stay in the trailers when they aren't rented."

"I'm sorry I took your bed."

"But you didn't," she said in a voice muffled because she was still facing his chest. "You didn't use it. You slept...I don't know where. But you didn't take my bed."

"Mmmm," was his only response. His hands slowly caressed her back, and with each stroke, she melted farther into him until she didn't think she could stand of her own volition anymore. He was the only thing holding her up.

"I'm scared," Dakota admitted in a barely audible voice.

Slade's arms tightened around her and Dakota finally turned her head, resting her cheek against his chest.

"You're not alone anymore," Slade told her confidently. "No one is going to get their hands on you."

"Promise?" She knew she shouldn't have asked. It wasn't like he could actually promise something like that, but the word came out before she could call it back.

"I fucking promise." It was a vow, and they both knew it.

They stood together for another long moment before Slade pulled back, kissed her on the forehead this time, and ordered, "Shower. Change. I'll be back in twenty minutes to walk you to the bar."

"I thought we were talking here?"

"We are. But you need some breakfast first. Real food, not just that," he said, indicating the cup she still held.

"You don't have to come back. I'll just meet you over there."

Slade lifted her chin with his index finger and said softly, "I'll be back to walk you over. I'm not taking any chances. I promised to keep you safe until Fourati is either captured or dead. You're going to have to get used to me being by your side twenty-four seven."

Dakota nodded. Right now, that sounded perfect. Oh, she knew in reality it would probably be a pain in the ass, but remembering what he'd said about only having a couple days lead on whoever Aziz sent to get her and bring her back to him, it was heavenly.

"Okay," she told him.

"Okay. Have a good shower. Drink your coffee. I'll be back."

Dakota watched as Slade turned and walked out of the trailer.

Her life had completely changed when she'd had the bad luck to be caught in the middle of a terrorist act, but she had a feeling it'd just done another one-eighty.

CHAPTER 5

*E*xactly twenty minutes later, Slade knocked on the door of the trailer. Even being apart from her that long was somehow painful. He kept imagining someone sneaking in through the other door and taking Dakota away from him. He might have been upset at his thoughts, except there was every reason for him to believe someone *might* do just that.

Until he could get Dakota out of Rachel and back where he had cell phone reception to call Tex and make sure they were still in the clear, he wasn't going to take any chances.

Instead of returning to the bar, Slade leaned against the side of the A'Le'Inn and kept watch over the trailer while Dakota showered. He might be going overboard, but he didn't think so. She'd been dead to the world when he'd opened the passenger door to her car that morning. She hadn't even twitched when he'd shut it, either. If he could sneak up on her that easily, so could anyone else. And the thought of Fourati or any of his followers getting their hands on her made him want to hit something.

"I'm ready," Dakota called out in response to his knock. "Come in."

Slade turned the knob and entered the small but cozy trailer. As far as accommodations went, it wouldn't win any traveler awards, but for this town it was downright palatial.

"I saved part of my donut for you," Dakota told him somewhat shyly.

If he hadn't already been halfway in love with her, that would've sent him over the edge. He knew how much she treasured those maple-frosted pastries...her dad had made it more than clear that no one touched her donuts. "You go ahead, sweetheart. It's been a while since you've had a treat."

She eyed him for a long moment and he thought she was going to either comment on the use of the endearment, or refuse to eat the pastry he could tell she wanted by the look in her eyes, but she finally shrugged and gave him a small smile.

"Thanks. And for the record, I was going to let you have it, but I'm happier that I can eat it all myself."

Slade chuckled. "I can see that." And he could. Her green eyes sparkled in the low light in the trailer and she'd already reached into the bag to grab the rest of the sticky donut.

"You ready to talk?" he asked her, pulling out one of the chairs to the small square table sitting next to the communal kitchen. "It's a pretty full house over at the restaurant."

"Yeah, people tend to get going early around here. At least the tourists. And while I really like Pat and Connie, they're the worst gossips. I guess it comes with not much to do or see out here," Dakota said matter-of-factly, and sat in the chair he'd pulled out for her.

They made small talk as she finished eating and when she licked the maple frosting off her fingers, Slade had to shift in his chair to give his dick room. He'd grown hard at the look of satisfaction on her face as she'd finished the donut, but when she began to use her tongue to catch every last speck of the sugary confection, he almost came in his pants.

"You said something earlier that I've been thinking on," Dakota said quietly, interrupting his inappropriate sexual thoughts.

"What's that?"

"You said that Aziz is foreign. Tunisian. What did you mean by that?"

Slade was puzzled for a moment. "What do you mean, what did I mean? I meant exactly what I said."

"But he's American," Dakota told him.

"Aziz Fourati is the leader of the Tunisian faction of the Ansar al-Shari'a terrorist group," Slade said firmly.

Dakota's eyebrows drew down in confusion. "Okay, then who was the guy at the airport?"

"Hang on, let's back up a second," Slade said, and he stood to go to the sink. As he pulled off a paper towel and wet it in the sink, he continued. "I'm part of a top secret task force assigned to find out all I could on

Fourati and take him down. He's gaining followers online. Quickly. I told you he's trying to replicate the LAX bombing all over the country in simultaneous attacks. No one is sure where he's getting the money to fund such an operation, but at the moment that isn't important. He's sneaky. He's good at staying under the radar, and the fact of the matter is that the government can't find him, partly because there are no known pictures of the man. Absolutely none."

He squeezed out the paper towel and came back to the table. As he continued to talk, he picked up each of Dakota's hands and gently cleaned them of the sugary mess the donut had left behind.

"Part of my goal, other than making sure you're safe, is to get a description of the man, maybe even a sketch, so the government knows who they're looking for and can put it into the facial recognition program. That way, if he ever steps foot inside an airport again, they can stop him."

Dakota put her hand over his, halting his movements. She looked into his eyes. "The man who pretended to be a hostage, and then ranted and raved for twenty minutes before he ordered the other guy to blow himself up, is American, Slade."

Slade's fingers gripped her own. "Are you sure?"

She nodded. "Positive. He had blue eyes and blondish hair. He also had what I'd say was a New York accent. I know people can fake accents and change their looks, but at no time did I *ever* think he was anything but American when I was around him."

"Did he ever call himself Aziz?"

"No. I didn't know his name until you said it, remember?"

"Then it might not be the same guy," Slade said more to himself than Dakota. "Tell me about LAX," he ordered gently.

"I was in the security line waiting just like everyone else. I heard yelling and screaming and turned to see what was happening. There were two men waving rifles around and shouting. They pointed their guns at a group of us in line and ordered us to follow them. We were herded through a door that said 'employees only,' I guess one of them had the code or a swipey thing to get in. I have no idea. Anyway, we all were marched down a hall and through another door into some sort of room. Maybe a break room or something for the employees?

"Everyone was scared and crying. One of the guys had explosives strapped to his chest. He handed that Aziz guy a pistol. He pulled me to my feet by my hair and held the gun to my head as he spoke. He had one arm around my chest and jammed the muzzle of that gun to my temple. He said that America was broken. That no one understood the meaning of spirituality anymore and that the Quran was the answer. He said it would take a grand act to make everyone face their mortality and turn to the revelations of God according to the Quran."

She was whispering now, and while Slade hated the fear on her face as she recalled the awful experience she'd been through, he let her continue to speak. He needed to hear what happened in that airport, and she needed to get it out so she could begin to heal.

"There was a younger hostage there, I hate that I don't even know his name, but he stood up and challenged the guy I now know was Aziz. And he just shot him. Took the pistol away from my temple, shot the guy who stood up for me, then pressed it right back against my head. The barrel was still hot and it hurt. Everyone began to scream and cry even louder as the man lay on the floor bleeding. Dying. And Aziz didn't care. He started talking about how every leader needed a woman at his side, supporting him. Having his babies to continue the dynasty."

Slade couldn't stand it anymore. He pushed his chair back a few inches, then grabbed Dakota's hand. He pulled her up and into his lap. She snuggled into him as if they'd done this exact thing hundreds of times. He was tall; at six-five, most furniture didn't fit him well, but he didn't give a shit at the moment if he was uncomfortable. He'd sit there and hold Dakota in his arms as long as she needed him to.

He put one of his big hands on the back of her head and held her tightly to him as she continued.

"I knew he was talking about me, that he wasn't going to martyr himself for his cause like I first thought. He rambled on a bit more and continually checked his watch as if he was waiting for a specific amount of time to pass. Then he nodded at the guy with the explosives, fired in the air, I think to make everyone scared of what was going to happen, then pulled me behind him as he quickly walked away. I knew if I didn't get away from him, he'd make me his sex slave and keep me locked up. So as soon as we exited the room, I attacked him."

"Good for you," Slade murmured, interrupting her for the first time.

"Not so good," she said with what he hoped was amusement. "I kicked him and he went down, but I didn't incapacitate him. I started to run toward the door that led back into the terminal, but he caught and tackled me. He kneeled above me and whispered, 'Good to know my future wife has courage. You're going to need it.' Then he bent down as if he was going to kiss me, but that's when the explosives went off. I don't know if the guy set them off too early or not, but I saw surprise and anger in the man's eyes before the ceiling fell in on us."

"His body protected you from the debris," Slade guessed.

She nodded against him. "Most of it, yeah. Knocked him out cold. Something hit my arm and broke it. I was so scared and the guy was deadweight on top of me, but I wiggled out from under him, hoping he was dead, and made my way out to the terminal. It was chaos, and no one realized that I'd come from the room the men with guns had entered. I was just another frantic person trying to get away from the building. I blended right in."

She fell silent then and Slade let her have the moment. A couple minutes and a few deep breaths later, she continued. "I thought I was good. That I'd gotten away. But I figured out pretty quickly that he didn't die."

"How did you know?" Slade asked.

"Because a week or so after I went back to work, I started to get presents delivered to my office. They were delivered anonymously, but I knew. Each one was addressed to 'My Future Bride.' There wasn't anyone else who would do that sort of thing. I'm not the kind of woman who has secret admirers. I quit the day one of the second-graders in my school brought me a box tied with a red bow. She said a man had given it to her outside the front doors and told her to bring it to me."

"What was it?" Slade prompted when she didn't continue.

"A plastic grenade," Dakota told him as she sat up a little straighter on his lap. "The bastard was not only threatening me, but all my kids as well. I called the cops, they took the threat seriously, but there wasn't much they could do. There weren't any prints and the little girl couldn't really describe the person who gave her the box."

"So you quit."

"I quit," she confirmed. "I didn't want to. But what else could I do? He wasn't going to leave me alone, I knew it. Heck, he *told* me. Then it got worse. My apartment complex burned to the ground. I know it was him. He wanted me scared out of my mind with no place to go and ready to agree to anything he wanted."

"But you're too tough for that."

She chuckled then. A sad sound that conveyed her hopelessness. "I don't know about that. I went to my dad's, said goodbye and told him to be careful, not to trust anyone who came to the door, then left. My first plan was to go to the East Coast, as far away from California as I could get, but I only made it to Vegas. And now here I am."

"Why Rachel?" Slade asked, genuinely curious.

"I wasn't planning on staying. I met some people who told me all about the area and how cool it was. I thought it sounded like a good place to hole up for a while, figure out what my next move was going to be. But I didn't take into account that when I got here, there wouldn't be any gas stations, and I didn't have enough fuel to get me to one." Dakota shrugged.

The chuckle began softly enough, but when she looked up at him and her own lips quirked into a grin, he couldn't hold it back. He threw his head back and laughed. She joined in and soon they were laughing at the randomness of life.

Through chuckles, she elaborated, "I quickly got that sorted out, but the more I thought about it, the more I realized that Rachel was a great place to hide. I'm paid in cash and can save up some money while not using my credit cards, and there aren't a lot of people out here, so I can keep watch on who comes and goes pretty easily."

Slade finally got himself under control and said, "I think staying out here was a really good idea. It's like you've been hiding in plain sight."

"I guess."

"I'm sorry you lost all your belongings in the fire."

"Don't be. It was just stuff. My dad still has pictures of my mom, so I don't even feel that bad about losing mine. I feel worse for the families and other residents who lost everything because some asshole thinks he can take whatever he wants. If you ask me, he's less a terrorist than a big baby."

"Can you describe him for me?"

"He's about my height. Five-nine or so. He's got short blond hair, at least he did a few months ago. Blue eyes. Pale skin. He was dressed really nice in the airport...slacks, polo shirt, and he was carrying a briefcase. I don't know if it was just a prop or not. He was fairly young. Probably mid- to late-twenties, if I had to guess. He was muscular and honestly looked like any other businessman on his way to a meeting." Dakota sat up straight on Slade's lap and looked him in the eyes.

"He looked like the boy next door, Slade. Completely harmless, which is what made what happened so scary. When he was on top of me in the airport and looking down at me, I swear to God I saw nothing but blackness in his eyes. I don't think he cares about religion at all. He just wants to kill people. He gets off on it."

Slade closed his eyes in both relief that Dakota had gotten away from him, and frustration that the search for the terrorist just got tougher. A man with his description could blend in anywhere in America.

"You aren't going to be able to find him, are you?" Dakota asked, obviously more attuned to him than he'd thought.

Slade opened his eyes and looked directly at her as he swore, "We're going to find him."

"But how? He—"

"Sweetheart, you're not going to have to worry about this guy for the rest of your life. I know people who know people who know people. They'll find him. Can I change the subject for a second?"

"Oh…well…yeah, I guess so," she said uncertainly, obviously not really wanting to drop the subject of Aziz.

Slade tightened his arms around her waist and asked, "You feel this?"

She hesitated for a moment, then nodded shyly, not asking what he meant.

"Yeah. I've been in your presence for less than twelve hours and I can tell you without a doubt that you've somehow become the most precious thing in my life. I've been married and divorced, I have nieces and nephew and I love my family. But *nothing* has ever made me feel like I do right this moment with you in my arms."

"We don't know each other," she protested.

"I know."

"And we're too old for this kind of insta-lust."

"Speak for yourself," Slade said with a grin. "I might be forty-eight, but I'm not dead, sweetheart. I spent four years married to my ex, and not once did I ever feel this way about her."

"What way?"

"Like if I take my eyes off you, I'll lose something precious. Like I want to hold you so tightly against me, until I can't ever remember what it feels like to not have you in my arms. Like if I don't kiss you right this second, I'll die."

He held his breath, hoping he hadn't just scared her away.

Instead of answering him or laughing at his words, Dakota slowly leaned toward him. Her eyes dropped to his lips, and the erection Slade had been controlling with sheer stubbornness sprang to life at the desire he saw there.

One of her hands came up between them and landed on the side his neck. Her fingers brushed against the sensitive skin behind his ear, and her thumb rested on the side of his face and caressed his beard.

"I've never kissed a man who had a beard before."

"Then I think it's about time you did," Slade told her, not moving an inch. He wanted her to take what she wanted. He wanted to make sure this was something *she* wanted to do.

Dakota pulled him toward her and kissed him.

She kissed *him*.

The second her lips touched his, however, Slade took over. It was enough that she'd made the first move, he couldn't hold back any longer. His head slanted, his hands came up to frame her face and he devoured her. This was no tentative first kiss, this was a claiming.

Slade's tongue pushed past her barely parted lips as though if he didn't get inside her in the next second, he'd die. Their tongues tangled together as they kissed. When Dakota pulled back to take a breath, Slade followed her, not giving her more than a second's respite before claiming her mouth again.

For what seemed like hours, he drank from her. She tasted like sugar and peppermint. It was a taste he knew he'd crave for the rest of his life. Slade learned that she enjoyed a little roughness, but melted into him when he lightly nipped and sucked on her lower lip. He brushed his cheek against hers, smiling when she made a whimpering sound deep in her throat as his beard made contact with her sensitive skin.

Sometime in the midst of their kiss, she'd turned into him and straddled his hips on the small chair. His cock was now flush against the cleft between her legs, and she was rubbing herself against his hardness in the same rhythm he was using to suck on her tongue.

When he finally allowed her room to breathe, he rested his forehead on hers and held her hips tightly against him as they both fought to catch their breaths.

"I think it's safe to say I like you back," she said with a small smile.

His lips twitched, but he remained serious when he said, "Good."

"I thought your beard would be scratchy. But it's really soft. It feels good."

"I'm glad you don't hate it. I've gotten kinda used to it."

"I don't hate it," she told him firmly. They sat still for a moment, then Dakota asked softly, "Should I be embarrassed about this?" She motioned to their laps with her head.

"Embarrassed that I can feel how hot and wet you are from only the touch of my mouth on yours? Fuck no. You can see and feel how much *I* liked it."

At his words, her hips nudged his hard-as-nails dick once more and he smiled at her.

"This is the beginning of us," he declared firmly. "I don't care what the future holds. I'm not giving this up. I'm not giving *you* up."

"It's probably the danger thing," Dakota told him. "You'll feel differently when it's all over."

"Wanna bet?" Slade asked.

"What?"

"A bet. I bet you fifty peppermint mochas and maple-iced donuts that when Fourati is dead, I'll still want you just as much, or more, than I do right this moment."

"Oh…uh…okay. And if it's just the heat of the moment?"

"It's not."

"But it's not a bet if you don't bet on both sides, Slade."

He smirked. "Fine. If, after Fourati is out of your life for good, I don't feel exactly how I do right now, like I want inside you more than I want my next breath, then I'll give you enough gift cards to set you up for life with your coffees and pastries. And if I do, then I'll personally deliver a coffee and donut to you in our bed every morning for the rest of our lives."

Dakota opened her mouth to speak—but Slade quickly covered it with his hand.

It was as if a switch had been turned on inside him. He lost the relaxed, teasing vibe he'd had when they were talking about the bet, and was suddenly all business.

"Shhh," he ordered urgently, easing them to their feet at the same time.

Dakota nodded and he took his hand away from her face, running his thumb over her lips in apology for how hard he'd been, even as his eyes swept the interior of the small space.

The soft noise came again at the other door of the trailer.

Slade didn't waste any time. He pushed her into the room she'd showered in, grabbing her backpack as he went. Closing the door silently, then locking it, he turned to Dakota and slipped the backpack over her shoulders without a word.

He stalked silently to the window and pried the top of the blinds apart a minuscule amount so he could see out. Seeing nothing alarming, he quietly pulled the cord to open them and pushed the window up. Thank God there was no screen.

Holding out his hand to Dakota, he said softly, "We need to go, sweetheart. Looks like our time has run out."

"Aziz?" Dakota asked in a whisper.

"Or his goons. But we're not going to wait around to find out."

Glad to see determination on her face rather than fear, Slade took hold of her hand and squeezed. "I'm going out first, then I'll help you. You need anything from your car that isn't in that backpack?"

Dakota shook her head and whispered, "I keep my stuff with me as much as possible. I always have a couple changes of clothes and a few personal items. Just in case."

"Good. My bike is parked to the side of the restaurant. I filled the tank with the gas I brought with me after we parted last night, so it's ready to go. We've got enough to get back to civilization. There's not much cover between here and my bike though, so we're going to have to make a break for it. You ready?"

She nodded, but pulled on his hand when he went to climb out of the window. "I've never ridden a motorcycle before, Slade."

He took precious seconds he wasn't sure he had to lean down and kiss her lips hard. "All you gotta do is hold on, sweetheart. I'm not going to let anything happen to you. Trust me."

"I do."

"Good. Then let's get out of here." Slade let go of her hand and quickly eased out of the window. Because he was so tall, his feet hit the ground before he was all the way out. He grabbed hold of Dakota as she began to climb out, and had her standing next to him in seconds.

Without letting go of her hand, Slade quietly moved to the side of the trailer and peered around the corner. Standing at the far door was a Middle Eastern man fiddling with the lock. Obviously not Fourati, if Dakota's description was correct, but certainly one of his flock. He briefly wondered how the man had found them, but didn't have time to ponder it. It wasn't relevant anyway. It didn't matter if this was the last trailer he'd checked, or the first, he was here now, and it was time for them to *not* be here.

He turned to Dakota and pulled her back the way they'd come. He cautiously peeked around the corner of the trailer and saw nobody. "New plan. See that truck?" He pointed to the rusted hulk of what used to be a truck sitting about twenty feet away from the trailer.

She nodded.

"Go and hide behind it. Do not come out no matter what you hear. Got me?"

"But—"

"Dakota. I was a SEAL. I got this. But I need you to help me. If I'm worried about you, I won't be able to do what I need to do. Please. I need you to hide. Hunker down and wait for me to come get you."

"Okay, but don't get dead," she whispered fearfully.

His lips twitched. She was kinda funny even when she wasn't trying to be. "I won't. Now go on. You'll hear me coming. Be ready."

"Am I supposed to leap on the back of your bike while it's moving like they used to do to horses in the wild west?"

He couldn't hold back his smile this time. Funny. "No, smartass. I'll stop. If we have time, you'll also put on the helmet I bought for you."

"You bought me a helmet?"

Slade rolled his yes. "Yes. Now go."

Without hesitation, she stood on her tiptoes, kissed him, then took off running for the rusted truck. Slade felt his lips tingling where she'd touched him, and licked them as he watched her disappear behind the dubious safety of the rusted vehicle.

Forcing himself to leave her, Slade headed back toward the front of the trailer. He waited until the man had entered to make his move. He had no idea if the guy was by himself—not likely—so he couldn't dick around.

Looking around to make sure no one witnessed him entering the trailer, and not seeing anyone lurking nearby, Slade slipped in behind the man silently. He needed to get Dakota out of town, but he couldn't just leave this asshole walking around free and clear. It wouldn't sit well on his conscience if he blew up the A'Le'Inn or killed anyone in town while looking for Dakota.

Five minutes later, the man was unconscious and tied up in the trailer, and Slade headed for the bar. He needed to warn Pat and Connie that there might be more terrorists lurking about and get them to call the police. It would probably take a while for help to arrive, but at least the asshole in the trailer wouldn't hurt anyone in the meantime.

Slade figured the man had a partner, or partners, somewhere, but couldn't take any more time to try to track them down. He'd warn the owners and make sure they were safe before getting the hell out of dodge.

The second the guy's partners realized he'd been compromised, they'd be hot on Slade and Dakota's trail. If they were going to escape, they needed a head start. It wasn't as if they could disappear in the small town, and there was only one road leading into and out of Rachel, with absolutely no cover whatsoever. As much as he didn't like it, his best option at the moment was to bolt, not track down an unknown number of terrorists.

He made one other quick stop before hurrying to his motorcycle. They needed to be far out of sight before the man, or men, knew which way they'd gone. His actions might buy them some time, but Slade had a feeling things were just getting interesting.

CHAPTER 6

*D*akota heard Slade before she saw him. She had stuffed herself as far under the rusted-out old truck as she could and hoped she couldn't be seen from the other side.

Her heart was beating wildly and she had to constantly force herself to stay where she was and not peek around the truck to look for Slade. He said he'd come and get her, so she had to stay in place until he did.

The morning had been intense, there was no doubt about that. But whatever weird connection she felt for Slade was obviously returned. She'd never felt as strongly about a man as she did him. She'd been scared for so long, it felt good to have someone care whether or not she lived or died.

Besides the physical attraction she and Slade had for each other, there was something more. Something almost divine. It was if her soul recognized him from the second their eyes met.

Dakota was a romantic. She knew it and didn't try to hide it. She read romances, watched sappy movies, and cried at the end of *Cinderella* every time. But she hadn't ever had that ah-ha moment she'd always felt so sure she'd experience when she met the man destined to be hers. At forty-three, she figured she never would. She'd been to sixty-seven weddings in her lifetime. Sixty-freaking-seven. When teachers in her school got married, they'd inevitably invite her and she'd go. To every one. And each time, it felt more and more like a stake in the heart as she watched her friends and colleagues tie themselves to their soul mates. Knowing she'd probably never have that, hurt.

But now here she was. On the run from a terrorist who wanted to make her his love slave, in danger, not knowing what her future would bring, and it had finally happened. Slade Cutsinger had walked through the door last night and she'd known he was hers with one glance.

The amazing thing was that apparently, he felt the same. But he was in danger while she hid like a coward. Suddenly staying put didn't seem like the best plan after all.

She sat up and began to brush off the sand from her legs, determined to do more than hide like a coward, when she heard a loud engine approaching.

Dakota held her breath and sighed in relief when Slade pulled up next to her on his Harley.

"Climb on, sweetheart. No time for a helmet right now. We'll stop in a few and get you all set. That's it, put your left foot there on the peg and swing your right leg around. Good. Watch that, it gets hot, don't let your calf touch it. It'll burn the shit out of your leg. Hold on. No...hold *on*. Good. Here we go."

And with that short intro to riding a motorcycle, he gunned the engine, sand spewed behind the tire, and they fishtailed for a few yards before Slade gained control of the huge machine between his legs and they shot forward.

Dakota squeezed her eyes shut and held on to Slade for dear life. She guessed that her fingers were probably white with the pressure she was exerting on his belly. Her chest was flush against his back and the wind blew her hair crazily around her head. The bun she'd put her hair in after her shower was quickly torn out as they raced down the road at what seemed like an insane speed.

She kept her eyes closed as Slade raced away from Rachel. Dakota had no idea which direction they were even going, but at the moment it didn't matter. Slade would take care of her...she had no doubt.

It could've been hours later, but was probably only fifteen minutes or so, when Dakota felt the bike slow. She waited until they were completely stopped before opening her eyes. Slade had turned his head and was watching her.

"You okay?"

She nodded shakily.

He put his hand around her fingers still clutched together at his belly.

"Come on, sweetheart. We can't stop for long, but I need to take care of you before we continue. Let go."

Dakota forced her fingers to uncurl, surprised at how stiff and cold they were.

"I've got a pair of gloves for your hands. I'm sorry I had to wait so long to pull over. I would've picked you up faster, but I had to take care of something."

"Take care of something?" she asked with a tilt of her head.

"I couldn't in good conscience let the asshole who broke into the trailer possibly take out his frustration at finding you gone on the residents of Rachel."

"Did you kill him?"

"No. But he certainly won't feel like doing much anytime soon. Come on, stand up, let me get you outfitted properly."

"Outfitted properly" included a leather jacket exactly her size, a pair of gloves, and a helmet. "I'm sorry I can't fit your backpack in my saddlebags. Are you okay wearing it?"

"Of course. It's no problem," she told him. "Were you that sure you were going to find me?"

"What do you mean?"

"You have a jacket for me...which fits perfectly, by the way. And a pair of gloves in my size. And the helmet."

Slade put his hands on her shoulders and turned her so her back was to him. He began to gently finger comb her long, tangled hair. "I was that sure I was going to find you," he confirmed. "Because I wasn't going to stop until you were safe."

Dakota swallowed hard at the feeling of his hands in her hair and said simply, "Okay."

"Okay," he agreed, then began to braid her hair.

"Why are you doing that?" she asked softly.

"Because we have a while to go. And it'll just continue to get tangled if I don't. And..." He paused dramatically and she felt him lean into her. "It gives me an excuse to run my hands through your hair."

She chuckled, but didn't protest. He quickly finished the simple braid and tied it off with her hair elastic. Then he turned her to face him and picked up her helmet. He gently placed it on her head and wiggled it a bit. "How's this feel? Too tight? Too loose?"

"No, it seems okay. Not that I'd know how a motorcycle helmet is supposed to fit though."

"Let me know if it pinches in any way when we get started." And with that, Slade buckled the strap under her chin and stared down at her for a long moment.

"What?" she asked nervously. "Does it look stupid?"

"No, Dakota. It doesn't look stupid. It looks great. *You* look great. I just can't believe you're here. On the back of my bike. I know the situation sucks, but I can't be sorry. I'm so happy to be here with you."

"I'm glad you're here with me too," she told him softly.

Then he tapped her on the end of her nose with his finger and smiled down at her. "We gotta get going. This time you need to open your eyes," he teased, then threw his leg over the Harley and settled in, looking back at her expectantly.

Ignoring his jibe about her eyes, she said, "Are you sure we won't be followed?" Dakota settled in behind him as she asked. Her arms tentatively circled his waist. Now that they weren't moving, she wasn't sure where she should put them.

Not even hesitating, Slade reached down and took a hand in each of his own and wrapped them tighter around his waist once more. He linked her fingers together, then pressed them against his stomach, giving her a nonverbal command to keep them there.

She was plastered against him once again, but now that she was wearing a leather jacket, she was warmer and could appreciate how his muscles moved under her hands and chest more.

He started the motorcycle and turned his head so she could hear him over the motor. "Followed by the guy I knocked out, no. But I'm not sure about any of his buddies. I did stop and pierce the gas tank of the only other car that hadn't been there when we entered the trailer though," he said matter-of-factly. "If there was more than one of them, they aren't going to be going anywhere for long in their piece-of-shit car. I bought us some time to get back to San Diego ahead of them."

Dakota's arms tightened involuntarily. "Back to California? Is that a good idea?"

Slade's eyes met hers, and the reassurance she saw there made her relax before he even said a word. "I want you on my turf. I've got people there who will have our backs. I can communicate with my friend, Tex, who will give me a head's up on what's happening with Fourati. I know it's scary, but I can end this faster if we're there."

"You won't use me as bait, will you?" Dakota asked quietly, her voice barely audible over the roar of the engine. It was a concern. She figured it was cowardly of her, but she wasn't exactly GI Jane. She was an elementary school principal, for goodness sake. The last thing she wanted to do was see Aziz Fourati again, even if Slade and his friends were watching over her. He scared the crap out of her.

"Fuck no," Slade bit out with a shake of his head. "There's no way I'd allow you to put yourself in danger like that. If there's even a one percent chance that something could go wrong, I won't do it. And since this Fourati guy is obviously off his fucking rocker, there's no telling what he'd do if he got his hands on you. So no, you won't be fucking bait."

Dakota thought it was somewhat amusing that the more emotional Slade felt, the more he used the f-word. Wanting to soothe him, she ran her hands up and down his stomach. "Okay, Slade. Good."

"Good," he agreed, and turned around to face forward once again.

But before he grabbed hold of the handlebars, he reached down and picked up her right hand. He kissed the palm before placing it back on his stomach.

Dakota's own stomach tightened at the tender gesture. She couldn't feel his lips since she was wearing gloves, but somehow her hand still seemed to warm.

As they took off, Dakota realized she still wasn't sure which way they were headed, but assumed north. They could take Route 95 down through Goldfield and into Vegas, then get back on Interstate 15. But at that moment it didn't matter. She was on the back of a motorcycle with a man she trusted down to the very marrow of her bones, and she felt safer with him than she'd felt in a very long time.

Ten minutes later, Dakota felt the motorcycle slowing. It was still early morning, but the the sun had come up, warming the chilly air enough so she wasn't freezing. Slade's body heat, the leather jacket, and the helmet went a long way toward keeping her body heat in as well.

"Why are we stopping?" she asked in a loud voice to be heard over the engine.

Slade was bent over a piece of electronics and didn't answer her immediately.

Giving him time, Dakota looked around. There was a mountain range in the distance ahead of them. She had no idea how far away it was because distance was skewed out here in the desert. It could've been two miles or twenty. Spatial reasoning wasn't her forte.

There were big puffy clouds in the sky, and it would've been beautiful if it wasn't for the fact they were trying to outrun goons who wanted to do her harm.

"How're you holding up?" Slade asked.

"I'm okay," Dakota said immediately.

"No. How are you holding up?" Slade repeated firmly.

Her brows drew down in confusion. "I don't know what you're really asking."

"You haven't ridden a bike before. It's chilly. You've been tense the entire ride. The morning has been stressful and I'd like to do whatever I can to keep that stress at a minimum for as long as I can. I'm sure your legs are probably beginning to get sore from straddling the seat and the vibrations of the bike. I'm asking how you're feeling so I can determine which route we're going to take to Tonopah."

"What are our choices?" Dakota ignored his incredibly accurate rundown of the morning. She would be sore later, no doubt about it. Slade's Harley was big...he was a big man, after all. The vibrations had started out feeling good, like a large erotic massager, but as they'd ridden on, they began to get irritating. Her teeth felt like they were still rattling even though they weren't moving. And forget about her girly parts being aroused, numb was more like it.

But she was beginning to understand Slade a little more. It was crazy, it wasn't as if she'd known him all that long. But she knew without a doubt that he'd put her comfort first...even if it wasn't the best tactical decision. She might not be the strongest woman in the world, but she refused to be a burden.

"We can continue on the blacktop road. It's probably another forty miles or so to Tonopah. The road heads north, then turns west directly to the small town. It's a straight shot. With no cover."

Dakota understood his concern. The desert was beautiful, but if she could see for miles, so could the people who were after her. If they managed to somehow catch up with them, there would be absolutely nowhere for them to hide.

"And our other option?" she asked.

Appreciating that Slade didn't treat her like a child, he laid it out. He pointed to his left. "This dirt road leads to the Tonopah Test Range Airport. It continues on to Tonopah itself. It's rough. *Really* rough. We won't be able to drive very fast because of the likely condition of the road."

"But it's safer," Dakota concluded.

"Yeah. Definitely. There's no way anyone could follow us…not in a regular car. They'd have to go the long way around," Slade told her.

"But they could go faster, right? Beat us to Tonopah?"

"It's a possibility," Slade agreed. "They won't be able to fix their gas tank, I put a big-ass hole in it. But if they were able to obtain another vehicle, they could drive like a bat out of hell and get there before us. But, it'll be much easier to hide, if we need to, once we hit ninety-five. There are small towns all along the way down to Vegas."

"Let's take the dirt road," Dakota said firmly. "If it's safer, we should do it."

Slade twisted around so he could see her better. "It's not going to be comfortable," he warned. "It'll be really dusty and I can guarantee before we're twenty miles down this piece-of-shit thing called a road, you'll be wishing we'd stayed on the blacktop."

"Probably," she agreed. "But there are a lot of things I've wished in the last couple of months. I wish I woke up late and didn't make it to the airport on time. I wish there was a longer line to check in so I wasn't in the right place at the right time to catch Aziz's eye. I wish I'd stopped to check to make sure he was dead before I ran. Taking the shorter road here seems like a no-brainer to me. The last thing I want is for us to be caught in the middle of the desert, with nowhere to go and no way to protect ourselves."

"I never said I couldn't protect you, Dakota," Slade said quietly. "I will always protect you."

She swallowed hard before saying, "I'm looking at this as an adventure. I've never ridden a motorcycle, and now's my chance. Just like I'd never kissed a man with a beard before…and that turned out okay."

"Just okay?" Slade asked with a smile.

"Maybe a bit better. I need more data to make a definitive decision," she teased.

He smiled at her response, then leaned in. "You need a break, don't hesitate to let me know. We have the time. We can stop. Let you walk around."

"I'll be fine," she told him, not sure she would, but trying to be strong. "Slade?"

"Yeah, sweetheart?"

"Do you think we might be able to find a hotel that has a Jacuzzi? If I'm going to be sore, it might be nice to have a warm soak."

"I'll make it happen," Slade vowed.

And somehow, she knew he would. Even if they were in the middle of nowhere, Nevada, somehow Slade would find the one hotel that had a Jacuzzi so she could soak her sore muscles.

"Here," Slade said, interrupting her thoughts. "Wrap this around your face. It'll help keep the dust out of your nose and mouth." He held out a handkerchief.

Dakota didn't know where he'd pulled it out of, but it didn't matter. She unbuckled her helmet and tied the cloth around her face. It smelled good. Like Slade. She might be uncomfortable and miserable, but she'd have Slade's scent in her nose. She could deal with that. As she buckled her helmet again, she noticed that Slade had donned a bandana around his face too, and, even though she couldn't see his mouth anymore, knew he was smiling at her by the wrinkles around his eyes.

"I'll make a biker babe out of you yet," he teased, then ran his gloved fingers down her cheek and turned to face forward again. "Ready?"

"Yup," Dakota chirped, trying to hide her trepidation. "Drive on, James."

Slade pulled her arms around him again, taking the time to lift her hand once more, pull down his bandana, and place a kiss in the middle of her palm. Once more, she couldn't feel his lips through her glove, but the tender gesture made her shiver anyway.

"Here we go," he told her as he gave the engine some gas. "Hold on."

An hour later, Dakota thought she was going to die, but she held on, determined not to be a wuss. Slade had warned her, had said it was going to be tough. She thought she'd be able to hack it, but it had become clear about ten minutes down the dirt road that she'd overstated her "hack it" ability.

She didn't want to be weak. Didn't want Slade to see how pathetic she was. But this riding-a-motorcycle thing was for the birds. She wanted off. At this point, she'd be willing to walk the rest of the way to San Diego if it meant not having to straddle the beast anymore.

Her inner thighs hurt from gripping the seat. Her head hurt from the noise of the engine. Her fingers hurt from clutching each other. Her arms hurt from squeezing Slade's sides. And finally, even her eyes hurt from squinting and trying to keep the dust and wind out of them.

She was miserable and ready for Aziz to find her and have his way with her just to put her out of her current suffering.

Dakota didn't even realize Slade was slowing down until he cut the engine and the silence of the desert washed over her. Picking her head up from his shoulder, where she'd rested it miles ago, she blinked and looked around in confusion.

"Are we there?"

"No, sweetheart. But you need a break."

"But we need to keep going."

He'd climbed off the bike, unbuckled his helmet, and had removed the bandana around his face. He spoke as he did the same for her. "You've held up wonderfully, but if we're going to make it to Goldfield tonight, you need to walk around. Take a break."

"I can keep going," Dakota protested, even though the thought made her wince.

Slade pulled her bandana to rest around her neck and hung her helmet next to his on the handlebars then leaned into her. "I have a feeling you could do anything you put your mind to. But you don't have to lie to me. In fact, I'd prefer you didn't. I appreciate your stubbornness, but I know without a doubt you need to stop for a while."

"How?" She hated that she was so easy to read.

"You were flinching after every pothole. You were gripping me so tight, I know you've got to be sore as hell…and we haven't even gotten halfway to Tonopah. You're wincing, so it's obvious your head hurts, and your legs are shaking as you're sitting there."

"Darn," Dakota murmured, looking down at her lap. Sure enough, her legs were trembling as her feet rested on the pegs on the back of the bike.

"Throw your right leg over the front of the bike and turn toward me. Then you can slide off the seat and have both feet on the ground at the same time. Hold on to me. I won't let you fall."

"This is gonna suck, isn't it?" Dakota asked rhetorically under her breath as she followed his orders. She went to scoot off the seat, but Slade stopped her by putting both hands on either side of her neck and tilting her head up toward him.

"I'm proud of you, sweetheart."

"Why? Because I can't ride more than an hour without wanting to cry like a baby? Because I feel so weak I know I'm not going to be able to stand by myself? Or because the thought of having to get back on this monster and continue makes me want to lie down right here in the dirt and cry?"

"Because you're feeling all those things, but you won't let any of them hold you back. You aren't the first newbie to be sore after riding, but I daresay others haven't been on the run from assholes nor ridden for an hour over the worst excuse for a road that they've ever seen. You don't have to worry about standing by yourself, because I'm right here and won't let you fall. And you might not want to get back on the bike, but you will. And that right there is why, with just one glance at your picture, I knew I wanted you for myself."

Feeling flustered and hot, Dakota joked, "And the crying?"

"You go right ahead," Slade told her. "I'm not afraid of a few tears. I hate that you'll shed them because that means you're hurting, but if they'll help release your emotions, then go for it."

Dakota closed her eyes tightly and took a few deep breaths. She didn't feel very strong at the moment, but Slade thinking she was went a long way toward making her feel better.

He moved his hands from her neck to her waist and gently lifted her off the seat to stand in front of him. As soon as her feet hit the dusty ground, her knees buckled. She would've fallen if he hadn't been holding her up.

"Easy, Dakota. Just stand there for a moment. Let the blood work its way back to your feet."

"I can't believe you do this for fun," she bitched as her legs tingled from the increased blood flow to her toes.

He chuckled in her ear. "I wouldn't say driving my Harley on roads like this is fun. This is more something I'd do on my dirt bike."

"Oh lord. Don't tell me. You've got a garage full of motorcycles at your house."

"Nope."

"Thank God."

"I live in an apartment. They're in a buddy's garage," Slade told her, grinning.

"Evil," Dakota told him, easing back a little, trying to stand on her own.

"Come on," Slade said, putting an arm around her waist and turning them to the side. "Walking will do you good. Get your blood pumping and your muscles working again."

"I think sitting would be better, or maybe lying down and never moving again," Dakota told him, wrinkling her nose at the pain when she began to move. She knew she was walking completely bowlegged, but Slade didn't say anything or make fun of her. She was going to call that a win in her book.

He helped her limp up the side of a small rise. It seemed more like a mountain when they were walking up it, but when they got to the top, Dakota saw that it really was just a tiny hill compared to the mountain range that stretched in front of them.

Slade helped her sit, then settled in behind her, pulling her back to his front and taking her weight. Dakota bent her legs up and put her feet flat on the ground in front of her, relaxing into Slade.

He pointed toward the mountains. "The highest point there is Kawich Peak. It's about ninety-five hundred feet high."

"Do people climb it?" Dakota asked, not really caring, but needing to talk about something to keep her mind off of how much her body hurt.

"Not much. It *is* out here in the middle of nowhere," he deadpanned.

Dakota chuckled. "True."

"But more than that, see all these scrub bushes around?"

Dakota nodded.

"I've heard the brush gets horrible the higher you go. It gets to a point that it's a pain in the ass to continue."

"You've talked to someone who climbed it?" Dakota asked, surprised.

"No, but I researched the area before I came out here. I wanted to know what my options were in case we needed to hide."

She craned her neck and gave him an incredulous look. "You were going to have us climb that mountain?"

He smiled back. "I'm not saying it would've been fun, but I'd be an idiot to follow you to the middle of the nowhere and not have a plan in case things went south."

"So you knew this road was here."

"I knew this road was here," he confirmed, then pulled her back against him.

Dakota relaxed as she looked out at the beautiful landscape in front of her. "It feels as if we're the only people in the world. It's so quiet and peaceful."

"Mmmm," Slade responded.

"You know, at night, the stars look so much brighter out here. I've never seen anything as gorgeous in my life."

"I've been in some pretty remote places myself, and I agree."

"I used to lie on the hood of my car at night, when it was warmer, and look up at the stars and marvel at the fact that we're so inconsequential. So small. But more than that, I was comforted by the fact my dad could be looking up at the exact same stars at the same time I was. It made me feel closer to him."

"I've done that," Slade admitted. "When me and my team were in the middle of some desert in the Middle East, I've looked up at the stars and wondered who was looking up at them at the exact same time. No one but the government knew where we were, but somehow those stars made me feel not so alone."

"Yeah, that's it," Dakota agreed. "Even though they're millions of miles away, they somehow bring me closer to my dad. To my old life."

Slade kissed the top of her head in response to her words.

After several minutes, Dakota asked softly, "What's going to happen when we get back home? I don't have any place to go. I literally only have the clothes on my back, no food. Hell, I don't even have my car anymore. I feel lost, Slade."

He squeezed her tightly, then ran his hands up and down her arms. "I can't imagine how you're feeling," he told her honestly. "But you said so yourself...things can be replaced. My plan, at the moment, is to stay with my friend, Wolf. He's a Navy SEAL himself, and he and his wife don't have any children. They have an apartment set up in their basement that's mostly private."

"Will you call and let me know what's going on?" Dakota asked, strangely disappointed that Slade wouldn't be taking her back to his place with him.

"You think I'm going to drop you off at a stranger's house and go about my business?" Slade bit out.

"Oh, well, I—"

"Dakota, I'll be there with you. I'd take you back to my place in a heartbeat, but I've been compromised. After this morning, they know you're not alone and most likely have someone who knows what he's doing helping you. It won't take long for them to figure out who I am and where I live."

"True," Dakota muttered.

"There's nothing I want more than you in my space. Cooking in my kitchen. Eating at my table. Sleeping in my bed. Watching the waves while we sit on my balcony together. But I won't knowingly put you in danger. We talked about you not being bait, and taking you to my place would definitely fall in that category. Caroline and Wolf will be happy to let us crash at their place."

"Won't that be dangerous for them?" she asked.

"No."

"Why not?"

"Because Wolf is in charge of a SEAL team. One of the best teams I've ever known. No matter what the danger is, he'll protect his wife and I'll protect you."

Dakota closed her eyes and took a deep breath. She heard the wind blowing through the scrub bushes surrounding them, but that was about it. There was literally nothing out there with them, nature, and the sky.

"I feel as if I'm a burden to everyone I meet."

"You're not a burden."

He sounded so certain. "What would you be doing right now if you weren't chasing me down?" she asked.

"I'd be sitting at my desk at the Naval base looking at boring-ass reports and trying to reconcile expenses for the government. I'd go home at the end of the night, make myself dinner, then eat by myself. Maybe watch a movie, or sit on my balcony and watch the surfers or the stars for a while. Then I'd go to sleep in my big bed by myself. If I felt like it, I might think about the woman I hoped was out there somewhere waiting for me and get myself off. Then I'd clean up, go to sleep, and get up the next morning and do it all over again. My life is good, but since I've retired from the teams, it's boring. That was nice at first, but now, quite frankly, I'm lonely."

Dakota tried to ignore the bolt of lust that swept through her body at the image of Slade lying on a bed stroking himself until he exploded…but she was having a hard time, especially since she was practically sitting in his lap. "You were married, though, right?"

"If you want to call it that, yeah. I met Cynthia at the grocery store, of all places. We got along. But she absolutely couldn't take what I did for a living."

"What do you mean?" Dakota asked. "She knew you were a SEAL when she married you, right?"

"Yeah, but that doesn't mean she really understood what it meant to be married to one. I think she liked the *idea* of it better than the reality. I was gone on missions a lot. And I couldn't talk about what I did with her. Most of them were top secret. I guess she thought she'd be able to brag to her friends about how I was off saving the world or something, but instead all she could say was that I was at an undisclosed location for an indeterminate period of time doing something top secret."

"How'd it end? If you don't mind me asking."

"I don't mind at all. In fact, I love that you want to know more about me. It wasn't all that dramatic, really. I came home from a mission. She'd packed all her shit, and told me she didn't love me anymore and was moving on."

"Ouch," Dakota said, wincing. "What a bitch."

"No, we just weren't compatible," Slade told her, not seeming at all affected by the actions of his ex-wife. "I'd fallen out of love with her years before. I was just going through the motions. She married a guy who worked in IT for a local university within a year. Last I heard, they had two kids and had moved to Seattle."

"Do you miss her?"

"Not like you're thinking. I miss having someone to talk to. I miss the simple joy of making dinner with another human being. Of sitting on the couch, holding hands, watching TV."

"Yeah," Dakota said, knowing exactly what he meant.

"What about you?" Slade asked.

"What about me, what?"

"You haven't been married, right?"

"No." Dakota wasn't sure she wanted to talk about this. But fair was fair. "I dated a few men I thought I could be happy with, but ultimately decided that wasn't what I wanted."

"To be happy?" Slade asked.

"To settle," she said. "I enjoyed being with them, but didn't feel a bone-deep need to see them. I didn't think about them in the middle of the day. I wanted a relationship like my parents had. Even though it grossed me out, my dad was always hugging and kissing my mom. They held hands wherever they went. All the time. They weren't afraid to say 'I love you' to each other."

"What happened to your mom?"

Dakota shrugged. "Cancer. By the time they found it, it was too late to do anything other than give her drugs to make her comfortable. She was gone almost four months to the day she got the diagnosis. It's been about ten years now."

"I'm sorry, sweetheart."

Dakota swallowed hard. "Me too, but I'm sorrier for my dad. He lost the love of his life. His soul mate. He told me once, not long after Mom died, that they truly believed they'd been together in a past life."

"He believes in reincarnation?" Slade asked.

"I guess so, yeah. I can't say I don't believe. It was uncanny the things they knew about each other when they met. Mom would sometimes say stuff out of the blue that she literally shouldn't have known about him. It was really cool. My dad has been so strong since she died, but I can tell there's a part of him that's missing. Every day is a struggle for him." She turned in Slade's embrace and looked up at him. "That's what I want, and I didn't feel that with any of the men I dated. I didn't want to settle."

"You shouldn't settle," Slade told her softly, running his fingers over her cheek lightly. "My parents are still together, and even though I know they love each other, I don't think they have the passion that you've described your folks having."

"It's so rare, most people never find it."

Slade's eyes seemed to pierce into her soul as he gazed down at her. "I've seen that kind of passion with my friends and their wives. I want it. I'm willing to give up everything I have to get it too. I'd fight and kill for it."

"Slade," Dakota whispered, shaken by the truth she saw in his eyes.

He ignored her unspoken plea and continued. "I see and feel that same passion with you, Dakota. I don't know what's going to happen tomorrow, or even later today. But I know without a doubt that time is precious. Every second I get to spend with you is a second that I'm a better man because of it. Your arms around me as we drive down this fucking excuse for a road are what keep me going. Wanting to find Fourati and end the threat to you is what's driving me. Not the love of my country. Not wanting to keep random strangers safe. I'm an intense guy, I get that, but I haven't waited almost half a century for you to come along to waste time now."

He stopped speaking, but didn't drop his eyes from hers. The look on his face was both tender and fierce. Dakota knew without a doubt he meant every single word. There was nothing she could say that would come close to telling him how she felt, so she showed him instead.

Licking her lips nervously, she rose stiffly to her knees and turned to face him. The ground was dusty and small pebbles dug into her skin through her jeans, but she ignored the pain. She leaned toward him, suppressing a groan as her muscles complained, and kissed him.

Slade immediately wrapped his arms around her waist and hauled her into his body, easing them backwards until he was flat on the ground and she was lying on top of him. Dakota could feel every muscle move and flex under her as she settled over him. His legs spread and her own fell between them. She felt surrounded and protected.

She kissed him with all the fierce passion pent up in her soul. The passion she'd never felt for any other man poured out of her as if she'd turned a faucet on high. She couldn't get enough of his taste, his mouth on hers, the way his facial hair felt against her own smooth cheeks. She wanted to inhale him and burrow herself into his chest at the same time.

Slade let her take control of their kiss. He lay still under her as her hands roamed his chest, as she nibbled on his bottom lip, even as she moved to his neck and began to suck on the tender skin there. It wasn't until her hands began to wander south toward the button on his jeans that he moved.

Grasping her fingers in his own, he stopped her, then sat up, manhandling her until she was straddling his lap. His hands went to her ass and he hauled her against him so there wasn't an inch of space between them. Then his hands eased upward, under her jacket and shirt, until his chilly fingers touched the warm skin at her waist.

He didn't stop when she giggled and flinched from his cool touch, nor when she breathed in sharply as he skimmed the undersides of her breasts. One hand went to her chest, where he cupped a breast in his large hand, and the other pressed against her spine, encouraging her to arch into him.

Dakota tried to breathe, but was finding it difficult. She couldn't tear her eyes away from Slade's. She felt his thumb brush over her nipple in a gentle caress. She pressed both her pelvis and breast into him at the same time. Wanting more. Needing more.

"Fucking beautiful," Slade said softly. "I knew you'd be like this."

Dakota closed her eyes then, lost in the joy of his hands on her.

"Did you mark me?" he asked.

Her eyes flew open. "What?"

"Did you mark me?" he asked again calmly. "When you sucked on my neck. Did you give me a hickey?"

Dakota giggled and glanced down at the collar of his shirt. Sure enough, there was a small bruise on the side of his neck, right where everyone could see it. "No," she told him in a tone that she knew he'd be able to tell she was lying.

He smiled and his hand moved down the front of her body and came to rest at her waist. He leaned in and ran his nose up the side of her neck. Dakota tilted her head, giving him room. "You smell so good," he told her, before latching onto her neck and sucking...hard.

Dakota moaned at the sensation, then giggled at what he was doing. She should be appalled. They were acting like teenagers, but she couldn't deny that she wanted Slade to mark her just as she'd done to him. As he sucked, his tongue licked and caressed her skin, once again leaving goose-bumps in its wake. When he finally pulled back, Dakota rolled her eyes at the look of satisfaction on his face.

She wrinkled her nose at him. "It's huge, isn't it?"

"Yup," he said immediately. The look on his face was smug and proud.

"I can't believe we just did that."

The hand that had been at her back came up and he tenderly smoothed it over her head. "I can. And I'm hoping for more when we get to Goldfield tonight."

At the reminder of how far they still had to go, Dakota groaned.

"How about this?" Slade asked. "As incentive for you, when we get to Tonopah, you get another kiss. When we get to Goldfield, you get more of my hands."

Dakota's eyes glittered. Now he was talking. He was great incentive, that was for sure. "And when we get to San Diego?" she asked.

"You get whatever you want," Slade returned.

"I want it all," Dakota whispered. "I'm scared, but I want it all."

"It's yours," he said, all trace of teasing gone. "Anything you want. Everything I've got. It's all yours."

"I'm ready to continue," Dakota told him, still whispering.

"Okay." But instead of standing, Slade wrapped his arms around her and crushed her to him. They sat on the ground for several moments, soaking up the residual feelings of passion, respect, and trust that had been garnered over the short time they'd known each other.

Finally, Slade pulled back, kissed her lips hard, and stood. He helped Dakota stand on wobbly legs, and they walked hand in hand down the short incline back to his bike.

As they set off once more, Dakota hardly felt the bumps and aching muscles anymore. She'd made a decision on that small hill in the middle of nowhere, Nevada. She was going to take a chance with Slade Cutsinger. The biggest chance of her life. If they could make it through whatever Aziz had planned for her, she might just be rewarded with a love like her parents had.

She smiled all the way to Goldfield.

CHAPTER 7

"$\mathcal{I}$t doesn't look like much," Slade told Dakota honestly. They were standing in front of the old Goldfield Hotel in downtown Goldfield, Nevada. He'd thought the small town was going to be bigger. There was literally only one place to stay, the Sante Fe Motel and Saloon. He considered driving back up to Tonopah, but knew Dakota was done.

She'd held up better than he could've hoped after their short break. He'd pushed through to Tonopah, where they'd grabbed a quick lunch. She'd told him she was going to wait for her reward until they reached Goldfield.

As they'd driven south toward the infamous mining town, Slade didn't see hide nor hair of anyone suspicious. He was going to call Tex when they were settled for the night. He was cautiously optimistic that they were safe for the time being.

Dakota had been talking in his ear for the last thirty minutes about the haunted Goldfield Hotel. He hadn't even heard of the place before, but because of Dakota, he was now an expert.

"Come on, let's go look inside," Dakota urged, tugging on his hand.

He'd parked his Harley around the corner, trying to keep their location on the down-low for as long as possible. Slade grinned as he allowed Dakota to "lead" him toward the large glass windows at the front of the building. She wasn't so much leading him as he was holding her up as she walked.

She was hobbling along, and every step looked like it pained her something awful, but she still had a beautiful smile on her face and did her best to pretend nothing was wrong. She might not think she was tough, but Slade knew differently. The more time he spent with her, the more she reminded him of Caroline. Understated beauty, thinking of others first, and a spine of steel.

He'd been on plenty of missions in his lifetime where the women they'd been sent to rescue had completely fallen apart at the slightest hint of danger. Others had been so traumatized they couldn't even walk. It wasn't fair to compare some of the situations he'd been in to what Dakota was going through, but he had no doubt if the shit hit the fan, she'd stand tall and firm and claw her way out.

They stopped at one of the large windows on the front of the building and Dakota dropped his hand, limped to the glass, and cupped her hands to peer inside. Her voice was muffled as she excitedly reported on what she was seeing.

"Oh my gosh, Slade. It's amazing! It's like time stood still. There are two black leather circle couch things. I can just picture people sitting around and waiting for loved ones. And the front desk is still there. There are little mailbox slots behind it where I imagine the keys would sit. Oh! And a staircase with red carpet leading upward to something. I can't see what. And a set of double doors with what look like pineapples etched in the glass. It's dusty, yeah, but it's like the place is just waiting for the front doors to be thrown open and guests to stream through."

She picked up her head and smiled at him. "Wanna see?"

"Yeah, sweetheart, I do," Slade told her. He walked up behind her and leaned forward, trapping her body between his own and the glass window in front of them. He felt every inch of her body against his as he peered inside. To him, it looked like an old, rundown abandoned room, but he wasn't going to burst Dakota's bubble.

When he leaned back, she grabbed his hand again and headed down the sidewalk toward another window. She repeated the same routine, peering inside, giving him a rundown of what she saw. This time she included some other information as well.

"The owner won't let anyone inside because he's afraid the ghosts will hurt them. The *Ghost Adventures* crew went in there in two thousand seven or eight, and had a brick thrown at their heads! They even got it on film. It was creepy, but so cool. Man, I wish we could go inside!"

"You're kidding, right?" Slade asked her.

"What? No! That would be awesome!" Dakota gushed. "There's supposed to be a ghost of a woman named Elizabeth who was handcuffed to a radiator, and she had a baby and the father of the child killed them both. And there have been a few people who've committed suicide in there, and they're supposed to haunt the place too."

"Only you would be on the run from terrorists, but not scared of ghosts," Slade said, shaking his head.

Dakota turned to him with her hands on her hips and demanded, "Look me in the eye and tell me you wouldn't be fascinated to see proof of ghostly activity."

Slade leaned forward until she took a step back, trapping her against the glass window. He put his hands on either side of her head and got close enough that their noses were almost touching. "I've seen my share of ghostly activity, sweetheart. I can't say any of them were great experiences."

"You've seen ghosts?" she breathed, her eyes wide. Her hands came up to clutch his sides. "Seriously?"

"Unfortunately, yeah. You don't spend as much time as I have overseas and avoid it. Although the ones I saw were mostly women and children. I don't know how they were killed. Maybe it was their husbands, maybe it was by bombs. Regardless, seeing them wandering the streets at o-three-hundred, lost and calling for their loved ones, isn't something I'll ever forget or want to experience again."

"Wow, I guess not," Dakota said, petting his sides unconsciously.

"You seen enough? Ready to check into the hotel, rest for a while, then grab something to eat?"

She grimaced and nodded. "Thank you for indulging me. I've wanted to see this place for myself ever since I saw Zak and Nick experience that brick flying across the room. Hey, maybe we can watch that episode together when we get home...err...sometime."

Turning and wrapping his arm around Dakota's waist and helping her walk back toward his Harley, Slade smiled. "I'd love to watch it with you when we get home," he told her, purposely using the word home. He loved the thought of them having a home together.

They made it back to the motorcycle without encountering any specters, much to Dakota's disappointment and Slade's relief. He loved spending time with her but hated to see the pain cross her face as she gamely climbed on the back of his bike again. He needed to take care of that for her.

"Hang on, sweetheart. I'll have you in a tub full of hot water as soon as I can."

She squeezed his waist and Slade smiled as he drove the short distance to the motel. He would miss having her arms around him twenty-four seven when they got to San Diego and he parked his bike in favor of his car. It was amazing how quickly he'd gotten used to her weight and heat at his back and her arms locked around him.

The motel had eight rooms, which weren't any more impressive than the trailers in Rachel. But they were clean, and had bathtubs, which were Slade's most pressing requirements. He wanted to get Dakota soaking as soon as he could. She'd held up better than he thought she would, but that didn't mean she wasn't hurting.

He requested a room on the end, and parked his Harley around the corner where it'd be harder to be seen from the street. He opened the door and peeked in, making sure it was clear before gesturing for Dakota to enter.

"Why'd you do that?" she asked.

"Do what?"

"Look into the room. I thought for a second you were going to push me out of the way to get inside first," she teased.

Slade didn't even crack a smile. He shut the door behind them and turned to her. "I know people have been conditioned to think it's the gentlemanly thing to do to open doors and let ladies enter first, but that doesn't fly in my world."

"But *isn't* it the polite thing to do?" Dakota asked, dropping her backpack on the bed and tilting her head at him in question.

"It might be polite, but it's not safe," Slade told her. "If there's someone waiting in the room for us, I absolutely don't want *you* to be the first one through the door. I'll always be the one to check out the room before I deem it safe for you to enter. On missions, I saw way too many times where men shoved women and children through doors before they entered. If there was danger, they'd either use them as shields or run when they were shot as they walked inside. So no, sweetheart, I don't care if it makes me impolite. I won't allow you to go first in any situation where there could be the smallest chance you could get hurt or caught in any kind of crossfire."

"I hadn't ever thought about it that way," Dakota said, limping toward him. Then she put her arms around him and hugged him. Hard.

Automatically wrapping his own arms around her, Slade asked as they stood together in the small motel room, "What's this for?"

"For all those women and children you had to watch get hurt," she told him softly. "I'm sorry."

Slade's throat closed up and he pressed his lips together hard. The things he'd seen and done for his country while overseas were a part of his past. He'd dealt with them, talked with counselors and hadn't thought about them much after retiring. But he definitely could've used Dakota's sweet sympathy and concern for him when he'd returned from a few of those awful missions. "Thank you," he finally croaked.

They stood together for a long moment before Dakota said, "If I don't move, I'm gonna fall asleep right here standing up."

Appreciating her attempt at lightening the situation, Slade chuckled and pulled back, keeping his hands on her waist in support. "Come on. Let's get you in the tub. I'll get some pizza, since that's apparently the only choice at the bar, and we can eat when you're done. Yeah?"

"Sounds heavenly. You think this place has hot water?" Dakota joked.

"If it doesn't, we're heading back to Tonopah," Slade returned immediately.

"I was kidding."

"I wasn't," Slade told her. "I promised you a Jacuzzi, and while I have to renege on that, I'm not budging on the hot bath. You need it. We've got a long day of riding tomorrow and I want to make sure you'll be able to make it."

"I'll make it," Dakota told him stubbornly.

He ran his hand over her hair and said softly, "Let me rephrase then. I want to make sure you'll make it with the least amount of difficulty possible. And that'll happen easier if you can soak your muscles tonight. I've got some painkillers in my bag and between those and the hot water, you should be okay for tomorrow. So if this place doesn't have hot water, I'm hauling your ass back up to Tonopah to one of the chain hotels where I know there will be some."

He saw the tears form in her eyes and frowned. "What did I say to make you cry?" he asked.

"Nothing. It's just that...it's been a really long time since anyone has cared about me like that. When I'm sick, I deal with it myself. I once tripped in my apartment and hit my head on the counter. I passed out and woke up about fifteen minutes later with a pool of blood under my head. I just...it's nice not to be alone."

Slade's teeth ground together at the thought of her lying unconscious and bleeding and no one knowing she was hurt. He took in a big breath through his nose and kissed her forehead. "Get used to it," he ordered, before helping her sit on the side of the bed.

He went into the small bathroom and turned on the taps. Fortunately for them both, hot water immediately began filling the tub. Trying to gauge the temperature and making it as hot as he thought she could stand, Slade returned to the room to see Dakota lying on her back on the bed. Her legs were still hanging off the end of the mattress and she seemed to be asleep.

"You awake?"

"Yeah," she mumbled.

Slade had gotten a room with two beds, not wanting to be presumptuous, and Dakota hadn't even commented on the fact that he'd rented only one room or the number of beds. He'd been prepared to argue against them sleeping in different rooms because of the danger, but as it turned out, he didn't need to. She accepted the arrangements as if they didn't even bother her. And it was obvious they didn't.

"Come on, up you go," Slade said as he grabbed her hand and pulled her to a sitting position.

She groaned and twisted her head back and forth as if working out the kinks. "I take it the water is hot?" she asked.

"Yup. And it's calling your name."

"Is that what I hear? I thought the mumbling I heard was the water mocking me for overdoing it today."

Slade chuckled, but didn't respond. He merely pulled her upright and helped her into the bathroom. He left her sitting on the toilet seat and went back out to get her backpack. She hadn't moved by the time he'd returned. "You need help?"

She looked up then and asked coyly, "In taking off my clothes? Definitely."

He smiled at her teasing, but said seriously, "You shouldn't tease about something like that."

"Who said I was teasing?" she returned softly.

Taking another deep breath, which he found himself doing a lot lately, Slade said, "If I thought you were up to it, I'd have you naked and under me before you could blink. But as much as I want to see, and hold, your naked body, you need hot water more. And food. And I need to call my friend, find out what's been happening while I've been offline."

Dakota nodded. "You're right."

"Of course I am."

"But that doesn't mean I've forgotten what you promised me if I made it to Goldfield," she said with a grin.

"And what are you gonna take as your reward?" Slade asked, not able to help himself.

"I want to sleep with you."

He about choked, but she hurried to finish her thought, as if he might protest.

"I know you got two beds, and that was sweet of you. But what I want as my reward is to sleep next to you. I haven't felt as safe as I did today with you in a long time. I'm not saying I want to have sex...but I've been snuggled up to you all day. I just...I want that tonight, too."

"Then you'll have it," Slade told her, knowing he had a full night of torture ahead of him. Lying next to Dakota, holding her in his arms, was going to kill him. But it would be the sweetest kind of hell he could ever imagine. "Bathe. I'll be back with pizza. Take as much time as you want. I'll call Tex after we eat."

"Why don't you use the time away from me to call him? I'm sure you want your privacy."

"I've got nothing to hide from you, Dakota," Slade said. "You've got just as much right to know what's going on as I do...more so. Besides, I want to introduce you to him."

"You're going to tell him about us?"

"If you mean am I going to tell him that you're important to me and that I see us having a relationship when the threat against you is neutralized...the answer is yes."

"Oh...um...okay."

She was cute when she was flustered. Slade leaned down and kissed her on the lips before straightening. "Make sure you check the temperature before you get in. I don't want you burning yourself." Then he turned and left the small bathroom before he took her up on her offer to help remove her clothes. He shut the door behind him and headed for the exit to go see about getting them some dinner.

CHAPTER 8

*I*t was an hour and a half later. Slade was lying on the bed, Dakota snuggled up against him. Her head was resting on his shoulder, one arm flung across his belly, the other bent up against her body, and she was fingering the sleeve of his T-shirt. She'd rested in the tub until she was a prune—her words—then pulled on a pair of sweat-pants and a T-shirt. They'd eaten the meat lover's pizza Slade had gotten from the small bar/restaurant at the motel, and now it was time to talk to Tex.

"Are you sure that line is secure?" she asked when he picked up his phone.

"What do you know about secure phones?" Slade asked with a teasing glint in his eye.

Dakota rolled her own. "It's the twenty-first century, Slade, anyone who's ever watched TV or gone to the movies knows about secure phone lines."

He chuckled. "Right. And to answer your question, yes. My phone is definitely secure. It was issued by the Navy, and I guarantee Tex's lines are all more than safe."

"Can I ask something?"

"Of course."

"What makes a line secure? I mean, I know abstractly what it is, but not how it works."

"A secure line has end-to-end encryption. It prevents someone from tapping into the line and listening. As long as both speakers are using a secure line, whatever is said will stay between those two people."

"Hmmm, so it's kinda like talking in code. Your words get scrambled as you talk, then unscrambled so the other person can understand you."

"Basically, yeah," Slade told her, smiling at the simple way she put it.

"Cool."

"Yeah. Now, you got any more questions, or can I call Tex?"

Her cheeks flushed, but she said simply, "I'm done...for now."

Slade grinned. He enjoyed her curiosity more than he could say. The fact that she wasn't curled into a ball scared out of her mind said a lot about her inner fortitude. And he liked it.

Slade leaned over and kissed her on the forehead to reassure her before dialing Tex's number. He clicked on the speaker button so Dakota could hear the conversation. He was honest earlier when he'd told her he had nothing to hide from her.

"Hey, Tex."

"Cutter. Where in the hell have you been?" Tex exclaimed grumpily.

"I told you where I was going," Slade told him without rancor. "Unfortunately, I didn't think about the fact there might not be cell service out there in the desert."

"Did you find her? Tell me you found her."

"I found her."

"Thank God."

Something in his tone struck Slade as wrong. "Why? What's wrong?"

"Fourati knows where she is. You need to get on the move. Now."

"We're already on the move, and yeah, we figured he found her when one of his goons broke into the trailer we were occupying. But what I want to know is *how* Fourati found her. Tex, she was in the middle of fucking nowhere. There was no cell service and there are only about fifty people living in Rachel. How in the hell did he track her down? Was it me? Did I lead them there?"

"I'm not sure," Tex told him. "She doesn't have a cell?"

"No."

"Could her car have been tracked?"

"Not likely, she's been there quite a while. They would've been out to snatch her long before now if it was."

"Two-way radio? Using her credit cards? Has she been sending letters to anyone back home?"

534

Slade felt Dakota shake her head at his shoulder. "She says no."

There was a pause before Tex asked, "She there now?"

"I'm here," Dakota said in a soft voice. "It's nice to meet you, Tex. Slade has nothing but good things to say about you."

"Well, shit, he's lying then," Tex returned immediately with a hint of humor. "You all right, honey?"

Slade's lips twitched. How like Tex to be in the middle of an interrogation, but pause to make sure a woman was good.

"I'm okay. Although I think Slade's Harley is trying to kill me."

Tex chuckled. "Give it time. You'll get your biker legs in no time."

"No offense, but I don't think I *want* biker legs," Dakota told him.

"You stickin' with Cutter?" Tex asked her.

"If Cutter is Slade, then yeah, I'd like to," Dakota said, blushing.

Slade grinned. He loved that she basically just flat-out confessed to Tex that she liked him. It was one thing to admit it to him, it was a whole other thing to tell someone else.

"Cutter is Slade," Tex confirmed, then said, "so you'll be getting your biker legs. Now...you talk to anyone back home while you were hiding out in Rachel, Dakota? Call anyone? Write anyone a letter?"

"Not really. I sent postcards to my dad, but I gave them to tourists and they mailed them for me when they got home."

"It's how I figured out I needed to start in Vegas," Slade interjected. "Two people didn't wait until they got home to mail them."

"Hmmm. Did her dad say anyone else had visited?"

"A couple of people who claimed to be with the government. He sent them all on their way without talking with them though. He was extremely cautious with me and didn't say anything about Dakota until he was sure of who I was."

"So the question is, what information does Fourati have? Were his people in Vegas for months looking for her and somehow made the same connection to Rachel that you did, Cutter? Or did he somehow get to her dad after you were there. Could you have been followed? Maybe one of his people saw you in Vegas and trailed you."

"Damn...we've got too many unknowns," Slade said with a shake of his head.

The line was silent for a moment as everyone pondered the mystery.

"I honestly don't think he could've known about me," Slade mused. "I'd only gotten the assignment from Lambert recently. There's no reason for him to have me on his radar at all or to link me to Dakota."

"You might not be," Tex countered. "Maybe he's been tracking her somehow this whole time. It's possible he had things he needed to take care of in his organization and wasn't ready to claim her yet. But when those things were done, her time ran out and he sent someone to fetch her."

"Pat and Connie, the owners of the A'Le'Inn, have wi-fi," Dakota said into the silence. "I didn't get on last night because I didn't have access to a computer, but I've been on it before, searching San Diego news sites and stuff for information on the bombing. Could he have found me that way?"

"It's possible," Tex mused. "If he doesn't have a tracker on you, he knows that pretty much the only directions you might've gone from San Diego are north and east. You could've gone into Mexico, but that would've been a long shot. So he probably had his eyes out for use of your credit cards and any suspicious internet activity. I'm guessing your searches could've tipped him off. He could've traced the IP address to Rachel. It might have simply taken him two months to hit on the searches and pinpoint your location. Which was lucky for us."

"I'm sorry," Dakota whispered. "I honestly didn't think he'd be able to find me if I did searches for general news stories. I knew I'd been there too long, but I wanted to save up a bit more money before fleeing again."

"It's not your fault," Tex said, before Slade could reassure her. "You weren't using your credit cards, and stuck to cash, that was all good."

"I guess I know what not to do next time," she said softly.

"There isn't going to *be* a next time," Slade said fiercely, squeezing her shoulders tighter. He looked down into her eyes and willed her to believe him. To trust him to keep her safe.

"What're your plans, Cutter?" Tex asked, interrupting the emotional moment.

"To get to San Diego as soon as possible," Slade said.

"Dakota, you gonna be able to handle the bike that long?" Tex asked.

Before Dakota could answer, Slade grumbled, "You think I'd push her past what she can handle, Tex?"

"It's okay, I can—"

Tex interrupted. "Just making sure I've read the situation right."

"I got this," Slade told his friend.

"Good. Once you get home, then what?"

Slade could feel Dakota staring at him, but he ignored it for the moment. "I'm going to call Wolf tonight. I'm hoping we can crash in his basement. I don't want to go back to my place in case that fucker *has* clocked me."

"You gonna let Wolf in on what's happening?"

"Yeah. I'm not supposed to, but I don't give a shit. He has a right to know, since I need him to help me look after Dakota," Slade said.

"He'll have your six."

And he would. Slade knew that. It was why he didn't hesitate to consider his place to crash while they figured out how to get to Fourati.

"What about my dad? Is he safe?" Dakota asked.

"I'll talk to Wolf. See if he can get some eyes on him. If needed, we'll hide him until Fourati is out of the picture," Slade told her.

She stared up at him with big eyes. "You'd do that?"

"He's important to you, so of course I would. I'm not going to sit back and let anyone hurt him, because hurting him would hurt *you*. So yeah, Dakota, I'm going to do everything in my power to keep him safe."

"Thanks," she whispered, clearly overwhelmed.

"You'll let me know what you find out?" Slade asked Tex, but his eyes were still on Dakota.

"Of course. You'll have your phone on tomorrow?"

"Yeah, although since I'm on the bike, I won't be able to answer it."

"I'll leave a message if I need to," Tex reassured him. "Be careful out there. I don't have any information on the guys who showed up to escort Dakota to their boss. I'll see what I can do to find them, but if Fourati is even a little savvy with technology, and it seems he is, it might not be as easy as I'd like."

"I will. Last I knew one is probably on his way to lock up, at least until he bonds out, and any others were stranded in Rachel, but I wouldn't put it past them to steal a car."

"They'll definitely improvise," Tex said dryly. "Dakota, it was great to meet you. And for the record, you couldn't have found a better man. Cutter has saved my life more times than I could tell you. If my wife and children were in trouble, there's no one I'd want looking after them more than him."

"Okay," she whispered.

"Talk to you later," Tex said, then hung up.

Slade clicked off the phone and hugged Dakota. "Don't worry about the wi-fi thing. You've done so many things right over the last couple of months, I'm impressed with just how well you've been able to stay under the radar."

She sighed. "I knew being found was bound to happen sooner or later. I'm just glad it happened when you were there. They would've had me if you weren't."

"Look at me, sweetheart." Slade waited until she met his eyes before continuing. "If for some reason, everything gets FUBAR'd, I want you to—"

"FUBAR'd?" she asked before he could finish.

"Sorry. I keep forgetting you don't know much about the military. Fucked up beyond all repair. FUBAR."

She giggled, but gestured for him to continue.

"If something happens and you somehow end up with Fourati, do not, under any circumstances, give up. I don't care what he does or what happens. You. Do. Not. Give. Up. Don't antagonize him into hurting you. Don't take crazy chances to try to escape. Because I'm coming for you. I'll get the entire US Navy to come for you if that's what it takes. But I need you to hang on and do whatever you need to do to stay alive until I can get there. Okay?"

Dakota bit her lip. "I'm really not brave."

"Bullshit," Slade countered immediately. "You're one of the bravest women I know. You didn't sit at home and wring your hands when the shit hit the fan. You didn't hide out at your dad's house and cry. You didn't stay at your job when you knew the kids could be in danger. Even without having the expertise, you managed to evade capture for a fuck of a long time."

"I ran. That's not brave," Dakota insisted.

"The hell it's not. Sometimes running is the smartest thing you can do. You got out of the situation you were in and bought yourself some time. Where do you think you'd be if you hadn't?"

"Probably chained to a bed in a basement, forced to do whatever that jerkface wanted me to do," Dakota mumbled.

"Exactly." Slade's voice gentled. "I made you a promise to do whatever I could to keep you safe. And I will absolutely uphold that promise. But shit happens. Unfortunately, I know this better than a lot of people. All I'm asking is that if shit happens to *you*, to us, you try to stay calm. Don't antagonize Fourati, but don't be a doormat either. Whatever happens, you hold the fuck on until I can get you out of there. All right?"

"Okay. But you'll...hurry, won't you? I can fake being brave for a while, but eventually I'll break."

"I'll do everything in my power to get to you as soon as I can and not a second later."

Dakota nodded, then looked down at his chest. Her finger made little circles there and she asked, "So…Cutter?"

He grinned and decided to go with the PG version of his name for her. She definitely didn't need to know about his throat-cutting skills. "My last name."

"Ah. That makes sense," she said.

Slade relaxed muscles he didn't realize were tense when he felt her melt into him once more. "I'm going to call Wolf now, that okay?"

"Sure."

He dialed Wolf's number and waited as it rang.

"Hello?"

"Hey, Wolf. It's Cutter."

"When are you coming back?" the other SEAL asked without any other pleasantries.

"Why? You miss me?" Slade teased.

"Fuck yeah. That guy who took your place at work is slow as molasses. I swear to God, I had to show him how to change the margins on a Word document today. How in the hell he ever got a government admin job is beyond me. Please tell me you're coming back. Where the hell are you, anyway? I heard you went to Vegas?"

Slade could feel Dakota smiling against his shoulder. Wolf sounded extremely put out. It was funny as shit. "I'm hoping to be back in town tomorrow night."

"Thank fuck."

"But not at work yet. My plate is still full with the reason I took the leave of absence in the first place."

"Damn."

This time, Dakota giggled.

"This a bad time to talk?" Wolf asked, obviously hearing the quiet giggle.

Knowing the man was trying to be both professional and nosy at the same time made Slade's lips twitch. "Not at all. Dakota, meet Wolf. Wolf, Dakota."

"Hi," Dakota said softly. "It's nice to sorta meet you."

"Same, darlin'," Wolf said. "How come I'm gettin' the feelin' it might be longer before you're back at work than I'd like, Cutter?"

"Need a favor," Slade said without answering his friend's question.

"Name it," Wolf responded immediately.

"I need a place to crash with Dakota for a few days."

"You got it."

"I don't know how long we might be there," Slade warned.

"Basement's yours as long as you need it," Wolf said.

"Thanks. Appreciate it."

"You know I have your back no matter what. But I gotta ask…is whatever you're involved with gonna have blowback on my wife?"

Slade hesitated. He wanted to say no but the bottom line was, it was possible. Until Tex found out more information about how Fourati had tracked Dakota, he wasn't sure. "We can stay at a hotel," Slade told Wolf.

"That's not what I was implying and you know it, Cutter," Wolf said in a low, hard voice, very unlike the easygoing tone he'd been using thus far. "I wouldn't give a shit if Osama Bin Laden was hot on your heels, I'd still open my doors to you with open arms."

"Isn't he dead?" Dakota whispered after Wolf stopped speaking.

Slade didn't even crack a smile even though she was cute as shit.

"Oh my God," Wolf exclaimed. "It's her, isn't it?"

Slade knew what he meant. They'd had a few conversations since they'd known each other about how Wolf had known from the moment Caroline had helped save his life that she was the woman he wanted to spend the rest of his life with, even though he'd tried to deny it. He'd even gone on to say that it didn't matter how old Slade was…he'd know when he saw his own woman.

"Yeah."

"Fuckin' pleased for you, Cutter," Wolf told his friend. "And to answer your question, Dakota, Bin Laden *is* dead, a team of Navy SEALs killed his ass. But even if he was a ghost coming back from the grave to haunt Cutter, I'd still let the man next to you stay in my house. All I need is a head's up."

"That sounds fair," Dakota murmured under her breath. Then said, "I bet Wolf isn't afraid of ghosts. He'd explore the Goldfield Hotel with me."

"Sweetheart, I'm not afraid of ghosts, I'd just rather not have a brick thrown at my head by one," Slade told her, squeezing her waist at the same time.

He felt her smile against his chest, but cleared his throat and told his friend what was going on. "Remember that LAX bombing? Looks like it wasn't a one-time thing."

"Already know that, Cutter."

"Dakota was there. She can ID Aziz Fourati."

Wolf whistled low and long. "He know where she is?"

"Unknown."

"Okay. I'll talk with the team. We'll set up rotating patrols around the house. I'll send Caroline to Cheyenne's house. She needs some baby Taylor time anyway."

Slade swallowed hard and closed his eyes, trying to get his composure back. Wolf and him had always been friendly. They'd shot the shit about some of the non-top-secret aspects of his missions and Slade had always offered his advice when asked. But for the man to not only readily agree to let them stay at his house as a place for him and Dakota to lie low, but to arrange for his SEAL friends to keep watch over them and send his wife away without even seeming to blink was almost too much. Slade knew he'd missed being a part of a team, but he hadn't realized until right this moment how *much* he'd missed it.

"Thanks, Wolf. If it's any consolation, Tex is on this. I don't expect this to drag on. I'm gonna end it sooner rather than later."

"Anything that gets your ass back in the chair behind that desk, I'm one hundred percent behind," Wolf joked. "I can't stand your temp replacement another day longer than necessary."

"I'll let you know when we're close to home," Slade said.

"Great. I'll give you the code to the alarm when you call."

"Wolf?" Dakota piped up.

"Yeah, hon?"

"Thanks."

"I'm looking forward to meeting you. And when things settle down, I know my wife and her friends will descend upon you en masse. Just a friendly warning."

"Can't wait."

"Heh. You say that now. Take care of Cutter for me. The office can't run without him. Later." And like Tex, Wolf ended the phone call without waiting for Slade to sign off.

"I think your friends like you," Dakota told Slade after he'd leaned over and placed the phone on the table next to the bed.

He shrugged.

"What is it that you do in the office that Wolf can't seem to get over?"

"Paperwork."

"It's gotta be more than that," Dakota insisted. "He can't stand whoever is there now."

"I'm good at what I do," Slade told her without conceit. "I have a knack for it. Maybe it's because of the years I spent on the teams, or that I don't put up with bullshit from anyone. But I get stuff done. One way or another."

"I can see how that'd be important."

"Yeah. Now, can we stop talking about my job? You need to get some sleep. Tomorrow's gonna be a long day."

"Can I say one more thing?"

Slade sighed in mock exasperation, but gave Dakota a squeeze, making sure she knew he was teasing.

"I like that you've got people who'll have your back."

"You don't have that." It wasn't a question. If she did, Slade knew she'd be with them now.

"Not really. I mean, I'm good friends with the secretary at the school, and some of the teachers and I get together at times for dinner or drinks. But those are more work relationships, if you know what I mean."

"I do know what you mean," Slade told her.

"I guess you and those men tonight are work friends too, but it's different."

And it was. When you put your life in the hands of another, bonds were formed. Unbreakable ones. Throw in several life-or-death situations and friendships for life were the result. "Yeah," he said softly.

"I'm relieved that you found me," Dakota said in a small voice. "I'm glad it was you."

"Me too. Now close your eyes. Sleep," Slade ordered.

"You don't mind me sleeping like this?" she asked, tightening the arm over his belly, indicating her closeness.

"Fuck no. I want you right here. It about killed me to sit next to you in your car this morning and not touch you. You looked so uncomfortable in that seat."

"How long were you sitting there before I noticed?" Dakota asked.

"Two hours."

At that, her head popped off his shoulders and she peered at him in disbelief. "Two hours? How in the world did I sleep though you shutting the car door? And you were there the whole time?"

"You were obviously tired. And yeah, the whole two hours," Slade said.

"What did you do?"

"Watched you sleep." He didn't even pretend not to know what she was talking about. "I sat there for two hours and watched you breathing,

542

wishing I had the right to pull you into my arms. I also devised a plan to keep you safe."

"Wow," she said, and dropped her head back to his shoulder. "I had no idea."

"If I was a threat, you would've known I was there," Slade told her definitively. "But because I wasn't, your body allowed you to stay asleep."

"I think you're giving me way more credit than I deserve," Dakota said. "I'm not that astute. I'd probably sleep through Aziz bombing a hole through a door to get to me."

"Sure you are. You've been on the run for months. You trusted me from the get-go."

"That's true," she agreed.

"Now...will you please shut your eyes and get some sleep?"

"Are you gonna lie here and stare at me if I do?"

Slade grinned. She constantly surprised him with her offbeat humor. "Maybe."

"Whatever. But you have to drive. And maybe shoot at people tomorrow if they find us. You'd better get some sleep too."

He knew she was kidding, but he would absolutely use the pistol he had in his ankle holster to protect her if he had to. "Shhhhh," he murmured, running his hand over the back of her head in a gentle caress. When she sighed in contentment and burrowed farther into his shoulder, he did it again.

"That feels good," she whispered. "No one has touched my hair like that since my mom died."

Her words hurt his heart, so he continued running his hand from the top of her head all the way to the ends of her hair in a rhythmic motion.

Within minutes, she relaxed against him completely. Dead to the world, but safe in his embrace.

Slade lay under Dakota, his hand petting her as he tried to relax enough to sleep. All his senses seemed heightened, just as they were when he'd been on the teams and on a mission. And he *was* on a mission, the most important one of his life.

As if all the times he'd been sent overseas for his country were dress rehearsals for this moment, Slade went over as many scenarios as he could think of for what might happen in the next couple of days. And every single one ended with Aziz Fourati dead, and Dakota free to live her life without fear...with him.

CHAPTER 9

"*Y*ou doin' okay?" Slade asked for what seemed like the hundredth time that day.

Dakota was *not* okay. She'd been on the back of Slade's bike for eight hours and was more than ready to get off the stupid machine. Her cooter was numb and her feet had been tingling for the last hour or so. The only thing that worked in her favor was the weather. It wasn't as cold as it'd been in the higher elevations of Nevada and she was quite comfortable in the leather jacket Slade had gotten for her.

She'd woken up that morning, stiff and sore beyond belief, but also extremely comfortable. She and Slade had shifted in the night, and she'd been on her side in front of him by morning, his large body curled around hers. His arm had been around her waist, and as she'd shifted, she'd felt his very large morning erection pressing into her ass.

"Mornin'," he mumbled, even as his arm tightened and pulled her closer to him.

She didn't say a word, caught in that half-aware state between being asleep and awake. But Slade didn't seem to care that she didn't return his morning greeting. The hand at her waist moved and slipped under her T-shirt. He caressed her belly, which she tried to suck in, but she promptly forgot about any excess weight around her middle when his hand kept moving toward her breasts.

He shifted behind her, propping his head up on his free hand. The morning light made its way through the thin curtains, giving the room a weird orange glow. When Slade's fingers made contact with her bare breast, Dakota inhaled sharply, which pressed her chest into his questing hand.

Taking advantage, his fingers brushed over one of her nipples lightly. Dakota felt it immediately tighten, as if begging for Slade's touch. He didn't disappoint. He tested the weight of her breast in his hand for a moment, then his fingers went back to lazily playing with her now rock-hard nipple.

He continued for several moments, before Dakota finally squeaked, "Slade?"

"Shhhh, don't panic. I'm not going any further than this," he said softly. "I just need to touch you. I'll stop if you're uncomfortable. Just say the word."

Dakota shook her head, not liking the idea of him pulling away from her. "No. I'm okay with this. More than okay with it." She could feel his erection, fully engorged now, pulsing against her ass, and she couldn't help but push back against him when he pinched her nipple. The eroticism of his movements overwhelming.

"You like that," he said, and repeated the action on the other nipple this time.

Dakota nodded, speech beyond her at the moment.

Slade pulled back, and when she was about to open her mouth and complain about losing him, he put pressure on her hip and she turned so she was lying on her back next to him. His face was inches from her own and he murmured, "good morning" again, then bent his head and began what was the most amazing good morning of her life thus far.

He kissed her forehead, then her nose. He skipped her lips and tasted her earlobe. Then he licked the side of her neck and leisurely kissed every inch of skin he could reach. In the meantime, his fingers went back to tormenting her breasts, much more accessible to him now that she was lying on her back.

Dakota wasn't sure what to do with her own hands, so she grabbed the sheet at her hips and held on. It wasn't until Slade moved down her chest and sucked one of her nipples into his mouth through the cotton of her T-shirt that she found her voice.

"Slade, God, that feels so good. It's never felt like this before. Never."

One of her hands came up to rest on the back of his head, and she tried to press him back to her breast when he lifted his head and murmured, "For me either, sweetheart. I swear I could come just from just sucking on these beauties."

"Me too," she told him dazedly, but with a smile.

He kissed her nipple, which was now clearly visible through the damp material of her shirt, then commented, "Slept like a log."

"What?" Dakota's mind was slow catching up to what he was saying. She was still lost in the sensation of his mouth and fingers on her body.

"Haven't slept that good in a very long time. I usually wake up a couple times a night...remembering some of the shit I've seen in my life. Last night, didn't wake up once. Slept like a baby. All night."

His hand was still beneath her shirt and his thumb was gently brushing back and forth on the underside of one of her breasts. The morning had started out erotic, but morphed into a gentle intimacy. She'd never experienced anything like it, and knew she'd crave this from him from this moment forward.

Dakota brought a hand up to his face and lightly brushed her fingertips over his beard. It wasn't long, it wasn't short. It fit him. The thought raced through her mind about what it might feel like against the sensitive skin of her breasts or inner thighs, but she stopped her thoughts before they went any further. The thought of his beard between her legs as he feasted on her was too much for the moment.

"Last night was the first since the bombing I didn't dream of Aziz," she said softly.

"What do you dream?" Slade asked.

"What *don't* I dream?" Dakota countered. "He's raping me, shoving his tongue down my throat, laughing as he shoots a child in front of me; he taunts me, saying that no one will ever find me, that I'll have his babies, which he'll raise to hate women and be killers."

"Jesus," Slade breathed, then lowered his head until his nose nuzzled the skin behind her ear.

"But I didn't dream of *him* last night."

"What did you dream about?" Slade asked, his voice muffled.

"You. Us. This." The three words were simplistic, but had so much deeper meaning, Slade inhaled sharply.

"I want you," he said as he lifted his head. "In my life. In my bed. I want to be the reason you're safe in your dreams."

"It's crazy, but I want that too," Dakota whispered back, scared, but at the same time surer than she'd ever been of anything in her life.

They stared at each other for a long moment and Dakota thought they'd get down to the business of making love, when Slade stated, "We need to go."

She must've made a pathetic noise, because he smiled in resignation. "I know, sweetheart. There's nothing more I want to do right now than pull off your shirt and feast on your beautiful tits. Okay, yeah there is, I want to taste your very essence. Inhale it and let it mark me. You're going to ruin me for any other woman, and I can't fucking wait. I *want* you to ruin me. But we need to get to Wolf's tonight. It's the safest place for you, and I won't do anything that will put you in any more danger than you're already in. Because of that, instead of lying here with you in this bed and planting my cock so deep inside you we don't know where one of us ends and the other begins, I have to get some painkillers in you and we need to head south."

Dakota liked everything about Slade's words. She could feel how much she liked it, on her inner thighs. She was soaking wet for him and wanted his mouth and fingers on her. She wanted to watch, and feel, as he emptied himself inside her…but he was right. They had no idea where the men were who'd tracked her to Rachel or if Aziz had sent more to try to intercept them.

"Okay, Slade. But can we maybe…" She trailed off, suddenly unsure about what she'd been about to ask. It was too soon.

"What? You can ask me anything. You name it, I'll give it to you," Slade said softly.

"You can say no, or that you'll think about it, but do you think…once this craziness is done…could we come back up here? Maybe spend some time in Rachel as just us? Come back to Goldfield and do this again, but without the need to make a mad dash home?"

"Absolutely," Slade told her with a small smile. "We'll take a week or two, maybe find some of those geocache things. We'll make love before we go to sleep, and I'll wake you up with my tongue on your clit and we'll start every morning with more than a bit of petting. I'll make sure you're completely satisfied before I get up and find you a peppermint mocha and maple donut."

Dakota stared at him for a moment, the longing for the picture he'd put in her head almost a physical thing. Needing to diffuse not only the lust in her body, but the intimate situation as well, she teased, "Do you think Wolf will give you the time off? I'm not sure he's gonna want you to leave anytime soon after you go back to work."

Slade chuckled. His hand, which had been resting on her breast, slid down her belly and moved to her side, his thumb caressing her hipbone. "Wolf's not my boss, sweetheart. I've got a ton of vacation time saved up." He shrugged. "Never had anywhere I wanted to go to use it."

"Okay then."

"Okay then," he echoed. He leaned down and kissed her lightly on the lips, then pulled back and said, "I'd give you a proper good-morning kiss, but I've got morning breath. Go shower. I'll see if I can't rustle us up some food. You can eat while I shower and we'll get on the road."

"Sounds good."

"Don't get used to solo showers," he told her sternly, his eyes sparkling. "When we're the 'us' I want us to be, that I hope we'll be soon, I want to start my day with you naked, wet, and writhing in my arms."

Dakota shivered from head to toe at the carnality of his words. Yeah, she wanted that too. She didn't even have the words to respond.

"Go on. Don't forget to take the painkillers before you shower. Unfortunately, you're gonna need 'em by the end of the day." And with that, Slade squeezed her waist and climbed out of the bed.

Dakota stared at him as he walked leisurely to the chair he'd draped his clothes on last night. The muscles in his long legs flexing as he moved. He was wearing a pair of boxer briefs, which did nothing to hide his muscular ass from her eyes.

She continued to stare at Slade as he pulled up his jeans. He turned to her then, his pants unbuttoned, his erection plain to see straining against the denim. "Dakota? We really do need to get moving."

"I'm going, I'm going," she mumbled, not taking her eyes off him. Slade might be almost fifty, but he was literally the sexiest man she'd ever seen. He was still in shape from his days of being a SEAL. She figured he must still work out because the muscles in his chest and arms looked solid, and rippled when he moved.

He chuckled and bent over to grab his T-shirt. Suppressing a sigh, Dakota watched as he pulled it over his head.

"I'm going. I adore your eyes on me, love, but I'll never get my cock to relax enough to ride if you don't stop eye-fucking me."

Dakota blinked, then blushed. She looked away from him then and said, "Don't mind me. Go on, find me some coffee and sugar. I'll be ready when you return."

She heard him stalking back to the bed, and it dipped as he rested his hands on the mattress and leaned over. "Love this," he declared, and didn't make her ask what. "Love that you can't keep your eyes off me. Never had it. My ex never cared enough about me to look at me the way you do. As if you want to eat me alive. And so you know, the feeling's mutual. The only thing keeping me from fucking you until neither of us can move is the hairs on the back of my neck standing straight up. Those assholes are out there just waiting for me to fuck up. And it's not gonna happen. Shower. I'll be back." Then he gave her a hard, closed-mouth kiss on the lips and stalked out of the room.

The memory of the morning had kept her occupied for most of the ride out of Nevada. Riding on the back of the motorcycle had been scary when they'd hit the traffic of Las Vegas, but Slade had somehow sensed her nervousness and had reached back and patted her thigh and shouted, "I got this, love. Close your eyes and trust me."

And she had.

But the long stretch of interstate between the California border and the small military town of Barstow had been brutal. There wasn't much to look at and Dakota kept imagining Aziz's goons driving up from behind and ramming them.

By the time they were headed down the Cajon Pass and into San Bernardino, Dakota was way over the whole motorcycle thing. All she wanted to do was lie down and stretch out all the kinks in her body. She'd never think that sitting in a massage chair was cool ever again. Her brain felt as if it had been rattling around for days rather than hours.

"Dakota, you doin' okay?" Slade asked when they were passing by the city of Escondido.

She sighed and yelled back, "Fine!" The word came out more irritable than she'd wanted it to, but whatever. She couldn't take it back now.

"Twenty minutes, tops," he told her with a squeeze to her hands on his belly.

Dakota nodded, even though she knew Slade was totally lying to try to make the last part of the trip easier. She knew Escondido was about thirty miles from San Diego. She rested her helmet-clad head on Slade's back and closed her eyes, letting her mind wander as they covered the remaining miles to Wolf's house.

She should've been nervous to be back in the town where her apartment had burned down and she'd been threatened by Aziz, but at the moment, all she could think about was Slade.

She tried to analyze why she'd fallen for him as quickly as she had. It probably had to do with the fact that she was in danger...although when she'd first seen him, she hadn't *felt* as if she was in danger. She'd been in

Rachel for so long she'd become merely cautious, rather than freaked out by the people who entered the small restaurant/bar.

Maybe it was because she hadn't had sex in so long...years. But she didn't think that was why she'd fallen for Slade either. She enjoyed sex, but didn't *need* it. Before everything she owned had turned to ash, she'd had a vibrator in her bedside table that she'd used on a regular basis. It wasn't the same as having the intimacy a man provided, but it worked for her. So yeah, she didn't think she was attracted to Slade simply because he was hot.

There was just something about him that made her feel...grounded. Yes, she felt safe with him. Yes, she wanted him. But it was more. Dakota knew the man wasn't perfect. He'd lived almost half a century; he would certainly have his own quirks, idiosyncrasies, and ways of doing things that would probably drive her crazy, just as she wasn't perfect. But she'd easily overlook his quirks if the contentedness she felt around him continued.

Was she crazy for imagining herself spending the rest of her life with him? For even knowing after two days that she *wanted* to spend the rest of her life with him? Probably. Dakota grinned. But who the hell cared. It wasn't as if she was getting married anytime soon. But she'd been cautious enough in her life. It was time to be spontaneous and go with her heart rather than her head. If she was crazy, so was Slade. And being crazy together sounded a hell of a lot better than being crazy by herself for the rest of her life.

Her thoughts were brought to an abrupt halt when Dakota felt the machine between her legs rumble as it slowed. She opened her eyes and lifted her head to look around. She saw they were in a neighborhood with small, cute houses. Slade eventually pulled into the driveway of a gray house with a small front porch. There were two cars already parked in front. He stopped the Harley and turned off the engine.

Dakota sighed in relief. The next time Slade wanted her to ride this beast, she was at the very least requesting earplugs.

As he'd done every other time they'd stopped, Slade immediately hopped off the motorcycle and turned to her. He'd already unbuckled his helmet and reached for hers. Dakota let him remove it; she'd tried to tell him earlier that she was perfectly able to take care of herself, but he'd only smiled and said, "I know, but it pleases me to do it for you." How could she deny him when he'd said something so sweet?

He unbuckled her helmet and hung it alongside his own on one of the handlebars. Slade gently massaged her head, magically homing in on the places where the plastic had bitten into her skull. He'd tenderly braided her hair again that morning before they'd set off and she decided his fingers felt like magic.

"You ready?"

Dakota knew he meant was she ready to get off the bike. And she wasn't, because she knew it was going to hurt, just like it had every other time he'd stopped and made her walk around. But she simply nodded, trying to hide her discomfort and anxiety from him.

Apparently, she did a shit job, because he sighed and said, "I'm sorry, love. I know you hurt, but you did an amazing job today. I'm proud of you. If I didn't know better, I'd think you've been riding bikes all your life."

"Yeah well, did I forget to mention my dad is a member of the Hell's Angels and I've been riding with the gang since I was a small child? Silly me."

His lips twitched, but he didn't laugh. "Thank you for joking about this and trying to make me feel better. But it won't work. I feel like shit for hurting you."

Dakota could see that Slade really did feel awful. Her heart cracked even more. Besides her parents, no one had cared this much about her... ever. She laid her hand on his arm and said softly, "You didn't hurt me, Slade. I'm fine. Yeah, I'm sore, but it's not like we had a choice. You're helping me, and that's something I'll never forget. Ever."

"I'm not doing this for your gratitude," Slade bit out.

"I know you're not," she returned. "But you need to stop getting all pissed off every time I thank you. I know better than anyone what Aziz has in store for me because he explained it to me in great detail. I can't stop being thankful to you for helping me, so getting upset with me doesn't do either of us any good. But just because I'm grateful, doesn't mean I don't feel more for you. I didn't jump on the back of any other guy's motorcycle who came through Rachel, and believe me, there were plenty. I got on the back of *your* bike. So cool it with the macho bullcrap and if I say thank you, swallow hard and say you're welcome."

She probably wouldn't have snapped at him if she wasn't so tired and sore, but it had been a long two days and Dakota wanted nothing more than to get clean, then sleep. In that order. She wasn't in the mood to deal with Slade's crap.

"You're right. I'm sorry," he said immediately. "And you're welcome."

Dakota blinked. Well. All right then. She'd mentally tallied a strike against the man for not wanting her thanks, but had to erase it when he'd so easily and quickly apologized.

"Good."

"Now...you ready to stand?"

Dakota grimaced. "No." But she threw her leg over the bike and prepared to do it anyway.

As he'd done every other time, Slade's hands went to her waist and held her steady as she stood. It took a few moments for her to get her balance, as usual, and she stayed still in Slade's arms until she felt as if she could walk on her own.

"I'm ready," she told him after several moments went by without him moving back as he usually did.

"Fuck, you're gorgeous," Slade breathed.

Dakota snorted. "I'm sweaty, dirty, windblown, and walking as if I've got something stuck up my butt. I think you need glasses."

"You're sweaty, dirty, windblown, and walking funny, but I can see you clear as day, love. And what I see is an unpretentious woman who is in the middle of a fucked-up situation, doesn't own anything but what's in a beat-up old backpack, but who can still somehow embrace new experiences, be open to a relationship with a retired old Navy fart, and who doesn't complain even once about feeling like shit after an eight-hour bike ride."

"Uh...okay, whatever."

"And *you* need to learn to take a compliment," Slade said, grinning.

His smile did something to her insides. Dakota loved when he grinned. It made her belly do cartwheels, especially knowing he was smiling at *her*.

"Is my retired Navy fart ever going to help me walk inside so I can get that shower?" she asked cheekily.

In response, Slade leaned down and kissed her. It wasn't short, but it wasn't long either. His tongue swiped over her bottom lip and when she opened for him, it ducked inside, caressed her once, then retreated. Dakota swayed toward him when he pulled back, and blinked.

"Come on, love. Let's go meet Wolf—who's been watching us for the last five minutes—and whoever else he's got inside."

"Oh geez, he's been waiting for us to get inside?" Dakota asked, frowning. "How rude of us."

Slade didn't respond, but turned her so she was tucked up against his side, which she was thankful for because she wasn't sure she could walk on her own, and steered them toward a door off to the side of the house.

Ready or not, it looked like she was going to meet Slade's friends. Briefly glancing up at the heavens, Dakota sent a short prayer upwards. *Please let the craziness of my life end soon. I really want to be able to spend time with this man without the threat of a terrorist hanging over my head.*

CHAPTER 10

*I*t was an hour later and Dakota had showered, taken more pain pills, and was currently sitting curled against Slade's side on Wolf's couch as her current situation was discussed.

"So Fourati is American?" Wolf asked.

"Yeah, I'm almost positive," Dakota said.

"Damn," the SEAL swore, running his hand through his hair. "No wonder the government wasn't having any luck finding him. Not if they were looking for a foreigner. This makes tracking him down more difficult."

"I know," Slade agreed.

"And how'd you get involved in this again?" Cookie asked Slade. Cookie was a SEAL on Wolf's team, and who Slade worked with all the time. He'd come over at Wolf's request so they could talk about security for Dakota. The rest of the team would eventually be brought up to speed as well, but for now it was just the three men, and Dakota, talking.

"Can't say," Slade told him. "But the bottom line is that it's a matter of national security to take Fourati down. And not just because he's after Dakota. Though that's my main motivator at the moment."

"How come the papers didn't report on the fact you were the lone survivor of that blast?" Cookie asked, switching topics easily. "Does anyone else find that odd?"

"It's not odd," Dakota piped up. "I was scared, and even though I hoped

Aziz was dead, I wasn't sure. I waited a day or two to see a doctor about my arm, just to be safe. And his speech about me being the mother of his future children who he'd train to be terrorists was fresh in my mind. It had been absolute chaos both inside and outside the airport, and I just wanted to go home. I didn't tell anyone I had been in there, so the press simply didn't know."

Slade tightened his hold on Dakota and glared at Cookie. He didn't like that his question had disturbed her.

"That makes sense…but you knew about her being at the bombing, right?" Wolf asked, looking at Slade.

"Yeah, but not until recently. My…contact told me about her. Said recruitment videos online talked about her, and even had a picture of her from that day," Slade informed his friends, hating how Dakota's body tightened further at his words.

"So everyone in his network knows about her," Wolf concluded.

"Seems so," Slade agreed.

"So we need to find this Fourati guy and take him out before this goes any further," Cookie added.

"No," Slade disagreed. "*I* need to find this Fourati guy and take him out. You and your team, Wolf, have nothing to do with this. This is off the record, and you will *not* be involved beyond protecting her while I get things sorted here. I'm retired. It's why I was specifically asked to take care of this."

"That's bullshit and you know it," Wolf growled. "SEALs don't work alone. No fucking way. We're a team."

"This is unsanctioned. I can tell you this much though, the job came from the highest fucking levels of the government. You cannot be involved."

"But we *are* involved," Cookie argued.

"Maybe I should leave," Dakota said. "If you guys could get in trouble, I should just go."

"You're not going anywhere," Wolf said.

At the same time, Slade and Cookie said, "No."

Slade put his finger under Dakota's chin and forced her to look up at him. He hated the look of uncertainty and fear on her face. "I'm going to fix this for you, love. I'll take Fourati down and he won't hurt you again. Soon this'll be just another story we can tell our friends and family when we're old and decrepit. Got it?"

"But—"

"No. No buts about it. You're not going anywhere."

The look of fear was replaced by irritation. "You're annoying."

"I know. But I'm the annoying old Navy fart who is going to make it safe to rebuild and live your life...hopefully with me beside you every step of the way."

"Fine."

"Fine," he echoed. Then he turned to Wolf and Cookie. "Your job in this is to keep your eyes on Dakota when I can't."

"We were gonna do that anyway," Wolf told him. "But you need to—"

"No offense, but no. I don't want to involve any of you more than you already are. If it makes you feel better, however, I've got Tex on this."

"Fuck. Why didn't you say so in the first place?" Cookie asked. "If Tex is on this, Fourati is as good as captured. Me and Fiona will expect you and Dakota to come over for dinner next week." He grinned, the natural cockiness of a man who was that sure of his friend's success showing through loud and clear.

"Done."

Slade could feel Dakota's head whipping back and forth between him and his friends, and it made him smile. SEALs could be crass and uncouth sometimes, but the men in front of him had hearts of gold. "Caroline get settled over at Dude's place?"

Wolf nodded. "Yup."

"And you guys still don't want any kids...even when she's dying to spend time with their daughter?" Slade asked Wolf.

Wolf shook his head. "Caroline loves children, but neither of us really want our own." He shrugged. "It's hard to explain."

"No need," Slade reassured him. "Once upon a time, I wanted a household full of rug rats, but something deep inside me knew Cynthia wasn't the one to have them with." It was his turn to shrug now. "Now I'm too old to even think about it." He mock shuddered. "I'd be almost seventy by the time they got out of high school. Can you imagine?"

Wolf's eyes flicked to the woman at his side, and Slade stiffened. Shit, had he offended her? Did Dakota want kids? They hadn't known each other long enough to even have sex yet, much less talk about babies. Had he fucked up?

He turned to look down at Dakota, and found her staring off into space with a wistful look on her face.

"You okay, sweetheart? I hope I didn't say something that'll make you rethink spending the rest of your life with me," Slade asked somewhat nervously.

One side of her mouth tilted up into a smile. "No, Slade, you're fine. I'm not exactly a spring chicken myself. About twelve years ago, I talked with my mom about this very topic. I was considering in vitro fertilization. I was single, but was at a point in my life where I thought I'd either need to have a kid right then, or never have one." She looked away from him then and continued.

"But after talking with her about all that she went through with me, and hearing what she had to give up, I decided that being a single parent wasn't something I wanted to do. I loved my job and sometimes worked until it was dark out. It wouldn't be fair to a child to work those kinds of long hours, and it wouldn't be fair to slack off on my job so I could be home with a kid. Don't get me wrong, my mom wasn't upset that everything changed after she had me, but it just drove the point home that my life would be completely upended if I had a kid, and I wasn't sure I wanted to do that."

She looked back up at Slade. "So you can relax, you didn't offend me and I'm not going to expect you to be a dad at fifty."

"Thank god," he breathed, and leaned down and kissed her forehead.

"But I wouldn't object to snuggling with other people's babies," she went on, and looked at Wolf. "Your friends have kids?"

"Yup," Wolf told her. "Jessyka will love you forever if you take a shine to hers. She's got a houseful of them and is always looking for a sucker… err…babysitter."

Everyone laughed at Wolf's good-natured teasing.

"On that note…I need to talk to Tex, and Dakota's about done in," Slade told his friends. "You ready to crash, love?"

She nodded. "Definitely."

"Do you mind if I talk with my friends for a bit?" Slade asked. He didn't want to keep secrets from Dakota, but he also didn't want to needlessly worry her. He wanted to talk schedules and let Wolf and Cookie know what his immediate plans were and when he'd be away from the house.

"Of course not," Dakota told him. "You'll be…um," she blushed and blurted, "coming down later…right?"

Slade leaned in and nuzzled the skin behind her ear and whispered, "Yeah, love, I'll be down later. Save me room in bed, okay?"

She nodded and her blush deepened.

Wolf and Cookie were considerate enough to look away from them as they spoke. But since they were both smiling, Slade knew they'd heard the short conversation.

Slade helped Dakota stand, knowing she wouldn't be able to do so gracefully by herself. He'd gotten his stuff from the bike and put it and her backpack in the basement earlier. He needed to stop by his apartment and grab more clothes, and he needed to pick up some stuff at the store as well. But for tonight, they'd get by.

He walked her down the stairs—slowly, because the muscles in her thighs were obviously sore—and kissed her long and hard before heading back up to his friends.

The next hour was spent discussing the logistics of making sure Dakota stayed safe in the house, and what Slade's movements would be the next couple of days. When they were done, Slade tried once again to thank his friends. "I appreciate this. I could drag Dakota around with me, but I think it'd be safer for her if she stayed out of sight. If Fourati doesn't know she's back in town—which is a possibility, though unlikely—it's better for her to lay low."

"You're beginning to piss me off," Wolf stated flatly. "If this was happening to Caroline, Alabama, Fiona, or any of our women, you'd help in a heartbeat."

"Damn straight," Slade confirmed.

"We take care of our own," Cookie chimed in. "You might not've fought on our team, Cutter, but you're as much a part of it as we are."

"Thanks," Slade said. "Seriously."

"Again, no thanks necessary. The sooner we get your ass back in the office, the better," Wolf grumbled.

"The new guy still not working out?" Slade asked.

"He's an idiot. Had no clue how to set up a secure browser today. I walked by his desk and he was using fucking Google to search for something. I thought Hurt was going to lose his shit. Sent him home early and told him not to come back tomorrow if he didn't have his head out of his ass."

Slade smirked. Commander Hurt was pretty easygoing, but when it came to the men on the teams he was in charge of, he wouldn't stand for anything less than perfection. The lives of the SEALs literally depended on it. He knew Greg Lambert probably had the best of intentions, but he'd clearly sent the replacement without knowing how clueless the man was with administrative matters. He'd have to give Lambert shit the next time he talked to him.

Thinking of Wolf's team, or some of the other men he worked with on the base being put in a position of vulnerability because of an incompetent contractor, made Slade's eye twitch. He'd been gone less than a week, but he missed it. It was crazy; who would've ever thought he'd miss a desk job? But he *liked* working behind the scenes to keep the men on the front lines safe. Sometimes it was only a matter of making sure they had fresh batteries before they went on a mission, but even that could literally be life or death.

Yeah, he was old enough and experienced enough to realize the excitement that came with being on the teams was for the young and enthusiastic. He was past that point in his life, and the only thing he wanted was to do his part to keep his fellow SEALs safe and go home to a loving woman. To Dakota.

The thought made him smile.

"And with that, I'm out of here," Cookie said with a smirk. "I'll talk with Abe and the others and let them know what's up."

"Don't forget Dakota's dad. I wouldn't put it past Fourati to try to use him to get to her," Slade said as they all stood.

"On it. If nothing else, maybe Dakota can convince her old man to move in with Benny and Jess. I don't know how he feels about kids, but their brood would keep anyone busy. We give them shit all the time, but those kids are some of the most well-behaved children I've ever met. They'd love to have another adult around to entertain them."

"Sounds good," Slade told Cookie. "If you guys think it's necessary, we'll make it happen. I'll talk to Tex and see if he's heard anything about Mr. James being in danger."

"Good. Later," Cookie said, and after a chin lift, headed toward the kitchen and the side exit of the house.

"You gonna call Tex?" Wolf asked.

"Yeah."

"All right. I'll leave you to it. I'm headed upstairs. I'll turn on the alarm," Wolf told Slade. He'd already shown both him and Dakota how it worked and told them the code.

Slade nodded. "I'm gonna try to sneak out of bed in the morning and get some errands done early. I'd like Dakota to sleep in, but with the way she climbs all over me during the night, I'm not sure I'll succeed," he told Wolf with a grin.

"It's a great problem to have."

"That's for sure," Slade agreed. "I'll see you in the morning?"

"Yup. I got approval to skip PT tomorrow. I'll be hanging around here with your woman until you get back."

Slade sagged in relief. "Thanks."

Wolf waved away his gratitude.

"Oh, one more thing. You got a coffee shop around here? And a donut place?"

"Yeah, about three blocks away. Your woman have a hankering?"

"Oh yeah. Big-time addiction. She's been without her peppermint mochas for a while now. Figured she wouldn't mind a surprise in the morning."

"She's gonna fit in with our women just fine," Wolf told him. "I've tried to tell Ice that she can make coffee here, but she insists that it's just not the same."

The men grinned at each other in commiseration. Then Wolf lifted his chin at his friend and said, "Later."

"Later, Wolf."

As soon as the other man had disappeared up the stairs, Slade called Tex. As he waited for him to pick up, he marveled at how quickly his world had changed. A week ago, he hadn't even known Dakota. Now he was literally imagining how to rearrange his entire life to make her fit. Making plans to get up early just so he could stop by the coffee shop to pick up a peppermint mocha for her. But it was the realization that he was actually excited for what his future would bring that made him sigh in contentment.

He'd been living his life as if on autopilot. He did the same thing every day, ate the same food, saw the same people. No, chasing a terrorist wasn't exactly the shake-up he'd wanted in his life, but Dakota was. He knew without a doubt that every moment with her would be exciting, and he was filled with anticipation for that to begin now. All because of her.

"Cutter," Tex said as he answered the phone.

"Tex," Slade returned.

"You at Wolf's?" Tex asked, not beating around the bush.

"Yeah. Made it here a few hours ago. Cookie just left."

"I'm sending a tracker for Dakota," Tex informed him.

"I don't think—" Slade began, but Tex cut him off.

"It's necessary. Fiona didn't think she'd be kidnapped by sex slavers.

Benny didn't think he'd be conked over the head and his woman would have to give herself to his kidnapper. Melody didn't think—"

"Point made," Slade bit out, stopping Tex's tirade.

"They're earrings. Had a set made for a friend's kid. I think they're pretty kick-ass, myself. I'll also send along a few of the others so they can be placed in her clothes too, just in case. They won't get there for a couple days though."

"No problem. We'll be careful in the meantime. What did you find out about Fourati?"

"Not much. I tried doing a few searches for a blond guy in his twenties who showed interest in terrorist leanings, and came up blank. Either he's completely new to the terrorist business and extremely lucky, or he's incredibly smart."

"What else has been posted about Dakota?" Slade asked.

Tex hesitated, and Slade's stomach cramped. "He's escalating in his determination to find her. There are new pictures being posted almost every hour on the Dark Web. Recruitment posters about how Fourati's woman will be the salvation of Ansar al-Shari'a, and how the babies she'll bring to the cause will be celebrated and revered for years to come."

"What kind of pictures?" Slade bit out, ignoring the last part for the moment. Fourati could say whatever he wanted, it didn't mean it'd come true, but pictures were another thing.

"They look photoshopped to me," Tex said calmly. "Pictures of her wearing a traditional Tunisian outfit, bustier, silk pants, beige shawl. Standing side by side with a man whose face is blacked out. On her knees looking up at a man."

"Okay, so he's getting pictures from the Net and altering them."

"Right, except…" Tex's voice trailed off.

"Except what?" Slade asked impatiently.

"There's one, posted a couple of hours ago, of Dakota on the back of a motorcycle. It's captioned, "If you see this woman, take possession until the Ansar al-Shari'a ruler can claim her.""

"Fuck me," Slade said. "Can you tell where it was taken?"

"It's grainy, as if captured from far away," Tex said, not answering the question.

"Maybe it's not Dakota."

"It is, Cutter. It's your bike. I should know, I was there when you bought the damn thing. It's definitely her."

"So he's put out an all-points bulletin on her," Slade concluded.

"Looks that way," Tex said silently.

"I need to find this Fourati guy and shut down his communication channels." Slade told Tex something he already knew.

"Shutting those down will be easy. All it'll take is me hacking into the main site he's been using to communicate with his followers and posting a cease-and-desist order supposedly from him. I can get creative and word it in a way that any of his potential recruits will think it's Fourati. But he has to be neutralized in order for it to work, otherwise he'll just start a new site. But it's finding *him* that's the tricky part."

"What if I egged him on?" Slade asked.

"Use yourself as bait?" Tex asked.

"Yeah. By now, he has to know she's with me. And if he's even marginally good at searching, he'll figure out who I am. He'll want to get rid of me to be able to get his hands on her easier. Let's face it, if I go off the grid with her, no one will find us unless I want them to. But I really don't want to take Dakota away from her life. She doesn't deserve that. I'd rather take him out now so she can be free of all this bullshit. If I set myself up as an easy target, he'll come after me to get me out of the way, and I can take him down."

"Risky," Tex commented.

"Yeah, but what other choice do I have? I could pass him on the street and have no idea it was him. If I control the where and how we meet, I've at least got a shot of stopping him and making Dakota safe."

"And preventing another attack on US soil," Tex added.

Slade was silent for a moment before admitting, "It might make me an asshole, Tex, but I couldn't give a shit about that right now. He wants to make Dakota his sex slave. Get her pregnant and take her baby away from her. He wants to use her for whatever his own sick perversions are. That is *not* going to happen."

"You could use her to—"

"No," Slade said before Tex could finish. "She is not going to be bait. She's scared to death of this guy, Tex. I'm not going to put her through that, not even if it means we catch him tomorrow."

"Okay, it was just a suggestion," Tex said calmly.

"A shitty one."

"I'm missing something," Tex said, moving on. "I don't know what, but it's important. Be careful, Slade. I don't like this. My shit's-gonna-hit-the-fan meter is pegged."

"Agreed."

"I know you got shit to do, but don't let her out of your sight if you can help it," Tex told him.

"After I get some stuff done, I wasn't planning on it. A couple of days, max, then I'm connected to her hip. But work fast, Tex. Help me end this."

"I will. If I figure out what we're missing, I'll call. Later." Tex hung up, obviously more interested in continuing the search for Fourati than being polite.

Slade didn't take offense. He glanced at his watch. It was late, but he had one more call he had to make. It was even later on the East Coast, but he didn't give a fuck.

He dialed the special number he'd been given and waited.

"Lambert."

"It's Cutsinger."

"Have you found Fourati?" the former commander asked, not beating around the bush.

"Not yet. But I found the witness. She's under my protection now."

"Good. She tell you what he looked like?"

Slade proceeded to tell Greg Lambert everything Dakota had said about that day at the airport, including her description of Fourati. When he was done, Greg was silent for a long moment.

"So he's American," he finally said.

"Seems so, Sir."

"You know, I never thought I'd see the day when I'd be fighting to keep citizens of our own country from blowing each other up. Gang wars are one thing. Drugs, guns, emotions running high…they're all one thing. But the likes of people like Timothy McVeigh and Aziz Fourati, if that's even his name, are something else altogether. I'll never understand how someone can decide killing their own fellow citizens is the right and just thing to do."

Slade agreed with him, but didn't respond.

Greg sighed. "Okay. I'll run the description past the experts here. Tell them that I have a source who ferreted out the information. If I find anything new, I'll let you know. In the meantime, you need anything, let *me* know. I'm not going to tell you how to do your job, but it's possible the only way we'll catch this asshole is to use the witness to—"

Slade tuned the man out. Why in the fuck did everyone think the only way to catch Fourati was to put an innocent woman, who had already been through hell, in more danger?

He realized that Lambert had stopped talking and said woodenly, "I'll keep that under advisement, Sir." He didn't know what the fuck the man had proposed but if it involved Dakota, it wasn't happening.

"I expect you to remain professional," Greg warned, obviously picking up on the fact that Slade wasn't happy with his suggestion. "One of the reasons I reached out to you is because you're known to be levelheaded and not fall for every fucking damsel in distress you've been sent to help. I can make your replacement at the base a permanent one if you go off the rails."

"I don't give a fuck if you take me off this assignment," Slade said in a low, deadly voice. "I'm going to catch that motherfucker and end his miserable life if it's the last thing I do. But don't you *ever* threaten me again. You want to get me fired? Go for it. The replacement you arranged sucks. He'll have every SEAL team under Hurt's command killed within the year. But I'll be gone. I'll take Dakota and go so far undercover you'll never find either of us again, and you won't have a shot in hell of finding Fourati. I know about your wife, and I'm as sorry as I can be that you lost her to cancer, but that doesn't give you the right to be a dick when it comes to other innocent lives and any relationship I might have."

"Fuck. You're right, I apologize," Lambert said in a quiet tone. "Do what you need to do. I'm counting on you to get this done, Cutter. The country is. I didn't mean to imply that Ms. James' life is worth less than the hundreds or thousands of people who could die if Fourati follows through with his plans. But I still have nightmares about those killed on 9/11. I see the people jumping from the burning towers every time I close my eyes. I don't want to see it happen again. Not when I'm around to stop it."

"Understood," Slade said in a slightly less edgy voice. "I'll call again if I find out anything else."

"Be careful," Greg said softly.

"Always," Slade returned. "Later."

"Bye."

Slade hung up and forced himself to relax. The urge to see Dakota crawled through him all of a sudden. Done with making phone calls, Slade went to the basement door. He took one last look around the small house. The lights on the alarm system were lit, indicating it was on and armed. Nothing looked or sounded out of place. Satisfied that for the moment they were as safe as they could be, Slade quietly slipped through the door and headed down into the basement. To Dakota.

He stood by the queen-size bed for a long moment, absorbing all that was Dakota. She lay on her side, one arm outstretched as if reaching for him and the other tucked close to her chest. She was once again wearing a T-shirt. Slade couldn't see what else she had on because the covers were pulled up to her waist.

Wanting to be in bed next to her more than he wanted his next breath, Slade quickly stalked toward the bathroom. The sooner he changed and brushed his teeth, the sooner he could be where he needed to be.

Within minutes, Slade was slipping under the covers and snuggling into Dakota's warm body from behind. The minute his legs tangled with hers, he stifled a groan. Her legs were as bare as his. Lifting the sheet and peeking down at her, he saw she wore a shirt and a pair of white cotton panties, and that was it.

His cock immediately surged with blood, ready and willing to do what God intended for it to do. Slade gritted his teeth and ignored the discomfort of his body, concentrating instead on how amazing Dakota felt against him.

The second he wrapped his arm around her waist, she turned sleepily to face him.

"All's okay?" she slurred, obviously more asleep than awake. Her forehead rested against his chest, her arms curled up between them, and her legs tangled once more with his.

He was surrounded by her warmth and scent, and the way she so trustingly curled into him made Slade's heart fill with love.

He loved her. Every inch. He hadn't seen her naked. Hadn't had the privilege of making love with her yet. Didn't know her favorite color or even when her birthday was. But he didn't need all of that to know she was now the most important thing in his life. More important than his job, his home, his siblings, his friends. She was his everything.

"Shhhh," he whispered. "All's good. Sleep."

"'Kay," she mumbled, and he felt every muscle in her body sag in her sleep.

His erection was nestled between them, hard against her belly, but Slade hardly noticed. All he could think about was how right Dakota felt in his arms.

CHAPTER 11

*T*wo days later, Dakota thought she was going to go stir crazy. She hadn't been out of the house since she'd arrived with Slade and she was beginning to feel as if she were a prisoner. The thought made her feel guilty, as she knew Slade and Wolf were only trying to protect her, but it was driving her insane.

Slade had left that morning to do some super-secret SEAL thing. He wouldn't tell her what, had only kissed her on the forehead and told her he'd be back soon. Not only was she feeling claustrophobic being locked up for her protection, she was about to self-combust from horniness.

For two mornings in a row, she'd woken up with Slade's hands on her body. This morning she'd practically been orgasming before she'd fully woken up. Slade's hand was down the front of her panties and his fingers had been coated with her juices.

All it had taken was one look into his lust-filled dark eyes as he'd deliberately and expertly flicked her clit and she'd exploded. The second her thighs had started to tremble and she'd arched up in ecstasy, he'd prolonged her pleasure by easing one long finger inside her body and groaning at the way her muscles gripped him. Seeing his excitement and feeling the insistent stroking of his finger against her G-spot, she'd come again, wishing it was his cock deep inside her instead.

Then he'd blown her mind even more when he'd removed his hand from between her legs and immediately sucked the finger he'd had inside her into his mouth. His eyes had rolled back into his head and he'd groaned at her taste.

He'd met her gaze, said, "Fucking fantastic," and kissed her until she didn't know her name anymore. Between her own musky flavor on his tongue and the feel of his beard against her face, she'd almost come again. When he pulled back, she'd tried to return the favor, wanting to see him up close and personal, but he'd stopped her hand when it trailed down his stomach toward the erection she could feel against her leg, kissed her palm and told her that he had to go, but he'd take her up on her offer later. He'd promised that he had to wrap up one last thing and when he returned, he'd be able to spend more time with her. He would still be hunting Fourati, but could do that with Tex's help and not have to leave her alone as much. Then he'd left her in bed, sated and sleepy, and ordered her back to sleep.

As expected, Slade had been gone when she'd finally roused enough to get up, shower and wander up to the kitchen. But surprisingly, Caroline was there. She'd met the woman the night before when Wolf had stopped by with her in tow. Apparently, she'd convinced her husband that she'd be safe in her own house as long as he or one of the men on his team was with her.

And now this morning, Caroline was in the kitchen when she wandered upstairs, with another SEAL, whose name was Benny.

After warming up the peppermint mocha Slade had left for her, Benny informed her over a breakfast of cheese omelets and bacon that, if needed, her dad would be moving into his house with him and his wife. They'd make sure he was safe, comfortable, and entertained.

Dakota had almost burst into tears of relief and gratitude, but managed to hold them back. While her life had been turned upside down, she'd done her best to keep her dad out of it. But with Fourati still on the loose, Slade wasn't taking any chances that the terrorist would use him to get to her.

"What do you want to do today?" Caroline asked from across the table. They'd been getting to know each other over breakfast and Dakota liked the other woman. She was down-to-earth, not pretentious at all, and they'd really clicked. It was nice to talk to a woman about something other than teachers, Common Core, and testing for once.

Dakota shrugged. "No clue. I'm about TV'd out, board games aren't my thing, and I'm not much of a cook. I'm open to any ideas you guys have."

"We could play a prank on Wolf," Benny suggested, a grin on his face.

Caroline rolled her eyes. "I can't believe you guys are still on this practical joke kick. What's the latest?"

The smile on Benny's face didn't dim as he looked down at his phone and searched for something.

Dakota couldn't help but be entertained by Benny. There were times that morning when he'd seemed like an immature little boy, but when he'd answered his phone and spoke with Wolf, she saw another side of him. The dangerous side. Apparently, Slade had been concerned because Tex had called and said Fourati had posted on his recruiting Dark Web site that his wife would soon be giving her own speech to their followers, and Wolf had called to give Benny a head's up.

Dakota didn't like the sound of that, because if Aziz was talking about her, then he'd have to *have* her in order for her to give a speech. But Benny had reassured Wolf that Dakota was safe and they had no plans to leave the house.

The determination on Benny's face was easy to see. And it wiped the playful boy right off his persona. It made her relax a bit and understand that while he might joke and kid around about some things, he was still a badass Navy SEAL.

But now he was back to being the entertaining host, trying to find something to make her smile and not feel as if she were a prisoner in the house. Benny turned his phone toward Caroline first and explained through chuckles what she was seeing. "So you know the new guy sucks, right?"

Caroline nodded. "Uh, yeah, Wolf hasn't stopped bitching about him since Slade took his leave of absence."

"Right, well the guy might be a good mathematician, but he sucks at computers. Time and time again, we've had to explain shit to him that he should already know. It's gotten really old. So, Mozart and Cookie distracted him this morning, asking if he'd come help them with something in another office, and Dude and Abe sabotaged his computer. They hooked up smoke bombs to certain keys on his keyboard. Apparently, Dude had seen this done before but hadn't had a chance to try it out. He prepped one at home and switched it out with Zach's while he was being distracted."

"What am I looking at, Benny?" Caroline asked, tilting her head to the side as if that would help her understand the picture in front of her. Benny leaned forward and pointed to the screen as he spoke.

"Zach came back from the other room, mumbling about what assholes

Mozart and Cookie were, and sat down and began to type. Smoke immediately started pouring out of his keyboard. He panicked and pushed more keys, which made more smoke come out! Instead of doing the smart thing, and getting a fire extinguisher or calling for help, he began to smack at the keyboard like a little kid instead. This picture is of the entire area around his desk filled with smoke," Benny informed Caroline.

He scrolled through a few more pictures, still chuckling. "See? It just kept getting worse. We were all laughing so hard we couldn't even tell him to stop. I could barely hold my phone steady enough to get pictures. It got so bad, Hurt came out of his office, mumbling about how juvenile we all were, and grabbed the keyboard away from Zach, hauled it into the hallway still smoking and slammed the office door. It. Was. Hilarious."

"It doesn't look like Zach found it funny," Caroline observed, her lips twitching.

"That's 'cause he's an ass," Benny declared, then turned toward Dakota. "And a big baby. He glared at us all, said we were pathetic, and left the office in a huff. When I left to come over here and relieve Wolf, he still hadn't returned. I hate people who can't take a joke. Look, Dakota, tell me this isn't funny as shit."

Dakota took the phone Benny offered and grinned, excited to see the results of the prank. It sounded hilarious to her.

The first picture was of the back of a man sitting at a desk, smoke rising from the keyboard in front of him.

For some reason, the hair on the back of Dakota's neck stood up.

She used her finger to quickly scroll to the next picture. The smoke was thicker in that one, but the camera was closer to the man sitting at the desk. She scrolled again—and her breath caught in her throat as she stared at it.

"Hilarious, isn't it?" Benny asked, misconstruing her reaction.

"T-this is Zach?" Dakota asked. "The guy who took Slade's place in the office?"

"Yup. Doesn't look like an admin guy, does he?" Benny asked rhetorically. "He was transferred over from another office, not sure which one, but he's completely hopeless. Hurt is about ready to boot his ass out, and the hell with whoever it was who pulled strings and got him the job. Before the smoke-bomb incident, the commander begged Cutter to come in this morning and show the guy how to do some simple shit. Of course your man agreed. He's such a perfectionist when it comes to his shit, and he was afraid Zach was fucking it up ten ways to Sunday."

Benny got up to refill his coffee cup, missing the stricken look on Dakota's face.

Dakota tried to school her features. The last thing she wanted was to look panicked in front of Benny and Caroline. She was ninety percent sure that this Zach person and Aziz were one and the same, but she didn't want to jump the gun until she was positive.

She looked down at the pictures in front of her once again.

There was a lot of smoke obscuring the features of "Zach," but when she studied them again, she knew without a doubt the man who was doing Slade's job was none other than Aziz.

The man they'd been looking for had been right under their noses all along.

"Did you talk about me in the office? Say anything about why Slade was on a leave of absence?" Dakota asked Benny shakily.

"What do you mean?" he asked. His voice abruptly changed, from the happy-go-lucky tone he'd been using when talking about the joke they'd played on Zach to one of intense scrutiny.

Dakota had no doubt the SEALs were close-lipped about the missions they were sent on, but were they about other things? She knew how the employees had been in her office, they gossiped about lots of things, even sometimes confidential information they shouldn't be discussing.

"Hurt got us all together and told us Cutter was taking a leave of absence, but not why. We never discuss anything about our missions where we can be overheard by anyone without a need to know," Benny said, his tone serious now, his eyes watchful.

"Did anyone mention V-Vegas?" Dakota stammered.

Benny sat back down and leaned toward her, all business now, and looked into her eyes. "No. We might gossip like girls around each other, but we'd never share anything inappropriately. Our lives depend on secrecy What's wrong, Dakota? Talk to me."

Dakota had heard Slade talking with Tex enough to know they thought Aziz had to be somewhat good at technology, in order to track her to Rachel via her web searches, but what if that's not how he'd found her? What if he'd somehow been able to track *Slade*? They hadn't talked about the possibility of Slade's motorcycle having a tracker on it, or his supposedly secure phone, but Slade or Tex would've checked for that...right?

She shook her head and tried to control the panic trying to consume her. According to Wolf, Benny, and the other SEALs, they thought this

Zach person knew nothing about computers. Either Aziz had help posting his anti-American and pro-terrorist stuff online, or he was one hell of an actor when he was at the base.

"Zach is Aziz," she whispered.

To give Benny credit, he didn't tell her she didn't know what she was talking about, that she was mistaken. He stared at her for a long moment, eyes narrowed, his jaw ticking, then looked down at the phone in his hand.

Just as he began to dial, the window over the kitchen sink shattered.

The security alarm immediately began shrieking, the sound ear piercing and painful.

As if in slow motion, Dakota saw Benny slump bonelessly onto the table, his phone falling face up with only three numbers keyed in.

Dakota noticed Caroline's mouth open and assumed she screamed, although she couldn't hear it over the noise of the alarm, and she saw her new friend whip her head toward the now-broken window.

Dakota never heard the man who broke into the house by kicking in a window in the other room. Never heard him approach as he came up behind her.

She'd just stood, her chair falling over with the force of her leap upward, when an arm wrapped around her neck, holding her tightly against a rock-hard body, and a hand with a chloroform-soaked rag covered her nose and mouth.

The last thing Dakota saw before losing consciousness was Caroline desperately struggling with a masked man who was dragging her into the other room.

CHAPTER 12

Slade looked around his apartment, wanting to make sure he didn't need to come back for the foreseeable future. He'd grabbed enough clothes to last him for the time he needed to be gone. As long as he had a chance to do laundry, he'd be good. He picked up his extra pistol and ammo and even grabbed a couple of his knives.

When he'd been on the teams, he'd been known for his expertise with the latter. Both throwing and using them in hand-to-hand combat. It had been a while since he'd needed to use them, working a desk job wasn't exactly dangerous, but something told him that he should grab them today.

It was partly because he wanted to be prepared, but it was more than that. Tex's report of the video Fourati had posted about his "wife" making a statement soon wasn't sitting well. He knew Benny and Caroline were at the house with Dakota, but he still wouldn't be satisfied until he joined them and could see for himself that all was well.

His eyes swept over his living room, the weight of the knives in holsters at his ankles, small of his back, and at his waist comforting. Slade could see the waves lazily crashing against the shore as children played and their parents soaked in the sun. There were a few surfers in the water, crazy motherfuckers…it was damn cold outside, and he knew from experience the water was downright frigid.

He'd emptied his fridge and pantry of anything that would spoil and set the timers on a couple of lights to make it look like there was someone occupying the space. He didn't have a newspaper delivered, and he'd had his mail forwarded to Wolf's house. The other man said he'd make sure bills were paid and any important mail was taken care of if he needed to bug out with Dakota at any point.

Taking a deep breath, Slade took one last look around. He wanted Dakota *here*. In his space. In his kitchen. In his bed. She didn't have an apartment to go back to when the threat of Fourati was over, so he hoped he could convince her to move in with him. It was insane, their relationship was extremely new, but deep down, Slade didn't give a fuck. He wanted her with him.

Nodding, and telling himself to stop fucking around, Slade abruptly turned and left without a backward glance. Wolf was already headed home and said he'd meet him there. He locked his door and double-timed it to his Harley. He couldn't wait to see Dakota.

* * *

DAKOTA CAME AWAKE SLOWLY. She groaned and turned her head. Her eyes opened into slits and she stared groggily at the sight before her. Caroline was lying on the concrete floor beside her. She was wearing a long black robe that covered her from her neck to her toes.

Seeing her new friend wearing such an odd piece of clothing was all it took for Dakota to remember exactly what had happened. She sat up and winced. Her head felt weird, probably a residual effect of whatever had been used to knock her out.

She looked down at herself and gasped in shock. She wasn't wearing a long black robe like Caroline; instead, she was dressed in what looked like some sort of traditional Middle Eastern dress. No, not really a dress.

She slowly stood, keeping one hand on the wall for balance, and glanced down at herself again. She was wearing a pair of beige silk baggy pants. So baggy it almost looked like she was wearing a skirt. Dakota fingered the material. It was soft and luxurious, and creepy as all get out. Covering her breasts—her naked breasts, she realized—was a bustier. It was elaborately embroidered with red and gold thread and had different kinds of gold sovereigns sewn into the pattern. A matching necklace with over a dozen of the small coins was around her neck and when she turned her head, Dakota could tell she had in a pair of earrings as well.

In addition to the necklace and earrings, each arm had at least six bracelets of varying widths and metals, and when she shifted where she stood, Dakota could feel the heavy weight of more adornments around her ankles. She was barefoot, and the concrete was cold against her toes. There was a beige bolt of silk on the floor next to where she'd been lying as well.

Dakota shivered. This could not be good.

Caroline hadn't moved, and Dakota shuffled across the small space to her, each step making the metal on her body clink together melodically. She kneeled down next to her friend and gently shook her. Caroline didn't respond.

Dakota looked around the room again. There was no furniture. It was simply a small room, concrete floors, and a rectangular window. The walls were white and, even as she strained to hear something, completely silent.

There was nothing to use as a weapon. Nothing that would help them escape. Nothing at all. Beginning to panic now, Dakota shook Caroline again, harder this time.

"Come on, wake up," Dakota begged in a whisper. "I'm scared."

As if her words were all the other woman had been waiting for, her eyes popped open as though she'd been faking sleep the entire time. Dakota could see recognition in Caroline's eyes, and was more relieved than she could remember being in a really long time when Caroline pushed up to a sitting position, put a hand to her head as if it hurt, and asked, "What happened?"

"I'm not sure. I think someone shot Benny, then they must've drugged us. The guys will be looking for us, right?"

"Fuck. Benny? God, I hope he's okay. Jessyka is gonna freak. But yes, I know the guys are looking for us," Caroline said confidentially. "Not only that, they'll be here sooner rather than later because..." Her voice trailed off as if she realized something vitally important.

"What? Why?"

"Where are my clothes?" Caroline asked.

"I don't know. When I woke up, I was dressed in this," Dakota said, gesturing to her elaborate and fancy outfit. "And you were in that robe."

"I'm completely naked under this," Caroline told Dakota. She fingered her earlobes. "And they took my jewelry."

Dakota didn't want to be a bitch, but worrying about some earrings and stuff was the least of their problems at the moment. "Me too," she told the other woman. "I mean, I'm wearing earrings now, but not the diamond studs I had on when we were taken."

"No, you don't understand," Caroline said gravely. "I had trackers on. I always wear those earrings because there are location trackers in them. In my bra, too."

"What? Why?" Dakota asked in shock.

"Because being the wife of a Navy SEAL isn't all fun and games. Me and my friends have had way too many close calls, and our guys had Tex make them for us. That way, if we're ever in trouble, we can be found."

She hadn't really understood *wanting* to wear a tracker, until right this second. "So no one knows where we are. They aren't coming."

"They are," Caroline countered. "But it's going to take longer than I thought because none of our clothes or jewelry are here. If they didn't change our clothes here, the trackers won't help our guys find us."

"Oh crap. Caroline, why are we dressed so differently?" Dakota asked, suddenly not liking her outfit at all.

"I don't know, but I'm thinking it can't be good." Caroline said exactly what Dakota had been thinking.

"Nothing about this is good," Dakota agreed. "What are we going to do?"

"What we *aren't* going to do is sit around like helpless females," Caroline said sternly and stood, shaking out the long black robe as she did. The garment swam on her frame. It didn't have a hood, but no skin other than her neck, face, and hands could be seen. "Look, as shitty as it is, I've been in this kind of situation before."

Dakota stared at Caroline in disbelief. "You have?"

"Yeah. And one thing I learned—okay, two things I learned are that we gotta be brave, and we have to do what we can to help ourselves."

"But there's nothing in this room. Nothing at all," Dakota countered.

"I see that," Caroline groused, wrinkling her nose as she looked around. Her eyes came back to Dakota's. "But *we're* in this room. We have to be ready for anything. I'm assuming Aziz is behind our little vacation."

Dakota nodded. "I'm so sorry. He's obsessed with me." A thought occurred to her. "Oh no."

"What?"

"He wants me to be his wife, to get me pregnant so I have a baby he can raise to be a terrorist."

"Fuck," Caroline whispered. "Are you wearing a wedding outfit?"

Dakota gulped and confirmed, "I think so."

Caroline grabbed her arm and leaned in, urgency clear in her tone. "Do you know my story?"

Not understanding, Dakota merely shook her head.

"Okay, we don't have a lot of time, but suffice it to say, I went through a lot of shit, but I got out of it, and we will both get out of this. Matthew and Slade will be coming for us. We have to hang on for them, and we have to be smart and help them find us if given the opportunity."

"I don't understand."

"One thing I learned is that assholes like to taunt our men. They like to show off the fact that they got one over on the SEALs. I don't know what's going to happen, but if Aziz dressed you up like that, he's probably going to want to record your so-called wedding for his followers. And that means a video. And that means he'll probably put it online so he can show you off."

Dakota shivered. She didn't want to be on film and she *definitely* didn't want to marry Aziz. She closed her eyes in despair for a moment, then squared her shoulders. If Caroline wasn't panicking, she wouldn't either. "What's the plan?"

Not knowing how long they had until someone came to get them, Caroline spoke quickly. Giving Dakota a brief history of what had happened to her and what she'd done to try to help Wolf find her. Neither of the women knew what Aziz's plan was, but they wanted to be ready for anything.

By the time the door opened and two men entered, they had a plan... of sorts. They'd been able to look out the window and make some observations about where they might be. They might not have a physical weapon, but they had their brains. Neither knew what curve balls would be thrown their way, but Dakota felt better knowing she wasn't going to simply cower in a corner and cry. She might not make it out alive, but she certainly wouldn't go down without a fight either.

* * *

SLADE PULLED up to Wolf's house, and the hair on the back of his neck immediately stood up. He whipped off his helmet and ran to the kitchen door. Wolf was in the middle of his kitchen crouched by Benny, who was lying on his back on the tan tile, unmoving.

"What the fuck?" Slade bit out, joining Wolf at his teammate's side.

"Dart," Wolf told him, motioning to the needle lying next to the unconscious SEAL.

Without a word, Slade stood and left the room. He searched Wolf's house from top to bottom, calling out for both Caroline and Dakota. He had hoped the women were hiding somewhere, but by the time he got back to the kitchen, he knew his greatest fear had been realized.

"How in the fuck did this happen?" he asked, running a hand through his hair in agitation. He'd failed Dakota. He'd told her nothing would happen to her. That she'd be safe. That Fourati wouldn't get his hands on her. And he'd been wrong on all counts.

"Window over the sink is broken. My guess is that whoever shot Benny, did so through it. His phone was lying on the table, the first three numbers of my cell punched in."

"Why didn't the alarm go off?" Slade asked, pissed off.

"It did," Wolf replied in a tone that said he was barely keeping his shit together. "But my motherfucking override code was punched in. It's why I wasn't notified."

"Who knows your code?"

"The team. Caroline. And you and Dakota. That's it."

"There has to be someone else," Slade insisted.

"There isn't," Wolf told him.

"What about the neighbors?" Slade asked. "Wouldn't they have called the cops?"

"Not necessarily. Sometimes Caroline doesn't get to the code fast enough to shut it off. The neighbors used to call the cops when it first happened, but they've learned not to by now."

"Fuck," Slade swore.

"Whatever happened, the women were incapacitated quickly. I've taught Ice self-defense. She wouldn't go quietly. She knows better. I'm calling Tex." Wolf clicked some buttons on his cell and brought it up to his ear.

Something Slade had seen when he'd been frantically searching the house clicked in his brain, and he rushed out of the kitchen to the front hallway.

There on the floor were two piles of clothes and accessories.

He recognized the jeans and T-shirt he'd bought Dakota the day before. She'd been so pleased with his choices of clothing for her. Slade heard Wolf come up behind him and say, "God *damn* it. Pick up, Tex. Dammit, pick up."

Slade looked down at the clothes the woman he loved had most likely put on that morning and felt his heart encase in ice. They'd stripped her. Taken all her clothes off and left them on the floor. They had plenty of time to do it too, especially since apparently, no one had alerted the cops. He had no idea why they'd removed her clothes. To rape her? To taunt him? Any semblance of the man he'd become after getting out of the teams, any softness he'd built up as a result of being away from the death and destruction men could do to one another, disappeared. All that was left was the highly trained killer the Navy had created.

Slade knew Dakota was probably hurt. Not only that, but Fourati had touched what was his, he knew that without a doubt. He'd been determined to kill the man before, but now the outcome of their meeting was a certainty. Fourati would fucking die. The pile of clothing before him was the catalyst.

"Tex? Wolf. Track Caroline now," the other man ordered tersely.

Seconds passed, but they seemed like hours to both men.

Slade's jaw ticked as he continued to stare at the piles of clothes on the floor. He tried to block out the thoughts of what Dakota was going through, but couldn't. Slade had seen too many broken women after they'd been in the hands of terrorists. He'd see too many rape victims staring into space, shells of their former selves. The thought of his Dakota being that way was abhorrent. The hate in his soul bubbled and festered.

"She's there in the house," Tex said through the phone speaker.

"No, she's not. We checked," Wolf bit out.

"All of the trackers are showing her location right there," Tex insisted. "What the fuck is going on?"

Without answering his friend, Wolf kneeled next to his wife's clothing and, using only his index finger, separated each item. Shirt, pants, underwear, bra...and on the bottom were her wedding ring set, a necklace she always wore, and a pair of earrings.

"They're here," Wolf said, standing up but still looking down at his wife's belongings. "All her trackers are here. How in the fuck did they know about them?" Wolf asked in an eerie tone. It was almost calm, but Slade and Tex could hear the absolute fury behind it.

Instead of answering, Tex asked Slade, "You get Dakota's trackers yet, Cutter?"

"No. But it wouldn't fucking matter if I did, because those fuckers took off not only every piece of clothing, but her jewelry as well. In case we're not making this clear, they stripped our women of every fucking thing they were wearing before they left this house. You need to get on your computer, hack into every fucking satellite, computer, and phone in a sixty-mile radius and fucking find them. Now!" His voice had risen with each progressive word until he was shouting the last.

"Fuck, I need to call Lambert," Slade added. "I know this job was supposed to be unsanctioned, but I swear to Christ if he doesn't get the VP and president involved, he'll be sorry."

"I'm on this," Tex reassured Slade. "*I'll* call Lambert."

"This isn't your job," Slade told his friend.

"Maybe, maybe not. But I gave your name to Lambert in the first place. I'll call and fill him in on what's going on and make sure you have all the assistance you need to find Caroline and Dakota."

"Fuck," Slade repeated, not sure he could come up with anything more coherent at the moment.

"If it makes you feel any better, Fourati doesn't want to kill Dakota," Tex tried to reassure his friend.

"Yeah," Slade said bitterly. "He only wants to rape her over and over until she's pregnant."

"And he might not want to hurt Dakota, but he doesn't give a shit about Ice. Why did he take her too?" Wolf added.

Both men could hear Tex's fingers clicking on the keys of his computer in the background. The sound was usually comforting, but at the moment it was anything but. Not when their women were in the wind.

"Call me back the second you have anything," Wolf ordered. "I gotta check on Benny. I've already called for an ambulance."

"What happened to Benny?" Tex barked. "Goddamn. What the *fuck* is going on?"

"That's what *we* want to know," Wolf said, then relented. "I found Benny facedown on my kitchen table, a dart in his neck."

"I'll be in contact," Tex said, and ended the connection.

Wolf and Slade looked at each other for a long moment. As if they'd worked together for years, the men turned at the same time and headed back through the living room to the kitchen.

They both noticed the broken window, obviously where entry was made into the house, but ignored it; not that it mattered now. They needed to get medical help for Benny and they needed to gather the team.

Slade thought about how Lambert had said the mission was to be a solo one and frowned. He'd definitely blown that to hell and back.

Screw it. He'd already told Wolf and some of the other guys most of the story. He needed as much help as he could get right now. Besides, it wasn't just Dakota on the line. Caroline was involved up to her neck right now too. There was no way Wolf's men would sit back and do nothing.

Slade didn't care if Lambert refused to pay him a dime. Nothing mattered but Dakota. He'd end the threat of Aziz Fourati to the American public, but more important, he'd end the threat to his woman.

Slade fingered the knife strapped to his waist absently as he kneeled down next to Benny. Fourati was going to get an up close and personal lesson on why Slade's nickname was Cutter. His knife would be the last thing the man ever thought about…as it severed his carotid artery and his blood spilled on the ground.

CHAPTER 13

*D*akota stood silent and still, eyes full of tears she refused to shed, and prayed for all she was worth.

Two men had come to collect her and Caroline, and they hadn't been gentle about it. Both women had struggled and strained against their captors' holds, with no luck. When Caroline had kneed one guy in the balls, her effort hampered by the voluminous folds of the robe she was wearing, he'd backhanded her so hard she'd stumbled backward and fell on her ass.

Seeing her new friend fall, Dakota lost it and fought for all *she* was worth, trying to gouge out the eyes of the man holding her. But he'd avoided her fingers and had turned, ramming her forehead against the nearest wall. She'd seen stars and had lost any advantage she might've had.

Both she and Caroline had been brought into another room, where Dakota saw Aziz for the first time since that awful day at the airport.

The man she knew as Aziz Fourati was definitely the same person the SEALs knew as Zach, she'd recognized him immediately in Benny's pictures. She had no idea how in the world he'd gotten a job as a contractor for the Navy, or passed the background checks, but ultimately it didn't matter. He had, and now she was back in his clutches.

Dakota shivered in fear. All of her nightmares were coming true, but she wasn't dreaming this time. Slade wasn't there to kiss her awake, to hold her tightly and tell her everything would be okay. Thoughts of Slade bolstered her. She remembered what Caroline had said. She had to keep it together so she could help Slade and his friends find her. That was the ultimate goal.

"Ah, beautiful Dakota, it's so good to see you again. Your wedding outfit is absolutely stunning," Aziz said. The man holding her stopped in front of Aziz so she had no choice but to look at him.

"I wish I could say it's good to see *you* again," she retorted snarkily.

He made a tsking noise, as if she were a recalcitrant child rather than a grown woman. "I was so hoping you'd come to your senses. I gave you time to think about what your destiny was and to come to terms with it. I'm disappointed that you're still fighting it, fighting me. You *will* become my wife today. You *will* have my children. And you *will* stop defying me. Those three things I guarantee you."

Dakota fought down the urge to throw up. She raised her chin and spat at him. The spittle didn't quite make its mark, but the feelings behind it definitely did.

The amused look on his face disappeared and Dakota got a glimpse of the killer she'd seen in the airport all those weeks ago.

"Your intended doesn't have many manners," someone said from behind her.

Aziz curled his lip in derision at her. "She will. Take a seat, my bride," he ordered in a gruff tone.

Dakota had no intention of doing anything he said, but she didn't have a choice. The man behind her manhandled her over to a chair and forced her to sit. He then held her down while two other men quickly zip-tied her ankles to the legs.

Her heart beat overtime in her chest. She really didn't like the feeling of being tied and helpless in Aziz's presence. At least if she was sitting, he couldn't rape her...could he? She glanced to her right and saw Caroline being held between two men. Each had hold of an arm and had wrenched it upward so she was standing awkwardly on her tiptoes. Dakota could see a bruise forming on her cheek where she'd been hit, and the small mark made her stomach clench in concern. They'd stuffed a piece of fabric into her mouth and taped her lips together. The noises she was making were muffled and weak.

Seeing Caroline helpless and in pain, hurt. She had to remember that it wasn't just her in this situation. No matter how often Slade had told her she was brave, at that moment, Dakota didn't feel brave. But strangely, having Caroline there with her made her feel better. If she'd been by herself, she would've been completely freaking out. She was scared shitless, there was no doubt about that, but she made a vow that she wasn't going to calmly do whatever Aziz said. She couldn't. The longer she could drag whatever this was out, the longer Slade and his friends had to find her and Caroline. She could take what he dished out.

"Here's what's going to happen," Aziz said, his calm demeanor once more at the forefront. "We're going to have a wedding ceremony. You'll sit there calmly and answer affirmatively when prompted. If you say or do *anything* that gives the impression you don't want to become my bride, you'll regret it."

"I won't marry you," Dakota said with less force than she wanted, tugging at her arms which were being held down by the two men who had restrained her ankles to the chair. "This is insane. *You're* insane."

Aziz didn't respond to her comment, but shook his head as if disappointed. "You don't want to make me angry, my bride."

"Why not? What are you going to do? Hit me? Blow up the building? Rape me? You're going to do the last anyway. Go ahead. Do it. If you wanted a docile wife, you picked the wrong woman."

"I was kind of hoping you'd be this way," Aziz said strangely. "I knew you had passion and spunk when I saw you in the airport. I watched you for a while, you know," he said conversationally. "I decided you were there at the exact time I was for a reason. To be mine. I followed you, making sure I didn't make a move until you were in my web. You tried to think of something to do that would stop the inevitable. It was brave of you, but too little too late, I'm afraid."

Dakota looked at him in horror. He'd followed her in the airport? He'd waited to take hostages until he knew he could take her too?

Wanting to think about anything but what he was saying, Dakota looked around. The men in the room with them were a mixture of American and Middle Eastern. They obviously knew Aziz wasn't Tunisian, but didn't care. They all looked to be in their late teens or twenties. Aziz was wearing what looked like something a traditional Tunisian would wear. Some sort of long shirt which went all the way down to his knees. It had a deep vee in front and he had on a maroon silk shirt under it. His pants were also maroon. If she wasn't mistaken, the same embroidery pattern on his long shirt was on her own clothing. He wore a pair of pointed leather slippers and a close-fitting red cap on his head made of what looked like felt, with a black tassel hanging from it.

Dakota's breaths came short and fast. Aziz also looked like he was dressed for a wedding. It wasn't that she'd thought he was bluffing earlier, but now that she'd had a moment to think about what he'd said and take in what he was wearing, it was obvious he really did want to marry her right this minute. Aziz wouldn't ever pass for a Middle Eastern man, no matter what he was wearing. The government had simply assumed he was, based on his website and posts. She flinched when he began speaking again.

"There will be a time when I'll encourage your passion. A time when I'll crave your fingernails in my skin. It'll only make my taking of you all the more…exciting. But, alas, today is not that day. Today I need you to be a proper Arabic wife. It's important to show my recruits that I am in charge of all things, including the woman who will be my wife." He stepped closer and knelt at her feet. His hands went to her thighs and he slowly but surely pushed them apart.

Dakota tried with all her strength to keep her legs together, but she was no match for Aziz's strength. His hands squeezed her thighs with enough pressure to make her wince, but she controlled it and didn't give him any outward sign that he was hurting her.

He smiled, a scary, wide expression that made Dakota shiver in revulsion.

"Your name is now Anoushka," he informed her. "It means lovely or gracious. From here on out, that is what I will call you and that is what you will call yourself. You will never answer to your heathen American name again. Your new life starts right now, Anoushka. You will be the revered wife of the leader of Ansar al-Shari'a. You will learn how to please and serve me. Everyone and everything you've known is now a thing of the past."

"I will never serve you," Dakota told him. "You can rape me, beat me, and lock me up, but when you least expect it, I'll stab you in the back. You'll never be able to drop your guard because I'll do anything possible to take *you* down."

"Such a pity," Aziz said without a trace of worry in his tone. "I mean, do you really think you, a mere woman, can take down a chosen one such as myself?"

"I'm not scared of you," Dakota said. "And you're no more a chosen one than I am."

"Will you cooperate for our wedding ceremony?" Aziz asked as if she hadn't spoken.

"Never," she vowed.

"Pity," Aziz repeated, shrugging. He squeezed her legs once more, hard enough that Dakota did wince that time, and smiled. He stood and motioned to one of the men standing against the wall.

"Not even if you're beaten?" he asked.

As soon as the last word left his mouth, the man he'd gestured to turned sideways and kicked out at her with the bottom of his foot. It made contact with her knee and Dakota shrieked in pain. It felt as if he'd broken something, or at the very least tore a tendon. She'd never felt such pain before in her life. For a moment, all she could think about was the radiating waves of agony from her leg. She forgot where she was and forgot Aziz had even asked her a question.

"Will you cooperate for our wedding ceremony? Aziz asked again.

The tears Dakota had been holding back fell down her cheeks, but she shook her head at him in defiance.

Aziz nodded at the man again, and he once again kicked her in the knee. The same knee.

Black spots crept into her vision and Dakota thought she was going to pass out. Welcomed the black void in fact. Aziz reached forward and grabbed hold of one of her nipples through the bustier, and twisted. Dakota struggled against the men who were holding her arms and tried to turn away from Aziz. His fingers pinched harder as he leaned toward her and put his face inches from her own.

"I can do this all night until you agree," he warned.

Even though the pain was worse than anything she'd ever experienced in her life, Dakota glared up at Aziz and panted, "I can take whatever you dish out. I will never marry you!" She hoped she sounded brave and strong rather than desperate and on the verge of giving in to whatever he wanted.

At her words, Aziz abruptly let go of her nipple. He stood in front of her, his hands clasped behind his back. One side of his mouth quirked up into a lopsided grin and he said, "That's what I thought you'd say. My woman is strong."

Dakota kept her eyes on his and refused to look down at her chest to see if her nipple was still attached. It was throbbing and literally felt as if he'd ripped it off. She breathed through the pain and tried to remember to be brave. Caroline had said she needed to be strong, and dammit, she was trying.

Aziz gestured behind him again—and this time the men who had been holding a squirming Caroline came forward with her between them.

Dakota's eyes widened. What was Aziz planning now?

"Since I knew you would endure whatever I did to you, I made sure to have a plan B," Aziz said. He walked over to a small table Dakota hadn't noticed before now. He stood in front of it so she couldn't see what lie on top. His back was to her, contemplating whatever was on the table top, and asked once more, "Will you cooperate for our wedding ceremony?"

"No," Dakota whispered, truly afraid now.

Without another word, Aziz picked something up from the table and turned. But instead of heading for her, he went to Caroline.

In horror, Dakota watched as he grabbed the hair at the back of Caroline's head and tilted it backward. She tried to kick and lash out, but a fourth man knelt behind her and wrapped both his arms around her knees, effectively hobbling her.

Holding the knife he'd picked up from the table, Aziz put it against Caroline's throat. He turned to stare straight at Dakota while slowly drawing the knife downward. The robe the other woman was wearing slit as easily as if Aziz was cutting a piece of aged and tender beef.

When he was done, Caroline stood exposed from her neck to her knees. She was completely naked under the garment and her body was now on full display for everyone in the room.

Dakota strained against both the hold of the men and the bindings around her ankles. Suddenly her knee didn't hurt at all anymore. He was going to hurt Caroline because of her. "Stop it!" she ordered breathlessly.

"I can't wait to sink inside your lush body, Anoushka. You will provide me with many hours of enjoyment. However, I am not a greedy leader. Once you carry the heir to Ansar al-Shari'a, I am willing to allow my most trusted and brave warriors to share in the bounty I have been given." Aziz's beady blue eyes met her own. "I see you understand. I like to share, my bride. I have no problem watching as each and every man who vows loyalty to me and our cause takes a turn with you."

"No," Dakota said in a voice barely audible. His words were too much to bear.

"Yes, Anoushka. Your only job from here on out is to please and obey me. In all things. You will go to your knees in my presence, you will allow me to take you whenever and wherever I want. You will spread your legs for anyone I give you to, willingly. You will not struggle when I want to film myself filling your body with the gift of life. And if you don't? I think

I'll keep this one around to make sure you understand what will happen if you disobey me."

Aziz let go of Caroline's hair and ran the tip of the knife between her breasts once more, a slim line of blood welling up in its wake.

"No. Stop it!" Dakota ordered, once again struggling to escape the grasp of the men next to her. "This is insane!"

"Will you cooperate for our wedding ceremony?" Aziz asked once again.

Dakota knew Aziz wasn't kidding. He knew she'd continue to refuse him no matter what he did to *her*. She'd rather die than marry him. But there was no way she'd be able to sit there and watch him torture someone else. He would keep Caroline around if only as a means to an end...namely, Dakota doing whatever depraved thing he wanted.

Apparently deciding she hadn't answered soon enough, Aziz went back to the table and put down the knife and picked up something else. He took the few steps back to Caroline.

"Wait, please stop!" Dakota begged.

Aziz ignored her and held up a small pair of needle-nose pliers. He grinned a sadistic grin then turned to Caroline once more.

"I'll cooperate," Dakota yelled desperately. "I'll marry you! I'll say whatever you want me to, just leave her alone!" she went on, trying to make him step away from Caroline. The other woman had already been through too much at the hands of another evil man. There was no way Dakota was going to make her go through anything like that ever again. Not if she could prevent it.

Without moving away from Caroline, Aziz turned his head toward her. "Ah, Anoushka, those are the words I want to hear. But how do I know you mean them?" He moved the pliers toward Caroline once more and her screech of fright was easy to hear through the gag.

"You knew I wouldn't let you hurt anyone else on my behalf. Let her go and let's get this over with," Dakota said as calmly as she could. She couldn't look at Caroline's face anymore, but out of the corner of her eye she saw the other woman shaking her head desperately. Dakota didn't know if she was saying no to the pain Aziz wanted to inflict on her or to her words. But it didn't matter. Aziz would torture Caroline until Dakota did what he wanted anyway. She would spare her friend the pain.

Dakota knew good and well Aziz wasn't going to let Caroline go after he married her. He'd flat-out told her he was going to keep the other woman around to use as incentive if he wanted her to do something. And she'd do whatever he said. She could handle pain, but she couldn't handle him hurting Caroline because of her refusals.

Aziz let go of Caroline and stepped back. He handed the pliers to one of his cronies and walked back to Dakota.

She held his eyes, hating him with everything she had.

"You've made me a very happy man, Anoushka," Aziz told her in what could've been a tender tone. "A word of warning, just to make sure you understand, if you do *anything* to bring dishonor to our wedding ceremony, I won't hesitate to pause and show little Ice over there what pain truly is."

"I understand," Dakota told him, not even questioning how he knew Caroline's nickname. He knew everything else about her and the SEALs, why wouldn't he know that too? She might have to marry Aziz, but she hadn't lost hope that Slade and his friends would find them. She just wished they'd do so before her wedding night. They had to.

If Aziz violated her, Dakota knew she'd never be the same again. Oh sure, she'd survive it, but something inside her would die. She'd never feel clean again and would forever lose her chance to belong to Slade.

I'm trying to be strong, she silently told the man who meant everything to her, *but I don't know if I can do this. Please, come get me.*

CHAPTER 14

Slade paced back and forth in Wolf's living room as they waited for Tex to get back to them. Benny was at the hospital. He'd still been completely out when he'd been taken away by the ambulance. His heartbeat was strong and the paramedics seemed to think he'd been drugged, not poisoned, as a result. They'd have to wait for whatever had been used to knock him out to wear off before they could get any information about what had happened right before the women were taken.

The other men on Wolf's team had assembled. Abe, Cookie, and Dude were in the kitchen. Mozart, the sixth man on the team, was holed up with the women and children. None of the men were going to risk anyone else being put into the line of fire. Even though Slade knew Mozart wanted to be with them, helping to rescue Caroline and Dakota and catch whoever had shot Benny, they all knew the other women and kids were just as important right now. The last thing they wanted was Fourati getting ahold of them too.

Commander Hurt was dealing with the police and keeping the authorities away so the SEALs could plan. He was a good man, one who knew when to bend the rules and to look the other way.

Slade didn't give a shit who was involved at this point. As far as he was concerned, the more the merrier. These men had been through this too many times to count. Their women had been in danger one too many times. Slade needed their expertise as warriors, and husbands, to help get

Dakota back. If he got in trouble with Greg Lambert, so be it. He was just so frustrated with the entire situation. All he wanted was Dakota, and Caroline, back safe and unhurt.

His phone rang and Slade answered immediately, putting it on speaker so everyone could hear the conversation.

"Cutsinger."

"It's Tex." He didn't wait for acknowledgement. "There's a new video being streamed. It's live."

Slade gestured wildly at Wolf and the man ran into another room and came back with a laptop.

"I've sent everyone a link to the URL. I'm not sure how stable or secure the site is, but for as long as it's up, I'm recording it."

Slade didn't respond, just watched impatiently as Wolf brought up his email, then clicked on the link Tex sent.

The room fell silent as what they were seeing sank in.

Dakota was sitting in a chair, some sort of beige silk shawl around her shoulders and head. Sitting in front of her, with his back to the camera, was a man. He also had a shawl over his head and shoulders. Not one inch of his skin or hair was visible to the camera.

Dude commented, "He's being very careful to keep his identity a secret."

"There's no way to tell what he looks like from this angle," Abe agreed.

Slade ground his teeth together and clenched his fists at his side. He didn't give a shit about Fourati at the moment. All his attention was on Dakota. She looked at the face of the man sitting in front of her, her back ramrod straight, and didn't move a muscle. Someone in the background was speaking, probably in Arabic, but Slade didn't hear any of it. He tried to figure out what Dakota was thinking instead.

She looked scared...and pissed. Seeing how angry she was made him relax a fraction. If she was upset, then she wasn't broken...yet.

"Where's Caroline?" Wolf asked no one in particular as the video continued. The camera didn't waver, as if it was on a tripod or some other sturdy surface.

Slade had no idea what a traditional Tunisian wedding ceremony was like, but when someone off camera began to speak in English, he figured it wasn't this.

"Do you, Anoushka, take Aziz Fourati as your husband? Do you promise to obey and follow his every command? Will you defend him over all others, even give your life for him and the cause of Ansar Al-Shari'a?"

"Yes," Dakota said immediately.

Slade frowned. Why had she agreed so easily? What had Fourati done to her to make her so compliant?

The voice off camera continued. "Do you promise your womb to the Ansar al-Shari'a cause? Will you freely and willingly take your husband's sacred fluid into your body to create the next supreme ruler?"

"Yes," Dakota said again.

Slade saw her flinch this time, but she kept eye contact with the man in front of her.

"Aziz, the woman in front of you is now yours to do with what you want. Yours to punish, yours to praise, yours to worship. She will give the cause their next leader and we will praise this day for years to come. This is the beginning of Ansar al-Shari'a's reign of supremacy. So it shall be."

The man sitting in front of Dakota bowed his head, then kneeled on the floor in front of Dakota. He did something they couldn't see because of the angle of the camera, and Slade wanted to reach through the computer screen and snatch Dakota away from him when her lip curled in disgust at whatever he was doing.

The voice off camera then began to speak in Arabic once more. The man Dakota had apparently just married moved sideways out of range without once turning his face to the camera.

The person speaking in the background went silent and the camera zoomed in on Dakota. She glanced to her left, winced again, then looked back at the camera. Then she began to speak. Her voice was flat and had no intonation whatsoever. It was obvious she was reading something held up in front of her, off camera, word for word.

MY NAME IS ANOUSHKA FOURATI. My husband, Aziz Fourati, is the leader, chosen by God, of Ansar al-Shari'a. I am honored to have been chosen to carry his offspring, the future of our movement. God willing, this child will be born to all of us in due haste. In the meantime, carry on the fight. Do not let the heathens of this country lead you astray. Our time is coming. We need more soldiers. I am willing to die for my husband, for my God, and for Ansar al-Shari'a. Are you? Will you ascend to heaven to be with our God, or will you spend the rest of eternity in the pits of hell with the other citizens of this country who don't believe? Stay tuned for more instructions. Long live Aziz Fourati.

DAKOTA REMAINED SEATED, her legs apart, her hands gripping the arms of the chair she was sitting in. Her face blank of all emotion. The last thing Slade saw before the screen went blank was Dakota's eyes looking off to the left of the camera once more, her head nodding once.

"What the ever-loving fuck?" Wolf exclaimed. "Where's Ice? Did we just watch Cutter's woman marry that asshole Fourati? Tex, you better have something," he finished in a cold, hard voice.

"I'm sending a copy of the video to all of you now," Tex answered.

"And?" Slade asked. "Where are they? Did you trace the feed?"

"It's untraceable," Tex said reluctantly. "They've got a really good tech person."

"Tex, *you're* a really fucking good tech person," Cookie said. "I can't believe you can't get a lead on this guy."

"Tex," Slade said softly with desperation in his tone. "We've got nothing. No tracker. Fourati made sure of that. We don't even have a picture of this guy. All we know is that he's blond and American. We need more. You *have* to find him."

"I'm trying," Tex told his old friend. "Swear to Christ, I'm trying."

"She just married him," Slade whispered. "He's going to rape her. I don't know how he's controlling her, but if we don't get there, fucking soon, he's going to hurt the woman I love. She won't be the same if he gets his hands on her."

"I don't have a definitive trace," Tex said, all business, "but I do know it's coming from your area. The signal is bouncing around like crazy, but it's pinging off all local towers and servers. He's not far. One, he didn't have time to get that far away, and two, he has to have an inside connection to you guys. He wouldn't have known about the trackers if he didn't."

Relieved now that Tex seemed to have his head back in the game, Slade sat back and listened as he spoke with Wolf and the rest of the guys.

"He'd need to use local power to be able to broadcast. The kind of thing he's doing can't be done with a simple modem. The camera set up they have is more sophisticated than a simple cell phone and broadcasting via Facebook Live. And wherever they are, it's not in the middle of nowhere," Tex said, talking more to himself than anyone else.

"The room they were in was concrete," Cookie added.

"And what about her clothes? Those aren't exactly found in the local Walmart. Maybe they were special ordered," Abe suggested.

"Yeah," Tex nodded enthusiastically. "I'll do a search for online orders of traditional Tunisian clothing."

"The camera equipment isn't shit either," Wolf noted. "The video almost sounded and looked professional."

"Got it," Tex said. "I'll look for purchases of video stuff too. Maybe we'll get lucky."

"We don't have a choice," Slade said. "We *have* to get lucky."

"Tex, we're going to review the footage. See if anything stands out. Can you take out the voices and see if there's any background noise that will help point us to their location? Vehicles, boats, planes, fucking birds, *anything*," Wolf said.

"Will do," Tex agreed. "I'll see if I can pick up anyone else talking behind the scenes as well. Sometimes people whisper behind the camera, thinking they can't be heard. I'll also see if I can pinpoint who else was watching the feed. Maybe some of his recruits have information and we can backtrack to Fourati through them. Later."

Slade clicked off the phone.

Wolf immediately sat on the couch with his laptop. "You guys remember when Ice gave us a huge hint as to where she was being held when the asshole who took her filmed a beating he gave her? She might've talked to Dakota and it's possible she did the same."

"Yeah, Caroline talked about gulls and boats, which led us to look near the coast. Dakota is smart, she could've done that too," Dude said softly.

The men gathered around the laptop, eager to watch and listen to the video again to see what clues they could find in Dakota's speech. At this point, it was all they had to go on.

Thirty minutes later, and twenty-two replays of the footage, Slade couldn't take it any longer. He'd been holding on to his composure by the skin of his teeth, but if he heard his Dakota call herself Anoushka Fourati one more time, he was gonna fucking lose it.

He pushed up from the couch and paced in agitation. "There's nothing there. She was reading word for word from a script. She was too scared to say anything outside of whatever he wrote down for her," Slade said in frustration, resisting the urge to punch the wall...barely.

"There has to be something. Did you see how she looked to the left immediately before she spoke and again before the tape cut off? Who or what was she looking at?" Dude asked.

"She could've been looking at one of Fourati's flunkies who was holding a gun on her, making sure he approved of her speech," Abe said with a shrug.

"Or she could've just been desperate to look anywhere but at the camera," Cookie suggested.

Slade tuned the men out. Wolf started the video for the twenty-third time. Slade knew the man was as desperate as he was to find something, *anything*. His wife was out there somewhere, just as Dakota was. At least Slade had seen with his own eyes that Dakota was physically okay for the moment. Wolf didn't even have that. They didn't even know for sure that Caroline was still alive. With every minute that passed, the women seemed to be slipping away.

Slade stood behind the couch and stared at the computer screen over the heads of the other SEALs. He couldn't quite hear what Dakota was saying, but it didn't matter because he had her fucking speech memorized by now anyway.

For a moment, something registered in his mind as he watched her, but the fleeting thought was gone almost as soon as it appeared.

He tilted his head and concentrated on the computer screen harder.

Dakota sat with her back ramrod straight in the chair. The beige shawl draped over her forehead rustled in a small breeze in whatever room she was in. He could see a faint blue mark on her head, the beginnings of a bruise. *Fucker put his hands on her. Hurt her. He'll pay for that along with everything else.*

Dakota's hands were in constant motion as she spoke, as if the hand gestures would help get her point across to the fuckers who were watching. It was odd. Slade hadn't noticed that she used her hands when she'd talked to him over the last few days. She was more likely to clasp her hands together when she told him something important, not wave them around distractedly.

That was it.

"Start it over," Slade ordered.

"But—" Wolf began to protest.

"I said, start it over," Slade repeated. "And turn off the fucking sound."

Without another word, Wolf did as Slade requested. The video began to play once more and Slade concentrated on Dakota's hand movements, staring at her with intense concentration.

"What are we looking for?" Dude asked into the now silent room.

"I don't know for sure," Slade said when the video finished. "It's just a hunch. Again, Wolf."

The other SEAL did as Slade asked and started the video over again.

Slade narrowed his eyes. He was missing something. But what?"

"Holy fuck," Cookie whispered. He turned to Slade. "Does Dakota know sign language?"

Slade shrugged. "I have no idea. Fuck, I don't know much about her at all. Don't know where she grew up, how old she was when she lost her virginity, what foods she doesn't like and what she does, if she—"

"I'm pretty sure she's signing," Cookie interrupted before Slade could go off on a tangent. "We've only had a couple of classes with Cooper, but I would swear what Dakota is doing with her hands looks an awful lot like Kiera and Coop when they're signing to each other."

"Holy shit, I think you're right," Slade said, wishing fervently they'd had time to have Cooper give them more classes in sign language now.

The five men turned back to the screen and watched with intense concentration.

"Fuck me," Wolf breathed. "She *is*. She's talking to us with her hands, not words."

Slade pulled out his phone and dialed.

"Hurt."

"I need Coop's number."

"On it," the commander said immediately. "What's up?"

"I'm watching a video of my woman, who just married fucking Aziz Fourati, and she sent me a message, but I need someone who knows sign language to tell me what the fuck she's saying."

"Hang on, I'm settin' up a group call," Hurt said, and the phone went silent.

Within a minute, the commander was back. "I'm here, and I have Coop and Kiera," he said.

"I need your secure email," Slade demanded of Cooper. The man might be retired, and spending his time with kids at the deaf school his girlfriend worked at rather than killing bad guys, but he hadn't lost any of his edge, if the immediate acquiescence was any indication.

Slade gestured to Wolf, and the other man slid the laptop over. Slade punched in the email Cooper had given him. "I'm sending a video," Slade told the soft-spoken woman and the retired SEAL. "Don't bother with the sound. It's irrelevant. She's using sign language. I need you to tell me what Dakota is trying to tell us."

"What happened, did—" Kiera started to ask, but was interrupted by Slade.

"I don't have time to answer your questions, and I'm sorry I'm being so abrupt. But while you pull up the video, I can tell you that we're dealing with a life-or-death situation. A terrorist kidnapped Caroline Steel. My woman was with her and was just forced to marry a really fuckin' bad man, but we have no idea where they are. I can get them back if you help me figure out what she's trying to tell me. Can you *please* help me?"

"Of course we will," Kiera said immediately. "Cooper is bringing up the video now."

The men in Wolf's living room heard keys clicking through the phone speaker and they waited as Kiera and Cooper watched the film.

"Well?" Slade asked when an appropriate amount of time had gone by for the video to have played all the way through.

"I'm learning quickly, but I think this is outside my expertise. I'll let Kiera take the lead on this one," Cooper told the men.

"Holy crap," Kiera breathed.

"What?"

"Wait, give me a second?" Kiera asked, sounding uncertain. "Let me watch it again to be sure. Some of the signs are slurred."

"How can a hand signal be slurred?" Abe asked quietly.

"She's not being precise with them. That's one of the first things inter- preters are taught. Signs should be crisp and unmistakable. Think of it as annunciating when you speak. She's not annunciating because she's trying to be sly and hide the signs in her wild gestures, they're not clear," Kiera explained.

"Deep breath, baby," the men heard Cooper say quietly. "You can do this."

After several moments went by, Kiera finally said, "It looks to me as if she's spelling something in the beginning when she first starts speaking."

"What?" Wolf blurted, his tone communicating how urgent the situa- tion was.

"Z-A-K is what I think she's signing in the first part. Three letters. She does it at least twice."

No one said a word for a long moment, and Kiera continued. "I don't know what she's trying to tell you though, sorry."

"Wait!" Cookie exclaimed, and sprang up from the couch and ran into the kitchen. He came back holding Benny's cell phone. He typed in the code—all the guys had the same password on their phones for cases just such as this—and closed the keypad to reveal the last thing Benny had been looking at before being shot with the dart.

He showed the picture to the group.

"Yeah, we know someone named Zach," Wolf told the woman on the other end of the line tersely. "What else?"

Slade clenched his teeth and tried to control the need to break something. He stared at the picture of Zach on Benny's phone. The man had been pissed off at the practical joke that morning and had left. Had their actions put the man over the edge? Fuck.

Before he could continue beating himself up, Kiera began to speak again. "The rest of what I think she's saying is confusing to me. It looks like she signed four things, other than Z-A-K, as far as I can tell. Three of them are the number eight, beach, and basement."

"Eight men?" Wolf asked, focused now.

"A number of a license plate or address?" Dude asked.

"I'm sorry, I don't know," Kiera said softly.

"They're just talking it out, baby, they're not asking you to tell them what she means behind her signs," Cooper told Kiera quietly.

"Beach is easy. She's somewhere near the ocean," Cookie said.

"Which means shit, as half of San Diego is near the fucking ocean," Abe grumbled.

"Yeah, but beach house narrows it down," Dude countered.

"What else?" Slade asked Kiera, not hiding the impatience in his voice. He felt bad. Taking out his frustrations on Kiera, who was only trying to help, wasn't cool, but he couldn't stop it.

"There was basement," Kiera reminded them.

"Which could mean they're underground or under a building, not necessarily in a house," Cookie pointed out.

"Or that they're in a fucking basement," Wolf bit out, his patience also obviously gone.

"The last sign I'm not a hundred percent sure about," Kiera said reluctantly. "It doesn't really make sense."

"What?" Slade asked.

"Tornado."

"What the fuck does that mean?" Abe asked no one in particular.

"I know, it doesn't make sense. But from what I can tell, she definitely made the sign for a tornado. But..." Kiera's voice trailed off. Then she said, "Hang on a second."

Slade impatiently waited for whatever Kiera was checking. Every second that went by grated on his nerves.

"I...I don't know. But it looks to me like she made the letter C, then made the sign for tornado. She did it twice, and each time looked the same. I don't think that C was an accident."

"A tornado and the letter C? I don't get it," Wolf said, running his hand through his hair in frustration. "C for Caroline? C for coast? C for fucking come and get me? It could mean almost anything."

Slade closed his eyes and tried to think. He vaguely heard the other men discussing what Dakota could've meant, but tuned them out. Tornado. C. C. Tornado. Beach, basement, eight and C.

It came to him then. It was as clear as if Dakota had screamed the word at him. "Coronado. Tornado was probably the closest spelling she could get to Coronado without finger-spelling it out. The fucker's right fucking here."

"It makes sense," Wolf said slowly. "Zach worked at the base. He's probably given himself access to the super-computers there. If he's as good at tech shit as Tex thinks he is, he probably hacked right into the mainframe. He could bounce the signal around to almost anywhere."

"There are quite a few houses on the beaches over there. Especially on the south side," Abe observed.

"I'll be in touch," Slade told Kiera, Coop, and Hurt, and didn't even feel the slightest bit bad when he hung up in the middle of whatever the commander was saying. He immediately dialed again and got Greg Lambert.

"Lambert here."

"He fucking worked beside the team when I took my leave of absence," Slade said in lieu of a greeting.

"What? Who?" Greg asked.

"Zach Johnson. The guy you had work in my place. We just watched a video of Zach, otherwise known as *Aziz Fourati*, forcing my woman to marry him. She used sign language to talk to us. She spelled his name. Zach is fucking Aziz!"

"Fuck me," Greg said softly. Then louder said, "His name was at the top of the list of trustworthy employees when I checked for your replacement. I didn't even question it. He was already there at the base, it seemed to be an easy decision."

"Fuck, we bought right into his 'I don't understand computers' act," Abe bit out.

"Something wasn't right when I was trying to help him this morning," Slade commented. "I couldn't put my finger on it at the time, but now it makes sense. It was as if he was trying too hard to look like an idiot when it came to the computer. Clicking on stupid shit anyone who has been alive in the last twenty fucking years would know not to click on."

"So he's actually a techie…how'd he get one step ahead of us? How'd he track Dakota down?" Dude asked.

"He didn't seem to be a real threat to her until Lambert asked me to take on the case," Slade said.

"So you're the key," Wolf surmised. "How?"

"My computer?" Slade asked.

Wolf shook his head. "Our computers are secure."

"He could've hacked into it once he had access," Dude said.

"Possible, but there's no way he would've found out some of the information about Dakota from there. My computer was clean. I don't use it to email anything remotely personal," Slade informed the group.

"What about the phones?" Abe asked.

Slade shook his head. "The only time I used the office phone was when Lambert called that first time…before Zach or Aziz or whatever the fuck we're calling him, took over my job."

"How about your cell?" Lambert asked.

Everyone was silent for a second.

"It's Navy issued," Slade said slowly.

"That phone is supposed to be secure," Cookie told the group something they all knew.

"Fuck me. Yeah well, Cookie, I'm guessing it isn't as secure as we thought," Slade said, shaking his head. "I've been using it the whole time. Updating Tex on my progress. Telling him where I was, where I was going. He talked about sending Dakota trackers like the ones the other women had. Hell, Wolf even gave me his security code when we were on the way to his house. Fourati most likely listened to every fucking one of those conversations. Could be listening right now. All he had to do was follow along. I delivered Dakota to him on a silver fucking platter."

"I'll get as much information as I can on Zachary Johnson," Greg told the now extremely pissed-off group of men. "I'll get all known addresses for him and anyone remotely connected to him. Parents, siblings, a fucking UPS man who happened to deliver a package. I'll get them all. I never meant for this to happen," Greg told Slade. "When I asked you to take this mission, I never expected this."

"I never expected Dakota either," Slade said softly. "And this isn't your fault. None of it. Just get us the info, like fucking yesterday."

"I'll be in touch," Greg said, then hung up.

Slade clicked off the connection and motioned to Wolf for his phone, dropping his own on the table as if it were poison. He glanced at the window and noticed how fast time seemed to be passing. Fuck, they were taking too long. He needed information and he needed it now.

With a grimace, Wolf understood and threw it to him.

"Don't have a choice, I'm takin' a chance that your phone is clean," Slade said, before punching in a number.

"You got Tex."

"Tex, it's Cutter. I need houses on the beach on Coronado. Someplace that has a basement, or something similar that's underground. That could be a long shot though."

"Fuck me, how'd you get that intel? Did Dakota say all that in her speech?" Tex asked even as he was clicking keys on his computer.

"I'll tell you later," Slade reassured his friend.

Wolf and the other men were already on the move, headed for the door. Slade followed along behind them, the adrenaline coursing through his body. He was more than ready to get this shit done. It had been way too long since that video had played. Who knew what Fourati was doing to Dakota.

"Okay, I pulled up the MLS listings of all the houses on Coronado. Um...right, okay it looks like there are thirty-three houses with basements near a beach."

"Is there unusual electricity usage for any of them? What about cars in driveways or parked nearby? Any boat docks? Any with an eight in the address?"

Tex's fingers were moving nonstop, and Slade could hear his friend muttering under his breath as he did the searches.

"Nothing stands out, Cutter."

"Fuck, Tex. There has to be something. Fourati is Zach. The guy who replaced me."

"What? I thought that guy was a fuckup."

"Obviously he wasn't as much of a fuckup as everyone thought," Slade said dryly. He got into the backseat of Cookie's SUV and held on to the oh-shit handle as the man backed out of Wolf's driveway as if the hounds of hell were after him. Slade approved. As long as they didn't catch the attention of a ticket-happy cop, he didn't care what it took, they needed to get to Coronado. "My phone was compromised. I'm using Wolf's. Bastard listened to every one of my conversations. Followed me right to

Rachel and back to San Diego. He knows everything about Wolf's team… and me. I led him right to Dakota. We need this info, buddy."

"Fuck," Tex swore. "Okay, hang on. That puts a completely different spin on this then. If that fucker hacked into your phone, he had to have left a trail. No one is that good. The Navy doesn't—oh yeah, there you are, you asshole…"

Slade listened impatiently as Tex did what Tex did best, use his computer knowledge to track terrorists…and find missing women.

"Got him. There's a house with a beach view owned by Dolores and Richard Johnson. You'll never guess what their son's name is."

"Address, Tex," Slade said impatiently. He'd worry about Zach's parents later.

"Right, after you go over the bridge, take a left on Orange Avenue. There's a housing development at the end of the street. The houses are centered around a park. Address is 418 Ocean Boulevard."

"You're sure?" Slade asked.

"Fucking positive. Fucker's not as smart as he thinks he is," Tex said.

"There's an eight in the address," Wolf commented, but Slade tuned him out. He didn't care *what* Dakota was trying to tell him. Address, license plate, eighty-eight fucking bad guys. He'd kill them fucking all if they did anything to hurt her.

"Thanks, Tex. We're already on the move," Slade said.

"I'm shutting his website down. He won't be able to post anything else."

"Good."

"And I'll be talking with the admiral out there at the base and letting him know there was a breach, and that he'd better fucking get on that or there'll be hell to pay," Tex swore.

Slade didn't give a fuck about that. His only concern at the moment was for Dakota.

"Call me when your woman's safe," Tex ordered.

"Will do," Slade told him, and clicked off the phone. He gave it back to Wolf and tried to concentrate on the upcoming rescue. All his focus was on retrieving Dakota and Caroline and putting an end to Zach—and anyone else who got in his way.

"What's the plan?" he asked the other men in the vehicle as they flew toward Coronado, racing the setting sun.

CHAPTER 15

$\mathcal{D}$akota huddled on the floor with Caroline. The two women had their arms around each other as they spoke quietly.

"Are you okay?" Dakota asked.

"Yeah. I'm good."

"I'm so sorry, I didn't—"

"This isn't your fault," Caroline said fiercely. "*He* did this, not you."

"But he hurt you," Dakota said sadly.

"Yeah. But you stopped him before he did something awful. Besides, I've been hurt worse."

"Are you still bleeding?" Dakota reached out and put her hand over Caroline's breastbone. At the other woman's inhalation, she realized what she'd done.

"Jesus, I'm sorry," Dakota told her, yanking her hand back. "I didn't mean to...I mean, we don't even really know each other, I shouldn't be touching you like that, and—"

Caroline reached out and grabbed Dakota's hand. She placed it back between her breasts and held it there. The two women sat like that for a long moment, drawing strength from each other, connecting in a personal and empathetic way.

"I'm okay," Caroline reassured Dakota. Her lips quirked up in a semblance of a grin as she said, "It's only a scratch, and thanks to you, he didn't hurt me worse. We need to figure something out before he comes back though." Caroline dropped her hand to her lap and Dakota grabbed it and held on tightly.

"I swear I'll do whatever he wants so he won't hurt you again," Dakota vowed. "I could probably hold out if he hurt *me*, but I can't stand to see him do anything to you."

"I'd like to tell you that it doesn't matter, but I can't," Caroline said in a soft voice. "One of us needs to get out of here. Get help."

Dakota motioned to her knee, which was swelling enough that an unusual bump could be seen even though she was wearing silk pants. "I can barely walk, much less run. That asshole really did a number on my knee. It's going to have to be you. It's probably better anyway; if you're out of here, Aziz can't hurt you to make me compliant."

Thinking about the terrorist she'd just married, Dakota shivered in revulsion. As soon as she'd finished the speech she'd been forced to make earlier, Aziz had motioned for two of the men in the room to cut the zip-ties holding her ankles to the chair. He'd hauled her up, putting his arm around her waist so she wouldn't fall to the ground when she put weight on her injured knee. "You did wonderful, my bride. Unfortunately, the consummation of our wedding will be delayed. Our marriage is big news and I have recruits I need to talk to. If you promise to be good, I'll let you stay with your friend."

He'd looked at her expectantly then, and Dakota had nodded and said softly, "I'll be good."

"I'm glad to hear that, Anoushka. I'd hate to have to hurt your friend. I do *so* hate the sight of blood."

Dakota had resisted the urge to roll her eyes, and stayed silent as she was helped into another small room with Caroline. This one had a dirty mattress on the floor and a wooden chair in the corner. There was no other furniture.

"Here you are, my bride."

"It's not exactly comfortable," Dakota said dryly.

"The more you show me that you can obey your wedding vows, the better your accommodations will be," Aziz said smugly. "Since I don't trust you yet though, no matter what you swore to God in our wedding ceremony, we will consummate our marriage here. Your friend Caroline will be in that chair over there," he pointed to it with his chin, "and will be accompanied by two of my most trusted followers. If you refuse me in any way, *she* will pay the price. Understand?"

Dakota had nodded immediately, horrified by what the evening would bring.

"Good. Get comfortable. I'll be back once I've secured the major funding I've been working toward." He kissed her gently on the forehead, as if he really was a loving new husband. "Our wedding was the one thing my backer was waiting on. Now that he knows I have done my duty, he will pay. And we'll be that much closer to our ultimate goal."

"Of?" Dakota asked, afraid to hear the answer.

"To make the LAX bombing look like small potatoes," Aziz answered readily. "Take a nap, relax." He leaned into her, grabbing her chin with a cruel grip and forced her face up to his. "I will be back. I will fuck you into submission, and when I'm done, I might just let my loyal followers take a turn as well. To reward them, you know. I honestly don't give a shit who gets you pregnant. It doesn't matter. In fact, it'd probably be better if the brat had dark hair anyway."

Then he ground his mouth down onto hers. Dakota had refused to open her mouth, but he bit her bottom lip until she gasped at the pain and his tongue swept inside her mouth.

After a moment, he pulled back but didn't let go of her. "You'll have to do better than that, my bride, if you want your friend to remain unmolested." Then he laughed. "On second thought, don't. I'd love to take a shot at her as well." And with that, Aziz had left them alone in the room.

Dakota shook her head, trying to remove the memories. "I'm not sure we'll even get a chance to make a break for it," she told Caroline in despair. "I don't think there's anything we *can* do."

"Bullshit," the other woman said, determination clear in her tone. "You sent the message like we talked about, right?"

"Yeah, but I don't know if Slade will understand it. I don't know much about him at all, other than he's got a Harley and is sexy as hell."

Caroline shook her head and squeezed Dakota's hand almost to the point of pain. "One of the guys will understand."

"Does Wolf or any of his teammates know sign language?"

"They're in the process of trying to learn it, but I don't know how fluent they are yet. But they have their own nonverbal signals they use all the time. Because of what I did when I was captured, they're going to know to look for a message of some sort," Caroline reassured her. "I know it."

"I hope so. It's been a while since I've signed, I hope I didn't screw it up."

"I know my husband and the others are on their way, but we can't sit around waiting on them. We need to help ourselves." Caroline pushed herself to her feet, swaying slightly before locking her knees and walking around the room.

Caroline explored their prison, even though there wasn't much to see. The window was nailed shut and wouldn't budge so they couldn't get out that way. The chair was impossible for them to break apart to make a weapon. There wasn't anything on either of their outfits that would pass for a weapon, and the barrettes in Dakota's hair were useless as a defensive tool.

Even with the odds against them, neither woman was willing to give up. Caroline sat back down on the mattress next to Dakota and they plotted and planned. With Dakota's bum knee and Caroline's robe—which was slit up the middle, exposing her if she wasn't holding it closed—they were somewhat handicapped, not to mention outnumbered, but both made a vow not to give up, especially after Caroline told Dakota her entire story. How she'd literally been on the edge of death in the ocean when Cookie had shown up with lifesaving oxygen.

"Don't ever give up," Caroline said. "Even when you think all is lost, hang on for one more second."

Dakota nodded. "You too."

"We can get through this. Our men will come for us," Caroline said firmly.

Dakota could see the absolute certainty in the other woman's eyes. She had no doubt whatsoever that her husband was on his way. "How long do you think it's been?"

"I have no idea. It's getting dark though, so several hours," Caroline said.

Dakota closed her eyes and leaned against the wall behind her. She and Caroline once more had their arms around each other as they waited for whatever was going to happen to happen.

I can do this, Dakota told herself. *Slade is coming. I know it. We might have just met, but he's coming.* The last week flashed through her memories. Slade sitting in the passenger seat of her car, watching her sleep. Slade holding her in the trailer of the motel in Rachel. Riding on the back of his bike as she held on tightly to him. Looking up at the stars before they'd gone into the hotel room in Goldfield. He'd taken her in his arms and they'd silently gazed upwards before Slade had kissed the top of her head and led her inside. Slade smiling at her as they ate pizza in Goldfield. And how good his hands felt on her body.

Yeah, Slade was coming for her. Her only job was to hold on until he got there.

* * *

THE FIVE MEN silently exited the SUV a block away from where they believed Zach was holed up with the women. The darkening sky aiding in their cover. They weren't sure how many followers he had with him, but assumed it was anywhere up to a dozen. Twelve against five didn't seem like great odds, but not only were the men silently stalking toward the house on the beach highly trained killers, the mission was personal.

"I contacted Hurt," Wolf told the others quietly. "He called in that new SEAL team under his command to back us up and watch over the coastline. I wouldn't put it past this asshole to be ready for anything."

"Are you talking about Gumby, Rocco, and their team?" Cookie asked. "The guys who helped us over in Turkey?"

"That's them," Wolf affirmed.

"Fuck yeah," Abe whispered.

Slade didn't give a shit who was covering what. All his focus was on the house and finding Dakota before it was too late.

"Abe, Cutter and I will go around the left. Dude and Cookie, take the right," Wolf ordered, taking command of the small group. "Take out any tangos you run into...silently. We don't want to give Zach any head's up we're here."

They'd been calling Fourati "Zach" since they'd found out who he was. The fact that the man had duped not only the Navy, but all of them, had pissed them off to no end. Besides, Aziz Fourati was simply a name he'd been using, it wasn't who he was. No matter how much he might want to be an international terrorist, he wasn't.

Zach was a spoiled rich kid who, for whatever reason, had decided to become a terrorist. Slade didn't give a shit how and why the man had became what he did. He was sure the man's entire history would come out after the women were rescued, but ultimately it didn't matter. He was a dead man for touching Dakota.

* * *

THE DOOR to the room opened with a crash and both Dakota and Caroline jumped in surprise. They'd become more and more wary and stressed as the time had gone by and neither Aziz, nor any of his followers, had returned.

The men moved fast once they burst into the room. Two men in black robes grabbed Caroline and another two yanked Dakota to her feet before they could do more than weakly protest.

Dakota struggled in the grip of the two men who'd restrained her earlier. Her knee throbbed and was excruciating to stand on, but she refused to go down without a fight.

"Looks like they still have some spunk in them, Aziz," one of the men drawled, clearly amused by their struggles.

Dakota glanced at Caroline and saw her doing her best to slip out of the grip of the men holding her, too.

"Tsk, tsk, tsk, Anoushka," Aziz murmured as he came up to stand in front of her, now dressed in a black robe like the other men around them. "I was so hoping you would've spent your time waiting for me more constructively." He leaned in and took her chin in his hand in a brutal grip. "I like it when my woman fights me," he said with a gleam in his eye. "It turns me on."

"Fuck you," Dakota bit out, wrenching her head out of his grip.

Aziz motioned with his head to another man standing in the doorway. "It appears if I want to beat any sense into you, I need to do so before you're pregnant. I don't give a shit about you, but I wouldn't want to hurt the future leader."

The man Aziz had signaled moved toward Dakota and, without a word, drew back his fist and hit her in the face.

The men holding her let go, and she fell like a stone to the concrete floor. Her hand went to her face and she tried to hold back the moans of pain that were in her throat.

Before she recovered from the strike, the man's boot hit her stomach. Dakota curled into a ball, trying to protect herself. He simply moved, kicking whatever he could reach as she tried to get away from him.

"Dakota!" Caroline cried. "Oh my God. Stop it, you're going to kill her!"

"Ah, maybe you think I should pay attention to you, huh?" Aziz asked as if he didn't have a care in the world. And with a tilt of Aziz's head, the man who'd been kicking Dakota turned to Caroline.

As if in a daze, Dakota watched as he reached for her friend. Then her vision was blocked by Aziz. He'd kneeled down in front of her and was speaking softly.

"You will learn that defiance earns you nothing but pain. I might like a little fight in my woman, but I do have limits. Don't worry, you'll learn how far you can push me, Anoushka. You'll submit to me sooner or later. But for now, I think you might need a little help relaxing, hmmmm?"

Not knowing what he was talking about, Dakota did her best to keep her eyes open. It hurt to breathe and her knee was screaming in pain, but she still managed to glare at the man in front of her. "I will..." She took a deep breath, and even though it hurt, it felt good to be defying Aziz. Her eyes narrowed as she finished her thought. "*Never* submit. You'll never be able to turn your back on me. You'll never be able to leave me alone. I'll spend the rest of my life doing whatever I can to escape."

Aziz grinned then. A nasty, evil grin that Dakota knew she'd see in her nightmares for years to come. "Oh, you'll submit to me, beautiful Anoushka. You're my wife. It's my right to discipline you as I see fit. It says so right in the Quran. But for now, I'm going to take the edge off of that passion and fight. We have to travel, and I'd rather not worry about you drawing unwanted attention to us. As a bonus, some men like their women to be completely unconscious when they take them, but me? I want you to know it's me, your husband, taking you. I want you to remember how you could do nothing but take whatever it was I give you. I will fill you with my seed until it overflows from your nether lips. Then I'll do it again, and again. I'll fuck you whenever I feel like it. You'll be pregnant before the month is out, even if I have to keep you drugged the entire time. Oh yes, Anoushka, you are mine. Forever...or until I tire of you. But..." He ran his knuckles down her bruised cheek, smearing the blood from her nose and bleeding lip as he went. "Mark my words, my bride. You will never escape me. Ever."

Dakota tried to push herself away from Aziz, but the men who'd held her earlier were there to hold her still. She struggled weakly as another man came toward her with a syringe. She shrieked in pain as her arm was roughly stretched out and held down on the floor. The man injected her with whatever drug was in the needle.

She glanced over at Caroline and saw another man inserting a needle into her arm as well. Dakota panted in pain and terror as she felt an unnatural lassitude take over her body. She sagged on the floor, almost boneless.

"There. That's much better," Aziz said with a smirk. "You are conscious. You know what I'm saying and what's happening, but you're too out of it to fight back. Exactly how I like my women." He turned to the others. "It's time to go. There are some Ansar al-Shari'a supporters waiting for us just over the border. We'll use the boats. Go get them ready."

Without a word, most of the men left the room to do Aziz's bidding, now that she and Caroline weren't a threat. Dakota felt as if she were floating. The good thing about whatever Aziz had injected her with was that she didn't hurt anymore. The pain in her knee was now a dull throb and she couldn't even really feel the injuries on her face and torso from the beating she'd been given.

Aziz was busy talking to a man over by the door, probably planning how they were going to leave undetected. Earlier, when she'd looked out the window, Caroline had said she could see the ocean and a beach, and that it seemed to her as if they were in a residential house.

Dakota rolled her head to the side and saw Caroline lying on the floor near her. Her robe was open and her body was on display, but she made no move to cover herself. Their eyes met and both women blinked. Caroline rolled her head away and stared straight up at the ceiling. Then she brought her hands up to her chest and made the sign for run. Then she patted her chest twice.

Dakota got it. The other woman was telling her that she was still going to make a run for it. She wanted to believe her. Wanted to believe that Caroline would be able to make a break for freedom when they were brought out to the boats, but she wasn't sure she could. Even though it should be dark outside by now, she didn't know if Caroline could do it. With the way she felt, Dakota wasn't convinced Caroline would be able to move any better than she could, much less break free from whoever would certainly be holding her and run away.

Feeling as if she were looking down at herself from high above the room, Dakota closed her eyes and let the feeling from the drug take over her body. At the moment, she didn't care what happened to her; as long as she didn't have to go back to the pain she'd been feeling five minutes ago, she was good. Everything was just super.

* * *

THE SEALS MOVED SILENTLY as they parted and surrounded the large, beautiful house. Wolf paused near a window and held up his hand for

Slade to stop moving. As they were waiting and listening, a commotion caught their attention.

Both men watched in disbelief as a group of men in oversized black robes exited through a door almost hidden under a large wooden deck at the back of the house. They began to walk in a huddle toward the beach. Slade didn't know where they were going, but was pleased they'd have fewer men to worry about when they entered the house to find Caroline and Dakota.

Just then, shouts went up and a figure dressed in a long black robe broke free from the group and began to stumble down the beach into the dark night.

A feminine voice Slade would recognize anywhere yelled, "Go, go go!"

He looked at Wolf, and without hesitation, all five SEALs shifted to Plan B and took off running toward the group at the same time.

Spotting the SEALs running pell-mell toward them, one of the men yelled, "Leave her! Get in the boats!" As a unit, the group of men began to sprint toward the beach, where Slade could now see four rubber boats waiting.

"Fuck, we have to stop them!" Slade bit out, and pushed himself to run faster.

The figure who'd broken away from the group fell onto her hands and knees, but immediately got up and began to make her way down the beach once more. But this time Slade could see that whoever it was—most likely Caroline, if Dakota yelling "go" was any indication—was weaving and moving as if drunk. She looked back toward the group who'd left the house, and what she was wearing clicked in his brain for the first time.

It was definitely a woman. And definitely Caroline. She was nearly naked, the robe she was wearing huge and flapping around her body as she ran. It was open down the middle, and her pale body was easy to see in the moonlight as she tried to flee.

"Fuck, Wolf," Slade exclaimed.

"I see her! It's Ice," the other SEAL returned.

"Go." Slade needed the man's help, but if it had been Dakota running away, half naked, panicked and in obvious distress, nothing would've kept him from going after her.

Without a word, Wolf turned left and sprinted toward his wife.

Slade turned his eyes back to the group of men and cursed. They weren't going to make it to them before they cast off from the beach.

They were entering the four boats now and pushing them away from the beach at the same time. His eyes roved over each one, trying to see which held Zach.

In one of the middle boats, Slade saw the man's blond hair, easily recognizable amongst his dark-haired friends and followers.

Dude and Cookie reached the edge of the ocean at the same time Slade and Abe did.

"They've got one of the women," Cookie said, not even breathing hard.

"You sure?" Slade asked.

"Yeah, I saw one of them toss her over his shoulder and throw her into a boat."

"Where are they going?" Slade asked, not taking his eyes off the boats, which were quickly putting distance between the beach and themselves.

"Mexico?" Abe guessed. "Where else would they go?"

"We need to stop them," Slade bit out in frustration.

Cookie had his phone to his ear and said, "Rocco and his team are two minutes away. Two boats will come and pick us up and two others will make chase and give us coordinates."

Slade nodded and paced impatiently along the sandy shoreline.

"Where's Wolf?" Dude asked.

"Caroline's the one who got away and took off. He's on her," Slade told the other SEAL succinctly.

"Thank fuck," Cookie breathed.

"Yeah," Slade said between clenched teeth.

"I didn't mean—"

Slade held up his hand, stopping his friend's words. He knew Cookie didn't mean anything by being happy Caroline was free from the terrorists. But *his* woman was not.

Within a minute and a half, the four men saw two boats coming at them at a high speed. Slowing only enough not to ram the boat halfway up the beach, the SEALs driving the high-speed vessels were backing out even as Abe, Cookie, Dude, and Slade were jumping inside.

As if they'd worked together on missions like this for their entire career, the men from three different SEAL teams moved in a kind of deadly harmony. Their focus was on catching up to and eliminating the threats from the other boats.

* * *

DAKOTA LIE on the bottom of the boat she'd been tossed into and tried to understand what was happening. She'd seen Caroline break away from the group. She had no idea where she'd found the strength, but was impressed. No one had been paying much attention to her because they assumed she was too far out of it to be able to defy them. But instead of running after her, the men had bolted toward the boats they'd obviously gotten ready earlier.

She was thrown over someone's shoulder and she'd bounced bone-lessly as they'd raced toward the surf. The water was cold as it splashed onto her face, making her only slightly more aware of what was going on. She was unceremoniously thrown into the boat, and Aziz began to yell to the drivers of the others.

"Once we're away from shore, separate. They must not know which boat I am in. The leader must escape! We'll meet up across the border. Long live Ansar al-Shari'a!"

"Long live Ansar al-Shari'a!" was shouted back, then the voices were drowned out by the motors being revved.

Dakota had a momentary thought that Aziz was the biggest coward she'd ever met. He'd basically ordered the others to do whatever it took to make sure *he* escaped. What a douche.

Her limp body was thrown against the back of the boat as the driver gunned the engine and raced away from the shore. She concentrated on trying to see who was at the wheel, but the farther they got from Coronado, the harder it was to see anything. The two men in the boat hadn't turned on any lights and the only thing she could see clearly were the stars twinkling over her head.

As her mind floated, Dakota stared up at those stars. She could see the Big Dipper and North Star. She recalled standing in Slade's arms and seeing the same stars in Goldfield. How long ago had that been? Yester-day? No...yesterday she was at Wolf and Caroline's house. Her brow wrinkled as she struggled to remember. After a long moment, she decided it didn't matter and closed her eyes.

The bottom of the boat hitting a wave jostled her back to reality as pain tore through her body, and she blinked. Dakota slowly pushed herself up to a sitting position and looked around in a daze. She saw the lights of Coronado twinkling as they raced southward.

"He'll never find me," Aziz yelled back to her as he stood at the front of the boat. "I've got new identities for both of us, Anoushka. I was right under his nose and he had no idea it was me he was looking for." He cack-led, long and loud, and Dakota winced.

"I've got everything I need to grow my flock, and within a year I'll have organized the biggest and deadliest terrorist incident on US soil they've ever seen. And you were my inspiration," Aziz told her. He took a step toward the back of the boat where she was sitting, but a large wave made him lose his footing and he had to grab the railing to keep his balance.

Obviously changing his mind about coming to the back of the boat where she was, he said, "Rest, my bride. And don't worry. I'll have you inside a warm home, safe in my bed, where we can consummate our marriage in no time. Close your eyes, Anoushka, sleep."

Dakota closed her eyes as he ordered, more out of frustration and terror than obedience. She couldn't allow Aziz to get her out of the coun-try. She'd be even more helpless than she was right this moment. It would be twice as difficult for Slade to find her then.

It was thoughts of Slade that gave her the strength and determination to both defy Aziz and overcome the pull of the drug coursing through her veins.

Seeing that her captor and the other man were busy trying to see where they were going by looking at the instruments softly glowing on the panel, Dakota slowly forced her uncooperative body up until her belly rested on the edge of the rubber boat. The lights onshore were swirling dizzyingly, but she didn't let that stop her. The noise of the engine and the waves crashing on the underside of the boat worked in her favor. As did the fact that Aziz thought she was incapacitated by whatever he'd given her.

Without a sound, Dakota held her breath and leaned over the edge of the boat, sliding headfirst into the frigid waters of the Pacific Ocean. The small splash her body made as it knifed into the water was indistinguish-able from the other sounds the vessel made as it raced toward Mexico.

CHAPTER 16

*S*lade stood with his feet braced apart, not even feeling the spray of the cold water on his face as the Zodiac's powerful engine pushed them closer and closer to their objective. The four boats that had left the beach had scattered in four different directions.

He and Cookie were in a boat with another SEAL named Rex. He was wearing a tactical headset and was communicating with his teammates on the other Zodiacs, then relaying the information to the others on his boat.

"Phantom and Gumby neutralized the tango headed north."

"Was Dakota or Zach with them?" Slade shouted to be heard over the engine and water.

"Negative," Rex said as he shook his head.

One down, three more to go.

"Rocco and your men, Abe and Dude, are coming up on another... they're in a firefight, but it looks to only be two men, and not any women onboard."

"Come on, come on," Slade pleaded in a soft voice as they continued to gain on the boat in front of them. *Please be the one Zach is on. I want to be the one to kill that fucker.*

"Second boat down," Rex informed them.

"Update on the third?" Cookie shouted.

"Ace and Bubba are closing in," Rex informed him.

Slade didn't take his eyes off the boat in front of them. It had no lights on, but Rex and Cookie were wearing night-vision specs, and he had on a pair of thermal-vision goggles, allowing him to clearly see the bright red and pink traces of warm air from both the boat and the people onboard.

He could only see two shapes, near the front of the vessel, but that didn't mean Dakota wasn't there. He didn't have a clear view of the bottom of the boat. If they were following Zach, it was likely that Dakota was there too. The alternative was unthinkable.

"Bubba says the female target is not in the third vessel. Repeat, she is not in the third boat."

Which meant they were following Zach, and Dakota *had* to be there.

Slade could see one of the two men look behind him several times, but he otherwise didn't move away from the controls. He had no idea if the terrorists could hear them coming or not, but it didn't matter. The men were as good as dead.

Rex shouted, "Hold on," as he steered the rubber Zodiac straight for the boat in front of them. He pulled up alongside the other craft and without hesitation, rammed it, both figures at the front flying off their feet at the collision.

Slade and Cookie were moving even as Rex gunned the vessel and pulled up alongside the boat again. They'd removed their goggles and jumped into the other boat as both continued to careen forward at a high rate of speed.

Cookie was on the driver before either of the men knew they'd been boarded. He'd reached around and slit his throat so quickly, he didn't have a chance to fight back.

Zach wouldn't be so lucky.

Slade grabbed the man and threw him to the bottom of the boat so hard, he gasped, trying to get air into his lungs. Slade was on him in an instant, crouched over him, his KA-BAR knife at his throat. Cookie slowed then stopped the boat, but Slade's attention was elsewhere.

Keeping the knife on Zach's jugular vein, he turned to look at the back of the boat.

Empty.

Dakota wasn't there. She wasn't fucking there! How could she *not* be there?

For the first time that evening, his heart rate increased. He'd been focused and stoic until now. Cold, ready, and willing to do whatever it took to end the threat to Dakota. But she wasn't in the boat. She was supposed to be there. Where the ever-loving fuck was she?

Shifting so that one of his knees pressed into Zach's breastbone, he snarled at the terrorist, "Where is she?"

An ugly sneer slid across Zach's face. "Who? My wife, Anoushka Fourati? Hidden where you'll never find her."

"Bullshit," Slade said putting more pressure on the knife, not caring that a line of blood welled at the man's throat. "Where is she?"

The pain was getting to Zach. He winced and tried to pull away from the knife at his throat, with no luck. "She was a great fuck. I love it when bitches fight," Zach unwisely boasted.

Slade was done. He wanted the man under him to die slowly and painfully, but Dakota needed him. He didn't have time to kill Zach the way he wanted. He leaned down until he was right in Zach's face and said softly, "You're nothing but a coward."

"Maybe so, but my name will be remembered forever. Like Timothy McVeigh and the Unabomber, my actions will live on in infinity," Zach choked out.

"Wrong. I'm going to make it my goal in life to make sure not one news outlet knows your name. Not one." And with that, Slade drew his knife across Zach's neck slowly and methodically, not even attempting to be merciful.

He was turning away from the man even as he gurgled and bled out at the bottom of the boat.

Rex's voice speaking to the men on the other boats sounded as though it were coming from a great distance. "Target not here. Repeat, target not here. Anyone got eyes on Dakota?"

Slade turned back to Zach's body, his blood spilling into the boat in a slow but steady pace, the man's hands at his neck not doing anything to staunch the flow from his jugular. He leaned down and took hold of the man's blond hair, lifted his head up high, and proceeded to slice his throat again. Then a third time, before dropping the man with disgust. "I killed you too quickly, motherfucker," Slade said in a cold, deadly tone.

Then he looked up at Cookie. "Where's my woman?"

"I don't know. But we're gonna find her, Cutter. We're gonna fucking find her."

* * *

DAKOTA FLOATED ON HER BACK, arms stretched out, legs spread, and gazed up into the night sky. The stars were as clear out here as they were in Nevada. She'd never seen so many in all her life.

When she'd first hit the water, her breath had left her at the freezing temperature. The water was frigid. It was enough to jolt her out of her drugged stupor for a while. She'd treaded water for a long moment, watching as the boat she'd been on raced away from her. Stupid Aziz hadn't even realized she was gone. Idiot.

Then she'd begun to swim toward the shore. She had no idea how far away it was, but it was most likely a couple miles. Distances were skewed at night, especially in her confused state. After a while, she stopped being so cold and realized she was tired. Really tired.

Happy for her natural buoyancy, and the fact that she'd been a competitive water polo player all through high school and college, thus learning how to swim and float better than the average person, Dakota turned on her back to rest.

She bobbed up and down in the water bonelessly. She'd just rest for a while, then she'd start swimming again. The night really was beautiful, serene. With her ears under the water she couldn't hear anything but the whoosh of the waves as they gently lifted her body up and down, and her own slow heartbeat.

As she stared up at the sky, a shooting star went sailing past her line of vision. Dakota smiled. It had been forever since she'd seen one. A wish. She had to make a wish. Closing her eyes and feeling more comfortable than she'd been in hours, Dakota made her wish.

* * *

"WE KNOW she was on one of the boats," Rex said into the headset. "We saw someone throw her into the bottom of one of them. She *has* to be out here somewhere. They might've thrown her overboard when they knew we were on their tails."

Slade blocked out the chatter from the SEAL at the front of the boat. He was kneeling on the side of the rubber boat, one hand fisted in the rope at the side to keep his balance, his eyes fixed on the blackness in front of him.

Cookie was wearing night-vision goggles, which gave him the ability to see about twenty feet in front of him, but Slade had put the thermals back on. He could clearly see birds soaring on the thermals in the night sky, and even a couple of flying fish as they jumped out of the water. But what he was looking for was Dakota. He knew the water was cold, which would quickly sap the warmth from her body, but it hadn't been that long. He should still be able to distinguish her body in the water. She had to be out here somewhere.

He refused to think about what Caroline had gone through all those years ago, when her captors had weighted her body down with chains before throwing *her* into the ocean. He refused to think about Dakota sinking to the bottom, struggling with her bindings before running out of air and instinctively taking a huge breath, which would fill her lungs with water instead of life-saving air.

No. He would not lose her now. No way. It had been less than a week since she'd come into his life, and it wasn't enough. It wasn't nearly enough. He wanted to know everything about her. Where she'd learned sign language. What her favorite color was. What she was like as a young child.

The tears came to Slade's eyes unbidden, and he forced them back. He had no time to lose it. He needed his vision to be clear. He needed to be able to find Dakota. She was out here and time was ticking away.

"Come on, where are you, love?" he asked softly, even as his eyes continued to scan the horizon for anything out of place. Any spec of pink that might indicate the warmth from her body. It was like looking for a needle in a haystack...no, a needle in a needle stack. Impossible, but he wasn't going to give up. No way. He would find her.

"Our boat had Zach, it's most likely she's in this area," Rex was telling the other boats. "Converge on our position and begin a grid search. We don't know when she might've been...err...put out of the boat. She could be anywhere between us and the beach."

Again, Slade tuned the man out. The hair on the back of his neck stood straight up as he scanned the waters.

"See anything?" Cookie asked from his left.

"Not yet," Slade said. "But she's here. We're close. I can feel it."

"Yeah, me too," Cookie said. Neither man looked away from the vast ocean in front of them, but Cookie went on. "I've got the same feeling I had the first time I met my wife. I was two steps away from leaving that shithole of a hut in the middle of fucking nowhere, Mexico, when something made me turn back. I shouldn't have. I had Julie and we needed to get the fuck out of there before the sex traffickers came back, but I hesitated, took one last look around and before I knew what I was doing, I was walking toward the back of that hut. Sure I was missing something."

"Fiona," Slade said with certainty.

"Yeah. I've got that same feeling right now."

"Come on, love. Help me find you," Slade whispered as he scanned the waves.

* * *

DAKOTA WAS DYING. She knew it. Had no idea why she was still alive as it was. She couldn't feel her extremities and knew there was no way she would make it to land. Aziz was long gone, and she didn't want to get picked back up by him or any of his followers anyway.

The stars twinkled merrily above her head as she floated, and she felt sad. Not for herself; once she was gone, she wouldn't be in any pain. She wouldn't miss her loved ones. She firmly believed her soul would fly free and know nothing but cocooned happiness until it was determined she was to reincarnate and come back to Earth.

She wondered for a moment what Slade thought about death. Was he religious? Did he believe in God? It was one more thing she'd never know about him.

Remembering why she felt sad, Dakota sighed. Her dad would take her death hard. After her mom died, it had taken him a long time to get back to a semblance of his old self. And Caroline? Did she make it to safety? Would she forgive herself if Dakota died? Would she spend the rest of her life wishing she'd done something differently?

And Slade. She'd known the man less than a week, but her soul had recognized his. She didn't talk about her beliefs with that many people, but the second she saw him, she knew they had to have known each other in another life. Knew they were meant to find each other in this one. And they'd had less than a week together. Less than a darn week.

Lifting her arm, not even noticing how much it shook, Dakota reached up to one of the stars. She wanted to touch it. To bring it down to Earth. To share it with Slade. But it remained out of reach. It looked like she was touching it, but when she closed her fist, she was left with nothing but air.

Dropping her arm in frustration, not feeling the water splash onto her numb cheeks, Dakota closed her eyes. She was so comfortable. The water wasn't even cold anymore.

* * *

"DID YOU SEE THAT?" Slade asked Cookie urgently.

"What? Where?"

"Eleven o'clock. It was a flash of pink in my goggles."

Rex was steering the boat in that direction without having to be told. Slade and Cookie repositioned themselves in the boat and aimed their gazes ahead of the Zodiac.

Cookie and Rex didn't even ask if Slade was sure. They didn't second-guess him. If Slade said he thought he saw something, they'd go and investigate. They were all aware of how much time was going by. Precious time that, if Dakota was alive, she didn't have.

Rex informed the other search boats that Slade thought he saw something and to hold for more intel.

As they got closer and closer to whatever it was Slade saw, he held his breath.

Please be Dakota. Please be Dakota. I need her. I can't lose her.

"Fuck me, it's her," Cookie murmured.

At the same time, Rex said into the headset, "We found her!"

Slade had already whipped off his thermals, not needing them to know what he was looking at. Dakota was lying on her back. The beige shawl she'd been wearing in the video was somehow still attached to her and floating around her in a mass of fluff. The silky pants were completely see-through and looked almost ethereal. Her hair around her head formed what appeared like a halo.

Her eyes were closed and her arms and legs outstretched. She looked as if she was taking a nap, except her lips were blue and her skin was an alarming shade of white. Whatever she'd done to catch his attention had probably taken the last of her strength.

Without thought, Slade ripped off his boots and slipped into the water, careful not to make any waves that would wash over her and possibly choke her. A part of him realized that Cookie was right there next to him in the water, but he didn't spare a glance for the other man, all his attention was on Dakota. Was she breathing? Was she alive? It certainly didn't look like it.

He was at her side with two hard strokes. He put one hand on the back of her neck, holding her still and making sure her head didn't slip underwater, and the other went under her, resting on her shoulder blades.

Slade knew Cookie went to her other side and put his hands under her spine and butt, but he couldn't take his eyes off of Dakota's face. She'd been beaten, badly. Her lip was split and there was still blood oozing from one of her nostrils. Both eyes were swollen and she had several visible cuts on her face. He couldn't see the rest of her body to check for injuries, but he had no doubt they were there.

But she had a half smile on her face and she looked serene. It was unbelievable, but Slade almost didn't want to disturb her. Almost.

"Dakota? Can you hear me?"

Not expecting any response, Slade was shocked when her eyes popped open into slits and she looked at him.

"Slade?"

"Yeah, love. It's me." It was an inane conversation to have in the middle of the fucking ocean after he'd just killed the terrorist who'd married her live on video, but he didn't care.

"You came." The two words were said with absolutely certainty. Not wonder or surprise.

The tears he'd held back earlier filled his eyes and spilled over. Not once in his entire SEAL career had he ever cried over a rescue. Not once. But this was no ordinary rescue.

"You think you're ready to go home?" Cookie asked from the other side of her.

Dakota's eyes moved from Slade's face to Cookie's, and now she did look surprised. "You have a thing for rescuing women from the ocean."

The other SEAL laughed. "I see you and Ice had time to chat, huh?"

"Yeah. She okay?"

"Why don't we get back in the boat and see?" Slade suggested calmly. He had no idea what had happened to Caroline, but figured she was probably good since Wolf had taken off after her and Rex hadn't said otherwise. He and Cookie moved in unison, shifting Dakota closer to the Zodiac. By that time, two other boats had converged on the area to assist. They made a triangle around the trio in the water, protecting them from rogue waves.

Dakota closed her eyes and nodded.

"Keep your eyes open," Slade ordered.

Obediently they opened.

"That's it, love. Keep looking at me. I've got you."

Throughout the entire production of hauling her out of the water, stripping her clothes off, Slade removing his as well, and the other SEALs wrapping them both up together in an emergency blanket, she never looked away from him once.

Slade lie in the bottom of the Zodiac as it raced back to Coronado and the Naval base, where Commander Hurt had medical personnel standing by waiting for them, and marveled at the feeling of having Dakota back in his arms. It was literally a miracle that they'd been able to find her. People fell overboard all the time and were never heard from again.

"Are you injured anywhere besides your face?" he asked into her ear as they raced across the water.

She nodded.

"Where?"

Slade put his ear to her lips as she quietly spoke.

"My knee. My side. My hips."

"Do they hurt?"

"I can't feel anything. I'm not even cold. Maybe it's the drugs?"

"What drugs?" Slade asked urgently, motioning to Cookie with his head. The other SEAL leaned down so he could hear Dakota.

"He did something to me. Gave me something. Caroline too. He wanted us conscious, but not able to fight him."

"Did he rape you, love?" Slade reluctantly asked. He needed to know. Not for his sake, but for hers. If she'd been violated, he'd get her whatever help she needed in order to get past it. She was his, and nothing would keep him from her side. Literally nothing. He didn't care if she was pregnant. He hadn't planned on ever having children, not at his age, but if by some fluke, Zach had been able to go through with consummating his fucked-up idea of marriage and get her pregnant, he'd raise her baby as if it was his own. A child who would be half hers, and he loved Dakota with all his heart. Any baby of hers would never know hate. Would know nothing but love from both its parents.

"No."

Slade wanted to believe her, but wasn't sure he could.

He leaned down and put his lips right near her ear, making sure she could hear him loud and clear. "Nothing that happened will make me leave your side, love. Nothing. You understand?"

She nodded and he pulled back. Her skin was like ice against his. He was shivering nonstop, quaking with it, but she lay over him unmoving and still. It wasn't a good sign.

"He was waiting until we got to Mexico. Wanted to take his time. Give me more drugs. He wanted me to be inpacasitated...incamasitated... unable to do anything while he and his buddies raped me. I swear he didn't touch me that way, Slade. I wouldn't lie about it."

He breathed out a huge sigh of relief, closed his eyes, and rested his

622

forehead against hers. "Thank fuck," he said, his lips brushing hers as he did.

Dakota struggled over him for a moment, and Slade loosened his grip so she could free her arms from between them. She wrapped them around him and buried her nose into the space between his neck and shoulder. Cookie was there to tuck the silver emergency blanket closer around her, making sure she was completely covered after she'd shifted.

Slade put one arm around her waist and the other on the back of her head.

"Did you kill him?" she mumbled into his skin.

"Yeah."

"Good."

And that was that. She didn't ask how. She didn't ask if Slade was sure Zach was dead. She merely relaxed against him. Her entire body going lax as she lay still in his embrace.

Slade looked up at the stars as they raced toward shore, marveling at how bright and clear they seemed. He'd seen the sky from remote places before, but it had never seemed as beautiful as right at that moment.

As he held Dakota in his arms and stared upward, a shooting star flew across his line of vision. It had been ages since he'd seen one. Slade closed his eyes and wished on that star as if he were a little boy instead of a hardened former Navy SEAL.

Please let her live.

EPILOGUE

"*A*re you looking forward to our trip?" Slade asked Dakota. They were walking along the beach near his apartment. He had his arm around her waist, letting her lean on him as her knee wasn't one hundred percent healed yet.

"More than you know," she said, looking up at him, the love easy to see in her eyes. "I can't believe Patrick is letting you leave so soon."

"It's been three months, love, it's not that soon," Slade protested.

She gave him a skeptical look, her eyebrows raised.

"Okay, yeah, having a homegrown terrorist working right under your nose would make anyone leery to let someone new in to take my place again, even temporarily," Slade agreed. He leaned down and kissed the tip of her nose as they resumed their walk. The physical therapist had said she needed to continue to take walks to build up the strength in her knee. She'd had surgery to repair the patellar tendon, which had torn when she'd been kicked by one of Zach's followers.

"Who did he finally approve?"

"It's another retired SEAL. Hurt said he will never work with another contractor who *hasn't* been a SEAL ever again." Slade shrugged. "Can't say I blame him. Not sure he can actually control that, but I wouldn't put it past him. Your dad okay with us taking off?"

Dakota nodded. "Yeah. He wasn't happy with everything that happened to me, but he's one of the strongest people I know. I'm so glad

Jessyka went and got him and brought him to the hospital so he could be there with me. I know she was freaked out about Benny, but she took the time to go and get him. Your friends' wives are amazing."

"They are, aren't they?" Slade asked with a small smile. "But love, you're just as amazing."

As he thought she'd do, she shook her head. "No, I'm nothing like them."

Slade bought their slow stroll to a halt. "Please tell me you're not still blaming yourself for what happened to Caroline."

Dakota slowly shook her head. "No." When he continued to look at her skeptically, she sighed and shrugged. "I know she doesn't blame me, and neither does Wolf. But thinking about how pissed he must have been when he realized she was practically naked and all of Zach's men saw her like that...I can't help it."

Slade took her face in his hands and kissed her briefly on the lips. "She got off much easier than you, love. Wolf got to her and she was fine. Bruised and out of it from the drugs, but fine."

"You swear Wolf doesn't hate me?" Dakota asked softly. "Or the other guys? I know they say they don't, but I can't help but think that if it wasn't for me, she never would've been in that position."

"They love you. They're in awe of you. No one blames you. You need to let it go."

She sighed. "I'll try. Promise."

"Speaking of the guys, Benny wants to know when you're going over to his place again. His kids had such a great time with you, and you managed them all so well, I think you're in trouble."

"They're great kids. I'm glad Benny is okay. I was so scared when he slumped over the table that day."

"Zach had it well planned. They darted him through the kitchen window, then it was an easy thing to break one in the other room and enter the house. I told you how he'd decrypted my phone and listened to all my conversations. He had the code for the alarm, and punched it in while two other men took care of incapacitating you and Caroline."

She shivered. "I'm glad I don't remember anything after that."

Slade thought about how Zach and his men must've stripped the two women, and silently agreed with her. He was glad she didn't remember either. "You might be interested to know that I found out the Johnson house was recently sold."

"That sucks."

"Sucks?"

"Not that the house was sold, but that Zach killed his parents. I mean, who *does* that? He chopped them up and kept them in a freezer. That's just sick."

"Love, this was the same man who laughed about that bomb at LAX and was planning on duplicating it all over the country."

"I know, but they were his *parents*. How could he do that?"

Slade kissed Dakota's temple and continued to walk with her. "Some people are just wired wrong."

"I guess. But saying they went on a cruise around the world was really smart. No one missed them and he was free to set up his terrorist shop right there on the beach." She bit her lip then said, "I'm kinda glad they weren't around to find out what a horrible person their son was." Then Dakota looked up at Slade. "And someone bought the house? I can't imagine living there. Talk about seeing ghosts!" she shivered.

"The city of Coronado bought it to tear it down and make it into a parking lot for the public beach nearby," Slade told her.

"Well, whew!" Dakota pantomimed wiping sweat off her brow. But then sobered. "It's still sad."

"You, my love, are simply incredible. I'm in awe of you. You have compassion for everyone you meet. Not only that, but you survived something that even today the doctors are still talking about. Your body temperature was ninety-one degrees, and that's by the time you got to the hospital. Most people lose consciousness at that point. They usually can't reason and are extremely confused. You defied all the odds. You not only weren't that confused, you were completely conscious and talking when we found you."

"It was the drugs," Dakota protested. "I have no idea how Zach knew about conscious sedation or where he got the Propofol, but it was certainly effective. I was helpless to protect myself from him, and he could've done whatever he wanted to me. I would've known he was doing it, but I couldn't have stopped him."

"No, love. It was you. You knew I was coming and you held on. For me."

"That's true," she conceded. "Caroline told me time and time again that you guys would be coming. She swore that you'd figure out my message and were on your way."

"She was right," Slade said. "But be that as it may, Caroline being kidnapped again wasn't your fault."

Dakota sighed and rested her head on Slade's chest, burrowing into his warm strength. "What happened to the bodies of Zach and his buddies?"

Used to her topic changes, Slade went with it. "Rex's teammates, Phantom, Gumby, Ace, Rocco, and Bubba, secured the boats and their bodies were taken care of."

"And?"

"And you don't need to know anything more than that," Slade told her.

"They're really all dead though, right? They're not sitting in Guantanamo Bay plotting revenge against us? You wouldn't lie to me about that to try and make me not worry, would you?"

"They're all dead. You have nothing to worry about," Slade said in a hard tone. He felt Dakota's arms squeeze him, but she didn't move out of his embrace.

"Do you think...that storm the next morning seemed to move in out of nowhere," she said. "It was supposed to be a beautiful day. Maybe it was a higher power cleansing the entire area, getting rid of the evil vibes that remained or something."

"Hmmm." Slade made the noncommittal noise deep in his throat.

"Whatever. I'm glad he's gone."

"Me too, love. And you don't have to worry about anyone from Ansar al-Shari'a coming after you again. Tex posted a note on the same underground site Zach had been using to say that you both had been killed. The movement pretty much died after that because there wasn't anyone around to pick up the cause. I'm not saying they won't regroup, but if they do, it'll probably be with a real Tunisian, not an American impersonating one."

They walked for a while, both lost in their thoughts before Slade spoke again. "Can I ask you something?"

"Of course," Dakota said, looking up at him.

"Are you really okay with not going back to work? You've been there a long time. The school board said they'd take you back in a heartbeat if you wanted."

She shrugged. "I know, but...it's hard to explain."

"Try."

"Bossy," Dakota said, but she was smiling when she did. "Slade, I've spent my whole life working. I quit for a valid reason, but I found that working at the A'le'Inn was a whole new kind of satisfaction. I didn't need a degree, it wasn't that stimulating but it was freeing. I didn't have to worry about paperwork after my shift. Once I was done working, I was done. No meetings, no pleasing parents, no worrying about test scores or politics. I met a ton of really neat people. And I enjoyed the freedom of doing what I wanted, when I wanted." She shrugged. "It probably makes me a bad person, but I like not working."

"It doesn't make you a bad person, love. It makes you human."

"I guess." Then she smiled up at him and put her hand on his bearded cheek. Her thumb caressed him as she said, "I hate lemons, but I love lemonade."

Slade filed away the random fact about her, just as he had all the others he'd learned over the months. "In a box at my mom's house is the very first uniform I ever bought when I joined the Navy. She wouldn't let me throw it away."

They smiled at each other for a long moment before Slade turned her in his arms and they slowly started back toward his apartment. They'd begun sharing small facts about themselves shortly after she woke up after her knee surgery and was coherent.

They both realized how little they knew about each other and set about fixing that as soon as possible. She'd learned sign language because one of the kids in her school was deaf. She'd wanted to be able to communicate directly with the child instead of going through her interpreter. If he'd known that about her, they could've figured out her message sooner and gotten to both women before the terrorists had left for the boats.

"If I had a choice between watching only Disney movies for the rest of my life or action/adventure, I'd choose Disney every time," Dakota said as they walked.

"Why?"

"Because there's always a happy ever after with Disney."

"You wouldn't get sick of the cartoons? Or the singing?" Slade asked, smiling.

"Nope. You know how much I love to sing in the shower."

He did. The first time she'd been allowed to shower without the home health care nurse with her, he'd heard a god-awful noise coming from his bathroom. He'd raced upstairs and burst into the room, a knife in his hand, ready to kill whoever was hurting his woman, and had realized the screeching he'd heard was actually Dakota singing. Or trying to. They'd shared a good laugh and he'd made her promise not to scare the shit out of him like that ever again.

Surprisingly enough, as much as he'd been reluctant to rush it, their love life was amazing. Even with her recovery and bum knee, they'd found ways to be intimate. Last month, she'd finally convinced him she wasn't in any pain and was ready to become his in every way.

He'd taken his time, learned every inch of her body with both his fingers and mouth, before slowly sinking into her hot depths. It had been an amazing experience for them both. They hadn't rushed, had taken their time, savoring the feeling of being one for the very first time.

Tomorrow they were taking off on a three-week trip through Vegas, up to Rachel, where they were spending a whole week, then down highway ninety-five, where they'd take their time and visit every haunted hotel and mine they could find. He had a bottle of peppermint syrup already packed in his bag. It wouldn't make her morning coffee taste like the specialty ones she liked, but it'd come close...he hoped. He'd bought one of those fancy coffee makers so she could have a cup of her favorite peppermint coffee every morning.

He'd made plans for them to stay at one of the super-expensive suites in Vegas toward the end of their trip, although Dakota didn't know about that yet.

Slade smiled when he thought about the ring he'd bought for her. It was at the bottom of his bag, and he was going to propose to her one night when they were in Rachel. It seemed appropriate that he ask her to spend the rest of her life with him in the same place they met for the first time. He planned to propose while they lay on top of his car watching for shooting stars. He couldn't ever look up at the night sky and not think of her.

Then he was going to see if he couldn't convince her to marry him in Vegas on their way home. He'd already made arrangements for her dad to fly out so he could be there if she agreed. There was no way she'd want to get married without her dad present, and Slade would never ask it of her.

But he wasn't willing to wait for anyone else. It was unfair of him, and selfish; she probably wanted the whole white-wedding-in-a-church thing, but he didn't want to wait. He wanted his ring on her finger and his name after hers. If she wanted a big shindig, he'd give that to her when they got home. In fact, Wolf and the rest of the guys would probably demand it, but he wanted to officially make her his as soon as possible.

"I'm sad we can't take your Harley," Dakota told him as they reached his apartment complex.

"I know, but we'll go out another time," Slade reassured her. There was no way she'd be able to ride the bike for long distances with her knee still recovering. He'd bought her a brand-new Subaru Outback to replace the car Fourati's goons had stolen from Rachel. When they'd figured out that their friend had been compromised, they'd left him there to fend for himself with the cops. It hadn't been hard for them to steal Dakota's Impreza since her keys were in the ignition. At least they hadn't killed anyone in the small town.

They hadn't had to rush after them though, because, thanks to the conversations Zach had overheard, Slade's plan to go back to San Diego and Wolf's house wasn't exactly a secret.

Later that night, after Slade had made them a delicious meal of steak and veggies, they showered together and slipped into his king-size bed.

Dakota lay on top of him, naked from head to toe, and played with his beard.

"When I was out there—you know, in the ocean—I thought about us," she told him quietly.

Slade was hard and more than ready to slip inside her hot, wet body, but he waited patiently as she worked through what she wanted to tell him.

"We'd only known each other for a short time, but I felt as if I'd known you forever."

"You know I feel the same way. From the first time I saw your photo, I knew I had to find you."

"Do you think...no, it's silly."

"What, love? Nothing you think is silly."

"It's just that...do you think we were lovers in a past life? That we somehow knew each other?"

Slade's heart stopped for a beat, then continued with its regular rhythm, albeit a bit faster. He hadn't really thought about it before, but it made sense. All his life he'd felt as if he was missing something. None of the women he'd been with had made him yearn for them as Dakota did. He'd thought he'd loved his ex-wife, but now that he'd met Dakota and realized what love really was, he realized that he'd liked Cynthia, but had never truly loved her like she deserved to be loved.

"I think anything is possible," he told Dakota.

"There's really no reason I should've survived," she continued, oblivious to the impact her words were having on the man lying under her. "I mean, with the beating, the drugs he gave me, being able to escape the boat without Zach knowing, and then being so cold...it's just not feasible I was that lucky. You know what I think?" she asked softly, leaning down and kissing Slade on the lips.

"What, love?"

"I think we were meant to be together. And even though it took us forever to find each other, whoever is in charge of souls decided we were gypped and it wasn't fair to break us up so soon. We'd found each other, but didn't have time to truly enjoy it. So we got a break, a second chance."

Slade was quiet as he considered her words.

"I told you it was silly," she said with a wrinkle of her nose. "Don't listen to me."

"It wasn't silly," Slade insisted. "I've had some close calls in my career. Times when I knew I should've been killed, but somehow wasn't. I was sitting right next to Tex when that IED hit. He lost his leg, and I came out with not even a scratch. I never understood why. Until now. It's because I hadn't met you."

"Slade," Dakota whispered, her eyes filling with tears.

It was his turn to frame her face with his hands now. "Call it God, call it the keeper of the souls, call it whatever you want. But I'll believe until we're old and gray that it's Fate. We were meant to find each other. Meant to spend our lives together. And you know what else?"

"What?" she asked.

"I think we'll find each other in our next lives too. And the next, and the next. A love like ours can't be confined to only one lifetime."

"I hope so."

"I know so," he countered. And with that he kissed her. A long kiss that quickly turned carnal. Slade carefully flipped them until Dakota was under him. Her legs spread and his hips notched into hers. One hand went from her face, down her body, stopping to play with her nipples along the way. When they both needed to take a breath, he moved his lips from her mouth down to her chest.

He licked and sucked at her nipples, as his hand continued to move south. He caressed her folds as he bit and nipped at her taut buds. She'd come a long way since the first time they'd been together after her ordeal. The first time he'd touched her chest, she'd freaked out. Slade had held her close as she'd told him about what Zach had done to her.

But now she was eager for his mouth, and she not only enjoyed, but craved a harder touch on her nipples. Loved it when he pinched her hard peaks as he played with her. Wanting to taste her, Slade moved down her body, settling himself on his stomach between her legs. He pushed them up until they rested on his shoulders.

"Comfortable?" he asked. Ever aware of her knee, he waited to continue until she nodded.

Once she reassured him, he dipped his head and lightly licked her distended bud, which was already peeking out from its protective hood. Using one fingertip, he teased her opening as he licked and sucked on her bundle of nerves.

It wasn't until she was shifting under him, pressing her hips up toward his face, begging for him to stop messing around, that he slowly eased his finger inside her. He'd never get tired of how hot and tight she was. It was as if her body was made for him and only him. He smiled at the feel of her copious juices easing the way. She knew what she wanted and wasn't ashamed of the way her body wept for him.

He licked harder at her clit as he curled his index finger inside her and found her G-spot. Dakota was the most responsive woman he'd ever been with, and he knew it was because they were meant to belong to each other. He smiled as she clenched against him and moaned as he set up a rhythmic stroking of that special spot inside her.

Able to read her body as well as his own, he loved the way Dakota's thighs began to shake and her hips pressed upward. She was close, and he couldn't wait to feel her explode. He didn't need to be inside her to glory in her orgasm.

He concentrated on licking hard and fast over her clit while at the same time increasing the speed of his finger against her G-spot. Within seconds, she was shaking uncontrollably and Slade felt a surge of wetness against his palm as she came.

He continued to lap at her clit until he felt her flinch away from his touch. He brought the finger that had been inside her up to his mouth and licked it clean. Then he crawled up her boneless body and kneeled over her. His cock was dripping precome and he couldn't wait to be inside the woman he loved.

"I love you," he told her.

"I love you too," Dakota responded immediately. Her eyes moved over his face, from his beard, which was soaked in her juices, to his lips, which he licked as she watched. He felt her shiver under him with increased desire.

"I need you," she told him without an ounce of shyness.

"I'll *always* need you," Slade returned. Then reached down and grasped his rock-hard cock and ran it up and down her soaked slit. She tilted her hips up as he got to where she wanted him and pressed her hands into his ass cheeks.

Moving slowly, Slade sank into her body. "Every time feels like the first," he said in awe. "Your body grabs mine and sucks me in."

"I love the feel of you inside me," Dakota told him.

"And I love the feel of me inside you," Slade said with a smile. It was a running joke between them, a ritual of sorts. He pressed inside her until he couldn't go any more, then put one hand under her ass, lifted, and was able to gain another precious few millimeters. When he felt his balls flush against her ass, she used her inner muscles to squeeze him.

Slade took a deep breath and squeezed her butt in response. "So greedy," he said with a smile.

"Always. I want all you can give me."

He pulled out slowly, looking down between them, watching as his cock emerged from her body, covered in her excitement. "I'll never get tired of this," he told her, not taking his eyes away from where they were joined as he sank back inside. "I love seeing you all over my cock."

Then he brought his eyes back up to hers, propped himself up with both hands on the mattress at her sides and began to make love to her.

In and out.

In and out.

He pressed in slowly, then pulled out quickly.

He gave her a few fast strokes, then slowed and moved inside her leisurely, making love as if he could last all night.

But Dakota wasn't in the mood for slow tonight. She bent both knees and wrapped her thighs high around his lower back. "Fuck me, Slade. I need it. I need you."

Knowing he was losing the precious control he'd been holding on to for all he was worth, Slade partially sat up and took hold of her ankles in his hands. He gently placed them on his shoulders, then leaned over her again.

Dakota was now almost folded in half and completely at his mercy. She moved one hand up to her head and grabbed a pillow from next to her. Slade helped her stuff it under her ass, then she raised both arms above her and held on to the slats of his bed.

She looked him in the eye and said softly, "Fuck me, Slade. Fuck me hard."

Her words released his iron control. He slammed into her, hard, knowing from the moan she let out that she loved it. He did it again. Then again. Each time she gripped him and thrust her pelvis up toward him.

Slade knew he wasn't going to last. With every thrust, it felt as if he could feel himself bottom out inside her. She was so tight, and so wet, the noises his cock made as it tunneled inside her were almost obscene. But he didn't care, and apparently neither did Dakota.

"Come inside me, Slade. Fill me up."

After another talk about children, Slade had undergone a vasectomy. He'd wanted the freedom to come inside Dakota and didn't want her to have to fill her body with hormones to prevent an accidental pregnancy. It was the best decision he'd ever made, because now he could fuck her without anything between them. It was messy, sure, but also intimate and exciting.

As if her words were all his balls had been waiting for, they let loose a monster load of come. He reached between them and thumbed Dakota's clit hard as he came. He felt her come a second time as he did. They jerked and thrust against each other, lost in the joy and pleasure of their bodies and being together.

Slade came back to himself before Dakota did, and he gently removed her legs from his shoulders, kissing each calf before carefully placing them back on the mattress, making sure not to jostle her still-healing knee. He kept himself lodged inside her, knowing he'd eventually slip out, and turned them until Dakota was once more lying on top of him.

"Mmmmm," she murmured, stretching against him like a contented kitten.

"You okay? Nothing hurts?" Slade asked.

"No. I'm great. Awesome," she said sleepily.

"I love you," Slade told her.

"Love you too."

A short moment passed, then Dakota said, "My second toe is longer than my big toe."

Slade smiled. He'd never, ever get tired of hearing her give him silly facts about her. "I don't have any tattoos because I'm scared of needles."

She lifted her head at that and looked at him incredulously. "Really?"

"Really."

"Hmmm. I felt awful when I was taken that I didn't know more about you, but I just realized that I knew the most important thing. Everything else is just fluff. Fluff I like, don't get me wrong, but we could go for the rest of our lives and still not know everything there is to know about each other."

"What was the most important thing, love?" Slade asked.

"I knew down to my very soul that you would do whatever you had to do to find me."

"Damn straight," Slade said, and kissed her hard. It was wet, and long, and he hoped it conveyed all that he was feeling.

It did.

"I love you," Dakota said as she lay her head on his chest and snuggled in for the night.

"And I love you, sweetheart."

* * *

GREG LAMBERT COULDN'T SLEEP. He'd re-read through the final report that Slade Cutsinger had sent him. It had been thorough and complete and he couldn't help but feel a twinge of pride that he'd had a hand in removing a terrorist threat that would've crippled the United States if it had been left unchecked.

But that didn't mean there weren't more threats looming. Slade and his friends might've ended one, but there were still plenty more.

The pressure of knowing there were more terrorists out there, plotting and planning to kill innocent American citizens, made it hard for Greg to sleep. Sitting up and throwing his feet over the side of his mattress, he decided that since he wasn't sleeping, he might as well get up and plan the next takedown.

He shuffled into his home office. Kissing his fingers and pressing them to the glass of the frame that held a picture of his late wife, Greg settled into the chair behind his desk. He pulled out the list of former Navy SEALs who'd been identified as candidates for the solo missions and tried to decide who to call, and which terrorist to take down next.

Running his finger down the page, he stopped at one name. Bingo. He'd researched this man and knew without a doubt he would succeed in what Greg was going to ask of him. The former commander glanced at his watch. It was too early to call right now, but in the meantime, he'd make notes.

One terrorist might've been taken down, but there was always more waiting in the wings.

Greg picked up the cold cup of tea he'd been drinking earlier and added a splash of whiskey. Then he held it up in a silent toast. *To Slade... and Dakota. May you live the rest of your lives free from the worries of terrorism. Love each other like there's no tomorrow, because you never know when there might not be.*

And with that, Greg slammed back the strong concoction and took a deep breath. Time to get back to work.

* * *

You know you want to read Greg Lambert's story, right? Well, now you can! It's FREE too! Get Lambert's Lady today!

Thank you to everyone for picking up this last book in my SEAL of Protection Series. I had to end it like I started it...with Caroline being snatched. :) But in this one, like in her own book, she comes through the ordeal stronger as a result...and in this case, Dakota really needed her to keep her calm and focused.
The SEAL of Protection series will continue with the team you met in this book. Gumby, Rocco, and the others get their OWN series...SEAL of Protection: Legacy. Look for the first book, Securing Caite, to be out in Jan 2019.

*

Find out who the Commander calls next. Make sure to pick up ALL the books in the Sleeper SEAL series. These can be read in any order and each stands alone.
Protecting Dakota by Susan Stoker
Slow Ride by Becky McGraw
Michael's Mercy by Dale Mayer
Saving Zola by Becca Jameson
Bachelor SEAL by Sharon Hamilton
Montana Rescue by Elle James
Thin Ice by Maryann Jordan
Grinch Reaper by Donna Michaels
All In by Lori Ryan
Broken SEAL by Geri Foster
Freedom Code by Elaine Levine
Flat Line by J.M. Madden

IF YOU HAVEN'T READ *Protecting Caroline* and read about how Caroline and Wolf met...you can pick it up for FREE.

* * *

JOIN my Newsletter and find out about sales, free books, contests and new releases before anyone else!! Click HERE

Want to know when my books go on sale? Follow me on Bookbub HERE!

Also by Susan Stoker

SEAL of Protection Series

Protecting Caroline
Protecting Alabama
Protecting Fiona
Marrying Caroline (novella)
Protecting Summer
Protecting Cheyenne
Protecting Jessyka
Protecting Julie (novella)
Protecting Melody
Protecting the Future
Protecting Kiera (novella)
Protecting Dakota

SEAL of Protection: Legacy Series

Securing Caite (Jan 2019)
Securing Sidney (May 2019)
Securing Piper (Sept 2019)
Securing Zoey (TBA)
Securing Avery (TBA)
Securing Kalee (TBA)

Delta Force Heroes Series

Rescuing Rayne
Rescuing Aimee (novella)
Rescuing Emily
Rescuing Harley
Marrying Emily
Rescuing Kassie
Rescuing Bryn
Rescuing Casey
Rescuing Sadie
Rescuing Wendy
Rescuing Mary (Oct 2018)
Rescuing Macie (April 2019

Badge of Honor: Texas Heroes Series

Justice for Mackenzie
Justice for Mickie
Justice for Corrie
Justice for Laine (novella)
Shelter for Elizabeth
Justice for Boone
Shelter for Adeline
Shelter for Sophie
Justice for Erin
Justice for Milena
Shelter for Blythe
Justice for Hope (Sept 2018)
Shelter for Quinn (Feb 2019)
Shelter for Koren (June 2019)
Shelter for Penelope (Oct 2019)

Ace Security Series

Claiming Grace
Claiming Alexis
Claiming Bailey
Claiming Felicity

Mountain Mercenaries Series

Defending Allye
Defending Chloe (Dec 2018)
Defending Morgan (Mar 2019)
Defending Harlow (July 2019)
Defending Everly (TBA)
Defending Zara (TBA)
Defending Raven (TBA)

Stand Alone

The Guardian Mist
Nature's Rift
A Princess for Cale
A Moment in Time- A Collection of Short Stories
Lambert's Lady

Special Operations Fan Fiction
http://www.AcesPress.com

Beyond Reality Series
Outback Hearts
Flaming Hearts
Frozen Hearts

Writing as Annie George:
Stepbrother Virgin (erotic novella)

ABOUT THE AUTHOR

New York Times, USA Today and *Wall Street Journal* Bestselling Author Susan Stoker has a heart as big as the state of Tennessee where she lives, but this all American girl has also spent the last fourteen years living in Missouri, California, Colorado, Indiana, and Texas. She's married to a retired Army military man who now gets to follow *her* around the country.

She debuted her first series in 2014 and quickly followed that up with the SEAL of Protection Series, which solidified her love of writing and creating stories readers can get lost in.

If you enjoyed this book, or any book, please consider leaving a review. It's appreciated by authors more than you'll know.

www.stokeraces.com
susan@stokeraces.com
www.AcesPress.com

facebook.com/authorsusanstoker

twitter.com/Susan_Stoker

instagram.com/authorsusanstoker

goodreads.com/SusanStoker

bookbub.com/authors/susan-stoker

amazon.com/author/susanstoker